Fated Genes

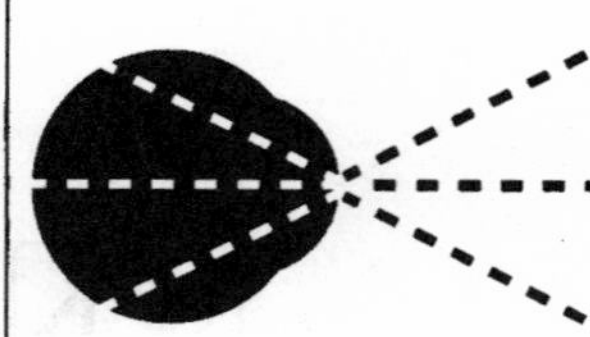

This Large Print Book carries the
Seal of Approval of N.A.V.H.

Fated Genes

Harry Lee Kraus, Jr., M.D.

Thorndike Press • Thorndike, Maine

This is a work of imagination. None of the characters found within these pages reflect the character or intentions of any real person. Any similarity is coincidental.

Published in 1998 by arrangement with Crossway Books, a division of Good News Publishers.

Thorndike Large Print ® Christian Mystery Series.

The tree indicium is a trademark of Thorndike Press.

The text of his Large Print edition is unabridged.
Other aspects of the book may vary from the original edition.

Set in 16 pt. Plantin by Minnie B. Raven.

Printed in the United States on permanent paper.

Library of Congress Cataloging in Publication Data

Kraus, Harry Lee, 1960–
Fated genes / Harry Lee Kraus, Jr.
p. (large print) cm.
ISBN 0-7862-1361-2 (lg. print : hc : alk. paper)
1. Pediatric surgeons — United States — Fiction.
2. Genetic engineering — Fiction. 3. Large type books.
I. Title.
[PS3561.R2875F3 1998]
813′.54—dc21 97-48788

For my sons
Joel, Evan, and Samuel

ACKNOWLEDGMENTS

As with any project like this one, many deserve special mention.

Thanks to Dr. Tim Kinney for all of the computer literature searches he did with undaunted enthusiasm. Any inaccuracies in the presentation of complex research topics are my fault, not his.

Thanks to all the editing staff at Crossway Books, the true unspoken heroes of this business. Thanks to Jill Carter, Lila Bishop, Steve Hawkins, Lane Dennis, and Leonard Goss, and also Ted Griffin who worked so hard to make this project a success. Thank you for keeping the vision alive.

My hat's off to Mark Schramm for his design work and to Brian Ondracek for his oversight in all phases of production.

Special thanks to my wife, Kris, my faithful support and, as always, my patient first-reader.

PROLOGUE

Tenwek Hospital, Western Kenya Highlands

Surgeon Matt Stone could tell by the Kenyan's eyes that he was smiling behind his surgical mask. *He should smile,* Stone thought. *He's doing good work.*

"Scissors." The doctor from Kenya requested the instrument with his right palm open, keeping his eyes fixed on the operative field. "Tie." The African surgeon's fingers blurred in a flurry of repetitive movements. With the knot secured, the last of the visible hemorrhage subsided.

Now Dr. Stone smiled too. *Just like I taught him.* He spoke his praise. "Well done. You could have saved this one without me."

"Oh, Dr. Stone, I'm glad you were here." The African would never take the credit he deserved. He shook his head and looked at the young, thin, dark patient on the table between them. "The tribal fighting has got to stop. This boy is only fourteen."

Matt Stone sighed. "I know." He pulled off his surgical scrub gown, its normal pale green now nearly obliterated by deep crimson stains. "I know." Stone went to the scrub sink and washed off his sterile gloves. In a land of little, they reused everything. He dropped the size 7 gloves onto a laundry rack to dry. He sighed again. *With all its frustrations, I'm going to miss this place.* Stone, an American missionary surgeon, looked younger than his stated age of thirty-six. His sandy blond hair stood out in contrast to the black hair of those he served.

"John . . ." Matt used the African's Christian name. The dark man pulled down his mask and smiled again. Stone's eyes met with those of his African brother's. "You are ready to take this work on without me."

The two clasped their hands tightly. The Kenyan spoke softly in plain English. "You have taught me so much. I will always be in your debt."

"You have taught me much as well," the surgeon reminisced. "I will never forget the insights you have given me into fighting the spiritual forces of darkness. It seems I needed to go a long way from home to understand how much I was missing by seeing things only with my natural eyes."

"We have seen some times!" The African sobered. "Some I wouldn't want to relive." He broke away and looked back toward the operating table where an assistant was dressing the incisions.

Matt Stone watched as the team finished up and gently moved the boy to a stretcher. He thanked each worker and stepped out into the star-filled African sky. Around him he heard the bustle of activity on the wards. Inside himself, he communicated with his Heavenly Father as he walked alone down the rocky path to his concrete and cinder-block flat. *Is this the guidance Linda and I have been seeking? Is the work you had for us here complete? Where next, Lord? Where next?* With his heart full of the peace he'd sought, he quickened his pace and looked ahead to the light coming from his apartment window.

CHAPTER 1

Paul Southerly slept peacefully, unaware of the two dark figures stealthily moving up the broad hallway to his bedroom's entrance. That the would-be Surgeon General could sleep at all was somewhat amazing, considering that his Senate confirmation hearings were set to begin in the morning. The role of the nation's highest health official had changed in recent years, especially since the government had become the administrator of the most expensive health care delivery system in the world. As Surgeon General, Dr. Southerly would not only serve as a spokesperson for health care issues concerning the American public, but would also administer the multibillion dollar budget that funded public medical care and research.

Sally Southerly, Paul's wife, had left the night before to avoid the media throng that had increasingly gathered and clamored around them, questioning and probing until her patience and her sanity demanded a timely vacation. Although she felt guilty for abandoning her husband on the eve of the Senate hearings, she knew it was best to avoid a potentially damaging situation. Her answers to the reporters had become terse, and she feared that she would soon lose control of her temper altogether. She left Paul with the same motherly advice she had given him daily since his health had waned a decade before: "Don't forget to take your medicine, dear. Remember to check your glucose level. And call Dr. Raines if there are any problems." He, of course, had nodded thoughtlessly, having learned that arguing with Sally bordered on futility.

Quietly, the larger of the two figures laid two broad leather straps across the sleeping form as the second silently lifted a down pillow from the head of the bed. Slowly he placed the pillow over the face of the sleeping physician. It took nearly thirty seconds before the victim's brain signaled an emergency need for oxygen.

Dr. Southerly snapped to full alertness. *I need air!* He struggled to lift his arms but felt a strong, oppressive grip holding both wrists to his sides. *I'm being smothered!* He attempted a kick but met only the same tight restriction, limiting his reaction to a few violent twists of his torso and shoulders. He fought for a breath but managed only to stick out his tongue against the pillow tightly plastered to his face. As he flung his head from side to side, his teeth cut a deep laceration into his tongue, and his mouth immediately filled with blood. *I'm choking! I'm dying! Father! Father God, I'm coming home* — His thoughts ceased as he began to seize; his consciousness was obliterated as his brain's oxygen level dipped to a critical level.

The two men looked on without alarm. They were relaxed, having hardly worked up a sweat in the struggle. The smaller of the two quickly inspected the room. Everything appeared in order. No overt signs of foul play, other than the blood draining from the victim's mouth, could be seen. That could easily be attributed to a tongue laceration obtained during a convulsion. The physician's hearing aid, a glass of water, and a prescription medication to prevent seizures sat undisturbed on the bedside table. After the restraints were removed, the scene would be difficult for even an experienced coroner to misinterpret: suffocation secondary to loss of airway during a seizure in a known epileptic.

As the younger of the two assassins glowered over their apparently perfect assault, the older and taller of the men lit a candle with a butane lighter. The candle, a small irregularly shaped cylinder, had been fashioned out of human baby fat. Thin, black smoke curled off the flame's tip as the distinct odor permeated the dark room. The fire cast off a small light that emitted an eerie glow onto the man's coarsely bearded face.

"What the —" The younger man's startled response was cut short by the chanting of his darkly clothed partner.

The older man remained oblivious and continued a repetitive prayer.

"What are you doing!" the younger man demanded in a hushed tone. "The priestess *paid* us for this! We are not performing sacrifices tonight!"

The older man continued as if in a trance, apparently not hearing his associate's objections. Then, just as the younger attacker turned to face the bearded man to issue a second rebuke, the smoke alarm above the victim's bed screamed its shrill warning as the smoke from the candle gathered near the dark ceiling.

The smaller, more agile assailant swore, then jumped onto the victim's bed, his hand extended into the dimness toward a small red light radiating from the smoke detector. Swiftly he found the button he sought and silenced the alarm. Meanwhile, the older man quickly ceased his worship and extinguished the flame between his thumb and index finger.

With the alarm silenced, the men listened quietly for evidence of any further sound. After two additional minutes of silence, the two figures exited the house quietly through a cellar door. They stepped out into the cool air in the richly wooded subdivision, unnoticed by the nearest neighbor who resided nearly the distance of a full city block away. In two more minutes, they sped away in a foreign luxury car — the younger man at the wheel, seething with anger at the actions of his partner, and the older man reclining in the backseat, oblivious in the afterglow of worship with his lord.

CHAPTER 2

Brad Forrest, M.D. looked compassionately at the helpless infant in the incubator in front of him. The small male child had been born with a hole in his diaphragm, allowing his intestines to push up into his chest, severely compressing and compromising the development of his lung function. After surgery on the first day of his life, he had been placed on E.C.M.O., a special machine that helped pump the infant's blood and fill it with oxygen. In essence, it served to function as an artificial lung and heart unit that would be withdrawn as soon as the baby improved. He was now on day 3 of E.C.M.O. and was showing few positive signs of recovery.

"Get better soon, young one," whispered the pediatric surgeon. "Uncle Sam won't let me continue this much longer." Brad stood an even six feet tall but somehow seemed taller. His thick, dark hair was dotted prematurely with gray at the temples, giving him a distinguished look that other doctors coveted. His olive complexion had come by way of his mother's Mediterranean heritage and gave him a tanned appearance belying the fact that he rarely had time to see anything except what was bounded by the hospital walls. He mentally reviewed the government's requirements for use of E.C.M.O., knowing that this case would be closely scrutinized by the review board, especially if the infant didn't make it, and even more likely if his overall bill exceeded the regional norm. *Age less than seven days, weight more than 2,000 grams, gestational age greater than thirty-six weeks, absence of renal failure* — His thoughts were interrupted by the vibration of his pager clipped to his scrub pants' waistband. He glanced from the infant's chart to the digital display — "431-2312" — and sighed. *Julie. I wonder what she wants now.*

The young physician scribbled a quick order dictating parameters for weaning the infant off of E.C.M.O. and checked the ultrasound report that was attached to the front of the chart. "Ultrasound, Head. Baby Boy Richards. No signs of intracranial bleeding." Each infant on E.C.M.O. required blood thinners to keep the blood fluid as it ran through the oxygenator and attached pump. The blood thinner, in turn, increased the risk of bleeding, especially within the infant's head, mandating a daily ultrasound for monitoring. Good. Brad sighed again. *This should keep the reviewers off my case for another twenty-four hours.*

His beeper emitted another short vibration, reminding him of his unanswered page. *O.K., O.K., I'm coming!* He depressed the button on the top of the pager to silence the recurrent message and then turned and walked quickly to the central nursing station in the neonatal intensive care unit. He looked at his watch as he dialed his home number.

"Hello." Julie's cheerful voice provided some needed sunshine in Brad's stressful day.

"Hi, honey. It's me." Brad leafed through a small pocket daily planner as he talked. "Did you need something? I've had a killer of a day."

When hasn't it been that way lately? Julie stifled her thoughts and answered politely, "Oh, nothing much. I just thought I'd see if you could pick up some soda on your way home. The Kutzes are coming for dinner, and I hoped —"

"The Kutzes!" Brad interrupted. "I was hoping for a quiet evening at home with just the family for a change." He paused and then continued as he closed his daily planner. "Besides, I'm taking trauma call tonight, and I'm not sure if I'll even get home."

Julie bit her lower lip. "Trauma call! Since when?" Her voice trembled slightly at this newest news.

"Since this morning. Steve has to present a paper tomorrow. He's really pressed this time. He promised to make it up next month. I told him I'd help him out this —"

"You knew we had plans! We discussed this last week!"

Brad looked back to today's date on his planner. He'd not made an entry for the dinner date. He listened to the silence on the other end of the line. "Look, Julie, I'm sorry about the dinner. I forgot." He sighed. "Carl and Karen won't mind. They're like family —"

"So you can let your surgical schedule tromp all over them just like you treat your own f-family!" Her biting words erupted with a sob, the emotions of the normally reserved doctor's wife now uncharacteristically uncapped.

"Look, honey . . ." Brad spoke with urgency in his voice, then lowered his volume and glanced around the busy nursing station. "I'll be there when I can. You know I agreed to cover for the trauma service when they needed me. That was part of my contract."

Julie wasn't interested in the facts. She wanted a supportive husband who knew his own family as well as he knew his patients. "You haven't seen Bradley awake for three days! He's becoming such a young man — but *you'd* never know it. You never even see him!"

The truth in his wife's words stung like alcohol in a fresh laceration. The surgeon sighed and stared into the receiver, his wife's sobbing apparent only to him as he stood in the noisy intensive care unit. His pager vibrated. Its digital display called him back to the work that had become a jealous taskmaster. *Emergency room. Now what do they want?*

The phone cord tethered Brad's pacing to a small arc within a few feet of the chart rack in the central nurses' station. He always paced when he talked, especially when he felt stressed. Now he remained in constant motion, almost wrapping the cord around a colleague before formulating his final reply. "I'll make it up to Bradley. This residency program will be over in another two months. It will be better then . . . I promise!" He checked his watch again and quickly added, "I love you. I've got to run."

Julie paused, then added without enthusiasm, "Yeah, sure. Bye, Dr. Forrest." She laid the receiver in its cradle, her eyes brimming with tears. She'd heard the promises a thousand times before. She'd long lost hope of having a full-time husband, hoping now only for little more than a part-time father for their son. Her inherent optimism had waned slowly through four years of medical school, seven years of general surgical training and research, a year of critical care fellowship, and now two additional years of pediatric surgery training. She and her husband would both turn forty next year, and they jokingly called each other the king and queen of delayed gratification. After this last residency year, which would end in several months, Brad would be free to pursue his first "real job."

Dr. Forrest hung up the receiver without further response. He shook his head slightly, promising himself that he would concentrate on his family problems later in the evening when, and if, he got home. Right now he needed to get to the E.R. to see what kind of fire demanded his attention there.

Brad stopped by the incubator of Baby Boy Richards for one last look before exiting the unit. *Please get better, little one.* It was more of a thought than a prayer. His prayers had become nearly nonexistent since embarking on his surgical career now almost a decade ago. Like so many other important areas of his life, his Christianity had been ignored, shoved to the back burner as he gave himself to his all-consuming love of surgery. As he paused to look at the child's vital signs, his thoughts turned to his own son, Bradley. His wife's words a few days earlier haunted him. *You don't even know your own namesake!* Their son had been born eleven years earlier, during Brad's last year of medical school, and Brad had insisted on passing along his father's name. His son, Bradley Jacob Forrest II had spent three weeks in a similar neonatal I.C.U. suffering from a variety of maladies commonly seen in the premature. He also suffered from a more lasting problem — Down's syndrome, a condition caused by the presence of a third chromosome number twenty-one.

Brad still remembered the pediatrician's surprise at Brad's insistence at naming the baby after himself. "He's retarded, son," the calloused pediatrician had said. "Save your name for your next boy." Brad's reply echoed in his memory as if it had been stated only yesterday: "His name is Bradley! My firstborn is my firstborn regardless of his

I.Q.!" The dark-haired surgeon now shook his head as if erasing the memory. He quickly exited the I.C.U., donned his long, white lab coat to cover his scrubs, and headed for the Bridgewater University Medical Center's emergency room.

Twenty miles south of the Bridgewater University Medical Center, nestled on a forty-acre wooded hillside, the Crestview Women's and Children's Health Center pulsed with activity. Its reputation for providing comprehensive prenatal, obstetric, gynecologic, and pediatric care stood unmatched by even its larger nearby university competitor. State-of-the-art equipment filled its rooms; the finest physicians walked its halls; its pharmacy carried the very latest in available chemotherapeutics. In short, it set the standard as the best money could buy. And in fact, even in the presence of the skyrocketing costs of new medical technology, Crestview Women's (as all the locals referred to their favorite hospital) had turned out two successive years of *decreasing* expenses.

Rationing had hit the health care delivery system, however, and the government's leading economists fielded tough questions on a daily basis. It was becoming obvious that treatment of every illness in every citizen was an economic impossibility. But who would be denied care? How would the rationing take place? Age criteria? Limitation of numbers of certain procedures? Harsh decisions were handed down. The first had come slowly and met with unprecedented public outcry. These cries had softened, however, in the light of the enormous federal debt and an even larger fear of economic collapse. So far the cuts had involved only the elderly and those adults whose medical needs placed "unfair" burdens on society as a whole. No one over sixty-five could be initiated on hemodialysis. If a patient's kidneys failed before age sixty-five, dialysis would still be offered as long as the patient desired. Severe restrictions for "extraordinary" procedures, such as cardiac, liver, renal, and pancreatic transplantation, also crept forward through tough congressional debate and were signed into law by the President. Government scrutiny by unyielding review boards became commonplace. Stiff fines were meted out to physicians who strayed from the guidelines.

Weber James Tyson sighed with frustration as he stared at the stack of charts on the teak desk in front of him. As chief of the Surgery Department at Crestview

Women's, he not only had to deal with his heavy patient load, but also had to maintain a critical eye on the budget and expenditures of the entire department. Fortunately for him, as a pediatric surgeon he had not yet been affected by the rationing of the health care dollar, although he knew that he must do all he could to keep his expenditures down, especially in the neonatal intensive care unit where rationing seemed eventually inevitable.

Dr. Tyson typified the excellence that Crestview Women's promoted to the public so skillfully. He had graduated *summa cum laude* from Harvard and then attended Duke University Medical School, graduating easily in the top 10 percent of his class. After a general internship, he served for two years with the national public health service in rural Arkansas to repay a government loan, then moved to Ann Arbor, Michigan, to do a general surgery residency for five years, followed by three years of pediatric surgery training in Philadelphia.

For the past fifteen years Weber Tyson had worked diligently at building the biggest and most successful pediatric surgery practice in the Southeast, Valley Surgeons for Children. He had skillfully succeeded in building a large, multi-state referral base for critically-ill newborns requiring surgery. This, of course, was to the dismay of the university pediatric surgery service. Until Dr. Tyson had come to town, the pediatric surgery patients were all referred to them. Now, however, the typical referral patterns were destroyed; every pediatrician within 150 miles knew where the best surgical care would be given to their patients: Valley Surgeons for Children, senior associate and founder, Dr. Weber James Tyson.

Dr. Tyson sorted through the patient charts in front of him, placing each one in a neat stack on his left as he finished reviewing it and dictating his consultant notes. In spite of the late-evening hour, and in spite of the fact that he was "off call," Web Tyson slowly and meticulously reviewed each case, noting every lab value and every X-ray test that he had ordered earlier in the day. For the next two hours he would memorize each chart and dictate letters back to the numerous pediatricians across the state who had referred the patients to him. He would also pay extra attention to two charts that had been flagged by reviewers as failing to meet requirements for further in-hospital care. For these, he carefully documented his reasoning for recommending continued in-patient care. As money became tighter, regulation had increased. As long as he could stay below the regional average for cost for patient care, the reviewers seemed content to look the other way. As soon as a case began consuming more than the regional average, however, the eyes of the review board returned unswervingly back to these "outlyers," and to the physicians in charge of their care. Weber Tyson took the reviewers seriously. He ran a tight, efficient ship. No one did it better than he did, and he knew it.

The evening for Brad Forrest passed in a blur of emergency room calls and new consults in the neonatal I.C.U. His thoughts of dinner at home with his family and a few close friends had vanished quickly as the daily routine flow of trauma patients demanded his attention. Part of the requirement of his coveted pediatric surgery fellowship included providing attending coverage for the adult trauma service. Because he was already board-certified in general surgery, he remained qualified to do both adult and pediatric surgery; but he only covered the adult service when absolutely necessary — when the normal general surgery staff had difficulty filling all the "call" spots. Fortunately for Dr. Forrest, his adult trauma skills and willingness to "cross cover" for the trauma service when needed had helped him land his pediatric surgery position. Unfortunately for Dr. Forrest, his inability to say no contributed to his lack of sleep, the lack of time spent with his family, and a strained relationship with Julie, his wife, and Bradley, his son.

By 9 P.M. Brad was exhausted and hoping for a break in the action that would allow him to slip home for dinner. He settled for a pack of crackers, however, when the chief resident on the trauma service, Gene Montgomery, called to notify him of another case. Brad inhaled his "dinner" and headed for the emergency room.

Brad entered quietly and observed his resident team in action. The chief resident was standing over an apprehensive male patient who appeared about twenty years of age. The patient was strapped to a backboard, his head held captive by a bulky cervical collar that kept his cervical spine immobilized. Three intravenous lines twisted from plastic containers suspended above the patient, two with clear electrolyte solutions and one containing Oxydel, a blood substitute. Brad noted the rate of the IV fluid administration without speaking: wide open. The last recorded blood pressure was visible on the black monitor screen above the patient: 80/58. The EKG tracing showed a regular rhythm with a rate of 132. Dr. Montgomery hurriedly instructed a second-year surgery resident on the interpretation of the ultrasound findings. He slowly moved a lubricated, handheld probe across the patient's upper abdomen.

"See, you can see the spleen here," Gene Montgomery stated as he pointed to the black-and-white shadow images on the screen beside him.

"He's got a crack right into the hilum near the splenic artery," Dr. Hanson replied.

"Exactly. He's got a lot of free fluid around the spleen as well." The chief resident applied more lubricant to the lower abdomen and reapplied the probe, directing it toward the patient's pelvis. "Lots of fluid down here as well."

Dr. Forrest interrupted. "Have you notified the O.R.?"

"Hey, Dr. Forrest, I didn't see you come in. No, I haven't called the O.R. yet. I was waiting to see what this would show." Dr. Montgomery nodded toward the ultrasound screen.

"Is his chest clear?"

"Three cracked ribs on the left. Nothing

else striking. Certainly no reason for his hypotension."

"Call the O.R., Gene. This doesn't look like a spleen we'll be able to watch without an operation," Forrest stated flatly. He then looked at the younger resident and added, "How much Oxydel has he received?"

"This is his first liter bag," Dr. Hanson replied.

"O.K., Keith. Give him one more liter of this and then get some real blood in him if his pressure stays below 100." He squeezed the pliable IV bag to accelerate the flow-rate of the fluid. In another minute Gene Montgomery was back.

"O.R. 3 will be ready in five minutes. Let's get him packaged for the trip," Dr. Montgomery snapped.

"Have his c-spines been cleared?" Brad looked at the latest blood pressure on the monitor. 94/64.

"C-spines and pelvis are both clear. An attending radiologist even looked at 'em."

"Good. I'll see you in O.R. 3," Brad replied. Then, looking at the patient, he spoke to him for the first time. "Looks like your spleen is busted up pretty bad. We need to operate to stop the bleeding."

The patient was apprehensive and very pale. "Do what you have to do," he replied.

He bit his lower lip. "Has anyone called my mother about this?"

Patty Rader, a veteran E.R. staff nurse, came to answer the boy's question. "I've tried your mom at home and at work. She's not answering yet. I'll keep trying," she added, squeezing his right hand. "Is there anyone else I can call? Maybe your father?"

The boy, James Tyson, replied with an expletive. "He won't care!"

Nurse Rader winced at the boy's language, then softened. "Maybe we should at least try. I'm sure he'd like to know that you're going to need some surgery."

The second-year surgery resident began edging the stretcher out of the trauma bay, anxious to get the patient upstairs.

"Fine. Call him then," the patient called out weakly. "He won't be at his home. C-call him at Crestview Women's and have him paged," the patient added haltingly as the pain in his abdomen stabbed through his left shoulder and shortened his breath.

Brad Forrest looked at the patient's armband for the first time. "James R. Tyson," he repeated, reading slowly. He raised his eyebrows with incredulity. "Is Dr. Weber Tyson your father?"

The patient clinched his teeth with pain and responded simply, "Yes."

Forrest shook his head in amazement. *The* Weber Tyson? He looked at the monitor as the systolic blood pressure alarm sounded. The patient's pressure was again falling. Brad Forrest looked at the nurse at his side. "Try to reach Dr. Tyson. I'd speak to him myself, but it doesn't look like we have that luxury now. This fella's tryin' to bleed out. We need to get him upstairs to the O.R. — and STAT!"

Weber Tyson stretched momentarily and tossed the now-cold paper coffee cup in the trash can under his desk. He then dictated a short letter that would be forwarded to several state congressional representatives concerning a bill to be considered in the upcoming week. In addition to his practice responsibilities, Dr. Tyson took an active role in state and local health care issues. After establishing himself as one of the premier pediatric surgeons in the Southeast, he naturally became a pediatric health care advocate, holding up the concerns of the young and advocating children's rights in the state government assembly on numerous occasions. As the official advisor to the governor on health care, he had helped to spark and fan to fruition the flame of the school-based clinic movement. Safe sex and condom distribution were well entrenched in all the school systems where Dr. Tyson's policies were touted and loved.

His quick mind made him a medical doctor; his quick hands made him a surgeon. Aging had improved his diagnostic and surgical skills, layering him with experience that only the halls of hard decision-making could bring. In spite of the massive explosion of technology that spanned his career so far, Dr. Tyson remained a practical technician, seeking to honor the fine art of physical exam and history-taking, applying an expensive test only when he knew it would change a patient's outcome. Now, facing the increasing crunch of escalating health care costs, he again relied on his practical, albeit callous, nature. He had known for many months that it was only a matter of time before the government would force him to ration expensive care. If rationing would happen in his field, he was determined to do it on his own terms and in his own time. He had been in charge for too long to tolerate acceptance of anyone's ideas other than his own.

Dr. Tyson had, in fact, instituted his own small form of health care rationing years before when he decided to concentrate his efforts on only those children who were

deemed “acceptable risks” for his delicate surgical interventions. The pediatric surgeon is often called upon to evaluate and treat the most severe of developmental abnormalities in young infants. Some infants whose abnormalities are complex present themselves as almost insurmountable challenges to the surgeon. On numerous occasions in the past, Dr. Tyson had risen to the challenge and had performed successfully. Many of his patients had thrived. A smaller number had not. As money became tighter, and as reimbursement of care for infants who lingered on in the intensive care unit lessened, Dr. Tyson had on occasion chosen to take a “conservative” approach to the treatment of some of his patients, allowing “nature to take its course,” and had withheld needed surgical therapy if he felt that the patient’s quality of life would be less than desired. In every such case Dr. Tyson had gently, and apparently compassionately, guided the parents of these infants into quiet decisions to “prevent the needless suffering” that would be caused by cruelly extending the infant’s life span. The physician was careful not to show his bias against those infants whose contributions to society would certainly fall below his standard expectation. A critical outside observer could

see the bias, but, as he was the head of his department and was given an almost universal respect by the hospital staff, his decision-making was never doubted.

The surgeon yawned and stood up, his paperwork completed for the night. *I still need to check on that pitiful Down's syndrome baby on 5 north,* Tyson muttered under his breath as he picked up his long, white lab coat. He exited his office at a brisk pace and took the service elevator to the fifth floor. He walked down the dimly lit hall to the last room, situated the greatest distance from the nursing station. He viewed a small, struggling infant, premature, weighing only four pounds, three ounces. The child, born two days before, had been moved up to this "observation room," away from the neonatal intensive care unit, late on the first day of his life. The baby, a male, suffered from Down's syndrome and duodenal atresia, a condition where the first part of the small intestine is absent or malformed and small, creating a complete bowel obstruction. The intestinal problem is easily remedied with surgical correction; the Down's syndrome is not, being associated with a lifelong mental disability, the degree of which varies significantly from individual to individual.

The child had a weak cry, soft enough

not to be of great concern to the Crestview nursing staff, most of whom spent the night hours closer to the nursing station where the child's whimpering could not be heard at all. Dr. Tyson had handpicked the staff on this floor, which had been devoted entirely to the patients of Valley Surgeons for Children.

Dr. Tyson had spoken to the patient's mother and grandmother on the day of the child's birth. "The child has multiple anomalies," Tyson had stated with apparent compassion. "He is severely retarded. His bowels are malformed. In fact, there is a segment that is absent altogether. We know that patients with this type of retardation have a shortened life span, and what life he can have will be complicated with illness. If you insist, I will perform surgery to see if the bowel problem can be corrected. I may only be prolonging this child's suffering. He will certainly not understand all of the pain that he will experience with this kind of major surgery." The teenage mother and the grandmother had expressed their concern that the child not be allowed to suffer. Dr. Tyson had urged them to consider the option of not prolonging the infant's pain, which would certainly be lifelong. The tearful teenager had been unable to reply. The maternal grandmother voiced their brief response: "Do what you think is right." Dr. Tyson had nodded with concern and agreed to transfer the patient out of the neonatal unit. The mother would never visit the child again.

Tyson looked down at the child, who was already wrinkled from dehydration. *If only your mother had the common sense to get prenatal genetic screening, you wouldn't be in this condition!*

Dr. Tyson's thoughts were interrupted by the appearance of the nursing unit's night manager.

"Up late tonight, Doctor?"

Web looked up. "Oh, hi, Tammy."

"I'm surprised at how long this one is lasting." The nurse spoke in a quiet tone. "When I saw how premature the baby was, I thought maybe he wouldn't make it the first night."

"It makes it worse for all of us," Web replied with a tight frown. The surgeon paused and sighed. He didn't feel like staying in the room any longer than necessary. He had seen that the child was still alive. Now he wanted to get out of there. He turned to go, then stopped at the doorway and turned back to his trusted nurse manager. "Make this one very comfortable."

Tammy paused, then replied softly and tersely, "Sure." She reached out and stroked the side of Tyson's arm, her hand coming to rest naturally in his open palm.

The unspoken deeper message was clearly communicated in the same way it had been many times before.

With the patient anesthetized, an assistant scrubbed his abdomen with a betadine solution as Dr. Forrest and his resident, Dr. Hanson, scrubbed their hands at the large porcelain sinks just outside O.R. 3. After they finished, they entered through the swinging door with their hands held so that the water would drip off their elbows. The scrub nurse handed Brad Forrest a sterile towel to dry his hands. He put on a sterile gown, and the nurse assisted him with a pair of sterile rubber gloves, size 7.

"Better double glove, Dr. Forrest," the resident suggested as he began placing sterile towels around the patient's abdomen, brown from the betadine paint. "Dr. Montgomery took a complete history on this patient. He's gay."

Brad nodded with understanding and put a second pair of gloves over the first. This would add one more layer of protection to prevent blood contact, blood that in this case was at increased risk of carrying the AIDS virus.

The two surgeons stood on opposite sides of the patient's abdomen. The patient was completely covered with sterile blue paper drapes except for the area that had been prepped with betadine. Dr. Forrest spoke first. "Knife," he stated, lifting his voice above the noise of the operating room. He pointed to the resident across from him as the scrub nurse lifted the instrument off of the surgical Mayo stand positioned over the patient's legs. Dr. Hanson held the knife securely and glided it across the abdomen, scoring the skin from just below the sternum to below the patient's umbilicus.

"Enough. Let's use the Bovie from here on," Dr. Forrest instructed. "We should minimize the use of all the sharps in cases where AIDS transmission is a possibility." The resident passed off the knife and continued opening the abdomen with the Bovie electrocautery unit.

The fascia was transected, and the peritoneum bulged outwards, indicating the buildup of blood from the internal injuries. Keith Hanson gently opened the delicate peritoneal lining.

"Packs!" The surgeons quickly placed dry sterile laparotomy sponges into each quadrant of the abdominal cavity to soak up the blood and tamponade off any ongoing hemorrhage. "More packs!"

"It looks like at least four units in here. What was his initial hematocrit?" Dr. Forrest inquired.

"Thirty-three, but that was before all of his IV fluid," Keith answered.

Carefully the surgeons searched the abdomen for other injuries. Finding none, they turned their attention to the left upper quadrant that was still packed off, tamponading the splenic injury that had been diagnosed by the ultrasound. After removing the packs, they gently mobilized and inspected the damaged organ. A stellate fracture deep into the hilum of the spleen produced a steady flow of blood.

Dr. Forrest gently wrapped the spleen in a dry pack and compressed it with his hand. "What should we do now?"

"Splenorrhapy or splenectomy," the resident answered.

"O.K., you know the options. You're the surgeon. What are you going to do now?" Dr. Forrest spoke in a normal tone, not a condescending one, in order to teach the junior resident.

As the resident paused for a few seconds, Forrest released the gentle pressure from the splenic capsule. Bright red blood rapidly saturated the surrounding pack. The attending surgeon reapplied the pressure. Looking over the "ether screen," Brad directed his next question to the anesthesiologist at the head of the table. "What's the blood pressure now?"

"Ninety, Brad, but it seems we're just catching up on all his blood loss," the anesthesia attending quipped rapidly.

Brad looked back at his quiet resident. "Well?" he prompted.

"I think we should take it out," the resident responded, viewing the badly lacerated and bleeding spleen.

"In someone so young?" Forrest chided, seeing if the resident would stick firmly to his decision.

"Yes," the young surgeon responded with more confidence than he felt.

"Correct. Let's do it."

The surgeons worked with coordinated precision. Within ten minutes the splenic artery and veins were ligated, and the spleen was floating in a plastic container of formalin.

"I think you can handle it from here," Forrest added, stepping away from the operating table. "Good work. You made the right choice. This patient would not have done well without you." He took off his gown and gloves, wadding both into a small ball and depositing them in a large trash bag labeled "Bio-Hazard." "I'll go look for some family."

Web Tyson looked at his watch. 11 P.M. After leaving 5 north, he had spent an hour in medical records signing overdue charts. Now, back in his office, he hung up his coat in preparation for his trip home. Just enough time to drop by Jake's Diner for some supper before heading home for a little —

The phone emitted an electronic chirp, startling Tyson from his thoughts. *What the — ? Who's calling on my private line at this hour?*

He interrupted the second ring. "Dr. Tyson."

"Web! It's me!" The voice on the other end was frantic and female.

"Libby?"

The caller didn't respond to his question, but her next statement confirmed he was right. He had heard his ex-wife this excited only once before.

"Jimmy's been in a wreck! I've been tryin' to page you but couldn't get through! You're not at home either!" Libby Brumfield exclaimed, stating what was only too obvious to the now-alarmed surgeon.

Tyson looked at the beeper clipped to his belt. The button on the side of the pager was in the Off position, just as it had been since 8 P.M. when he'd checked out to one of his junior partners. He was immediately defensive. "I don't even have my pager on. I'm not on call!" He shook his head, refocusing on the more important news. "Tell me about Jimmy."

"He's just out of surgery. The surgeon says he had to remove his spleen."

"Surgeon! Where is he?"

"Bridgewater University Medical Center. It was the closest place."

Web sighed from relief, not from frustration.

Libby misinterpreted his audible exhalation. "I suppose you don't think they're qualified?"

"No, it's not that. I —"

"The surgeon, Dr. Bradley Forrest, was quite knowledgeable. He explained everything to me."

"I don't doubt his competence, Lib." He paused, thinking, *Since when did you become an expert on surgical knowledge? You'd like any doctor that smiled in a compassionate way.* Tyson continued, "In fact, I'm glad he's at the U. If Jimmy were here, news about his other problem would certainly get around." He paused again, then added, "No, I'm quite certain it's best that he stay up there. He'll be less likely to attract all the attention that having my son in the hospital at Crestview would stir up."

Libby stifled her desire to reply, *All you have ever cared about is your reputation. If you'd have shown the boy a little love once in a while, perhaps he wouldn't have his little "problem" as you call it!* She managed to return to her previous thought-train. "He's in the intensive care unit, Web." *At least you could ask how he is!* "Dr. Forrest said he'll need to be monitored closely for bleeding."

Dr. Tyson paused and lowered his voice. "How is he, Lib?"

"They say he's going to be O.K." She wanted so much to be strong in front of her former husband. She bit her lower lip to stop its quivering. "He looks so helpless, Web. He still isn't awake completely from the anesthetic, so he hasn't responded to me yet."

"I'm sure he'll be fine. Do you want me to come up?" The surgeon sighed and put on his overcoat, balancing the receiver between his left shoulder and ear. "I'm not sure he'd want to see me tonight."

"I don't need you," Libby replied curtly. "But it might be nice if you'd show up for Jimmy's sake." She paused, looking blankly at the large automatic doors that led to the surgical ward where her son was located.

"Look, Lib. It's after 11," Tyson replied with a sigh. "He's not likely to even know anyone before morning." *She's too emotionally wrapped up in this to understand my professional objectivity,* he thought silently. "I'll come by in the morning before rounds. My first case isn't until 9:30 A.M., so I should have a brief window to see him then."

You sound like you're scheduling a patient visit. This is your only son, remember? Libby Brumfield squelched her thoughts. She sighed and replied with obvious irritation, "Fine."

"Good-bye, Lib." Dr. Tyson spoke in a condescending, sing-song tone. *Spare me the emotional garbage, woman! That's one thing I'm glad not to have to deal with since you left.*

Click! Libby hung up the phone with more force than she'd intended. She then turned and fell into the supporting, strong arms of John Brumfield, her youthful husband since the previous autumn.

CHAPTER 3

Lenore Kingsley knew the value of worship. Even though this was only to be a brief planning session involving the inner circle, she wanted to set the tone by making it very clear who was to be praised for the success they had experienced thus far. The meeting had been called on short notice, too short for the preparation of any sacrifices. That didn't worry Lenore. She would enhance the session with ritual desecration of her enemy's holy symbols.

The group of four stood quietly on the bank of the Wanoset River, their faces dimly lit by the full moon that pierced through a thin fog that had settled in a few minutes before, at 2 A.M. The wind, which before had been steady, had fled, allowing the participants to keep their candles at arm's length without fear of the flames blowing out. All was quiet except for the gentle lapping of the waves of the Wanoset. The nearest highway was rarely traveled at this hour, and even that stood a full half-mile from the river's edge, with the distance in between thickly forested with tall southern pines.

Lenore Kingsley led the session with practiced majesty. Her flowing, deep purple hooded robe disguised her slender frame as she slowly circled a small wooden table while lifting her hands in obvious tribute to her lord. She began singing softly, chanting praises of thanks to the one who owned her. She pirouetted quickly, the skirt of her robe lifting slightly as she turned. The priestess continued, elevating her voice so that the men who were with her could hear and understand her intention for them to join her.

The men echoed her prayers into the dark fog.

Lenore hissed softly and bowed low with her hands outstretched.

The three responded with matching volume and movement.

The men mirrored her actions, kneeling before a six-inch-thick stained wood table that sat just off of the sandy shoreline in a grove of pines.

The leader slowly stood and stepped forward to the wooden altar in front of the others, who remained motionless in adoration. On the thick, scarred wooden table sat a silver goblet, a loaf of bread, and a small, inverted wooden cross. She ascended two small steps that led to the stained tabletop, lifting the skirt of her garment as she stepped.

The men arose spontaneously, invigorated and ready to hear the reasons they had been called.

Julie Forrest yawned and looked at the alarm clock. 6 A.M. The covers on Brad's side of the bed had been turned back by the sleepy surgeon thirty minutes before. Brad had gently kissed his wife's golden hair and hurried back to the University Medical Center for a pediatric surgery conference. Julie stretched beneath the worn quilt that had adorned the Forrests' bed since their wedding fourteen years ago. Her hand searched the space beside her that was normally occupied by Brad and sighed. The sheets were cool, the heat from her husband's body long gone. She tried to remember talking to him the night before. It had been past midnight, and she'd been too tired to be mad. She had kept her informal dinner party plans, but the evening had been spoiled for Julie, who had planned on leaving the grilling to Brad. Bradley had spilled iced tea all over the dining room rug, Julie burned the grilled pork chops while cleaning up the tea spill, and their German shepherd pup chewed up her best pair of Nike running shoes. By the time Brad had come home, she was too exhausted to acknowledge his arrival. Too tired to talk, she had feigned sleep when he tiptoed in and collapsed beside her. Now she seemed wide awake. Hearing Brad's grandmother downstairs, she slipped on her robe and quietly descended the steps to the kitchen below.

Julie stopped on the last step and viewed the white-haired woman sitting in the rocking chair beside the woodstove. At age eighty-two, Grandma Forrest had experienced some of life's best and worst. She was strong, a true warrior in the spiritual sense, spending at least an hour each morning in that very rocker, with her Bible open in her lap, praying over her family and the concerns that were brought to her by a dozen different sources. The old saint was sure her gift of intercession had not been wasted, and as far as Julie knew, Grandma Forrest had never missed this part of her morning routine. Julie rolled her eyes unconsciously, her body language reflecting the fact that this kind of personal relationship with a loving, communicating God was foreign to her own experience. Although she wasn't really jealous of the older woman's devotion, Julie felt gently convicted every time she witnessed her grandmother-in-law's daily faithfulness.

Grandma Forrest, or Belle as everyone called her, sat unaware of her observer. She quietly and steadily vocalized her requests and listened for several moments before opening the worn leather cover of the book in her lap. "Belle" was short for "Annabelle," the name given her by her own grandmother. As long as she remembered, she'd been known by the shorter name, and everyone, even her great-grandson, called her that. It was the name Julie used to greet her as she stepped into the room now.

"Belle, you're up early," Julie said quietly.

"I couldn't seem to rest this morning."

"Not another vision keeping you awake, I hope."

Belle ignored the younger woman's jab. "No, child," she replied. "A burden for prayer. Someone needs my support this morning."

Julie didn't seem interested in comprehending Belle's communication and went about busily fixing her morning beverage. "Coffee?" she said as she placed a cup on a saucer and held it out toward Belle.

"Thank you," Belle replied, motioning for Julie to set the coffee on the kitchen table. She then stood and walked to the front door of the old Victorian home. The *Valley Daily News* struck the oak door just as she opened it. "Good shot, Sammy!" the white-haired woman called out after a wiry teenager who was already heading for the next house.

"Morning, Belle!" the paperboy yelled as he threw the neighbor's paper against the front door with a thud.

Belle's wrinkled hands deftly undid the rubber band around the paper and began scanning the front page, holding the paper out at arm's length to read. "Oh me," she moaned softly. "My, oh, my."

Julie looked over at her. "What's up, Belle?"

"Take a gander at this." The elder woman spoke with an accent that pinpointed her southern country roots.

SURGEON GENERAL APPOINTEE SOUTHERLY FOUND DEAD

Paul Southerly, M.D. was found dead yesterday, the day his confirmation hearings were slated to begin. Dr. Southerly, the only pro-life appointee of the Blackburn Administration and a known diabetic with epilepsy, apparently died in his sleep. An investigation and coroner's report is pending, but at this time no foul play is expected. Funeral arrangements . . .

Julie read the article as Belle emptied an artificial sweetener packet into her coffee. "It says a congressional aide went out to his home when he failed to show up for the hearings. He called the police when Southerly's car was found in the driveway and no one answered the door."

"He seemed like a good man. I think he knew the Savior," Belle said slowly, stirring her coffee.

Julie didn't respond. She turned to the comic page and pushed the remainder of the paper across the table toward Belle. Finally she stood and headed back to the stairs. "I'm going to get Bradley up. He only has school for a half-day today because of parent-teacher conferences. Can you watch him for me this afternoon?"

"Sure," Belle replied. "Maybe I'll even go down to the bridge with him today. He's been wanting to show me the fishing hole his dad discovered."

Julie shook her head as she climbed the stairs. *Just where does she get her energy?*

Web Tyson entered his access number on the keypad on the dashboard of his new

Mercedes. The decorative steel gate at the end of his driveway opened, and Tyson pulled out onto the quiet, tree-lined cul-de-sac. He yawned, took a sip of black coffee from the large cup beside him, and pressed the accelerator toward the floor. The houses in Tyson's neighborhood were massive and widely spaced, each with three or more garages hiding foreign luxury cars or a sport utility vehicle or two. No one else left this street before Tyson, who rarely left his residence after 6 A.M. This morning he hurried along a full forty-five minutes ahead of schedule, determined to visit his son before beginning his routine operating day. Normally he listened to his favorite classical music on CD. Today he traveled in silence, quietly wrestling with his own thoughts.

He thought about Jimmy, his only son, lying in a hospital bed . . . again. He had been hospitalized once before, just the previous winter, with pneumonia, the result of a poor nutritional state and alcohol abuse, having aspirated his own vomit during a drunken stupor. Web had not spoken to his son since that time. He suspected that his son had AIDS, but the serum tests had been unexpectedly negative.

Web thought back over his broken relationship with his son, the son he found impossible to love. Born during the decade of Web's surgical training, Jimmy had little to no contact with his father during his first eight years. He spent some time with a male butler, but really had no strong male role model to help shape his identity. Once Web began private practice, the little extra time he had at home to spend with Jimmy was ruined by Web's continuous perfectionist criticism. Jimmy drew even farther from his father during his teen years, and he spent every summer at an exclusive New England camp, glad only to be away from his demanding father. It was there he found love and acceptance from an older, gay camp counselor. After two summers of "love" with Dave, Jimmy finally told his parents about his homosexual feelings.

Web winced at the memory of his own response. After a fiery shouting match, he had grounded his son for two weeks. Later Web forced his son to ingest an old trunk full of heterosexual pornographic magazines that he had secretly kept hidden away since his college days. "This ought to straighten you out," Web had stated flatly after depositing the trunk in the middle of Jimmy's room. Instead, Jimmy was only further confused and repulsed by the distorted stereotypes he saw portrayed within the glossy covers. He withdrew and didn't speak to his father for a month. After two additional years of noncommunication with his father, Jimmy moved out, settling in with a friend across town and working nights serving tables in a gay bar.

Now Web had only regrets, feeling deeply the loss of the relationship for which he had once hoped. At first Web felt responsible, even guilty, for raising a son who would make such choices. He would later deny the possibility that his dysfunctional relationship with his son could have affected Jimmy's sexual preferences. He would insist that the search for a gay gene would show without a doubt that his son was born that way, that his outcome was merely a reflection of his DNA. Regardless of the cause, the relationship had never healed, and now, Web feared, it never would.

It's good Jimmy isn't at Crestview, Web mused to himself. *Everyone would be talking. He's so open about his lifestyle, it's embarrassing.* The surgeon glanced at the digital clock on the dashboard. *I've got to make this quick, so I can get back to Crestview in time for my first case.* He thought for a few seconds more and spoke a message for his car phone: "Dial Bridgewater University Medical Center." The phone worked perfectly, responding to the verbal command. A few seconds later he heard the line pick up.

"Bridgewater University Medical Center. How may I help you?" The female voice was pleasant.

Dr. Tyson didn't feel like offering pleasantries. "Page Dr. Forrest. This is Dr. Tyson."

"Yes sir, Doctor. Can you hold the line?"

"I'll wait," Tyson grumbled, signaling to turn left onto University Boulevard.

Dr. Brad Forrest sipped the black coffee slowly as he listened to the chief resident on the pediatric surgery service drone on and on about tracheoesophageal fistulas in the neonate. *How many times have I heard this discussion?* he thought sleepily. His head had just begun to nod when his pager emitted its vibration, startling him to alertness. He looked at its message: "222-5000." The "222" stood for physician waiting. The "5000" was the operator's extension. *Who could this be?* Brad slipped out of the conference room, picked up the phone on the nurse's desk across the hall, and dialed the operator.

"Operator."

"Dr. Forrest. I was paged."

"Thank you, Doctor. I'll put you through to your call."

Brad listened a moment as the line was connected.

"Dr. Forrest? Dr. Web Tyson here. I'm on my way to see my son, Jimmy Tyson. He's a patient of yours, I understand."

"I helped take care of him last night." *Dr. Tyson! I can't believe he's calling me!*

"How is Jimmy?" Tyson asked while turning into the hospital parking deck.

"He's fine. He lost quite a lot of blood before his surgery, but he had a stable night. He looks like he will be okay." *You've got to be the best pediatric surgeon in the state. And you're calling me to find out how I treated your son.*

"Good. Good," Tyson repeated nervously. "Say, Dr. Forrest — there's something about Jimmy you should know. I'd appreciate it if you'd keep this quiet." Tyson pulled into a parking slot and turned off the key, pausing in his conversation to look at himself in the rearview mirror. He straightened his tie. "Jimmy's gay."

Brad was taken back by the statement. He knew the patient was gay. He hadn't really thought twice about it. *Is this why you're calling me?* "I am aware of that. Is there anything else we need to know?"

"No. I just wanted to be sure you were aware of the AIDS risk."

"Jimmy has the AIDS virus?" Brad thought back to the operation, trying to remember if there had been any direct blood contact.

"No. That is, not that I know of. I think testing for the virus would be appropriate, though."

"Sure," Brad nodded. "I'll pass this information on to the trauma team. I was really only covering for the trauma service to fill in for someone else. Dr. Braxton will be handling his case from now on."

"Please don't pass this information on to anyone but those involved in my son's case. You know how people like to talk — especially about those of us in the limelight so frequently."

"Of course, Dr. Tyson. It's a matter of medical confidentiality. I'll treat it like any other medical information that I gather about my patients."

That seemed to satisfy Tyson. He didn't care to have his own solid reputation tarnished by his only son and the gossip that surrounded him. "Thanks, Dr. Forrest. I'd like to thank you in person sometime."

"I'm glad to help, sir."

Tyson was just about to hang up, then

added, "You say you were only filling in for someone else? What is your normal role around the university?"

"Pediatric surgery fellow. I'm in my last year and am already boarded in general surgery. Because of that, I fill in on the adult general and trauma surgery services on occasion — like last night."

"Pediatric surgery?" Tyson was taken back. "Like me?"

"Like you, sir."

Tyson shook his head. "I will have to meet you someday, Dr. Forrest. Perhaps I'll run into you at one of the weekly teaching conferences."

"I-it would be my honor, sir," Brad stuttered incredulously.

"Thanks for your time. And thanks again for your part in helping Jimmy."

Brad Forrest was about to say, "Thanks" when he heard a *click* followed by the dial tone.

At United Biotechnical Industries, everyone called Lenore Kingsley "Doctor." She was, in fact, ready to sit in defense of her doctoral thesis in pharmaceutical chemistry, but had little time or need for it. Though she had not obtained a Ph.D. degree, she cared little about pursuing it, and she had long ago stopped correcting her employees when they honored her with the title "doctor."

"Morning, Doc!" Sam, the security officer, called out as Lenore passed his desk in the plush lobby of UBI.

"Hi, Sam." Lenore walked through a set of heavy metal doors at the rear of the lobby. Immediately she looked into a small blue box mounted on the wall to her right. She stood still, her gaze fixed on a pinpoint of red light emitted by the retinal scanning device. In a fraction of a second, a second set of double doors were unlocked as the scanner recognized the specific pattern of blood vessels crossing her retina and identified her as Lenore Kingsley. The computer screen beside the scanner displayed the message, "Welcome, Dr. Kingsley." Even the security computer called her "Doctor."

Lenore read the second message printed below the first. "Please see Randy in Lab 62." *The human genome lab. Maybe Randy has finally made some headway in our latest project!* The thought excited Lenore, and for a moment she forgot how tired she was because of last night's "planning session" of the inner circle.

Of course, very few at UBI knew about the inner circle. Lenore intended to keep it that way. Her tiredness would be attributed to late hours researching her latest projects.

Lenore stood for a moment contemplating the screen's message, then punched the Received button and pushed through the now unlocked double metal doors to the offices and laboratories beyond.

She stood five feet, ten inches tall, her build slender, her nature a composite of drivenness and tact. She wore her hair long, often in one simple, black braid while she worked in the lab, just to keep it out of her way. She had been with UBI for fourteen years, since nearly completing her Ph.D. program at Fulkner Institute. Her father, Gardner Henry Kingsley, had founded UBI a few years before that. But the company had thrived because of the work of his only daughter, Lenore. Gardner Kingsley had devoted his life to the development of safe, over-the-counter medications for treatment of hay fever. He first worked for another firm in Arkansas, then moved his family north when the opportunity to start his own company arose. Lenore had brought needed diversity to UBI. Her crowning achievement had come just four years ago in the development of a product known as Oxydel.

Oxydel, an artificial blood substitute named for its ability to deliver oxygen, had virtually changed the need for blood transfusions overnight. Oxydel contained a synthetic hemoglobin molecule within a microscopic biomembrane capsule. It carried none of the infection transmission risks that come with human red cell transfusions, did not need to be crossmatched, and had a significantly longer shelf life than human blood. Its use had become so common that now the only time real blood was transfused was in cases where additional molecules responsible for clotting were needed. These clotting factors were not yet available in the Oxydel solution; so in cases where massive blood loss was encountered, Oxydel was given to substitute for lost red cells, and real blood or plasma was given for clotting or coagulation factors.

With the incredible reception of its product, United Biotechnical Industries quickly became a multibillion-dollar corporation. Gardner Kingsley rewarded Lenore by making her the president, while he maintained the position of C.E.O. UBI's financial success freed the company from reliance on government grant money for research and allowed Lenore to pursue riskier research endeavors. She had steered a large portion of the company's research and development monies into production of a wide line of genetics testing materials. Paralleling the development of new genetics tests, UBI had entered into the race of identifying and patenting human genes. As a new gene was discovered, UBI would quickly produce a prepackaged lab test that could test for the specific gene that had been discovered. These test kits could be marketed to labs, hospitals, and physicians who provided genetic screening to their patients. It would only be a matter of a few years before the entire human genome or DNA content would be known, and UBI fully intended to capitalize on this knowledge.

Lenore walked past her receptionist and her administrative assistant without speaking. She wasn't in the mood for light conversation; she had some thinking to do, and she didn't want to be distracted. Ms. Kingsley slid in behind her antique teak desk and entered an eight-digit code on her computer keyboard. She quickly accessed a file that brought her daily planner onto the screen. When she saw the day's date, she sighed. *The first of the month again! Time is slipping by so fast. Oxydel's patent isn't going to last forever. When that expires, this place had better be ready with another chart-breaker or be ready to face a bleak economic future!*

A tight-lipped smirk crossed the woman's

face. She thought back to the planning session held on the shore of the Wanoset. *But we'll be ready. I'll see to it that the money keeps right on rollin' in. People will know that UBI is here to stay. And I'll take all the credit. My master wills it that way. He has promised.*

Patient report had taken longer than usual. The youthful-appearing nurse completed the sign-out information to the next charge nurse coming on for day shift, grabbed her gym bag, and made a purposefully noisy exit toward the main elevators. She then silently entered the stairwell and descended one flight. She walked the length of the nearly empty orthopedic ward to the back stairwell and climbed up again to 5 north. Pausing to catch her breath, she listened for sounds of anyone in the back hallway. Hearing no one, she silently pulled open the metal door. The back stairwell was situated just across from the last patient room, which was a good seventy-five feet from the nurses' station.

The nurse entered the last room and closed the door behind her. Quickly she turned over the struggling infant and located the heparin lock, a small IV that had been capped off and flushed with an anticoagulant to keep it open in case access to the patient's blood was needed. The heparin lock was located in the baby's upper left arm. Slowly she pushed a needle into the heparin lock and pushed in two cc's of clear fluid. She noticed the skin over the IV site swelling a little when the medication was injected. *It looks like this IV has infiltrated! Oh well, this will be effective even if it's not given directly into the vein.* The infant cried once, then ceased moving altogether. In two minutes there was no respiratory effort at all. The nurse stared at the lifeless form for a few moments before stepping slowly away and reaching for the closed door. The door flew open quickly just as she was about to touch it. Suddenly she stood face to face with an elderly woman delivering breakfast trays.

"Oh! —"

"Scared you, didn't I?" The gray-haired woman smiled at the obviously startled professional. When the smile wasn't returned, she added, "I didn't mean to alarm you. I'm just here with breakfast."

"Breakfast? This patient doesn't get anything by mouth!"

The aide looked at the card on the food tray she had in her hand. "Room 524," she read slowly and then, looking directly above the nurse's head, said, "and this is . . .

Room 525. Well, what do you know! I'm going into the wrong room!" She turned and took the tray into the room next door. "Breakfast time!"

Behind her, the nurse stealthily slipped back into the stairwell and closed the heavy door. She leaned against the wall and focused on quieting her breathing. She wiped her forehead with her white coat sleeve, her thoughts spinning. *What's wrong with me! I'm doing the right thing!* She instinctively reached for her own radial pulse at her wrist and looked at her watch. *120. Get ahold of yourself, girl!* The stairwell was quiet except for her respirations that came in rapid, shallow gulps. The temperature was notably warmer, as the stairwell was not air-conditioned. *You've never reacted like this. Why were you so scared? It was only Dietary. She didn't see anything! Besides, you are only doing the right thing — eliminating suffering.* "Eliminating suffering," she whispered, breaking the silence of the damp air around her. She nodded her head in response to her own affirmation. *I don't want to let Web down either.*

She waited a few moments longer, her fingers still monitoring her own pulse-rate. *There, down to 96. I've got to get out of here!* She straightened suddenly, descended the five flights to the ground floor, and exited at a near jog into the parking lot beyond.

Dr. Web Tyson stepped slowly into the critical care cubicle where his son slept. He silently pulled back the curtain bordering his son's bed. Above his head, a tangle of IV tubing and cardiac monitoring wires hung motionless. Below him, the containers of his body fluids, one for urine, another for gastric secretions, were easily visible for making careful recordings of his outputs for each hour. At the foot of the bed a pneumatic compression pump whirred softly, inflating the small bladders held against Jimmy's lower legs, to prevent dangerous venous clots from forming. In the center of it all, Jimmy seemed almost suspended, his breathing slow and regular, his pain anesthetized with a narcotic that also clouded his ability to receive and interpret sensory input. Dr. Tyson had seen hundreds of other patients in conditions much worse, but the emotion he felt now . . . This puzzled him, and he wanted to divert his eyes away from the evidences of his son's condition.

Web reached out but stopped short of taking his son's hand. He had never been much for physical displays of affection. He leaned closer to the head of Jimmy's hospital bed.

"Jimmy . . ." He found his voice weak, almost a whisper. "Jimmy . . ." he repeated with a deliberate increase in volume.

Jimmy moaned softly, his mind dulled by the last dose of morphine that had been given only moments before his father's arrival. He slowly opened his eyes but did not speak. A barely perceptible increase in his heart rate on the monitor was the only witness that Jimmy recognized his unexpected visitor. The pediatric surgeon sighed, looked at the clock on the wall above his son's bed, and walked to the central nurses' station.

"May I see my son's chart?" It was not a request.

The clerk behind the counter was taken back. "Sir, it isn't customary to release the patient information to anyone except the patient or his caregivers."

"I happen to be a physician. Really, I just want to check on his progress. He is too sleepy to wake up and talk to me." He walked around to the small chart rack behind the counter.

The clerk understood that it was not in her best interest to stand in his way. She remained seated and pretended not to notice.

Dr. Tyson scanned the chart, paying particular notice to the detailed dictation by the attending physician, Dr. Brad Forrest. Tyson was impressed by the completeness and organization of the note. It was easily apparent that his son was in competent hands. Tyson grunted. He was used to this kind of work coming from himself and was ultracritical of many of his associates for doing incomplete workups. He could muster up none of his routine complaints for the way his son was being treated. He knew the work at Crestview Women's to be topnotch. But now he was seeing that Bridgewater University also had some talented professionals. Honestly, he was slightly surprised, and he immediately felt a twinge of jealousy, an emotion that he felt rarely. With his handpicked staff at Crestview, that was an emotion he hoped to keep at bay indefinitely. Slowly he noted and memorized his son's vital signs, urine output, hematocrit, and other morning labs. Everything appeared in order.

Tyson checked his watch again, closed the chart, and strode quickly to the automatic doors to exit the unit.

Julie Forrest exited the red-brick school building and walked slowly to her car, a

1978 Chevy Nova. The right rear tire sagged visibly lower than the other three. Julie saw it as she slipped in behind the steering wheel. *Great! That's all I need.* She ran her hand over the torn upholstery of the front bench seat and sighed. *If only Brad had time to maintain the cars like he should!*

She drove two blocks to Willard's Exxon and pulled up to the open bay. A short, bald man responded with a smile and said, "Morning, Ms. Forrest. Looks like you've picked up a nail or somethin'."

Julie looked back at the man, who had a black grease spot right at the top of his rather pointed head. *He must have stood up under a greasy car,* Julie mused as she returned his smile. "Can you fix it for me?"

"Just pull 'er into the open spot there."

Julie obeyed, then, eyeing the small park across the street, said, "I'll be back in a few." With that, she headed across the street and began to walk a paved fitness course that was empty except for an older man in a gray jogging suit.

The small incident with the tire had opened up a small torrent of thoughts for Julie, all centered around Brad and the current state of their sagging relationship. *That tire isn't the only thing around here that's lost some air,* she mused, stopping to pick up a small, rounded stone. *The life seems to have left my relationship with Brad, too.*

The light filtering through the large pine trees highlighted her golden hair that hung shoulder-length, thick and naturally wavy. Julie McIntyre Forrest had inherited more from her Irish grandmother than the few freckles that graced her small nose and high cheeks. She possessed a fierce independence, the sort that made her worry if any marriage relationship would ever work for her. However, her independence had proved beneficial during the last decade of her husband's training. Without Brad around for more than a waking hour or two every few days, Julie had pretty much mastered the life of a surgery widow.

Julie thought about the early days of their courtship and marriage. *We were so in love then . . . and so young.* They had married midway through college and had struggled together to balance work, school, and their commitment to each other. Somehow neither their financial status, the endless diet of rice, beans, and potatoes, or the pressures of their schoolwork could dampen their enthusiasm for the love blossoming between them. Julie smiled when she remembered how Brad would leave poems hidden inside the box of her favorite cereal. Julie never considered herself a "morning person," but this juvenile trick of Brad's always brought a giggle or two. *He was so silly! He would do anything for me . . . for us! He was . . . is,* she corrected herself, *so handsome.* Neither she nor Brad had ever suffered for lack of potential dates, but the competition for Brad's eye had not been particularly difficult. Once she had caught his attention, Brad had fallen hard — lock, stock, and barrel, and the two were bound by a love that, by anyone's guess, would last forever.

Medical school, surgical residency, research, and now pediatric surgery fellowship had provided long years with little time for Brad to renew his love for Julie. Now Bradley, Jr. required so much of Julie's time that she felt she had little to give to anyone else. The love that everyone thought was an eternal bond had gotten lost in the daily shuffle of life's pressures.

Do I love him anymore? She threw a stone against a nearby tree. Julie couldn't seem to answer her own question. She finished a lap on the fitness course and looked across the street at her green Nova. *All of our college friends moved into nice homes long ago. They have new cars and savings accounts. All I have is an old Chevy Nova and a husband whose training seems to go on forever.*

Her thoughts were interrupted by Mr. Willard's calling her from across the street. "Ms. Forrest!" He waved a greasy red rag toward her car. "She's all fixed up again."

If he could only do the same for my marriage! Julie bit her lower lip to keep it from quivering as she crossed the street.

CHAPTER 4

Although Lenore Kingsley still ruled the research teams in the labs at UBI, she found herself continuously pulled away into business-related concerns, especially when it came time to chart the company's future. This day was no different as she sat in her plush office sorting through her in-box.

Barb Peterson, Lenore's secretary, spoke softly through the intercom. "Bill Stedman's on the phone. He wants to speak to you. He's being too vague about the reason. What should I tell him?"

Lenore sighed. *It's starting, and it's not even 9 o'clock yet.* "I'll talk to him." Bill Stedman was one of forty-six attorneys employed full-time by UBI. Most of them worked at smoothing the occasionally rough legal climate associated with new pharmaceutical products; others worked in malpractice issues; others managed the retirement plans of the employees. Increasingly, Lenore Kingsley used them to fight important civil rights battles that applied directly to the application of UBI's products.

UBI's president picked up the phone. "What is it, Bill?" she snorted.

Stedman was undaunted by her lack of a salutation. He hadn't gotten as far as he had by allowing small things to offend him. "Good morning, Lenore." Stedman paused. Lenore ignored him, so he went on, "I think I've found a case that might interest you. I'd like to get a team on it if I can guarantee UBI's backing."

"Look, Bill, I'm busy. If this is just another —"

"Hear me out, Lenore! It's a wrongful-life suit — the kind you said you said you'd love to support!"

Lenore shifted in her seat. She was listening now and picked up a pen to jot down an idea or two.

Stedman continued, "It's a kid over in Green County — just over the mountain from here. He's suing the obstetrician who delivered him. It turns out he's blind and has cystic fibrosis. His life sounds like one big ball of suffering. His sister had CF as well."

"I'm not sure what this has to do with —"

Stedman interrupted again. "The obstetrician didn't offer the mother prenatal testing, Lenore! The kid says his mother will testify that if she would have been given the opportunity to have the child tested before birth, she would have had him aborted." The lawyer paused, and again Lenore kept silent. He went on, "Both of his conditions could have been detected before birth, Lenore. He is arguing that he should have never been allowed to live in the first place — that his is a 'wrongful life.' I know it sounds like it has little to do with us, but the potential benefits to us could be enormous. Even if we lose, the media can be manipulated into their usual frenzy, and we will have obstetricians all over the country running scared and ordering prenatal genetic testing on every pregnant female around, just to avoid potential lawsuits."

"Tests that are developed and marketed by UBI," Lenore replied with a thin smile.

"Bingo."

"Bingo," Lenore echoed.

"Does this mean I can pursue it?"

"Listen, Bill, I know it sounds a lot like cases I said we'd like to support, but there've been at least a dozen important cases we've ended up backing in the last quarter. We need to be selective." She paused. "And we need to act from behind the scenes. No one is to know that UBI is supporting this."

Stedman winced. "Of course, of course. Secrecy has always been rule number one." He was growing impatient. "If it makes any difference, I found this out through my brother. The kid has hired someone from his firm to handle this. I just thought I might be able to spring a couple of our rookies free to do some legwork for them. We'll end up being served by this one, win or lose."

"Is the *Harris vs. Boland Biomedical* case complete?"

"It will be next week."

"O.K. If we have the manpower to help him and our other work is still being done, let them have a few of our guys for a while. But remember to get some info to the media. This case needs some public hype to work for us. Just keep UBI's name clean. Understood?"

"Completely."

Lenore paused. "Thanks, Bill."

Stedman was relieved by her acceptance of his proposal. Just as he was about to hang up, he added, "You know, Lenore, as good as you are at manipulating public opinion, maybe you should see what you can do about swinging the government's policies in our favor."

Kingsley laughed heartily, then became

suddenly sober again. "We could use a few people in Washington who understand the need for the type of work we do, couldn't we?" *If you only knew what plans I have already made — and executed.* She stifled her thoughts, knowing she could not share her plans indiscriminately outside of the inner circle. "Goodbye, Stedman."

"Goodbye, Lenore."

His family's mood was celebratory even though Brad Forrest wasn't home for dinner . . . again. A four and a half pound catfish had been skinned and filleted, and the aroma of the frying fish permeated the air. Belle lifted homemade hush puppies from the pan, and Julie filled a ceramic bowl with coleslaw. Bradley set the table, or at least attempted to do so while still carrying around his fishing pole that he had refused to set down since returning to the house nearly two hours before. He had shown up with the fish in one hand, his pole in the other, and a very out-of-breath Belle dragging in behind him.

"That would be easier if you just put the pole down for a while," Julie said with a smile as she dodged the end of Bradley's fishing pole.

Bradley frowned.

"Look, you can't hold it while you eat the fish anyway. I'll draw the line there. You can put it beside your chair so it will be close by."

That seemed to satisfy him, and he carefully put the pole down beside his chair and emphatically stated, "There!" Because of his thick tongue the word actually came out sounding like "Dare!"

Bradley went quickly back to his "job." To assist him in table setting, his mother had used an old wooden tray on which she traced the outline of a plate, fork, knife, spoon, and drinking glass. Bradley first carefully put each item on the tray, as if he were completing a puzzle, and then carried the tray to the table and took each item off one by one to reproduce the table setting on the old oak table. He repeated this four times so a place was set for him, his mother and father, and Belle. "When can we eat?"

"I'm almost done, Bradley. I just need a plate for these fillets." Belle put the fish on a ceramic serving plate and set it on the table. "Supper's on."

Bradley sat down with a bump and reached for his lemonade. Suddenly he stopped and looked at his mother. "I want to say the prayer. Belle's been teachin' me."

Julie looked at Belle.

Belle encouraged him, "Go ahead, son. You know how."

Bradley bowed his head and clasped his stubby fingers together. "Dear F-father God, thank you for my f-fish." He stopped momentarily and opened his eyes and then continued until he had named every food item on the table. Julie began to shift in her seat. Their German shepherd pup barked at the back door. Bradley was undaunted. He continued by listing the people he was thankful for, beginning with his mom and Belle and his teachers and last of all his father. Brad slipped in the kitchen door just as Bradley concluded, ". . . and help Daddy find a job so he can eat at home."

Bradley looked up at Belle, who prompted him, "In Jesus' —"

Bradley finished rapidly, ". . . name, amen!"

"Amen," Brad added from his position just inside the screen door.

"Daddy!"

Julie looked up with a smile. "Just in time."

"Daddy, I caught a f-f-fish!"

Belle motioned for him to sit down. "Bradley set a place for you. We're just about to begin."

Brad sat as instructed and proceeded to

enjoy firsts and seconds of the best catfish and hush puppies he'd tasted in years. It was the first time in two weeks that he had been home for supper with the family. In addition to eating, he listened to Bradley tell about catching the fish at least seven times. Julie finally reminded her son of his fish lying untouched on his plate. Bradley reluctantly turned his attention to devouring his catch and allowed the rest of the family a chance to talk.

It wasn't until late in the night, before retiring, that Julie brought up the subject of Bradley's prayer. "Did you notice your son praying tonight?"

"He was cute. I thought he might not quit there for a minute."

"He was more than cute, Brad. He was serious! He wants his daddy home for dinner more often."

Brad began his usual protest, "Julie, I —" and then stopped when he saw the moisture in Julie's eyes. He turned his eyes to the floor and then slowly walked to the bathroom to brush his teeth. Julie followed.

"Did you give Dr. Dixon your acceptance?" Dr. Dixon was the chairman of pediatric surgery at Bridgewater University. He had asked Brad to stay on after his residency was completed. As an assistant professor in the department of surgery, Brad would take on a new role as pediatric surgery attending.

Brad knew Julie wasn't crazy about him staying at the university. She had grown very jealous of all of the demands his work there had put on their lives so far, and she didn't look pleasurably at the idea of more. Brad also knew it was the best offer he had. Private practice jobs in pediatric surgery were few and far between. Most were in big cities, places where neither Julie nor he wanted to live. The university offered job security as long as he was willing to do additional research within his field.

Brad spat his mouthwash into the sink. "I haven't given him a final answer yet." Brad still avoided eye contact. "He said he needs to have a word by the middle of next month."

Brad wasn't up for a fight, but Julie was. "I don't even care much about me anymore, Brad. You know, I've learned to fend for myself by now. But I'm concerned for Bradley. Don't disappoint his prayers! He needs to have you at home at least once in a while." Brad sighed. Julie continued, "Did you see how he brightened up tonight while you were here? This is the happiest he's been in weeks."

Brad offered a weak protest. "He was excited about catching a fish."

"He was excited about having you home!"

Brad sighed again. "Look, Julie, I'm tired. You know we agreed not to start serious conversations after 11 P.M. We never solve anything when we're tired."

"It's the only time you're available anymore."

"O.K., O.K., I give. What do you want?" Brad hoped his passive stance would take the fire out of Julie's fight.

"Just give Bradley's prayer for a different job a chance to be answered."

"And when did you start taking such an interest in prayers?" Brad's words stung, and as soon as they were out, he turned his head to the floor again, regretting the lack of restraint in his own tongue.

Julie didn't flinch. Instead, amazingly, she softened. "I — I don't know, Brad. It's just that . . . Well, maybe I wish I could believe that his prayer could be answered — that just maybe there can be a happy balance between this mistress of yours and your family."

Brad looked Julie in the eyes for the first time since the conversation started. "I'll delay telling Dixon my decision. He wants me. I'm secure in that. The job's mine if I want it. And it is a good job, Julie," he added, still maintaining a steady gaze into her brown eyes. "I'll put it off until he absolutely needs to hear. If by some miracle something better comes up before then, I'll be waiting right here to take it. If not, I'm not giving up the chance to work for Dixon." Brad paused. "Fair enough?"

Julie nodded. "Fair enough."

Web Tyson felt exhausted. After making the rounds of his post-op patients, he stopped to see a consult on a three-week-old firstborn male who had been projectile vomiting. He carefully examined the upper abdomen of the infant and easily felt the "olive" that represented the enlarged muscle mass blocking off the stomach. "This baby has pyloric stenosis," he said confidently.

The staff nurse asked, "Shall I schedule an ultrasound or barium upper G.I. X-ray to confirm?"

"Not necessary in this case. I've seen all I need to see. Schedule him for a pyloromyotomy this afternoon, to follow my morning cases. Make sure you maintain his IV, and don't let him try anything more by mouth until after surgery." The nurse nodded. "Any family of this one around?"

"The mother is eating breakfast in the

cafeteria. I haven't seen the father here yet."

"Get the mother to sign an op permit. I'll be up to answer her questions after my first case."

"Yes, Dr. Tyson," she called as he disappeared through the double doors at the end of the hallway.

Tyson finished his morning cases, signed charts during his lunch break, attended a hospital steering committee meeting, put in an IV on a one-thousand-gram preemie, and returned to the O.R. to do his add-on case, the pyloromyotomy.

As he scrubbed his hands, his long-time first assistant, Helen Briggs, looked on with concern. "Did you stop for lunch today?"

"No time today, Helen." He gave her a look that communicated, *No more questions.*

Helen ignored the unspoken message. "I heard about Jimmy. Is he O.K.?"

"Jimmy will be fine." He didn't feel like elaborating. "Let's see if we can get this done by 4. I've got a ton of paperwork waiting at the office."

"Why not let one of your partners do some of the add-on cases? It's not a crime to give yourself a needed break once in a while." Helen had taken on a mothering tone.

Tyson scrubbed his forearms faster, the

lather falling off his elbows and into the sink. "Latner is in O.R. 3 doing a skin graft on a burn victim. Davis is running our afternoon clinic." He paused, then turned to push the door open with his foot. "I should be there helping him."

"Maybe you should hire more help." Helen's comments rebounded off the swinging door.

The baby was anesthetized before Tyson entered the room. He quickly draped the abdomen that had been painted with betadine solution. He made a short transverse incision in the upper right abdomen, then carefully divided the enlarged or hypertrophied muscle making up the pylorus, which had effectively kept the infant's stomach from emptying. That deftly accomplished, he reapproximated the fascia and skin and walked from the room to find the patient's mother.

After a brief talk with the parent, he headed back to his office to finish up. After working for two hours on his in-box, he reached the last item, a handwritten message from his receptionist, Jolene: "Call Tom Yearling, reporter for the *Washington Post*. He wants to set up an interview with you. He is doing a story on the search for a new Surgeon General. He won't give me any more details." A number was written for him to call. Below the message was his receptionist's initials, "J.M." and the added note, "Is there anything you aren't telling us?" with a smiley face after that.

What is there to hide? I don't know anything about this. Maybe he just wants my suggestions to help guide the search. That's all I need, more work to do. He reflexively pulled out his daily planner and looked at the following day. *Whew! And I thought today was bad. Tomorrow looks like a zoo. Maybe Helen is right. Maybe I should look into hiring more help.* With that thought he jotted down a short note to his office manager.

> Call the pediatric surgery department at Bridgewater University. See what you can find out about a fellow, Dr. Brad Forrest. Maybe they will even fax us a *curriculum vitae.* Be vague. Just tell them Dr. Tyson wants the credentials of anyone involved in his son's care. That should satisfy them.

Below this, he signed his name, from which all anyone could make out was a "T" followed by a line.

Lenore Kingsley looked on with approval

as Randy Harris showed her the results of his latest effort at DNA splicing. They were in lab 62, an advanced lab dedicated to the elucidation and mapping of the human genome, the actual molecular sequences of each gene, determining every human quality from eye color to intelligence to the likelihood of development of future disease states such as diabetes mellitus or bowel cancer. Actually Dr. Harris had stepped far beyond just figuring out which gene sequences were responsible for particular traits; he now sought innovative ways to clone and introduce new DNA or gene segments into the nucleus of a cell.

They were looking at a row of metal cages, each containing several yelping Dalmatian pups. "Here is a picture of the mother and father. I have them housed downstairs in the animal storage facility. I just don't have enough room up here anymore," Randy stated flatly as he gestured to the cluttered lab counter to his right.

"Is that a hint?" Lenore smiled faintly. She then turned back to staring at the caged animals in front of her and looked at the picture Randy had handed her. "Are you going to tell me what I'm supposed to be getting out of this, or do I need to guess?"

Randy Harris, Ph.D. took on the air of a

smug professor. "Look at the hair color of the dogs in the picture."

Lenore obeyed. She looked at him, her eyes saying plainly, *Stop playing games with me, Randy.* She spoke up only to say, "So?"

"So look at the pups in the cage in front of you. All of them have black coats. Neither parent carried a gene for that hair color. They were strictly purebred Dalmatians." The doctor continued, seeing he had caught his employer's interest. "Not only are these dogs expressing a new gene that we spliced into their genome, but they will grow to approximately twice the size of their parents, due to the presence of an additional growth hormone gene that will be expressed later in their development."

"Will these characteristics be passed on to the next generation of pups?"

"Of course. We've altered the very core of the genetic material. All of their cells show evidence of the gene therapy we've accomplished."

Lenore looked puzzled. She liked to stay on top of all of the lab projects, but hated to admit this particular lab was moving beyond her area of personal expertise. "How did you do this?"

"I actually had quite a few helpers on this

one, Lenore. The folks at our animal in-vitro fertilization lab helped me quite a bit." Randy paused. "Basically, we took Dalmatian egg and sperm and combined them in the lab to create Dalmatian embryos. I then grew the embryos to an early stage and separated off a few cells. I grew these cells, embryonic stem cells, in culture until I had enough genetic material to analyze. I confirmed the presence of the normal genes for size and coat characteristics. I then used a virus — a retrovirus — to introduce several new genes into the DNA of the stem cells. I took these modified cells and put them back into the Dalmatian embryos. I radiated the embryos before putting the cells with the new genes back, so that the only cells that would reproduce would be those with a modified genetic message."

Lenore was sorry she had asked the question. "Spare me the details, Randy."

Dr. Harris could see he was giving her more than she wanted to hear. He continued anyway. "Hear me out. This is the good part. We then take the modified embryo and implant it into the uterus of a surrogate mother Dalmatian and presto — a new breed of animal with the coat of a black Lab, the brain of a Dalmatian, and the body build of a Great Dane!"

Lenore brightened, then looked at the researcher and squinted. “This is germ cell line manipulation! You are creating changes that will be passed down through future generations.”

“Exactly.” Randy smiled.

Lenore began pacing around the laboratory, tapping a pencil against her temple as she thought. After a few moments she stopped and verbalized the question that haunted her even as she spoke. “What’s to stop us from trying this in humans?”

The doctor looked at the face of UBI’s president. His voice quivered slightly. “Are you serious?”

“I’m just asking a question, Randolph.” Lenore whirled around, walked to the far wall of windows and peered down at the town below. She looked back and locked eyes with her researcher. “Sure, I’m serious.”

“We mustn’t rush into this. We still have the safety issues to work through. I’ve not had a chance to carefully examine the DNA of the modified puppies to be sure they haven’t suffered any ill effects of the viral mediated gene transfer.”

“Insertional mutagenesis?”

“Right. I’m not sure we haven’t caused any other genetic mix-ups. All I am sure of is that the new genes we spliced in are working. There are several billion other nucleotide sequences that may have been affected in some unpredictable way."

"Wait a minute, Harris. A moment ago you were as proud as a young parent watching his offspring take his first steps, and now you are downplaying the whole project. If I understand this correctly, we are about ten years beyond everyone else who is attempting this kind of embryo manipulation —"

"At least ten," Harris replied, regaining some of the pride he had displayed earlier. "Some others have had success at making transgenic mice, but this has never been done in higher mammals — and certainly not in humans." His countenance changed back to a somber stare, and he walked over to the bank of windows where Lenore Kingsley stood. "Then there's the matter of funding. It will take hundreds of human embryos and money beyond belief to get a project like that off the ground." He looked out the window. "The money's here for us now, Lenore, but without another breakthrough soon, and with Oxydel's patent running out, we could be in for some —"

"This could be the breakthrough we've been looking for!" Kingsley interrupted. "Don't you see? If we are the first company to accomplish germ cell line manipulation in humans, we could combine with any in-vitro fertilization program and virtually guarantee a concerned couple that the baby they have will be a perfect child — a child completely screened of genetic defects, the sex of their choice — perhaps even with special-order features that we could splice in —" She tapped her pencil against the glass pane in front of her. "We wouldn't need to think about money for a long time, Randy." Her eyes locked on his with an icy stare. "If we could capitalize on this, we wouldn't need to think about ever needing government grant funding again."

The researcher seemed undaunted. "What about the government? The N.I.H. hasn't been too thrilled about funding for this kind of research in the past. And even if we don't need to depend on them for funding, the Council for Responsible Genetics has strongly cautioned —"

"@#$% the C.R.S.! Those ethicists wouldn't know the difference between a high school chemistry lab and what we are doing here! And as for the N.I.H., they have looked favorably on other forms of embryo research. But who cares about all that anyway? We are the ones on the cutting edge here. Governmental support or not, I say we proceed. It's not our fault that the government doesn't know enough to regulate us. Policy will follow research breakthroughs if we play our cards correctly." Lenore smiled smugly.

Randy looked on incredulously. He couldn't discern her thoughts. He wouldn't have liked them if he could have.

Lenore stared out the window and continued the rhythmic tapping of her pencil eraser against the pane before her. *He will never know just how much I've already done to be sure the government looks favorably on our research efforts. Once our new Surgeon General is in place, we won't even have to quibble over whether the government will approve. In the future, work like ours will be admired and required. And my master will relish in the glory of it all.*

UBI's young president sauntered toward the door of the lab. Before she exited she called back over her shoulder, "Oh, nice work, Randy. Put some thought into trying the same thing with human embryos."

She exited before she heard his hesitant response. "Yeah, sure."

CHAPTER 5

At 6 A.M. the halls of Crestview Women's were quiet. Over the next few minutes, however, activity would pick up, beginning with the last-minute patient checks by the nurses finishing the shift, accelerating with the appearance of the phlebotomists gathering the morning blood samples, and culminating in an efficient roar as the breakfast trays were delivered and physicians carrying their own coffee mugs began sifting through the patients' charts at the nurses' stations. Dr. Tyson often rounded on his patients early, just to avoid all the confusion that so frequently characterized the time around nursing shift change.

Tyson closed the last chart in front of him and stood to leave the 5 north nursing station. As he walked away, the charge nurse called out, "Dr. Tyson, can you fill out these papers for me?"

Tyson turned and inspected the papers that were held out before him. "What are these?"

"The new death certificates. One set

needs to be filled out by the attending physician within twenty-four hours of a death on the ward. This is for the Down's baby with duodenal atresia who died early yesterday morning."

"Oh," Web mused as he signed his name at the bottom of the sheet.

The nurse chatted on, unaware that the physician had focused his entire attention on the form in front of him. "These deaths don't really get to me," the nurse said matter-of-factly. "The ones that get to me are the ones I don't expect."

The last phrase jarred Tyson back into the conversation. He looked up. "You expected this death?"

"Well, kind of," the nurse replied slowly. "I mean, with the patient being a Do Not Resuscitate and all —"

"Oh, sure — I guess you are able to anticipate which patients aren't likely to make it, aren't you?" Tyson felt some relief. At first he thought that this nurse really knew just how the baby had died. Even though he felt strongly about the compassion that motivated him toward the nontreatment of certain disabled infants, he knew he couldn't let it get out that he sped the dying process in many of his sickest patients. *For a moment there I thought Tammy must have told you how the infant died. The public just wouldn't understand. Not yet.*

Dr. Tyson finished filling out the paperwork and walked toward the elevators. As he walked, he mused to himself, *Just what was my response when they called and told me the child had been found dead? I hope I sounded surprised. I've got to be careful not to sound too calloused. Until the government approves open euthanasia and infanticide, I must continue to appear to be doing the politically correct thing. Hopefully, soon they will formally recognize the greater good that can be served by giving physicians wider latitude in these matters. Until then, I'll continue to do the humanitarian thing even though it isn't in the center of Uncle Sam's approval.*

Belle Forrest was usually up as early as Dr. Weber Tyson, but for different reasons. She now rocked slowly in her chair by the kitchen table, the early-morning light shining in through the venetian blind onto the worn, leather-covered Bible in her lap. This morning, like many others in recent months, she was not alone. Draped in an old quilt to ward off the morning chill sat a captivated Bradley, Jr. in the chair next to Belle. There he sat, morning after morning, listening to Belle pray and tell exciting stories from the Bible, or perhaps one of the many stories of how Belle had seen her Heavenly Father move in her life or the lives of those around her. Mostly Bradley would listen; occasionally he would say a simple prayer himself. He didn't understand all of what Belle said, perhaps not even most of it. He did know that it was during these times with Belle that he felt most at ease. He couldn't explain why; his handicap limited his ability to articulate what he felt. He only knew that in the morning times with Belle he felt happy. It felt good to hear her speak about God.

This morning Bradley had awakened when he heard his father leave at 5:30 A.M. After a few minutes he heard Belle stirring; so he wrapped his quilt around him and headed for the kitchen. There he hastily fixed breakfast for himself and Belle: a blueberry Pop-Tart and a glass of milk. Belle passed on the milk but accepted the Pop-Tart with a smile.

Bradley ate noisily as Belle began to read. She read from John chapter 1: "But as many as received him, to them gave he power to become the sons of God, even to them that believe on his name." She rocked forward and planted both feet on the floor in front of her. She looked at the face of her great-grandson. His features were characteristic of Down's syndrome; his nose was slightly flat, and his eyes slanted gently. He seemed happy to be eating his breakfast pastry. "Did you hear what I read?" she asked softly, her wrinkled hands reaching over and smoothing down his blond hair.

Bradley looked at the elderly woman and smiled. "Yeah."

"Many believers in Jesus never act as if they really understand this verse. They walk around feeling unworthy or depressed, constantly defeated." Belle paused for a moment, took a small bite of her Pop-Tart, and wiped her chin with her hand, displaying a slight tremor. "They just don't understand who they are. We are the children of God, Bradley. It says so right here," she said, returning her index finger to the underlined verse in the book in her lap. "Don't let anyone ever convince you that you are worthless, son. You are a son of the King. You are of great value, Bradley, because he made you and because he saved you."

The young boy listened with unusual intensity a moment longer. He then began to repeat the phrases he had heard from Belle many times before. "Bradley is valuable," he said, with the last word sounding more like "vowable" because of his characteristic pronunciation difficulties. He said it three times, haltingly at first, and then added, "God loves Bradley" and "Bradley, God's son," spoken with his plump right hand closed in a fist over his heart.

The elderly woman's eyes glistened as she heard the young boy speak the truth. "Don't ever forget it, son," she said softly. "Never forget it."

"I won't." Bradley paused, then added, "Want another Pop-Tart?"

"Not this old woman, son. Here," she added, reaching out her hand, "help me out of this chair."

Bradley obeyed and helped pull Belle to her feet. She walked to the coffeemaker and poured a cup of fresh coffee. She turned back to face Bradley and lifted her mug toward him with a gesture they had repeated hundreds of times before. He knew what was coming next and lifted his milk glass in response.

"Cheers!"

Mary Jacobs sighed and crumpled the electives request form in her hand. She stood in the dean's office of the Bridgewater University Medical School for the third time in a week. She glanced at her watch. She had eight minutes to get back up on the adult medicine ward and make it to attending rounds on time. She looked at the middle-aged woman sitting at the desk in front of her. Mary didn't know her full name. Everyone just called her Ms. G.

Mary cleared her throat. "I didn't know sorting out your fourth-year schedule was supposed to be this hard."

"I'm sorry, Mary. It's just that we've had too many requests for the same electives." She handed Mary a list of the services that still had openings for medical students. "You only have one more month to fill. Pick from this list."

Mary sighed again. *I haven't even prayed about this.* She read the options silently and slowly, one at a time. *I haven't even had time to eat, much less pray! Lord, help me make the right choice.*

The administrative assistant looked at the medical student. The schedules were supposed to have been finalized the day before. "Look, Mary, why don't you give yourself a break?" She lowered her voice and glanced at the open door behind her. "Why not give yourself a break and take the dermatology consult elective? All the students are out after 2 o'clock rounds. You look like you could use some rest."

The student wrinkled her nose at the suggestion and continued to stare at the list in front of her. She wouldn't think of taking an elective just because it was a breeze. No one could ever accuse her of that; she had principles to uphold. She wouldn't take the easy road even if she was exhausted, though she did need some rest. She'd been up since 5 A.M. the morning before, her call night on the medicine service having consisted of three new patient workups, the last of which came in at 3 A.M. with a gastrointestinal bleed. She looked very much the part of a third-year medical student. She wore a short white coat that was overflowing with supplies. Her stethoscope hung limply around her neck, and her long blonde hair had not been washed in three days. She stood five feet, seven inches tall; her enviable figure had been maintained easily during her medical school years because her fascination with learning and her busy schedule took priority over regularly scheduled mealtimes.

Mary ran her finger over the list. She paused halfway down the page. "What's this one all about?"

"Pediatric Surgery at Crestview Women's?" Ms. G sounded incredulous. "It's an off-site elective with Dr. Tyson and his associates. They are awfully busy, Mary. I hear they work you night and day."

The information seemed to bounce off Mary without penetration. The administrative assistant tried again. "You've got some tough residency years following medical school, Mary. Why don't you look at something easier for a month?"

"You don't rest when training for a race — you run," Mary replied quickly. She looked at her watch again. "I've got to get to rounds. Sign me up for the elective at Crestview Women's. Maybe getting away from the 'U' for a month will do me some good." She turned and left before the woman could utter a response.

Ms. G shook her head, filled out the paper, and sighed.

Lenore Kingsley spent the afternoon in the seclusion of her richly paneled office. She had left specific instructions with her administrative assistant: she was not to be disturbed. She had spent the last three hours poring over the data sheets from Dr. Harris's embryo research. She stood and stretched, drank a cup of coffee, and then returned to her teak desk and stared into the sixteen-inch color monitor of her desktop computer. She then typed a proposal mirroring the research project she had just studied — with the exception that the embryo genetic manipulation would be with human subjects.

Since leaving the human genome lab a few days earlier, Kingsley had slept little and thought much, her ideas flowing at a near-manic pitch, pushing even the thoughts of slumber to a remote back burner. The obstacles to manipulation of the human germ cell line by gene splicing in an early embryo seemed formidable, but Lenore thrived on a challenge, particularly one with the potential to boost her own personal empire. She had spent hours staring into her computer screen, running literature searches to find out exactly what others had accomplished in the area of human germ cell line manipulation. From what she could see, the results Dr. Harris had accomplished in the Dalmatian pups was a first. If other labs had made the jump into successful human germ cell line manipulation, they had done it quietly — outside the published literature and without government funding.

After working for another hour, Kingsley reread her proposal. She looked critically at the wording and made necessary changes, carefully avoiding the use of the word "embryo," choosing to use the term "pre-embryo" or "fertilized totipotential cell" instead. *This ought to keep those pro-life crazies off my back! I won't even use words that will offend them. Not that any of them will ever have a chance to read about my research — until we have gained the wide acceptance of the government and the scientific community.*

Several problems remained. First, she needed access to human embryos to use for the project. Second, she needed female volunteers to use as surrogate mothers for carrying the embryos for a few months. For this project, the babies would be aborted after twelve weeks and their DNA examined carefully to see if the gene splicing had worked. Lenore and Randy would also examine the remaining portion of the child's DNA content to see if there had been any unexpected complications of their genetic manipulation. *As long as we intentionally abort the babies during the first trimester, no one will complain that we were actually experimenting on humans without their consent. After all, it's been well established that the fetus has no rights during early pregnancy,* Kingsley mused

For the first problem, Lenore called a close friend at the Crestview Women's Hospital. John Beardson, M.D., a gynecologist specializing in the treatment of infertility, said he could assure her a steady supply of embryos from the in-vitro fertilization clinic. "We always have a few leftovers after each successful IVF," he had said slowly. "Eighty percent of our infertility patients sign a waiver giving us permission to dispose of the embryos in any manner we see fit, including use of the embryo for research as may benefit medical science." Lenore nearly beamed at the news. It seemed that little could stand in her way as long as she persisted.

As for the second obstacle, Lenore knew this would be potentially explosive. If word got out that a protocol required abortion, the public outcry would potentially dampen enthusiasm for development of the techniques that could lead to the ability to determine the traits of human offspring. *Our surrogate mothers need to be extremely dedicated to this research. Where can I find such women?*

Lenore pondered those thoughts as she poured another cup of steaming black coffee. Slowly a dark voice within her pressed for recognition. An eerie dread passed over her, and she felt the hair on the back of her neck rise. She felt as if she might vomit, and she put her hand to her mouth. After a few seconds the wave of nausea passed, leaving her with a dull, empty pain in the pit of her stomach. Suddenly she understood. She would be the chosen carrier. *Where else could I find someone with such dedication to the project?* She would be the first surrogate mother. Certainly this was the best answer. Others would later follow her example. She touched her forehead, glistening with beads of sweat. Lenore stood up and turned down the thermostat that hung on the far wall. As she did, the clarity of her master's plan for her became even clearer. *I have used my womb for my master's bidding before; now I will do it again.*

It was Wednesday morning, and that meant one thing for Brad Forrest: inguinal hernias. Pediatric hernias were so commonplace that the university pediatric surgery service ended up dedicating a whole morning each week just to get them all done. For Dr. Forrest it was nearly routine. A quick "hello" to the anxious parents, a six-minute hand scrub while the anesthesiologist put the baby under, a twenty-minute operation, and another conversation with the parents. Over and over. Every Wednesday morning the same. Well, almost the same.

Brad's pediatric surgery attendings had stopped coming to the O.R. on Wednesday mornings months ago. It was Brad's job to help the surgical intern who was on the pediatric surgery service do the operations. In July, when the interns were fresh out of medical school, the cases were slow, and the explanations of how to do the basic techniques tried the patience of the resident and attending teaching assistants. After a few months the cases proceeded along at a faster pace as the lubrication of experience smoothed the flow of the caseload. For the surgical intern, being taught to do hernias was the biggest reward of the rotation. Most of the cases were much too complicated to be handed down to the intern and were handled by a senior resident or the pediatric surgery fellow. For the intern, Wednesday morning seemed like heaven, a needed reward for the countless hours of scut work assigned to them in the daily care of the sick children on the wards and in the I.C.U. For the pediatric surgery fellow, Brad Forrest, Wednesday seemed nearly mindless. He had done this hundreds of times before.

Brad looked up from the operative field. The intern had just begun suturing the skin to finish a right inguinal hernia. "How about some closing music, Nancy?" Brad directed his comment to the circulating nurse.

"Sure, just let me finish this sponge count." The circulator counted the last of the four-by-four gauze sponges, with the scrub nurse managing the sterile table watching and confirming the count. "I've got three here," she said as she lifted three blood-tinged gauze pads with a long instrument and laid them out on a blue towel so they could be numbered easily. ". . . four, five . . . and one on the field . . . six, seven, eight, nine, and one on the back table makes ten." She stopped and recorded the sponge count as "correct." She then looked at Brad Forrest and stated mechanically, "Sponge and needle counts are correct."

"Counts correct. Thank you," Brad answered with the routine required acknowledgment of the correct instrument, needle, and sponge counts.

Just as the nurse turned on a CD filled with "oldies," the anesthesia resident grumbled, "Boy, these crazy forehead temp monitors are for the birds!" He pulled the small probe off the male infant's forehead and pitched it in the small kick bucket at Brad's feet. "This thing reads 105 degrees Fahrenheit!" He looked at the trash bucket in disgust. "Must be some new cheap government substitute! 105! @#$%!"

Brad looked quickly at the EKG monitor above the anesthesiologist's head. The heart rate was up, with occasional irregular ventricular beats. He glanced back down at the open wound that the intern was repairing. Dark blood had begun oozing from the cut skin edge. Brad snapped to action. A mental warning flare tore through Brad's mindless humming of the song on the boom box. Brad voiced his concern in a controlled, authoritative manner. "This child is showing classic signs of malignant hyperthermia. Stop your anesthetic gas now, and get some dantrolene for injection."

The anesthesia resident laughed. "You aren't going to believe this fifty-cent piece of junk, are you?" he added, picking up the pliable, plastic temperature probe from the trash.

Brad did not respond to the anesthesia resident. He spoke instead to the circulating nurse. "Get the crash cart in here STAT! There is dantrolene on the cart to counter the hyperthermia. Do it now!"

The anesthesia resident looked back at the patient and touched his head. It was hot — profoundly hot. He began believing that Forrest just might be right. "#@#$!"

"Turn off your anesthetic now! This case is over. Get us a skin stapler. We need to finish this yesterday!" The scrub nurse responded, and Brad clipped the skin closed and tore back the sterile drapes. With the drapes off, the baby lay exposed on the operating table. The infant appeared mottled and cyanotic. Brad looked at the intern, who had backed slowly away from the table, stark fear visible on his young face. Brad raised his voice. "Get us some ice. Let's pack the child. And get us the fan!"

The cardiac monitor began showing signs of increased cardiac irritability. This decayed rapidly to a fast, ineffective pumping rhythm known as ventricular tachycardia. Brad felt for a pulse in the groin and, feeling none, began chest compressions with the first two fingers of his right hand. Overhead, the O.R. loudspeaker sounded out the call, "Code Blue! Room 4! Code Blue! Room 4!"

Nancy Stutzman, R.N. pushed the code cart through the door, crashing the sterile instrument tray to the floor in the process. She quickly opened a prefilled syringe of dantrolene and handed it to the anesthesia attending who had just arrived in response to the overhead call.

"We need some procainamide and bicarb!" Brad spoke loudly because of the noise in the room.

Within minutes the male infant was surrounded by ice packs, and a fan was positioned to blow air across his small frame.

Minutes passed. The anesthesia staff injected drugs. Brad continued chest compressions. A nurse drew the child's blood for STAT blood tests to confirm the diagnosis. Brad's mind blurred. He thought of the quick "hello" he'd had with the parents of the baby boy only minutes before. "Take good care of Tommy," the mother had expressed with a choke of emotion, "he's our miracle baby." Brad hadn't asked her to elaborate. He had only wanted to get the day started.

Arterial blood samples were drawn and sent to the lab, and the anesthesia resident hyperventilated the child in order to fight the acids that were being produced.

Brad continued the rhythmic pumping of the infant's chest, watching the heart monitor for any signs of changes. Again his mind blurred from his present state. For the second time in twenty-four hours his thoughts turned to prayer. This time he wasn't thinking about Bradley's prayer, but one of his own. *God . . . help me. Help this baby. Save this baby.* Brad looked at the monitor. Ventricular tachycardia persisted. *This is useless. My prayers don't seem to go beyond the wall.*

At that moment the fast heartbeat ceased. Electrical activity of the heart seemed to have stopped. Three seconds, then four went by. Time seemed suspended. Brad stopped breathing and cursed inwardly, embarrassed by his turning to prayer in a seemingly hopeless situation. *Obviously prayer didn't help this little one.*

A normal electrical complex appeared on the monitor. After a single-second pause, a normal sinus rhythm returned. The intern slid his fingers over the femoral pulse. "I have a pulse! . . . Uh, the baby has a pulse!"

Brad stopped chest compressions and looked at the intern. "Still there?"

"Yes. There's a pulse without chest compressions."

Relief broke across the room like a crashing wave. Nancy Stutzman heaved a sigh. "I thought we'd lost him."

The intern clenched his fist and pounded the back table, striking it as he yelled, "Yes!"

Brad Forrest put his own fingers on the femoral pulse to confirm the good news. He looked at the nurse. "Get some STAT blood gases and a serum C.P.K. and potassium." To the intern he said, "Get an intensive care unit bed for this one. Better check the serum and urine for myoglobin. We'll have to watch him closely for a few days." The pediatric surgery fellow looked around the room. Clutter was everywhere.

At least eight additional people had responded to the code, including Brad's attending, Dr. Dixon.

Brad briefly explained the situation to his attending surgeon, who had the ultimate responsibility for the case. Then he and Dr. Dixon turned to leave to talk to the child's parents. Before he left, Brad turned and pulled down his surgical mask. "Thanks," he said. "Thanks to everyone," he added shaking his head in disbelief. *That child was dead!*

The two surgeons walked slowly to the waiting room, where they would find the infant's parents nervously paging through year-old magazines. As Brad contemplated what to say, his thoughts crowded out the small voice pushing for recognition in his mind: *I answered your prayer!*

CHAPTER 6

Dr. Web Tyson alternately stared at the menu in front of him and then at his watch. He sipped slowly at the mixed drink in his hand. He didn't want to get too relaxed. He still wasn't sure what he was doing here.

He sat alone at a spacious table at the Evers' Country Inn, a bed-and-breakfast outfit that was known for its excellent service and its delicious menu. A bay window next to his table provided a view of the Wanoset River that was both expansive and peaceful. He had agreed to meet Tom Yearling, the *Washington Post* reporter who had requested an interview. The reasons for the interview were not entirely clear to Web. However, his love for Evers's food and the chance to relax for an hour looking at the river seemed appealing; so he said yes to the interview without much thought. Now he wondered again just what he was doing when his thoughts were interrupted by a tall, lanky man holding a black briefcase.

"Dr. Tyson?" The man's shirt appeared wrinkled from his long trip, his tie loosened enough to allow two buttons of the white button-down shirt to be undone. He extended his hand in a friendly greeting. His grip was noticeably strong.

Web stood to greet the tardy reporter. "Yearling?"

"Yes, sir." The reporter immediately felt self-conscious in front of this surgeon who was impeccably dressed in a three-piece dark suit and silk tie. Tom Yearling looked down at his shirt and fumbled with his tie. "Sorry I'm late. You were right about that last right-hand turn. The sign is almost completely hidden by the willow branches."

"Sit down. I've taken the liberty to order for you. The food here is out of this world."

"Thanks for taking the time to meet with me. I know how busy you must be." The reporter opened his briefcase and took out a small, handheld tape recorder. He noticed the look of curiosity on Tyson's face and added, "This is all routine. I use it so I don't have to take so many notes. I'll only quote you if you give me permission."

The curiosity on Tyson's face didn't change. "Just why do you want to talk to me anyway?"

A pudgy woman of about sixty quietly put a basket of steaming homemade rolls in front of Dr. Tyson and then quietly stood waiting, not wanting to interrupt. Web knew her by name, at least the name everyone called her. "Thanks, Mama Evers."

She responded with a proud smile, looking at the guest across from Tyson. "Can I get you anything to drink?"

"Some iced tea would be fine." Tom looked at Web and explained, "I've got a long drive ahead of me tonight." Mama Evers scurried off, and the journalist continued their previous conversation. "I'm here to talk to you about the search for a new Surgeon General candidate."

Tyson remained pleasant but direct. "I know that much from our previous conversation on the phone yesterday. What I'm still not sure about is, why me?"

This guy really doesn't seem to have a clue! Tom began wondering if he was the mixed-up one. "We do personal interest, general background stories on all of the candidates. It's just a matter of giving you some broader exposure so the public can feel a part of the selection."

Web put down the drink in his hand. His head shook slowly in surprise. "Me?"

"You weren't aware that you are being considered or at least investigated as a possible replacement for Dr. Southerly?"

"I am? Well, I . . . No . . . no, I wasn't

aware . . ." stammered the normally smooth-tongued surgeon.

Tom began mentally reviewing the events leading up to this interview. *Lenore urged me to do this story. How did she put it? "You know you owe me at least this much." But why all the secrecy? "Don't let him know that I asked you to do this." He doesn't even seem to know about the search for a new Surgeon General at all! You don't suppose that Lenore just set me up?* Tom mentally corrected himself. *No. I called the White House press office, and they supplied a new list of potential candidates being considered — and Web Tyson had just been added the day before.* He broke from his thoughts and back into the conversation with Tyson. "Well, I can tell you that you are on the official list. I talked to the White House press office myself."

"This is interesting," Tyson replied, shaking his head again.

"I only assumed that you'd been informed."

Tyson paused and let the idea sink in. *Me? Surgeon General of the United States? Incredible!* He paused without speaking and swirled the glass in front of him.

Tom Yearling continued, "I do know that you were one of the most recent names added to the list of possibilities. The White

House is going slow this time. They said they did not have a clear deadline for replacing Southerly. Maybe they are going so slow they haven't gotten around to asking if you'd even consider it." He spoke again after a pause, thinking that his chances to get a good interview out of Tyson were getting slimmer. "I guess this may not be the best time to talk to you. I thought you would have at least had a chance to process the idea and have some thoughts about what you'd like to do."

"I guess I'm a little surprised by all this. I just thought you must want to see what physicians would actually like to see in the Surgeon General, that's all. I never imagined that you wanted a story about me as a potential candidate for the position." He paused again and sipped his drink. "Just how did you get this assignment anyway? How do you guys in the media find out about this before I even know I'm being considered?"

"I had a tip — from a fan of yours you might say." Tom thought again about Lenore's warning: "Don't let him know I'm behind this." He didn't know her well, but he knew enough to know he needed to obey her urging. Besides, he did owe her. His mind drifted further away as he paused to look out at the Wanoset River through the window. *I guess Dad would be dead right now if it wasn't for Lenore Kingsley and the creation of Oxydel. No one thought a man could lose so much blood and still live without a transfusion.* For a moment he was back at his father's bedside in the strange environment of the I.C.U. His father had bled massively from a stomach ulcer and yet because of his personal religious beliefs had refused all blood transfusions. His father was so weak that he'd been placed on a ventilator. All Tom could do was squeeze his father's pale, cold hand and pray. And that's when Lenore Kingsley appeared and offered an experimental new blood substitute. She'd studied it extensively in the lab, but never in human subjects.

Tom knew it would be his father's only hope. He signed what seemed to be a dozen papers relieving the hospital and doctors of all responsibility just so the experimental drug could be given. The F.D.A. had approved its use in limited human trials only the week before. Frank Yearling would be the first to receive it — and the first miracle recovery attributable to Oxydel. Tom snapped back to the present when Tyson responded, "And just who is this fan?"

Tom looked up and decided to stick to the promise of secrecy he'd made to Lenore, a promise he didn't really understand. He replied only, "A reporter never reveals his sources."

Tyson let it pass just as Mama Evers arrived with two Caesar salads with her own homemade Parmesan dressing. This was soon followed by grilled lamb basted with a lemon-and-butter herb sauce and wild rice. The two men ate quietly, making occasional small talk about the food and their surroundings.

Eventually Tom turned his attention to the real reason for their meeting. "Would you mind if I asked you a few questions? I can understand if you'd like some more time, since you just found out about this."

Dr. Tyson felt uncharacteristically relaxed. "Fire away. I'm O.K. with all this. If I'm not prepared to answer something, I'll let you know." He looked at the tape recorder in Tom's hand.

Tom noted Dr. Tyson's uncomfortable look. "Hey, this is just because of my lousy memory, remember?" His eyes met momentarily with Web's. "You don't have anything to hide, do you?" Tom laughed.

Web lightened up but didn't join in with the laughter. "No, of course not. I'm just not used to this sort of thing."

"Look, we'll keep it general — background sort of stuff. You know, your education, your work in this state — stuff like that. I know you haven't had a chance to think about government health policy yet."

The two men talked for the next two hours. In that time Tom consumed not one but two pieces of Mama Evers's homemade chocolate-covered cheesecake. Dr. Tyson answered questions, drank four cups of black coffee, and shook his head, watching the thin reporter inhale more calories than most people do in a day.

Long after the moon had risen high over the Wanoset, Dr. Tyson stepped out of the Victorian-style inn and sighed. Tom had sped away in an old Pontiac with a doggy bag of lamb chops and homemade rolls by his side. Web looked up at the moon as he opened the door of his silver Mercedes. His mood was somber in spite of his ego-building interview. The news that he was being considered for the job of Surgeon General stood prominently in his thoughts. Deeper, however, an old anxiety had been stimulated by Yearling's jesting: "You don't have anything to hide, do you?" Tyson shook his head, slid into his Mercedes, and sped into the night.

* * *

Brad Forrest rarely walked anywhere slowly. It just seemed too time inefficient. In fact, he never took the hospital elevator system, even when going up. It was just too slow. Tonight Brad could have cared less about speed. He had spoken to Julie just thirty minutes before — after missing yet another dinner with the family. She sounded as if she could use a little time to cool off. What does she expect? *I don't have a predictable 9 to 5 job.*

Brad decided to check on the child who had experienced malignant hyperthermia in the I.C.U. He completed his assessment, left the unit, and sauntered toward the stairwell. Behind him he heard a voice. It belonged to Dr. Pete Harston, an intern on the trauma service.

"Dr. Forrest!"

Brad turned to see the intern and a nurse escorting a thin, young male in a hospital gown pushing an IV pole. Brad turned and faced the trio. "Hi, Pete. Light night on the trauma service?"

"Only two hits since 3 P.M. The fog's keeping the helicopter grounded," he replied. He looked at the patient to his left, then back to Brad. "Remember this guy?"

Brad looked back with a blank look on

his face. Before he could reply, Pete continued. "He's Jimmy Tyson. You helped out on his case the night he came in."

Forrest brightened and extended his hand, "Oh yes, I remember. You were pretty busted up. How are you getting along?"

"I'm O.K. They tell me I should be getting out pretty soon."

"Great." Brad turned to go. "It looks like you've got a pretty good team watching over you. Best of luck."

"Dr. Forrest?" The voice belonged to Jimmy.

Brad paused with his hand on the door to the stairwell. "Yes?"

"Do you know my father?"

"I've talked to him before, but know him? I figure everyone knows about Web Tyson — at least everyone in medicine."

"I just wondered. He came by to see me the other day. We never were very good at communication, but it seemed after a while that all he wanted was to find out about you."

Brad was surprised at Jimmy's words and responded with a laugh. "Well, what do you know." He didn't say anything else, so the nurse responded by steering Jimmy's IV back toward his room.

"I think you've had enough walking for one night. It's time to get you back to bed." The nurse helped him keep from tangling himself in the IV tubing as he executed a turn.

Brad watched the patient and his helpers for a moment longer before heading into the empty stairwell.

Brad quickened his step back up to his normal pace. *Web Tyson was asking about me? Maybe he just wants to know everything about whoever has treated his son. Surely he doesn't know I'm looking for a pediatric surgery position?* A few minutes later Brad skipped across the hospital lawn to the parking deck. *Maybe I'll delay giving Dixon my final decision for a few weeks, just in case another job offer comes in at the eleventh hour. Wouldn't Julie like that!*

Lenore Kingsley knew that any successful project at United Biotechnical Industries would at least need a nod of approval from the C.E.O., Gardner Henry Kingsley. He wouldn't get too caught up in the details like his daughter, but he liked to at least know the goals and basics of his lab's projects. Lenore had grown skillful at feeding him just the right amount of information to keep him satisfied. For some projects she kept him well informed. For others . . . well, Lenore felt some things were best left unsaid.

Tonight she would entertain her parents at her own posh suburban apartment. Tonight she would present to her father the basics of a new project that would lay the foundation for splicing human DNA. She knew that for this one, she would have to stay away from the details and focus instead on long-range planning, presenting the humanistic goal of helping people who are known carriers of certain genetic diseases, such as diabetes or colon cancer, to become parents of children guaranteed to be free of the same diseases their parents carry. She would make no mention of the need to discard hundreds of human embryos in the process. She would certainly not mention her desire to be the first surrogate mother to be used in the project. She knew her father well. He would like what she said. Since her work on Oxydel, he seemed only interested in "the big picture." Lenore would let him understand the "virtuous" goal; she wouldn't want him to be upset at the "minor details."

Lenore set the table while sipping wine from an old silver goblet. *I need to relax. I hate it when Daddy and Mommy come over.*

I have to be so "proper" when they're around.

As she busied herself fixing a large green salad, she suddenly remembered the need to put away some of the more prominent evidences of her commitment to the occult. *I can't risk Daddy thinking I'm not completely in line with his standards!* Her involvement in Satan worship had been a touchy subject in Lenore's early years, resulting in a complete separation from her parents for nearly three years following her graduation from high school. She had progressed quickly from her success with tarot cards and Ouija boards into a deeper involvement with a local coven, where her "gifts" were recognized and rewarded. She eventually left home altogether and immersed herself in the search for supernatural power. After obtaining new status as a high priestess, a regional high priest urged her to heal the relationship with her parents and reenter college. Her influence for her lord could be greater if she became educated, they explained. She obeyed implicitly, returned to her home, and practiced her worship of Satan covertly, so as not to disturb her parents. By this time she had grown so used to lying to everyone around her that it bothered her little to practice this continual deception.

She quickly glanced at her watch. Her

parents were due any minute, but would predictably arrive fashionably late. She set down the paring knife she was using and walked into the living room. She picked up several old volumes of witchcraft lore and a copy of a Satanic bible. She put these under her arm, grabbed an old candelabra with the other hand, and carried them back to her bedroom. *They won't come in here.* Lenore walked back to the kitchen and retrieved two more candles, a silver cup, and a large flask filled with fluid. She stored these in her bedroom closet. Most of her occult paraphernalia was already in her bedroom anyway and would not be out where her father could view it. There! Lenore thought with a smirk. *I can appear as straight and narrow as anyone.*

The doorbell rang. Lenore viewed herself in the hallway mirror, practiced a sincere smile, and pulled open the door.

"Dad, Mom, I'm so glad you could come," she lied.

Julie Forrest kissed her son good night and tousled his blond hair. There would be no stories tonight. She just didn't seem to have any strength left to quiet her own heart, much less the restless heart of her eleven-year-old. As she turned to leave,

Bradley asked her for the tenth time when Daddy was coming home.

"Bradley, I said I don't know!" Julie regretted her shouting tone immediately.

Bradley, having no idea what his mother was thinking, felt hurt. His mother's temper had been getting shorter for quite a while now. He laid his head on his pillow and faced the wall.

Julie softened. "I'm sorry, Bradley. I shouldn't yell."

Bradley didn't respond.

Julie rumpled his hair again. "It's just that maybe I miss him, too." She turned on a small seashell night-light that was plugged into the wall outlet. "Good night, son."

Bradley stayed quiet. Julie left the room and slumped down on her own bed in the room across the hall. *Maybe the girls at the fitness center are right. Maybe I should cut my losses while I'm still young enough to start another relationship — this time with someone who will be around to help out for a change. Any relationship would be better than this! Brad is never even home long enough to see how lonely I am. He doesn't come around enough to know we have communication problems — as if he cares anyway. His whole life is surgery, surgery, surgery!*

Julie stood up and changed into her nightgown. She picked up her wedding picture from the top of the dresser. *Maybe things will be different after this training program is done. When Brad gets a real job, maybe things will be different. At least that's what he says.* Julie smiled. *Maybe I can give it one more chance.*

She laid in bed awake for over an hour, her mind full of thoughts of the past and hopes for the future. Finally, at just after midnight, she closed her eyes and slept, her husband still at the hospital serving his other love.

CHAPTER 7

Web Tyson stumbled into his house at 1 A.M., tired, yet invigorated by the latest development in his amazing life. *I am being considered for Surgeon General!* After leaving Evers' Country Inn, he had stopped for a nightcap at The Downtown Cafe. He knew it would take more than warm milk to induce sleep after an evening like he'd had.

His thoughts flowed rapidly. *Just look at what I've done for this community, this state! Maybe I'll have a chance to influence the whole nation. But can I give up clinical medicine for politics? What about my practice? What about the needs of Crestview Women's and this community? Who will take my place?*

Web poured himself a small glass of brandy. He rarely imbibed, but this was a special night, and he didn't have any surgery scheduled for the next day. After his drink he retired to his master suite and slumped into a large, flowered easy chair beside his king-size bed.

It was there that an uneasy memory surfaced again, birthed by an unseen presence and fueled by the alcohol he'd consumed. *What was it that Yearling said? "You don't have anything to hide, do you?"* A gnawing sensation gripped his abdomen. Web arose and went to his medicine cabinet. *Two Tagamet ought to quiet my acid stomach. I should know better than to eat so much.*

The surgeon undressed and slipped into bed. The medicine quieted his stomach but couldn't suppress his dreams. As he drifted into a restless sleep, his mind replayed events long buried, events he had desperately wanted to lie dormant and undisturbed. The year was 1970, and Web Tyson, M.D. served as a general practitioner as a part of the National Health Service in rural Arkansas. He only had one month to go to complete his obligation prior to entering a surgery residency program at Ann Arbor. It was late one night, and raining . . . again.

Tyson squinted to see the route signs, the windshield wipers on his Dodge Dart ineffectively fighting the rain that threatened to stop his progress completely. Tyson cursed audibly. *Why do babies insist on coming into the world on nights like this?* He downshifted and turned left onto a gravel road flanked by a thick pine forest. Thankfully, the rain seemed to slacken, or was he just sheltered by all the trees? Slowly he traveled up the lane, which seemed to be half gravel, half puddles. Ahead he could see a clearing. The house was a small, brick flat with a broad front porch. It was surrounded by an unusual number of cars. This must be the place. There isn't another house on this road for a half a mile! The house emitted a dim light. *What's that in the window? A candle! No electricity tonight — this is just great! Obstetrics by candlelight!*

Tyson's Dodge skidded to a slippery stop. He didn't even have an umbrella. He gathered his supplies and waited for a moment until he detected a brief respite in the rhythmic dropping of the rain. *Well, here goes! This is what I get for borrowing from Uncle Sam for my education.* Web ran for the front porch, holding his leather instrument bag above his head as he slid along. Once there, he wiped his face with his sleeve and glanced back toward his car. Barely visible from the front porch was a light coming from the barn next to the house. Web could see the faint outline of two shadowy figures as they passed quickly into the barn from an old truck parked beneath the barn's hayloft. *Were they wearing robes?*

Tyson began to squint to get a better look when the door to the house swung open.

Web whirled around in surprise. A tall man flanked by two others greeted him. "Doctor Tyson?" There was concern in his voice. A shorter, stocky man gripped the tall man's elbow. A painful scream bellowed out from a room in the back of the house.

Web extended a wet hand. "Hello. I thought I'd never find this place. Mr. Landers?"

A limp hand met Tyson's. "Your patient is in the bedroom. Sorry 'bout the lights. Electric's been off for an hour."

Tyson followed the three men down a dark hall to a room with two other men, the patient, and two additional women. It seemed unusual to have so many people around, even for a home delivery. The patient seemed young, very young. She had long, black hair, and her forehead was beaded with sweat. She alternately moaned softly or screamed loudly. Occasionally she uttered words that to the young doctor sounded like a foreign language, one he couldn't identify, one he was sure he'd never heard before.

Tyson looked around the dim room. He identified a gas lantern in the corner. "Bring the lantern over here. Who's going to be my assistant?"

A young woman with a blank stare

stepped forward without speaking.

The doctor began, "I need to see how far along she is." He looked up at the men in the room. "If you'll excuse us, I think we can take it from —"

"She wants us here!" The interruption came from the stocky man, who still gripped the elbow of the man who had greeted Tyson.

Tyson wasn't in a position to argue. He sighed. "Is there a place where I can wash my hands?"

"Down the hall," grunted Tyson's self-appointed assistant.

Web washed his hands and returned to the room. His eyes were adjusting to the dim light. He positioned the patient on her back. She cooperated with him and seemed to understand his English, but continued to speak in a language that was incomprehensible to Tyson. He gently palpated her abdomen with both hands. *At least this one is head-down. All I need is to do a breech delivery in the middle of nowhere in the dark!* "I need to see how far along you are. How long have you been in labor?" From the looks of the bed, her water had broken prior to his arrival.

The patient declined to answer, responding only by arching her back and emitting a deep moan. Tyson felt immediately chilled, although the temperature in the room was easily above eighty. The assistant answered for her. "About four hours, real strong. This isn't her first baby, you know."

Tyson hadn't known, of course. He opened his bag and retrieved a package of sterile exam gloves and a spray bottle filled with betadine. With appropriate exposure he sprayed the woman's perineum and waited for the next contraction. As it started, he examined her cervix. "One hundred percent effaced and ten," Tyson reported mechanically to no one in particular. He looked up. Each of the men in the room clutched a solitary lit candle with both hands without speaking. He felt a distinct unease, almost a fear, grip him. *What's going on here?*

"It's time to push." He reached for his bag and brought out a syringe, a needed painkiller he was preparing to administer to the girl writhing on the small bed in front of him.

"Doc," the stocky man said, "there will be no medicines given here."

"It's only a mild narcotic. It will make her more —"

"No medicines, Doc." The man took a step toward Dr. Tyson and spoke again.

". . . and no records!"

Tyson looked beyond the short man and into the hall outside the room. This time he saw two hooded men in robes. He was sure this time! *Just what is going on here?* He was in no position to argue. He knew the baby's birth was imminent. He'd just have to do his best — on their terms!

The doctor looked back at the patient. She seemed wild, nearly uncontrolled. As she shook violently, the old bed creaked with the woman's pain. Tyson tried to calm himself and the young girl. "When the next contraction starts, I want you to hold your breath and push. O.K . . . er . . ." He looked at his assistant, realizing he didn't even know the patient's name. "What is her name?"

The assistant stole a look at the stocky man. "Call her Delilah," he said solemnly.

Tyson was puzzled by the response but didn't have time to question. The baby was crowning.

"O.K., Delilah, push!" The girl responded and silenced her moaning. "Good, good," Tyson coached. He examined the perineum during the contraction. *This one won't even need an episiotomy,* he thought, *as if "Stumpy" would allow that anyway!*

The contraction passed, and Web relaxed

for a moment. "Relax, Delilah. You're doing great. A few more pushes — oomph —" Tyson choked on his own words as a sudden and deep dread filled his mind. *I've got to get out of here! I'm going to die!* He didn't understand his reaction. He tried to rest his hand on the young woman's abdomen to detect the next contraction, but it trembled as he extended his hand, and he immediately withdrew it and clasped his hands tightly in an effort to calm himself again. Then, for the first time, the patient began talking in a language Tyson could comprehend. Slowly and softly she began, lifting her hands to the ceiling: "I bear this son for you. For you I give my life." She repeated the phrase several times in an exhausted monotone.

She must be a religious nut! The patient stared off as in a trance. "Delilah?" No response. *Great! Right when I need her to cooperate, she goes off to another world!* Tyson had no comprehension of how close to the truth he was. He repeated her name, hoping to bring her around. "Delilah . . ." Again no response. He tried again. "Delilah, this is Dr. Tyson. I need you to push again! We need to —"

Tyson stopped as the woman locked eyes with his. Her eyes were wild and bulging, her neck veins full, her countenance twisted, as if she had aged twenty years in a moment's time. A guttural voice unlike her own bubbled from her lips. "I know who you are!"

Tyson felt completely exposed. He sat on a stool beside the bed. *Or was I pushed?* The woman continued to describe Tyson's own birth, the result of an affair his father had with a local barmaid. *How can she know these facts?*

The baby came with the next contraction. Tyson's mind whirled. He never remembered cutting the cord and handing the baby to . . . the mother? Or was it to the stocky man? He barely recalled the conversation that followed. He wanted to fill out the birth certificate. They refused. When he insisted that it was the law and in the interests of the child, they reminded him of old Doc Glover. *He died in a car accident, didn't he?*

In the end he conceded. He delivered the baby off the record. As he left the house, he thought he saw one of the men running to the dimly lit barn with a blanket in his arms. *The baby? What are they going to do with the baby?* Tyson turned and ran for his car. He didn't notice the rain. He felt only the urgent need to get away. Away from this place!

He drove for what seemed to be an hour before the pounding of his heart ceased and he could begin to process what had happened. A thought pierced his conscience: *That baby is in trouble!* He pulled his Dodge off into a service station with a phone booth. *But who can I tell?* His thoughts turned accusatory. *You can't tell anyone! You have no records! No one will believe you! You violated the law! You will lose your license! You will never be able to practice medicine again!* Tyson pounded his fist into the dashboard. *You never delivered that baby! This never happened!* He angrily stomped the accelerator to the floor, spraying gravel against a metal sign with a tiger on it. He sped away from the phone, away from his conscience, away from the small voice that beckoned him to confess the truth.

In the weeks that followed, Web was able to piece together exactly what happened at that rural Arkansas farmhouse. A state policeman stopped at the local hospital and warned the medical staff of some complaints, mostly dealing with animal sacrifice. "Be forewarned," the officer stated, "we have seen a rise in satanic occult groups before. Before long some crazies will want a little help with doing human deliveries without records, so the children can be used in occult rituals. The real Satan worshipers call these girls 'breeders.' They consider it a real honor to bear a child for sacrifice. If anyone hears about anything of this sort, please contact me right away." The large uniformed man passed out his calling card to the physicians who had assembled. "Believe me," the officer added, "to cooperate with these folks could get you into a lot of trouble."

Tyson had swallowed hard and kept quiet. Over the following weeks he kept his lips sealed about the incident. After a month he moved to Ann Arbor and began a new life as a surgical resident, with all evidences of that fateful night suppressed and hopefully forgotten.

Dr. Web Tyson sat up in bed with a start. He fought for a moment to collect himself, to orient himself to his surroundings. He coughed nervously and got up to go to the bathroom. He rubbed the back of his neck. *If that's what a little brandy before bed does to me, I think I'll do without!*

Sally Southerly, Paul Southerly's widow, sat staring out of her bedroom window. The thoughts that had plagued her since her husband's mysterious death drove sleep to the far corner of her mind. Paul's death seemed mysterious only to her, it appeared, as everyone, including the police, had ruled it an open-and-shut matter. They said Dr. Southerly had died peacefully in his sleep secondary to asphyxiation during an epileptic seizure.

At first she had taken everyone else's word. Their explanation seemed to make sense. Or did it? She grieved profoundly for days, blaming herself at every turn for abandoning her husband on that fateful night. Slowly, however, her guilt and incessant weeping gave way to other thoughts: *What if they were wrong?* Other thoughts tumbled along behind, as if linked like cars on a coal train. *Why a seizure? The autopsy reported his Dilantin level was therapeutic. The only other time he'd had a seizure in the last twenty years, his Dilantin level was low after a severe bout with the stomach flu. And why on the eve of his confirmation hearings? Coincidence? He was so looking forward to serving his country in this way — and the country badly needed a man with a solid moral and Christian foundation. That's certainly a rarity in politics today. Did that have anything to do with anything?*

Sally stood and paced around the spacious colonial bedroom, praying aloud as she walked, as she had often done with her husband in years gone by. "Lord, what am I to make of these thoughts? Is there truth that has yet to come to light? I do not desire to continue to hang on like this, Lord. I want to move on. Paul is gone. I can't change any of that now." She listened quietly and continued to pace. More questions surfaced — more questions without answers. She remembered the eerie feeling of evil that pervaded her house for the first days after Paul's death, a sense of darkness that lifted from the house only after she had gathered her prayer group to intercede. *What was the meaning of that, Lord?*

Another isolated fragment fell into her memory, a fragment she could not yet fit together with the others: *What about the smoke detector? Our security system recorded that an alarm had sounded in our room on the night of Paul's death. What can that mean?*

Over and over Sally pondered the meaning of her thoughts. Finally she laid them in the hands of her Lord and left them there. "Here," she said audibly, "I'm exhausted from mulling this over. This burden belongs in your capable hands." Like so many times before, when Sally truly placed something in the hands of her Savior, a sense of peace prevailed and she found her mind at rest once again.

Sally slipped into bed and closed her eyes. The time had come to stop worrying and to start trusting. Her deep breathing signaled the onset of sleep within two minutes.

Mary Jacobs lived the life of an M-3 to the extreme. M-3 stood for medicine, year three, the first immersion baptism into clinical medicine. It meant late nights, early mornings, and days filled with new patient workups and endless questions volleyed from the attending and resident staff. As far as glamour and prestige, there were none. Even the nursing staff told the medical students where to walk, where to find everything, and when it was O.K. to talk. If the students were smart, they listened; if they were proud, they learned the hard way. One person described the position of the third-year medical student as the part of the totem pole that is pushed into the ground. There were days when Mary felt that to be only too true.

She had arrived back at the dorm at 10, actually early for her, on a non-call night. If she'd have been "on," she wouldn't have left the hospital at all. Now, after a quick, cold supper of pita bread, peanut butter, and raisins, she sat on her single cot poring over her medicine texts to prepare for the next day's attending rounds. At attending rounds all of the new patients were presented by the assigned med student, who would then be "pimped" or questioned by the attending physician. The whole process was quite unnerving for the timid; for Mary, it had become a natural place for her eloquence to shine.

Mary looked at Kim, a D-3 (dental school, year three) who had been her roommate for the last two semesters. "Have you ever seen a patient with Bell's palsy?" Mary wasn't really looking for an answer, only someone who would pretend to listen while she continued her nightly oral recitations in preparation for the next day's rounds. "Did you know there are eight common causes of seventh nerve paralysis?"

Kim grunted compliantly and studied the dentures in front of her.

Mary continued looking at her text. "How about this one? Leprosy is in the differential diagnosis of possible causes of facial nerve paralysis!" Her blue eyes danced above her nose that turned up slightly at the end.

Finally Kim looked up and sighed. She added in an exaggerated yawn, "Only a third-year medical student would find that remotely interesting."

"Look who's talking. I once listened to

you explain that early oral carbohydrate digestion products lead to dental caries!" Mary announced with a friendly verbal jab.

"You were listening, weren't you?" Kim looked up as if in surprise.

"O.K., O.K., I'll cut out the play-by-play action and study quietly." Mary did a miserable job of trying to look hurt. "I promise." She studied for a minute longer and closed her books. She looked back at Kim, who still appeared engrossed with the teeth in her hands. "This whole M-3 routine's gonna be a thing of the past in a few weeks anyway. M-4 is just around the corner."

Kim looked up and echoed her own sentiments. "Yeah! D-4, here I come!" She paused as an inquisitive furrow wrinkled her brow. "You mean I won't have to listen to this nightly cram session for attending rounds?"

Mary smiled. "You know me better than that. I'll always let you know what I'm learning." She began brushing her thick, wavy blonde hair. "It looks like I won't be around much for the first elective, though. I couldn't get matched into a Bridgewater rotation for that spot."

"Where are you going?"

"Crestview Women's and Children's Health Center. It's just south of here, about twenty miles. I hear they even have call quarters for med students doing electives."

"How will I ever get along without you?" Kim laughed. "How will I ever keep abreast of the causes of Bell's palsy?"

"Give me a break!"

CHAPTER 8

On Friday morning, true to predictions, a two and a half column article appeared in the *Washington Post* introducing a newcomer to the national scene of health care politics: Dr. Weber James Tyson. The article was just what Lenore Kingsley wanted to see. Apparently Yearling had done all she'd asked, his pen yielding such lofty statements as "a real thinker," "a real physician with impeccable credentials," and "a Harvard grad with a true sense of call — a visionary, yet a public servant with his feet planted firmly on mother earth and holding an established track record for practical health care policy in his state."

Tyson liked what he saw as well. He practically devoured the article before a light breakfast and continued scanning it during his drive to work, his Mercedes drifting dangerously close to the soft shoulder of Route 783 on three occasions. Finally he closed the paper and drove ahead in silence, looking forward to the reactions of the Crestview Women's attending staff.

I can't wait to see George Latner's face when he reads this! George had been a partner in Valley Surgeons for Children for six years. He liked to work hard but had been feeling the same pressure Web had to get more help. They were just too busy. *Old George will really sweat if he thinks I might bail out for a few years and leave him with all this work!*

Tyson slowed down momentarily as he thought about all this, and a young woman driving a red convertible roared past and cut back in front of him. Web cursed the woman audibly and slapped his hand on the steering column. He didn't like to be passed by anyone. He especially didn't want to be passed by a woman. He fumed for a minute longer, intentionally riding the convertible's bumper to vent his anger. The sleek car eventually turned, leaving Dr. Tyson to cool off on his own.

His thoughts returned to the manpower shortage Valley Surgeons for Children had encountered. *Even if I stay on and don't end up as Surgeon General, we could sure use some additional help.* He thought over the information he'd covertly gathered on Brad Forrest. *He seems to be our kind of man — self-styled and confident, quiet, and not likely to make too many waves in our smooth practice*

— independent, but enough of a yes-man that he'll likely go along with whatever I deem appropriate.

Tyson thought too about his secret practice of infanticide. He would never use that term, of course. He preferred to think in terms of appropriate use of expensive life-saving treatment for those who have a chance to contribute to society — as he saw it, certainly. He saw no problem with shortening the life of someone who would only be a burden to society as a whole. It was mainly an issue of simple economics for Tyson; with a limited amount of resources, expensive care should be given only to those whose lives will benefit the overall societal good.

It will take a special man to fit in with my style of thinking. The men Tyson had added to his practice over the years had all come to him in the same way: Dr. Tyson investigated them and sought them out. No one that came asking for a job was ever given serious consideration for a permanent position at Valley Surgeons for Children. *Yes, it will take a special man indeed. It wouldn't do to have someone come along and call my moral reasoning into question now, would it? I think I'll talk to Latner and Davis about this Forrest. It seems that he may be just the kind of man we need around Crestview.*

Tyson pulled out his card to open the entry gate to the doctors' parking deck at Crestview. He parked his Mercedes in the space reserved especially for a man of his caliber. A small sign — "Reserved for Chief of Surgery" — warned off others who might be tempted to use the conveniently located spot.

Tyson cracked a thin smile and grabbed the paper from the seat beside him. *Just in case they haven't seen the* Washington Post, *I'll put this in the doctors' lounge for my associates to see. I can always get Jolene to order a few extras for my private collection.*

Lenore Kingsley had the floor in the plush conference room on the top story of United Biotechnical Industries. Most of the board of directors listened intently as she spoke. Several of the younger members had a hard time getting their minds off of Lenore's striking physical presence.

"As you know, we are sitting comfortably at the forefront of the pharmaceutical world." Lenore looked around at each of the men at the table. Several murmurs of self-congratulation could be heard following her pause for effect. Kingsley injected forcefully, "Pushing ahead, breaking new ground is where UBI has got to be! Sitting comfortably in the lead today is sure to find us looking at someone else's dust trail tomorrow!" The murmuring ceased, and the boardroom was quiet.

Lenore opened a copy of *USA Today* and spread it out on the table in front of them. "This is a full-page ad in today's paper. This ad signifies our full institution of phase 1 of my plan for UBI's future." Each member leaned forward for a closer look. A smiling infant in the arms of his mother could be seen taking up a prominent position in the center of the page. Below, the words "He's so perfect" formed the bottom border of the picture. In smaller letters below this was centered the slogan, "United Biotechnical Industries: Guaranteeing A Better Future For You And For America." The small print at the bottom of the page was more difficult for those around the table to read: "If you or someone you love is concerned about possible birth defects, call our toll-free number for more information. We can help you prepare your own perfect future. Lines are open 24 hours a day." A bold-print 800 number followed.

"Ads like this one have appeared in all of the major city newspapers across the U.S. in the last week. Our 800 number operators are giving out the names of the closest medical facilities that currently use our genetic screening products." She looked around the room. Everyone seemed to be paying attention. At least everyone was staring in her direction. She continued, "We have fielded thousands of calls from people who will be asking their doctors for the genetic testing UBI provides, tests that we will continue to expand and distribute as our researchers elucidate more of the human genome on a daily basis."

Gardner Kingsley beamed. He was finding it hard to sit still. He wanted Lenore to get on with an explanation of phase 2. Finally he interjected, "Tell them about phase 2!"

Can't he control himself for once? Lenore smiled through clenched teeth. She turned away from her overanxious father and continued, "What he is referring to is the ability of UBI to develop the technology to actually act on the information we obtain in genetic screening in a positive way, so that when a genetic defect is discovered, we can act on it and change it or remove it to prevent the imperfect condition from ever occurring." Several members looked puzzled by her last statement. "What you need to understand at this point is the big picture. What we're able to do now is provide parents with important genetic information about their offspring in time for them to abort the fetus legally. That's the essence of phase 1 of UBI's plan for the future. In today's push for fewer and fewer offspring, parents want the peace of mind that they will have normal, healthy children. We've been able to contribute to that peace of mind by the development of our genetics testing products. Everyone with me so far?"

There were scattered nods across the room. Gardner smiled at his daughter proudly.

Lenore went on, "O.K., now for the introduction of phase 2. We screen for genetic defects, and then, instead of aborting the babies, the genetic code is altered to correct the defect, perhaps even enhanced to give the parents exactly what they want, right down to sex and hair color." Lenore bit the inside of her lower lip. *I shouldn't have mentioned that yet! I've got to sell them on correction of disease states before we move on to enhancement of normal genetic makeup.* After her silent rebuke, she asked for questions. Fortunately the board had a paucity of scientists, and they seemed content with an overview and didn't ask about many of the specifics. Lenore was careful not to mention that the work would likely involve the sacrifice of thousands of human embryos.

"What about the other work UBI is doing? Have we forgotten the development of synthetic blood products and pharmaceuticals?" The question came from long-term board member Michael Dubner.

Lenore didn't take offense. She answered with the coolness that had become the signature of her business style. "Mr. Dubner, we are not abandoning our other research interests. What I am encouraging us to consider is the challenge of the future. As you know, our patent for Oxydel will be up in a few years. We need to position ourselves now to prevent a potential loss of significant income for UBI. If we fail to pursue other research interests and broaden our research base, we could find ourselves in the middle of a long, dry slump. Believe me, gene research and genetic therapy is the wave of the future, a wave that I believe UBI should be riding the crest of, Mr. Dubner."

Dubner remained silent and stroked his well-groomed, gray beard. After a few more questions, the meeting was adjourned by the C.E.O., Gardner Kingsley. Lenore departed quickly after gathering her supplies. Michael Dubner caught up with her in the hall. "Lenore!"

Lenore focused her attention on the tall executive without speaking.

Dubner approached the topic cautiously. "What do you know about the government's feeling about embryo research? This is a hot topic in the public arena, Lenore. It might not look so good for —"

"This administration is very open to this sort of thing, Mr. Dubner. The N.I.H. has liberalized their policies quite a bit in the last few years." Lenore seemed instantly tired of their short conversation.

Dubner reached for her arm to detain her for a moment longer. "It's just that in today's unstable political climate, it might not be so good to push into such a controversial area — what with the Surgeon General spot vacant and all. You never know who will be controlling all of the research money in the next few years. It may serve us well to wait and see if the next health care administrator will look favorably on research of this type."

Lenore sighed audibly. *These guys in the outer circle just don't get it, do they? Who do they think opened up the vacancy in the spot for Surgeon General? They are naive to believe all they hear and see.* They have no idea that all of this is already under my control. "Listen, Mr. Dubner, we have a very powerful lobby in Washington. I'm sure we can influence the choice for a Surgeon General who will cast us a favorable glance now and then." *I will own the man — and he won't even know it!* Lenore was careful not to give away too much of her thinking. "Mr. Dubner, I have another meeting to get to. Can we talk another time?"

Dubner persisted. "Just remember the Reagan-Bush era, Lenore. Remember the federal ban on fetal tissue research? One wrong man in a key position like that of the Surgeon General could set research like this back a full decade — or more!"

Lenore tried to interrupt. "Mr. Dubner, really, I —"

"All I'm saying is that we should pursue less controversial areas of research. This is too hot an issue politically for us to put so much money into."

"Just remember where this money came from, Michael," Lenore snapped, emphasizing his first name in a condescending manner. "Oxydel began and ended with me!" She whirled around and then called over her shoulder, "And it has carried this company for the last three years." She turned and stomped toward the elevator.

Dubner shrugged and returned to the boardroom for his briefcase.

As she waited for the elevator, Lenore

fumed. *When Daddy's gone, I'm cleaning out the dead wood around here! The members of the inner circle seem to be the only ones I can really trust to make reasonable decisions. At least I understand where I stand with others who serve the same master. These idiots can't see beyond their own noses. They have no idea who is controlling all of this.* She tapped her foot impatiently and pushed the Down button two additional times. *I can't wait until all of UBI is in sync with the only real power.* With that thought on her mind, the elevator opened, and Lenore descended to her office.

The doors to the Oval Office were closed. The President of the United States, Thomas Blackburn, didn't like to be "the last to know."

"Sam, give me the latest on the search for a new Surgeon General appointee."

"Well, sir, I —"

The President didn't wait for a reply. "And who is this Weber James Tyson? Why wasn't I briefed on him before I read the morning paper?"

"Well, Mr. President, I —"

"I can't stand finding these things out this way!" The new President stroked his graying temple and sighed. He looked around the room at his most trusted advisors. "Don't you realize what happened to us the last time we failed to communicate on an 'important government appointee'?"

No one answered the President's question.

The President continued to vent his frustration by reiterating what they already knew. "Let me remind you then. We almost got a pro-life Surgeon General! You know what that would have done. We would have looked like we were riding the fence again. 'One for the right. One for the left. Let's keep everyone happy!' " The sarcasm in his voice bit deep. "I've got too much support in the pro-choice camp to commit political suicide like that!"

"I really thought he was a moderate, sir," Dan Stevenson offered.

"Who?" the President shot back.

"Paul Southerly, sir."

The President shook his head in disgust. "That's just it! We hadn't done our research well enough. Except for a weird twist of fate, we would be stuck with Southerly right now. Can you imagine what he would have done at the helm of a multibillion-dollar health care budget? He'd probably be throwing money to the Christian conservative right to fund abstinence programs or some such nonsense!" He shook his head again. "Ooooh, my friends, we lucked out, but next time? That's why we're having this little talk. There's not going to be a next time. No more mistakes. I want complete background checks and all the cards on the deck when it comes to an appointee's past voting records and current political views."

The room remained silent. The President opened the *Washington Post.* "Now, what does anyone know about this Dr. Tyson? How did he get on the list?"

Sam Wetherby spoke up first. "He's only been on the list of potentials for a few days."

Dan Stevenson added, "We've been taking a look at quite a few possibilities that have been compiled by our staff."

The President reiterated his question without raising his voice. "How did Dr. Tyson get on the list?"

"How does anyone get on the list, sir? A suggestion is made, and we consider all leads seriously until we see something that raises a red flag or —"

"Who suggested him?"

The men stared at each other and then at the floor. The President waited.

"Doesn't anyone have any idea how he got on the list?"

No answer.

"I suspect we had better find out, gentlemen. This is probably how the fiasco with Southerly started. A name is suggested, the list is leaked to the media, they write about him, the public grows to like him, Congress gets a chance to confirm him — need I say more?"

"Mr. President, I'll get right on it," Wetherby blubbered.

"We need to go exceptionally slow about this. I'd rather that the media say we're dragging our heels than rushing ahead uninformed. The media can make the public see that barging ahead with such an important decision could spell disaster for U.S. health care policy."

Heads nodded around the room.

"Good. Find out all you can about everyone on this list. I want to know about it all before this —" The President looked at the article. "— before this Tom Yearling, staff writer, whoever he is, does."

Every Friday morning at 9:30 A.M. seven faithful prayer warriors from Patterson's Nursing Home gathered in the rec room for prayer. Almost every Friday, Belle Forrest prayed with them too. The gathering had actually been Ben Kreider's idea. Now in his eighties, Ben had spent most of his life in foreign missionary service in Israel. He had lost a few inches in height in the last decade, but he still stood a slightly bent six feet tall. He had a warm smile and wiry, white hair that reminded people of an old Albert Einstein.

"We've got our minds, friends," he had exhorted the small group of believers that had found camaraderie in the west wing of Patterson's minimal care wing. "We may not be able to be out there doing great works for God," he gestured with his hand toward the window, "but we can make significant inroads on Satan's territory right here on our knees."

"Not on these knees!" Florence Tutweiller had responded with a chuckle. "I talk to the Lord sitting right in this chair," she said, her arthritic left hand stroking the arm of her wheelchair. An octogenarian herself, she was no baby when it came to spiritual warfare either. She had thin, white hair and perfect, white dentures that seemed almost too prominent because of her frequent smile.

That particular conversation had occurred over two years ago when the group formed. At that time there where just four participants: Ben Kreider, Florence Tutweiller, and Craig and Sandy Nesselrodt. The Nesselrodts were retired from a family-run drugstore. Craig stood only five feet, five inches and had a waist the size of his generous heart. Craig had loved the pharmaceutical business he'd inherited from his father all of his life, and he frequently reviewed all of his neighbors' medicines on the west wing of the home and gave out unsolicited advice about everything from Tylenol to beta-blockers. Sandy was the same height as her husband, although Craig always insisted he was meant to be much taller because of his weight. Sandy had raised four sons while balancing the books at the corner drugstore and in general providing the glue that kept the Nesselrodt family together. Although faithful church attendees all of their lives, an active personal prayer life had remained an illusion to them until they met Ben and Florence. They had, however, taken up their charge quite seriously once they embraced it, and Craig had led the group last winter in Ben's absence when he'd been hospitalized with pneumonia.

Richard and Alice Yoder joined the prayer army six months after they began their weekly assembly. The Yoders attended the first week they moved into Patterson's. They had left a similar group behind when they moved into the Green Valley area and had prayed steadfastly for God to bring them back into contact with a group of like-minded believers. The transition into the Patterson way of life was not an easy one, especially for Richard, who had complained for two months about the single beds in their room. "It just doesn't feel right without my Alice beside me." Alice stayed quiet about the matter, however, and was relieved she could now sleep through the night without Richard waking her up during his twice nightly trips to the bathroom. Regardless, the prayer group had solidified their love for the place in general, and soon even Richard had stopped whining about his sleeping arrangement.

Jennifer Slabaugh had joined the six most recently and remained the group's only new convert. Jen had committed her life to the Lord one morning after weeks of conversation with Ben, Craig, and Richard. "Ben thinks he talked me into the kingdom, Craig thinks he prayed me in," confided Jen to Sandy one evening, "but it was your friendship that made the love of God real to me in a way I could touch." A diabetic, Jen had lost one leg to gangrene only eight months ago, and it was Sandy who went with her every day to physical therapy for three months without missing a day. Until her amputation, Jen had been able to function independently at home. But in the absence of her husband Bruce, who had passed away after a massive stroke two years before, she yielded to the pressure of her two sons and entered Patterson's care facility. "Just until I'm back on my feet again solid," she had asserted confidently, holding on to the hope that she could someday move back into her own home.

Belle Forrest, the only outsider in the group, had been a longtime friend and supporter of Ben Kreider. He had known her support both financially and spiritually during the years he served the church in Israel. Today they gathered as they always did, in the rec room on the west wing. They met just beyond a Ping-Pong table in front of a wall of windows that looked out over the large, green lawn leading down to a thick forest bordering the Wanoset River. As far as they knew, no one had ever played Ping-Pong in that room, but the table served many other purposes. Today it held an old tea service and a few diabetic cookies, compliments of Jen Slabaugh.

They began with a prayer of dedication and commitment of their time, led by Ben. Florence had always insisted on a praise song or two, and today the room could hardly contain the uninhibited worship of these elderly saints who cared little about what others thought and more about what mattered to the One who would be their Father for eternity. The songs were joyful always, in tune mostly, and rang with a rhythm inherent of those smitten with a slight case of Parkinson's disease.

After the songs, Ben opened an old cloth-covered notebook that chronicled both their requests and answers to their prayers. "Who's got a report or concern?"

Around the room, one by one, answers to prayers were shared and concerns were raised. When a personal request was made, the group gathered in close, with wrinkled hands clasped in unison or gently laid upon a shoulder of the requesting member.

When it came time for Belle to speak, she unfolded that morning's *Washington Post* and turned to the article on Weber James Tyson. She passed it to Richard, who sat on her left, and he to Alice and then to Florence, and on around the circle until they had all read snatches of the article. "I'm not sure what has bothered me about this," Belle began slowly. "It's just that I had such a sense of loss at the passing of Paul Southerly, and now to see Dr. Tyson as a potential replacement, I, well . . . you have all seen his prominent liberal views pushed in our own state — early sex education, condom distribution, health care rationing for the elderly . . ." Belle faded out, the others listening intently. "I'm not sure exactly what my request is, except that I want God's will to be done in this whole thing. I think we need to pray for a leader with a heart for the family, a person who will stand up for Christian moral standards."

"Doesn't he work down at Crestview Women's?" Ben asked, somewhat incredulously. He stole a silent look at Florence who shook her head as if to say, "Who would have believed this?"

"I've heard Brad speak of him often. He's the chief of surgery there. He's held in quite high esteem, it seems," Belle answered.

Ben looked at Florence again. "This is sure interesting in light of something that happened to Florence and me this morning." He paused and directed his next question to Florence. "Do you still have that *USA Today*?"

"It's on my dresser. Door's open."

Ben hobbled off and returned with the second newspaper to be passed around the group that morning. "Just look at this ad."

He was met with curious stares, except by Florence who had talked about the ad that very morning.

"This thing reeks of humanism — man as the controller of his destiny — you know, the subtle lies that our enemy is using to convince us that man is supreme," Ben explained.

Richard interjected, "Aren't you reading a little too much into this thing?"

Alice chimed in, "And how does this relate to Belle's prayer request?"

"O.K., O.K.," Ben retreated, "I'm not sure it's related at all. It just came to mind when she mentioned Dr. Tyson. He works at Crestview Women's Health Center, right? Well, when I saw this ad, I just had to call that 800 number to see what they were after. I talked Florence into doing it for me because she sounds so much younger over the phone. And get this — when she called, they informed her of all the genetic screening tests offered to pregnant women today. They referred her to Crestview Women's Health Center here for more information regarding genetic screening. They said she could get appropriate abortion counseling there! They thought Flo was pregnant!"

The group giggled for quite a while after that. Finally Craig brought the group back to focus on the issue at hand. "All right, what's this all got to do with us and our prayer time?"

Ben answered solemnly, "All I know is that if this is what they're peddling down at Crestview Women's and Dr. Tyson is one of their big wheels, I'm not sure he'll tout the kind of philosophy as Surgeon General that we'll be comfortable with, that's all. Basically, I'm just affirming Belle's request that we commit this important decision into the Lord's hands."

Ben offered his open palms to his neighbors, who followed his example. Together, in a circle of prayer, they began a new battle, asking that the truth would be exposed and that the powers of the enemy would be turned back.

CHAPTER 9

Tammy James looked much younger than the thirty-seven years she had reported on her Crestview Women's application form. Her life had changed voluminously since leaving New York seeking to escape a bad relationship and a directionless life seven years before. For five out of the last seven years she had worked at Crestview Women's and in the last two years had settled nicely into her role of 5 north's night nurse manager. Her search for direction led her on a circuitous path through a local palm reader who eventually led her to the ever-broadening coven of Lenore Kingsley. She feared Kingsley but was unmistakably drawn by the power Kingsley possessed.

It was Tammy who, quite accidentally, brought Web Tyson into Lenore Kingsley's plans. Tammy had wanted advice on directing Web into her life. She had fallen hopelessly for the surgeon, who seemed to have little time for interests outside his love for medicine. As she described Tyson to Lenore, she told of her admiration for him as a pioneer, an independent thinker who did not let the current law dictate his every move. Eventually Lenore was able to draw out the whole story of Tyson's involvement in state health care policy and even his secret infanticide of debilitated infants. Tammy thought that perhaps she had shared too much, but reasoned that Lenore could read her thoughts, even the unspoken ones, anyway. Lenore instructed Tammy on several spells that she could use to get Tyson's attention. In the meantime, Tyson had gained Lenore's full attention, and she knew he would be the one to open the way for the research that she planned.

Tammy looked at herself in the full-length mirror in the women's bathroom behind the nursing station. She wore her chestnut hair in a french braid, as she often did on the job. A small gold chain with a single crystal adorned her neck, her blouse open at the collar to expose the stone against her tanned skin. As the shift drew to a close, she knew that Web Tyson would be rounding soon. She freshened her lipstick and smoothed her white blouse. *Fortunately "sterile white" is a good color for me.* She smiled at her comely reflection and went back to her small office to complete her shift's paperwork. She glanced at the calendar, which served as a constant reminder that she had to do next month's staffing schedules. Sighing, she filed the bedside chart papers in her out-box. She personally inspected and initialed all of her staff nurses' work. The patient list had been high, and her compulsive scrutiny over the floor details would detain her past her appointed off hour.

When she looked up, Web Tyson stood in the doorway. "Morning, Tammy."

"Good morning, Web." She had used his first name now for six months, since the time he had allowed her into his secret "treatment" of "hopelessly ill neonates."

Web lowered his voice and stepped into the small cubicle. "Thanks for helping out with that Down's baby the other morning."

Tammy looked up at him, trying to discern his thoughts. Her eyes locked with his in a soft exchange. After a few seconds, she replied in a hushed tone, "You know you don't need to —"

"Yes, Tammy, I do," he interrupted, raising his voice only slightly. "I have been very careful to keep this between us. I know it creates a stress you don't particularly care to add to all of this." He struck the pile of paperwork in her in-box.

She stood and eased the door closed behind him. She took his hand from where it rested on the papers on the desk. She caressed his hand slowly, noting the callus-free texture of the surgeon's skin. "Sometimes doing the right thing creates a little stress, Web."

"You don't have to convince me of that. I'll just be glad when the rest of the world recognizes it, too."

Tammy pressed his hand into a fist and placed it against his chest, releasing it after an additional squeeze. She felt in total control of the emotional flow in the cramped office. She returned to her chair, then brightened as she remembered the news from the previous week. She raised her voice to move away from her sultry tone. "I hear that you may be just the man to convince the rest of us that your private policies are exactly right . . . Surgeon General!"

Web looked down and smiled. "It's still quite a long shot, Tammy." He opened the door. "Well, I've got rounds to make."

"And I've got to get a schedule made up."

Tyson stopped short of leaving the office and looked back at the nurse who had already returned to her work. "Hey, what do you say we go out and celebrate this new possibility sometime?"

Tammy looked up casually, not wanting

to appear too anxious. "What do you have in mind, Doctor?" she taunted playfully.

"Eat dinner with me."

"Is that an order?" she replied coyly. "I always follow the physician's orders, you know."

Tyson smiled again. "It's an order then. I'll give you a call tomorrow. Let's aim at Friday." With that he turned and hustled down the hall, grabbing the bedside chart out of the wall rack as he entered the room of the first patient he needed to see that morning.

Tammy sat at her desk for a minute longer before pushing the stack of papers on her desk aside, unable to concentrate on her assignment. *I'll work on this tomorrow,* she thought. *Maybe Lenore's advice is paying off after all.* She unconsciously clutched the crystal around her neck, stood and locked her office, and left for the day.

The next two weeks spun rapidly with activity. The dizzying pace in and around Green Valley raced on in ironic contrast to the peaceful forested mountains that provided a lush retreat to so many seeking an escape from life's pressures.

Lenore Kingsley and Randy Harris laid precise plans to begin human embryo gene splicing. Lenore was able to push beyond Harris's initial objections and persuade him to cooperate. He understood that his job stood on a precipice, and he could fight the determined Kingsley only to a point without endangering his position.

A romance budded between Dr. Web Tyson and the night nurse manager, Tammy James. One dinner had turned into two, and that had ended in a trip to Tammy's apartment. Web had added one more commitment to his expanding schedule, and Tammy began entertaining the initial fantasy of a life married to a national political figure.

As for Julie Forrest, a description of her relationship with Brad would hardly begin with the word "romance." On the few nights that Brad had gotten home before 10 P.M., the air had been heavy enough for a surgeon's scalpel. Their nightly "discussions" of what the future held and what direction Brad would pursue had turned icy. Julie had finally clammed up altogether. To her, Brad seemed closed to options other than university practice; and Julie seemed sure that the future would look very much like the present. Brad finally admitted his secret hope that Dr. Tyson's apparent interest in him would materialize into a job option, and Julie held on to a slim hope that things would change.

Jimmy Tyson was discharged from the hospital. His mother had insisted he come home with her for a few days. Web Tyson had even offered his place along with a full-time, hired home-health nurse. Jimmy had declined both, preferring his small apartment and the support of the gay community.

Ben Kreider developed pneumonia and missed the Friday morning prayer group for the first time in a year. The others met in his absence, but the heart of the group seemed subdued, and they broke up early for the first time ever.

The Blackburn Administration began full background checks on all potential Surgeon General candidates, including Web Tyson. In spite of an unsure start, the picture of Tyson that emerged seemed very much in line with what the President desired. Still, the administration wanted a thorough investigation, and anything done with that type of completeness in Washington took time. No progress reports were provided to the media other than the daily press release: "All possibilities are being investigated. The administration is committed to the timely nomination of a suitable Surgeon General candidate."

Mary Jacobs conquered her final oral exams for the third year of medical school, internal medicine. She deftly outlined a twelve-step approach for a workup of fever of unknown origin, provided a complete differential diagnosis for each of six cases she was presented with, and even enumerated seven side effects of the anticoagulant, heparin. Bridgewater University had steered away from traditional letter grades for clinical rotations, so she had been awarded "Honors" instead of an "A" for her stellar performance. She had only one four-week rotation in neurology left before M-4.

Sally Southerly couldn't quite stop thinking about her misgivings about her husband's death and contacted the sergeant who had headed the police investigation. He reviewed the file to get her off his back and politely informed her that everything seemed to be in order and that he deemed further research into the matter to be unnecessary and a waste of taxpayers' money.

As for Valley Surgeons for Children, two deaths were recorded at Crestview Women's and Children's Health Center. One, a premature infant with respiratory failure and a hernia in the diaphragm, was allowed to suffocate because he weighed too little to fit the government's newly imposed standard for use of E.C.M.O. A second infant, a female with mental retardation and spina bifida, died at the hands of Dr. Tyson after he explained to the parents that any aggressive treatment to surgically cover her exposed spinal cord would only prolong her unbearable suffering. A stealthy injection of a paralyzing agent stifled the infant, whose death was recorded on the death certificate as sudden infant death syndrome (S.I.D.S.).

Finally, for Brad Forrest, his unexpressed wish appeared to be materializing. Just as things at home became intolerable, events unfolded to reveal an opportunity to meet with Web Tyson to discuss "matters of extreme importance to both of our futures." If the government's scrutiny of Tyson was thorough, Tyson's behind-the-scenes inspection of his potential business associate was more so. Forrest seemed impeccable. Tyson wanted him. They arranged a meeting for 8 P.M. Thursday for dinner.

"Come on, Julie!" Brad snapped, looking at his watch. "We're going to be late!"

"We still have plenty of time. I'll only be a minute longer," Julie called from behind the locked bathroom door.

Brad heaved a sigh, straightened his tie for the fourth time, and sat down on the bed in a huff. The evening hadn't started out well, and it threatened to get worse if Brad didn't lighten up. He'd carefully arranged cross-coverage so he could get home early to get ready for his meeting with Dr. Tyson. He arrived home in plenty of time, only to find the Nova in the driveway with a flat right rear tire. He deftly put on the spare, but his generous time cushion had been eroded by twenty minutes. His internal clock pushed him to pester his wife until she could stand his questions no more and locked herself in the bathroom to finish her preparation without her husband's inspection. Now Brad realized he'd better collect himself or he could destroy the whole night.

Brad set his internal clock back five minutes and told himself to relax. He even took off his coat and carefully stretched out on the old wedding-ring quilt on their bed. He positioned himself on his back so any wrinkles caused by his action would be covered when he put on his suit coat. *Just chill out, Forrest,* he chided himself mentally. *You should know by now that acting this way will only make things worse!* He closed his eyes momentarily and counted to ten, a method he had practiced since childhood to deal with his anger. The slow count brought back an unexpected flood of memories from his childhood.

One . . . two. He was an active little boy of four dressed in his Sunday best except for a red football helmet that stood out prominently on his head. "A hyper child like Brad needs to wear this at all times," the doctor had said firmly. "Until the skull fracture has healed, it is too risky that he will reinjure it." *Three . . . four.* "I'm gonna start counting!" His mother's shouting was muffled as Brad hid deep in the closet behind all of the family's winter coats. "You'd better be down here by five, young man! One! Two! Three!" *Five . . . six.* "Brad, you have to go to church! Daddy is the preacher!" *Seven.* The scene changed, and Brad was in the center of a sea of chanting Sunday schoolers. "Brad wears a helmet to church! Hey, Brad, wanna play football? Hut one! Hut two! Hut three!" *Eight.* "You'll not ride that bicycle again until you're at least eight years old, and that's final!" The words were his father's words, which he would always obey or else! *Nine . . . ten.*

Brad sat up and shook his head. *Whoa! Where did all of that come from?* He hadn't even noticed that his wife had emerged from the bathroom and now sat beside him on the edge of their bed. Brad felt strangely and suddenly subdued by the memories his count had evoked. Julie looked beautiful. It had been too long since he had taken time to look at her and really take in . . . really appreciate . . . her loveliness.

Julie broke into his private thoughts. "I'm ready, Dr. Time-conscious. Did you forget our appoint—" She stopped, suddenly noticing the steely look in her husband's dark eyes.

"J-Julie, I . . ." Brad stuttered. "I'm sorry for the way I acted. I've paid more attention to the clock than I did to you."

Julie returned his stare and remained quiet.

"You look radiant."

She softened and kissed her husband tenderly. "Hey, I know this night is important to you — to us." She corrected her sentence carefully. "I'm a little nervous about this myself."

The couple stood together, and Brad rather sheepishly checked his watch again. "Come on." He coaxed a weak smile. "We still have twenty minutes until we meet Dr. Tyson. We've got plenty of time."

To Lenore Kingsley, Randy Harris seemed insistent on sticking his neck in the way of her newest project proposal.

"I'm really only concerned about your safety, Lenore," Randy pressed on with real anxiety showing in his voice. "Why don't you just let me do the gene splicing, grow the embryos in tissue culture, and then sacrifice them for DNA analysis?"

"Randy, we've been over this all before. I know you are concerned, but believe me, I'm the one calling the shots in this deal. We can never get the information we need just by growing the embryos through a few divisions in-vitro. You know we need to implant the embryos so we can get an old enough fetus to really see if what we're hypothesizing will work. We just can't get the information any other way."

Randy stroked the side of his smooth-shaven face, then folded his hands across his chest in exaggerated body language. "But why you? Why do *you* have to be the surrogate?"

"Just where do you suggest I find another willing carrier?"

"With your kind of money and influence, I'm sure you could find and pay someone enough to do it."

"There is also the matter of breaking this to the scientific community in a controlled fashion. We can't have the word going out about this work until we have established a successful, reproducible way to alter the genes of our offspring." She smiled smugly. "I can be the most tight-lipped individual in the world if I need to be."

Randy started to protest again, but halted when he sensed that Lenore's patience was thinning. "I just —"

"I'll have no more discussion about this, Dr. Harris. You do your thing, I'll do mine." She paused and looked around the lab. "And by the way, I've arranged for my gynecologist to do the implantation. She works as an infertility specialist at Crestview Women's. She's ultra-smart, and she has agreed to do it here in one of our labs — to avoid the documentation that would be required if we did it at the hospital."

Randy surprised himself at his own reaction. "Oh, fine. You're being tight-lipped about this and you've already told your gynecologist."

Lenore pointed her finger at her researcher. "For your information, she won't know any of the details about what goes on with the embryos before implantation. She thinks I want to carry a baby for an infertile couple. Besides . . ." Lenore looked at Randy and decided to tell the truth. ". . . she's in my coven. She knows what would happen if she mistreated me." Lenore laughed heartily.

Dr. Harris looked at her with concern, then joined in with a forced laugh of his own. "That's not such a funny joke, Lenore. Some people might be crazy enough these days to believe a statement like that."

Lenore laughed deeply for a moment longer, then opened her briefcase and retrieved a small card with a date on it. "From my temperature charts and the regularity of my menstrual periods over the last year, I should be ready for implantation in another ten days." She sobered and stated in a very businesslike command, "You can get all the human embryos you need from Alice Roberts over at Crestview Women's in-vitro fertilization lab. It's all been approved. Have you decided what gene manipulation you want to try first?"

Randy was taken aback at the date on the card he held in his hand. Lenore was pushing ahead at an alarming rate. "I — well, I was expecting more time for a clear decision, but, uh, well — if I have to do it this soon, I guess I'll splice in an additional growth hormone segment — and a hair color marker so we can have more than one way to see if the retrovirus did its job."

"Good." Lenore turned and walked to the

lab's exit. "Oh, thanks for staying late so we could talk about all this. I hope I didn't foul up your social life too much."

"Oh, no," Randy mumbled in return. Lenore didn't hear. She had already left. Randy sighed and looked at the lab that was empty except for him and a group of caged Dalmatian puppies. He wondered if Lenore's jab at his "social life" was intentional. "I need a drink," he spoke aloud to the closest canine. "I need a drink real bad." His countenance changed as he decided to reward himself. *I'll go down to Anthony's.* He had not been to his favorite gay bar for over two weeks because of the extra work Lenore had demanded. *I think that's exactly what I need after a week like I've had.*

Dr. Tyson had spared no expense. The restaurant, although not five-star, was the closest thing the valley could support. The champagne, at $120 a bottle, tingled their palates and lubricated their conversation, which was both piquant and probing. The steaks were thick, the bread homemade and steaming. By the end of the evening, Tyson had concluded his research.

As they sipped dessert coffees, Tyson began his offer. "As you know, I founded Valley Surgeons for Children over fifteen years ago. The practice is the most respected in the tri-state area and is world-renowned for its expertise in the surgical treatment of critically ill neonates. We work hard. We publish. We educate. Our physicians are respected authorities held in equal regard to any of this country's great university surgeons. In many ways our practice sets the tone for the excellence that personifies Crestview Women's and Children's Health Center. Many have wanted to come and work with me. I have added only two other surgeons since this practice was founded — Mark Davis and George Latner. Both typify the devotion, clinical excellence, and loyalty that make this practice click."

Brad and Julie sat quietly. Tyson's personality was electrifying and captivating. Brad squeezed Julie's hand in a silent message of excitement. Julie pumped back her quiet, affirmative response.

"I've taken the liberty to ask Bridgewater University's department of surgery for your C.V." Tyson paused and swirled his coffee. "I want you to join me, Brad. I believe you have what it takes to carry on the fine tradition that I've established."

"What about the Surgeon General position? Will you still practice?"

"The possibility exists that I will be asked

to serve in that position. That remains very much in a possibility, not probability, stage at this point. Certainly it has made me think more seriously about adding someone to this group. But in all honesty, if I never set foot in Washington, we are still busy enough to need you onboard."

"I — I'm honored to be asked, sir. I — I almost don't know what to say."

Tyson took out a business-sized envelope and handed it to Forrest. "Here are the facts of the offer in outline form. If you are agreeable, I will have my attorneys draw up a full contract."

"I'll need a few days. I've promised to talk to Dr. Dixon at the university this week. I guess you know he wants me to stay on."

"I know more than you think," Tyson offered with a wink. "Take a few days. Talk over the offer. Call me with your response when you know. I am confident you will make a wise choice."

The bill was delivered and easily conquered by Tyson's Visa Gold Card. As the Forrests stood to leave, Tyson offered even more encouraging information. "By the way, Latner and Davis have also reviewed your file. As founder, I have complete and sole responsibility for hiring the right people; but I want you to know that my associates are in complete agreement with my assessment. Davis is operating tonight or he'd be right here with us. Latner is presenting a paper at the Southern Surgical Clinical Congress or he'd be here as well."

Brad extended his hand. "I'll give you my answer within a week."

With that, they left without another word.

Randy Harris slipped into his favorite booth in the back at Anthony's Place. It was dark, and it took him a few minutes to get his eyes adjusted to his surroundings. He ordered a Mexican brew and sipped slowly while he looked around the room. After one beer he relaxed a little more and ordered a European beer, followed by a Chinese beverage. It occurred to him that he should just drink himself around the world, and he smiled at this little plan and tried to locate an Australian stout on the extensive list in front of him.

After an hour and a half he found it quite difficult to concentrate on the menu and decided it best to eat something and sober up a touch before driving home. Although he had not come with intentions of leaving alone, his desire for a companion had not materialized. Anyway, he didn't seem to be handling his geographic alcoholic survey in the way he intended. He ordered a steak sandwich in hopes that some solid consumption would cure the dizzy feeling in his head, then sat back and closed his eyes.

A commotion at the entrance startled Randy's eyes back open, and the thirty-five-year-old researcher looked toward the door. Tony, the bar's owner, had a piercing tenor voice that cut through the noise of the restaurant. "Jimmy! I didn't expect you! You look great!" Hugs were exchanged, and the young man took a seat at the bar.

Tony filled a frosted mug from the tap and set it in front of the well-groomed customer. "Thanks, Tony," Jimmy responded. He seemed rather subdued in contrast to the owner who continued his exuberance.

"Everybody! Look who's back! A round on the house to celebrate!"

Jimmy Tyson turned around and nodded to the restaurant-goers. Scattered well-wishers lifted their beers toward him. Across the room Randy could hear their comments. "Good to see you again, Jimmy." "Are you here to work?" "We're glad you made it." "How do you feel?" "Take it easy, Jimmy." "You look like you never left." Randy watched him as he stood, walked slowly around the room, and greeted his friends.

Dr. Harris ate his steak sandwich in solitude. He felt better, and his dizziness left him as he dined. After a few more minutes he walked over and paid his bill, then sat down next to Jimmy Tyson, who remained at the bar. He extended his hand. "Hi, Jimmy. I'm Randy Harris."

Jimmy looked up and shook his hand. "I know you, Dr. Harris. I've seen you here before."

"Hey, call me Randy. That Dr. Harris stuff is for the lab, not this place." He smiled, then added, "I heard about your accident. You look like you've made it through O.K." Randy touched Jimmy's arm tenderly.

Jimmy sat quietly for a moment. He wasn't in the mood for a pickup.

Randy responded to the silence and tried to open conversation another way. "Looks like you're destined for the limelight, huh?"

Jimmy looked at him curiously without speaking.

Randy continued, "You know, your old man being Surgeon General and all."

"Oh, that," Jimmy sighed. Everyone always wanted to talk about his father. "That's pretty premature yet, uh, Randy." He took a sip of his beer. "He's never even talked to the White House. It still looks like a long shot to me."

"That's not what I hear down at UBI. Lenore Kingsley talks like he's already in. It's almost strange, you know. She's his biggest fan. I've heard her talk about him to some of the other bigwigs down at the lab. She acts like it's already fact — like she knows he's going to get it or something."

Jimmy took the information in without commenting. The last thing he wanted was to be thrust into the public eye because of his father. Randy continued talking nervously to cover Jimmy's silence. "Lenore talks like his policies will be a boon to the future of research genetics and —"

Jimmy interrupted, not so much out of interest, but out of the desire to quiet his intruder's babbling, "Who's Lenore?"

Randy was taken aback. He thought everyone around the valley knew Lenore Kingsley. "Lenore Kingsley. You know — the president of United Biotechnical Industries. She invented Oxydel."

Jimmy brightened. "She did?" He finished his beer with a gulp. "You know, I got some of that stuff — that Oxydel. They used it on me because I lost so much blood in the accident."

The researcher winced. "Man, you must have been hurt pretty bad."

"They say so." Jimmy sighed with fatigue.

Randy stood and extended his hand. "I'm glad you're back."

"Huh? Oh . . ." Jimmy shook his hand again. "Thanks."

Randy turned to leave. "See ya."

Jimmy mumbled, "Sure."

CHAPTER 10

"Linda! Linda! The letter came! Our answer's here!" Matt Stone yelled as he ran up the rocky clay path to his cinder-block apartment.

Linda Baldwin Stone greeted her husband in the tribal language of the Kipsigis, the Africans they had served for the past three years. She often practiced her language skills on her husband, but today reverted quickly to English. "Have you opened it? What does it say? Where are we going?"

"Hold your fire, matey." The breathless Stone held up his hand and used a thick, overdone Irish accent. "Let me catch my breath," he panted. "I didn't open it. I wanted you to find out the same time I did. I ran all the way from the post office."

The letter, postmarked two weeks before in the United States, contained the return address insignia of Physician Placement Services, a company that specialized in filling temporary practice vacancies for physicians. The young surgeon's hand trembled slightly as he loosened the edge of the envelope. The couple had considered their options prayerfully over the last six months since the arrival of a new missionary surgeon at the mission compound in the highlands of western Kenya. Matt wanted to start or join an established general surgery practice in the States, but searching for the right position from the other side of the world had proved frustrating. Then the opportunity to consider a temporary position had come. "It's a chance to return to the States, save a little money perhaps, and look for a more permanent position," Matt had consoled his young wife. "A good opportunity to seek God's guidance and plan for the next step," he stated with the confidence that characterized his living faith.

The plan seemed right. They tested it with the "rule of peace." Yes, it seemed like God's hand at work again. Matt had written over six weeks ago that he would be available for an assignment in July. That gave them two weeks to get out of Kenya and back to the U.S. Just exactly where that would be was yet to be determined. But hopefully the letter in Matt's hand contained the information they had prayed about for months.

"I can't look." Linda covered her eyes playfully.

Matt couldn't not look. He slipped the folded sheet out of the envelope and began scanning the type. ". . . filling in for Dr. Jack Stevens who will be on extended leave for personal reasons . . . apartment provided . . . hospital nestled in fertile valley . . . patient caseload predominantly focused on the treatment of breast diseases . . ."

"Where is it?" Linda interrupted.

Matt kept reading the highlights. ". . . also managing general surgical and critical care needs of surgical intensive care unit . . ."

Linda raised her voice. "Where is it, Matt?"

Matt looked at the address at the bottom of the page. "Hmmmm." He scratched his head, went to his bookshelf, and pulled out a well-worn U.S. road atlas. He thumbed through the pages, finally pointing to the exact location. "Here it is." He held the map up to Linda, who anxiously held her breath.

"Look, Matt, we could drive to your mother's place on the Eastern Shore in one day."

The young surgeon kept staring at the paper in his hand. "Sounds like a strange patient mix. Listen to this. 'Ninety percent of patients are female between the ages of fifteen and seventy-five.' "

"Why only women? They haven't got you mixed up with a gynecologist, do they?" Linda smiled.

"I've done enough OB/GYN right here to last me a while," Matt chuckled. In the Kenya bush just about every physician became a generalist out of necessity. General surgeons did C-births, pediatricians treated adult TB, and dermatologists treated malaria and AIDS. Overwhelming needs create the perfect environment for the adaptable to improvise and the super-specialists to broaden — or crack.

"I seem to remember a certain general surgeon doing a little emergency obstetrics back in residency," Linda chided.

Matt sobered. "I don't think I'll ever forget that emergency room c-section — not in this life anyway." His memories of that night and of the larger controversy that had brought him into confrontation with a morally misguided surgeon, Dr. Michael Simons, brought tremors of apprehension into his mind. He shook his head before looking back over the practice profile sheets. "Evidently this Dr. Stevens has enough general surgery to do at this one women's hospital. Looks like a large referral base from three states. This hospital must have some reputation."

"What's the name of the place?"

"Crestview Women's and Children's Health Center. I start in two weeks."

Julie Forrest smiled. It seemed almost too good to be true. Brad Forrest, associate, Valley Surgeons for Children. The most respected pediatric surgery group in the state — bar none!

Brad had told Dr. Dixon, his chairman, of his decision only that morning. That afternoon he had signed a three-year contract leading to full partnership with Drs. Tyson, Davis, and Latner. Tonight was a night for celebration.

"With three partners sharing the call, I expect I can take your picture down from the refrigerator. Bradley will see you enough that I won't have to remind him who you are," Julie teased.

"Very funny." Brad poured two goblets of champagne. "Here's to our future."

Julie lifted her glass and clinked it gently against her husband's. They sipped the bubbling liquid slowly.

"Let's go out on the porch," Julie said quietly. Brad picked up the bottle and followed his wife. He instinctively checked his beeper, still attached to his belt. Julie watched him. "You're not on, are you?"

He switched the beeper to Off. "Not tonight. Steve's covering. He owed me from the adult trauma call I took for him," Brad replied with a sigh. "So tonight I'm yours, no strings attached."

"I think your champagne has gone to your head." Julie sat down on a wooden porch swing. Like most of the home improvements at the Forrests' old Victorian home, the porch swing had come because of Julie's, not Brad's, elbow grease. She'd found the old swing at a yard sale the previous fall and stripped off the old paint before recovering it with a white that matched the house's trim.

Her husband sat down beside her and refilled the glasses. He put his arm around her, and she responded by snuggling closer. She rested her head on his shoulder. They enjoyed the night together, neither speaking for a few minutes. Belle and Bradley slept inside. Brad and Julie were alone, listening to the symphony of summer night sounds.

In a few minutes Julie interrupted the crickets' song. "I'm gonna miss this old place."

"Yeah, and I'm gonna miss every night call too," Brad responded with buoyant sarcasm.

"Brad, I'm being serious. I know this old

place has a lot of memories for you, too." Julie pushed harder against her husband.

"I know." Brad swirled his glass. "At least we won't be forced to move right away. It's only a thirty-minute drive to Crestview. We can take our time finding just the right place."

Julie sighed contentedly and lifted her golden hair over her husband's arm. "It looks like it all might pay off after all, Dr. Forrest." Julie enumerated the years of training she had endured. "Four years of college, four years of medical school, seven years of general surgery residency and research, three —"

"Enough already." Brad nudged his wife playfully. "You're making me feel old." Julie laughed. The champagne was catching up with her. Brad sat quietly a moment longer, then spoke softly, as if trying to keep someone nearby from hearing, even though they were alone. "Did you realize that Tyson will be paying me two and a half times what Dixon offered?"

Julie was well aware of the figure. "I saw," she responded with a whisper and nibbled her husband's ear. "I saw."

Brad shivered. He wasn't sure if it was Julie, the champagne, or the salary. "Maybe we should look for a place over at Cedar

Point. They have a few homes with a great view of the Wanoset River. Bradley could even go fishing."

"How about replacing the car first? I think a BMW is required for entrance over there, you know."

Brad chuckled. "I guess we would look pretty funny driving that," he said, nodding his head toward the old car in their driveway.

Julie closed her eyes. It felt good to dream. She so hoped that their new life would be different. She almost felt that she was on the edge of reclaiming her husband from the black abyss of medicine that had taken him away for so many years. *It will be better now,* she thought. *We will actually have money! And time together!* Julie kissed her husband's neck tenderly. *I've got the chance to take you back again.* She felt a sudden chill, an unexpected intrusion on the warm night. *One more chance to make this relationship work.* She didn't share her thoughts with her husband, who seemed preoccupied with dreams of his own. Instead, they rocked slowly without speaking, the squeak of the swing adding a tenor note to the crickets' choir.

Dr. Web Tyson liked being out with

Tammy. She made him feel so young — so alive. She caressed his hand as they sat in their favorite riverside cafe, DeAngelo's. It was a small place that specialized in Italian cuisine and sat nestled along a small inlet on the edge of the Wanoset River. The decor was mediocre, but the location more than made up for what was lacking in decorative amenities. It was surrounded by a massive wooden deck and had a pier leading out into the water. The surgeon and his new friend were sitting at an outdoor table on the deck. From where they were positioned they could see the lights of the Nickel Bridge, which had been named for an old bridge toll, long since abandoned.

"More wine?" Web held up a bottle.

"No more for me. I've got to work tonight, remember?"

"I have to go home alone?" he pouted.

"You'll survive," Tammy drawled in her finest southern drawl.

Web loved her accent. *Why didn't I notice how attractive she was all these years at Crestview?* He looked at her longingly for a moment and then out to the Nickel Bridge in the distance. A waiter came and served their dessert, two dishes of Italian ice cream and chocolate shavings. Web looked back at the nurse, who was ten years his junior.

His demeanor changed to serious. "Dr. Forrest has signed to come on and work for the practice."

"I heard. News at Crestview travels at record speed, you know." She spoke in a sultry voice. "The lowdown on 5 north is that he is smart and . . . handsome," she said slowly, watching for Web's response. *Had he diverted his eyes? Jealous already, dear?*

Web didn't respond. He just changed the subject. "You know, Tammy, I've been thinking about something you said a few weeks ago — about being able to influence the thinking of a nation. Maybe I'm starting to get over the novelty and pride at even being considered for the Surgeon General position. Now I'm starting to think a lot about the responsibility — the power." His voice faded.

"With the way they've restructured health care, it's definitely a position of increased importance," Tammy responded.

Web lowered his voice unconsciously. "There are the ever-debated issues of abortion, euthanasia, and infanticide. The next decade will be pivotal in deciding the future of American medicine." He paused. "Perhaps I should notify President Blackburn that I would like to change my status from 'interested' to 'seeking,' " he said. "I would rise to the challenge of enlightening the ignorant public concerning the answers we have found for these distressing problems. It takes a real leader to convince the masses to make the right choices, no matter how difficult they may seem."

"I, for one, think you are the perfect man for the job," Tammy said softly. "You don't have to convince me that we are in desperate need of some policy changes. I know it would be a relief to get some of this out in the open."

"From what I understand in talking to Blackburn's front men, they are very open to decriminalizing euthanasia and infanticide. At the very least, that's a start. I think the right Surgeon General may just be able to swing their thinking enough to get Congress to consider the next step."

Tammy raised her eyebrows. "The next step?"

"Active protocols for physician-assisted suicide, and in the case of minors or infants, increased parental rights so debilitated infants won't have to live on as needless burdens on an already overtaxed society."

"What about the elderly? Those with dementia or Alzheimer's disease?"

"The same rules could apply. A power of attorney could interact directly with physicians to allow death with dignity as every American's right. It would certainly streamline the system to keep the courts out of it. With legalized euthanasia, there would be no need to tie up the judicial system. It would be every person's right to interact only with their physician to determine when the proper end of life should be."

Tammy nodded with understanding and agreement as she ate her ice cream. Tyson continued at a low volume. "I know we have been careful to cover our tracks in the past in regard to our special treatment of debilitated infants. It will be doubly important for us to do so in the future. I'm sure that public inspection of my life and my practice is going to increase, the closer I get to being Surgeon General."

"It sure wouldn't look good to have accusations about infanticide surface," Tammy whispered slowly. "Regardless of what is morally right, it is still technically against the law."

"I prefer to think of what we are doing as 'in front of the law' rather than 'against the law.' It is only a matter of time before the humane compassion that we are showing becomes the law. Eventually it will be recognized as completely acceptable to painlessly and compassionately put society's good above the individual rights of a congenitally malformed infant who will only be a burden on the taxpayers." Tyson chuckled nervously. "I guess it all boils down to the bottom line in one way or another — money. We live or die by the dollar, Tammy. Like it or not, the almighty dollar seems to run the world."

Tammy looked at her watch. "Well, it's running me, that's for sure. I've got to get to work. Can you drop me off at the hospital?"

Tyson laid enough cash on the table for the bill and tip. "Sure." He stood and kissed her cheek. "Let's get out of here."

Randy Harris sighed both from fatigue and satisfaction. Lenore had been true to her word. A special courier had delivered the human embryos, the "leftovers" from Crestview Women's in-vitro fertilization lab, and Harris had worked on them for more than 100 hours. The fertilized eggs were allowed to divide through three cell divisions. He then separated several cells off of the early-stage pre-embryo and grew them in-vitro until he had enough DNA to analyze. He determined the absence of genes responsible for blond hair color, used a retrovirus to introduce a new gene for blond hair, used a segment of complementary DNA to negate the black hair color gene that was present in the pre-embryo's normal genome, and then repeated the process to add additional human growth hormone to the newly modified genes. These modified cells were then reintroduced back into the embryo in preparation for transfer into the surrogate uterus.

There! Randy thought as he stared at the petri dish containing three newly modified embryos. *This has not proven to be much more difficult than the experiments I did with mice during my Ph.D. thesis work. The hurdles I conquered during my work with the Dalmatians have translated directly into my ability to modify the human genome.*

Randy carefully entered his observations in the lab's computer, data that Lenore Kingsley could review from the desktop computer in her office. Randy finished his work, then exited the computer, carefully moving the data into a file accessible only to Lenore or himself.

He felt both elation and anxiety. *I just wish Lenore had allowed me to complete the DNA analysis of the dogs before proceeding with the human experiments. Since the dogs are relatively young, I still don't know if there were changes in the genes we were unaware of that haven't been expressed yet.* He held his head in his hands and sighed. *She seems obsessed with being the first to accomplish this work in humans — at any cost! Tomorrow's the implantation. At least I'm not responsible for that part.*

He walked to the windows of his lab and looked out on the lights of the city below him. *At least we know that the human embryos will never be brought to delivery. I won't have to worry about that. That could be a disaster! I'll at least have the luxury of examining the fetuses after a few weeks in utero to see if there have been unexpected detrimental effects of our gene splicing.*

He turned out the lights, locked the door to the lab, and headed down the hall. Except for UBI's security force, the researcher was alone. A surveillance camera recorded his exit but couldn't read his private anxieties that registered as a dull gnawing in his upper abdomen. *At least it's carefully documented in my private journals that Lenore is the one insisting on proceeding without knowing fully if the experiment is completely safe.* He sighed again. *It's her body. Why should I care?*

Randy exited the building and walked to the parking deck. He slipped into his 1969 Triumph TR-6, revved the engine, and turned up the volume of the radio. *Maybe this will quiet my mind,* he thought as he squealed the tires and sped onto the highway. *It always has before.*

The following morning Belle gathered with the seven west-wing believers at Patterson's Nursing Home. She was troubled in her spirit and had risen even earlier than normal to "pray through." She had come to a point of peace, but still didn't quite understand her burden and looked forward to the fellowship of her brothers and sisters in Christ to help shed some light on her situation.

The meeting proceeded as it normally did. Ben was back and moderated with his usual dry wit. The praise songs were enthusiastic, the prayer was fervent, and the snacks were diabetic. After an opening prayer, Belle began to share her burden.

"I'm concerned about my grandson, Brad. You've heard me speak of him on many occasions." She looked at Jen Slabaugh, who had a puzzled look on her face. "You know — he's Bill's boy." The puzzled looks resolved as the members recalled the stories of Reverend William Forrest's tent ministry and fiery preaching. Belle continued, "He's a children's surgeon." She nodded her head with confidence. "I'm sure I've told you about him." Craig, Ben, and Richard nodded in unison.

"Well, a few weeks ago we prayed about the new Surgeon General candidate, Dr. Tyson. Now, believe it or not, my grandson has landed a job with this same surgeon. He's very enthusiastic about it. He has nothing but good things to say about this apparently very well-known pediatric surgeon. All I could think of when he told me about the job was the information we came across about the work at Crestview Women's. Remember the genetic testing and abortion services they offered to Florence?" A few smiles registered on the old believers' faces. "All I know is that every time he mentioned his new job at Crestview with Dr. Tyson, I wanted to tell him my misgivings, but each time I started, I just couldn't speak — almost as if I just couldn't talk at all."

"Now that's a first." Ben chuckled.

"O.K., laugh if you will, but I'm serious about this." Belle's voice trembled slightly as she continued, "I even thought I might be havin' a stroke the first time it happened. I just couldn't get my words out. Soon, however, I realized that it wasn't that, because I could say other things. I just couldn't talk about Dr. Tyson or Crestview Women's Health Center."

Craig thought for a moment, then tapped Ben on the arm. "Now that may be a miracle, Belle not being able to talk —"

Florence spoke sharply. "Just a minute, boys." At her age Florence called everyone, regardless of their age, "boy." "This may just be the hand of God in action. We prayed about this Dr. Tyson, right? Maybe, just maybe this new relationship with Belle's grandson is part of God's plan for both parties."

Ben scratched his wiry, white hair and looked at Belle. "Does your grandson know the Lord?"

Belle sighed. "I'm not sure how to answer that." She wrung her wrinkled hands. "He knows about God —" She paused. "But he doesn't know him the way we understand him, that's for sure. His father was a preacher, unfortunately a very busy one. I think Brad may have been lost in the shuffle, so to speak." Belle paused and wiped her eyes with a tissue. "Don't get me wrong. He's a good boy, but, well . . . he had a fallin' out with his father when he was a teenager. Brad went off to college, a big secular university, and it just broke his father's heart. Bill had wanted his son in the ministry. Brad wanted to become a doctor. It seems like such a small thing, but the fight just poured alcohol on the fresh wound of bitterness over the neglect from his father. Brad left home declaring he'd never serve the God who stole his father away. Unfortunately, they never reconciled before Bill's death two years ago. I think Brad's buried it all pretty well now. He's given his life over to medicine and never talks about his father. He doesn't seem to object to my faith, but he doesn't seem to see the necessity of it in his life."

Ben opened the prayer notebook. "I'm adding Brad's name to the list. Starting today we need to pray for this young surgeon's salvation. It sounds like he needs a real encounter with the truth. And he's gonna need some protection workin' in a place like Crestview Women's if that place is anything like I discern."

Several "amens" reverberated around the spacious rec room. Belle looked at her friends and smiled. *A burden shared is a lighter burden,* she thought as she closed her eyes and joined her partners in prayer.

CHAPTER 11

Matt Stone looked at his watch and sighed. 3:30 A.M. *My body thinks it's 10:30 A.M. and I shouldn't be in bed.* "Awake?" he whispered softly at the motionless body next to his.

"Yeah. I can't sleep either." Linda moaned and threw back the top cover. "Might as well get up and make some coffee."

"Coffee?" Just the thought of hot black coffee was enough to bring Matt to his feet. It had been rare to get good coffee in Africa. Now they had been back in the U.S. for less than twenty-four hours, and he couldn't wait for his first cup of the straight, black, American-style wake-up juice.

"Yeah, Matt. You remember! Hot, black stuff you drank by the gallon as a surgical resident," Linda said with a smile.

Matt looked at his wife and laughed. She looked good with her dark hair and deep African suntan. "Don't remind me of those days."

"Why? It's when you met me! Remember?" Linda kissed her husband teasingly.

Matt returned his wife's kiss. "I'll have to admit, you were the best part." He paused and looked at Linda's green eyes. "But you and your friends almost got me fired, remember?"

Linda imitated her husband's comment. "Don't remind me of those days." They both laughed.

Over coffee they began to unpack their meager belongings and orient themselves to their new apartment. The apartment was furnished, had two bedrooms, and sat one block from Crestview Women's and Children's Health Center where Matt would be working for the next few months.

"When do you have to meet with Dr. Stevens?" Linda called from the center of a room of unpacked boxes.

"Not until tomorrow. I hope to be better oriented to the time by then."

"Good idea. I don't guess your patients would like to be disturbed by you rounding at 4 in the morning."

"Very funny," Matt replied. He looked at the box in Linda's arms. "Here, I'll take that. It's books for my study." He smiled cunningly.

"Your study?" Linda replied playfully.

"The second bedroom. I thought I could

just camp out in there with all my surgical books."

Linda looked around the small apartment. It was little by most people's standards but seemed spacious to the Stones, as they were used to almost no space at all back on the mission compound in Kenya.

"We've been blessed, Matt."

Matt looked around with Linda, then reached out and squeezed her hand. "Yes, we have. We really have."

Dr. Suzanne Feinberg looked around the procedure room where she would do the implantation. "Everything is in order, Lenore. Your facilities here rival what I have to work with at Crestview."

"At UBI we pride ourselves in being second to none. Besides," Lenore added with a smile, "I knew it would be the only way I could talk you into performing the procedure right here."

"Here, put this on," Dr. Feinberg said as she tossed Lenore a flimsy patient gown. "Just because we're on your turf doesn't mean we're not going to do this by the book."

"Yes, Doctor," Lenore added, stepping into a dressing cubicle and pulling the curtain behind her.

"Is Dr. Harris going to be involved today?"

"Not for this part," Lenore called from behind the curtain. "If you need some help, I can get one of our female technicians to come up from the next lab. It's just that Randy and I have such a close business relation—"

"Say no more. I understand. I've done this so many times, I think I can manage by myself," the gynecologist added, folding a sterile towel that had covered a tray of instruments. She looked at the containers that Randy Harris had laid out before leaving moments before. Lenore reappeared from behind the curtain. "I'll need you up here, on your back."

Lenore cooperated by getting up on the procedure table and putting her legs in the stirrups. Dr. Feinberg sat on a stool in between the patient's legs. The doctor made small talk as she began. "Whose baby did you say this is?"

"Uh, an old friend of mine from college. We're like sisters. She's even more of a career woman than I am. Her last pregnancy nearly killed her. She had an emergency hysterectomy after she bled from a botched c-section, but they really want another kid and, well . . . if you only knew what all she did for me . . . it's the least I could do." Lenore chattered nervously for a moment longer.

"But why all the secrecy, Lenore? Why do the procedure here?"

"That was part of my condition, Suzanne. I've gotten to be such a local celebrity, as the president of UBI, that I want to keep as low a profile as possible," Lenore lied.

Suzanne Feinberg thought that Lenore's reasoning sounded a little eccentric, but the money was right, and the deal was processed as "cash only." *Besides,* she thought, *with the setup she's provided for me, this should be no problem at all!*

"I'm going to examine you now." The doctor talked in soothing tones. "I'll be putting a speculum in now." Lenore winced slightly in reaction to the doctor's exam. Dr. Feinberg spoke in surprise. "Lenore, I thought you reported that you had borne no children. This cervix shows clear signs of previous delivery."

Lenore hadn't realized that she could be caught in the lie. *I didn't know she could tell!* She felt vulnerable. Exposed. She cleared her throat. "Yes, I . . . well . . . what I meant . . ." She had a sudden idea. "I never had a live child. I — I had a stillborn child when I was just a girl myself," she lied. "I

— I didn't realize that counted."

"Don't be alarmed. It shouldn't affect your success as a surrogate mother."

Lenore closed her eyes and tightened her fists. She reacted out of anger, not out of pain. *I have to be more careful! I can't risk raising any suspicions about what is going on in this lab until I can reveal our success to the world.*

The doctor completed the procedure without problems in the next few minutes. Neither the doctor nor the patient spoke again until the procedure was over.

"There. I'm all done."

Lenore opened her eyes. "So I'm pregnant?"

"We'll know if we've had success in another week or two. We will need to do a blood test to determine your beta-H.C.G. level."

"I don't feel any different."

"Just wait."

Lenore hopped off the table and stretched. "In fact, I feel great."

"Easy, Lenore. I want you to stay quiet for a few days. No vigorous physical activity of any kind. No lifting — and no sex." Feinberg smiled, but Lenore stayed quiet. "And you'll need to stay on the hormone supplement regimen we discussed earlier."

"Uh, sure, no problem there."

"I'll schedule an ultrasound for three weeks from now. I want to make sure that everything is beginning as it should. If your beta-H.C.G. level or the ultrasound shows any evidence of pregnancy loss, we'll stop the hormone replacement."

"We have ultrasound capability here," Lenore interrupted. "I'll not be going to Crestview Women's for my care, remember?" Her steely blue eyes locked on Suzanne Feinberg's.

The gynecologist felt suddenly threatened. "O-O.K., O.K.," the doctor choked. "Can you at least take pictures?"

"Sure."

"Just send me the ultrasound pictures then. I'd like to follow the progress." The doctor seemed incensed but knew she had little leverage against a patient like Lenore. She had been paid well, easily double what she normally received for a surrogate implantation. Dr. Feinberg collected her things and walked out without speaking.

Brad Forrest dressed in a white button-down shirt, a striped silk tie, and a dark, solid jacket. *It's time to dress the part,* he thought as he readjusted the knot in his tie. *My first day with a "real job."* He checked his watch. 5:30 A.M. *Plenty of time to eat and get to Crestview by 6:30.* He kissed his sleeping wife, then crept down the stairs and out to his car. In similarity to his wife's aging Nova, Brad drove an old foreign car, a Datsun, made by Nissan prior to their name change.

As the young surgeon traveled, he thought back over the past few days. Julie's joy over the prospect of his spending more time at home was shaken when he'd insisted on starting at Crestview on Monday, after finishing his pediatric surgery fellowship on Friday. "Why can't you take a little break? Let's take a few days off and take Bradley to the lake," Julie pleaded. Her concerns went unheeded as Brad's excitement over his new position kept him from thinking about anything else. Now as he drove across the Wanoset Nickel Bridge, he felt a twinge of guilt for putting his job ahead of his family again.

Brad shook his head as he remembered their biting words. "Your driven behavior is ripping this family apart!" Julie had shouted. "Who are you trying to please? Isn't it enough to have accomplished all you have? Look at you, Brad! You're a pediatric surgeon! How many people ever accomplish anything close to that? And now you've landed the best job in the world, and you're still pushing! Your addiction to perfection is going to ruin everything!" Brad's protests had seemed shallow. He wasn't able to face the truth in Julie's words.

Now as he drove, her words haunted him again. "Who are you trying to please?" He turned on the radio but didn't really hear the words of the popular tune. His thoughts turned to his father. *Dad. The man with all the time in the world — for his flock. The man I could never seem to satisfy. You should see me now. Maybe now you'd be proud. I've landed the job of the century, Dad. Prestige. Money. Influence. I told you it would pay off someday. I'll show everyone who laughed at the little "P.K." I'll show you, Dad.* Brad rubbed his temple. Julie's words had opened a small window of understanding in his mind. *"Who are you trying to please?"*

He stopped at Jake's Diner and ordered sausage, grits, and coffee. The food was quick, hot, and southern. Jake came out from behind the grill when he saw Brad. "Old Doc Tyson told me you're joinin' up with him. He comes in here all the time since him and the missus broke up." Jake smiled broadly and extended his hand. Brad pumped the owner's plump palm.

"Thanks, Jake. It looks like a great opportunity for me," Brad replied. He looked back at his plate and stirred his grits. He didn't really feel like talking.

"Word's out that old Tyson might even make Surgeon General." Jake wiped his greasy hand on his white apron. "Wouldn't that be something?"

"He's not in yet, Jake. We'll just wait and —"

Jake seemed distracted and ran toward his grill to turn some hotcakes.

Brad returned to his food and his own thoughts. *Tyson's divorced? I guess I didn't really ask him about his home life, did I?* He ate the rest of his breakfast in silence and left his payment on the counter.

He arrived at Crestview Women's fifteen minutes early. He walked to the O.R. doctors' changing room, where he found his full-length locker next to the other surgeons' in his group. A gold-lettered nameplate stood out against the light green locker door: "Brad Forrest, M.D. Pediatric Surgery." Inside he found a new stethoscope, a digital pager, and a white lab coat with his name embroidered on the left front pocket, followed by "Valley Surgeons for Children." Two new Parker pens were in the pocket, which also contained a neatly folded patient list. On a shelf below sat a new three-volume set of *Glen's Pediatric Surgery* and a new surgical atlas. Below this, a pair of medium scrubs had been folded and placed in his locker, ready for his use later in the day. Brad could barely contain his surprise and excitement over each new item he found in his locker. He lifted the starched white coat and gently ran his fingers over his embroidered name. *Man! These guys really know how to treat a new surgeon.*

Brad slipped off his sport coat and put on the long white lab coat. The buttons were cloth after the manner of classical clinical tradition. He looked at himself in the mirror and smiled. As he continued to admire the coat, Dr. Tyson walked in behind him and went to his own locker. "Ahhh, Dr. Forrest. You've found your locker, I see."

Brad, startled, answered hesitantly. "Y-yes, sir." He turned away from the mirror. "Thanks a lot. How did you know my size?" He wasn't really curious but didn't know what else to say.

"I make it my business to know everything about the surgeons I work with," Tyson replied with a wink.

Brad shrugged and let the comment fall without a verbal response.

"Let's go to the conference room. I told Latner and Davis to meet us there at 6:30."

Brad followed the graying surgeon obediently. At the conference room, checkout began promptly. George Latner had been on call, so he led the verbal accounting of each patient on the Valley Surgeons for Children's census. "Everyone should have a patient list," he began. He looked at Brad and explained for his benefit, "Our office assistant, Jolene Martin, puts a copy of the updated list in each of our lockers every morning. After checkout we each go to our assignments. Every day it will be a little different, depending on who has office hours, who is operating, and who is on call. After all the work is done for the day, you may check out with the call man and turn your pager off."

Tyson added, "We run an efficient ship here, Dr. Forrest, and we're proud of it. Today you will take new consults and make rounds on the patients on our list. Learn them well, so that if the nurses call you for information, you will be ready."

After that Latner gave a detailed checkout of all the patients on the census. They adjourned, and Brad again followed Tyson into the corridor. Tyson turned back to his new doctor. "Follow me. I'll introduce you around on the wards and in the O.R. This will be a light day for you, since you won't have to operate unless we have an emergency." He handed him a thick, yellow manila envelope. "Here are the outlines of the chapters of *Glen's* textbook that you will find in your locker. After your work is completed on the wards each day, we should be able to find you in the library that is on the second floor. No one in this group has ever failed to pass the board exam in pediatric surgery," he said slowly. "Judging by your in-service prep scores, you will have no problems."

Brad weighed the bulky envelope in his hand by raising and lowering it several times. *He sure seems to know a lot about me.*

Tyson continued, "Our very own Dr. Davis has sat on the board as an oral examiner for the last six years. He will be meeting with you periodically to hone your oral examination skills. Your first mock exam is next Friday and will cover the first four chapters in *Glen's*."

Brad nodded again.

"By the way," Tyson added, "we will be sending you to Chicago next month." He handed Brad a plane ticket and a small, colorful brochure. "This course is run by the best pediatric surgeons in the country. It will provide a helpful review before your board examination."

"Thanks." Brad shook his head in amazement. Everything seemed so regimented. *I thought I was out of residency! Daily library visits? Mock exams?* Brad's head was spinning when Tyson broke back in on his thoughts.

"Come on. I've got some people on 5 north I want you to meet."

Being a surrogate mother was certainly not going to stand in the way of Lenore's work performance. In fact, she was determined that no one at UBI, except Randy Harris, would even be told about her voluntary surrogacy. *No one needs to know,* she reasoned, *especially not my father. He would only worry. Besides, I'm going to abort before anyone can tell I'm pregnant anyway.*

Lenore sat in her office, taking mental inventory of her feelings since receiving the embryo transfer earlier that day. *I don't feel any different. Maybe a little tired, but that's probably due to all the late hours Randy and I have been putting in.* Her thoughts were interrupted by her secretary.

"Dr. Kingsley? Randy Harris is here to see you."

Lenore sighed. *I told her not to call me*

"doctor." She punched the intercom button forcefully. "Send him in."

Randy came through the door holding a vase of flowers in one hand, his briefcase in the other. He smiled sheepishly and held up his gift. "Congratulations, mom!"

Lenore rose and closed the door behind him, looking cautiously into the entryway beyond. "Remember, no one is to know about this! Keep your voice down!" She softened when she saw Randy's smile.

"I couldn't help myself. Besides, I know what a wreck that hormone therapy can make you. I thought you might like something to cheer you up." He set the bouquet down on the desk corner.

"Thanks, Randy." She looked down. "Is this why you came? I thought you said earlier you had something to say."

"I do. Good news on the embryo supply front," he said matter-of-factly. He slid a stack of articles out of his briefcase. "I figured out our needs for embryos in the next year. If things go as well as we think, we will easily outstrip the supply of Crestview's infertility clinic." He looked up at Lenore. He had hoped that his little revelation would at least raise a concerned comment by the UBI president. Instead, she remained quiet. "That's where this information will come in handy," he continued, striking the stack of articles. "These describe the technique of harvesting eggs from aborted female infants' ovaries."

Lenore sat back down at her desk and sniffed the flowers in front of her. *Sometimes Randy can be so thoughtful — and sometimes so bothersome,* she thought.

"Lenore, are you listening?" Randy raised his voice. "The supply of embryos has always been the limiting factor in my germ cell research. Sperm is never in short supply, but eggs are a different matter entirely. If we can duplicate the experience of these researchers, it looks like our supply problems will be solved. One aborted female infant can be the source of hundreds of eggs, each of which can be fertilized with sperm from our bank to make embryos."

Kingsley brightened. "Now all we need is to show the scientific community that this gene splicing will work. With appropriate financial backing, we will have all the surrogate mothers we want. UBI will be in the catbird seat for the next decade and beyond. If we can perfect our techniques on the human genome, we can patent the whole process. Everyone will be bowing to us, Randy. Everyone will want what we control. UBI will assume world prominence as the only company to be able to control what is passed on from one generation to the next. Even governments will seek our help. With Uncle Sam paying everyone's health care bills, it will become mandatory to screen and eliminate every faulty disease state we can find. In many ways we will control the destiny of the world." Lenore had stood again and paced as she talked. She faced Randy and repeated the phrase, "the destiny of the world."

"I think this whole surrogacy thing has affected your head." Randy laughed. "This hormone manipulation is giving you grandiose delusions."

Lenore seemed put off by the researcher's statement. *He doesn't realize how serious I am. He has no idea . . .*

Just then Lenore's secretary, Barb, cracked through on the intercom. "Dr. Kingsley? Bill Stedman is on the phone."

Randy leaned down and spoke softly to Lenore, who was behind her desk again, "I've got to run, really. I just wanted you to have the flowers. I really couldn't help myself." With that, he scurried off, leaving Kingsley to her phone call.

The president punched line 3. "What is it, Stedman? I hope you have good news for me."

"Hello, Lenore. Well, yeah, good news and bad, I suppose."

"Isn't that the way it always is with you lawyer types?" Lenore chided.

"Funny. Real funny. The bad news is that we lost the wrongful-life suit over in Green County. The good news is that no one knew that UBI had anything to do with backing the case, and the media exposure was strong. The obstetricians have all heard about this one. In terms of their sensitivity to ordering genetic screening tests, I suspect a loss in this case will be almost as effective as a win. All the doctors will be running scared, ordering every conceivable genetic test on the market just so they won't get slapped with a lawsuit."

"Just as we'd hoped." Lenore smiled.

"Just as we'd hoped," the attorney echoed.

Brad looked at his watch. 9:30 P.M. It had been a long day. In between getting to know his new floor patients, he had seen three consults, started an IV on a thousand-gram premature infant, and admitted a young boy with a closed head injury and a facial laceration — and he still hadn't had a chance to visit the Crestview library. He was back on 5 north reviewing the final few charts so he would be up on all the patients. Tonight he was off, but he knew Julie would understand if he didn't get home right away. After all, it was only his first day.

He picked up the final chart. It was for Room 525. The chart was different from the rest. It wasn't very thick, and displayed prominently on the front was a red sticker emblazoned with the message: Do Not Resuscitate. *Hmmm. Unusual for a pediatric patient.* Brad opened the cover. Quickly he scanned the chart. No IV fluid orders were present in spite of the order to give nothing by mouth. He scanned the H and P (History and Physical) note. The patient had been admitted only the night before. The diagnosis caught his eye. Infant with Down's syndrome. Heart murmur. Vomiting with suspected bowel obstruction. He looked carefully for the orders for diagnostic tests and treatment plans. He found none.

On the second page of the progress notes he found a notation about the parents' wishes that the child not be allowed to suffer. He read carefully the handwriting of Dr. Web Tyson. "In light of the severe incapacitating and irreversible illnesses, the family has elected to pursue comfort measures only. No surgery that would only prolong the child's suffering will be offered." Brad continued to review the chart contents carefully. *Other than the Down's syndrome, there are no other irreversible problems that I can see. There is no documentation of any other organ system dysfunction. Perhaps Dr. Tyson is aware of test results that are not yet noted on the chart. Certainly he wouldn't deny this child the necessary surgery just on the basis of Down's syndrome, would he?*

Brad scratched his head and yawned. *I've got to get some studying done. I can ask Web about this tomorrow. I bet he gave a verbal order for an IV for hydration, and the nurse just hasn't written it down yet.* He shoved the chart back in the rack and walked to the elevators. Tonight he was bushed. He wouldn't walk the stairs.

He exited on the second floor and quickly found the library. There he opened his new pediatric surgery textbook and began to read. Within fifteen minutes his head was bobbing, so he closed the book. He drove the thirty-minute route with the radio blaring, mostly to keep him awake. When he arrived home, he found Julie in bed just as he'd left her early that morning. With Julie asleep, he checked on Bradley. He stroked his son's hair and pulled the covers up over his shoulders.

Brad returned to his room, dropped his

pants on the chair, hung his coat in the closet, and crashed on the bed beside Julie. In minutes his deep and regular breathing signaled the onset of much-needed sleep.

Brad hadn't noticed the light on in Belle's room. There she sat quietly, apparently alone to those unfamiliar with God's guiding presence, fighting an unseen battle for the lives of her family. She prayed with a sense of urgency, not really understanding the deep burden that troubled her. Down the hall Brad and Julie slept undisturbed, unaware of the need for the prayers she made for them. At midnight on a damp summer night in the green southern valley, one light remained on in the Forrest home.

CHAPTER 12

Matt Stone had grown up in more ways than one since completing his surgical training at Taft University Medical Center and engaging in spiritual battle with Dr. Michael Simons and his allies.

His surgical skills had been tested and refined. His faith had been challenged and nurtured. The rough environment of the rural African mission had strengthened his reliance on a hefty, daily dose of divine grace. His encounters with the tribal religions had lifted his awareness of spiritual warfare to a new level. Matt returned to the U.S. an innovative, faster surgeon, but more importantly, a humble Christian warrior who knew the priority of moving in the strength of God's Spirit.

Matt slipped from bed at 5:30 A.M. *One good thing about adjusting to the new time clock is that getting up early isn't so hard,* he thought as he added water to the coffeemaker. As the coffee began to drip, he thought back to his last hospital experiences in the U.S. *What if I've lost my touch? It's been a while since I practiced good old expensive, defensive, high-tech, American medicine. I've been reading the current journals to keep up, but still, it's a lot different really doing it. Africa is a long way from here — in more ways than one.*

The young surgeon quieted his anxieties with a prayer, committing himself and his work to his Lord. He slowly sipped his coffee, opened his worn New Testament, and read over the highlighted passages.

In a few minutes Linda emerged, unusually early and obviously still undergoing time clock adjustments. She sang an African chorus and poured herself a cup of coffee before depositing herself on the couch next to her silent husband. "Morning."

Matt squeezed his wife's slender shoulders. "Morning."

Linda, too, opened her Bible and began to read. Neither spoke as they began their day as they often did, in this comfortable and necessary routine.

Eventually they ate and washed up, and Matt prepared for his first day at Crestview Women's. He met Dr. Jack Stevens, a middle-aged general surgeon whom he would be replacing temporarily. Dr. Stevens expressed relief at seeing Matt but seemed edgy, and Matt sensed he was hiding an unspoken anxiety.

Stevens looked older than his stated age and walked and talked slowly as he showed Matt around the hospital complex. His shoulders were stooped, and he spoke in fragmented sentences, often jumping from one subject to the next without apparent connection. Matt listened closely as Stevens described the record-keeping and dictating equipment and introduced him to his office staff and his daily schedule. By midday Matt had seen it all — the state-of-the-art equipment, the latest diagnostic instruments, and the largest operating theater he had ever imagined for a private hospital. As they were about to part ways in the parking lot, Matt gently probed for the reasons Stevens had decided to take a break.

"Thanks a lot for the tour. I'm sure I'll get along fine." Matt extended his hand.

Dr. Stevens opened his hand and took Matt's, hoping his tremor would not be noticed. "If you have any questions, just talk to the office manager, Tina. She has kept me straight for a long time."

"So," Matt paused, "why are you taking a break? Everything here seems so ideal — the best equipment, a great facility . . ." His voice faded as he saw Dr. Stevens look toward the concrete sidewalk.

"I — I —" the surgeon stuttered. "It's

just time for a break, that's all. My life has seemed a bit unraveled lately. My wife left . . . Well, my wife . . . she's not well. She needs me, that's all."

Matt knew to let it drop. *Something really has this guy stressed out!*

"Thanks again."

The surgeon walked away, leaving Matt standing on the sidewalk in front of the office complex adjacent to the hospital. After watching him for a moment longer, Matt turned and went to the general surgery office on the fourth floor to prepare for his afternoon surgery clinic.

Brad Forrest arrived at work early, stopping at his locker to put on his white coat and pick up a new patient list and his pediatric surgery text. *I have thirty minutes to read before checkout.* He focused on the patient list, running his finger down the patients' names, mentally reviewing as many diagnoses as he could remember. Room 525 was no longer listed. Brad made a mental note, remembering that there was a young Down's baby to check on. He thought about how he felt when his son was born. He scratched a note on the bottom of the page to see why the child had disappeared from the list and hurried off to the library.

At checkout, Brad learned that Tyson was in Washington and that he would be substituting for him in his post-op clinic. He asked about the baby in 525 and received only a shoulder shrug from Latner and Davis.

Davis said, "Tyson was on call. He gave me checkout this morning. I don't really know the details. Web admitted the patient himself. If it's not on the list this morning, the baby must have died or was discharged. Web didn't mention it when he called this morning to tell me about the list."

"If it's not on your list, you're not responsible for it," Latner chuckled.

Brad shrugged it off as well. "It looks like I've got a clinic to run." He smiled.

The other two surgeons slapped him on the back. "Time to swim. Call us if you have questions."

With that, Latner and Davis left for the O.R., and Brad headed for his outpatient clinic with two volumes of *Glen's* under his arm for support.

As the next days stretched into weeks, Julie Forrest's frustrations began to multiply. Brad's schedule had gone from bad to worse as he spent his few precious free moments poring over his new pediatric surgery texts in preparation for his mock orals with his senior associates. The only thing Julie did enjoy was the new paycheck. As she deposited the generous check, she wondered if her excitement over the freedom from their tight budget would prove to be as fulfilling as she hoped. *It doesn't seem to make up for Brad always being away.*

It was Saturday, and although Brad was off, he had gone to Crestview to spend "a few hours" in his office for undisturbed study time. *Is that what he thinks of his home — a disturbance?* After leaving the bank, Julie stopped at the local grocery store. As she worked her way through the cereals, an old familiar voice called from behind her. "Julie!" The voice belonged to Becky Goings, an old college friend.

"Becky?" Julie was surprised to see her there. "What brings you to the valley?"

The two friends hugged affectionately. "I moved here three weeks ago. I got a job working for UBI."

"That's great." The two faced each other holding hands at arm's length. "I can't believe this. You look great. You haven't even put on a pound since college!"

Julie pulled her friend's left hand up to her face. "What? No wedding ring? I thought for sure that you and Tom had —"

Julie stopped when she read the expression on Becky's face. Her frown stood in sharp contrast to her attractive appearance.

Julie's friend completed the sentence for her — ". . . that you and Tom had married by now?" Becky paused and pulled her hands free. She looked down the aisle, away from Julie. "We *were* married. Six years. Not much to say, really."

Julie looked back into the eyes of her old friend. Were her eyes glistening? "I'm sorry. I —"

"Hey, don't be sorry. I'm not. It's all for the best. I just couldn't compete anymore. Tom's job became his whole life. He spent more time at his computer store than he ever did with me." She looked back at Julie. "Eventually he ran off with his business partner, Jordan Green. The business was six months old before I ever met his partner. My teeth about dropped when I realized Jordan was a woman!" Becky managed a nervous laugh. "Anyway, she won't have any better luck with him than I did. He's driven to the point of perfection."

Julie smiled as her friend laughed. "I know what you mean. Brad's the same way. I never see him anymore. I suppose it's been that way for years, actually," she added slowly.

Becky brightened. "Hey, why don't we do lunch?"

Julie glanced at her watch. "Well, Brad's not home anyway, and Bradley's with Belle, so I guess so. Why don't you let me treat you at DeAngelo's? We can sit out next to the river and catch up."

"O.K. Let me put this ice cream back. It's the only thing that won't keep."

Julie did the same, following her friend over to the long freezer against the far wall. After they checked out, they both jumped into Becky's new Bronco. Julie's eyes widened. Becky just winked. "It was part of our divorce settlement. I gave him his freedom — he gave me the Bronco and half the house."

In twenty minutes they were sipping cool drinks and enjoying a view of the Wanoset River. For the next two hours the two old friends caught up on old times. Julie laughed, cried, and poured out her own story of frustrations with life with her surgeon husband.

As they stood to leave, Becky added, "How about coming with me to Lisa's on Friday? She's having a few friends over for dinner. I'm sure she won't mind." She paused and raised her eyebrows. "Steve Harrison will be there."

"Becky! I —" Julie began to protest.

"He's newly single again, you know," Becky interrupted. "From what I remember, there was a time when he couldn't keep his eyes off of you."

"Becky!"

"Hey, I'm not suggesting anything. I've heard your story. Your relationship sounds as dead as mine." She paused. "Don't let me rush you. You don't have to talk to him. I'm sure Lisa would like to see you too."

"I don't know." Julie smiled. *Steve Harrison . . . We really had some good times.* "I'll think about it."

"Julie," Becky emphasized her friend's name as she grabbed her hand, "do something for yourself sometime. You've spent your whole life giving to everyone else."

Julie shrugged. "I'll think about it."

"Call me."

"I will."

Sunday morning came with a vengeance in Lenore Kingsley's abdomen. She sat on the side of her king-size bed with her head in her hands. Her head was swimming again. A plastic trash container beside the bed contained the evidence of her nausea. *I don't remember this with my other pregnancies. It must be the hormone replacement therapy.*

She got up and staggered to the bathroom sink. She spat repeatedly and gargled with a medicinal mouthwash. "Yeeuuk!"

She ran her hand over her lower abdomen in an effort to sense the onset of the next wave of morning sickness. She paused, noting the bulge in her lower abdomen. *What? I can't be showing already! I'm only three weeks along!* The thought was enough to send her retreating to the commode, her head brought low in preparation for the violent retching that followed. When she finished, she slowly stood back to her feet and looked at her unnaturally perspiring reflection in the gold-rimmed mirror.

I've got to talk to Dr. Feinberg. Maybe we can change the strength of the hormones or something. I can't take another nine weeks of this, she thought, looking ahead to her abortion date. *I guess this means I don't need that beta-H.C.G. test Feinberg wanted. I've got all the evidence for this pregnancy I need. I'll be getting an ultrasound soon anyway.*

In another hour the nausea had lessened. Lenore nibbled a few saltines and dressed for work.

Brad pulled the pillow closer to his face. Something had pushed him to just this side of wakefulness, but not so far as to be recognizable. He grunted and returned to his dream. In a few seconds his mind again alerted him to a stimulus pushing for attention.

"Dad."

Bradley?

"Wake up. I'm all ready." The chubby boy held a fishing pole in his hand. "Don't wake up Mom." He pulled his dad's hand and pinched his cheek.

Brad sat up, now completely alert and startled. He sought to orient himself. "Bradley? What time is it?" He looked at the illuminated red digits on the clock radio. *5 A.M. Sunday morning. My only day to sleep in!*

"You promised to take me."

Brad sighed and tried to remember the promise long forgotten. His son's eyes were visible in the dim light of the room. The eyes told the exhausted father he could not say no.

Slowly he climbed out of the comfort of his nest and put on his blue jeans. He made some instant coffee and inhaled it. The idea of a morning at the river began to grow on him as he stepped out onto the porch and breathed in the cool, damp summer air. The sky in the east showed the earliest hint of dawn. *This might be just what I need.*

Brad packed a sack of sandwiches and threw in a box of oatmeal cream cookies. He stuffed six root beers into the ice of his small cooler, grabbed his tackle box, and joined Bradley in the Datsun where he had sat waiting for the previous ten minutes.

In twenty minutes they pushed an old aluminum johnboat from the sandy shore of the Wanoset. The boat belonged to the father of a former patient of Brad's. He had an open invitation to use the old boat that otherwise would have sat completely idle. Not that Brad had used it much. But the several times he had worked up the energy to come out, he had lost himself in the solitude of the river and swore he would do it again soon. It was a promise to himself that he rarely kept, a reward he needed but often overlooked.

The sun had just risen over the tree-lined ridge as Brad stopped rowing and began preparing the lines. They fished as they drifted with the tide, the fish and an occasional heron their only companions. The bass enjoyed the grasshoppers that Bradley had collected the day before. By 10:30 they were hungry and had drifted as far as the Nickel Bridge. They attached a rope to a bridge piling and stepped out onto a small wooden platform that sat just six inches above the water at the present tide. The structure appeared to be the last remnant of a scaffolding used in building the bridge and had long since been abandoned to the use of curious fishermen. The platform was five feet wide and was located far enough under the bridge that it was barely visible to those on the road above, and therefore provided a private spot that the two Forrests used for eating and resting. Bradley refused to eat when he fished because he never wanted to divert his attention from his line. Stopping the boat seemed to be the only reasonable way for Brad to nourish his son on these outings, and so this spot on the Nickel Bridge had become the turnaround resting point for Brad and the lunch spot for Bradley, Jr.

The two were quiet as they ate. Brad looked at his son as he counted and recounted the fish. *This has been so rare lately. I've almost lost touch with him completely. He hardly seems like the same little boy I used to bring out here.* He looked out onto the water. *I've turned into the same driven man as my father. His work always came first.* He shook his head. *But I just need a little time to establish myself as a reliable surgeon. Then I can cut back a bit and pay more attention to Bradley — and to Julie.*

His thoughts were broken by Bradley, who had counted the fish for the tenth time. "I ca-c-caught six, and you caught four!"

"You've outfished me again, Tiger."

Bradley smiled, his cheeks pushing his eyes into narrow slits bordering his flat nose. Brad smiled as well. *This was a good idea, son. A good idea indeed.*

CHAPTER 13

Mary Jacobs had no time for fishing on Sunday. She spent the time organizing her pediatric surgery lecture notes to prepare for her next rotation. She collapsed into bed early and rose before the sun on Monday morning.

She looked at herself in the mirror. *Private practice, here I come!* Her thoughts of her first day at Crestview Women's were broken by Kim's voice.

Kim sat up in bed and squinted in the direction of her roommate. "Since when did you start putting on makeup for a clinical rotation?"

Mary looked up with a start. She turned back to the mirror and ignored the comment. "What do you think, Kim? Is this lipstick too much?"

"You look very professional, but what's the deal? New leaf or something for Ms. Honor Student?" Kim smiled.

"I'm starting my rotation at the private hospital up in Crestview — pediatric surgery." Mary adjusted her collar. "Just thought I'd lose the sleepy med student look for a while. We private-practice physicians must look the part, you know." She finished her sentence with an innocent giggle. She did feel a bit different; but then again, she knew first impressions were important.

Kim yawned and glanced at her watch. "It's awful early, you know."

"I'm supposed to be there by 7 A.M. I don't want to be late on my first day."

"You've still got an hour," her roommate grumbled sleepily before pulling the covers back over her head. "We dental students must get our rest."

"I'll be out of here in a second." Mary picked up her bag. "I'll likely be staying up at Crestview for a few days — at least until the weekend. They have a call room there for me to stay in."

"Have fun."

Mary turned off the light and slipped into the hall. She stuck her head back in the room momentarily. "Kim? Pray if you think about it. I'm kind of uneasy about all this. It's my first outside rotation."

"You'll do fine." Kim's voice was muffled from the blanket on her head. She pulled the cover back when she realized Mary still hadn't shut the door. She looked at her roommate. "I'll pray — I'll pray." Kim sighed and laid her head back on the pillow. "First I'll sleep, and then I'll pray," she grumbled softly.

Mary hadn't heard. She was already creeping quietly down the empty dorm hall.

Brad had fallen into a comfortable routine. Off to work early with a coffee cup in his hand, then a short stop at Jake's for another cup and a homemade sausage biscuit to go that he consumed during the remainder of his drive to Crestview. After a half hour in the library, he donned his white coat and joined his associates for checkout.

"Morning, Brad." The professional monotone belonged to George Latner.

"Morning, Doctor." Brad shook the man's hand and smiled. He always greeted George in this way. It was part of his routine.

"Brad," George responded, "we have two surprises for you this morning." Brad sat down and looked at the first one, an attractive blonde woman in a white coat laden with medical supplies and booklets. She smiled sweetly and waited for an introduction.

"The first one is here," George continued, lifting his hand toward the young student. "Mary Jacobs has been assigned to our group for a fourth-year medical school rotation. We get these students from Bridgewater occasionally, and we take their interest very seriously. She will be under your direct supervision. She will be taking call right along with you. Teach her, and involve her in rounds, the office, and the O.R." His tone of voice reflected the non-negotiable nature of this new assignment.

Mary lifted her hand to Brad's. "Nice to meet you, Dr. Forrest."

"Hello," Brad replied with brevity, still trying to process this new responsibility.

Latner went on without delay. "The second surprise is a slight alteration in our call schedules. Tyson is out of town again for an interview. We will all be picking up the slack for him. You have been assigned his call for tonight and Friday. You will still be responsible for your previously assigned calls on Tuesday and the weekend."

Brad stared at the paper in front of him. *It seems like I'm going to be here a lot this week. Julie is sure to love this new development!* He paused and looked up at Latner. He knew he needed to be careful not to show his disappointment. He looked at his newly assigned student. *Teaching always slows me down, too. It seems to double your rounding time!* He spoke not to Latner, but to Mary.

"Seems like you and I are in for a long week."

She responded with an oft-quoted surgical quip. "Oh well, you know the only thing wrong with every other night call is that you miss half of the good cases."

Latner chuckled and proceeded with checkout. Brad added relevant notes to his patient list. His mind drifted as Latner continued to drone on about electrolyte values and radiograph reports. *At least with all this time on call I'll be spending it with a little support — even if it is a medical student. I hope she's half as helpful as she is attractive.* He stole a glance in Mary's direction. She seemed to be concentrating on the list in front of her.

Brad sighed and refocused his attention on Latner's voice. "Room 522 is Evan Jacobsen, a four-year-old with a fractured spleen from an M.V.A. on Friday. Room 523 is Joel Thomason, an eight-year-old in for post-operative pneumonia after a resection of lower extremity sarcoma at the 'U.' Room 524 is Samuel Harris, a two-year-old with . . ."

Matt Stone saw quickly that he hadn't lost his touch. In spite of the absence of the technology in Africa, his laparoscopic surgery skills came back to him just like he'd used them all along. *Just like riding a bike,* he thought as he looked at the video screen in front of him.

He carefully dissected the gallbladder away from the liver bed, rarely taking his eyes off the image projected on the screen positioned on the patient's right. The whole room looked like something from a *Star Wars* movie. The monitors and video screens provided the room's only light since the overhead surgical lamps had been turned off for better visualization of the TV images. The surgery was easily accomplished using special instruments inserted into the patient's abdomen through small sleeves. A video camera, passed through one of the sleeves or portals, allowed Matt to see what he was doing without looking down at the patient. After twenty additional minutes he deftly removed the gallbladder through a one-centimeter incision in the upper abdomen. He then removed the trocar sleeves and sewed up the three small stab incisions.

After talking with the patient's family, Matt nearly jogged to his small apartment where he found Linda sitting on the front porch. "Hi, honey."

"Hi, Matt," she responded before she

kissed her husband generously. She followed him into the front room. He hung his white coat on the rack behind the door and collapsed onto the couch.

"What a day!" He sighed. "I couldn't wait to get out of there." Matt looked around the room, which had obviously changed from that morning. Matt smiled. Linda always rearranged the furniture when she was bored. She had done it no less than monthly when they were in their small flat in Africa. "Bored again?"

Linda smiled sheepishly. "I just couldn't quite resist." She sat down beside Matt on the newly repositioned couch. "So tell me why you were practically running up the road. Are things really that bad over there — or couldn't you wait to see me again?" She giggled softly.

Matt sighed again. "I'm not sure what it is, Linda." He looked at his young wife, who had detected a quiver in her husband's voice. She stopped smiling and returned his gaze. "It's like a darkness hovering over that place. I sensed it for the first time when I talked to Dr. Stevens as he showed me around. It was almost as if he had been beaten down by an unseen weight that drove him to near-exhaustion. I haven't quite been able to put my finger on it. It's almost too perfect. Everything is so clean, so sterile, so first-class."

"Aren't you just experiencing a bit of old-fashioned culture shock? You're not in Africa anymore, Matt."

"I don't know why, but I think it's more than that. It's as if Crestview Women's stands out as a tribute to man's accomplishments and successes. They are so proud of everything over there." He looked down at his hands. "It all seems so empty without God in the picture." Linda stroked his sandy hair and listened. "It really hit me hard today when I took a short tour of the GYN facility at the request of one of their fertility specialists, Dr. Suzanne Feinberg. I met her in the cafeteria this morning. She knew things were a bit slow for me and offered to take me around. What she showed me made me sick. She proudly revealed their new emphasis on genetic screening during the pre-embryo implantation phase of their in-vitro fertilization process. They're screening the embryos for genetic problems before putting them into their mothers' uteruses. If they find anything at all awry, they just discard the embryo, no questions asked. She even smiled when she told me they gladly do sex selection for the parents if desired. She then showed me the vast amount of information they can obtain by amniocentesis or even just maternal blood testing of a pregnant mother. They are fairly confident of the diagnosis of Down's syndrome just from a blood test of the mother's serum. I pushed her for the statistics a bit. She finally admitted that over half of the women who come in pregnant for genetic screening are given information that influences them to have abortions."

"They do the abortions there?" Linda winced. She remembered only too well the horrors of the abortion industry that she and Matt had stumbled upon a few years earlier in Fairfax, Kentucky. The visions of the evil Dr. Michael Simons that came into her mind made her shudder even now. It was only with divine assistance that Simons's plot had been defeated.

"Crestview does abortions by the hundreds every month." Matt shook his head. "It's a big business." He paused. " 'Come to the perfect hospital. Have the perfect doctors. Have a perfect baby.' Neat. Clean. Sterile. Expensive. Deathly so."

"I don't like what I'm hearing, Matt."

"It's as if that philosophy has invaded the whole staff. Everyone walks around as if they are God's private gift to medicine. Of course, God is never mentioned. Man is supreme. Man is in charge."

"Could you be overreacting to what you saw in one small area of the hospital, Matt? Think of all the children they're helping. You said yourself that they're known all over the southeast U.S. for their work in pediatric surgery. They've got to be helping hundreds of sick kids over there."

Matt stood up and stretched. "Maybe you're right. Maybe I just let it get to me." He walked into the kitchen. "Thought about supper at all?"

"We're having something healthy, Matt. Stay out of there until it's done. I'll let you try it in another twenty minutes."

Matt came back out eating a Hostess Twinkie.

"Where did you find that? They were supposed to be a surprise!"

"You always hide them above the refrigerator. It's been over two years since I've eaten one of these. Boy, this brings back memories." He stuffed a second yellow cake into his mouth in one large bite. "Ahhhhh!"

Linda shook her head in exasperation. She would never understand the questionable nutritional standards of her physician husband. She refocused on their previous conversation. "Matt?"

"Yeah?" he asked in a muffled tone.

"Let's ask the Lord for spiritual discernment. I think this a spiritual fight you are sensing. Maybe you're right on target with your thoughts. Maybe you're right about the darkness hovering over Crestview. Maybe, just maybe, I spoke too soon and you weren't overreacting."

Matt walked out onto the little front porch and looked over at the medical complex. Silently he asked for his spiritual eyes to be opened. He looked back at Linda. "Maybe we're onto something. It's time to pray."

And that's just what they did.

Lenore Kingsley stepped out of her red Corvette and stomped across the preferred parking area used by the executives at UBI. Her heels clicked loudly against the concrete sidewalk as she strode determinedly through the front lobby, past Sam, the security officer, and into the restricted hallway beyond. After a quick look into the retinal scanner, an electronic tone signaled the door unlocking in front of her. She pushed her way in and nearly leaped to the women's restroom halfway down the long corridor. She spent several minutes dry-heaving over the commode, splashed some water on her face, then crept at a slower pace to the elevators. In another minute she fell into the leather chair behind her desk. Slowly she laid her head on the desk. After a few minutes of stillness she felt better and sat up without feeling the now consistent morning nausea.

Her assistant, Barb Peterson, came in carrying the morning mail. She looked at Lenore, who appeared pale and perspiring. "Are you O.K.? You look washed out."

"Just the flu, Barb. Thanks," Lenore quipped.

"Can I do something for you?"

"Find a restaurant that does chicken noodle soup takeout."

Barb looked at her curiously. Lenore continued, "It's the only thing I've kept down for a few days."

"Why don't you take the day off? I'm sure that —"

"No thank you, Barb!" Lenore said with obvious irritation. Barb knew not to argue back.

"Here's your mail," she said, laying a stack of letters on the desk.

Lenore looked up, "Er, oh . . . thanks, Barb."

With her assistant gone and her next wave of morning sickness yet to pound the beach, she picked through the mail with indifference. *The way I feel, I should be at home. It's hard to concentrate on anything anyway.* She picked up a letter from Crestview Medical Labs. A slip of paper giving her beta-H.C.G. level fell to the desktop. The value was high. The pregnancy test result slip had a red circle around the word "POSITIVE" at the top. *Tell me something I didn't already know,* Lenore thought sarcastically. *I told Dr. Feinberg we didn't need to bother with stupid tests to confirm what I already know. Oh well, maybe getting the test like she wanted will show her that I'm not the most difficult patient in the world. Besides, I still need her to cooperate with me in this thing. Just wait until she finds out I need her to abort this baby!*

She dropped the paper into her briefcase so Barb would not see it. *We can't let this get out around here. So far Randy and I are the only ones besides the gynecologist who know I'm pregnant. It's only been three weeks, and already I can't wait for this to be over!*

Lenore was too distracted by her gastric distress to read the fine print at the bottom of the lab slip. "This value indicates a pregnancy of approximately six weeks gestation." With the date discrepancy unnoticed, Lenore shoved the lab slip beneath a stack of papers in the back folder of her briefcase.

* * *

Days fell upon nights in endless busy routine for Brad Forrest as he circled from the library to checkout to rounds to the O.R. to clinic and back to the library before heading home for the night. For most of his waking hours, Mary Jacobs became a near-continuous presence in his shadow. Brad found her to be a welcome break from other disinterested medical students he had instructed. He had forgotten that most of them were fulfilling requirements by doing a surgery rotation. Mary had chosen to do this rotation as part of her elective time. On Monday and Tuesday, Brad had probed her intellect and tested her interest and enthusiasm by asking her to help with mundane scut jobs such as patient transports and phlebotomy or drawing patient blood tests. When she consistently responded with willingness, he backed off and began to take an interest in teaching her the ins and outs of his special love, the field of pediatric surgery.

On Monday night when Brad filled in for Web Tyson, the work wasn't done until 11 P.M., thanks to two cases of appendicitis and a motor vehicle accident (M.V.A.). Brad ran for home and Mary to her call quarters for a few hours of sleep before an early morning library rendezvous followed by patient checkout. By Tuesday night, Brad's regularly scheduled call night, Brad and Mary were sleep-deprived and punchy. The night fell fast upon the day, and it was soon 10 P.M., with still another new patient to evaluate.

Brad made a quick call to Julie, who listened quietly to his "good night," knowing he would be home long after she was in bed.

"Good night, Brad," Julie said without enthusiasm.

Brad hung up the phone and looked at Mary. She seemed so full of life. Julie seemed so tired. "She's not too excited about my schedule." He shrugged his shoulders.

Mary looked back. "She must be pretty special."

Brad didn't seem to hear. He was already heading for the emergency room to see a new patient. His faithful shadow followed obediently. In the E.R. they found a two-year-old male who was screaming and a mother who looked as sleep-deprived as the surgeon. The father seemed to clutch to the mother as tightly as the child. He was tall, his hair was tousled, and he spoke rapidly in broken sentences.

"You got to do something, Doc! He's screaming. Pain comes and goes. Got to do something. Old Doc Shubert sent him right over when he saw it," he said shoving his wife's hand forward.

His wife obediently held up a disposable diaper. "He passed this after his last screaming fit," the woman nearly yelled to get her voice above her crying son.

Brad unfolded the diaper. Mary wrinkled her nose. "Come on, Dr. Jacobs," Brad prodded. He held up the diaper. "You need to see this. It's part of the diagnosis. You'll never forget this."

The med student looked in. It contained a deep-red "currant jelly" stool.

"O.K., Doctor. Without touching this child, just with what you know, what's the diagnosis?"

The child screamed again. The father clutched the mother. They both looked helpless. The father was in no mood for questions. "Do something!"

Mary seemed distracted by the crying. Brad persisted for a moment. If he was right, he knew the child would settle down shortly. "It's a classic presentation, Mary. You may never see one so much right out of the textbooks."

The patient's cries softened to a whimper.

Brad gently palpated the baby's abdomen. There seemed to be a sausage-shaped mass just below the belly button.

"We can help." He looked at a nurse who had just arrived. "Let's get this child some pain relief. Morphine will do. Tell the radiologist on call that I have a stat barium enema for him to do." He looked at the parents, now a little calmer since their son had stopped screaming. "Your son has . . ." He paused and looked at Mary, giving her one last chance.

". . . has intussusception," Mary finished. She stole a quick glance at Brad, who smiled with approval. "The intestine or bowel has telescoped on itself, turning a short segment inside-out within itself," she explained. "Here — I can draw you a picture." She quickly sketched a cartoon of the bowel with intussusception and held it up for the parents.

"We will get a special X-ray study, a barium enema, to see if we can correct the problem. If it doesn't work, we'll need to operate — tonight." The parents responded together with a solemn nod.

After securing an IV line, the child was swept away for his enema, and Brad and Mary talked in the plush doctors' lounge across the hall. After watching the headlines on CNN, Brad looked at his watch. 11:35 P.M.

"Good job with that diagnosis, Doctor." Brad spoke with friendly candor. "I thought for a minute I had you stumped." Brad threw a Velcro ball at a large dartboard on the far wall. It struck an outer circle with the words, "Malpractice suit filed, -50."

"For a minute I was," Mary admitted, taking up the challenge and heaving a Velcro ball toward the red board. She struck the third circle entitled, "Correct diagnosis, +40."

"You dog!" Brad picked up another dart.

"You really gave it away when you ordered the barium enema. That's what reminded me." She watched Brad throw the ball into the second circle with the words, "Patient Recovers, +50."

Brad stuck out his chest. "Beat that, young doctor!"

Just then Dr. Rohrer, the radiologist, stuck his head in the lounge door. "Brad? I thought I might find you here. The barium enema was a success. The intussusception looks completely reduced. You can run for home now. I've talked to the parents. The child should be up on 5 north in a few minutes," he said, looking at his watch and sighing.

"Thanks, Joe," Brad replied, not taking his eye off the student, who was winding up for a shot of her own. The radiologist shrugged and left without speaking.

Mary fired a shot into the center of the fabric, a circle with the words, "Payment Received, +100." She looked up with a sly grin, not knowing what to expect from her competitive mentor.

Instead of running for home as the radiologist had suggested, Brad retrieved the balls from the board. "Give me another chance," he said laughing. "One more chance."

By the time Friday had rolled around, Julie felt sure she deserved a break. Brad had been home during her waking hours only briefly Wednesday and Thursday night, and then he seemed so tired or distracted that their communication was superficial. Now as she sped toward her friend Lisa's place, her mood had lightened considerably, and she decided to put all of her parental worries and responsibilities behind her for the night. Bradley was with Belle. Brad was at work. She needed a break.

She parked her Nova in front of the elite condominium complex and walked around to the pool where the party was already in full swing. Becky spotted her first.

"It's about time you showed up, girl," Becky said, placing a colorful glass of punch in Julie's hand.

"Hi, Becky." Julie looked around. People crowded around the poolside, which was bordered by tiki torches for the occasion. Jamaican music filled the air, causing people to lean close in order to communicate. She recognized a few faces — a few college friends, her real estate agent, Becky, Lisa, and . . . Steve Harrison.

Julie sipped the drink she'd been given. *Whew! This is potent stuff!* After a few minutes of small talk, she wandered over to a table for some food, to slow the absorption of the punch's kick. She spent an hour meeting people and talking to Becky and her new circle of friends.

"It seems like forever since I've done something like this," Julie said in Becky's ear. "I can't remember the last time Brad and I went to a party."

Becky frowned. "You need to pay more attention to what's right for you. You can't just give, give, give, you know. You deserve a little fun, too." She glanced toward a patio table a few feet away. She grabbed Julie's arm and tilted her head to the side. "Come on. I want you to talk to Steve."

Julie followed without resistance. "Steve," Becky bubbled, "I'm sure you'll remember this old friend." Julie and Becky sat down at the table beside the athletic-appearing man, who wore a white shirt that accentuated his deep tan.

Steve Harrison smiled. "Of course. Nice to see you again, Julie," he said extending his hand first to her and then to Becky.

"Hi, Steve." Julie looked at her old boyfriend. "You haven't changed at all, have you?" She laughed. She didn't know what else to say.

Steve laughed, too. In a few moments they were swept into a whirlwind review of the last decade of their lives, and Becky quietly excused herself to mingle with the other guests. Julie didn't even notice. Her eyes were focused on the handsome face leaning toward hers.

By midnight most of the the guests had left, and Julie had forgotten her misgivings about being out on her own. She glanced at her watch and then at Steve, who had been her shadow for the previous two hours. *We always did communicate well, didn't we?* "I've got to run. I can't believe the time."

Steve reached for her hand. "It's been wonderful seeing you again." Their eyes met. He leaned close to her face. Julie stiffened and turned away. He kissed her cheek softly. "Can I see you again sometime?"

Julie felt suddenly uncomfortable. She looked back into his eyes. "I don't know." She turned away again. "It's just that —"

"Hey, I'm sorry, I didn't mean to push, I —"

Julie squeezed his hand, still in hers. "Don't apologize. If I hadn't wanted to see you, I wouldn't have come," she admitted honestly.

Steve brightened. "Becky told me all about your relationship with Brad. I know you need some time."

"She doesn't mind her own business very well, does she?" Julie forced a thin smile.

"Not really." He shuffled his feet. "She's been through this before, Julie. Maybe she cares more than you think."

Julie shrugged. "Maybe so. Look, I've really got to go." She turned and walked toward her car.

"Maybe I could call?"

Julie looked over her shoulder and looked at the man silhouetted by the torchlight behind him. "I need time to think."

CHAPTER 14

Julie collapsed onto her bed alone, her head spinning from a thousand new thoughts. Thankfully, she didn't have to share her thoughts with anyone since Belle and Bradley had been asleep for hours. *Just when I thought we had it made, everything seems to be crashing down around me.* She looked at the wedding photograph on the dresser. *We seemed so happy then.* She got up and moved quietly to the bathroom where she prepared for sleep. She stared at her reflection in the mirror, her own image distorted by the tears brimming in her eyes. *You've worked so hard for this! Why aren't you happy now?* Her own thoughts accused her. *For all these years I've supported Brad, and look where it's gotten me!* She let out a sob. *Now he has prestige, and the money is starting to flow, but what about us? He doesn't even have enough time to make a relationship look right, much less actually be right. Even if he had the time, he seems so preoccupied.*

She walked back to the bedroom and slipped beneath the old quilt. As she did, her thoughts shifted to the newest relationship in her life. *What about Steve? Am I really that hungry for attention? Who am I kidding? He's so handsome. Of course, I'm hungry for attention like that.* She closed her eyes tightly, as if that might slow her runaway thoughts. *What am I to do? Could I really give up on Brad after all we've been through? Do we even have a relationship left to save?* Her tears began flowing freely, her pillow soon wet from the evidence of her pain. She cried for what felt like an hour, her mind circling each argument over and over and over. In the end she lay exhausted from the emotional battle and didn't fight sleep any longer.

After a few minutes Brad crept in, tiptoeing softly past Bradley's open door and into his own room. Laying his pager on the bedside stand, he inched into bed beside Julie, careful not to disturb her apparent restful state. He slept unaware of his wife's emotional turmoil, his rest uninterrupted for four hours until the shrill call of their clock radio forced him back to alertness again. Julie slept, too, the cloak of sleep a thick blanket hiding the unseen turbulence within.

A few weeks later Dr. Suzanne Feinberg

found her frustration with keeping tabs on Lenore Kingsley growing. Lenore had called no less than a dozen times in the last two weeks since her positive pregnancy test, each time wanting advice, but being careful to stay out of Dr. Feinberg's Crestview clinic so as to keep official records to a minimum. Every day, it seemed, brought a new question from Lenore, most of which were left with Feinberg's office nurse, who forwarded them to the obstetrician. "The nausea is debilitating. Can we alter the dose of the hormones again?" "I'm gaining so much weight. Can you send a diet plan?" Just when Feinberg decided to insist on examining Lenore, the questions slowed, and a large cash payment from Kingsley arrived.

Now, as Dr. Feinberg sifted through her morning mail, she came across a copy of the ultrasound that Kingsley had promised her. *At least she's starting to cooperate a little.* She opened the folder and slipped out the ultrasound pictures. *I've got to hand it to her. They certainly seem to have state-of-the-art equipment at UBI. These ultrasound pictures are as good as those taken by the latest generation of ultrasonography machines at Crestview.* She reviewed the pictures carefully, noting the size and other details. *How old is this baby now? This picture would date it at almost ten weeks.* The obstetrician looked at her calendar. She hadn't marked the date that she did the implantation procedure, beginning Lenore's surrogate motherhood. *When was that? Could it have been that long ago?* She opened her compact electronic daily planner. *Not marked here either. I guess I just let the time get away from me.* She smiled. *Lenore certainly has asked enough questions for a ten-week pregnancy. It must have been longer than I thought.*

"Your next patient is here, Dr. Feinberg." A short nurse spoke from the door of the office.

"Thanks," Suzanne replied, taking the chart from her hand. "Let's see what we have here."

"New infertility workup," the nurse replied before heading back up the hallway.

Suzanne reviewed the new patient data. *Hmmm. Thirty-seven. No children. Two abortions. Previous history of both herpes and syphilis. Hysterosalpingogram shows both fallopian tubes blocked.* She thumped the back of the chart with her fingers. *The sexual freedom revolution certainly has helped boost my infertility practice,* she thought to herself.

It was time for evening rounds. Brad checked out to Web Tyson, who was "first call," and headed for the library. Mary looked in Brad's direction as if to say, "Am I free to go?"

Web answered her question for her. "Why don't you make rounds with me? You've been spending enough time in the library." Dr. Tyson enjoyed having admirers around, and students seemed so easy for him to impress.

Mary answered politely, "Sure, Dr. Tyson" and followed as he took the elevator to 5 north. Dr. Tyson paused at the nursing station and asked the evening shift manager, Ellen Pearson, to join them. When Web rounded, he liked the convenience of having a nurse join him so that he could just give verbal orders on the patients and not stop to write everything down.

Slowly they walked from room to room checking patients, talking to parents, advancing diet orders, and following up on tests ordered on morning rounds. Mary observed the routine and stole a glance at her watch. *8 P.M. and I'm still not home on my day off. Rounds are more interesting with Dr. Forrest because he makes an effort to teach.* She attempted to yawn inconspicuously, but her eyes met Dr. Tyson's in the middle. Tyson winked flirtatiously. Mary focused her attention on a patient's bedside clipboard.

After seeing the patients on 5 north, they headed for the neonatal I.C.U. There they were greeted by Dr. Richard Hart, a neonatologist who looked up from a small isolette where he was busy starting an umbilical vein catheter on a newborn. "Dr. Tyson . . ."

Web walked over after donning a clean gown over his street clothes. Mary followed.

"What can I do for you, Richard?"

"It's this baby," he said looking at the infant in the incubator. He sighed deeply, both from lack of sleep and frustration. "It looks like esophageal atresia. I'll need you to fix this one for me."

Web looked at Mary and explained, "The esophagus is underformed. It causes a complete obstruction, a complete inability to eat. Without an operation, the child will die." Mary nodded her head. She resented being talked down to. She knew what esophageal atresia was.

"Unfortunately, that's not all, Web," the neonatologist moaned. "It's another cri du chat baby."

"Uh oh." Web shook his head. This time Mary wasn't so sure she understood.

"Cri du chat?" she inquired.

Dr. Tyson responded, "A syndrome that is caused by a deletion of the short arm of chromosome number five. It is associated with a number of problems, including mental retardation. The infants have a characteristic sounding cry," he added, listening as the infant shrieked, "like a cat."

"Once you've heard one of the babies with this syndrome, you'll never forget the name," Dr. Hart said soberly.

"Cri du chat," Mary repeated, nodding her head.

"Have you talked to the parents?" Web's tone of voice had changed from educational to stern.

"Once. We just got confirmation of the chromosomal problem today."

"Let me talk to them," Web offered. "You should transfer the patient to my service. The esophageal atresia is a surgical problem."

"Whatever you think best, Web," the neonatologist replied. Most of the physician staff at Crestview held Web Tyson in such high esteem that they would never think of questioning his medical judgment.

Web walked off in search of the parents, muttering under his breath. Mary could just hear his parting comments. ". . . with proper genetic screening, this kid wouldn't be here for us to . . ."

In another two minutes Mary and Dr.

Tyson were surrounded by the immediate and extended family of the cri du chat infant boy. With all of the apparent compassion of a lifelong missionary, Dr. Tyson explained to the family the situation at hand as he saw it. He stressed the expense and suffering involved with surgery and the sadly debilitated life that the retarded infant was sure to experience. In a matter of a few moments he convinced them that the best, most loving approach possible was to offer no surgical treatment at all, but to allow the infant to die in peace. Everyone believed him. Everyone nodded. Everyone but Mary.

The child was moved from the I.C.U. to 5 north, Room 525. Mary left the hospital, heading back to Bridgewater for the night. She didn't want to spend the night in a Crestview call room if she didn't have to. Not tonight. As she drove, her mind tried to make sense of the situation as she'd experienced it. *Until Dr. Tyson knew that the child was retarded, the situation was clear.* His words echoed in her mind: "Without an operation, the child will die." *Is this what it's all about? Treating only those whose lives are in some way valuable in his eyes?*

Mary sped on across the Nickel Bridge on her way to the Bridgewater University campus. A light rain began to fall, and she turned on the windshield wipers. *What about the intrinsic value of human life, value simply because we are created in the image of God?* Mary had encountered the first major values clash of her young career. Her faith was strong. Her Christian values provided a solid foundation. She needed time and space to process this new challenge.

Her mind seemed as clear as her rain-streaked windshield. She needed answers. She began to pray as she turned into her dormitory parking lot. *Lord, how am I to respond? What am I supposed to do?*

Jimmy checked his watch. Quitting time! He walked over to the tap and filled a frosted mug with his favorite golden beverage. Tony didn't want him to drink when he served, but he always let him have what he wanted when his shift was complete. He walked to the back of the restaurant and approached Randy Harris, who was dining alone. Since his conversation with him a few weeks earlier, Jimmy had wanted to ask him a few questions. "Mind if I sit down?"

Randy smiled sweetly. "Be my guest."

"I asked my father about UBI. He said you guys are getting pretty heavy into genetic screening products."

Randy raised his eyebrows but said nothing.

Jimmy continued, "Evidently he's familiar with them because Crestview uses so much of that stuff."

Dr. Harris nodded. "We've made great strides in elucidating the human genome."

Jimmy's expression changed to reflect his lack of understanding of the term. Harris continued. ". . . the entire genetic makeup of the human species. Soon we will have it all mapped out. In a few years we will be able to tell everything about everyone just from their DNA, the molecules that make up our genes."

Jimmy nodded. "That's what I thought."

"Why do you ask? Are you interested in the research? I could show you the lab sometime."

This time the young waiter shook his head. "I don't think so. I'm not into that sort of thing." He looked away. "I'm not so sure I support that kind of thing."

Randy put down his drink and looked at Jimmy. "What are you getting at?"

Jimmy paused, looking at his beer. In a moment he began speaking again, his voice barely audible over the noise of the crowd. "Do you think it's in our genes to make us what we are?"

Randy squinted and leaned closer.

Jimmy looked up. ". . . to make us gay?"

That's what this is about! Randy thought and chuckled to himself. He paused and looked at the youth in front of him. *He really seems troubled about this.* After a few moments he replied, "What does it really matter? We are what we are."

"It seems to make a big difference to my father."

"In what way?"

"He's never accepted me the way I am. He feels guilty for raising a gay son. I think he takes comfort in thinking it had nothing to do with him, that I was destined to be gay because of my genes."

Randy wasn't sure how to respond. He just sat staring at Jimmy, who had returned his eyes to the table in front of him. Finally Randy asked another question. "What if he's right? Why should it matter?"

"It doesn't really matter to me, I guess. What bothers me is thinking that if it is true, if being gay is determined by our genes . . ." Jimmy lifted his eyes, filled with accusation, to the researcher before him. ". . . then what's to stop people from screening for gay genes as well?"

"I guess I hadn't —"

"And if a parent doesn't want a gay son,

what's to prevent them from aborting it on the basis of the genetic screening?"

Randy was beginning to see the raw nerve that had been exposed. *This is what's bugging him?* He squirmed defensively and remained silent.

Jimmy went on, "Don't you see? We've seen this kind of discrimination before. Remember Hitler's eugenics program to create a superior race?"

Dr. Harris thought about his response, looking around the room to see if anyone else was listening to their conversation, which had slowly grown in volume to be heard above the background noise. "Hey, wait a minute, Jimmy . . . For one thing, we're not even close to locating a gene responsible for homosexuality, if one exists at all." He leaned closer to Jimmy so he could lower his voice. "Between you and me, the research that has even suggested such a possibility hasn't been reproducible and carried a heavy bias. I've never seen any convincing study that showed us that a gay gene exists at all. Even in studies of identical twins, with exactly the same DNA makeup, when one twin is gay, there is an equal chance that the other twin will be straight. That certainly doesn't make it look like it's in the genes."

From what his father had told him, Jimmy knew that the researchers at UBI were far ahead of the rest of the world in genetic research. He respected Harris's opinion. "What about the work UBI is doing? Any evidence there?"

Randy shook his head slowly. "None yet."

Jimmy gulped at his beer and wiped his mouth with a cloth napkin. He had calmed down a bit. He stood to go. He looked at Randy. "Thanks. I was just wondering, that's all."

Randy watched him walk away. He returned to eating a steak sandwich, his regular fare at Anthony's Place. His mind, however, was far from registering the taste of the large plate of food. His conversation with Jimmy had sparked some new questions of his own. *What if we do eventually locate a gene like Jimmy mentioned? Would it really lead to discrimination? Would someone try to splice it out, if they could, just like I have with genes for growth hormone? Who's to say what the perfect child would be? Who has that kind of authority? Parents? Government?*

He took a large bite of the rare meat hanging from the edge of the toasted bread in his hand. *On the other hand, who's to say that married gay couples wouldn't want to select for gay babies preferentially? Most lesbian cou-*

ples are turning to sperm banks for help in having children anyway. Maybe we could help by screening for sperm with a gay gene to guarantee the type of child they want to raise. The question of discrimination seemed to push forward in his mind as a troubling stimulus. He burped quietly, his dyspepsia a reflection of his unsettled thoughts. He rose and walked to the register at the bar.

Tony greeted him. "Everything O.K.?"

Randy felt exposed, as if he must be carrying his feelings on his sleeves. "Fine." He didn't feel like talking. "Everything's fine."

As he left, his discomfort from the conversation remained, but he tried to pass it off in a shallow justification. *I must have been eating too fast,* he mused as he walked to his Triumph. *I hope I have some Tums in my car.*

Mary Jacobs managed to crowd in five hours' sleep after a late-night trip to the Bridgewater University medical library. There she had looked up all she could on the cri du chat syndrome and esophageal atresia. She dragged herself from her single bed, showered, dressed, and hurried south to Crestview Women's and Children's Health Center. Arriving five minutes early gave her enough time to check on the infant who had been moved to Room 525 on 5 north. She stopped at the nurses' station and checked her watch again. *I need to talk to the parents of the child in 525,* she thought as she glanced toward the dayroom where many of the parents spent their time when they had children in the hospital. Only one man was present, and he was still sleeping on the long leather couch along the far wall. She whirled the circular chart rack around to the slot marked 525. It was empty. She looked for the chart along the countertops that framed the nurses' station. No chart for 525 could be found.

She looked at the unit secretary, who was busily adding up the "ins" and "outs" columns of each patient on the unit. "Have you seen the chart on 525?"

The secretary continued working without looking up. "I've already broken the chart down. That patient died last night."

"Died?" Mary gasped. "So quickly? Why?"

The clerk looked up. "Look, I'm just a ward clerk. I really don't know what happened."

"Where's the nurse assigned to that room? Maybe she would know."

The ward secretary seemed annoyed at the interruption and spoke aloud the numbers she was trying to add before answering the question. "Twenty plus seventy plus thirty-two . . . 122," she said as she wrote the total at the bottom of the page. She looked back at Mary. "No nurse was assigned to that room on this shift. The patient in that room died the previous shift. Talking to a nurse who is here now won't answer your questions either."

Mary sighed as the woman returned to her work. *It's time for checkout anyway. Maybe Dr. Tyson will report what happened then.* She hurried to checkout and took her seat at the conference table beside Brad Forrest. Dr. Tyson was already briefing his associates on the patient list. Brad made an exaggerated look at his watch when his eyes met with Mary's. *Brother! It's only 6:32! These guys are punctual to a fault.* She stayed quiet for the remainder of the morning report. It didn't seem the right time to ask any questions. *Maybe I can talk about this with Dr. Forrest,* she thought.

The time came after morning rounds were completed on the fifth floor. Brad looked at his shadowing student. "What gives, Mary? You sure are quiet this morning."

Mary looked down the hall toward Room 525. "What do you think about withholding treatment of an infant on the basis of quality of life?"

Brad tried to read her thoughts. He looked at his watch. "You want some coffee? Why don't we hit the cafeteria before clinic?" He turned and headed for the elevators. Mary followed. He turned to her as they waited. "I'm not ignoring your question, Mary. What exactly are you getting at?" She shuffled her feet, so he continued, "Sure, sometimes we make difficult decisions regarding who to treat and who not to treat. There is a difference between treating someone who is going to die regardless of what you do and treating someone who has a reasonable hope of full recovery. In one case you are giving life. In the other you may just be prolonging death."

Mary nodded as the elevator opened. They descended with several others, so she stayed quiet until they sat down in the hospital cafeteria, each with a cup of steaming coffee. It was the one item on the breakfast menu that Brad never missed.

As Mary began to tell the story of the infant with esophageal atresia, Brad listened without interrupting. Finally she concluded, "It just seemed strange that Dr. Tyson seemed inclined toward surgery until he found out that the baby had cri du chat syndrome."

"Look, Mary, I know that most of the patients with that abnormality normally live beyond infancy, but perhaps there were other things that Tyson knew that made the surgery hopeless. We shouldn't operate on everyone just because we can. It's like offering life-sustaining treatment to a terminal cancer patient. Sometimes you are just increasing suffering rather than doing good."

Mary shook her head. "I heard everything that Dr. Tyson did. I don't think he knew more about the child than I did."

"But," Brad interjected, "the child died in only one night, right? That in and of itself speaks of other problems. Maybe you are having trouble with objectivity here. It's no fun losing a patient, especially a child."

Mary frowned and sipped her coffee quietly. She had other suspicions about why the child died in only one night, but she kept them to herself. She could see that Brad held Dr. Tyson, his employer, in such esteem that he found it very difficult to question his practices or judgment.

In a few minutes the two stood up. "Time to stamp out disease," Brad joked.

Mary smiled weakly and followed him to Crestview's outpatient clinic building.

* * *

Julie answered the ring of the cordless telephone in the den where Belle and Bradley played with a large box of Legos. As soon as she heard the voice on the other end of the line, she walked intentionally into the kitchen, away from the earshot of her grandmother-in-law.

"Julie?" The voice was deep, strong, and unmistakably Steve Harrison's.

"This is Julie, Steve. I don't remember giving you permission to call." She smiled but was hesitant to show her excitement at hearing from him.

"When I didn't hear from you, I bugged Becky until she gave me your unlisted number. I hope you aren't angry. I've been thinking about you a lot lately. When am I going to see you again?" His approach had always been a direct one. Julie remembered that about their relationship before. He was never very good at hiding his feelings.

Julie sighed and hesitated to answer. She had tried, unsuccessfully, to steer her thoughts away from her old friend. She began slowly. "I've been thinking about you, too," she confessed honestly. With that easy admission behind her, her bottled emotions seemed to flow without restraint. "I want to see you again, Steve. I'm so lonely lately,

I can hardly keep my mind on what I'm doing. I keep thinking back to college days when we —" She stopped suddenly as if her breath had been stolen. She put her hand to her mouth as if to catch the throb of emotion that had choked away her speech.

"Julie?"

She exhaled slowly. "Sorry. My emotions seem to be riding a roller coaster. I think I just went over a bump."

"That must have been some bump. I thought we'd been disconnected or something."

Julie paused and cast a concerned glance back toward the den.

Steve began again. "So can we get together next week? How about dinner some night?"

Julie put her finger over the following week on the calendar on the kitchen bulletin board. In red letters it said, "Brad. Chicago pediatric surgery board review." *Brad's not even going to be in town!* She bit her lip. *I suppose it would be all right just to go out as old friends, wouldn't it? Just to talk. He seems to understand me so well.* "I don't know, Steve. I want to see you, but — I'm not sure I should. I-I'm not sure I'm ready."

"It would be all right to just go out as old friends, wouldn't it?" Steve urged, his argument identical to her thoughts only a second before. Julie stared at the receiver with an expression of shock. He continued, "Just to talk. You seem to understand me so well." Julie again looked at the receiver and shook her head in amazement.

Finally she spoke, "Sure. It would be O.K. that way, I'm sure." She looked back to the den. Belle was standing up. "Can you call me next week?" she added, turning her back toward the elderly woman who had begun walking toward the kitchen.

"Sure. You mean I have your permission?" Steve added playfully.

"Yes." Julie smiled and said, "Goodbye." She looked up at Belle, who had bypassed the kitchen and was slowly climbing the wooden staircase. Julie's mind went immediately to the conclusion of her conversation with Steve. *It was as if he could read my mind. He said exactly what I thought.* She shook her head again and smiled.

She turned and walked back toward the den, unaware of the dark force that had been sent to give her the same message as that delivered to her old friend.

CHAPTER 15

By Friday Brad had pushed more work into a week than he thought humanly possible. He had expected his first few months at Crestview to be slow as he gained status as a new attending and earned the respect of the referring pediatricians. He soon found, however, that the name Valley Surgeons for Children meant instant respect, instant referrals, and instant work overload. Somehow he managed to convince Dr. Davis to move up his mock oral exam to Thursday, leaving a narrow opening in his Friday afternoon schedule. Brad made plans. His surprise for Julie just might work out after all.

He jumped in the Nova, the car his wife normally drove, and headed for Wheatman's, the area's best-known dealer for foreign luxury automobiles. His idea had grown out of a conversation he'd had with the car dealership's owner, just after fixing Mr. Walt Wheatman's grandson's hernia. "Stop in and see me sometime," Mr. Wheatman had said with a thousand-dollar smile. "I'll do for you what I did for your associates." *Julie will flip out when she sees what I have in store,* he thought. *It's about time I did something just for her. Heaven knows she hasn't gotten much from me lately — except my new paycheck.*

After his arrival Brad browsed around the showroom, feeling the shiny paint and smelling the fresh new-car scents. Mr. Wheatman joined him, his smile flashing as soon as he recognized the young surgeon. Brad shopped for cars like he shopped for clothes. See it. Try it on. Buy it. There just wasn't time enough to waste on comparative appraisals. And so within an hour Brad took a red, two-door convertible BMW for a spin and left with the keys in his hand and his signature on a two-year lease. He left the Nova on the lot. It was part of the deal. Mr. Wheatman had taken the car as a down payment only because he felt obligated to help the man who had helped his grandson.

Brad sat in the driver's seat and inhaled deeply. *Now maybe Julie can drive around town without hanging her head. A surgeon's wife should be treated like one. She deserves it after all I've put her through. This ought to make up for some of the stuff she's had to endure over the years.* He drove around town for a few minutes, enjoying the responsive handling of the car and the way it made him feel. *If only Dad could see me now. He'd know I made the right choices.* Brad looked at his watch. *I can't wait to see Julie's face when I drive up in this.*

Julie knelt on her knees as she weeded the mulched shrub bed in front of the Forrests' old Victorian farmhouse. Working around the yard occupied much of her time in the summer months, time that she fortunately enjoyed, as proper upkeep of the sprawling green yard and the shrubbery and flower beds demanded at least weekly, if not daily, attention. Bradley played on the back swing set as she pulled one undesired weed after another from the rich brown mulch. She first noticed the red convertible driving into the lane as she battled with a particularly tenacious thistle. *Who could this be?* She wiped the perspiration from her forehead and took off her gloves. As she walked up to the car, she could see a man smiling from behind the wheel.

"Steve?"

"Hi, Julie. I hope it's okay that I stopped by. Becky told me where you lived."

"I can't believe you just dropped in like this. I'm a mess. I —"

"You look fine — beautiful, in fact." Steve looked at Brad's Datsun in the driveway. He squinted his eyes with apparent concern. "Brad home?"

Julie followed his gaze to the old car. "Are you kidding? It's only 6:30. I never see him before 8:00 on his nights off."

"Isn't that his?"

"Yes, but for some reason he insisted on taking my Nova to work today. He leaves so early, I was too sleepy to protest. Besides, his Datsun is a year newer than my Nova." She paused, self-conscious again about her gardening clothes. She was about to apologize about her appearance when Steve interrupted.

"I shouldn't have stopped. It's just that since we talked, I just can't get you out of my mind. I must have driven past your place a dozen times." With this admission, Steve also found himself feeling self-conscious.

Julie returned his gaze. She was unsure what to say. "Would you like to sit down?" She motioned toward the porch swing.

"I guess I could." Steve smiled. "But just for a minute. I really should have called. I want to respect your boundaries. I know I wasn't invited."

Steve seemed edgy. Julie grabbed his

hand. "Look, if you're worried about Brad, he never comes home this early." She led him to the swing. "Don't apologize. I'm glad you came." She squeezed the hand she still held.

Steve relaxed and sat on the swing beside her. *She really looks nice in those shorts.*

Behind the couple, Belle looked on through a bay window. Her spirit was deeply troubled, and she began to pray.

Lenore Kingsley thought her problems with her pregnancy were over. Since the last adjustment in her hormone supplements, she hadn't vomited once. Now, as she readied herself for an evening on the town, she paused, vaguely aware of some mild abdominal discomfort that whispered but did not yet scream for attention.

Tonight she would dine with Dr. Web Tyson and Tammy James. The dinner date, which Lenore had been planning for months, had actually been suggested by Tammy earlier in the week. Knowing that Lenore seemed to be a big fan of Tyson's, Tammy suggested that they meet for drinks and dinner. Lenore had, of course, been following Web's progress toward the Surgeon General position. She had initiated — behind the scenes — several key interviews that had nearly guaranteed Tyson a favorable public opinion. Now that it looked like he was in the short list of front-runners, Lenore knew it was time for her to move into a whole new level of influence with Tyson. Before now she had always moved from outside his knowledge, arranging publicity, photo-ops, and interviews by manipulating a few of the many people over whom she held control. Now she would meet him face to face, and conveniently it would all appear to be planned by someone else.

"Aauugh!" Lenore huffed audibly as she tried to button her teal dress slacks. *I can't even get these things buttoned anymore! I'm not supposed to be showing yet!* She cursed loudly, pulled the slacks off, and threw them into a corner of her closet. "@#*$%!" She looked at herself in profile in the full-length mirror on the far wall. *I'm going to have to be pretty good at hiding this tummy if I've got to carry this thing for another six weeks!* Hurriedly she pulled out another outfit, this one a rose-colored pantsuit with an elastic waistband. "There," she whispered. "No one can even tell." She fluffed out the billowy top and stared at herself in the mirror. She buttoned up the blouse, then intentionally unbuttoned two buttons and put a small golden chain around her neck.

She stared at her reflection in the mirror and pushed her lips into a pucker, kissing the air with a smack. She looked very attractive. She knew she did. As Surgeon General, Web Tyson just might hold the future of genetics research in his hand. *Looking like this, I may be able to gain another level of control over him. Just wait until I let him know who is behind his sudden rise to fame.* She laughed out loud and blew out several small candles burning on her nightstand.

She finished touching up her makeup, hastily exited her apartment, and slid into her red Corvette for a dash across town to meet Tammy and Web.

Julie rocked slowly in the porch swing next to Steve Harrison. Just being next to him evoked so many old memories.

"What ever happened to us?" Julie spoke in a timid voice.

The question seemed to catch Steve offguard. He said nothing at first, then slowly answered, "I've regretted a few things in my life. The way our relationship ended certainly tops my list." He stopped, startled by movement over his right shoulder. He instinctively turned to the motion.

Julie followed his gaze. "It's just Belle —

Brad's grandmother. She's been with us nearly six years. She's great with Bradley."

Steve nodded. "Oh." Seeing someone else seemed to startle him a bit. His thought train was definitely broken. "Listen . . . I really better get out of here. How about next week? Is Wednesday night O.K.?"

Julie sensed his discomfort. "Brad never comes home this early, Steve. Relax a little."

Steve avoided her comment. He didn't want to acknowledge the accuracy of her judgment concerning his nervousness. *She always read me like an open book!* "You didn't answer my question."

She smiled. "Wednesday should be fine. I'll ask Belle to keep Bradley. I can tell her I'm going out with Becky."

"You sneak!" Steve laughed nervously. He wrote her name in a small black daily planner he had in his hand. He looked over his shoulder again and seemed relieved not to see Belle. He looked back and met Julie's gaze, his hands fidgeting over the little leather notebook.

"Relax!" Julie felt strangely confident and in control. *Steve has always been the one pursuing me, and now he's the one who seems edgy. Maybe it's about time I stopped worrying about Brad and started thinking about what makes me happy for a change.* She reached over and patted Steve's leg. "We'll take this nice and slow. Let's just see what happens. No commitments. Just good old-fashioned friendship. I hold you up — you hold me up. That's what it's all about, isn't it?"

Brad downshifted and signaled for a left turn onto Grayson Street that would take him the back way home. He didn't want to chance being seen by Julie if she happened to be looking out the front of the house. *Coming in this way,* he thought, *I'll have a better chance of arriving unnoticed.* He smiled to himself. *I've never been known to be extravagant, but maybe that's because we've always been strapped. Now that things are loosening up, I'm going to treat Julie the way she deserves.*

He tapped the steering wheel with nervous excitement. *Almost home. She is going to freak when she sees this!*

Randy Harris finished the last line of data entry and pressed Save on the desktop lab computer. From his location he could see the clock on the far wall. 6:30. Quitting time! He moved carefully around the lab counters and stopped at the animal cages near the entrance to his lab. Even with all of the normal items required in the gene sequencing lab, Lenore had insisted that Randy house all of the animals involved in gene splicing (the hybrid genome animals) within the laboratory, to be taken care of by him alone. It wasn't that there wasn't space in their huge animal care facility. She just didn't trust the technicians with the care of these extremely valuable animals.

As Randy checked the water supply, he noticed one of the pups lying still in the back of his cage. Although they all had similar black coats because of their gene manipulation, Randy knew each dog by its other characteristics and personality. The still pup, which Randy had always called Guy, normally greeted him at the front of the cage. "Guy! Night, boy!"

Randy turned to leave but looked again at the apparently sleeping dog, puzzled by the lack of his normal enthusiastic response. "Guy! What's the matter, boy?" He unlocked the door and stooped to enter the small housing unit. He reached out his hand to stroke the thick, black coat. "Hey, fella, what's the matter —" His voice choked as the reality of the situation dawned. *What!* He pulled the dog onto his back by the redundant skin on the back of his neck. The dog weighed easily twice as much as a normal Dalmatian of the same age, due to the increase in growth hormone production. *He's dead!* Randy eased the animal out onto the tile floor in front of the cage door. *He's getting stiff. He must have been dead for an hour or more. I can't believe this!*

He went to a nearby cabinet and returned with a large red bag. With some effort he managed to slide the dog into the bag and heaved it onto a large metal cart. *What could have happened? He seemed so healthy. I've got to get this to one of our veterinary pathologists for an autopsy right away! I'll need lots of fresh tissue samples to do DNA studies.*

Randy made a call to the veterinarian on night call at UBI. Because of the number of live animals kept for research, UBI employed three full-time veterinarians, at least one of whom was available day or night.

"Hello. Curt speaking."

"Hello, Dr. Scaggs. This is Randy Harris. I work in the human genome and DNA splicing lab. I've got an animal I need an autopsy on ASAP."

Dr. Curt Scaggs sighed audibly. "I was just on my way out. Can't you put it in the morgue refrigerator until morning? I'll hop on it first thing."

"I need this immediately. This is one of Lenore's pet projects . . . pardon the pun.

I know she'll want answers on this right away."

The vet wanted to protest again, but stopped short after hearing Lenore's name. The surest way out of a job at UBI was to cross Lenore Kingsley. *There goes my date with Bev Jantzi!*

Randy continued after the silent pause, "Look, if it's any consolation, I need to be here too. It's a gene splicing animal, a genetic hybrid. I'll be setting up fresh samples for DNA typing for most of the night."

Scaggs looked at his watch. "I'll meet you in the pathology suite on the fourteenth floor in ten minutes."

Click. Randy looked at the receiver and shrugged. *Time to go to work.*

Julie sat on the porch swing looking straight out toward the road. In her hand was the little leather calendar book that Steve had been holding only moments before. He had left quickly and absentmindedly left the little book on the swing behind him. *It is so unlike him to seem edgy like that,* she thought. *He must really be falling for me again. He's losing his head.* She smiled to herself. It felt good to see someone act like that around her.

She looked up to see a red convertible

driving into the lane. *Steve! He's returned for his date-book.* She walked toward the car. "You silly! You forgot your —" She stopped and gasped. "Brad!" She put her hand to her mouth. "What are you doing?"

The young surgeon just smiled. He handed her a set of car keys and opened the door, then jumped out and kissed his wife on the cheek. "It's all yours!"

Julie walked around the car. New thirty-day tags adorned the rear license bracket. The upholstery smelled of rich leather. The paint gleamed a brilliant red. "Have you lost your mind?" She stroked her hand over the car's surface. "Brad!"

Brad stood smugly without speaking, enjoying his wife's surprise.

Julie's hand returned to her mouth. "I can't believe this! What have you done?"

"Happy anniversary, honey."

Julie looked at him sharply. "Our anniversary isn't for another month!"

"Just think of it as one month early." Brad smiled.

"More like eleven months late," she responded playfully.

Brad exaggerated a pout and added sheepishly, "I did miss last year, didn't I?"

Julie came over and put her arms around her husband. "Yes. When did you realize it?"

"Now?" Brad's voice came out in a squeak. They both laughed.

Julie looked back at the car and then at her husband. "I can't believe you. It's beautiful." She kissed him noisily.

"Jump in and take it for a spin." Brad walked around after holding the door so Julie could slip into the driver's seat. He didn't notice the small black date-book that was barely visible in his wife's left rear pocket.

For Lenore Kingsley, the evening on the town was strictly business. It was time to confirm what she knew about Web Tyson and to strengthen her unseen choke-hold on his future political decisions. For the first hour Lenore, Tammy, and Web sat on the back deck at DeAngelo's enjoying mixed drinks and the quiet lapping of the Wanoset River on the shoreline. Their conversation centered on shallow events of the day and Lenore's admiration for Dr. Tyson's work for the community and the state. Eventually the chill of the night air and growing hunger prodded the trio inside to a table where the chatter turned serious. Lenore probed Tyson's positions on a variety of topics, including genetic screening and germ-line genetic research.

"In fact," Dr. Tyson continued, "I would support a mandated genetic screening program, or at least stepping up the current available genetic screening programs. As Uncle Sam continues to pick up the bill for universal health care coverage, he will realize the economy of picking up diseases before birth, so they can be dealt with expediently with abortion. That way a bundle can be saved by avoiding costly health care throughout life on individuals who are predestined to overutilize the health care dollar." He paused as he meticulously dissected the fat from the edge of his prime rib and began to eat.

As Lenore watched Dr. Tyson devour his prime rib, she smiled pleasantly. *He thinks just the way I do! I will have to see that Tammy gets rewarded for suggesting his name. He will make the perfect Surgeon General. His policies are sure to be a boon to embryo and genetic germ cell line research.* "Dr. Tyson, I do —"

"Please," he interrupted, "call me Web."

Lenore paused. "O.K., Web. I do think that you should come by sometime and see what we have been able to accomplish in our human genome lab. I think you would be quite interested in the advances we've made."

"I'd love to," Web responded sincerely. He returned Lenore's gaze warmly.

Tammy followed his gaze into the deep eyes of UBI's president. Lenore broke off the eye contact with Tyson as her eyes shifted to Tammy's. *Too bad you won't be able to keep this one, honey. It's just not in the master's plan.* Lenore smiled innocently and forced Tammy to avert her eyes.

Tammy, suddenly feeling jealous, slid closer to Web and put her hand on his leg. "How's your dinner?" she asked, wanting to change the subject.

"Marvelous. This was a great idea. We've all got to come here again," Web said after taking a long swallow of red wine.

As they chatted on, Lenore again became aware of a vague discomfort in her lower abdomen. *I must watch how much I eat.* She started to order dessert, but decided against it when another wave of pelvic pressure suggested otherwise. Just then her pager vibrated. She lifted the black beeper up to read, "Call Randy at UBI." *Can't he get along without me for one night? He knows I'm out. I'll call him tomorrow. I'm in no mood to talk to him now.* She ignored the message and returned to gazing at the distinguished surgeon opposite her. As she slowly reached her foot out to contact Web's lower leg, a sharp pain ripped through her uterus and ended her flirtatious advance. She immediately blanched and took a slow, deep breath. She hoped no one had noticed. She tried desperately to maintain composure and found relief after only a second or two of cramping. A few moments later she excused herself to the restroom and left Tammy and Web alone, talking among themselves.

In the restroom Lenore quickly locked herself into a toilet stall. She first noted the blood when she sat down. *I'm spotting! @#%$&!* She sighed heavily. *At least the pain has subsided — for now. I'll need to let Dr. Feinberg know about this first thing in the morning.* She didn't have any appropriate pads, so she shoved a handful of toilet paper into her underwear, washed her hands, and returned to the table.

Sally Southerly felt happy about the way she was dealing with the passing of her husband. It had not been easy. Paul had been a strong man, and she had depended upon him a great deal for many things. It had taken three months for her to feel comfortable in the house again. For two of the three months she had vacationed, first staying with her sister and then with her oldest daughter. Now, at the urging of her family, she had moved back into her colonial home, determined to keep her emotions in check and move on with her life. For the first two nights back in her house, she had slept, somewhat fitfully, in the guest bedroom. Tonight, driven partly out of motivation to conquer any fears over sleeping in the bed her husband died in and partly out of the lower back pain that resulted from spending too much time in the guest bed, she had returned to her own bedroom.

As she opened the door to the master suite, a musty odor greeted her. She realized that the door hadn't been opened since the first week following Paul's death. *What this room needs is a thorough cleaning. That might even help to drive away some of those old memories of Paul.* She looked at the clock. 10 P.M. *Oh well,* she thought, *no time like the present! I'm not tired anyway*. She walked to the hall closet and returned with a spray bottle of furniture polish and a cloth, an old T-shirt of Dr. Southerly's. As she dusted, she hummed the tunes of old favorite hymns. She carefully picked up each item on the dresser and nightstand, dusting each item with a gentle swipe of her cloth.

When she began dusting the footboard of their antique poster bed, her hand ran across a roughened area on the inner surface of the crossbar. Her eyes went to it, and she instinctively rubbed the roughened area with a bit more vigor. *What's this?* A greasy, waxy substance appeared to have been spilled or to have dripped onto the inner surface of the wooden cross-beam. *This looks like candle wax.* She rubbed the substance between her fingers. *It's so greasy, though. Funny. We never kept candles around the house because of Paul's allergy to smoke.* She shook her head as she recalled her husband's delicate state of health. Diabetes, seizures, multiple environmental allergies. It was a gift of God that he lived as long as he did. She looked at the yellowish substance she rolled between her fingers. She walked to the bathroom to wash off her hands when a thought interrupted her plan. *Save it!* Sally obeyed the inner prompting and went to the kitchen for a small container. *I've got to talk to our housecleaner about what she's been using for furniture polish. Maybe she will know what this stuff is.*

Randy Harris sighed, both from frustration and fatigue. He had spent the last four hours getting tissue samples ready for further histological and DNA sequencing studies. He had given up on contacting Lenore after two unanswered pages. *Oh well, maybe it's best, after all I've seen, to get a little more data before I tell Lenore about Guy. After all, she will just breathe down my back until the answers are available.*

Just then Curt Scaggs walked in. He looked washed out. Randy spoke first. "Done?"

"Yeah." He didn't elaborate. Randy stared at the veterinarian. *These guys sure get moody if you ask 'em to work late.* "Well? Did you see anything in the cranium that made a difference? The rest of the autopsy sure hasn't given us much to hang our hats on."

"Actually, yes," he answered slowly. He enjoyed keeping the researcher in suspense.

"Well?" Randy spoke a little louder.

"The dog died from an intracranial hemorrhage from a large pituitary tumor. It's easily the biggest one I've ever seen."

"Pituitary?" Randy began to pace. @#$*%! *The pituitary gland is the normal site of growth hormone secretion. Our added gene segment for additional growth hormone must have turned on an oncogene that stimulated tumor growth as a side effect!* Randy didn't share his thoughts with Scaggs, who didn't know the full details of the experiment they were running. He glared at the veterinarian. "Can you get me a piece of the pituitary? I'll need it for DNA studies."

The vet left without speaking further. Randy cursed again silently. *Things were going so well. No apparent side effects — until now. Maybe it's just a freak!* He walked to the animal cages along the wall. *Are you guys next? I wonder how many of you have the same problem.* He looked at the phone and thought of calling Lenore one more time. *No. I'd better wait until I have the full scoop on this. I can't have her overreacting if it's not necessary. Too much excitement for a pregnant woman can't be good.* @#$*%!

CHAPTER 16

Lenore stumbled to the front door of her apartment as another contraction launched a painful message toward her cranium. The pain had ceased for the previous hour, giving her ample time to confirm her feelings about Web Tyson. But then, coinciding exactly with her departure from DeAngelo's, the contractions cruelly resumed and further hindered Lenore's alcohol-impaired driving skills. She cautiously manipulated her Corvette through the sparse late-night traffic and cursed as she felt the evidence of the resumption of the bleeding. "@#$*#!" she muttered as she unlocked her thick oak door. *I've got to talk to Dr. Feinberg! I must be having a miscarriage!* Slowly she moved to the kitchen, clutching her lower abdomen.

As she grabbed the phone book from beneath her cordless phone, a second obnoxious stimulus interrupted her task — nausea! She dropped the book and grasped the edge of the large stainless steel sink and vomited her undigested gastric contents. After a few moments she slumped into a chair by the kitchen table. She concentrated on taking slow, deep breaths and allowed the sickness to ebb. She found the number for Suzanne Feinberg in the Yellow Pages and dialed.

"Crestview Reproductive Services answering service." The voice sounded mechanical and female.

"I need to talk to Dr. Feinberg," Lenore stated as strongly as she could.

"I'm sorry. Dr. Fitzhugh is taking calls for that group tonight. Can I page him for you?"

"I really need to speak to Dr. Feinberg," Lenore pleaded.

"Dr. Feinberg will be back on and available after 8 in the morning. If you have an emergency, I'll be glad to page Dr. Fitzhugh for you."

"L-listen," Lenore stuttered with despair, "I am the president of United Biotechnical Industries! I'm sure Dr. Feinberg would want to talk to me."

"I'm sorry, ma'am. I'm only allowed to page the physician on call. If you would like to call back in —"

Lenore ignored the rest of the message and slammed the phone onto the formica tabletop. *This has got to be kept secret! Fein-*

berg is the only physician who agreed to help me without all the bother of medical documentation. She ought to, with the amount I'm paying her! She lifted herself out of the kitchen chair and leaned momentarily against the counter. *Maybe I can just wait until morning.* She went to the medicine cabinet in the bathroom and swallowed four ibuprofen tablets in hopes of easing the pain. She then exchanged the wad of toilet paper in her underwear for two large absorbent pads, cursing as she saw that her undergarments had been profusely soiled with her own blood. *This bleeding . . . !* She dropped the wet underwear into the trash and limped into her bedroom.

She stumbled as the room began to swim. She grabbed for the air in a clumsy attempt to keep from fainting and finally collapsed onto her king-size waterbed in the center of the room. *I've got to make it a few more hours. Then I'll call Randy and have him take me to Dr. Feinberg. Or better yet, I'll have him bring Dr. Feinberg to me.* Another contraction followed, interrupting her thoughts, and Lenore concentrated on slowing her breathing again. In a moment she dozed, the effects of the evening's alcohol and her own exhaustion demanding the brief renewal. As she rested, an ever-widening warm ring expanded beneath her, coloring the white quilt with a brilliant red. When she awoke with new pain only minutes later, she screamed at the sticky evidence of her pregnancy's imminent loss. She fumbled with the phone at her bedside and called Randy Harris.

Harris, who had arrived home only minutes before, answered the phone on the third ring. "Hello."

"Randy, you've got to help me! I'm bleeding!" Lenore's voice erupted in a weak gasp.

"Lenore?"

She strained to remain conscious. The room had begun to swim again. She foolishly sat up on the edge of the bed to speak into the phone. "I think I'm having —" Lenore's voice trailed off as Randy began to scream at her.

"Lenore? Lenore!"

UBI's young president slumped to the floor, her blood volume now insufficient to maintain consciousness in the sitting position. As she fell, her head struck the edge of the glass nightstand, lacerating the edge of her forehead through the temporal artery.

Randy stared into the phone, a dull thud on the other end the only response to his persistent pleas. "Lenore!"

* * *

Web Tyson gasped as he fought to bring himself to full alertness. A dream of evil long buried had haunted him and brought fitfulness to his sleep. He sat up on the side of the bed, rubbing his eyes and his neck, trying without success to recall the source of his troubled emotional state. He felt his forehead, which dripped with the evidence of his anxiety, and tried to remember. As his heart pounded in his thorax and in his ears, he instinctively moved his right index finger over his carotid artery and looked at the clock. *One hundred forty! What's wrong with me?* He shook his head slowly and steadied his rapid breathing. He could not recall the dream but recognized the emotion that he had experienced only rarely before: fear!

Silently he reasoned with himself. *Come on, Web, think! It was only a dream! A dream you can't even recall! What is there to be afraid of?* He slid quietly from the bed so as not to disturb his sleeping companion, Tammy James, and walked to his bathroom. As he washed the perspiration from his face, his thoughts turned to Lenore Kingsley. *What is it about her? Does she have anything to do with my dream?* He stared at his own reflection, remembering how open he had been with her. *I felt so invincible around her — and so . . . so powerful. Was it just me?*

He walked over to the sliding glass door that led to the expansive deck behind his house. He looked at the silver moon, his thoughts fixated on Lenore. *There's something about her — something drawing me. Are my feelings just the wishful fantasies of midlife? Certainly Tammy has taken care of that, hasn't she? Perhaps she has only helped awaken me again. Lenore . . . Lenore . . . what is it about you? Something mysterious, dark, almost familiar —*

A hand on his shoulder broke into his thoughts. Tammy hugged him gently and followed his gaze at the moonlit sky. "Are you O.K.?"

Web would not betray his own secret thoughts. "Sure." He sighed slowly. "I just needed to use the bathroom," he lied. "Evidence of my age, I guess."

Tammy didn't reply. She sensed a deeper insecurity. "Come on, let's get some sleep. You've got a busy day tomorrow." She nudged him toward the bed. Web obeyed and resumed his sleeping position. His mind, however, failed to yield to the slumber he needed so desperately. As Tammy slept, Web's thoughts continued to center around UBI's mysterious president. *Why does she seem so powerful — so familiar?*

Brad Forrest muttered under his breath as he groped in the darkness to shut off his alarm clock. *4:30 A.M. I ought to have my head examined for arranging such an early flight.* He sat up on the side of the bed and collected his thoughts. He needed to be at the Green Valley Regional Airport by 6 A.M. to catch his first flight on the way to Chicago. He looked over at Julie and sighed. *She seemed so distant last night. I guess my little surprise must have really overwhelmed her,* he thought as he slipped from the bed and began his preparation.

After taking a quick shower and getting dressed, he carefully added his toiletries to the suitcase that he'd prepared the night before. He fumbled about silently in the dark, so as not to disturb his wife. Julie, however, having been aroused by the alarm, found herself unable to return to sleep, her anxious thoughts pushing slumber into the realm of the impossible. Brad closed the suitcase and kissed Julie gently on the cheek. In the darkness he did not recognize her alert state — or her silent tears.

He stepped into the hallway and intercepted his bleary-eyed son, who was clad in his fishing hat in addition to his pajamas.

"Where goin', D-dad?" he stuttered. "L-let's go f-f-fishin'!"

"Morning, son," Brad whispered. "I'm on my way to the airport. I have to go to a meeting, Bradley. Dad can't go fishing today." He put down his suitcase and hoisted the boy into his arms. "Uugg!" he strained. "You are getting too big for Dad to handle."

"I want to ride on a plane!"

"Someday, Bradley," Brad replied softly. "Dad can't take you today." He set his son down in the hallway. "Want to help me with my suitcase? I need someone awfully strong for this."

Bradley strained with the old suitcase, dragging it to the stairwell. Together they bumped the overstuffed bag to the bottom of the stairs.

At the bottom they were greeted by Belle, who stood to receive Bradley with a hug. "You boys make enough noise to resurrect the dead," she scolded with a chuckle. Father and son just looked at each other mischievously.

"You're up early," Brad said, greeting his grandmother with a kiss.

"The morning's always the best time for me," she replied.

Brad glanced at the clock on the far wall.

"I've got to run. I've got a ticket on the 6:30 puddle-jumper to Atlanta." He leaned over and gave Bradley a hug. "See ya Friday night, sport."

"Bye, dad," the boy replied, giving his father a squeeze. "Can I have Pop-Tarts for breakfast?"

Brad looked at Belle. "Sure, son." He opened the door. "Bye, Belle. I'll see you at the end of the week."

With that, he disappeared. From the window on the second floor, Julie watched him go. *I know your conference is just business, Brad, but at least you could have asked me to go with you.*

It took Green Valley Fire and Rescue Unit Number 1 only eleven minutes from the time of Randy's frantic 911 call until they reached Lenore's locked door. Her apartment was not on the ground floor, so a window entry was impossible. Kimball Young, a paramedic, pounded on the door and listened briefly for a response. He tried the door handle once more with a vain grunt. "Get the axe, Doug. We've got no choice."

Doug Reames ran to the truck and returned with a large, very sharp fire-axe. Kimball and the other members of the paramedic crew moved to the side. After five blows the hollow door was split away from the dead bolt. After two additional swings Kimball pushed through the rough entrance and unlocked and opened the door. A quick survey of the room revealed no problems. He followed a light from the bedroom and headed to the open door. A sickening scene greeted the experienced paramedic. Bloodstains covered the central portion of a large white quilt. "In here, guys."

He rushed to the side of a woman wearing a silky, rose-colored pantsuit. She was facedown on a rich gray carpet that was also stained heavily with bright red blood. Kimball Young looked at his help. "Let's logroll her to her back." The team quickly placed a wooden backboard on the floor beside Lenore, prior to gently and slowly rolling her onto it. Young assessed her airway and performed a jaw thrust by gently pushing forward on the angles of her mandible. "She's breathing! Let's get a mask and some oxygen."

"I've got a weak femoral pulse, but no radial," Reames replied. A third paramedic looked at the blood pressure dial as she listened carefully with a stethoscope on Lenore's arm. As Diane Edinburg let down the blood pressure cuff, she sighed nervously. "Pressure's 60 systolic."

Young continued his assessment. In addition to clotted blood in the hair, there seemed to be additional blood on the patient's pants. The only obvious immediate source for the bleeding was a large laceration on the left side of the forehead. "Let's get some IVs started," he instructed slowly. "One of lactated ringers and one of Oxydel." He moved his hands away after securing an oxygen mask. He peered at the laceration and gently lifted the skin away from the forehead. Pulsatile bleeding greeted him, spraying blood into the air above the patient and onto the carpet. "Whoa!" he yelled, returning the skin-flap to its original location. "Let me have some four-by-fours. We need to get some pressure on this cut!"

Diane Edinburg started a sixteen-gauge IV in Lenore's right forearm. She looked from the distribution of blood on the patient's clothing to Kimball Young, who was leading the squad. "Kimball, look at this girl. You don't suppose she was raped, do you?" The squad leader returned her concerned gaze. "Just look at this blood on her pants!"

Young finished applying a pressure dressing to Lenore's forehead and then stood up and looked anxiously around the room. "You may be onto something, Diane." He looked back at the patient. "She has her clothes on, though."

Doug Reames spoke next. "If she was attacked, whoever was responsible may still be around! That dead bolt can't be locked except from in here!"

"Come on, guys!" cried Diane. "You're making me scared! I don't want to stay any longer than we have to!"

"Calm down." Kimball Young steadied his voice to disguise his own concern. "Let's get the IV fluids running and get another pressure and then get out of here." Just then Lenore began to moan softly. Young lowered his face to hers, then looked at Reames. "What did the caller say her name was?"

Reames looked at his clipboard. "Lenore — Lenore Kingsley."

"Lenore! Lenore!" The paramedic repeated her name, hoping to get a response. "What happened?"

Lenore only moaned.

"Diane, call the police! We've got to tell them about our forced entry — and about the possible rape. We'll get the victim out to the ambulance."

Diane picked up the cordless phone that

was lying on the floor next to Lenore. As she saw her partners pick up the backboard and begin carrying the patient toward the door, she ran after them, dropping the phone back to the floor. "Hey, I'm not staying in here by myself!"

"Fine," the squad leader replied. "We can call from the unit. Let's get out of here."

Outside, as Kimball and Doug loaded the patient, Diane called the police. She relayed the message and hung up, so she could call ahead to the nearest emergency facility, Bridgewater University Medical Center.

"Hey, guys!" she shouted. "Guess what, Doug? The dispatcher told me two units are already on their way. Some neighbor heard you break the door down and thought we were burglars!"

Six miles away at Bridgewater University Medical Center, Mark Alty's trauma alert pager sounded. The young surgeon had been chief resident on the trauma team for only one night. So far his initiation had been a baptism by fire with two motor vehicle accident victims and one gunshot wound to the left lower extremity; now he was facing a "trauma alert," a term that was only used when a patient was hypotensive (low blood pressure) or unstable in some way and demanded immediate attention. He hustled to the emergency room to await the next patient. Once he was in, the head nurse in the E.R. filled him in on the details.

"We're expecting a woman, age approximately thirty-five, who has suffered a lacerated scalp and a possible pelvic wound. The details are sketchy, Dr. Alty. The patient is a possible victim of assault, maybe even rape. She was found hypotensive and unresponsive by our paramedic crew just a few minutes ago."

"IVs?"

"Two. They've started Oxydel per our field protocol for hypotensive patients with blood loss."

"Good." Alty shook his head and checked his watch. *If this patient needs an operation, I hope I can get her ready before the attending surgery coverage changes. Hodad's coming on at 7:00!* ("Hodad" was the nickname the residents gave to Alty's least favorite attending surgeon, who had a reputation for getting into trouble in the O.R. The acronym stood for "*H*ands *O*f *D*eath *A*nd *D*estruction.)

Dr. Alty walked to the front of the first trauma bay. Bay 2 was empty. Bay 3 contained the last motor vehicle accident patient. Two stretchers lined the hallway adjacent to the trauma bays. Both contained sleeping intoxicated patients sobering up after minor laceration repairs, the yellow coloring in their IV lines a telltale sign of the vitamin supplements they were receiving.

Alty assessed the team members. Two interns, a third-year resident, a respiratory therapist, two nurses, an X-ray technician, and a nurses' aide had all assembled. Alty gave the instructions. "Dave, I want you to handle the airway. Sandy, you should do the complete secondary survey. Joan, I want you to get initial vital signs and be sure the blood is drawn for the trauma lab survey."

In eight more minutes the patient arrived. Kimball Young gave the report as they transferred the patient onto the trauma stretcher. "She was found unconscious with a scalp laceration and some blood on her pants. She revived a bit with oxygen and some Oxydel. We've given 500 cc's en route. Her last B.P. was 90 systolic."

As Dr. Ed Turner took a detailed history from the paramedics, the team jumped into action. Alty assessed her airway and breathing, listening to her anterior lung fields with a stethoscope. A nurse to the patient's left called out the first recorded blood pressure and set the automatic blood pressure cuff to cycle every two minutes. "Pressure 97 systolic."

A second nurse was assisted by an intern in cutting off the patient's clothes. Alty turned to his third-year resident. "Dave, I want you to keep the patient's neck immobilized," he cautioned, touching the patient's forehead with his gloved hand. "With a wound like this, we have to assume she has a cervical spine fracture until we can prove differently." He looked at the X-ray tech. "Let's get a quick chest film and a lateral C-spine."

The tech responded promptly, positioning a film under the patient's back and yelling, "X-ray!" The warning sent the team scattering for a second until the film was taken.

With the ABCs (Airway, Breathing, Circulation) under control, Alty performed a quick assessment of the patient's neurofunction. Her pupils were equal, round, and reactive to light. She was unresponsive to voice but opened her eyes to painful stimuli and made purposeful movements. He glanced at her now fully exposed body, noting the large amount of blood on the legs and perineum. "Give me a hand here," Alty instructed the team. "Let's get a quick look at her back to be sure we don't miss a penetrating injury responsible for all this blood." The team acted by log-rolling the patient and thoroughly inspecting her back and buttocks. "There's nothing here. Let's get a closer look at her from the front."

"One liter Oxydel and one liter lactated ringers in," the surgical intern reported.

"B.P. 110 systolic," the nurse shouted.

Alty searched for the source of all of the blood below the waist. There was no injury to the legs or pelvis. "It's all vaginal," Mark Alty reported to Sandy Jamison, the surgical intern. "Give the O.B. resident a call. This may be out of our league. Maybe this was a rape after all," he added, twisting his face into a distasteful grimace. "Let's cover her up and keep her warm for now." Turning to his third-year resident, he asked, "Can you help Joan repair the forehead laceration? Make sure it's not an open cranium. From the looks of all that blood in her hair, you'll need to tie off the superficial temporal artery."

Alty stepped back and watched his team work. "If she doesn't come around rapidly, let's get a quick C.T. scan of her head." He paused, looking up as the O.B. resident arrived. "Hi, Herb."

The gynecologist, a sleep-deprived man of thirty-two, omitted the salutations.

"What've you got here, Mark?"

Mark briefed him on the history and the physical findings. Herb Appleby pulled the curtain, shutting out the rest of the E.R., keeping an intern and a nurse for assistants. In a few minutes he emerged, asking for a specimen container. He looked at the chief resident, who was dutifully updating his patient list. "She's having a miscarriage, Mark. No signs of rape as far as I can tell. There sure is a lot of blood, though. I think we should get her on up to the labor hall and start some pitocin. Her cervix is wide open. There's no saving this one. We just need to get the bleeding under control."

Mark nodded. "We just need a few minutes to finish sewing up her forehead. I'd like to C.T. her head just to be sure we aren't dealing with any intracranial bleeding as well."

The O.B./G.Y.N. resident looked back toward the drawn curtain. "Fine, but if it's O.K. with you, if all that checks out fine, I'd like her on my service, so we can follow her progress."

"Sure, but let me clear her head and neck first," Dr. Alty responded.

In a few minutes, with Lenore's laceration repaired, the intern wheeled her up to the C.T. scanner. After only five minutes the scan was completed, and she was taken to labor and delivery.

Lenore Kingsley didn't regain consciousness fully until noon.

CHAPTER 17

The next day as Randy Harris walked into Lenore's private room, he almost bumped into a large, uniformed detective from the city police force. The officer excused himself and left. Harris looked at Lenore and cocked his head. "What was he doing here?"

"You tell me." Lenore was back to her normal feistiness. "I know I didn't call them. The last thing I want is official police records of my pregnancy."

"They were at your apartment this morning when I went by. Must be something to do with the fact that I called the rescue squad after talking to you on the phone. I didn't know what had happened. One minute you were talking, the next minute all I hear is a thud." Lenore looked at him curiously. "You do remember talking to me, don't you, Lenore?"

"The last thing I remember is throwing away some bloody underwear. I remember going to the bedroom to get some sleep. The next thing I know, I'm in the hospital."

Lenore shook her head. "It seems so unreal." She changed her expression and frowned. "The officer said he needed to file a report because someone on the rescue squad thought I had been raped." She sighed. "I don't remember anything like that. The doctor told me there were no signs of external trauma or rape." She made eye contact with her visitor. "The doctor told me that I lost the baby. He told me it was a little girl."

"I'm sorry, Lenore."

"Don't be. This was an experiment, remember?"

Randy looked away, avoiding eye contact again. "Sure."

"The doctor said it looked approximately sixteen weeks old."

"No way," Harris responded. "We only started this eight weeks ago, max," he added looking at his watch.

"I don't think he was mistaken, Randy. I think the gene for extra growth hormone must have kicked in much earlier than we thought."

"I'll need to check it all out. Where's the specimen, anyway?"

Lenore remained quiet. Randy looked on with curiosity, which changed to anxiety when Lenore didn't answer. "You did get the fetus, didn't you? You didn't let them throw it away?"

"Randy, I was unconscious until a few hours ago. Give me a break!" She softened a bit. "I'm embarrassed to say I hadn't even thought about it."

Randy cursed loudly. "This baby may be our link to understanding human germ cell line manipulation, Lenore! What did they do with it?"

"I don't know." Lenore paused. "We can get it back, though."

"Right. I'm sure they will just give us the specimen. All that stuff is considered a biohazard, you know."

"We'll just have to get it, and that's that."

"Just how do you propose we go about it?" Harris questioned.

"I'll just tell them it's my baby and I want to have a funeral for it and provide a proper burial for it." Lenore smiled coyly. "They should be used to crazy requests like that from all the mountain folks they treat here."

Randy thought back to the Dalmatian and the large pituitary tumor that had been found. *I'll need to check the fetus's brain carefully to see if the human experiment had any signs that the same problem was encountered there.* He looked back at Lenore, not yet willing to share his thoughts with her. *No use in worrying her about this just yet. She needs to recover from this for a while.* "Yeah, I guess so." He paused. "Do you think you can get it soon? I'd really like to get started on that DNA analysis."

"I'll tell my nurse to look into it today." Randy shook his head resolutely and said nothing. After a short silence Lenore brightened and spoke again. "Oh, guess what?" Randy shrugged his shoulders. "They gave me Oxydel. One doctor swore it saved my life. Evidently I lost quite a bit of blood."

"I guess that means you saved your own life, in a way." He reached for her shoulder and stroked her gently.

Lenore responded soberly. "I always knew it would make me rich. I just didn't know it would save my life."

The President of the United States acted uncharacteristically warm. Dr. Web Tyson marveled how at ease he felt in his presence. "I hope you will remain understanding about our need to proceed quite cautiously and slowly in our selection process, Dr. Tyson."

"There is no need to explain that, sir," Web responded in kind.

"I feel I must explain, though," President Blackburn insisted. "You must know that you are one of only a few finalists. The kind of detailed investigation we have handled in this search has been quite extensive. We are glad to see that your positions on the main health care issues are identical to mine. I think philosophically you would work out fine." The President stood up and walked to the windows of the Oval Office. "But so much is at stake here — the directorship of a major part of our federal budget for health care and research funding, to mention only a few. You must understand that we feel we must pick a man not only capable of promoting our political views worldwide, but also a candidate who can handle a multibillion dollar budget and the stress of media and public scrutiny."

"I understand completely, sir," Tyson added. "I look forward to the final selection process."

The President approached him, his hand outstretched. Tyson grasped his hand. The energy of the moment was high for Tyson. *Surely I am on my way to worldwide influence!*

Julie glanced at her watch nervously. She didn't want to be early. It seemed to be an appropriate occasion to be fashionably late. She downshifted and turned onto a winding two-lane road that bordered the river, slowing slightly to read the sign, "Evers' Country Inn, 2 miles." Below the fading letters, a large red arrow pointed the way. She had insisted on driving. She just didn't think it would look appropriate to Belle for Steve to pick her up at the house. *Besides,* she thought, *I want to drive my new car — and this will give me a chance to be alone. Maybe a drive in the country will help clear my head.* As she drove, she could see the moonlight dancing on the water's surface, its reflection wrinkled by the steady westward breeze.

The thirty-minute drive did little to clear her thoughts. In fact, she was truly enamored by the new car, which continually reminded her of Brad. *Just when I'm ready to give up on you, you go and do something crazy like this,* she thought as she struck the steering wheel. *Not that creature comforts will heal this relationship. What I really need is a caring husband, not a new car.* Her thoughts skipped to her friend Becky and her recent divorce. Julie remembered the new vehicle Becky had gotten in the settlement. "It's not really so different with me, Becky," she whispered. "I've got a great new vehicle, just like you. We just don't have husbands to enjoy them with."

She turned into the parking lot of the Evers' Country Inn, the bed-and-breakfast where Steve had reserved a table for two. She saw his red convertible parked at the far end of the lot. She parked beside his car and glanced at the restaurant's front entrance. She walked toward the steps, then stopped, slipping the wedding band and engagement ring off her finger, a twinge of guilt causing her to pause for only a second. *I don't need anything reminding me of my empty relationship now,* she thought as she stepped into the Inn's inviting interior.

Dr. Curt Scaggs had been a veterinarian for twelve years, teaching at the Bridgewater School of Veterinary Science before coming on to work full-time for United Biotechnical Industries. His life had been devoted to teaching some of the country's finest young minds about veterinary medicine. He had thought that he would stay and teach until his retirement, but the lure of the finest new diagnostic equipment and a hefty doubling of his salary proved too attractive a job offer to pass up. He'd left Bridgewater University and joined UBI just three months before. Now he sat in his office and wiped his forehead, which was beaded with sweat. His office overhead light had been turned off, and the X-ray view boxes behind his desk provided the room's only illumination. In all of his days of academic veterinarian medicine, he hadn't run into a cluster of cases like those he was examining now.

It had been a busy week. First Dr. Harris had insisted he do a late-night autopsy. Then he'd been required to oversee the M.R.I. brain scanning of twelve additional dogs from Dr. Harris's lab. This required him to transport the dogs to the University Vet School. As sophisticated as UBI was, the one thing they didn't have was a magnetic resonance imaging scanner. Scanning the twelve dogs took most of the day. Each dog was sedated and carefully strapped into position for the special head scans. He had been so busy monitoring the dogs that he hadn't had time to give a detailed reading on the scans — that is, until now, as he sat alone in his office. As he completed the reading on the last of his "patients," he began to wonder exactly what he'd stumbled onto.

Just what is Dr. Harris doing with these . . . Dalmatians, he called them. They certainly don't look like any Dalmatians I've ever seen. He carefully finished the last of his report forms. Three additional dogs from this litter had M.R.I. evidence of previously undiagnosed pituitary tumors. *I've never seen anything like this before! Familial pituitary adenomas? Just what are they doing to these poor animals?*

Dr. Scaggs sighed, stacked the report forms, and checked his watch. *I just might catch the last half of the Nebraska-Miami game if I hurry.* He remembered what Dr. Harris had said: "Please get the information to me as soon as possible." On his way out, Curt stopped at the human genome lab. The lights were off. *Nice guy! Expects me to work weekends while he's out having fun. Probably out with Lenore Kingsley. Rumors are out that they've been seen together.* Dr. Scaggs slid the manila envelope through a slot in the door and hurried to the elevator. *I'm out of here!*

Lenore Kingsley rang the nurse call button and waited. She rubbed her eyes vigorously until she was sure they looked irritated and red. She then dropped several saline eyedrops into each eye until they spilled over onto her cheeks. She returned the drops to the top drawer of her night table. Moments later the nurse, a tired, graying woman of about fifty, entered with a strained smile. "What do you need, Ms. Kingsley?"

Lenore clutched the blanket into a tight knot beneath her chin and sobbed, "I — I want to see my b-baby!"

The nurse leaned down and put her hand on the apparently distressed patient's shoulder, "There, there, it's going to be O.K." She waited, giving Lenore time and space to quiet her own sobs. "Ms. Kingsley, you're feeling a lot of emotional pain right now." She paused again. "I'm not sure it would be advisable to let you see the baby. Dr. Appleby estimated her age at only sixteen weeks. That's very small, and if you are not used to seeing such young —"

"I want my baby!" Lenore interrupted with a new outburst of emotion. She buried her head in her pillow and moaned. She pulled the pillow away and faced off with the nurse. "It's my child. I want it to have a funeral and a proper Christian burial."

Oh, great, the nurse thought, *another right-wing fundamentalist crazy! She has no idea what she's asking.* The nurse could see that Lenore was determined, so she changed her demeanor and proceeded with the facts. "The truth is, hospital policy makes it impossible for us to release any bodies to anyone except a fully licensed funeral home."

"But I want to see her," Lenore lied dramatically. "I just need to be near her again."

"If you give us the name of an acceptable

funeral home, we will cooperate in any way we can."

"It's my child!" Lenore shouted hysterically. "This hospital can't just keep her from me! I want to see my baby!"

I don't have time for this. I have other patients to take care of. "Ms. Kingsley, your baby was very premature. Looking at it would only distress you even more. I'll check with the doctor to see if we can get something to calm your nerves —"

"I don't want any medicines! I want my baby!"

The nurse heaved a sigh of frustration and left. A few minutes later she returned, finding Lenore resting quietly, her episode of feigned hysteria passed. "Here," she said, holding out a small white tablet and a glass of water. "This will help calm your nerves."

Lenore recognized the pill as a common tranquilizer. She looked away, avoiding eye contact with the nurse. The nurse set the tablet on the night table along with the water. She turned and walked away, relieved that her patient was calm and quiet again.

Lenore snatched the pill off of the table and popped it into her mouth. *At least I can get a little buzz out of this,* she seethed. *Now how am I going to get that fetus?*

* * *

Throughout the evening Belle felt a prompting to pray. The thoughts pressed in with such intensity that she excused herself from Bradley's presence and isolated herself in her small bedroom, attempting to discern the source of her vehement burden. *Pray for Julie!*

Slowly and with many tears, she unloaded her burdens into the hands of the Lord. When she arose, thirty minutes had passed. She still did not have a fix on the exact problem. In the fifteen minutes that followed, she put in a call to Ben Kreider and Jen Slabaugh. They in turn spoke with the others who gathered each week to pray. With the prayer warriors of Patterson's west wing notified, the battle began to heighten. With intercession initiated, Belle returned to a game of checkers with Bradley.

Julie gazed across the table at Steve Harrison, who smiled back and took another sip of his dessert coffee. The evening had quickly passed in a whirl of food, drink, memories, conversation, and laughter. Except for one heart-sinking moment when Julie thought she saw Belle across the crowded room, she had enjoyed herself and her company immensely. For a brief second or two after her fear of being seen by Belle, she shuddered, sensing her grandmother-in-law's disappointment. After another second she shrugged the feeling away, passing it off as her own paranoia, telling herself that Belle couldn't possibly know what was going on.

Steve took another sip of his coffee. Up to this point, the evening had gone according to plan.

Julie took a sip of the coffee in front of her. She giggled. "Wow! What do they put in this stuff?"

"It's a specialty coffee, Julie. It will help put a cap on this whole wonderful evening."

She smiled at his strong face and looked in his eyes. "If I drink this, I'll not be able to drive anywhere."

"I've got that all under control," he said with his voice just audible above the noise of the dining room. He pressed a room key into Julie's receptive palm. "This is a bed-and-breakfast inn, you know," he added, emphasizing the word "bed."

Julie shivered. It was as if the key was on fire. She dropped it immediately to the table. She felt suddenly cold and in need of fresh air. The room closed in around her, and stark panic surfaced. *I'm going to vomit!*

Steve hadn't anticipated this reaction at

all. Neither had Julie. Until now the evening had been perfect! Steve looked across the table at a very pale Julie Forrest. "Julie, are you O.K.?"

"I just need some air," she gasped. The room circled. Her stomach flipped.

He put his hand gently on her arm. "I didn't mean to —"

Julie stood up quickly, spilling her alcoholic coffee over the linen cloth. She tore free of Steve's hand, staggering toward the front desk and the door beyond. *I've got to get some air!* She picked up her pace and put her hand to her mouth. She broke into the parking lot outside and deposited her supper in the bushes. She didn't even care if other customers saw her. After a minute the nausea passed, and her head cleared enough to see Steve still sitting at their table. *What is wrong with me? Isn't this what I wanted?* She thought about returning to her table but decided against it when she saw her splattered blouse. "Great," she muttered.

With fresh tears overpowering her eyes, she turned, hopped into her new BMW, and sped into the night.

Randy left Anthony's Place at 10 P.M. The restaurant had been crowded, but the faces were new, and Randy didn't feel like talking to strangers. He drove his TR-6 like he always did, with the top down. He maneuvered through the Saturday-night traffic, heading for UBI to pick up some papers and check on the dogs. *I'm too wired for sleep anyway.*

He pulled into Lenore Kingsley's parking spot and waved defiantly to the video surveillance camera. He trotted across the lot and into the plush lobby, which housed a chandelier the size of a Volkswagon Beetle. He walked past the security officer and held up his hand in a passive wave.

"Little late to be coming in on a weekend, isn't it, Dr. Harris?" The rotund man chuckled and looked back at the console of video monitors in front of him.

"Some things won't wait, Sam," Randy answered, removing his glasses so he could use the retinal scanner. After he had looked into the eyepieces, the doors in front of him unlocked. He was on his way through when he heard Sam, the security guard, call out behind him.

"I hope Dr. Kingsley don't find you parked in her spot. She can get pretty upset about —"

The doors snapped shut, muffling the rest of his sentence. *I really doubt that Ms. Kings-*

ley is any shape for that now! Dr. Harris exhaled noisily with a sigh. He quietly despised it when others called Lenore "Dr." He had worked hard for the title and resented people throwing the term around so loosely.

He took the elevator to his human genome lab. He unlocked the door and nearly tumbled over the reports that had been dropped through the mail slot. He flipped on the lights and anxiously began going over the M.R.I. scan results. He looked over the first seven. All normal. The eighth, eleventh, and twelfth animals had abnormalities similar to that of the Dalmatian that had died. All were seen to have large pituitary adenomas. He felt a chill of fear. $#*@%! *I used this same technique to splice in extra human growth hormone in the fetus that Lenore carried! I need to examine that baby to be sure we didn't cause a similar problem! What if . . .*

He walked to the table and put the reports in his briefcase. He looked at the dog cages, then cursed audibly. *I've got to get that fetus!*

CHAPTER 18

The following morning Randy Harris met Gardner and Martha Kingsley coming through the lobby at the Bridgewater University Medical Center. He was just coming, and they were just leaving after seeing Lenore. Their plastic smiles did little to disguise the stress on their faces.

Martha, Lenore's mother, spotted him first. Although not ordinarily talkative to Randy, she knew him to be a close associate and friend of Lenore's. When she saw him, she broke from her husband's supportive hold and threw her arms open to Dr. Harris. Martha was old enough to call everyone at UBI by their first name. And as the wife of the founder, she did what she wanted anyway. "Randy," she called, hugging him closely, nearly to the detriment of the bouquet he carried, "our Lenore —" Her words were quickly choked with emotion.

Randy gave her a supportive hug and smiled meekly. "I was just on my way to see her." He looked helplessly at Gardner through the stranglehold Martha had placed around his chest.

"Oh, Randy!" Mrs. Kingsley sobbed. She loosened her grip as her husband patted her shoulder.

"Now, now, Martha. She's going to be fine," Gardner said, the scarlet color of his earlobes reflecting his embarrassment over his wife's emotional display.

Randy directed his question to Gardner. "Dr. Kingsley, how do you feel Lenore is doing?"

"She's going to be fine," he repeated soberly, looking in his wife's direction. It seemed as if he thought that saying more might set off another round of tears from Martha.

Mrs. Kingsley wadded her hands into a knot and gave Gardner a look that said, "Tell him the truth!" When he remained silent, she spilled the news herself. "The nurse told us there was concern that Lenore may have been raped!" She lowered her voice and looked around the lobby. Fortunately, no one else seemed to be listening.

Randy snapped his head back, his eyes widening. "What did Lenore tell you? Did she say that?"

Gardner was obviously upset that Martha had shared this news with the first person she saw, but now that the word was out, he made some attempt at containing the rumor. "Lenore doesn't deny it, but she doesn't remember it either," he cautioned.

Martha tightened her lips. "It's a protective mechanism, Gardner. Many women don't remember that kind of abuse."

Randy could see that he didn't belong in the argument. He merely stood back and shook his head slowly. "My, my. That would be terrible. My, oh my."

Gardner nudged Martha toward the front doors. "Come on, Martha. We need to get home."

She reluctantly followed, after giving Randy yet another hug. "Goodbye, Randy."

Randy took the elevator up to the eighth floor and quickened his pace to Lenore's room. He entered after a brief knock and handed her the flowers. "Hello."

"Hi, Randy." Lenore looked pleased to see him. "You shouldn't have."

"I know," he added, taking the bouquet back and positioning it on the windowsill. "How are you feeling?"

"Fine. But I really need to get out of here. I think they'll let me go tomorrow."

They made small talk for a few minutes until Randy blurted, "I saw your parents in the lobby."

"Oh?" Lenore showed a thin smile and

looked away nonchalantly.

"They looked a wreck, Lenore." Randy pushed the door to Lenore's room entirely shut. "Why did you let them believe the rape story?"

Lenore continued staring out of the window. "I can't help what the nurse told them. I didn't tell them it was true."

"Yes, but you know they will worry about it. More importantly, you didn't tell them it wasn't true."

"I can't help what they believe. Besides, it will serve well to let them believe the story for a while. I can't have them finding out the truth about the research or my pregnancy. Gardner Kingsley wouldn't see it the way I do. He'd shut down the whole project if he realized I almost died from it."

Randy raised his voice as he walked in front of the window. "Just listen to yourself, Lenore! You almost died! Don't you think it's time we stepped back and reevaluated this project?"

She met his gaze with icy eyes. "Reevaluate, yes. Cancel it, no. Look, Randy, it's time you realized the high cost of staying on top. Let Gardner be diverted by his thoughts that I was raped! By the time he's got it figured out, he'll be gone."

He looked at her incredulously.

Lenore continued, "He's taking retirement as of January 1st, Randy." She let a thin smile escape to her lips. "And then who do you think will take over as president *and* C.E.O.?" She paused for effect. "And when I'm at the helm, research like this will be given the number one priority. All I'll need is a few cooperative policymakers down in Washington to keep the way open."

Randy hadn't heard of the upcoming retirement. He suspected that it wasn't company knowledge yet. He shook his head and sighed. "Lenore, we have a lot of reevaluating to do." He sat down. *I might as well tell her now. It's as good a time as any.* Randy exhaled slowly. "Lenore, there's a problem with the Dalmatian litter that I used in the gene splicing experimentation."

Lenore looked up. "A problem?"

"I found Guy dead in his cage. The autopsy showed a large pituitary tumor."

"So what are you suggesting?"

Randy knew he would need to explain. Lenore's expertise was pharmacology and biochemistry, not anatomy or physiology. He sat down and explained the role of the pituitary in the production of growth hormone. "Don't you get it, Lenore? Our retrovirus must have caused some unexpected mutation in the DNA that caused not just additional growth hormone production but tumor growth in the pituitary itself."

"Come on, Randy. A single case doesn't confirm your hypothesis. Have you done the DNA analysis yet?"

"I'm working on it. Nothing has shown up yet." He began to pace nervously around the hospital bed. "It's not just a single case, Lenore. I had M.R.I. head scans done on the rest of the dogs in the experiment. I've found three others with pituitary tumors just like Guy's."

UBI's president squirmed a little with the reception of this new information. "What would happen in a human? Did you read about that?"

"A human with a pituitary tumor? A lot of things, I guess — headaches, development of tunnel vision because the tumor pushes on the nerves leading from the eyes . . ." Randy paused, trying to remember what he'd found out in his research. "Weakness, symptoms of diabetes maybe. If the tumor produced a hormone, you would see symptoms of that hormone in excess."

Lenore wrinkled her brow.

Randy tried to explain further. "If the tumor made growth hormone, you might see growth of tissues like the tongue, hands and feet, and forehead."

"Why wouldn't *everything* just grow?"

"It would in a child, but not in an adult. Once the bones have fused, certain tissues are resistant to the effects of the hormone. The soft tissues of the face can still grow in the adult, so the patients suffer from a coarsening of their facial features."

"What happened to the dog?"

"Guy? Dr. Scaggs said it looked like the fragile blood vessels supplying the tumor had ruptured. Too much pressure must have built up in his brain."

"And that could happen to a human?"

"Sure."

They were both solemn for a moment. They both shared a common thought: *We've got to get that fetus for examination!* In a few minutes Kingsley began to formulate a plan.

With Brad Forrest in Chicago, Mary Jacobs continued her rotation with Valley Surgeons for Children with the remaining three surgeons — Tyson, Latner, and Davis. Mostly she followed whoever had the most interesting cases; but more and more she found herself avoiding the practice's founder, Web Tyson. On her assigned call nights, she worked with whichever surgeon took the same night. Tonight, unfortunately, the assignment fell to Tyson, and Mary tagged along for evening rounds.

They walked from room to room, with Tyson smiling sweetly and taking compliments from the parents of his patients. Mary felt ignored. Tyson certainly wasn't making an effort to teach her anything. The med student cast a longing glance at the door at the end of the hall. *I feel like a window dressing.*

Dr. Tyson pulled out his stethoscope. He handed his coffee cup to Mary, so he could use both hands. He listened to the patient's chest and pocketed his stethoscope again. "Thanks, dear," Tyson said, retrieving his coffee.

Mary attempted a smile. *If he calls me "dear," "sweetie," or "doll" again, I think I'll barf right here on his shoes.* That thought really made her smile. *What is it about him that repels me so?* Her thoughts turned sober. *Is it just his mannerisms? His arrogance? Or is it something deeper . . . something darker?*

They continued rounds, passing by Room 525, which was empty. Mary thought back to the cri du chat baby. *Is that why I feel so ill at ease around Tyson? Because of the way he decides to treat some but not all?* She watched Tyson as he interacted with another patient and a nurse. *Everyone seems to love him. But there's something here that just doesn't feel quite right. Am I just imagining it, Lord?* She threw the thought heavenward. *Or am I really discerning something that is displeasing to you, too?*

"Mary . . ."

She startled slightly, her prayer interrupted and her thoughts now focused on Dr. Tyson, who appeared ready to leave the floor.

"Come on, doll," Tyson quipped. "Let's look at the O.R. schedule for tomorrow."

Mary inwardly cringed. "Sure," she replied and followed him to the stairwell.

Julie couldn't seem to keep her mind on anything for more than a few minutes. Ever since her date with Steve Harrison, focusing on life's day-to-day activities had been an arduous mental discipline. This morning she had prepared Bradley for school but promptly forgot his lunch. Fortunately, Bradley reminded her just as they climbed in the new convertible. She quickly threw together a sandwich and gave in to his request to add a Pop-Tart to the hastily prepared lunch. She didn't have the energy to argue with him about nutrition.

Now as she cleaned up the kitchen, she

began again to process her relationships. *Why did I react the way I did with Steve? I've never been like that before. It was as if I totally lost my cool.* She had been surprised by his offer, yes; but the sheer panic she felt in response to it surprised her even more. She sighed and picked up a wet mop. *I just can't believe he would come on to me like that.*

The phone rang. Julie leaned against the mop and picked up the portable phone. "Hello. Forrests'."

Becky didn't identify herself. She knew Julie would know her voice. "Hi, Julie. How's it going?"

Julie didn't feel ready to process her problems with her old friend. "Oh, hi, Becky." She paused.

Becky interrupted the silence after only a few seconds. "Aren't you going to tell me about the other night? How was he? Did you have a good time?"

"It was fine. We had a nice talk," Julie answered quickly.

Becky sighed. "Come on, Julie. I know the whole scoop from Steve! He said you dropped out of sight like a shooting star or something. He thinks he must have scared you pretty bad. He seemed pretty broken up about it to me."

Steve talked to her! Can't I have any secrets

around here? Now Julie took a deep breath. "I'm confused about it myself. One minute I was feeling fine, having a great time. The next, I was fighting for air like some claustrophobic animal. My head was swimming, my guts were in knots, I —"

"Sounds like love to me," Becky interrupted.

"Love? I was sick!" Silence followed. Finally Julie added, "I guess I was pretty surprised by his offer. Did he tell you that, too?"

"Sure."

"Becky, it was our first real date."

"Come on, Julie — things have changed since we found our first husbands. Everything goes now. You've got to see if you're compatible."

Julie shook her head. Becky certainly had a way of cutting through all the superficiality. *My first husband? I've never really thought of Brad like that before!* She felt a rising tide of discomfort. Things just seemed to be moving too fast. "Look, if you don't mind, I'll take this all at my own speed. It's all too confusing right now. I'm not sure I'm ready to talk about this anyway."

"Look, I'm only interested that you don't miss out on a good thing, that's all."

Julie picked up her mop and plunged it

into the bucket beside her. "Thanks. Look, I really have some things I need to do —"

"Say no more. Call me when you want to talk about it, O.K.?"

"Sure," she responded without enthusiasm. "Bye."

As Julie mopped, she tried to concentrate on the dirty floor — without success. Her thoughts were a circle of bewilderment, an ever-widening quandary of distraction. *When was the last time Brad tried to surprise* me like Steve did? It is nice to think that someone still finds me attractive enough to pull a stunt like that, even if it did send me into o*rbit!* She thought back to Becky's words: "Things have changed since we found our *first* husbands." *Maybe she's right. Maybe I'm just hanging on to an outdated mind-set. Maybe I should call Steve. Perhaps I'll get another chance. But is that what I really want? Maybe I should just chill out and see if Brad can change. Or is it too late for that?*

She stumbled around the circle of confusion again and again. As she mused, she mopped. As she mopped, she moped, groping with the questions, but not really seeking in the right place for the answers she needed so desperately.

The two men approached the door of the

Bridgewater University Medical Center morgue with some apprehension. They had never been asked to do anything quite like this before. "What if they ask us where the hearse is?" The younger, more agile man squinted as he talked.

"Look, we've been over this — we'll tell them we only use it for larger bodies. Lenore said the baby we are after is small enough to put in a jar." The older man stroked his coarse beard. "Do you have the papers?"

"For the sixth time, yes!" The smaller, younger man rang the doorbell buzzer on the side of the black door. The morgue entrance couldn't be seen from the highway. Its location beside the central supply loading dock, however, meant that just about every day someone accidentally walked in, expecting to be in the large supply storeroom and instead finding themselves in a large, cool room with a concrete floor and three metal autopsy tables prominently located in the center. Because of that, the doors had recently been locked and a new red label affixed to the door: "Morgue."

In response to the buzzer, a voice cracked through a small speaker located just above the buzzer. "Deliveries are to be made next door."

The older man looked at the speaker. He hoped someone was listening on the other end. "We're not here to deliver anything. We're from Kyger's Funeral Home. We've come for a body."

The electronic lock on the door made a snapping sound. "Sorry. So many people find us by mistake," the voice responded through the speaker. "The door's unlocked now. Come on in."

A thin man around fifty came toward the two men who had slowly entered the hospital's morgue. A row of silver-colored doors lined the far wall. "You guys say you're from Kyger's?"

The younger of the two looked at the papers in his hand. On the top was the name. "Uh, yep, Kyger's, that's us."

"You here for the Ewing body? I think Mr. Kyger just called about this one." The man pointed to a naked body on an autopsy table a few feet away.

The older man stuttered, "N-no. We've just come after the Kingsley baby."

"Might as well take that one too, then," the man said bluntly. "Mr. Kyger would want you to save a trip."

The smaller man squinted again. "I told you we should have brought the hearse," he whispered. He turned from his partner and looked at the pathology assistant. "We'll just have to come back. Here," he said, handing him the papers from Kyger's.

The man looked at the papers and handed them back. "You keep these." He handed him a clipboard. "Sign next to the 16." He walked over to a silver cabinet door, opened it, and retrieved a sealed plastic container. "Here you go."

"This is it?"

"That's it. I can't believe some people want to have funerals for these." The graying man took back the clipboard.

"You might feel differently if it was yours." The response came from the older man and resulted in a stern look from the smaller, younger partner.

"Well, maybe so." He walked with the men toward the door. "If you're coming right back, I'll leave Mr. Ewing out. It's always a pain getting them into the refrigerated cabinets."

"Sure."

With the door closed behind them, the two men scurried off. The younger held a small container in which floated a small, female fetus. In another twenty-five minutes the container was sitting in front of Randy Harris in his human genome lab at UBI. In another twenty-four hours a perturbed driver for Kyger's Funeral Home picked up a room-temperature body from the Bridgewater University Medical Center morgue, cursing the pathology assistant for allowing the body to sit out overnight.

Brad Forrest smiled when he thought about Julie's reaction to the BMW. *It's about time she smiled again. She's seemed so distant lately.* He checked his tickets for a last time and approached the desk at O'Hare International Airport. He had talked to Julie only twice since leaving a week ago. He had tried twice more, but both times Julie had been out. When he had spoken to her, she sounded tired and hadn't mentioned the car.

For the most part Brad remained oblivious to his wife's pain. His long hours provided not only the fuel for Julie's malcontent, but also the anesthesia to keep him from discerning the true anguish his family felt. Nevertheless, as he settled into his seat for the trip home, he looked forward to seeing his family again.

In the past week, away from his practice responsibilities, he had looked hard at his relationship with Julie. He certainly didn't grasp the seriousness of the situation, but it didn't take a rocket scientist to sense her dissatisfaction with his work schedule. To Brad, his job remained the sum total of the problem. He had not yet understood the role his own insecurities played in the way he pushed himself to achieve unobtainable perfection. *Maybe I'll take the family out for dinner tonight for a change. I can't remember the last time we did something like that.* Brad sighed and leaned back in his chair. It felt good to be returning home. *Maybe once I get my board exams out of the way, we can go out on a regular basis. As it is now, I barely see the family at all. Oh well, such is the life I've chosen. Sacrifices need to be made in order to reach the goals we've set for ourselves.*

He closed his eyes and smiled. *I've finally arrived, haven't I? I've landed a job with the most prestigious practice in the whole Southeast. I've got a great salary, a new car, a beautiful wife. If only Dad could see me now.*

Mary Jacobs looked over Dr. Tyson's shoulder as he reviewed the records of a new patient transferred to his care. "Another Down's syndrome child?"

Tyson grunted an affirmative response and continued flipping through the record.

"I didn't realize the incidence was so high. It seems you see so many of them here — and ones with so many congenital problems, too," Mary added.

Tyson looked up from the chart he was studying. "What you don't take into account is that we have a wide referral base. We see babies here from all over the Southeast U.S." He paused and shut the chart. "And the routine Down's syndrome patients aren't sent to Valley Surgeons for Children — only the ones with other congenital surgical problems."

Tyson sighed and looked at Mary. "This is another unfortunate case . . . a Down's syndrome infant born with Hirschsprung's disease. Do you know what that is?"

"Sure. The patients are born without the proper nerves in the lower bowel, causing a functional bowel obstruction."

Tyson stiffened. "In simple language, you're right. Specifically, the children don't have ganglion cells in their distal colon."

That's what I said, Mary thought.

Tyson continued, "This infant male has a special case, complicated by enterocolitis. Without treatment it is highly lethal. The surgical treatment after stabilization is to do a colostomy to bypass the area of the lower colon without ganglion cells."

"Will you do the surgery tonight?" Mary smiled. He's actually teaching me something for a change.

"Not tonight. It depends on the parents. If they are reasonable, maybe I can convince them of the futility of treating this child at all."

Mary raised her eyebrows. "What do you mean?"

The surgeon stared ahead coldly. "Simply this: in a day of diminished health care dollars, we should be treating only those who might someday make a contribution to our society. Sure, a colostomy is a simple operation and is lifesaving, but then what have you saved? Some retard with a bag! One that's going to need more surgery in the future to correct the underlying problem. Is it really fair to saddle the parents or society with that kind of a burden?"

Mary couldn't answer his question. She couldn't believe the candor with which he spoke. *He's going to let the baby die just because he has Down's syndrome?*

Tyson stood up. "It's time for a family conference. I had the nurse put the parents in the conference room so we could talk."

Mary felt it wasn't her place to openly question his decisions. She merely shook her head and followed along behind Tyson, whispering a prayer as she went.

He led her to an intimate conference room with thick carpeting and several nice paintings on the wall, the kind with ornate, carved, gold-colored frames. In the center, at a broad cherry table, sat a man and his wife. The woman appeared to be older than the man, and she sat clutching his arm with one hand, a Kleenex in the other.

Tyson held out his hand. "Mr. Strabinski? I'm Dr. Tyson, chief of pediatric surgery here at Crestview."

The man stood. "Mike Strabinski," he said flatly. "And this is my wife, Darlene."

The woman added, "We've heard so much about you, Dr. Tyson."

Web smiled faintly. "Let's get right to the issues at hand. Please sit down." The four sat, with Mary taking a seat against the wall where she could see all the others.

"I've reviewed your son's case. I've just come from the I.C.U. where he is currently. The work done at the referring hospital is all in order. I agree with every diagnosis they've made. The rectal biopsy they did confirms the diagnosis of Hirschsprung's disease, and the genetic studies we have performed also confirm the suspected diagnosis of Down's syndrome." He paused, looking at the parents. "Do you understand the situation so far?"

The parents nodded without reply. Tyson went on to explain the treatment options of

Hirschsprung's disease. To Mary, it seemed he stressed in great detail the inconvenience of the colostomy bag instead of the fact that it was a simple, life-saving procedure and a measure that was only temporary. He then explained the many associated anomalies that can be seen in cases of Down's syndrome. "None of which have been confirmed in your child!" Mary wanted to add but kept quiet.

"Regardless of what you decide for us to do, the surgical treatment of the colon problem will never solve the underlying mental retardation. The child will never be able to understand the treatments we are forcing upon him." Web paused again. He could see that the parents were nodding understandingly. "Do you have other children?"

"Two. One boy, four, and our little girl just turned two," the father answered.

"You must also take into account how a new disabled child will affect your family as a unit. Almost all of your attention will be taken from your other two children to care for the new one."

In the end Mary could see that the parents were completely convinced that the only "compassionate" choice would be no treatment at all. To put the unfortunate neonate through surgery would only prolong the misery of a retarded child with the potential of other serious medical anomalies, and that would jeopardize the entire family unit. They agreed to pain medications to keep the child from suffering, but no other measures would be taken.

Tyson went home satisfied that resources had been allocated properly. The parents left to console themselves in the presence of their other children. The baby was transferred from I.C.U. to Room 525.

Lenore Kingsley closed her eyes, but sleep remained elusive. *All I've done for a week is lay in this bed! It's no wonder I can't sleep.* It wasn't late, but Lenore thought that sleep might make the next day, the day of her discharge, arrive sooner. She had been ready for discharge days ago, but then developed a fever associated with generalized muscle aches, runny nose, cough, and diarrhea. It looked all the world like the flu and was likely nothing serious, but her doctors wanted to keep her until it resolved, just to be sure. The fever, they explained, might be due to infection left behind in her uterus. She needed to be watched closely. In the end they said it was just a virus and nothing they could treat anyway. She could go home, they said, tomorrow.

Tomorrow — the day that never comes. A year couldn't have sounded farther away to Lenore.

I can't believe I had to stay here extra time just because of a little virus! I have to get back to UBI to check on Randy Harris and my baby — uh, my experiment. If everything has gone according to plans, he should have the specimen by now.

Lenore opened her eyes and sighed. She punched the call button. "Can I have a sleeping pill?"

Brad finally landed back at Green Valley Regional Airport at 9 P.M. — two hours late because of a thunderstorm. When he finally arrived home, Bradley launched a full frontal attack. "Dad's home!" he yelled, nearly knocking him back through the door with his hug.

He greeted Julie and examined the refrigerator for leftovers. Belle was in bed, and after fifteen minutes Bradley was too. It was when Brad and Julie finally sat down at the kitchen table together to talk that the phone rang.

Brad picked up the receiver after the first ring. "Forrests'."

"Dr. Forrest!" The voice was female and

frantic. "This is Mary Jacobs. I'm so glad I've caught you!"

Julie watched Brad frown, nod, and grunt through most of the one-sided conversation. After listening for a few minutes, she noted her own attitude souring. *Come on, Brad. You're not on call. I haven't seen you for a week.*

In a few minutes Brad hung up the phone. He looked sheepishly at Julie. "Look, something's up at Crestview. I know it's late, but I've got to go down there for a few minutes. Our med student is concerned that a patient's family is making a terrible decision. I've never heard her like this before. She's normally very levelheaded. She literally begged me to come down and talk some sense into the parents."

Julie looked at Brad and said with a huff, "I can't believe you're going to do this!"

Brad held his breath. "Julie, don't start —"

Julie walked into the next room, ignoring his words.

Brad followed her. "Julie, it's about a Down's syndrome baby." He looked to see if that information softened her exterior. It didn't. Brad went on, "Mary hoped that with my personal experience with Bradley, I might be able to talk the parents into allowing surgery to save the child."

Although the new information struck a personal chord with her, Julie was in no mood to see Brad arrive home just in time to return to the hospital. She saw her last-chance hope of salvaging a communicative relationship with Brad vanishing in his commitments to medicine once again. Julie faced her husband. "Who's on call? Why don't they do it?"

Brad looked down. "It's Web. The student's convinced that he's part of the problem. She thinks he has colored their perception of the situation in such a slanted way that the parents will refuse any surgical care." He sighed. "She just wants someone with another opinion to at least talk to the parents to be sure they understand."

"Oh fine, you go and butt into the situation. What's Dr. Tyson going to think about that? Don't you think he has the situation under control? He has a lot more experience than you, Brad. I can't see your boss being any too thrilled with you doing this. You could be jeopardizing the job of a lifetime, Brad."

Her words stung. "Julie!"

"Have you considered that your intrusion might not be so welcome? Just think of the parents. Remember how we felt?"

Brad protested, "But what about the baby?"

"But what about us?" Julie raised her voice. "I haven't even seen you for a week!"

The young surgeon shuffled his feet. "If the situation turns out as Mary explained it, a simple surgery would save the child. But the parents are refusing surgery because Tyson recommended doing nothing, which means the child will die. And according to Mary his advice was based purely on the fact that the infant suffers from Down's syndrome."

"What if the little medical student isn't seeing the whole picture? Have you considered that? I seem to remember you being a little naive when you were a student."

"What if she's right?" Brad picked up his stethoscope and jacket. He exhaled slowly. "Look, Julie, I'm just going to go assess the situation for myself. It's the only way to know for sure. It really shouldn't take me that long."

"Fine! Leave! What could be more important?" Julie's sarcasm bit to the bone. She stomped toward the stairs, then stopped and looked at her husband for a last time. "I'm not sure I'll ever understand you, Brad. You've got everything; but your great job might not last if you step on your boss's toes — and your family can't take much more of this either." With that, she ran up the stairs.

Brad started after her, then stopped, looked at his watch, and headed out the door for Crestview Women's.

"5 north nursing unit."

"Hi, babe." The voice was smooth and masculine.

"Web!" Tammy seemed exasperated. "I can't believe you said that. What if I hadn't answered the phone?"

"I could recognize your voice anywhere." Tyson laughed. "How are you?"

Tammy sighed. "You should know. You must have admitted twenty new patients today. We're swamped." She paused. "Anyway, why did you call? Business or pleasure?"

"Do you have time for both?"

"Not really."

"O.K.," Tyson sighed, "in that case I'll just stick to the business at hand. We've got another comfort-measures-only child in 525."

"The Down's kid?"

"Yes. The parents are reasonable people. They aren't interested in a long, drawn-out affair here. Let's not let the family suffer very long with this one."

"Sure." Tammy understood exactly.

Tyson paused. "Coming by tomorrow before work?"

Tammy brightened. "I thought I told you this could only be business or pleasure! You're out-stepping my rules, Doctor."

Web played along. "I couldn't help myself."

Tammy looked at the stack of charts in front of her and then at her watch. "Listen, love, I've really got to go. I'll stop by tomorrow."

"O.K. I'll see you then." Web hung up the phone and took his patient list out of his pocket. He drew a line through the name "Strabinski."

CHAPTER 19

Brad spent a full hour going over the patient's chart and examining the Strabinski infant. Mary hovered in the background, alternately looking over Brad's shoulder and looking in on the infant in 525. As Brad studied the case, Mary prayed silently that he would have wisdom and courage. Fortunately, the night was uneventful for Dr. Tyson, and he spent the night at home, away from Crestview. At least Brad and Mary didn't have to concern themselves about his reaction.

When Dr. Forrest finished, he spoke with quiet resolve, the volume of his voice low enough only to be heard by Mary. "Everything I see here is straightforward, Mary. I'm afraid your assessment is exactly right. I can see no reason not to treat this infant. To do less seems . . . Well, it's just wrong, that's all! Sure, the infant has Down's syndrome, but I can find no evidence of any other congenital abnormalities other than this correctable Hirschsprung's disease."

"So what do we do?" Mary pulled up a

chair next to Brad's.

"I guess I'd better call the parents. I'll just feel them out, give them another opinion. I'll see if they are open to having the child treated."

"If not?"

The young surgeon sighed. "We'd better hope that's not the case."

"I'll be praying."

Brad looked at her curiously. "You sound a lot like my mother and father," he muttered as he looked up the parents' phone number. He dialed and waited. After three rings, a sleepy Mike Strabinski answered.

Brad explained everything — who he was, why he was calling. He wanted to know if they might consider allowing therapy to save the little boy. Mary watched. Brad winced, then frowned. He explained some more, offering a personal note of how much Bradley had enriched his own life. Brad tightened his brow, then held the phone back from his ear. Finally he placed the receiver back into the cradle and looked at Mary. "He hung up on me. He was outraged. He accused me of butting in where I'm not asked to be."

"But you're only interested in doing what's right for the child!" Mary protested.

"That doesn't seem to matter. They respect Dr. Tyson's opinion." Brad imitated the voice of the father: " 'The child should not be allowed to suffer.' He repeated that to me over and over. He's their responsibility, and they are not interested in 'prolonging his suffering.' "

"Maybe you should talk to Dr. Tyson. Maybe he could convince them."

"Like he'd be willing to do that!" Brad lowered his voice again as a staff nurse sat down at the nursing station with them. "And even if he was willing, the Strabinskis seem to have their minds set in concrete."

"O.K. then, what now?"

"We have one more option, but it's one that's almost sure to bring this whole ugly thing out in the open. It could mean trouble for me." Brad fidgeted nervously with the buttons on his white coat. Mary looked at him without speaking. "I could contact the juvenile court judge and have another guardian appointed for the child. If we can convince him that the parents are not acting in the best interests of their son, he may be willing to do just that. Then we could do what we need to do to save the child regardless of the parents' wishes."

Mary looked at Brad, her eyes straining to read his thoughts. "You've got to do what's right for the baby, Dr. Forrest."

Brad looked at the medical student in front of him. He did want to do what was right. *Dr. Tyson would understand that, wouldn't he?* He took a deep breath. *I'm not sure why I'm letting you talk me into this.* "Come on," he said, standing up, "let's find a phone in a private place, away from the nursing station. If we're really going to do this, the sooner the better."

The Honorable F. William Hennipot II slept soundly, the result of his physical exhaustion and a hefty dose of his favorite Kentucky bourbon gulped several hours before retiring. He had been the juvenile court judge in his district for twenty-two years. Everyone knew him. He demanded, and deserved, respect. When he finally became aware that the phone was ringing, his wife, Selina, had elbowed a bruise on his rib cage that would take ten days to resolve. "Ooouch! $%@#!" He rolled over and fumbled for the phone.

"Hello."

Brad Forrest introduced himself, apologized, and briefly stated the situation at hand.

"Who did you say you were? Do you know what time it is?" The judge looked at his alarm clock. 1:05 A.M.

Forrest reintroduced himself and tried to state his case again.

The judge cut through the story and interrupted, "Is this child going to die tonight without surgery?"

"Well, no, not tonight, sir. It may take several days for the colon to expand and eventually burst without surgery, but I thought that —"

"You thought you'd just wake me up to discuss it!" Hennipot carried the phone over to a decanter in the corner of his room and poured himself another drink. "Did you say you are with Valley Surgeons for Children?"

"Yes, sir. I've been with them for —"

"What does Web Tyson think about all of this? He and I have dealt with these problems before. I suggest you talk to him!"

"Well, sir, I was just —"

"Have Web call me in the morning! Or better yet, I'll call him. If life doesn't hang in the balance tonight, I'd suggest we address this when we've all had a little sleep, which I was enjoying, thank you very much!"

"I'm sorry that —"

The judge interrupted again. "If Web feels it's appropriate, I'll set up a guardianship hearing in the morning." He paused.

Brad was speechless.

"Good night, Dr. Forrest!"

Brad looked at the phone with contempt as he heard the line disconnect. He looked at his watch and sighed. He remembered his feeble promise to Julie: "It really shouldn't take me that long." He looked back at Mary. *How'd I ever let you talk me into this?* He talked with her briefly, then headed for a call room. *I might as well stay here for the night. It's practically over anyway.* He hung his head as he walked down the hallway. The foundation of the young surgeon's too-good-to-be-true life had begun to shake.

The following morning Lenore Kingsley awoke as a barely perceptible throb of pain in the back of her head clawed for recognition. She sat up and looked at the curtains that held back the light of the morning. Her breakfast tray had already been delivered.

Every other morning she'd been awakened by the resident staff making rounds. She looked at her watch. *What? 6:30 A.M. and Appleby and his band of residents haven't interrupted me yet? Must be a conference morning,* she thought sarcastically.

"Ooohh," she moaned quietly as she rubbed the back of her neck. She looked at the tray and lifted the plastic plate-cover.

This time she raised the volume. "Ooohhh!" The rubbery-looking eggs were slippery with grease. She quickly replaced the lid. Just then the team arrived. A chief resident, a senior resident, two interns, and three medical students filed into the room.

Kingsley looked at them and forced a smile. *I'd better do this right if I expect to get out of here today*. "A little late this morning, aren't we?" she quipped.

"We had tumor conference," the lone female in the group explained. A medical student grabbed the bedside chart and began to read Lenore's vital signs in a less than excited monotone.

Herb Appleby stepped to the bedside. "Feeling better?"

"I'm fine," Lenore fibbed. "I feel great." *I'd better not mention this headache.*

"Any more discharge?"

"Just a little spotting. It's definitely slowed down."

"Would you like to go home?"

Lenore smiled. "You know I would."

Appleby looked at the female intern. "Make sure you fill out her discharge paperwork before coming to the O.R. this morning. I don't want any delays for Ms. Kingsley." He looked back at Lenore. "I'm putting you on some iron supplements. I don't need to tell you about the half-life of Oxydel. Its effect won't last forever, so we just want to help you build up your red cell stores as quickly as possible. Your last hematocrit was still under twenty, but stable. You'll need to get it checked again in a week to be sure it's coming around with the iron therapy."

Lenore's head bobbed obediently. "Sure, sure."

With that, the team turned to go. From the door the intern looked back. "I should have things ready for you to leave by 9."

Just get to it! Lenore smiled pleasantly again, covering her thoughts. *I've got to get out of here so I can get something for my head.*

When Brad showed up for checkout rounds, Tyson was red-faced. George Latner and Mark Davis were chatting nervously but stopped suddenly when Brad appeared. Evidently they knew what was coming.

"Have a seat, Brad." Tyson nodded toward the empty chair. Brad sat without speaking. *He must have talked to Hennipot!*

"I've had two interesting phone conversations this morning," Tyson began. "One with Mr. Strabinski, whom I called to give the unfortunate word that his son had passed away in the night." He paused. Brad sat straight up. *Passed away!*

Tyson continued, "I believe from my conversation with Mr. Strabinski that you had some interest in the case?"

"Well, sir, I thought it might be helpful to provide —"

"Let it be understood right now," Web Tyson steamed, "that I'll not tolerate you going behind my back to speak to any of my patients or their family members!"

Brad hung his head. "I just thought —"

"The next phone call I received," Tyson interrupted again, "was from Bill Hennipot — Judge Hennipot to you, Dr. Forrest. He told me about your conversation. Let me make this clear . . . Have you lost your mind! What's the idea — going behind my back and the backs of these loving parents to force a guardianship issue? The decision they made was certainly valid. The death last night only goes to prove that! Obviously the child was much worse off than in your estimation. This has only proven that your diagnostic skills must still be in a developmental stage. The judge and I discussed this, and he is willing to forget the whole matter. Obviously without a child there is no guardianship issue to be determined."

Latner and Davis kept their eyes on the floor. Brad did the same. Eventually Tyson concluded, "You will be given leave with pay until the partners can decide if your future includes Valley Surgeons for Children."

Brad was too choked up to speak. In a few minutes the associates stood, signaling an end to the meeting. As Brad opened the doorway into the hall, Tyson called out behind him, "We will call you at home within the week."

Brad nodded numbly, closed the door, and stumbled into the hallway.

For Julie, Brad's trip into the hospital on his night off sealed her decision. It was time to go. His going into work on his night off was stress enough. The fact that he did so after being gone for a week made it even worse. Not returning home for the whole night seemed unforgivable. Julie pulled the large trunk out of the back of the hall closet.

A home without Brad will be better than the continuous disappointment we experience now. She started packing right after an early-morning phone call from Brad. "I'm sorry I didn't call. The time got away from me," he'd mumbled. Julie had thought about leaving for a long time. Slowly, over the weeks, a plan had emerged. *It is time to follow through,* she thought.

After packing her clothes, she added Bradley's things. It was all she could do to answer his questions without crying.

Before leaving the house for the last time, she laid a letter on the kitchen table. In it she put her attorney's business card. "You may contact me through her," she wrote to Brad. She had nearly softened at the last minute and considered leaving another number, but in the end she bitterly adhered to her plan. *The separation has to be complete!*

Belle watched from her rocking chair. She didn't lift a finger to help her daughter-in-law pack. Silently she prayed, alone. *As soon as Julie leaves,* she thought, *I'll alert the others.* "How long will you be gone?" She stood and went to the door with Julie and her son.

"I'm not sure, Belle," Julie replied, diverting her eyes to the floor. "I'm just not sure."

Randy Harris watched as Dr. Kim Yakama carefully dissected the fetus that Lenore Kingsley had carried. Dr. Yakama, a pathologist with Crestview Women's, had done several consulting jobs for Lenore Kingsley in the past. In each case the money seemed abundant enough to help him with his agreement not to say anything about the tasks that he performed at UBI. Today's task was unlike any before: to autopsy a miscarried infant. As he worked, his mind filled with questions, ones he had enough sense not to ask. *What is a pharmaceutical firm doing with an aborted fetus?*

After a few additional minutes, Dr. Yakama summarized his findings. He talked in a mechanical tone, almost as if he were dictating. "It looks to be a female. Approximate date by size characteristics, sixteen weeks. The only abnormal finding is a tumor that protrudes from the base of the brain, about the actual size of the brain itself. I can't be sure until I do the microscopic examination, but by its location it certainly might be pituitary. It's so large that it is distorting the surrounding tissues, so I can't give you a definite on that yet." He looked over at Dr. Harris, who seemed to hang on every word. "I've put the tissue specimens you have requested for DNA studies in these individually labeled specimen containers."

"Thanks. When will I be able to get the results of your microanalysis?"

"In a day or two. If it turns out to be pituitary, I'll need to do some special stains to see if the tumor was producing any hormones."

Randy wanted to say, "Like growth hormone maybe?" but held his tongue. He knew from the Dalmatian experiments what he was going to find. His worst fears about the human project were playing out. *We caused serious problems by trying to change the genetic code, didn't we?*

Dr. Yakama gathered his supplies in preparation for his departure. Randy helped him gather the specimen containers and put them on a metal lab cart. As he watched the doctor leave, he pondered, *I wonder what other effects our gene splicing may have caused that we can't see. It may take months before I sort through all this DNA data. I'm not sure Lenore will want to wait that long before we try again.*

Brad drove around in his old Datsun for two hours before finally heading for home. He somehow couldn't bring himself to face Julie with the failure he felt he'd become. As he drove, his mind swirled. *How could I sit there and not even make a defense? Last night I felt so confident that I was doing the right thing. Now I can't seem to see anything clearly. Could I have been that erroneous in my assessment?*

Was there more wrong with that baby than I realized? He sighed. *I looked like a fool — to Tyson, to the judge, to Mr. Strabinski, to Latner and Davis, and now even to myself!*

He turned into their lane, then slowed

and backed up to the mailbox — anything to delay his encounter with Julie. He flipped through the mail. Two catalogs and a bill from Wheatman's Motor Company. Brad winced. *That's all I need today!*

Brad didn't seem to notice the absence of the BMW in the driveway. He walked through the back door deep in thought. *I might as well get this over with!* He shouted, "Julie!" Then he saw the yellow note sticking to the refrigerator. It was a note from Belle:

> I've gone to Patterson's. I'll be back for supper.

It was then that he turned and noticed the envelope on the kitchen table. His name was written on the outside. As he read the note, his hand began to tremble. Tears welled in his eyes, and the knot of anxiety in his gut tightened into a searing knife. Soon he slumped into a kitchen chair and collapsed forward onto the table, not caring that his forehead absorbed the impact. He clenched his fists, striking them over and over on the old oak surface. *My family! My job! My reputation! God, I can't take much more!* For the first time since his childhood, the strong, young surgeon began to sob. *I can't take any more!*

CHAPTER 20

Around the circle sat the regulars, minus Richard and Alice Yoder who were out visiting with their oldest son. Belle Forrest had shown up earlier that same day with a pressing concern. The others had agreed. Why agonize and theorize when you can pray?

Ben led the session with confidence. "Belle has come with concerns about her grandson's family. I think we all know about them from our sharing times before." He looked at Belle. "Perhaps you should give the group a briefing, so we can know how to pray."

"We need to pray for my grandson, Brad, and his wife, Julie, and also for their son, Bradley. I think you've all heard me speak of them before. Julie and Brad are separating. They've been together for fourteen years," she said, biting her lip. "Julie just left this morning."

Craig and Sandy Nesselrodt leaned closer. Sandy squeezed Belle's arm. Craig concerned himself with the strategy of their prayers. "Are there any known strongholds that the enemy might have in their lives that we should know about?"

Belle was familiar with this type of question. "Yes," she said slowly. "I really don't think either Brad or Julie are walking close to the Lord or even know him personally. They are both familiar with the Gospel from their childhood. I think both of them are dealing with strongholds of independence — and low self-esteem. Brad has been trying to prove himself for years, pushing himself further and further in his field, capturing the most competitive surgical fellowship, the best job, almost as if to prove that he can succeed without the religion of his father." She paused and refolded a tissue in her hands. "Julie has been forced to raise her son on her own. I sense that she has been quite bitter about her lot in life and has grown, over the years, to trust more and more in her own abilities. She doesn't see her need for God or a relationship with him."

Florence Tutweiller leaned over and spoke quietly to Jen Slabaugh. "Are you with us here? You look confused."

"I'm getting so forgetful!" she whispered back. She put her index fingers together as if to count. "Brad is Belle's grandson, right? He's Bill's son. Bill was the preacher?"

"You've got it all straight." Florence patted the back of Jen's wrinkled hand with her own. "Bill died a few years back. Betsy, Bill's wife and Brad's mother, went to Florida after Bill died, to be with her family."

Jen nodded. Craig was anxious to pray. After a few seconds' lull in the chatter, he broke in. "Let's get to it. There's a battle going on. I think we all know it. We need to pray for salvation and for restoration of a relationship."

Ben added, "It sounds as if both Brad and Julie need an encounter with the truth." He looked at the others and opened his hands. The others followed his lead.

At the very moment that Brad Forrest agonized over the apparent senselessness of his losses, the small group at Patterson's Nursing Home began to intercede for him and his family.

That same evening a group of fifteen medical and dental students from Bridgewater University gathered in the home of a local cardiologist for a potluck dinner. Together they formed the local student chapter of the Christian Medical and Dental Society. Tonight, after eating, they would hear from Dr. Matt Stone, who had been invited to share his experiences as a missionary surgeon. Mary Jacobs had invited Stone two weeks earlier, after meeting and talking with him in the Crestview Women's cafeteria.

"I'm glad many of you have brought your spouses," Matt began. "I brought my wife, Linda, because together we can give you a more complete picture of what service in a Third-World setting is like."

Over the next thirty minutes the Stones talked and showed slides of the work being done in western Kenya. They emphasized medicine as only a small part of a larger plan to reach the world for Christ and urged each student to see their patients' physical problems in light of their emotional and spiritual needs.

It wasn't until everyone else had left that Mary had her chance to speak with Matt and Linda. "Could I talk to you —" She hesitated. "— about something you said — about recognizing the spiritual war that is going on all around us. I wonder if you could shed some light on a situation for me."

The trio sat on a large, overstuffed couch while the host couple cleaned up the kitchen. Mary explained in detail her feelings about working with Web Tyson, about her suspicions as to why some of the D.N.R. infants were dying so quickly, and about the last incident that had happened only the night before and what had subsequently happened to Brad Forrest.

Matt Stone knew Web Tyson from working on the staff at Crestview. He had even talked with him briefly at a surgical staff meeting that Tyson ran as the chief of surgical services. Matt shook his head slowly. The allegations that Mary hypothesized were serious ones. Failing to treat an infant just because of a mental disability smelled of evil; active infanticide couldn't be interpreted otherwise. The whole situation brought back familiar feelings to the Stones, who had been involved in uncovering a dark research plot during Matt's residency. He shuddered at the memory of having to face and defeat the evil plans of Dr. Michael Simons. If it hadn't been for God's help . . .

"You may very well be onto something here," Matt replied cautiously. "What is needed is careful documentation." He looked at Mary. "Have you ever examined the records of these infants after their deaths?"

Mary shook her head. "No. The only two that I've known about occurred at night — the Down's baby last night and the cri du chat baby I mentioned. By the time I learned of the deaths, the charts and the patients had been taken away. I don't really even know the figures. I'm not sure how many more there might be."

Linda chimed in. "You say these deaths were attributed to S.I.D.S.?"

"I think so."

Matt scratched his head. "What about autopsy reports?"

Mary shrugged her shoulders again. "I guess what I need is more data."

The Stones nodded together. "Let me do this much for you," Matt urged. "Since I'm on staff at Crestview, I can select medical records to be placed in my box for review. Maybe the clerks can even give me the data on how many in-hospital infant deaths have taken place over the last year. Those charts might be a good place to start. It should tell us if your suspicions are based on fact or fear."

"Great. I'd welcome the chance to disprove my gut feeling about Tyson."

The mention of Tyson's name prompted another response from Matt. "Look, I'm sure I don't need to tell you this, but Tyson is a very powerful man. He's chief of surgical services and probably the most respected surgeon in his field in the whole Southeast. And now rumor has it at Crestview that he's going to be the next

U.S. Surgeon General. I think it would be best if we could conduct our little chart review without his knowing it."

"Yeah," Mary sighed. "It wouldn't do to have Dr. Tyson thinking we are investigating him. Just look what happened to Dr. Forrest when he dared to offer a differing opinion."

"Exactly," Matt responded. He looked around. Linda and Mary seemed in complete agreement on that point. "Why don't we lay this before the Lord? If you are anywhere close to correct, we may be in for a fight."

Linda squeezed her husband's arm. "Good idea."

With that, they closed their eyes, and Matt began, "Most holy Father, we come as your children . . ."

Tammy gazed across the table at Web. "I'm glad to have you all to myself tonight."

Web's brow furrowed into a question. Tammy explained, "The last time we were here, Lenore Kingsley was with us, remember?"

How could I forget? She seemed so . . . powerful. "Sure," Web replied, hiding his true thoughts.

They ate and made small talk for a few

minutes. Tammy could sense that her date was faraway. "Is something troubling you, Web?"

Web sighed and lowered his voice. "It's the whole thing with the Strabinski kid." He filled Tammy in on the details of Brad's involvement and his placement on suspension by the practice.

"What did Brad have to say about it?"

"Not much. He was pretty quiet," Web added, refolding his napkin for the third time. "I gathered most of the information from the judge and the patient's father." He sighed. "I just can't have someone looking over my shoulder questioning how I do things, especially not in this area. Until now things have run smoothly. I treat who I want, I don't treat who I don't want, and, yes, some babies' deaths are accelerated so they won't suffer once we've decided not to treat them. Is that so bad? If Latner and Davis have known about the euthanasia, they've acted as if they didn't care. They've always looked the other way. But Forrest — I'm concerned about his reaction to this whole thing. Of course, he doesn't know about the way the baby died, but it was certainly apparent that he felt the child should have been treated in the first place. He may turn out to be just the type to make a big deal over this."

"You believe in what you're doing, right?" Tammy asked, stroking his hand.

"You know I do."

"I think you need to continue doing what you think is right even if everyone else doesn't agree — even Uncle Sam." Tammy continued eating for another minute and then brightened with a new thought. "You know, it isn't really surprising to hear that Brad objected to not treating that child, what with his son like he is and all."

Web looked at her curiously. "What are you talking about?"

"His son, Bradley." Web's puzzled expression didn't abate, so Tammy continued, "His son has Down's syndrome. It's no wonder he wanted the Down's syndrome infant to have surgery."

"His son? His son has Down's?"

"Come on, you knew that!"

"No, I didn't. I can't believe this slipped past our evaluation of Forrest. I thought I knew everything there was to know about the man!" Tyson shook his head incredulously. "Come to think of it, I know a lot about Forrest himself — and his wife, for that matter; but all I knew about his son was that he bore his father's name. How did you find this out?"

"Brad showed some of the nurses his son's school pictures. I saw them. It's obvious."

"I'm not sure that this encourages me too much. I had hoped Brad would fit in well. We need the extra man badly. But having a son like that may just cloud his vision enough to keep him from being objective about tough decisions involving mentally deficient patients."

Tammy nodded her head slowly. "Really."

"It could be disastrous to have him bring this debate to the public. That's all I need — someone questioning my ethics. My hopes for the Surgeon General position would evaporate for sure."

"Let's not think that way. Things will work out. You said yourself that Blackburn's men told you that you're the top pick."

"Yes, but you know as well as I do that it only takes one scandal to derail a promising political career."

Tammy nodded her head again and sighed. "Let's just not let him get in the way of our future. I know there are others who would die for the chance to work for Valley Surgeons for Children." She looked at her watch. "I've got to think about heading to work. Want to come to my apartment for a few minutes until I have to leave?"

Tyson smiled for the first time since their conversation began. He fished for his favorite gold-colored credit card and lifted the small folder containing their bill. "Just let me take care of this first," he replied. "I'll be right with you."

For the next few days, Brad walked around in a state of emotional numbness. Clouding the clarity of his thoughts, the unknown seemed to loom over him like a fog. *Where is Julie? Why did she leave? Is it more than my schedule? Will I be able to work for Valley Surgeons for Children anymore? Is my career hopelessly marred?* He tried in vain to contact Julie. Her attorney would only advise "giving her some space." She said that Julie would contact him in a few days and refused to give out information that she claimed was confidential.

On the first day, Brad stayed inside. He really didn't feel like going anywhere or seeing anyone. Finally, at Belle's urging, he went out on the second day to get groceries. Even then, when he did get out of the house, he felt his shame intensify at being seen in town during working hours. Julie had always done the household shopping before.

Belle watched him sink lower into an incommunicative depression. Finally she convinced him to call his mother, Belle's daughter-in-law, Betsy, to fill her in on his life. "She cares about you, son. She'll want to know what is happening," Belle implored. "You've got to share your pain with someone."

Brad's relationship with his mom had always been strong, but it had seemed to intensify over the past few years since his father's death. Their conversation now became a purging for Brad as he confessed openly to his mother how he had always put medicine before his family.

His mother's reaction impressed and surprised him. She listened without judgment. Finally she spoke, her voice steady. "This is partly our fault, your father's and mine. You're a lot more like your father than you'd ever admit, Brad. He was a very driven man. Sometimes his family suffered because of it. He loved you, son. I know he was very demanding, and sometimes that hindered him from really showing you his affection."

Brad listened without interrupting. His mother continued, "I will be praying for you. You know I always do. I know your grandmother is praying as well."

Brad nodded as if she could see. He had strayed far from the faith of his parents. His father's overcommitment to the church had planted seeds that flourished into the bitterness Brad felt against God for stealing his father from him.

A few minutes later a very somber, defeated man hung up the phone. Somewhere deep inside, however, a spark of understanding began.

The following morning Tyson, Davis, and Latner squared off to decide Brad Forrest's professional future. Tyson, while fearing that Brad would upset his climb to national fame, did not want to share his reasoning with his partners. He didn't want to raise the issue of euthanasia. He preferred to keep his work under the table. If his partners knew about it, they had cooperated by looking the other way. He knew that if Forrest needed to be removed, it would have to be for reasons other than his disagreement with Tyson over this issue.

"I'm uncomfortable with someone looking over my shoulder, questioning my judgment. I think we need to show enough respect for each other that we don't get into this behind-the-back examination stuff," Tyson said, opening the issue for discussion.

Latner and Davis nodded. "He certainly could have at least called you to find out what was going on before coming in on his night off," Latner responded.

"Maybe he just wanted to spend some extra time with our little medical student," Davis added with a sly smile. Tyson and Latner looked at each other blankly in response to Davis's comment. Davis defended his statement. "O.K., act as if you two hadn't noticed her. I've seen you both practically drool during morning checkout!"

Tyson responded, "Let's be serious."

Davis huffed. Latner stared at the wall. Finally Latner spoke. "Look, Forrest might not be everything you were looking for, but he has been excellent in the O.R., and, well," he said, looking at Tyson, "with you being gone so much to Washington, we need some help around here. If you leave altogether to be Surgeon General, Mark and I are sunk. I never get home as it is."

Davis looked up. "Yeah, you can say that again. I think even if he doesn't work out for the long haul, we should keep him to fill the space until the next group of pediatric surgery fellows finish their residencies."

Tyson shook his head. "If we keep him, there had better be some pretty strict guidelines for watching his behavior." He struck his hand on the table. "If Judge Hennipot and I hadn't been friends, my reputation would have been on the line! I can't have someone out there questioning what I do in the public arena. No one looks over my shoulder to question what I do! No one!"

Davis answered, "Let's try to be a little objective. He has done extremely well on his mock board exams. This kid really knows the book answers. Maybe all he needs is a bit more experience."

Latner nodded again. Tyson just shook his head. George Latner faced his senior partner. "Look, we have to make this decision based on what's best for the group. If you're going to stay and work and give up your political aspirations, I say —"

Tyson interrupted. "You know this kind of opportunity only comes once! You know this Surgeon General position is important to me."

"O.K.," Latner responded. "If you go, I say we keep Forrest to help out — at least until he can be replaced. I'm just not up to running this practice with two doctors."

Davis backed up Latner's position. "Come on, Web. You've got to at least let us keep him temporarily. It's not fair to George or myself to fire him and then take an extended leave yourself. We would be drowning back here."

Tyson stood as if to close the argument. "O.K. I'll write up some conditions. He can stay temporarily. But if he so much as questions my actions again, he'll be history. Understood?" He walked toward the door. "You can tell him to come back to work next Monday."

George Latner and Mark Davis agreed with a silent shrug and stood with Tyson to leave.

Randy Harris swallowed a Tums and chased it with a long swig of Maalox. *It can't hurt to take both,* he thought, pondering the side of the medicine bottle in his hand. *Maybe I'm just letting all this get to me. Maybe I should take a break.*

He picked up the analysis sheet in front of him as he sat at a desk in his lab at UBI. The tumor in Lenore's special baby was definitely pituitary, and it stained heavily for growth hormone. The genetic manipulation had produced definite, uncalculated changes in the child's DNA. Instead of just inducing more growth hormone production, the gene splicing had somehow stimulated cancer cell growth. *I wonder what other effects were caused that we can't even see? It may take months before I can have all of the DNA sequences figured out.*

Randy dreaded revealing the information to Lenore. *If I'm correctly predicting her response, she will want to push ahead again before I have all of this figured out. She seems to be obsessed with UBI's being the first company to successfully manipulate the human germ cell line. What was it she said? "If we can patent a successful method for changing the human genetic code, we will rule the future. The makeup of future generations will be in our hands."* Randy shook his head in hopes that the antacid would quiet the burning agitation that gnawed at his upper abdomen.

Ever since his conversation with Jimmy Tyson, he had found it increasingly difficult to silence his doubts about the research. He stood and looked out the window, rubbing the back of his neck. Lenore was due to arrive anytime. He sighed audibly. *It's not that I think Jimmy's fear of finding a gay gene is correct. I don't think there's any good evidence for that. But what if other genetic traits are discovered? Traits that parents may or may not want in their offspring? Will that result in discrimination?*

He looked at the clock on the wall, reminding him of Lenore's scheduled visit. *And Lenore — what about the safety of this whole experiment? Lenore almost died!* Randy tapped the side of his head, as if trying to snap his thought train. He heard Lenore's heels in the hallway. *Maybe I just need a little vacation. I'd be a fool to stop working with Lenore. She pays me more than double what I could make anywhere else.*

Every time the phone rang, Brad's heart raced, anticipating hearing Julie's voice. *I've got to tell her I'm sorry — that I have been so wrong.* He jumped when the phone jangled in the mid-afternoon.

"Hello."

"Dr. Forrest?"

Brad sighed. The voice was masculine — definitely not Julie's. His caller continued, "I'm Matt Stone — Dr. Matt Stone. I've been talking with an acquaintance of yours — a student doctor, Mary Jacobs. I hope I'm not calling at a bad time."

"Uh, no." *Mary! What is she up to now?* "What can I do for you?"

"Well, I've heard about your situation at work. I am employed at Crestview as well. I'm a general surgeon." Matt paused, praying a silent prayer. "Listen . . . Mary and I have been doing some searching through the medical records department over the past few days. I think we might have some interesting information to show you."

Oh, great. What can all this be about? Hasn't Mary gotten me in enough trouble already? Brad was immediately suspicious. "What's this all about?"

Matt wanted to talk to Brad in person. "Let's just say that your diagnostic skills concerning the Strabinski infant may not have been as off-base as Dr. Tyson claimed."

"What are you talking about?" Brad raised his voice a notch.

"Look, there are a lot of things we should talk about face to face. Can we get together to talk?"

"I guess you know my calendar is rather open," Brad responded despondently.

"Perhaps you and your wife could join me for dinner. My wife is —"

"No! Uh, I mean, no thanks. I don't think that's possible. My wife . . . well, she left me." Brad frowned. *Why am I telling this to you? What do you care?*

"I'm sorry. I had no idea. I had the impression from Mary that —"

"Look, uh . . . Matt, this is all new. Mary has no earthly idea what I've been through. I may have just lost the job of my dreams, and when I came home to break it to my wife, I found an empty house and a Dear

John letter." Brad sighed from frustration and fatigue. "I don't know why I'm even telling you this. You don't care about this."

Matt stared blankly into the phone. "It sounds as if you've had a pretty rough week."

"The worst of my life," Brad added slowly, without exaggeration.

Matt didn't want to press. "Look, I can see you've got a lot to deal with now. Maybe we can talk later." He paused, then added, "I realize I don't know you very well, but I want to assure you that ever since I heard of your difficulty the other evening you have been in my prayers."

Now Brad was the one staring blankly into the phone. *First Belle, then Mary, my mother, and now you! What is it with all these people praying anyway?* He remained silent a moment longer, then responded, "Hey, Dr. Stone, I really need something else to think about right now anyway. Maybe you could stop over and show me whatever it is you think would interest me so much. Bring your wife. Bring Mary for all I care." He paused again. "The truth is, I could use a little company. I've been going a bit stir-crazy. I'm not used to being at home."

Matt looked at his watch. "Do you like Chinese food? Why don't you let us bring dinner? We've just discovered a great new place that does takeout."

"Why not?" Brad smiled at the thought of not having to cook for Belle.

"Great. I'll call Mary and make some arrangements. I'll give you a call in an hour to set a time."

Brad shook his head incredulously. *I can't believe this.* "Sure. I'll be here. Bye."

"Goodbye."

CHAPTER 21

"Lenore, you've got to be out of your mind!" Randy was exasperated. "Good news? How can you consider this a step forward?" The research scientist shook his head. "I've just told you that the child had a massive pituitary tumor. Our gene manipulation went out of control!"

Lenore stood her ground. "Yes, you heard me right! This is not just good news — it's great news! Don't you see? This just proves that it's possible. Sure, every detail didn't work out like we'd hoped, but still, it shows that with our current state of science we can make changes in the human genetic code!" Ms. Kingsley strutted to the window. "This is the essence of life, Randy, and United Biotechnical Industries will show the world how it's all done. The ability to change destiny, Randy — that's what this is all about."

"What good is it unless we can make accurate, predictable, reproducible changes without unwanted side effects?"

Lenore huffed with impatience. "It's a

goal, Randy. It won't happen overnight." She faced him. "Remember Oxydel? There were months and months that I thought I'd never make it work." She beamed proudly. "And now look! The profits from that one breakthrough alone were enough to bring us to the crest of the next wave."

Randy stared at the floor. He knew he could only push his friend and boss so far. "Let's just be careful, Lenore. I'll respect your leadership, but I don't think I want to repeat what we've just been through." Randy looked up. "The thought of losing you scared me pretty bad."

Lenore softened and returned his gaze. "I never did thank you for coming by while I was in the hospital. Other than my folks, you're the only one I even told that I was there. Everyone else just thinks I finally took a vacation. Thank you." Lenore went back to staring out the window. "Now, what was it you said you wanted to show me?"

Randy went to the desktop. "I guess you saw the *Washington Post* this morning."

"I saw it," she replied without apparent concern.

"Doesn't it even bother you? We could be shut down completely — or worse yet, back in search of the world's greatest hay fever medication." He opened to the story in question, "NIH Decision Awaits New Surgeon General":

> Approval for a new series of controversial embryo experiments will require the nod from the new Surgeon General, the NIH revealed Thursday. The new administration in Washington is expected to make an announcement this week, and the new Surgeon General could be in office as early as six weeks from now — that is, if Senate confirmation can occur rapidly. The government's newest health administration official will face a growing budget to provide universal health care, as well as an expanded role in policy-making, such as in the case of the embryo experimentations that the NIH is proposing.

Lenore looked at the article again. "Relax, Randy. Everything's going to work to our advantage." *If only he knew just how much of this I have already taken care of, he wouldn't be so worried.*

"How can you be so confident? It only takes one key person in Washington to louse everything up for another term."

The president of UBI sighed. "Look,

Randy, I have the inside scoop on this, believe me. I make it my business to know these things. Web Tyson is a shoo-in. I've talked to him before. I know how he feels about this kind of research. Believe me, UBI is not going to be bothered by restrictions by this administration." *When I get through with Web Tyson, he'll know where his allegiances need to be. When the time is right, I will show him who is responsible for his climb to fame. I will own the man — professionally, emotionally, and spiritually.*

Randy could see a distant look in her eyes. "Lenore?"

She snapped back to the present, her thoughts interrupted. "What are you doing for supper?" She changed the subject quickly.

"I was just heading down to Anthony's Place."

"Nonsense! This little news about our gene splicing experiment deserves a celebration. I'll treat." With that, Lenore headed for the exit. Once at the door, she turned and spoke again. "Coming?"

"Right behind you," Randy responded, turning off his computer console. He shook his head. *Just when you think some news is going to upset her, she wants to celebrate. Go figure!*

* * *

After they ate, Belle excused herself, leaving Brad, Matt, Linda, and Mary to talk. They cleared the dishes, and Matt came back to the table and opened his worn, leather briefcase. "Here, Brad, this is what we wanted you to see. Mary and I were able to get quite a lot of information using the medical records computer. Since they've entered all the diagnoses, getting printouts like these is just a matter of knowing what questions to ask." He spread out several data sheets in front of them.

Mary was excited but controlled. "Here — look at this data on deaths due to S.I.D.S. There have been twelve deaths in the hospital that can be contributed to S.I.D.S. in the last year alone. That's more than fifty times the national average!"

Brad wasn't sure where they were going with their explanation. He merely nodded and kept quiet. Matt continued, "What is interesting is what we see in the next column, labeled 'Attending Physician.' All but one of these babies were patients of your practice, Valley Surgeons for Children."

"And look at the next column," Mary added, " 'Associated Diagnosis.' Nearly all of them had other disabilities. Eight of them had associated mental retardation. Two had spina bifida, and . . ." She paused, running her finger down the page. ". . . eleven out of the twelve were classified as 'Do Not Resuscitate.' And all eleven had correctable surgical problems like duodenal or esophageal atresia or Hirschsprung's disease."

Brad squinted. "It would seem pretty normal that most of the infant deaths would be in infants with disabilities and also that the deaths would be in patients of Valley Surgeons for Children, because we take care of the sickest children. Just what are you getting at?"

Matt answered, "Just that there are too many similarities to attribute these deaths to chance alone."

Brad stared straight ahead. "And if they aren't by chance, what are you suggesting?"

"Before we answer that," Mary chimed in, "let me show you something else I've discovered." She took out another paper with some hand-tabulated data. "I had them pull the last twelve charts on this list. It's apparent that in all but two, the children who died were in need of surgery of some sort, and yet none of these children underwent surgery. In almost every case the last entry before the death notation in the physician's progress notes is a short scribbled note by Web Tyson basically explaining that the child is destined to have a low quality of life and that the parents are refusing surgery and that they desire comfort measures only to be instituted."

"O.K., let me get this straight. All of the babies who were on Web's service whose parents refused surgery died of S.I.D.S.?" Brad looked confused.

"Exactly. That's the way they're listed in the medical records," Matt reported.

"And get this part," Mary added. "In all but one case, once the decision not to treat was made, the children were dead within twenty-four hours."

Matt looked sober. "Even without surgical treatment, it would be rare that the infants would die that soon naturally."

Brad looked uncomfortable. He wasn't sure he wanted to hear any more. "So what are you thinking? Just what is it you're trying to say?"

Before Matt could answer, the phone rang. Brad looked at the phone. Mary could see that the conversation between Matt and Brad was heating up. Instinctively, she stood and walked to the phone.

Two hours to the south, Julie looked at a picture of Brad. Tears filled her eyes again, and this time she didn't resist the urge to call. Slowly she dialed the number.

After three rings a female voice answered, "Hello. Forrests'."

Julie was taken aback. Startled and unsure of what to say, she just hung up. *A woman! A young-sounding one at that! That definitely wasn't Belle — and there wouldn't be any sitters, because Bradley's with me! Brad!*

Mary put down the phone. "Hmmph," she said softly and shrugged her shoulders. "Must have been a wrong number."

"What I'm suggesting is this," Matt stated. "There are way too many similarities in these cases to be chance alone. The children all have the same doctor. They all needed surgery. The parents refuse — and then the children die within twenty-four hours, and the attending calls the deaths S.I.D.S. It just doesn't add up."

Brad wanted the bottom line. "What is your explanation?"

Matt looked him in the eye. "My theory, and it's just that, is that Tyson is involved in infanticide." He paused. "It all makes sense with what Mary is telling me. Tyson convinces the parents of these infants that the life isn't worth saving, maybe telling them that the life will be filled with suffering. The parents tearfully agree and ask that the child be made comfortable. Tyson then has the child killed, maybe by a lethal injection, because he doesn't want to drag out the process of letting nature take its course."

Mary looked at Brad. "I've heard Dr. Tyson say what Matt is describing on at least two occasions, just since I started this elective."

Brad stood up and began to pace. He thought back over the past weeks as he had worked along with Tyson. There had been several times that he had marveled over an infant's dying so quickly. Maybe there is something to what they are telling me. *Maybe, just maybe, my assessment of that Strabinski kid was O.K. Why should he have died in only one night? Hirschsprung's disease shouldn't have taken his life that quickly.* He looked back at the Stones and Mary. "But why call the deaths S.I.D.S.? You said that most of the children had surgically treatable diseases."

"Exactly," Stone quipped. "That makes it look like the deaths were not due to the surgical problem that needed treatment. By coding the deaths as S.I.D.S., the death rates for surgical problems such as congenital intestinal atresia or Hirschsprung's disease remain normal and don't attract the attention of the government's reviewers."

Brad held his forehead. "But what about the reviews that go on in the hospital? Certainly the surgical case review committee would pick up on any suspicious death patterns, wouldn't they?"

"We thought of that," Mary added. "But when we reviewed the minutes of their last year's meetings, only one of the dozen S.I.D.S. deaths was even reviewed. The other interesting fact is that Web Tyson is chairman of the committee. It's no wonder his cases aren't chosen for critique. It appears that he is so high up, no one is looking over his shoulder anymore."

Brad shrugged. "Look at what happened to me when I just offered a second opinion, one different from Tyson's."

Matt, Linda, and Mary nodded slowly. "Case in point," Linda said with a sigh.

Brad continued to pace around the kitchen. "Have you looked at the autopsy reports?"

"Yep. Not all of them had them. In those that did, only one pathologist was involved. A Dr. Yakama signed out the immediate cause of death as 'unexplained,' all consistent with the diagnosis that they were given: sudden infant death syndrome," Matt explained.

"Yakama?" Brad pivoted when he

reached the refrigerator. "Tyson told me about him. He brought him here personally. He said it's so important to have a strong pathologist versed in pediatric surgery that he recruited him especially to work with him on difficult pediatric cases. The pathology department actually falls under the jurisdiction of the Department of Surgical Services at Crestview. It's a unique setup that Tyson seemed to be very pleased about when he showed me around. He lured Yakama away from a full professorship at a big university with the promise of big bucks. He told me himself that what Crestview pays him is more than he could make anywhere else. Tyson is very proud of him."

Matt raised his eyebrows. "Another coincidence?"

"I don't know. Yakama is a subspecialist in pediatric surgical pathology. It would be routine for him to do the pediatric autopsies. What about drug screens? Any toxicology data on the dead infants?"

Mary responded, "I looked. There doesn't seem to be any evidence that toxicology screens were done."

"If anything shady is going on, those involved have been pretty careful about covering their tracks," Matt commented.

"O.K., I agree. Everything you've shown

me has raised my eyebrows a bit." Brad paused. "To be totally honest with you, I guess I have felt uneasy about a few cases in the past two months myself."

Mary looked at Matt Stone. "So where do we go from here?"

"Everything we have is circumstantial. What we need is some solid evidence to prove our gut feelings," Matt responded.

Linda had been quiet during most of the conversation. When she spoke now, her words reflected her heartfelt need for God's guidance. "I think before we proceed further, we need to seek God's wisdom." She looked at Matt. "If Matt and I have learned anything from our involvement in situations like this before, it's that often there are deeper spiritual battles that are being fought, battles that are only reflected in what we can see." She looked at the others in the room. Brad looked down. "If this Dr. Tyson is as influential as we think, this search could be very tedious to say the least. I think it is imperative that we fight this battle first on our knees."

Matt looked at Brad, who stared quietly at his shoes. "Would that be O.K. with you, Brad?"

"Uh — uh, sure," Brad stuttered. "I don't see why not." *These guys sure are different*

. . . *like my parents . . . like Belle.* He brightened suddenly. It had been a long time since he had prayed, but he knew Belle would be familiar with it. He looked at Linda. "Do you mind if I get Belle, my grandmother? I know she prays all the time."

"That would be great!" Linda smiled.

Matt smiled too. Brad even smiled, even though he wasn't sure why. "I'll get her," he said, disappearing up the old staircase. "Belle!"

Early the next morning Web Tyson toiled with a recurrent nightmare, the memory of a dark Arkansas night providing the stimulus for a fresh wave of turbulent fear. Eventually the dream nudged him from sleep altogether, but not before his restless tossing shoved the sleeping form next to him into full alertness. Tammy responded with a whisper, placing her hand on his wet forehead. "What's the matter, honey?"

Web sighed and stared at the ceiling. He remained quiet for a minute, not sure if he should share his secret memory. Methodically he gathered his thoughts and attempted to calm his racing heart.

Tammy remained quiet as well, not wanting to disturb the man she wanted so badly to call her own. She knew she had given herself too completely. She had determined months before that she would do anything for this man. And she had, too, completely adopting his personal positions at work in spite of her own initial misgivings. She had become exactly what she set her heart upon — an extension of this powerful man, acting on his wishes, carrying out his bidding, first at Crestview and now beyond. *I owe Lenore for this,* she thought and held the silent surgeon close.

Eventually Web's defenses crumbled, and he exposed the story he had buried for so long. Tammy listened without speaking. *It's going to take time for you to accept the power you seem to fear the most. But you will, with my help,* she thought. *You don't seem to understand what made it possible for us to be together.* After a moment she whispered her soothing message: "You couldn't have done differently, darling. You were in the presence of very powerful people."

"Pretty weird people, if you ask me." Web sighed. The burden was out.

You have a lot to learn. "It's history, Web. It's over."

"It's only haunted me again recently. Maybe it's all this public scrutiny stuff. Everyone wants to dig into the private baggage of public figures."

"It's buried, honey. No one will ever know." She kissed his ear.

"I know, baby, I know," Web responded with a low volume to match Tammy's. "My dreams for the future just haven't caught on yet." He hoped he sounded more confident than he felt.

Tammy closed her eyes. Web continued staring at the ceiling, with sleep remaining elusive until just before the alarm sounded at 5:30.

CHAPTER 22

Brad Forrest slipped from bed before the sun rose. He had only slept for four hours, having stayed up until well past midnight talking with Matt Stone. His mind was full, and even his lack of sleep couldn't force his eyes to shut or prevent his thoughts from racing. In the pit of his despair, a small glimmer of hope had surfaced. He could see that Matt, Linda, and Mary had more than just a shallow religion. He thought back to the night before when they had all gathered for prayer. *When was the last time I saw something like that? High school? They talked like they really expected some personal guidance. They prayed for me! Why should they care about someone they don't even know?*

Brad walked to the bathroom and began to shave, pondering the reflection of his own image looking back at him. *Now look at you. Who are you now? A surgeon? A father? A husband?* He felt like he deserved the name Failure more than any other title he'd used over the past decade. He had spent all of his time building walls of self-reliance, but the very walls he used to rely on were now crumbling around him. And now for the first time in a long, long time he could see that the walls that protected him also held the love of God at arm's length. *What was it that Stone had prayed? That I would experience God's love in a new way? Could it be true? Could they be right? Could my father have been right all along — that God really loves me?*

He continued to think as he prepared for the day. Just getting ready, even with nowhere to go, somehow eased the anxiety of having nothing to do. He thought back to his conversation with his mother. He thought about the anger and jealousy he felt toward God for his father's commitment to Christian ministry. Now, with the loss of his own family, he saw that he had come from the same mold — driven to perfection even when it meant sacrificing family and other responsibilities. Slowly the bitterness that had kept him from looking toward the Cross began to recede. A crack in his defenses widened. The bitterness he held toward his father had become a shallow excuse not to deal with the reality of his own need for God in his life.

He thought about Julie. Oh, how he missed her! Her voice, her beauty, her presence! He fought to remember the way she would inflect her words when she spoke about the things she cared about most. Her laugh! He remembered coming home one day to find her and Bradley giggling under a homemade tent made out of two chairs, a broom, and a blanket. Her touch! *When was the last time I held you?* He sunk into an old chair by the window next to the bed. "O God, I've messed things up pretty bad." He spoke in a quiet, emotion-choked whisper. "I'm so mixed up!" He looked at the ceiling, wondering if his plea was even getting beyond the confines of the small room. *Maybe it doesn't have to,* he thought. *Maybe God's love is right here, reaching out to me, just like Stone said.*

He paused, then decided to try again. Haltingly, he continued, "God, I've never relied on you before. Maybe I've never thought I needed you in my life. Help me. I've always wanted to do everything my way. Maybe it's time I opened up and gave you a chance." He looked around the room. *This seems so dumb!* He chastised himself with the thought. *I'm a preacher's son, and I don't even know how to pray!* He leaned forward and held his head in his hands. "I don't even know how to start! Sh-show me the way, Lord."

His anxiety faded as a new feeling settled into his wounded soul: *peace.* Only a moment later, the shrill sound of the phone interrupted his newfound calm. *Julie?*

He lunged for the phone. "Hello."

"Brad? It's Mark Davis calling. I hope I'm not catching you too early."

Brad looked at his watch. "No problem. I was up."

"Look, Brad, I know the group has let you hang for a few days. Things have cooled down a bit with Web. George and I have convinced him to let you come back. Things are so hectic with Web running to Washington all the time." He paused. Brad stayed quiet. "We could really use your help. I hope you'll consider coming back to work."

Surprised at the new turn of events, Brad stuttered his response. "S-sure. I-I'll help out."

Dr. Davis paused again, then added, "Do you think you could come over this morning? Both Latner and I have 8 o'clock starts in the O.R., and there are twenty post-ops to see in the clinic. Tyson's gone to Washington again to speak to Blackburn's frontmen and —"

"Say no more," Brad interrupted, looking at his watch again. "I can be there by 6:30 checkout."

"Great. That takes a load off my mind." Davis started to hang up, then spoke a final word of warning. "Hey, Brad, I guess I hardly need to say this, but . . . well, Tyson is a very proud man. You can't cross him more than once and survive in this job. He will be watching you. Any more attempts to alter the plans he outlines for his patient's care will end your career with Valley Surgeons for Children."

Brad swallowed hard.

Mark Davis went on, "He has a lot of respect in this field. I don't need to tell you that getting fired by Web Tyson could end your career in pediatric surgery."

Brad nodded his head as if Davis could see him. "I understand."

"I'll see you in a few minutes."

Click. Dial tone.

Brad took a short mental inventory. The peace that he'd felt only minutes before was still intact. *Maybe there's something to this prayer stuff,* he mused, thinking of how soon Davis had called to offer his job back after Brad had asked for God's guidance. *Maybe Dad was right all along. Maybe the things that Belle has always said are true. Maybe Matt Stone is right. Maybe God does care, after all!*

A few days later Lenore Kingsley swept

into her office past her receptionist. "Hold my calls," she ordered with teeth clenched. "I don't want to be disturbed."

She eased into her plush desk chair, trying not to jar the dull throbbing she sensed beneath her temples. She unlocked a side drawer in her desk and took out a bottle of Tylox, a potent narcotic mixed with a common pain reliever. These controlled substances were not hard for her to obtain from within the pharmaceutical industry. Certainly she had enough contacts there, though these particular pills were prescribed for the crampy pain she'd experienced during her recent miscarriage. She generally used the medication only rarely, but recently she had relied on it more frequently due to an increasing number of early-morning headaches. *The plain Tylenol and ibuprofen didn't seem to help. Maybe this will take the edge off this pounding!* She swallowed two of the red tablets. She hated the drowsiness they caused, but looked forward to the buzz that accompanied the pain relief.

She looked over the day-planner and picked up the morning paper that had been placed on an antique coffee table in the corner of her office. She found what she was looking for on the top of page 2. The headline caught her eye right away. "Blackburn

Chooses Weber Tyson As Next Surgeon General." She scanned through the article, smiling at the news in spite of the pain in her skull. She read, "No one in the Blackburn Administration seems exactly sure how Tyson's name appeared on the search list, but the President seems quite convinced of his candidate's capabilities." *These idiots were just too easy to manipulate!* She tightened her thin smile into a smirk. *Hmmm. Senate confirmation hearings will begin soon. Only one more barrier. It's time to move a step closer in my influence over Web Tyson and his future policies.*

She closed her eyes a few minutes and attempted to relax. After her brief rest, she felt better. The Tylox was working. She was actually beginning to feel quite good, almost euphoric. She picked up the phone and dialed Crestview Women's.

"Crestview Women's and Children's Health Center. How may I help you?"

The female voice was pleasant and sounded about fifty.

"I need the paging operator," snapped Lenore.

"I can help you. Who do you need?"

"Dr. Web Tyson please."

The operator looked at the call schedule in front of her. "I have Dr. Latner on for that group. Are you a patient?"

Lenore grew antsy. "I'm a personal friend. I don't want whoever is on call. I want to speak to Web!" She thought using his first name would sound more convincing.

"One moment, please. I'll page."

Elevator music filled the receiver. Lenore hated elevator music. After a few minutes the operator broke back onto the line. "I have Dr. Tyson. Go ahead please."

"Web?" Lenore spoke with a touch of insecurity in her voice.

"Yes. Dr. Tyson here." He spoke in an authoritative tone.

"Hi. It's Lenore Kingsley. I hope I'm not bothering you."

Lenore, you've been on my mind! But why are you calling? "Lenore?"

"Yes — Lenore Kingsley. We dined together the other week. I hope I'm not intruding."

"No, no. Not at all! I know you." *How could I forget you?* "What a delight to hear from you." Tyson smiled, still wondering just what would prompt the influential beauty to call him.

"I just wanted to congratulate you. I saw the wonderful news in the paper this morning."

"Thanks. Sometimes I can't believe this is all happening." Tyson shook his head. Although he'd known of the decision for a few days, he still beamed with the excitement of the appointment.

Lenore softened her voice and changed the subject. "I really enjoyed my time with you the other week."

"Yes," Tyson reflected. "Tammy and I enjoyed ourselves too."

Lenore spoke pointedly but in a sultry tone. "I don't recall mentioning Tammy." She paused. "I enjoyed being with *you*."

Web's ego inflated rapidly. "Well, y-yes," he stuttered. "I-I enjoyed b-being with you."

"Perhaps you would like to join me for a celebration of your success?"

"Why, sure, I don't see why —"

"A private celebration, Web. Dinner perhaps?"

"Well, well. This is a surprise." He paused. "Yes, I think I'd like that, but —" He halted again, thinking about his schedule. "I leave for Washington again in the morning. I'll be back in a few days. I could call you and —"

"What about tonight?" Lenore interrupted again. "I want to celebrate while the news is fresh!"

Web stared at the phone in partial disbelief. *I can't believe this! A private dinner with Lenore Kingsley? Tammy is working tonight, so that shouldn't pose a problem.* "Sure. I-I need to get things wrapped up here at Crestview. I should finish around 7 o'clock. Is that O.K?"

"Sure. Why don't you call when you're done. I'll be at UBI. Call me there."

"O.K. I'll do that. Goodbye."

Lenore hung up the phone and smiled. Everything was working according to plan.

A few floors below, a very proud scientist looked on as Jimmy Tyson looked around the human genome laboratory. "Man! This is the stuff of science fiction!"

"No," Randy Harris objected, "this is the stuff of science — it's truth!"

Jimmy continued his wide-eyed viewing as Randy explained the experiments. He gave just enough specifics to be sure that Jimmy would be impressed.

Jimmy walked to the edge of the lab where the genetically altered Dalmatians were housed. "So there are really no other dogs like this anywhere. You've created a brand-new breed."

Randy smiled. "Exactly." He tapped a pencil on the edge of the lab table. "You can see the great potential for improving our future right here."

The young man looked at the large animal in front of him. "I've never seen a Dalmatian this big before."

"I told you, Jimmy. Only his mother was a Dalmatian." Randy opened the cage and brought the dog out in front of them, inspecting the animal as if he were a grand champion show dog. "He's a Dalmatian with an altered gene pool. He has twice the growth hormone production of an animal with only Dalmatian DNA. Feel his shoulders."

Jimmy felt the massive, solid frame under the sleek, black coat. He began to lift the dog up to feel the weight of the animal when he felt a stabbing pain in his abdomen. He dropped the dog and grabbed his stomach. "Ow!"

Randy looked startled. "What's up? Are you O.K.?"

Jimmy stood up straight, his hands still cupped over his lower abdomen. "I think so. That dog's got to be the heaviest thing I've tried to lift since my accident. Maybe I just overdid it a bit."

"You should take it easy."

"I'm O.K. I just stretched my old incision, that's all. I'll be fine."

Randy put the dog back in the cage. He turned and faced Jimmy. "Well, what do you think?"

"It's all pretty amazing, really." He looked away toward a group of windows in a sober stare. "I'm still not convinced that all of this knowledge about our genes is a good thing. What if someday we do know everything about our DNA? There might be some things better off not known."

Dr. Harris twisted his face in a question. "Are you still thinking about a possible gay gene? I told you, we really don't have any evidence of that."

"Not just that. I guess I've thought a lot about that since I talked to you over at Anthony's Place. What about diseases? What if you had two children and only enough money to send one to college and you knew from the DNA screening that one would develop Huntington's disease or something — which child would you send to college?"

"You think that knowledge about our future might lead us to discriminate against certain gene carriers?"

"Something like that." Jimmy nodded.

"I've not spent a great deal of time thinking about all of that, truthfully. I'm more interested in the next step, that of changing the genes once we've identified them. If you don't like what you've got, alter it." He paused and walked around the animal cages again. "It's not really that simple, though. It's taken us months to get this far."

"My father would like this stuff."

"Lenore Kingsley seems to be counting on just that," Randy replied with a thin smile. When Jimmy returned a curious look, Randy explained, "When you're working with such a sensitive area, politics can make or break your research. If anyone would know about that, it's Lenore. She seems to be a real supporter of your father being the next Surgeon General. She thinks he will keep the research pathways uncluttered by needless federal setbacks. She has promised billions of dollars to be channeled into this research. She's betting the entire corporation's future on this. She says that the first company to perfect these techniques in the human species will be able to coast into the middle of the next century." He paused. "She's not likely to support any politician who isn't partial to her way of thinking."

"Did you read this morning's paper?"

Randy shook his head. "I left for work too early to see it."

"Tell Lenore to relax. It looks like my dad's a shoo-in. I wouldn't know it from him, of course. I had to read it in the paper myself." He looked at his watch. "I've really got to go. I need to get groceries before going to work. Thanks a lot for showing me around." As he turned to leave, he reached instinctively for his abdomen.

"Are you sure you're all right?" Randy looked concerned. "Maybe you should have your father check you."

"No thanks," he laughed nervously. "See you." As he walked down the hall, another twinge of pain near his old incision prompted his thoughts. *I shouldn't have ever tried to lift that dog! Maybe Randy is right. It couldn't hurt to have a doctor look at me. Maybe I could just drop by Crestview's clinic and see Dr. Forrest. He helped operate on me anyway.*

Matt Stone finished rounds and headed for the west wing at Patterson's Nursing Home. Ever since the other night when he had prayed with Belle and the others, he'd felt an instant bond with the old warrior. She had mentioned having some information that might enlighten him further and make his prayers more pointed and had invited him to join her in a morning of discussion and prayer. He stopped by his little apartment first, picked up Linda, and then sped off in their Toyota rental to meet with

Belle and a few of her friends.

Matt and Linda traveled silently for a few miles. Both of them sensed there was more to Dr. Tyson's actions than the natural eye could see. His distrust of Brad and his defensiveness of his own position seemed to be deeper than they could understand. They had encountered a battle with far-reaching spiritual implications, but just how far, they didn't know. And just what were the forces motivating Tyson? Was there an unseen, satanic enemy pushing for more and more ground? These concerns had dominated the Stones' prayers since their encounter with Mary Jacobs and Brad Forrest. They cried to God again and again for their eyes to be opened. They knew they needed proper discernment to move safely and effectively. This was spiritual war, and they knew they needed to wage the battle with weapons seen and unseen.

When they arrived, Belle made the introductions. Ben Kreider, Florence Tutweiller, Craig and Sandy Nesselrodt, Richard and Alice Yoder, and Jennifer Slabaugh all attended. They received the Stones warmly. Their hands were spotted and wrinkled, but their handshakes were firm and conveyed a sense of family.

Belle looked at the group, now seated in

their familiar circle in the rec room. "We've been praying for my grandson, Brad, and his family for a long time. We've also been praying for Dr. Tyson and the hospital where he practices, especially since he has been touted as a possible political leader in our country."

"We've watched with even more interest since he hired Belle's grandson," Ben added.

"Anyway," Belle continued, "when I saw that you had some of the same concerns, I thought it would be good for you to join us." She looked at Matt and Linda, who nodded their heads in silent agreement. Belle opened an old manila envelope. "I thought you might be interested in these," she said, standing up to spread the contents out on the Ping-Pong table. "I always clip articles that seem to relate to our prayer concerns."

Matt and Linda looked at the assortment of articles, most having to do with Tyson and his past influence on state policies, and several having to do with the search for a new Surgeon General to run the national health care program. There were also several ads for Crestview Women's and Children's Health Center dealing with the "availability of genetic screening."

Matt shared with the group some of his feelings about Crestview Women's, especially the way he felt after the tour he'd gone on with Dr. Feinberg. "I'm not sure if any of this relates to our present concern," he added, shaking his head.

"The whole thing smells funny to me," Craig Nesselrodt said solemnly.

His wife, Sandy, broke the seriousness of the conversation with a chuckle. "You haven't smelled anything for years." She looked at the Stones to explain. "He was a pharmacist. I think the chemicals killed every smelling cell he ever had," she reported, stroking his hand.

"I'm serious, honey. All I mean is that I wouldn't be surprised if this whole mess isn't connected somehow." Craig lifted a cookie from a plate in front of him. He closed one nostril, held the cookie under his nose, and sniffed firmly. He repeated the process, holding the other nostril shut.

"Careful, dear, you don't inhale them!" Sandy looked at her husband with friendly concern.

Craig shook his head in disgust. "Can't smell a thing!" he said suddenly. "Might as well not have a nose at all!"

"Don't be silly." Sandy patronized him with a gentle pat on the back of his hand.

"You need to set your glasses somewhere, you know!"

Even Craig chuckled at that one. He settled back down in his seat and pushed his glasses back up on his nose.

"Can we get back to the discussion at hand?" Ben prodded the group back into focus.

Belle spoke next. "I think the point is this — we aren't sure if all of these things fit together somehow. Maybe they aren't even pieces of the same puzzle. What we need is to continue to lift up those we know who have needs — Brad, Julie, and his boss, Dr. Tyson, Crestview Health Center, and those we know who are working there — especially Matt Stone and Mary Jacobs. They need additional wisdom to know how to deal with the situation at hand."

Together they formed an irregular circle and spoke an earnest, heartfelt prayer for guidance, wisdom, and God's will. Matt and Linda both contributed. After the session, Linda gathered up the contents of Belle's manila envelope. "Mind if we borrow these? I'd like to examine them further."

"Be my guest," Belle responded with a smile.

With that, the Stones excused themselves,

and Matt hurried back to Crestview for an afternoon clinic.

Later that evening, Lenore sat at the end of the counter at Jake's Diner. She tapped her painted fingernails lightly on the counter while she waited for Dr. Web Tyson. *Why did he ask to meet me here?* she thought as she looked around the place, which served breakfast and lunch, but after nightfall served mostly drinks and finger foods. *Certainly the clientele of this place is unlikely to recognize me, or Web Tyson for that matter.* She fidgeted with her diamond-studded watchband and checked the time again. *He's late. Maybe he had an emergency.*

"Can I bring you something, Dr. Kingsley?" The voice was on edge and belonged to the rotund diner owner, Jake Thompson.

Lenore seemed shocked to be recognized. "Sure. I'll have a Diet Pepsi." She looked at the corner of the diner by the window. "I'll be in that empty booth by the window. If you see Dr. Web Tyson, send him over." She smiled tersely and slipped off the padded bar-stool.

"Sure thing, ma'am. He comes in here all the time. I'll be right back with your drink."

Web comes in here all the time? As Surgeon General, he'll have to show a bit more class.

* * *

Web Tyson pushed the accelerator toward the floor. The smooth engine responded faithfully as he pulled out of Crestview on his way to Jake's Diner. *I can't believe Lenore wanted to pick me up at the hospital! Tammy would be sure to see me if I did something foolish like that.* He had asked her to meet him at the diner instead, thinking they could just meet in the parking lot and decide where to go from there. The restaurant was close to the hospital and near a number of more suitable eating establishments, so Tyson had used it as a meeting place before. He checked his watch. *I hope she's not impatient.*

Julie Forrest sat on the edge of the bed and bit her lip, her hand trembling slightly as she tore open the letter with a single word in the return address corner: "Home." *Nothing works as simply as I'd hoped.*

She'd moved into the downstairs apartment in the home of an old college friend, who agreed to watch Bradley while she looked for a job. So far that search had only landed her a part-time position at a public library, where the silence only magnified the loneliness she felt. Her friend, Sophie Mitchell, had been gracious enough to open her home, but she had a husband and two boys of her own and couldn't possibly be expected to give much more. Julie had found a school for Bradley easily enough, but he missed his old special ed teacher, and some of the lower-functioning children in his class kept the teacher so busy that she gave Bradley little attention at all.

Julie had begun the separation with a strong resolve, the ties with Brad being severed completely. *I'll show him for treating us like he has,* she'd thought. Now, however, with her dreams of a better life proving elusive and Bradley complaining bitterly of missing his father, she felt her resolve weakening. Several days before, she had finally given in to Sophie's advice and called home. She came away from that experience even more lonely and confused. *Why should I care if he had a woman over?* she had chided herself. *I'm going on with my life. Why shouldn't he go on with his?* She'd promised herself that she wouldn't get involved with anyone for a while, until she had things sorted out. But lately, during her evenings at home alone with Bradley, she found herself thinking more and more about Steve Harrison. *Maybe he could drive down for a visit, she thought.*

Then Sophie invited her to church, and

she'd given in just to avoid another day home alone with Bradley. Sophie and her husband, Gerald, had found a new life, she'd bubbled. Julie smiled and went along for the ride. It was the least she could do for them for opening up their home so graciously. Then, as she listened to the message and watched the members singing so sincerely, she softened and wondered if there could be more to life than what she was experiencing. Over the next week, in the solitude of the library, she found herself dwelling on the words the pastor had spoken. *Could it be that God cares for me personally?* This basic message was certainly not foreign to her, but she had shut it out, layering it under her desire to master her own life.

She had been to church as a child, but college, her marriage to a surgeon, and taking care of Bradley had quelled any sparks of interest she might have had. For a long time she hid behind her husband's distaste for the church, resenting the people who stole his father away. Later, when Bradley was born, she held a secret anger toward God for allowing her son to be mentally handicapped. Still later, she felt subtle, unintended pressure from Brad's perfectionist father. She felt she could never be the mother or wife Brad wanted her to be. Now, with time on her hands to think and no one else to blame, she began to see that her excuses were just that — shallow reasons to keep her from seeing her own need for a loving Savior.

Now, with the letter open, she began to read.

My dearest Julie,

I find it difficult to say what is in my heart. I only know that I have driven my only source of happiness away. How I reached this point, I'm only beginning to discover. In my own selfish quest to prove myself, I have ignored the people that matter the most — you and Bradley. Can you ever forgive me for the pain I have caused?

I have had many hours to think about us, about me, and about my career. I have been off for a week now. The day you left, I was suspended from my job for questioning Dr. Tyson's judgment. The whole story is too bizarre and agonizing for me to write. In a way, I think the timing may have been a God-send — his way of redirecting my thoughts back to the things that matter the most.

Julie paused. *Since when does Brad care about God's direction?* She continued reading.

I've met some new friends. They are very different and very real. They are praying for me. They say they are praying for you as well. I am starting to believe that what they are telling me might really be true. I've been running for a long time. I've never been interested in God before, but now, honestly, I don't know where else to turn. Without you, without Bradley, without my career, where am I? I've certainly not done a very good job of running my own life.

I really only want you to know that I love you. The other stuff can wait. Can we talk? I miss you. Please tell Bradley that I love him.

Love,
Brad

Tears welled up in her tightly clenched eyes. She couldn't stop them. She didn't want to.

Jake pointed toward the front corner booth, and Web Tyson responded with a wink. Since Lenore was already seated, and drinking, Web ordered a cocktail and took off his coat. Jake watched with suspicion as the couple imbibed a second and then a third round of pre-dinner enjoyment. They whispered, laughed, and eventually left hand in hand to climb into Lenore's Corvette.

They ended up at The Overlook, a four-star restaurant in the next county. The owner recognized Lenore and seated them immediately at a corner table. During the rich dinner Tyson shared openly about his recent run-in with Brad Forrest. "He should be thankful that pediatric surgeons are in short supply or he'd have been gone in a minute," he boasted.

Lenore listened with real interest and probed for more information. *Brad Forrest,* she thought, *is a threat. If he raises questions in the earshot of the public, Tyson's confirmation as Surgeon General could be compromised.*

Web smiled at Lenore. *Why am I so open with you? I'm usually not so revealing about my personal actions. You seem so . . . so powerful.* He was definitely drawn by something, and yet at the same time a distant uneasiness surfaced. *Maybe I'm just worried about Tammy. How will I ever explain this to her?* Lenore diverted him from his private thoughts with a light touch of her hand.

Unlike her last dinner with Web, when Tammy was present and her own well-being was hindered by her impending miscarriage, Lenore found no impediments to her advances, and little resistance by the intoxicated surgeon. She looked back at him and returned a thin smirk. *You'll make a delightful puppet, darling. You will serve my master's bidding and you won't even know it.*

After another hour the couple, now arm in arm, slowly strolled toward Lenore's red car. It wasn't until 2 A.M. that Lenore delivered Web back to the parking lot at Jake's Diner. There they said goodbye again, and Web sped off to pack for an early trip to Washington.

In the shadows of the diner's back door, Jake fumbled with his keys. He looked up at the couple saying their quiet goodbye, sighed, and shook his head.

CHAPTER 23

Tyson crashed into sleep like a hibernating bear. The alcohol and the late hour had taken its toll, and he remained alert for only a few seconds after his head struck his down pillow. Soon, however, his evening with Lenore stimulated a fresh wave of his most recent nightmare. This time every detail appeared in an exaggerated form — the shadows, the flickering candlelight, the screams of the laboring woman, her eyes, and her long black hair. She arched her back, accentuating her bulging abdomen that glistened with perspiration. She called his name, her guttural voice spitting out her hidden revelation. "I know who you are!"

In spite of his desperate need for the renewal of sleep, he found himself sweaty, with eyes open, staring at his sculptured ceiling. He threw off his blanket in frustration, trying to make some rational sense of his overpowering fear. *Why does this dream keep returning? I know the past is buried and gone. Tammy is right. I couldn't have done differently. Why am I troubled by this irra-*

tional, recurrent nightmare? Maybe it's just the stress of the upcoming Senate hearings and my new relationship with Lenore. I've certainly got enough reasons for tension in my life. It's just surfacing in my dreams, that's all.

He tossed for a few moments longer, then got up to empty his bladder. *I'll just try to focus on something else. Something enjoyable — maybe the pleasant face of Lenore Kingsley.* With that, he closed his eyes and sought elusive rest.

His new focus, however, only brought on the nightmare again and further disrupted his already shortened respite.

The next morning Brad Forrest left the house early and stopped at Jake's Diner on the way to Crestview. Jake was smiling and serving coffee — smiling, that is, until Dr. Forrest walked in.

"Morning, Jake," Brad called out as he sat down. Jake walked over. "I'll have the sausage biscuit and some cheese-grits."

Jake poured his coffee and said nothing. He walked over to the short-order cook and handed her Brad's order. A few minutes later he walked over with Brad's food. It was early, and there were only two other patrons, both sitting in the red booths. Jake looked at the young surgeon with concern.

Brad looked at him curiously. "What's the matter, Jake? Did I forget to button my collar or something?" He quickly felt his tie and his collar.

"No, no . . . It's not that." Jake looked around and lowered his voice. "Mind if I have a seat?" Jake fumbled with his apron and sat down. "Look, Brad, I've served a lot of people in this town. I know just about everyone. I've catered to all of your partners, and since old Doc Tyson's divorce, I must have fed him a million times." He paused. "And since I started stayin' open late and serving booze, well, I must know just about everyone's secrets anymore."

Brad squinted at him. "What are you getting at, Jake?"

"I guess I just wanted to know something from you, that's all. How much do you know about Web Tyson and Lenore Kingsley?" Jake's voice was barely above a whisper.

Brad put down his fork. "Dr. Tyson I know, of course. Lenore Kingsley? I've heard of her because of her work in pharmaceuticals. I've certainly used a boatload of her products, but . . . What do you mean, Web Tyson and Lenore Kingsley?"

"Exactly that. What's their relationship?"

Brad squirmed. "I stay out of Tyson's private life. I wouldn't know . . ."

Jake leaned even closer. "They were here together last night — quite cozy together, you might say."

"Look, Jake, I'm really not into gossip," Brad interrupted. "I'm not really comfortable with —"

"This is not gossip. If I wanted everyone to know, I'd raise my voice," the diner owner insisted. "I want you to warn him!" His voice was urgent.

Brad could see the sweat on Jake's forehead. "Jake, what are you talking —"

"I told you, I've seen and heard a lot of things working here. You've got to warn him about her!" He paused, and when he continued, his voice began to choke. "I owe a lot to Doc Tyson. He saved my little boy." Jake collected himself. "Doc Tyson is a wonderful man. I just think he doesn't know who he's tangling with."

Brad nodded but did not reply. He sipped his coffee while Jake blew his nose.

Jake continued, "I've heard enough recently about some pretty weird goings-on down by the Wanoset." Brad looked confused.

". . . some kind of strange cult," Jake whispered. "Some say even sacrifices and Satan worship."

"Come on, Jake, you don't believe —"

"Listen to me!" Brad's eyes met Jake's and locked. He could read the sincerity there. "All I know is what I've heard tending this very bar," Jake said as he rested his hand on the counter. "More than one person has told me that Kingsley is right in the center of all that action. She demands a lot of respect, Brad. Why, one night two of our Green County deputies were sitting at this very counter when the sheriff came by. 'Lenore says it's all clear,' he says. 'You can go back to patrolling along the Wanoset.' I don't think he knew I was listening. I'm not sure what he meant, but I could see that Kingsley seemed to be calling the shots that night."

"Why are you telling me this?"

"You work with Dr. Tyson. You can warn him about her." Jake was serious. "I'd give him my right arm if I could, after what he did for my son."

"I'm sure Dr. Tyson knows what he's doing." Brad returned to eating his sausage biscuit. "Besides, if you're really concerned, why don't you tell him?"

"I've been servin' this guy for fifteen years. I know his type well enough to know he won't listen to the owner of a small diner. He needs an equal he can respect."

Another customer entered and sat down at the counter. Jake raised his voice. "Any more coffee, Doc?" He looked at Brad. His face was stone-cold serious. What else did Brad detect? He wasn't quite sure. *Are you afraid, Jake?*

Jake walked away. Brad looked at his watch, took a large gulp of coffee, and put his money on the counter. He shifted his thoughts to the day ahead. *I've got to hurry if I'm going to get in any studying before check-out.*

Lenore Kingsley awoke with a familiar dull throb in her temples. Another morning headache! She grunted an audible curse and fumbled for the Tylox on her nightstand. After taking two red capsules, she closed her eyes for another twenty minutes before stumbling into the bathroom. She struck the doorway with her shoulder, sending a searing new message of pain for her brain to process. *I didn't even see the door-frame! Must be these pills.* She held her hand out straight in front of her, then moved it slowly to the side. *This stuff must be giving me tunnel vision.*

As she began dressing for the day, she reviewed her conversation with Web Tyson the night before. Her thoughts returned to

Brad Forrest. *All it takes is one opponent to set off a public outcry. Tammy told me all about Web's practice of infanticide. That's one reason he's been chosen for this task. But we can't have some self-righteous upstart bringing this practice to light, now can we? That must be avoided at all costs.*

She began to hum along with the radio as she applied her makeup, but her mind was not on the song. *What I need is some way to keep Brad Forrest silenced until after Web is solidly in the Surgeon General's spot. What shall it be? An affair? A scandal? A malpractice suit?* In a few moments she smiled. An answer had come. *Sometimes my brilliance makes it too easy,* she thought as she puckered her lips to apply her lipstick. She kissed a tissue to remove the excess and walked to the telephone. *Tammy will be perfect for this. Just perfect.*

Matt Stone was home for lunch. It was definitely to his advantage to live so close to the hospital. He walked over to the kitchen table where Linda was studying the articles from Belle's collection. Linda looked up. "Not eating lunch with Brad again today?" The two surgeons had eaten together regularly at Crestview cafeteria since Brad had started back.

"Not today. Brad has an afternoon clinic. Any revelations, Sherlock?" Matt kissed her cheek.

"Very funny." Linda kept scanning and sipped on a cup of mint tea. In a few minutes she looked up. "You know what's interesting? No one seems to know for sure how Tyson ended up in the running for the Surgeon General's spot. In the first article I can find about him, here in the *Washington Post*, it says the administration had no comment about how Tyson's name got on the list. Listen to this." Linda lifted the page and began to read.

> When asked how Tyson had come into consideration, Richard Kern, a White House aide, returned a blank stare. "I honestly don't know," he finally replied with an embarrassed smile, "but I can assure you that we are certainly not ruling anyone in or out of contention at this point." When asked what he knew about Tyson, Kern, who is supposedly heading up the new Surgeon General search force, again shrugged his shoulders. The Blackburn Administration seems to be dogged by a poor communications network. In fact, when I approached Dr. Tyson

about this interview, after seeing his name on the list of potential candidates, he himself had not yet been contacted by the administration.

"Hmmm. Sounds like a fumble by the Blackburn boys. Does the article judge Tyson as harshly?" Matt asked.

"Not hardly. The article talks like the writer wouldn't be surprised to see Tyson walk on water anytime. There's not an unkind judgment here," Linda replied, slapping the paper with the back of her hand. "It's all praise — pure and unadulterated."

"Wow. That's a rarity." Matt paused and looked at the article. "You say this is from the *Washington Post*?"

Linda looked up. "Yes." She twisted her expression. "Is that important?"

"Didn't Anne Caudill get a job with them after leaving Appalachia Christian University?"

"That's right," Linda responded. "She works as an assistant editor for the weekend health section, I believe."

"Maybe you could call her — see if she knows this —" Matt picked up the paper and read the author's name. "— Tom Yearling, whoever he is. Maybe she can get the inside scoop on what motivated the story."

Matt took a sip of Linda's tea. "Whatever it was, it seems to have launched a very positive public image for Tyson."

"Maybe he just likes Tyson."

"Maybe so," Matt replied. "But it might be fun seeing if Anne knows any of the inside Washington scoop on things."

"O.K. I'll try to call her this afternoon." Linda returned to reading another article.

In a few minutes she looked up again. Matt noisily opened and shut his fourth cabinet in search of a desired food item.

Linda got up and walked to the pantry, pushing aside the flour and sugar containers. She tried to suppress a smile. "Looking for these?" She held up a Twinkies twin-pack.

"Hey, where'd you get that?" Matt spun around sheepishly.

"There are very few foods that you will search for so diligently. I just figured —"

"You just figured you could hide them from me?" Matt interrupted with a piggish snort.

"Just protecting the man I love," she said, holding the treat just out of Matt's reach.

"Come on, Linda." He paused. "How about if I eat a carrot stick too?"

"It's a deal." She imitated a hog's grunt as she pitched the snack to her husband.

★ ★ ★

Brad Forrest did a double take when he looked at the chart of the next patient's age: twenty. *It's not often I see someone in the clinic older than thirteen.* He did his second chin-drop when he read the patient's name: James R. Tyson. Brad opened the door. Jimmy sat motionless on the middle of an exam table.

"Hi, Jimmy. When they told me I had a work-in, I had no idea I'd be seeing you." Brad looked at him with concern. "What's up?"

Jimmy began a rambling story of his uneventful recovery since leaving the Bridgewater University Medical Center. He finished by telling about his trip to UBI, where he lifted a dog and experienced pain in his incision.

"That's really why I came. I just thought someone ought to make sure things are O.K."

"Any more pain since the episode you had while lifting?"

"No, but I really haven't tried picking up anything heavy."

"Have you felt a lump in your incision? Perhaps a lump that came when you lifted that subsequently went away?" Brad picked up his stethoscope. "Can you pull this up for me?" He tugged on the patient gown. "Let me examine you with you sitting up first." He gently palpated the skin near the scar. "Bear down for me." Jimmy cooperated. "Cough . . . Good."

Brad repeated the exam with Jimmy lying on his back. "Does this hurt?"

"Not really." Jimmy looked embarrassed. "But it sure hurt yesterday."

"When I heard your story I was concerned that you might have developed an incisional hernia, but I can't find any evidence for it on your exam. I suspect you just had an abdominal muscle strain. I'm sure you're not quite at 100 percent abdominal strength yet."

"That's a relief. I thought I might have torn something." Jimmy fumbled with his gown nervously. "Say, Dr. Forrest, I'd appreciate you not saying anything to my dad about this. He and I don't —" He paused suddenly, then continued, "We don't communicate very well. He might be upset that I didn't just ask him."

"This is entirely confidential, Jimmy. You've got my word." He smiled at the young man. "Besides, *I* operated on you, not your father, right?"

Jimmy smiled. "Right."

Brad headed for the exam room's exit,

then turned back. "Say, what were you doing at United Biotechnical Industries anyway? You working for Lenore Kingsley now?"

"No. A friend is a research doc over there. He was just giving me a tour."

"Interesting place, I'll bet. They invented Oxydel. In a way they helped save your life."

Jimmy nodded his head in sober agreement. "They do a lot more than that now," he added.

"Like what?" Brad was curious, and as a pediatric surgeon he was enjoying a rare, meaningful conversation with a patient.

"They are heavy into genetic testing products, gene therapy, and even gene splicing. My friend even hopes to work out human embryo DNA problems. According to him, Lenore Kingsley is promising billions for the development of new techniques."

From the reports I've seen on Oxydel sales, that could well be possible, Brad thought. "I've been told that Ms. Kingsley is a very powerful person."

Jimmy grabbed his shirt from the rack behind the dressing curtain. "Just another power-monger wanting a piece of my father." The comment was made under Jimmy's breath, but it was heard clearly by Forrest.

Silence followed. Brad stood for a moment longer, then turned to leave. "Take it easy, Jimmy. Why don't you avoid any lifting over twenty pounds for another week. Then work back up slowly over a few weeks until you're up to speed."

"Sure, Doc. Thanks."

By the close of the work week, Brad was exhausted. Fortunately Latner was on for the weekend, and Brad would have the weekend to rest. He planned to eat dinner Friday evening at the small apartment of Matt and Linda Stone. As he entered, Linda greeted him with a smile.

"Hi, Brad." She hung his coat in the closet. "Make yourself at home."

Matt came over. "Hey, bud, good to see you. So you survived another day at the salt mines." He shook his friend's hand firmly. "Sit down." Matt motioned to the chair.

Brad was well-primed for this meeting. For days, every time he sat still for more than a moment, his mind had filled with questions — questions about God, about prayer, and about the relationship that Matt and Linda seemed to have with the Lord. He didn't want to ask Belle. Somehow he needed to hear it from someone outside the family.

For the next two hours, including the supper hour, Brad pumped Matt and Linda for information. At the conclusion Brad needed no coercion. He knew he needed a Savior! Matt led Brad through a heartfelt prayer. When Brad left the Stones' apartment, he had a brand-new life.

Later at home, in spite of the late hour, he penned a second letter to Julie.

My dearest Julie,

I can't begin to tell you about all the changes that are taking place in my life. I've been reinstated in my work. But more important, I've stopped running. I always thought that I might try out Belle's Christianity — my folks' Christianity too, the Christianity I always spurned — when I got a little older. But I've finally seen my desperate need for God right now.

Remember the new friends I mentioned? They have helped me find God, Julie. I no longer think he's some far-off, uncaring entity. I sense his presence here with me now. This all sounds so silly to write it, but I haven't stopped crying since I left the Stones' (my new friends') apartment earlier tonight. My sins are gone! God has forgiven the sins of my self-centeredness and pride. I only pray that you will find it in your heart to forgive me too.

My thoughts are racing too fast for me to write. I've got something new, Julie — peace. Peace with God.

My dad was right all along. I was just too proud and angry to see it.

I'm beginning to understand my insecurities. And I am rejoicing in the new life I have received from above.

I love you! Please call me — please!

Your husband,
Brad

CHAPTER 24

Two nights later Matt, Linda, and Brad sat around the Stones' kitchen table.

Linda looked at Brad. "Have you heard from Julie?"

Brad looked at his hands. "Not yet."

"I've been praying for her, Brad," Linda said softly, then added, "Every day."

Brad nodded. "I talked again to her attorney. At least no formal papers for divorce have been filed." He paused. "Not yet anyway." He looked up at Matt and Linda. "She got my first letter, but evidently she's sticking to her original resolve to stay away from me entirely for a time — and that means not even talking to me while she's working this thing through. I think I've hurt her so many times in the past by making empty promises that things would be better, now she's reluctant to give me another chance."

"Give it some time, Brad. She's not apt to believe you've changed overnight," Matt added.

"I know. It's just that so much is happening, and so fast." Brad sighed. "All in all I'm beginning to see that some good has come out of all this blackness. After all, I doubt I would have ever taken a serious glance at my own life if it hadn't been for all this — at least not any time in the near future." The Stones nodded. "Anyway, what's the deal with you and Mary?" Brad asked, changing the subject. "Have you come up with any more information about Web Tyson?"

Matt cast a glance toward Linda. *Should I tell him?* Understanding her husband's look, Linda nodded.

"I've carefully reviewed all the medical records we talked about when we first came to see you. I'm more and more convinced that things just don't add up the way they should. Disabled babies are dying at an alarming rate — and, I fear, not just from nontreatment. They die much too quickly to be dying of dehydration."

Brad's eyes locked with Matt's. "You think the deaths are physician-assisted?"

Linda answered for him. "That's being polite. It looks like Mr. Surgeon General-to-be is involved in infanticide. He makes the choice who should live or die, then accelerates the process."

Brad released a heavy sigh. "Even if what

you suspect is true, we have no concrete proof. No witnesses. No complaints from parents. Nothing. Only suspicions based on my experience and a review of the records."

"What is needed is a direct observation of the dirty deed," Matt acknowledged.

"It might not even be him," Brad added. "Ever think of that? Maybe someone else does it for him. Or maybe someone else wants Tyson's patients to die." The list of possibilities seemed to grow longer the more Brad studied it.

"You're right," the Stones chimed in together.

The group fell silent. Eventually Linda began again. "For what it's worth, I did a little background check on Tyson's bid for the Surgeon General job. To me it looks like it all started with this one article in the *Washington Post.* I talked to a friend of ours, Anne Caudill, who works for the paper. It turns out that she knows the guy who wrote the article. She's worked with him on a few projects before. Anyway, she pumped him about the story, how he picked it up, where he got his info — that kind of thing, and it looks like he did the whole story as a favor to Lenore Kingsley."

Brad's eyes widened. Linda continued, "He confessed the whole story to Anne. Evidently he felt he owed a favor to Miss Kingsley because she invented a blood substitute that helped save his father. He felt a bit used, Anne said, but he did call and confirm that Tyson's name was on Blackburn's list of possibilities, so he did the story. She said the reporter who did the story seemed a bit relieved to tell her about it."

"This is too weird!" Brad said intensely. "All I hear lately is Lenore Kingsley, Lenore Kingsley, Lenore Kingsley. First down at Jake's Diner, then from Jimmy Tyson, and now from you."

Matt and Linda looked at each other and shrugged.

Brad told them the details of his conversations with Jake and Jimmy.

Matt pushed back from the table and stood up. He always paced when he was excited. "Wow! If Jake is right and this Lenore Kingsley is a Satanist, and if Jimmy's right that she is out to influence his father, then —" He stopped suddenly.

"Then what?" Linda asked.

"Then she wouldn't be too happy with anything or anyone who might derail Tyson's chances of becoming Surgeon General," Matt added.

"I guess I hadn't thought about that much. If Tyson is involved in illegal infanticide, bringing that to the public light could be a fatal political blow," Linda said soberly.

"But if he is, don't we have an obligation to try to stop him?" Matt responded.

After a moment, Brad asked the obvious question. "So what now? It's not like we can watch him twenty-four hours a day."

"I've been praying about this very thing," Matt answered. "I think it's time to get more help. I think we need to register our suspicions with the authorities."

Brad remembered what Jake had said about Lenore's influence. He related the story Jake had told him about the Green County deputies. "It might not be so wise to involve the local authorities if Lenore really has that kind of power."

"Man! If all of this is true, it sounds like Satan might have big plans for Dr. Tyson. He's not going to be any too happy if we interfere with his orders."

"There's definitely more going on here than what natural eyes can see — a spiritual battle, for sure," Linda added.

Brad's eyes widened. Things were moving too fast!

Linda sensed his anxiety. "Satan is not someone we fear, Brad. As Christians, we know he's a defeated foe and that we can conquer him through the authority given to us by Jesus through his blood sacrifice. Spiritual warfare is a normal part of the Christian walk."

"This is a bit overwhelming. War . . . Satan . . . I'm not sure I knew what I was in for," Brad added meekly.

Matt smiled. "It's certainly not a primrose path. You can ask Belle about that. She's a true warrior from way back." He paused and slapped Brad's back. "Welcome to the fight, brother."

Matt picked up his pacing again. He walked the length of the small apartment and returned to the kitchen. "What about the F.B.I.?"

"The feds?" Linda asked quickly. She and Brad both looked incredulous.

"I'm serious. If we think the locals might be corrupt, we've got to tell someone about our suspicions. Why not the feds? This may even be more in their ballpark. Remember the Baby Doe regulations of Reagan's administration — something about a Down's syndrome child who was starved and deprived of a necessary operation? The new law made such action a federal offense — discrimination based on an infant's disability, I think."

Linda brightened. "Maybe they would

have special interest in this just because of who we think might be involved. Web Tyson is a nominee for federal office, right?"

Brad looked at the Stones. "I don't know, guys. This is pretty serious stuff here. Don't you think we ought to be sure?"

"Look, I say all we do is report our suspicions. It's not like we're telling them pure facts or anything. I just think we should let them know things smell a little fishy around here." Matt looked at the others.

"What if we're wrong, Matt? What if Tyson's completely innocent and he finds out I was involved with calling the feds to investigate? I might as well kiss my job goodbye forever," Brad replied.

"The stakes are pretty high," Linda acknowledged. She paused. "Why don't we pray about this again before making a decision?"

The others agreed. They sat around the table, linked hand in hand. While the Stones prayed aloud, Brad prayed along, talking to his newfound Lord. *What if we're wrong, Lord? What should we do?* He paused, listening to Matt's prayer for wisdom and direction. *But what if we're right? Who will speak out on behalf of the helpless children?* For the first time he could remember, Brad prayed a specific prayer. *What am I to do about this, Lord?* He waited, listening to the others. In the quietness, a simple answer provided the peace that Brad sought: *Trust me!*

Randy was relieved when Lenore told him he could move the animal cages back down to the regular animal housing facility. His lab was crowded enough, and he wanted his space back. He took the animals, one by one, down to UBI's basement where the remainder of the lab animals were kept. When he finished, he saw that one cage nearby was unoccupied. He read the tag that still adorned the front of the door. "Dalmatian bitch, 2201." *What! This was the surrogate used for my Dalmatian gene splicing experiment. Where could they be housing her?* He called over an older man who had charge of the facility. "Hey, Maxwell, what's with the empty cage?"

A balding man of sixty strolled up and looked at the cage. He picked up the tag and ripped the string that secured it. "Sorry about that, Dr. Harris. This animal's gone. I just hadn't removed the tag yet." He mumbled something to himself and began to walk away.

"Wait a minute! What do you mean, 'gone?' "

The man looked back. "Dead. I found her myself last Thursday."

"Dead?" Randy nearly screamed at the assistant. "Why wasn't I told?"

"Look, Dr. Harris, the paperwork's in the office here if you want to see it. No one said anything special about notifying you if an animal dies."

"Not just any animal — this animal! This animal was part of a special project!"

"I assumed all the special ones were housed in your lab upstairs. I certainly didn't mean to upset you." He began to shuffle away again. "As I said, I filed a report. It's in the office."

Randy sighed. "Is the animal available for autopsy?"

"That animal was incinerated the next day. It's UBI policy. We can't have unpreserved dead animals around. It's an infection risk."

"*%#$#@!"

Randy took the elevator back to his lab. *Great! Just great! First I find some of the pups have pituitary adenomas, with one already dead, and now I find out their surrogate mother has died as well! But from what? It couldn't be from the same thing. No, that's not possible,* he reasoned. *The virus used to adjust her pups' DNA couldn't have lived on and been passed* *into the mother's circulation to cause similar problems. No, that's never been reported.* Randy scratched his head. Then he had a sickening thought. *Of course it's not reported! No one else has had this much success yet.* Randy began to pace. *Be reasonable. That virus should have been long dead! There's got to be another explanation!* "*%#$#@!"

Brad finished up his evening charts on 5 north and looked at Mary. "Why don't you take off? You're not on tonight, are you?"

"Not me. But I've got to finish this progress note. I'll see you tomorrow at checkout."

"O.K. See you," Brad said as he headed for the elevator. The hall was quiet except for Tammy, who was pushing a large supply cart toward the service elevator. Brad looked at her curiously. "Short of help tonight?"

"Not really," she panted. "Lizzy just has some extra deliveries to make, and I had an extra minute, so I volunteered to take this to the basement." She grunted again conspicuously.

"Do you want some help? That looks pretty awkward." Brad smiled.

Tammy smiled too. *Lenore assured me this would be easy.*

They pushed the cart into the small, empty service elevator. Tammy inserted her key into the control panel and turned it to the right. Slowly the doors closed, and the elevator began to descend. The two stood face to face in the cramped space beside the large silver cart. Tammy smiled again, then spoke quietly. "I'm so excited about Web being the Surgeon General," she bubbled. "He's talking about taking me with him to Washington, you know." She winked.

"I've seen that you've grown quite close," Brad replied. He felt suddenly uncomfortable and edged a step closer to the back wall.

Tammy's demeanor suddenly changed. "I'd hate to see anything disturb his chances at becoming the Surgeon General. That wouldn't just destroy his future — it would destroy mine as well." Her eyes — two cold, steel daggers — caught Brad's. He was definitely uneasy now.

Brad eased further back until he was tight against the far wall. He made no answer to Tammy's strange words. *God, what is going on?*

Suddenly sheer panic crossed Tammy's face. She began to hyperventilate and made several choking sounds as she gasped, "I've got to . . . get some air!" She began to claw feverishly at her blouse, eventually pulling open the collar, sending her top four buttons flying.

Brad watched for a moment with increasing alarm. *Oh boy, she's having a claustrophobic panic attack!*

She turned and pounded furiously at the control buttons. In her fury, she snapped the key to the Off position. The key skidded across the floor beneath the supply cart. The elevator lurched to a halt, sending Tammy sprawling to the floor. Her arms flew madly about, further opening her blouse and smearing her red lipstick way up onto her left cheek.

Brad's concern about her previous comments melted, and he leaned over her to see if he could help. "Tammy . . ."

She continued to flail. Brad tried gentle restraint, but she managed to secure her hands around his neck in a choke-hold, smearing more red lipstick, this time on Brad's white shirt. Brad pulled back, but not before she had scratched a jagged mark into his lower neck.

"Ow!" Brad touched the scratch. *I've got to get that key! Maybe if I get this door open she'll settle down.*

"Need . . . air . . . Need air!" she urged. "Help me!"

"I'll get the door!" Brad spoke slowly, hoping to calm her. He reached for the key, which lay just beyond Tammy's right thigh.

Slam! Tammy's fist came down on the back of Brad's hand like a rock. He pulled his hand away without the key, which was now clutched tightly in Tammy's palm.

Brad looked at the woman, who was now heaving deep, quiet, rhythmic sobs. Tammy pushed herself up slowly, so that she was sitting against the door and buried her face in her arm. After a few moments Brad inched forward slightly. He spoke her name gently. "Tammy?"

She looked up, her face flushed with sheer terror. "Don't touch me!"

Brad rubbed his hand and slowly edged back to the rear of the elevator again.

Tammy looked at him coldly. "You tried to rape me!" she cried, then buried her head in her arm again. Her mascara flowed from her cheeks mingled with her tears.

"Tammy, I —"

"#@#$%!" She interrupted his soft reply.

"You're having some sort of panic attack, Tammy. I've done nothing but try to help you!"

Tammy sat quietly for a minute, the silence broken only by her occasional sobs.

Finally she looked up. "Just look at me!"

She spit at him. "Who would you believe?"

Brad did look at her. Her hair was tangled, fallen from its neatly fixed position. Her torn blouse was open, and her legs sprawled awkwardly. Lipstick covered her left cheek, extending from the corner of her open mouth. Brad felt his own neck, then looked at his hand. *I'm bleeding!* He took out a handkerchief and blotted the scratch.

Tammy whispered his name. "Brad. Brad?" She spoke with a slowly rising volume. "Do you remember what I've said to you?"

Brad looked at her without reply.

Tammy reminded him coyly, "I'd hate to see anything disturb Web's chances at becoming Surgeon General."

The young surgeon started to see the picture clearly. *She planned this whole thing to trap me!*

Tammy looked off into space. "So I had a panic attack, did I? Clawed feverishly at my own blouse — or was it done by a love-starved married man without a wife?" She flashed a glance at Forrest who sat motionless, leaning on the back wall of the elevator, and continued, "I just needed air. Everything closed in around me. I just panicked! Yes, that's it!" she mocked. "I just panicked." She looked at Forrest, who returned her icy stare. "I've got the story straight now, don't I, Brad? You self-righteous little boy! But just the same, I think I'll head back up to 5 north before I freshen up, just so all the others can see what I did to myself today." She paused. "Then if anything ever happens to jog my memory and I'm unable to suppress the traumatic memory of this sexual abuse, they will all be there to confirm my little story."

Tammy stood up and reinserted the key that she'd clutched so tightly. "Now, where were we?"

The elevator again started its descent, but Brad interrupted it by pushing the next available floor. He straightened his tie, smoothed his white coat, and exited without a word into a crowd of people waiting for the main elevator. He cringed as he heard Tammy's sobs resume and then fade as the door shut again. He pushed through the crowd, hoping not to be recognized, holding his white coat to cover the lipstick on his collar. He walked to the stairs at the end of the corridor, quietly lowered himself to a sitting position, and cried.

Later that evening Matt Stone hung up the phone and shook his head. "Oh boy," he said solemnly. "Boy, oh, boy."

"What's up? Sounded like a pretty heavy conversation you were having there," Linda called from the kitchen. "Want some tea?"

"Sure," Matt responded.

Linda walked in and sat on the couch next to Matt, handing him a cup of herbal tea. "That was Brad, wasn't it?"

"Yes. He was pretty upset. He wants to call off any notion of investigating Tyson."

He sighed and shook his head. He told Linda the entire story about Brad's elevator ride.

"She sounds positively evil," Linda responded.

"She may just be a pawn in a bigger battle," Matt said slowly.

Linda stroked her husband's blond hair. "So what did you tell him?"

Matt paused and looked at his beautiful, young wife. "I told him the truth. It's too late."

"Too late?"

"I talked to the F.B.I. this morning," Matt responded mechanically.

"Oh." The two sat in silence for a minute, sipping their tea. "Know what?"

"What?" Matt looked curious.

"The battle's on." Linda's eyes met Matt's.

Matt nodded his head and repeated his wife's words. "The battle's on."

CHAPTER 25

John Beckler had been with the Bureau for twelve years. He hated it when politics interfered with his work, and he despised taking orders from a liberal White House even more. But such was life in recent months as the F.B.I. and C.I.A. both cooperated with the White House for "special projects" at the discretion of the new Commander-in-chief. John swallowed the remaining cold coffee from a Styrofoam cup and looked at the picture of his wife and kids on his desk. *Looks like I'll be away from you for a few days*. He held the picture of his wife for a moment, until his thoughts were interrupted by the voice of his younger associate, Conrad Shanaberger.

"Why the short notice, boss?" Conrad held an overstuffed suitcase in addition to his briefcase.

"Politics, buddy, politics." John tightened his belt a notch. *New Year's resolution must be working,* he mused, patting his slim frame.

"More information on Dr. Tyson? What

gives?" The young investigator put down his luggage.

"Yesterday we got a call from a physician who works in Tyson's hospital. He's concerned about some observations he's made — even talked about Tyson being involved with possible involuntary euthanasia, that sort of thing." He looked at Conrad, who had plopped his large bottom down on his suitcase. He appeared to be making himself comfortable for a long story. John went on, "Anyway, he's got no real proof — just suspicions. It's the kind of thing that in a normal situation I would have just blown off. But they routed his call to me since I had done a background check on Tyson for the Blackburn Administration. I have strict orders to refer all info about the candidates to the director. He took it to Blackburn. 'Get on it now!' the President said."

John looked at the suitcase beneath his ample assistant. It seemed to be straining. "Evidently with Tyson's confirmation hearings right around the corner, they want to do everything possible to avoid a potentially embarrassing situation. If there's dirt to be found, they want us to find it, and find it in time for Blackburn to derail the confirmation."

"What do you have in mind? Setting up a sting?"

"No stings! We've got clearance only to observe. We have no proof of wrongdoing here, so we have no warrant for that kind of operation."

"Phone taps?"

"Yes, but not the stuff we can use for criminal prosecution. We are merely on surveillance detail. If we happen to uncover something good, we'll have to regroup with the director."

"Surveillance!" The former college football standout slapped his fist against his palm. He knew what that meant — hours of boredom, and sometimes moments of terror. Surveillance could mean sitting in a cramped communications van for days. "Come on." John picked up a light jacket from behind the door. "Let's go down to supply. We need to gather a few things for this one."

Lenore swerved violently back across the dotted white line, narrowly missing a large, blue truck that occupied the next lane. A horn blared, and the male owner of the truck screamed a curse loudly enough for Lenore to hear it.

@#%$! I didn't even see him. These Tylox*

are going to be the end of me! She rattled her purse containing the medication that she now used around the clock.

She slowed down to force the other vehicle ahead of hers, but the truck driver slowed momentarily and continued his "blessing." Lenore stared straight ahead, fuming. Eventually the man pulled away, leaving her to appreciate his diesel exhaust.

She was still irritated when she arrived at UBI twenty minutes later. She stomped past the security desk without speaking. She looked into the retinal scanner and waited. The box beeped, and the computer screen issued a message: "Unidentifiable pattern. Please press the 'Clear' button and stare at the red dot again." Lenore cursed and followed instructions. The machine issued a second beep and sent a warning to Security. The computer screen message angered Lenore even more: "Access denied. Subject not identifiable. Pattern not on record."

Sam, the security officer, walked up. Lenore glared at him. "Fix this! You know who I am!"

Sam shrugged his shoulders and put his own eyes up to the eyepieces, focusing on the red light. The door unlocked, and the screen printed his name. He looked at

Lenore. "Seems to be working fine, Dr. Kingsley."

She huffed and moved to the door. Sam touched her arm. "Must be a foul-up in the system somewhere. You didn't just get contact lenses or anything, did you?" he asked, looking in her eyes.

"No." She turned to leave, but the door had sealed again. "Let me in this place."

"I guess I'd better see your I.D. badge, just in case."

Lenore growled. "Let me guess. Protocol, right?" She dug for her I.D. in her small handbag.

While she looked, Sam rambled on. "You know, you might want to get your eyes checked by an eye doctor. I can remember a few years back when your father had that small retinal bleed. It did the same thing to him then."

"My retinas are fine." Lenore raised her voice, holding up her I.D. badge to within an inch of Sam's nose. "Get the machine fixed!"

He crossed his eyes and backed up. "O.K.," he added sheepishly, "you can go in." He stared into the retinal scanner again. The door unlocked, and Lenore pushed past the security officer without another word.

* * *

"Mark? Can I talk to you for a minute?" Brad Forrest looked at his colleague. He looked exhausted. His scrubs were wrinkled, and he had dried blood on his shoe-covers.

"Sure. Sit down." Davis motioned toward the couch in the doctors' lounge outside the O.R.

"I've been doing some heavy thinking lately." Brad paused. "I guess you've heard that Julie left."

Mark Davis looked up. His wife of eighteen years was gone, too. He sighed. "Yep, I heard." He closed the chart in his lap. "Pretty common problem in our business, Brad."

"I know." He folded his hands. "I'm not here to unload my problems on you, but I think you may be able to help me out." He looked at his associate, who now slumped back in his chair. "I finally spoke to Julie last night. She's not even been willing to do that for the last few weeks." He paused. "I'm really doing some changing, Mark. This whole thing at home and at work has caused me to take a good look at my priorities. I've got to stop putting everything else in front of my family." He sighed. "Anyway, Julie will hear my words, that I'm different, that I've changed, but she's not convinced yet that there's any substance to it. She wants practical proof."

Dr. Davis shifted in his seat. He seemed antsy.

"That's where you might be able to help. What if I delayed taking my board exam for a year? You and I both could take a break from the mock exams for a while, then pick it up at a more relaxed pace when things settle down. We'd both have more time to devote to outside interests." He looked for signs of a positive response. Davis looked tired but showed no response yet.

Finally he spoke. "Look, Brad, why put off your boards? Both of us know you're ready. I bet you could pass 'em without any more work. We've both been doing the mock board thing because of Tyson. That's the way it's always been at Valley Surgeons for Children. That's the way it will always be. I say we take a break from it. Tyson doesn't even have to know. It looks like he's not going to be around much in the near future anyway. If he finds out, I'll handle him. You spend more time at home and lay off the books. You know this stuff cold already." For the first time in the conversation he smiled.

Now Brad smiled, too. "Thanks, Mark." He stood up.

Mark extended his hand and shook Brad's firmly. "I hope it works out for you. I only wish I'd have reoriented my own life before my marriage exploded."

Brad didn't expect the candor. He nodded his head without speaking and squeezed Mark's palm a second time. Dr. Davis sighed, turned away, and walked back into the main O.R. corridor.

Web Tyson looked out the window at the evening sky and swirled the drink in his hand. He listened quietly as he balanced the phone against his ear.

Tammy bit her lower lip and tried to keep her voice from trembling. "But I have the weekend off, honey. I thought you wanted me to go."

Web frowned. "It's really going to be a quick trip. No frills. Just a public appearance or two, some pictures with Blackburn, maybe a talk show. Maybe next time, O.K.?"

Tammy sighed heavily into the phone. "I could look for a place to stay. I won't get in the way."

Web shifted on his feet. "You know I want you there, babe, but really, I think it's best —"

Tammy tried a playful angle. She interrupted him, saying, "We could stay together at the Ritz. You know what a delight we had when —"

The surgeon raised his voice. "Look, I'm sorry. Blackburn says it's a public image thing. No girlfriends in the public eye until after the confirmation." Silence. "I didn't want to have to tell you." He paused again and took a swallow of his drink. "But I guess it's best you know."

Tammy pouted but remained silent. Finally she added, "O.K., darling. Have a good trip. Call me when you come in. I'll wait up." She sighed heavily into the phone. She lowered her voice teasingly. "I love you."

Web looked at Lenore, who was waiting with her overnight bag over her shoulder. He lowered his voice. "You too," he responded in a whisper.

His eyes met Lenore's. Her unspoken message was clear: "Let's go!" Web nodded.

"I've got to run. I'll call. Bye." He hung up the phone as Lenore tugged playfully on his sport coat.

She spoke the message that her eyes had been communicating. "Our jet's waiting, darling." She winked. "Let's go."

Randy Harris dined alone in a secluded

booth at Anthony's Place. He ate his regular fare — a steak sandwich and fries — and drank an imported beer. In a few minutes Jimmy came over with a second draft. The restaurant was nearly empty, so Jimmy sat down. "You seem bummed. What gives?" he asked.

"Another setback in my research." Randy took a long swallow of the golden beverage.

Jimmy looked curious. "Setback?"

"An animal died," Randy snapped. He put down his beer. "It's really nothing."

Jimmy persisted, "That's it? An animal died? You look like you lost your last friend."

Randy sat quietly for a minute longer, then responded, "I guess it is more than that, Jimmy. Maybe it's what you've been saying, maybe it's just the late hours getting to me, but —" He stopped and looked at his plate.

"But?"

"I've been wondering if maybe all this embryo research shouldn't be looked at a little differently. I've been so excited about what technology has allowed us to do. I'm always pushing the envelope — if it can be done, let's try it." He fell silent again. "I really haven't given much thought to what *should* be done. I've spent all my energy on what *could* be done."

"Maybe you need a vacation." Jimmy smiled and stood up to serve a new customer at the bar.

"Right. Like Kingsley would just give me a few days off." Jimmy walked away. Randy finished his sandwich in silence and drank another beer. He shifted his thoughts back to his current situation. *I'd better find out what I can about our surrogate Dalmatian's death before I tell any of this to Lenore — and definitely before she volunteers to carry our next experiment.*

"Mom, ph-phone's f-for you!" Bradley screamed louder than the small basement apartment required.

Julie walked out of the bedroom. "Thanks, honey. Who is it?"

"Deve!"

Julie squinted. *Deve?* She picked up the phone. "Hello."

"Hello, Julie. It's me . . . Steve."

Steve! How did you get my number? I moved to get away from everyone for a while! She paused and collected her thoughts.

Steve spoke again. "Julie?"

"Yes, I'm here. I guess I'm just a little surprised to hear from you, that's all."

"I guess so," he chided. "You barely said

goodbye to anyone. I had to chase Becky down just to find out where you were hiding."

Becky! I should have known. She paused again. "Look, Steve, I came down here to collect my thoughts as much as anything. I needed time away from Brad —" She paused. "— from you, from Belle — everyone. I needed to get out of Green County altogether for a while. There are too many memories back there to cloud clear thinking."

Steve nodded his head, even though Julie couldn't see. "Lonely yet?"

Julie sighed and nodded her head in return. "Terribly."

Steve shared the real reason for his call. "Want me to settle that problem? I'm going to Atlanta for the weekend. I could stop by on my way —"

"I don't know, Steve. Maybe we shouldn't." She paused. "I finally talked to Brad. He wants me back, Steve. Maybe a second chance would —"

"Remember the lonely times?" he interrupted.

"I remember." *Why am I explaining this to you?* "He seems different — committed to change —"

"Julie, listen to yourself! You know how hard change is."

Julie sighed. "Maybe you're right. I don't know — I've still not made a final decision."

"Look, Julie, I've been through all of this with my former wife. I just don't want you to set yourself up for another fall." He paused. "I've seen it before, Julie. Some people are addicted to bad relationships. They return to those who mistreat them over and over and over."

Julie listened to Steve's smooth voice. *He's making some sense, I know, but still —*

Steve interrupted her thoughts. "So what do you say? Should I stop in? Maybe you'd even like to come to the big city with me?"

"Steve, I don't know. I —"

Steve persisted impatiently, "It will be fun!" Silence. "Look. You think about it. Atlanta's a great city. I'll call you Friday."

"Well — O.K."

"Great. See you!"

Click. Julie stared at the receiver, then quietly put the phone on the table.

CHAPTER 26

Sunday evening two men dressed as maintenance personnel entered Room 525 on 5 north, Crestview Women and Children's Health Center. The room was unoccupied, as was the adjacent room, Room 523. The two made swift work. When they were finished, no one would detect the changes.

On Monday morning Elizabeth Grandby arrived with her parents, Ted and Janet. The patient, a mature fourteen-year-old, was checked into Room 523. Elizabeth had a bandage over her right lower quadrant and an IV for medications. According to Dr. Brad Forrest's note and orders, she had been operated on for a ruptured appendix with abscess and would likely need to be hospitalized for a week for antibiotics. All of her paperwork appeared in order. She arrived on the floor precisely at nursing shift change; to save the recovery room staff from checkout, Dr. Forrest volunteered to do it for them. The patient spent most of her time listening to a Walkman tape-player with earphones. Her father, Ted Grandby, was an ex-football player turned executive who spent many hours in the room with his briefcase open and his cellular phone on. Her mother, Janet Grandby, devoted her time to reading magazines. She was a trim woman of forty-two, and her only apparent physical malady was barely noticeable — a snug hearing aid in her left ear. They appeared to be the model overprotective parents as one of them stayed with Elizabeth all the time, including the night shift when they took turns sleeping on a hospital cot beside their daughter's bed.

Down the hall, in the lounge opposite the 5 north nursing station, the parents of a new baby in the neonatal I.C.U., the Snyders, began a hospital vigil. The father read magazines or any number of different books that he kept in a large brown briefcase by his side, while the mother did crossword puzzles and told everyone who would lend an ear about their sweet little Katie, who was born two months premature. "They say she might be here for a month. We just can't leave when things are so critical," the mother explained over and over to anyone who would urge them to go home. "Frank insists we stay up here. The lounge by the N.I.C.U. is so crowded. And besides, the

TV reception is better in this one." So there they camped, each leaving every two hours "to see Katie and promote bonding."

Web Tyson arrived for his Monday morning clinic at Crestview looking tired. "Rough weekend, captain?" The voice belonged to his office manager.

"The usual stuff, Amy," he huffed. "How's the schedule for this morning?"

"Thirty patients — seven new, eleven second visits, ten post-ops, and two work-ins."

"Not bad," he mused as he looked over the list. Web headed for his desk. "Tell the nurses I'm here. Let's get started."

As he turned, Amy spoke again. "Oh, Dr. Tyson, let me have your beeper. A representative from USA Communications stopped by this morning with this loaner." She held up the small black pager. "They want yours for routine servicing."

Dr. Tyson pinched the clip holding his current pager to his belt. "This one works fine. I don't need a loaner."

"It's part of a new service. The guy insisted you get the loaner this morning. Evidently it's already programmed to get your pages. He wanted to stay and give it to you personally. I nearly had to chase him off." Amy chuckled. "Anyway, I promised I'd give it to you and give yours back to them. They should have your old one back to you in a week or so."

Tyson reluctantly surrendered his beeper. He wore it everywhere, even in the O.R. He clipped the new one on his belt and headed for his desk again.

Outside Crestview, John Beckler sat in command central, an inconspicuous white van parked in the main parking lot. As Dr. Tyson switched on his new pager, John turned the knobs on the silver panel in front of him. He adjusted his headset. *There!* John smiled. *Just like being in the exam room.*

Samuel Falls sat at the security console at UBI. He carefully scanned each screen on the panel in front of him. From the desk he had access to the more than one hundred video surveillance pieces scattered throughout the offices, labs, and parking facilities. Every seven seconds the screens changed to a new image, transmitting from a new camera location. Sam looked at the images carefully. As a view of Lenore's preferred parking came up, he remembered the incident on the previous Friday morning. *I'd better reprogram that retinal scanner before Lenore gets here. She'll have my hide if she can't get in again.*

He tapped a keyboard with a series of commands, eventually entering the security net program that controlled the employee screening throughout the complex. There were only three people with computer access to alter the program — Gardner, Lenore, and Sam. He had been with Gardner Kingsley since the first day he opened the doors many years before. He had earned the trust of the powers that be by his faithful service since that time.

The computer screen displayed the message, "Security Net Access Restricted: Please type in user identification."

Sam responded by entering his secret identification code — "Mad Dog," a nickname he'd inherited from his past professional softball days. He worked through a series of commands to recall Lenore's retinal image that was unidentified by the program. He then reprogrammed the scanner to accept the new rejected image as Lenore Kingsley.

There, he thought as he exited the program. *That should keep Her Highness happy!*

He scanned the console of screens in front of him, then pressed a remote control to forward screen 3 to the parking lot.

There he observed Lenore's red Corvette. *Just in time,* he chuckled to himself, then wiped his forehead with a cloth handkerchief. *Just in time.*

"Morning, Dr. Kingsley," he called out as she passed.

Lenore walked by without speaking, her right thigh clumsily colliding with the security counter as she passed. "@#%#@!"

Julie picked up the mail from the corner of the card table that served as her desk and kitchen table. Sophie always put the mail there, as she didn't have a special box for the basement apartment. *Another letter from Brad.* Julie sighed. *Why does Sophie always put it on top?* She lifted the letter, which had been forwarded by her attorney. *Maybe it's time I gave him my address. It's not like he'd come right down now that he's back at work.*

She opened the refrigerator and retrieved her favorite diet pop. A yellow sticky-note on the door reported Bradley's location. "Bradley is upstairs playing with the kids. Mail's on the table." A smiley face adorned the corner of the note. It was simply signed, "Sophie."

Julie opened the letter in her hand and began to read.

My dearest Julie,

I was so glad to speak to you the other night. My mind is so full that I find I can hardly say what I need to say in just a few minutes. Perhaps a pen will help to clarify my thoughts.

I am continuing work in full swing at Crestview while you are gone.

"While I am gone? Boy, he's optimistic," Julie muttered to herself, then continued reading.

I have made some arrangements that will increase my time at home, however. I spoke to Dr. Davis, who has been running my mock oral board exams. He's agreed to cancel them for now; so that will relieve quite a bit of study time, most of which I was doing down at Crestview. That's a real answer to prayer. I asked with a bit of trepidation, but Dr. Davis responded so positively, I couldn't believe it! He even mentioned being sorry he hadn't changed his priorities in time to save his own marriage. That is what I intend to do — preserve my relationship with you!

There is another issue that is heavy on my mind. It also relates to my job, and to Web Tyson. It would take forever for me to write the details, but I have reason to suspect that some of Tyson's practices may not be above board. Matt Stone, a fellow surgeon and friend, is convinced from reviewing the records that Tyson is involved in infanticide! I think Web is convinced he is doing what is right and humane. The cases in question have only to do with babies with disabilities. At first I didn't want to believe it, and I would have done anything to preserve my prestigious job at Valley Surgeons for Children. But now I'm not so sure. I have come to understand that I must follow what I think God wants me to do, regardless of the cost.

I have reason to believe that some very powerful dark forces are supporting Web professionally and in his bid for the Surgeon General's job. I haven't done anything rash, but I've gotten the message loud and clear from several sources that messing with Web Tyson could spell disaster! Anyway, I have decided to do what I sense is right, even if it means I could lose my present job.

I know this is confusing, but I can explain it all later, face to face. I remember now what Bradley said about prayer — "Belle's been teachin' me!" Ask him to pray for Daddy, that God will protect me. Tell him I love him. Have him call on Thursday evening. I'd love to talk to him again.

I love you, Julie. You are the focus of my love and of my prayers.

Brad

Confusing is right! Julie felt a chill. *What have you gotten into, Brad?* She reread the letter aloud. ". . . powerful dark forces . . . message loud and clear . . . messing with Web Tyson . . . disaster!" *What are you talking about? Is someone threatening you?*

Julie slumped into an old rocking chair and studied the letter again, this time focusing on the more positive messages. *It looks like he really may mean business about spending more time at home,* she thought hopefully. *And this talk about prayer and wanting what God wants . . . That's not my old Brad!*

She put the letter inside the cover of a well-worn Bible given to her by Sophie. She stroked its smooth leather. *What about me, God?* She rocked, folding her arms around the Bible, clutching it to her chest as if she were hugging a small child. *What about me?* She rocked in silence. *I want to know you, too. I want to know what you want.* "I want to know. I want to know," she whispered quietly, her voice choked with emotion.

She continued rocking for a minute longer, crying for her lost hope and her broken marriage. "I'm so lonely, God," she sobbed. "I'm so confused."

She heard Bradley calling from upstairs. "Mom!"

She wiped her tears and set the Bible aside. Before responding to Bradley, she whispered, "Brad, I miss you."

Ted Grandby looked at his watch. "The nurse will be in soon to take your temperature."

Elizabeth nodded with understanding. She took a small foam earpiece attached to a battery pack with a switch. She inserted the black, cone-shaped piece into her external ear canal. It was decorated to look like a small radio. She flipped a switch, activating a small, battery-powered heater. The soft probe quickly heated her external ear to 102 degrees Fahrenheit. She rubbed her cheeks vigorously with her hands. Ted stood and pulled the curtain. After a minute, Elizabeth repeated the process in her other ear. While she waited, her father moistened a washcloth with hot water and placed it on her forehead for a moment.

Two minutes later a staff nurse came by to take vitals and give a dose of antibiotics. The nurse looked at Elizabeth. "How do you feel?" She laid her hand on the girl's forehead. "You look flushed."

"I'm freezing," the patient complained.

The nurse inserted a small temperature probe into the patient's ear. After only a few seconds, the tympanic membrane temperature was reported: 101.7 degrees Fahrenheit. "Oh dear! You have a fever. I'll hang these antibiotics and notify Dr. Forrest." She hung up the small plastic bag that contained a clear fluid. On the side, a label indicated the name of the medication: Unasyn 1.5 gm. Into the bag the nurse spiked a sharp, sterile connector that hooked to the tubing carrying the medication to the patient's arm. The other end was connected via a needle inserted into the IV near Elizabeth's hand. The nurse carefully adjusted the drip and left.

Ted followed the nurse to the door. "Is she going to be O.K.?"

"Oh, sure. It's just a little fever. That's pretty common after ruptured appendicitis. I'll be notifying Dr. Forrest," she replied before heading back up the hall to the nurses' station.

Ted's gaze continued until she rounded the corner. He then returned and helped Elizabeth disconnect the IV long enough to let the medication run out into a small container, which Ted quickly discarded into the trash. He then took a stroll in the hall, walking slowly around the floor, pausing to say hello to Frank Snyder, who was camping in the lounge while his daughter Katie recuperated in the N.I.C.U.

"Web!" Tammy ran up alongside the surgeon who strode at an athlete's pace.

He paused momentarily. "Hi."

She grabbed his arm and kissed him lightly on the cheek. He looked rushed. "I'll walk with you. You have a case to do?"

"A case? Try six! Every mother wants their baby operated on before I leave." He shrugged.

Tammy pouted. "I was hoping we could eat lunch together."

"Not today." Web resumed his pace.

Tammy stumbled along. "I was hoping you'd call me last night. How's life in D.C.?"

Web seemed taken aback. "Oh that! Same as always. Interviews. Policy meetings.

Budget discussions. I'm not even in yet, and Blackburn wants me to review all the figures."

Tammy squeezed his arm supportively. "You can do it if anyone can." She paused. "Did you look for a place to live?"

Web looked at her. She was radiant. *I'm not going to like breaking your heart.* "No, Tammy. It was all business," he lied.

He turned to head toward the operating rooms. She faced him and grabbed his hands. "Can I see you later?" Her eyes met his, then locked on his hands. On his right ring finger sat a ring with an unusual crystal. She rubbed it with her finger. Web tensed.

"Look, Tammy, I brought a ton of work back from Washington. I —"

"Where did you get this?" She raised her voice and rubbed the ring again.

"This? I've had it for so long I don't even remember," Web lied again.

Tammy looked at it for a moment longer. *Haven't I seen this stone before?*

Web spoke again. "Look, I need to run. I know we have to talk, but . . ." *Soon,* he promised himself. *I've got to tell you how I feel.*

"Call me." It wasn't a request.

"Sure, babe." He leaned down and accepted another kiss on his cheek. "See you later." He turned and disappeared behind the double doors labeled, "Operating Rooms, Authorized Personnel Only."

"What's the status on our second run?" Lenore asked Randy Harris, who sat nervously on the edge of his desk chair. She was referring to another experiment using human embryos for DNA splicing.

"Lenore, we've got to slow down and look at the data. It's not possible to analyze the DNA sequences that quickly. There are literally billions of base pairs in every chromosome to —"

Lenore rolled her eyes and interrupted, "There are literally billions of dollars at stake! Think of the future! The perfection of these techniques will change our whole concept of childbearing. No more risk. Get what you want."

"I want to finish analyzing the data from our first experiment!" Randy raised his voice in a rare moment of defiance.

"Look, Randy, it's all one big experiment. There's always a data gathering phase and a data analysis phase. Let's not jump to phase 2 too quickly."

This time Randy rolled his eyes. *Look who is jumping ahead too quickly. You're making me look like I'm the one pushing ahead.* He kept his thoughts to himself and kept listening.

Lenore continued, "I say we make at least six to ten embryo gene manipulations to test our technique and perfect our methodology. Then we can sit back and use the DNA sequencers to help us figure out all of the small, exact changes."

Randy sighed heavily. "What about the failure of our first experiment? That baby had a pituitary adenoma as big as her whole head!" He glared at Lenore. "And what about your safety? Are you planning to donate your womb again? I don't think we can get anyone else to do it, not after what happened to you. I wouldn't feel right about that."

Lenore softened and turned away. She closed Randy's office door for added privacy. "Being a surrogate may not really be so dangerous to others, Randy. Maybe the idea to carry the experiment myself wasn't such a good idea." She lowered her voice. "I've had several abortions in the past. Maybe that set me up to miscarry our experiment. Maybe I'm just not a good surrogate choice. Willing, yes. Dedicated to the cause, yes. But physically? Maybe we just made a wrong decision, that's all."

Randy shook his head. "No way. You had

a miscarriage because the baby died from its brain tumor! Your losing the baby had nothing to do with you! It's a part of nature." He paused. "Just the same, I don't think we've worked out all the safety issues. We can't ask other young women to be surrogates when we're not sure it's safe."

"Look, Randy, I had trouble with the pregnancy from the beginning. I had cramps and spotting way before I lost the experiment. Maybe a young, fresh womb is what we need — not an irritable, old, used one like mine." Lenore sat on Randy's desk, pushing a stack of papers aside.

Randy had not yet shared with Lenore about the loss of the Dalmatian surrogate. He knew he didn't have reasons — only doubts. *She will refuse to change her plans unless I have firm data,* Randy mused. "I don't feel good about this."

"I don't pay you to feel good. I pay you for results." Lenore winked. She knew she needed to bolster his ego. "By the way, don't think I don't know that you are the best in the world at this type of work. No one has reported getting this far. No one."

Randy sat quietly without responding. *At least she realizes that!*

UBI's president went on, "You just work at setting up the new embryo manipulation.

We must have fifty frozen embryos in the freezer since linking with the infertility clinic over at Crestview. Let's not let 'em go to waste." She looked directly at Randy. She wasn't making a request. "Do your part. I'll do mine. You do the gene splicing. I'll find a suitable surrogate where we can grow it until harvest."

"What will you tell the potential surrogates?"

"What we always do. It's cutting-edge research. It could be dangerous, even life-threatening. They will have to sign the informed consent forms just like always."

Randy looked unconvinced. "Where will you find women willing to do that?"

"I can find them. Pay people enough and they will risk anything." Lenore walked to the door and looked at her watch. "I have to go." She exited without further discussion. The issue was closed. Randy knew he wouldn't bring it up again.

John Beckler yawned and ate another chocolate-covered cookie. He patted his abdomen. *Much more of this and I'll be competing with Conrad.* The screen in front of him showed a vision of Room 525 from the view of a fly on the central light above an empty patient crib. No action there.

He turned up the volume on his headset, picking up the sound through Tyson's beeper. Beckler wanted to hear the music playing in the background in the O.R. Tyson always played music while he operated. Unknown to the F.B.I. agent, the doctor's beeper hung on the phone cord against the wall. He clipped it there before each case, so the nurse could retrieve any messages and make the calls for him.

Not realizing that Tyson had removed the beeper, John adjusted the volume again to compensate for Tyson's voice, which sounded distant. *Maybe the sterile gown is muffling the sound waves.* Just then the phone in the O.R. rang. John tore the headset off. *Man! Where's he got that thing — sitting on the phone?* He turned down the volume again and sighed. *Now I can't hear him talking!* He edged up the volume once more. *There.* He listened attentively. The anesthesiologist told a coarse joke. *I can't believe they talk like that while they're operating!* In a few minutes the phone rang again, sending the needle on John's machine bending into the red zone and John into a frantic flail to remove the headset. "Ow!"

John sighed. *Take that blasted thing away from the phone!* He looked around his cramped quarters. *I should have taken an inside job on this one.*

The staff nurse returned to Room 523 and handed Elizabeth a sterile urine cup. "Here. Use this the next time you need to pee. Because of your fever, Dr. Forrest has ordered a urine culture. There are some instructions on this paper. Do you need me to go over them with you?"

Elizabeth contorted her mouth into a distasteful frown. "No thanks. I've done it before."

"A phlebotomist will come by to get cultures of your blood."

More frowns from Elizabeth.

"Doctor's orders," the nurse responded. "I'm sorry." She squeezed the patient's calves. "Any pain here?"

"No."

The nurse looked at the IV site. "No redness here." She took an insentive spirometer out of a sealed plastic covering. "This is an instrument to help you take deep breaths and exercise your lungs. Sometimes when you have had an operation, your lungs aren't expanded all of the way, especially if you are reluctant to breathe deeply because of pain." She held it up in front of Elizabeth. "Seal your lips around this mouthpiece and inhale as deeply and strongly as you can."

Elizabeth obeyed.

"Good. Slide this gauge up as you get stronger." She pointed to a yellow tab on the side of the spirometer. "Use this every hour while you are awake."

The patient nodded and stayed quiet.

"Dr. Forrest didn't want me to check your incision. He said he'd do that himself on evening rounds."

"Great," Elizabeth responded sarcastically.

The nurse left as the phlebotomist arrived. A gentle man with gray hair, he prepared for his duty silently. Finally when he was ready, he spoke quietly, "You'll feel a little bee sting."

"$%@#!!"

The phlebotomist continued working. "That's some language for a fourteen-year-old."

Ted Grandby looked at Elizabeth sternly.

"That's some $#@% bee sting!" she reacted sharply.

The man finished his work and put a Band-aid on Elizabeth. He walked slowly back to the lab, shaking his head. *I haven't heard words like that since I was in the service! And right in front of her father, too. Young people just aren't like they used to be.*

CHAPTER 27

"When c-can I see Dad?" It was only the hundredth time Bradley had asked the question in the last two hours.

He sounds like a broken record. Julie looked at her son. *Poor child. He is broken. What am I doing? Even Brad was better than no father at all.* "Soon, Bradley. We'll go home soon."

"When? When? When?" Bradley danced around the room like he was riding a horse.

"Whoa, partner!" Julie gathered the scampering boy into her arms. "You're getting too big for me!" She paused and straightened his collar. "There are a few things Mommy needs to do first. I hope it won't take too long." Bradley squirmed. "Now, I know one little boy who needs a bath and a bed!"

"A baf! A baf!" Bradley broke into his dance again. Julie chased him down the hall into the little bathroom. For the next thirty minutes Bradley "snorkled" in the tub. She put out his pajamas and let him dress himself. Slowly, carefully, he accomplished his task. A few minutes later Julie stroked his blond bangs and kissed him good night. "Mommy?"

"What, son?"

"Belle says I should pray."

"Go ahead, Bradley. You can pray," Julie prompted.

Bradley folded his stubby fingers. "Dear God, fank you for the day. Help us get home s-soon." He stopped.

Julie waited. Finally she prompted with a whisper, "Amen."

"Amen!" Bradley unfolded his hands and grabbed his pillow in a tight stranglehold.

"Amen," Julie said softly. It was her prayer too.

There were praises and thanksgiving all around the circle. Everyone in Patterson's west wing had heard the news: Belle's grandson, Brad, had become a believer! Everyone felt like singing. Richard Yoder felt like eating. "Let's eat the cake!"

Alice, his wife, cast him a sharp look. "Richard, you know your sugar —"

Craig looked at Alice and came to Richard's defense. "Let him go, Alice. He's a big boy. Besides, we've got a reason to celebrate. This is an awesome answer to prayer!"

Richard looked back at his Alice and winked. “I’ll just have a small piece.”

The cake, a chocolate cake with white frosting, had been baked by Belle the day before. Jen Slabaugh looked at the cake and moaned. “With my diabetes, maybe I should pass.”

Craig gave her the push she wanted. “Just take some extra insulin. Get the aide to check your glucose level in a few hours.”

Sandy rolled her eyes. “Leave it to the retired pharmacist to give out drug advice.”

“O.K., everybody, before you dig in, let’s bless the food.” Ben Kreider wobbled to his feet. Silence fell across the small group. Ben began, “Almighty Lord, we come to you with our praise and thanksgiving today.”

“Yes,” Belle whispered.

“For a soul has been delivered from hell, and a victory has been won!” Ben continued.

Craig Nesselrodt lifted a spotty hand to the Lord and shut his eyes.

Belle began to cry. Alice Yoder blew her nose, and Jen Slabaugh pounded her fist into her hand.

“How can we say thank you? We honor you who has been made known to us through the gift of your Son. Your Son’s blood provided the way for us to enter into life.”

Richard Yoder nodded his head in agreement as Ben continued, his voice punctuated by a rising fervor, "And your love has rescued another life from sure destruction! Thank you, Father, thank you!"

"Thank you, Lord"s reverberated around the circle.

The group fell silent again. Ben prompted, "All the people said . . ."

The group followed in unison: "Amen!"

John Beckler sat patiently. Today marked day 5 of surveillance. So far, nothing. Dr. Tyson was the model doctor. Compassion marked his words; confidence and direction punctuated his actions. So far everyone that encountered him trusted him, including the F.B.I. *I wish I'd have known about this guy a few years ago when Crystal was sick.*

John adjusted the volume control in front of him. *Another phone conversation! I get a bit tired of these one-sided conversations. If we have to do this much longer, I'm going to ask to tap his home phone, too.* John listened as Tyson spoke.

"I'm leaving again in the morning. The President would like me to be in town for a few days before the hearings begin on Monday."

A pause followed.

Tyson lowered his voice. "I'd like that."

Some papers rustled, and Tyson's breath was punctuated by a sigh. "No."

Another pause without sound, other than Tyson's breath.

"She's expecting to come. I — I don't want to bring this all up until after the trip."

The wood flooring creaked. *He must be pacing. Nervous, Dr. Tyson?* John Beckler smiled.

"She won't be there! I'll take care of that. The nursing coordinator is my friend and is going to help. I've told her that Tammy has become obsessed with me, that she needs to be let down gently, that she needs to have responsibility that she can't pass off during the hearings."

More steps over a creaking floor.

"She won't be there! She's tied up." He paused again.

"Why did you have to disrupt my life?" He chuckled.

More quiet laughing.

"Oooh. Uh-huh." Tyson breathed deeply.

"I can hardly wait." He paused. "O.K. I'll see you then."

The creaking floor abruptly stopped.

"You know I do." One final deep breath. "Bye-bye."

Click.

* * *

Leroy and Alta Gaines looked at the small infant in front of them. This was to be their last baby. Alta was forty-four. This baby, Jordan Michael, had come a month premature. The infant, the first boy of five children, carried his grandfather's name. His life was a total surprise. Alta had stopped taking birth control pills three years before and had not had a regular menstrual cycle since. The baby's first day of life came just two days before his transfer to Crestview Women and Children's Health Center. The child suffered from Down's syndrome and a high intestinal obstruction.

Dr. Web Tyson had spoken to the referring physician the day before and reluctantly accepted the patient in transfer from another facility seventy miles to the south. The child had just arrived. The staff nurse checked the child in with a few verbal orders by Dr. Tyson, who had not yet examined the infant. The child's room number was 525, by special request of Dr. Tyson.

Things were spinning at an incredible pace for Leroy and Alta. Their baby Jordan had been born Wednesday morning. From the start he seemed fine, but the pediatricians felt that his characteristic facial features mandated screening for Down's syndrome. When the test came back positive, the Gaineses wept. But Alta remained committed and cuddled the child close. Her milk was coming in, and she wanted to feed him. After his first successful feeding, the child began to vomit — more than just the typical little spit-up after a meal — true, voluminous, across-the-crib, projectile vomiting. The first time was disturbing enough, but when the episode repeated itself after the second and third feedings, the Gaineses grew increasingly alarmed. Something was definitely wrong! X-rays confirmed it. A bowel obstruction mandated a surgical consult. Dr. Tyson was the best in the state. For the Gaineses, the decision was easy. Their pediatrician arranged a transfer for the following day.

Leroy, a six foot, four inch welder, cradled the baby in one ham-sized palm. Since Alta had been discharged just the day before, a plastic I.D. bracelet still adorned her wrist.

She looked over her husband's shoulder and hummed softly while the baby slept. "He looks fine when he's sleepin'," Leroy whispered.

"Sure does," Alta responded. "Maybe they won't have to operate after all."

"Maybe Doc Norfleet is wrong. Didn't

Jennie throw up like this, too?" Leroy asked, thinking back to his oldest daughter.

"Oh, they all did a little," Alta reflected. "But nothing like this little fella. I've never seen anything like he did before."

Leroy grunted his response. A few minutes later he spoke again. "I'd forgotten what this is like." His eyes met Alta's.

Alta nodded. "It's been eight years since Lilly was born. Where did the time go?"

"When's the doctor coming in? Do you think they'll operate tonight?" Leroy looked at the time through a watch crystal so scratched you could barely make out the digital display.

"Oh, Leroy, maybe they won't have to," Alta said wistfully. "Maybe I should try feeding him again."

"You know what the nurse said, honey. Nothing until we talk to Dr. Tyson."

She held her hands to her breasts. "I've got to do something soon."

Leroy shrugged. After a few minutes he handed the baby to Alta. "Maybe I'll check with the nurses. They might know something." He lumbered out into the hall and up to the nurses' station. In a few minutes he was back. "Could be just about any time, she said. Might be soon, might not. Evidently this doctor is pretty busy."

Alta sighed. After another thirty minutes, the baby began to squirm and cry. She tried to rock him. After a few more minutes, she gave up. "I can't stand this anymore," she said. "I'm gonna feed him."

Leroy looked at her and shrugged again. "You know what the nurses —"

"I know, I know. But they don't feel like I do either."

"You know what happened the last time," her husband added timidly.

"Maybe it won't happen again. He looks O.K." Alta looked up. "Shut that door, Leroy — and make sure no one is comin'!"

Ted Grandby nodded politely at the hulk of a man closing the door to Room 525. The man appeared slightly distressed. Ted walked into Room 523 and opened his briefcase. The empty bed was scattered with teen magazines. *How can they read this stuff?* he thought, pushing a magazine to the side to make room for his briefcase. "Elizabeth?"

"I'm in the bathroom," came the muffled response.

Ted turned his attention to the contents of his briefcase. He took out a small Walkman and put on a set of earphones. After adjusting the volume, he closed his eyes. *There! I can hear everything perfectly.*

Inside the small cubicle of a bathroom, Elizabeth struggled to follow the instructions for gathering a sample for urinalysis. She maneuvered into position. "I've seen bigger bathrooms on airplanes," she muttered under her breath. When she was done, she opened a small vial containing a creamy white substance. Using an eyedropper, she slowly added three drops to the fresh specimen. She held it up and swirled the yellow fluid. *There. That ought to buy me a few extra days.*

Dr. Tyson introduced himself to Leroy and Alta Gaines. The patient, Jordan Michael, was sleeping in a small crib in the center of the room. "I've spoken at length with Dr. Norfleet. He's an excellent pediatrician, and I have no reason to doubt his diagnosis. I would, however, like to ask you a few questions and examine the child before I give you my opinion."

Alta nodded. Leroy responded, "Sure, Doc." He cast a wary eye toward his sleeping son. *He sure ate a lot.* He shrugged. No signs of trouble yet.

Dr. Tyson asked many questions about the patient, especially about his feeding patterns and his symptoms. He asked additional information about siblings, parents, and grandparents. In just a few minutes Dr. Tyson knew just about everything there was to know about the Gaines family. Alta looked at her baby and smiled. *He seems so content. He ate so well.*

"I'll need to examine him." Dr. Tyson smiled and lowered the crib rail. He put on his stethoscope to listen for bowel sounds. As he gently pushed the diaphragm of the stethoscope down onto the infant's abdomen, he turned his head away from the child for a brief moment. "When's the last time he had anything to — ahhh!"

His words were halted in mid-sentence by a volcano of freshly ingested milk. The warm liquid struck Tyson on the left cheek, showered his glasses, and dripped from his earlobe and chin. The surgeon jumped away from the child, who continued his vomiting onto Tyson's shoes. He opened his mouth to curse, but the taste of the milk on his own lips caused him to spit instead.

Alta stood, grabbed a burp-cloth, and began dabbing Tyson's forehead and face.

"My, oh, my!"

"*@&%$#!" Tyson ripped the cloth from her hand and spat into it. He wiped the tops of his leather shoes, collected his thoughts for a moment, and walked out. "I'll be back in a few minutes." Once he was in the hall, he literally ran to the staff restroom, where he repetitively spat into the sink. He looked at himself in the mirror. *I've got to get a shower.* He sighed and walked slowly to the O.R. changing area.

In Room 525, Leroy chuckled. "I told ya so, Alta. I told ya so."

Brad Forrest and Mary Jacobs sat at the central counter in the recovery room. Brad had just operated on a five-year-old boy who had lacerated his pancreas in a bicycle accident.

"That was pretty amazing," Mary commented.

"It looked like his pancreas had been severed by being pinched between his vertebral column and whatever impacted his anterior abdominal wall." He stood up and walked toward a Dictaphone. "Why don't you write the orders while I dictate the operative note?"

Mary looked surprised.

Brad spoke again. "Don't worry. I'll check them as soon as I'm done." After Brad dictated his note, he finished going over the orders with Mary. He looked at his watch. "It's getting late. You'd better catch up with Dr. Tyson. He's on tonight."

Mary nodded. "See you later."

★ ★ ★

Linda finished clearing the table and looked at Matt, who was loading the dishwasher. "I still can't believe how decisively the F.B.I. responded."

"I guess we just happened to push the right buttons. Evidently the present administration in Washington has been leaning on them pretty hard concerning this Surgeon General search. If it would have been anyone else, I think they'd have laughed in my face," Matt responded soberly. He closed the dishwasher. "I can't believe how quickly I've become dependent on this thing," he added, twisting the dial and punching the Normal Cycle button.

Linda smiled. "Missionary surgeon meets the twentieth century."

Matt's thoughts returned to Tyson. "Tyson's Senate confirmation hearings begin Monday. I doubt the F.B.I. will stay around after that. It sounded like they weren't really interested in uncovering any dirt in little, insignificant Green County — only in observing Dr. Tyson."

"It all seems so secretive," Linda responded. "Almost like a movie or something."

"Which reminds me," Matt added, "not a word of this, even after it's all over — not to anyone, including Mary. The feds specifically instructed us on that."

"Mary doesn't know?" Linda looked curious.

"Only me, because I made the inquiry, Brad, because they needed an inside contact, and you. I don't even think Brad told Julie. They forbade us from letting it out any further."

Linda walked into the next room and sat down. Matt hung a dishtowel over the sink and looked at the calendar Linda had put up next to the refrigerator. He looked to see if she had written anything for the following week. "Honey," Matt called, "what does this little red circle around the fifteenth mean?"

Linda smiled to herself and pretended not to hear. When he asked again, she shared the smile with him. "Just a little something I wanted to keep track of."

Her husband spoke in a high pitch, mimicking her as he walked in and sat next to her on the couch. "Just a little something I wanted to keep track of."

Linda giggled and kissed her husband on the forehead. *It never hurts to keep accurate records,* she thought as she folded back the cover of the magazine she was holding. Matt wouldn't see the title until the following day, when the clue would bypass him again: *Christian Parenting.*

Mary caught up with Dr. Tyson as he stood attentively viewing Jordan Gaines's X-rays. "See this?" Tyson tapped the X-ray film. "The large air bubble here, as well as the total absence of gas in the remainder of the abdomen, indicates a bowel obstruction." He sighed. "It looks like another Down's baby with duodenal atresia." He pulled down the films and shoved them into the large paper jacket. "We must see every baby like this in the whole South."

Mary nodded without speaking.

"These parents have no idea what they're in for. This kid might grow up, but he's always going to be a baby here!" He pointed to his forehead. "Let's go talk to them."

As they walked, Mary tried to lighten the conversation. "Congratulations on your new appointment."

"Thanks," Tyson responded tersely. "Let's get this over with. I leave early in the morning for D.C."

Mary followed him into the room. Dr. Tyson quickly introduced her to Leroy and Alta and their son, Jordan. "I've seen the X-rays." He paused. "And the results of the chromosome study." He shook his head and lowered his voice. "I've seen this combination of problems many times before — perhaps more than anyone else," he began. He continued with a detailed description of the multiple possible problems that are seen in patients with Down's syndrome. He talked about surgery, but only as one option, and emphasized the suffering and pain associated with recovery. He did not even mention the possibility of controlling the pain with medications.

Finally he stopped, and Leroy responded, "What are you suggesting we do?"

"As I see it, you have three options." Tyson raised a finger to emphasize his first point. "One, you can take the child home and do nothing. The child will want to eat, and if you feed him — well, you've seen what will happen." He paused and held up two fingers. "Two, you can put him through expensive and painful surgery, with the realization that we may only be prolonging his agony. You must understand that he may have other congenital problems that we have not yet discovered. And we can never cure his retardation." He held up three fingers. "Or three, we can leave him right here, in the comfort of his hospital crib. We won't prolong his suffering with surgery. We'll keep him comfortable with pain medication and just let nature take its course." He paused. "Death is a real relief for most of these kids," he added slowly. "It usually doesn't take long when there are so many problems." He looked at the couple in front of him. *These simple people aren't capable of making an objective decision.* He spoke again softly. "He could even die tonight."

Alta looked at Leroy with tears in her eyes. "I don't want him to suffer, honey."

Leroy's glistening eyes met his wife's. "Maybe just leaving him in God's hands would be best. Maybe he'll do a miracle."

Mary looked at the couple, who were arm in arm and wet-faced. She wanted to scream, "It's only a simple operation! He might not have any other problem — just mental retardation. It's not right to let him die just because of that!" But she bit her lip and stayed quiet. A burning sensation in her upper abdomen shortened her breath.

Leroy looked at Tyson. "Can we think about it overnight?"

"Sure." Tyson turned to go. "I'll be leaving for Washington. One of my associates will check with you in the morning." With that, he was gone.

Mary stumbled into the hall and followed Tyson, who was maintaining a surgeon's pace. *Why didn't I speak up?*

When they got to the nurses' station, Web turned to her. "Why don't you take off? It's Friday night." Tyson winked. "Med students have better things to do than hang out here."

Mary's face reflected her surprise. "It's my assigned call night. I'm here to help."

"Take off! You've worked hard." Web sighed and looked at his watch. "You know, so have I." He picked up the phone, then looked at Mary and raised his voice a notch. "Go on!" He turned his attention to the phone. "Operator, page Dr. Forrest for me. There's been a change in the call schedule. He's on tonight. Thanks." He hung up the phone and watched Mary disappearing through the front entrance.

In a minute the phone rang. "Brad? Tyson here. I'm sorry to grab you on short notice like this, but Latner must have really screwed up this call schedule. I'm supposed to be in Washington, and now I see I'm supposed to take call tonight."

Brad didn't wait for him to ask. Without Julie around, he had no reason not to volunteer. "I'll take the calls. Just let the operator know."

"Thanks, Brad," Tyson responded. *That was easier than I thought.* He told Brad about the new patients and hung up the phone.

He sat down and dictated an admission note on Jordan Michael Gaines. After he finished, he scribbled some additional admit orders, beginning with "Do Not Resuscitate." He looked down the hallway. *Where's Tammy?* He found her moments later in her office.

"Hi, babe." He kissed her and sat on her desk.

Tammy smiled. "Rough day?"

"Routine."

She pushed her paperwork aside. "I'm off at 11:30." She smiled again. "Want me to come by?"

Tyson shifted uncomfortably. "I'd love it, but I've had a schedule change. I'm heading for D.C. tonight." He paused. "Forrest is taking my calls. That's why I've come. I wanted to say goodbye."

Tammy looked unconvinced and stayed quiet. Tyson spoke again. "Are you coming up next week for the hearings?" He knew the answer.

She sulked. "No. The supervisor has chosen a great time to enforce a new leave policy!" Tammy reported sarcastically. "She won't let me go because I didn't request the time four weeks in advance. She's an idiot! She knows I didn't know about this four weeks ago!"

Tyson cursed. "I could talk to Administration."

"Right. I'm sure that would put me in good graces with her."

Tammy took Web's hand. "You know, I have half a mind just to quit." She paused, stroking his palms. "I won't be needing this job after you're sworn in anyway. It's too long a commute from D.C."

Web squeezed her hands. "I — I wouldn't do anything drastic." He sighed. The air seemed thick and uncomfortable. After another moment, he changed the subject. "There is something else I need you to do."

Tammy looked at him suspiciously. *I thought you just came by to say goodbye!*

"You've seen the new admit in 525. I saw your initials on the nursing notes." Tyson added, "The parents are simple. I'm sure they will do whatever I recommend."

He paused, and Tammy sighed. "What are you saying, Web?"

John Beckler glanced at the tape. It was rolling. He turned up the volume again. *Yes, Dr. Tyson, what are you saying?*

In spite of his strong convictions Web Tyson would never say, "Assist the death," "Kill the patient," or even "This is an infanticide case." Instead, he said what he always did: "Make this one very comfortable, Tammy." He turned to go. "Let's not allow this to drag out. The parents are good people."

Tammy looked at him sharply, then softened. "Sure, Web. I'll do what's right." She pulled him away from the door and kissed him passionately. "I'll see you next week."

"Come on, Alta," Leroy said softly. "Let's go to the motel. We can't do him any good stayin' here."

Alta resisted. "I want to be with him." The tears flooded over her cheeks again. "You heard what he said," she sobbed. "He could die . . . tonight!"

Leroy persisted, "It's not gonna help him none for us to be sick from lack of rest. You stayed up all night on the night he was born, and you didn't do much better last night. You need to sleep, honey." Leroy sighed and put his hand on her shoulder. "Look at him. He looks fine."

Jordan Michael slept quietly in his crib.

Leroy urged again. "Come on, honey. It's for the best. Let's go."

Alta stood. She knew she needed rest. She turned to Leroy. "Oh, baby, what are we going to do?"

He gripped his wife's shoulders. She had always been the strong one. Now Leroy knew he needed to hold her up. "We'll talk about it in the morning. Everything will be clearer then." With his shoulder wet from Alta's tears, he took her by the hand. "Let's go."

Next door, in Room 523, Elizabeth Grandby took off her Walkman and dried her own tears. *Get a grip, girl! Don't let 'em see you like this!* She looked at the clock on the wall. *It's almost time for vital signs again.*

CHAPTER 28

Mary shuffled her feet along the empty sidewalk in front of the main hospital building at Crestview. *Why didn't I speak up!* She looked up at the sky, which was rapidly losing the last hint of daylight. *I blew it, God! I blew it!*

She walked around the clinic building and into the large employee parking lot that bordered a dense woods. She needed time to think, and the night air seemed to clarify her thoughts. *This child is like all the rest Matt and I looked at. Once the parents tell Tyson they don't want surgery, the child will be doomed!* She bit her lip, which trembled from regret and anger. *I can't believe how compassionate and smooth Tyson acts. After he finishes with them, the last thing they would decide is to "prolong their child's agony."*

Mary felt a chill. The temperature was dropping with the nightfall, and she wasn't wearing a coat. Mary looked back up at the hospital from the edge of the forest. It seemed to loom eerily, with a thousand lights streaming from the windows into the darkness. She thought back to what Tyson had said. "He could even die tonight." She shuddered. *What is that, Dr. Tyson? A warning? A threat?* Suddenly she knew what she would do — what she must do. She turned and ran toward the hospital entrance.

Web spoke to Lenore from his car phone. He used the speaker so he could keep his hands on the wheel. "Yes, I'm serious. Let's go tonight! I've had enough of this place! I'm on my way home now to get my things."

"Tonight? Web, I thought you were on call."

"Forrest volunteered to take my call." He paused. "I'm a free man."

"Web, I can't —"

"Come on, babe. We can have our own private celebration. I've already called ahead and extended my reservation."

Lenore sighed. *I need to keep this guy wanting me like this — at least for a while.*

"I'd like that, Web, but I've got things to tie up at UBI," she lied. She gripped her forehead, which had begun to pound . . . again.

This time Web sighed. His little plan wasn't working like he'd hoped. "I've got a presidential suite, one with a whirlpool. We could get some champagne and —"

Lenore raised her voice and interrupted. "I can't, Web. It all sounds nice, but I'll have to take a rain check." She paused. "I'll see you up there tomorrow evening."

Web remained silent for a moment. "O.K.," he sighed. "I'll see you tomorrow. Just ask for me at the desk."

Lenore hung up the phone and folded a long, hooded robe. She then placed it in a small carry-bag and walked to the closet. *It's in your own best interest, Web,* she thought, *to be without me tonight. What I have planned is far more important to insure your future — and mine.* She walked to the window and looked at the moon. The sky was clear. *The Wanoset will be beautiful to-night — I just know it.*

"Bye, ya'll. Work hard! I'll see ya tomorrow!" Tammy's shift had ended, and she made her exit in a prominent fashion through the main doors across from the elevator. Instead of riding to the ground floor, she slipped off on the fourth and used the back steps to ascend slowly to 5 north. The doorway opened just across from Room 525. She steadied her breath. *Why do I get so nervous doing this?* She stood on the fifth-floor landing in the stairwell and looked through the window in the door. Nobody was in the hall. She gasped a deep breath and took out a syringe filled with clear fluid. *I want to get this over with. I wish Web was in town. This doesn't seem to bother him at all.* Silently she opened the door and slipped out of the stairwell and into the hall. In a second she stood in Room 525. She closed the door behind her and crept toward the crib. The lights in the room were off, the only illumination coming from the glow of a call button on the wall. Tammy squinted her eyes and located the infant's IV line. *There,* she thought. She pulled out the syringe and uncapped the needle. In the darkness she felt for the injection port so she could inject the medicine.

"Conrad, you'd better get in there!" John Beckler spoke with firmness but without raising his voice.

"Ted Grandby" got up and walked for the door, his "Walkman" still in place.

A hand pulled sharply on the tangle of strings on the wall near the head of the infant's crib. In the darkness and haste, the call button string and the fluorescent light were flipped on. "Ahh!" Tammy dropped the syringe to the floor. "You nearly scared me to death!"

"Sorry. I thought you might have needed some light," Mary responded.

The baby cried, awakened by Tammy's scream.

Tammy hid the syringe under her foot. "What are you doing in here?" she demanded.

"I'm a medical student. I helped Dr. Tyson work the baby up earlier today." She realized she hadn't answered Tammy's question. She certainly hadn't explained why she was sitting in the corner with the lights off.

Just then a voice cracked over the intercom. A nurse was answering the call button. "Can I help you?"

"It's O.K.," Tammy snapped. "I've got it."

The intercom squeaked again. "Tammy? I thought you left. Shift's over, girl. Get out of here." The night unit secretary certainly was feeling punchy.

"On my way," Tammy responded.

"What are *you* doing here?" Mary turned the question back to Tammy.

"I was doing a final IV check."

"In the dark?" Mary proceeded boldly.

Tammy faced her. "I didn't want to wake the baby!" She took the light cord out of Mary's hand and pulled firmly.

Under the cover of darkness, she quickly retrieved her syringe. She turned to go.

"Coming out?" Tammy asked innocently.

"I'm going to stay and see if I can get the baby back to sleep."

"Suit yourself," the frustrated nurse said. She jumped into the hall and ran into Ted Grandby.

"Excuse me," Ted offered.

Tammy huffed a curse and kept walking.

"Blast it all!" John whispered aloud. *That med student messed everything up! We just about had something going down, and she pops up and stops everything!*

John pressed the button on a small, hand-held radio transmitter. "Conrad, Garry, see if you can figure out a way to get that med student off the floor. Buy her some coffee. Anything! Just get her away from the baby long enough for the nurse to return."

Conrad radioed back, using a cellular telephone. "What's going on, John?"

"I'm not exactly sure. A nurse came in. It looked like she had a syringe. I think she was about to inject something into the child's IV. I'll review it on the tape and see. Just when she was starting, the lights came on, and the med student interrupted everything."

Conrad lowered his voice to a whisper. "It's the student who reviewed the charts with Dr. Stone, John. I think we'd better let her in on the gag so she'll stay out of the way."

"Use your own judgment on that one. I'm out here, you're in there. Just get her away from that baby!"

Garry Sanders, alias Frank Snyder, whispered into his cellular phone from beyond the doorways to 5 north. "I've had a chance to sneak a peek at the Gaines chart, and Deb looked at the med list when the nurses were away from the station. There are no orders for an IV medication for that patient, John. If you can definitely identify a syringe on that tape of yours, it may mean something really was up after all."

"Good pickup, Garry. You'd better get back to your location. See if you can hear any conversation at the nurses' station."

Mary patted the crying infant on the rump. When that didn't work, she tried rocking him. When that failed, she opted for a walk. With the IV, it was a bit cumbersome. But somehow she managed to hold the newborn cradled like a football in one arm and the IV bag in the other. She slowly exited the room and began a lap around the floor.

Behind her, Ted Grandby set out "to stretch his legs."

As she started up the hall, she could hear Tammy's voice at the nurses' station. She slowed down and listened. "I forgot to check the schedule for tomorrow. I just came back to check. I used the stairs for exercise," Tammy babbled nervously. "Anyway, when I saw that call light go on, I just responded."

She's lying! Mary thought. *She came in before the call light ever went on. She wasn't coming in to respond to a call light. So why was she — ?* The answer hit Mary like a spear. *All along I was waiting for Tyson, and maybe he wasn't coming in after all! He has someone else do it for him!*

Mary stepped up her pace, holding the infant close. She watched Tammy cautiously as she passed. *Now what do I do? She's like a vulture waiting to strike! I can't just leave him here!* Tammy looked at her suspiciously as she passed. "What are you doing? Dr. Tyson didn't authorize this!"

"I'm just taking the child for a walk, to settle him down," Mary responded with more calm than she felt.

"Put the child back in his crib. He's too sick to be up and around with his IV!" Tammy wasn't making a request. "Besides, it's time you got some sleep. Medical students aren't needed up here now," she taunted. "The nurses can care for him."

Mary slowly turned and walked back toward Room 525. As she walked, her discomfort with the situation continued to grow. *I can't just leave the child here! But I can't stay here either. And she's likely to return as soon as I leave.* When she got to the doorway, she looked back up the long hallway to the nurses' station. Ted Grandby stood beyond Tammy, who stood gazing at Mary as if to see if she would obey.

Mary's eyes locked momentarily with Tammy's. *I've got to save this baby!* She turned so that her back shielded the infant from the nurse's view. Slowly she placed the IV bag on top of the cradled infant to free her right hand. Then, with one fluid motion she bolted through the stairwell door. She could hear Tammy screaming behind her.

"Hey! Where do you think you're going!" Tammy ran down the long hallway. "Bring back that baby!"

Ted Grandby easily outstrode Tammy to the back stairwell. The Snyders moved quickly through the main entrance doors and hit the front stairs at a full run. Tammy screamed for Security. In all the commotion nobody noticed Elizabeth Grandby pushing her IV pole onto a main elevator.

Mary descended two flights of stairs and exited onto a quiet orthopedic floor. Above her she heard her name shouted into the stairwell: "Mary! Come back!" *Wasn't that Ted Grandby? What does he want?* She knew him from making rounds with Dr. Forrest on his daughter Elizabeth. She walked quietly past the nurses' station and through the swinging front doors of 3 north. She then paused at the entrance to the main stairwell to listen. A man and woman thundered past. When she heard no more noise, she slipped into the stairwell behind them. She descended to the basement and walked back to the rear stairs. *What do I do now?* She looked at the small, sleeping infant in her arms. *At least he's calm. My heart's in my throat! O God . . .*

She listened again before entering the stairwell. She then climbed slowly to the second level and sprinted through the empty hallway to a sheltered connecting overpass that led to the Crestview outpatient clinics. *This IV is a dead giveaway! If I can only get to the clinic!* The connecting walk was lined with tinted windows giving a view of the roadway beneath. Mary didn't bother to look. She felt only the push to get away, an inner drive to take the infant to safety.

The walkway opened onto a broad waiting area on the clinic's second floor. It was quiet, uninhabited, and dimly lit. Mary walked past the reception desk and through the doors leading to the exam rooms. There she paused to let her eyes adjust to the darkness and tried to slow her racing heart. *Think! What do I do now?* She walked to the counter. *I've got to get in touch with Dr. Forrest. He'll know what to do.* She dialed his number. One ring, two, three, four . . . *Come on! Answer!* Mary pinched the phone between her ear and shoulder, bounced the infant with one hand, and held the IV in the other. Five rings, six . . .

"Hello." The voice was thin, and female.

"May I speak to Dr. Forrest?"

"I'm sorry. He's not in. May I take a message?"

Mary sighed with frustration. *Now what do I do?*

When she didn't speak for a moment, Belle spoke again. "Hello?"

"Belle?"

"Yes."

"This is Mary Jacobs calling."

"I remember you."

"I really need to talk to Dr. Forrest."

"He hasn't returned from the hospital yet. You know Brad. Can I have him call you?"

"I'll be hard to reach. Maybe I'll try later. Thanks." Mary sighed again. After a moment she spoke again. "Belle?"

"Yes, dear."

"I'm in some trouble," she blurted. "I can't explain it now. Will you pray?"

"Of course."

"Bye." Mary tried to squelch a sob. *O God, what have I done?* She sank into a chair. *What now? I can't have Dr. Forrest paged. He's not on call. Tyson would answer. That's all I need.*

The infant began to cry. Mary did too.

"Find her!" Tammy hissed. "Don't just stand there!"

A dark-haired, young man in a tan hospital security outfit spoke into a hand-held radio. "This is a Code Orange. An infant's been kidnapped. Suspect is a blonde female around twenty-five years of age. She's wearing a dark skirt and carrying a sick infant with an IV."

John Beckler pounded his fist into his hand. "What are you doing, Conrad? Talk to me!"

"Ted Grandby" picked up his cellular phone. "I've got nothing here. The girl vanished into the stairwell. By the time I got there, she had disappeared! I've been up and down. No one at the nursing stations on the north wing remembers seeing her at all."

"Garry?"

"Frank Snyder" responded, "Nothing here either, boss. We've got the front lobby and the physicians' entrances covered. She's not been through here."

John spoke firmly. "We need to get to her before Security finds her. If the locals get to her first, she'll spill her suspicions, and this whole operation will be useless."

He sighed. "Let's get to her and get that infant back in Room 525!"

Mary could hear the hospital intercom issuing the repetitive message. "Code Orange! A Code Orange is in effect!"

She put the baby on the table in the center of the room. She then frantically opened cabinets until she found the supplies she needed. She quickly unwrapped the infant's little arm and removed the IV.

Overhead, the message boomed. "Code Orange. Repeat! Code Orange in effect."

She gently pulled out the intravenous cannula and held pressure over the stick site. After a minute she put a Band-aid over the site and threw the IV supplies into the trash.

Just then the room was flooded with light.

All over the clinic building daytime lighting had been reintroduced.

"Code Orange! Code Orange!"

It looks like it's just you and me, little one. Let's get out of here!

She scooped the child into her arms and ran to the back stairs. Once she reached the ground level, she instinctively pushed through a door marked "Emergency Exit." She stumbled into the night air as an alarm sounded behind her. *Oh great, announce your exit to the world,* she scolded herself. She had exited at the rear of the building. *My car! I've got to get to my car.* She was parked on the opposite side of the complex, in front of the main hospital.

Mary ran straight for the woods in front of her. Once inside the cover of the trees, she edged around the hospital's perimeter toward the front parking lot. The lot was well lit, but she was hidden by the thick forest. A branch stung her cheek. *Slow down,* she thought to herself as a twig snapped into the night's solitude. *They'll hear you!* She edged closer. *There! I parked just beyond that white van.* She paused behind a tall pine to quiet her labored breathing. As she prepared to run, she set her eyes on her small economy car.

Her heart sank. *Security!*

CHAPTER 29

As the minutes ticked by, Tammy's agitation escalated. *I guess I need to tell the attending physician. I wish I could speak to Web. If only he hadn't left town!* She sighed. *I suppose I'll let Dr. Forrest know. He's on call for Web tonight.* She picked up the phone and pressed 0. "Page Dr. Forrest." She slammed the phone down.

In a few moments the phone chirped. "Five north, Nurse Manager," Tammy stated flatly.

"This is Dr. Forrest. I was paged."

Tammy filled him in on the situation. "Dr. Forrest, I must inform you that the medical student has taken one of the patients off of the floor without authorization."

"Mary?"

"Yes."

Brad shook his head. "I don't understand. What are you saying? What did she do?"

"Exactly what I said, Doctor. This — this student doctor has left the floor with one of our patients — an infant — without permission."

"An infant? Who?"

"The Gaines baby in 525 that Dr. Tyson admitted earlier today — uh, yesterday," she corrected, looking at her watch. "She was hanging around the baby's room all night. Then suddenly she just snatched the child and ran."

Understanding began to dawn for Brad. He nodded his head. "That's the Code Orange?"

"Now you're getting it, aren't you, Doctor?" Tammy responded spitefully.

"Have you told the parents?"

"Not yet. I'm following protocol. I'm to notify you first."

"Good. I'll take care of the parents. I'm the official attending."

"Thank you, Doctor," Tammy retorted. "Goodbye!"

Brad hung up the phone. He quickly signed off the emergency record in his hand and handed it to the E.R. unit secretary. "Tell these parents the child is free to go. I'll see her again in the office to remove the sutures in a week."

"Thank you, Dr. Forrest."

Brad turned and skipped to the exit of the emergency department. *I've got to talk to John Beckler!*

John looked at the screen in front of him

and listened to the hospital's security radio transmission. He relayed the information to Conrad.

"Conrad, get to the rear of the clinic building. An alarmed exit door has sounded."

"Shouldn't we cover her car?"

"No. I can see it from here. It's too late. Security is everywhere! Our only hope is to intercept her before she gets to her car."

Web Tyson sat on the side of the bed, his soul dark, his mood oppressed, and his eyes far from sleep. *What's wrong with me? I'm on the verge of the opportunity of a lifetime. Power. Prestige. I've got it all — and it's all come by my own hand.*

He smiled thinly at that thought. He chided himself, *Why are you so blue? Just look at what you've accomplished — and from such meager beginnings. And now,* he thought, *the women are even lining up at my door.* He thought about Lenore. *What a beauty she is!* He sighed. *So why do I feel so depressed, so empty, so weighted down?* He stood up and opened the small refrigerator in the plush hotel room. *There. Maybe this is what I need to break out of this funk.*

He poured himself a drink and turned on the TV.

* * *

Lenore felt renewed vibrancy — new power. She always felt that way after meeting with the inner circle. She jumped as the phone rang. *Who could it be at this hour?*

On the other end, Tammy had retreated away from the busyness of the nursing station to use the phone in Room 525. *Nobody can hear me so far from the desk,* she thought.

"Hello."

"Lenore, this is Tammy. Something's up. I wasn't sure who else to call."

Lenore twisted her face as she listened to the story. @#$%! After a few minutes listening to the nearly hysterical nurse, Lenore interrupted. "Look! It's beyond you now. Call the Green County sheriff's department! They can assist the search. Try to keep this under wraps. Downplay it with the parents! We don't want anything exploding that will cast a public shadow on Tyson!"

She listened to Tammy's concerns again. "You say this was the student who was working with Forrest?"

"Yes," Tammy replied. "They were together almost constantly."

"He's behind this, Tammy. I know it."

"@#$%!"

"You need to get out of there. With you hovering around, you'll only bring more suspicion back on yourself."

"No one suspects anything, Lenore."

"Just the same, get out of there. Call me when you're home."

"Lenore, I —"

"Do it!"

Tammy bit her trembling lower lip. "O.K."

"We have some more work to do."

John Beckler put in a new cassette and pressed Record. *What is going on around this madhouse?*

Mary edged deeper into the cover of the trees. Slowly she picked her way through a tangle of briars and underbrush. The moon provided just enough light for her to make out the next step or two. The parents! *If I could only get the infant to the parents! I could explain everything, and everything would be —*

"Waaa! Waaa!" The infant's cry penetrated the quiet night. Although it was weak, it sounded like a scream to Mary. She pushed her index finger gently through the baby's lips. Silence returned as the baby began to suck. Mary sighed with relief. *Quiet down, little one. I'll get you to your mommy soon.* She bounced him for a few seconds longer and then began stepping slowly through the forest again.

When she reached the edge of the tree line, she could see Crestview Street, a divided highway with a grass median. *What now?* She looked toward the north. *There! Why didn't I think of it sooner? A bus stop!* She stayed off the sidewalk and next to the trees. Twice as she walked the distance of a hundred yards she stopped in the shadows to watch a county police car pass. *Great! I can guess who they're looking for!*

She waited in the shadow of a tall bush until she saw the bus coming. The bus stop had a small shelter with a bench. Twisting her left ankle as she ran across the uneven ground, she sprawled awkwardly onto the grass.

The bus driver slowed to see if anyone was in the shelter. Not spotting anyone, he signaled to pull back into the traffic.

He doesn't see me! There won't be another bus through here for an hour!

Mary lifted her hand in a frantic wave and screamed, "Stop!"

The bus slowed to a stop. *Thank you, God!* She gathered up the baby, brushed the grass off her skirt, and climbed into the bus labeled "University B."

The sheriff protested, "Look, Lenore, if

she goes back to her dorm, that's really outside my jurisdiction. Outside the county, we let the city police —"

"I'm not asking you, Robert!" Lenore snorted. "Just find her, even if you have to go outside the county!"

"The city cops will raise a stink if they see us," he whined.

"Just tell 'em you're out for a joy ride. Tell 'em you're off. Tell 'em whatever you want to. That's your problem. Just do it — and keep it out of the official police record!"

The sheriff sighed. "I don't like it, Lenore. The men are asking —"

Lenore interrupted again. "There's still the issue of that $25,000 car and your new boat, isn't there, Bob? How did you ever afford that on your salary?" She paused for effect. "And I'd hate for the media to start asking questions about your trip to Atlanta. Barbie sure had a bundle of fun on that trip, didn't she? And —"

"O.K., Lenore," the red-faced officer shouted. "O.K.!"

Lenore hung up the phone. *I knew he'd come to his senses. He always has before.*

The parents should be at the Crestview Manor. That's where most of them stay — if they're not camped out in the waiting rooms at the hospital, Mary thought. She looked at the small infant in her arms. *He seems O.K. No apparent injury from our little fall.*

She studied the map on the wall of the bus. *It looks like we'll stop just beyond the motel. I hope the parents understand.*

The bus rumbled on. Mary checked her watch. *1:30 A.M. I've been on the run for two hours!* She stared out the window. She could see the lighted yellow sign for the motel in the distance on the left. She had a sudden sinking thought! *What if Tammy called the parents and they're back at the hospital? I'd have to go back!* She swallowed hard. *I can't do that. No way.*

The bus stopped at a traffic light just short of the bus stop. Mary looked at the motel. A large man was standing in front of a motel door. The door opened, and Leroy Gaines stepped out into the night. *That's him! That's Leroy!* Mary squinted through the bus window. *But who's that? Ted Grandby? What's he doing here?* Mary's concern escalated. *He ran after me before, didn't he? I can't stop with him there! The snitch! He'll tell them I stole the baby!*

John Beckler looked out the window. A single security officer leaned against Mary's car. John returned to the back of the white van. He checked the various F.B.I. radios. They were all silent. Hospital security had every entrance under scrutiny.

He looked at the monitor. Room 525 was quiet.

He put his headset back on, still tuned to Dr. Web Tyson's pager. *What is he watching? That sounds disgusting!* He looked at his watch. *Doesn't our future Surgeon General ever sleep?*

Richard Yoder kicked over the trash can on the way to the bathroom. "Sorry, dear," he whispered.

Alice Yoder sighed and looked at the clock. Almost 2! "I wake up when you wake up even when we don't sleep in the same creaky bed." She chuckled, then admitted, "I've been awake for a while anyway."

"Is it your back again? Want some Tylenol?" Richard asked softly.

"No, no, it's not that." She paused. "I have the oddest feeling that someone's in trouble."

"Hmmm."

"I think we're supposed to pray."

The bus crossed the Nickel Bridge and turned toward Bridgewater University. *I guess I'll just take the baby back to the dorm and call Dr. Forrest. He has to be home by now!*

She looked at the baby. *He's getting dehydrated. He needs an IV and soon, or I'm going to be accused of something a whole lot worse than kidnapping!* The thought sickened her and tightened her gut into a tense knot of anxiety.

As she rode on in silence, she whispered a prayer. "Help me, God. I want to do the right thing." The knot in her stomach loosened slightly, and she leaned her head against the cool windowpane. "Help me find Dr. Forrest."

She exited the bus two blocks from her dorm. The street was empty except for a rescue squad vehicle parked outside the Bridgewater University Medical Center emergency department. She crossed the road and passed the large brick medical library. *Almost there,* she thought, *one more block.* She looked ahead to the dorm. Her room faced the street, and she squinted to see it.

My light's on! What's Kim doing up at this hour? She halted instinctively and moved into the shadow of a large oak tree to collect her thoughts. Then, ahead and beyond a row of cars parked along the street, she saw not one but two Green County police cars.

They're waiting for me! She froze and pressed herself against the tree. *I've got to get out of here! But what now? This baby needs some medical attention — and soon!*

She turned and walked slowly away, taking care to shield the baby from possible view by the police. Once she got to the end of the dormitory, she ducked behind a large hedgerow and collapsed. She was exhausted. The baby aroused and let out a weak cry. She looked at the little face and began to cry. *O Lord, I don't know what to do!* She thought about the bus and looked at her watch. *No, they don't run but once an hour until 6 in the morning. I can't sit out here for an hour! And my car is at Crestview.* She sighed. *My car is probably still surrounded by those crazy security guards!*

Suddenly she hurried to her feet, stirred by a new idea. *Kim's car! I can use my roommate's car to get away!* She edged along the side of the building until the parking lot behind the dormitory and Kim's blue Mazda were in view. She ran the forty yards to the car and opened the unlocked door. She put the baby on the floor in front of the passenger seat and frantically searched beneath the floor mat for the extra key. *Thank you, God!* She put the key in the ignition and pumped the accelerator. *Start, car, start!* After a few cranks, the car roared to life. She slowly pulled out of the lot with her lights off and turned up an alley leading behind the medical library and away from her dorm.

Suddenly a figure sat up in the seat behind her. A hand touched her shoulder.

Mary shrieked and slammed the brakes. "Ahhh!" She reached for the car door as the intruder flipped on the dome light.

"Mary, wait!" A strong hand restrained her.

In the mirror she could see him. "Dr. Forrest! Am I glad to see you!"

Forty-five minutes later Leroy and Alta quietly strolled up the hallway on 5 north. Alta carried their little son, and Leroy held up the IV bag. They moved along in slow synchronous strides so as not to stretch the IV tubing. As they neared the nurses' station, a staff nurse came running to greet them. Before she could speak, Leroy exclaimed, "I hope it was O.K. We took him for a walk."

"Walkin' seems to quiet him down some," Alta added. "Nothin' like a long walk to settle a colicky baby, I always say."

The nurse slowly closed her mouth. "You mean you —"

"Could you pass along a message for the surgeons?" Leroy interrupted. "Tell them we have decided to let them operate."

"We want them to fix him," Alta beamed, "so we can take him home to the family."

Brad Forrest and Mary Jacobs walked up the sidewalk outside the main hospital at Crestview. Behind them the moon formed a perfect circle.

"I still don't know how you knew I'd get in Kim's car," Mary said, shaking her head.

"Call it a hunch." Brad laughed.

"I'd call it the Lord's leading."

Brad nodded in agreement and kept walking. "Say, why don't you get out of here? I'm just going to see a patient in the E.R. You've had a long night."

"Like you haven't?" Mary kept walking. They stepped into the main lobby. The county police were waiting. Two tall, uniformed men looked their way. "There you are!" They walked toward the duo.

"Look," Brad started, "Mary's with me. She's done nothing. I can explain everything."

The two officers looked at each other and then at Brad. "I don't know what you're talking about, sir. We've been waiting for you."

Brad blanched.

"You *are* Dr. Brad Forrest? You need to come with us."

"Why? What's this all about?"

"Don't play stupid! You're being taken in for questioning!"

"On what charge?"

"Sexual assault and battery."

CHAPTER 30

"The confirmation hearings begin the day after tomorrow. The likelihood that we find anything out about Tyson before then is nil." John Beckler sat in a booth in Jake's Diner.

"If anything was going to go down, it looks like that medical student pretty well nixed our chances of seeing it," Garry added with a sigh.

"Let's pull out. We'll keep Tyson's beeper bugged so we can hear his conversations, and we'll leave the video unit in the ceiling in 525, but we're wasting our time keeping manpower back here. Dr. Tyson's not going to be back to work if these hearings work out like everyone thinks," John added. He looked at his watch. "Where are Conrad and Rachel?"

"Workin' on her discharge from the hospital." Denise smiled.

"I'll expect everyone at the usual time on Monday. We've got quite a few tapes to go through," John reported without enthusiasm.

"Let's go."

* * *

"I don't care what the rules are — I'm leaving!" Elizabeth Grandby faced off with a nurse the size of a professional linebacker.

The nurse stood between her and the exit and glared at her father. "What do you say, Mr. Grandby?"

"The girl says she's goin'. I'm not about to stand in her way." Ted shrugged.

"Can't you wait until the attending comes in?" The nurse tapped her foot uneasily.

"I'm all packed. I'll see Dr. Forrest next week if I have any trouble." Elizabeth looked at Ted. "Daddy! Do something!"

"There is still the matter of your urinary tract infection. Without your prescriptions, you could get quite sick. The infection could spread to your kidneys."

The nurse looked at Mr. Grandby again. "Since she is only fourteen, she's still your responsibility. She can't leave unless she's discharged by an attending physician or you sign the 'Against Medical Advice' discharge form."

Elizabeth gritted her teeth. "Sign the form, Daddy!"

"It could be risky!" The nurse didn't budge.

"Give me the form. I'll sign it so we can be on our way." Ted smiled at the R.N.

She held the A.M.A. form out at arm's length. "Sign here."

Ted scribbled an unintelligible signature.

Elizabeth skipped past the nurse, carrying her overnight bag. Ted followed at a fast clip.

The nurse watched the two disappear through the double doors. *She sure didn't act sick! And she sure had her father wrapped around her little finger. I wouldn't let my fourteen-year-old get away with that!*

The interrogation hadn't gone well. Brad answered the questions as well as he could, reporting the facts of the elevator scene.

When he was done, the officers had only smiled at each other. "That's just what she said he would say," Brad overheard as they left the room a final time.

Now he was back at Crestview. He had asked them to return him to his car. At least they paid him that courtesy. He looked at his watch. It was afternoon already. Although he hadn't slept since Thursday night and it was now Saturday, he needed something else more than he needed sleep. He headed down the street to the Stones' apartment to find it.

When he knocked on their door a few minutes later, he was greeted by a very relieved Linda Stone. "Brad! You're O.K.!"

Brad dragged himself into the apartment as Matt and Mary stood to their feet. Brad collapsed into a Matt Stone bear hug. "I'm beat." He slid onto their faded couch.

Linda followed him in. "Mary told us about the police."

Matt looked at Brad, who had removed his tie from his wrinkled, white shirt. "Do you want to tell us about it?" He paused and looked at Mary.

"I didn't know where else to go, Brad. I knew we had to pray," Mary explained. "I came over here as soon as they took you away."

Brad sighed from exhaustion. "It's been a bad night."

"It was Tammy, wasn't it?" Matt asked.

"Bingo. Just like she said she would do." He propped his head in his hands. "The problem is, it sounds as if they believe her." Brad looked at his friends.

"It's her word against yours. They can't do anything. They don't have any proof!" Linda stated firmly.

"They have pictures," Brad stated flatly.

"Pictures?" Matt's chin dropped.

"Not of us together or anything, but pictures of Tammy. She must have gone to the police right away." He paused. "I've given my explanation. I have to admit, it sounded pretty stupid." Brad shook his head. "It felt like a nightmare. They kept holding up photographs asking me to explain again and again how the blouse was torn, how her hose was run, and how the blood — my blood — stained her skirt."

"Your blood?" Linda questioned.

"She scratched my neck pretty good while she was flailing around. I guess I must have touched her when I tried to settle her down."

Matt stood up and began to pace. "You shouldn't answer any more questions. We need to find a lawyer."

"I thought I could clear the whole thing up by answering a few questions. I never imagined they wouldn't believe me," Brad added with a shrug.

"Believe it," Matt responded. "Remember what Jake told you about Lenore Kingsley? This could all be part of the same fight! Somehow they must have found out about the F.B.I."

"Or maybe just because I ran out with the baby — maybe they know we're on to Tyson's infanticide operation," Mary said soberly.

"And they don't want anyone messing with Tyson's chances to be Surgeon General." Linda swatted her hands together.

"I don't get it." Mary twisted her expression. "Why does Lenore Kingsley care about Web Tyson?"

Brad scratched his head. "Web's son says she's heavy into research using human embryos — gene splicing, that sort of thing."

"The very kind of potentially lucrative research that requires the favorable eye of government to continue," Matt surmised.

"So if Tammy ran to the police right after the alleged attack, why did they just pick you up now?" Linda began pacing, too.

Brad shrugged again.

"Did they arrest you?" Matt asked.

"No. I asked them that very thing. They just said, 'Not yet' and finally let me go."

"That's it? What's next?" Matt probed.

"All I know is that a charge has been made and a report filed. I'm not sure it will ever go further, unless someone else pops up with more evidence." Brad shook his head.

"This is getting out of hand." Mary looked worried. "I've messed everything up. What I did may cost you your reputation and your job."

Brad looked up. "Fortunately, I just worked through losing all that," he added with an unexpected chuckle. "And I found the most important thing of all in return." He looked at his friends.

"Why don't we pray?" Matt pounded his fist into his hand.

Brad nodded. "That's why I came."

The foursome joined hands. "There's a battle going on," Matt said soberly, "and we may have just seen Satan's first volley."

Lenore sipped from a silver goblet and looked beyond the raindrops on her kitchen windowpane. *Brad Forrest will get his due for suspecting Dr. Tyson of any wrongdoing. He has no idea what he's up against!* She walked to her bedroom and began to pack a small suitcase and a garment bag. She checked her watch. UBI's Lear Jet should be ready in an hour. She folded a blouse and packed her cosmetics.

As she worked, a looming threat continued to gnaw at her. She placed her hand on her temple again as another headache blossomed into a continuous throb. She reopened her cosmetics bag and took out two Tylox. She took a long drink from the silver goblet and swallowed the pills. *It must be another tension headache. I'd feel better if these pills didn't affect my vision.* She pressed on her eyelids firmly and tried to relax.

She stared at the bottle in her hands.

Am I losing my mind? Is there something wrong with me besides all this stress I've been under? She felt a chill of fear ripple over her. *What is the problem?* She shook her head, still hopelessly bound in denial. *It's just the medicine, girl! Relax! You're just pushing yourself too hard!* She exhaled slowly. She put the Tylox bottle back in her cosmetics bag and reminded herself to look up the side effects of the painkiller. She sat on the edge of her bed and sought an answer to her anxieties as the fear of real illness bubbled to the surface again. *Is there something wrong with me?*

She silenced her own thoughts and stared at the ceiling. An inner impression soothed her fears: *We will take care of you.* Trusting the false promise of peace, Lenore Kingsley unknowingly became even more ensnared by the forces of darkness.

She remained quiet for a moment longer until her thoughts returned to Brad Forrest. As she focused on his image, a sickening dread returned.

What does all this mean? Is there still a threat? She stretched out on her bed to wait for a further message — desirous of a mental respite, but tortured by the nagging demons who accepted her surrender to them. She focused her thoughts. *Maybe I should talk to the inner circle. Perhaps another sacrifice?* She looked at her watch again. *No, there's no time for that! Tyson's hearings start Monday, and nothing can stop his confirmation. We have made all the necessary preparations to assure a complete victory. My research and a secure fortune will be safe.* She continued to stare at the ceiling and probed her own mind. Her thoughts seemed to carry minimal reassurance. *What am I missing?* She breathed heavily for a few minutes with her eyes closed.

As the Tylox began to work, a new demonic message screamed into her consciousness. *Forrest is praying! Jacobs is with him!* She remained motionless. *Forrest is angry about the accusation. He still poses a threat! If his reputation is soiled already, what's to stop him from bringing Tyson's practices into public question? What does he have to lose? And what about the girl? Even if Forrest heeds the warning to remain silent, what is to keep this little snip from coming forward?*

Lenore moaned, deeply entranced in her personal turmoil. *Remove the threat! Remove the threat!* Lenore sat up. She understood the plan.

She moved to the phone and dialed slowly. A thin smile appeared upon her face. *Nothing will stop us now.*

* * *

Meanwhile, Tyson, now in Washington, was speaking to Latner and Davis via a conference call.

"It's all over the hospital, Web. The buzz about this sexual assault thing is already out of hand," George Latner reported with a heavy sigh. "I was just beginning to think that things would work out for Forrest and Valley Surgeons for Children."

"I can hardly believe this, Web. I just talked to him a few days ago. He really seemed to be working to get his act together. He badly wanted to get his wife back and get his life in order," Davis added.

"Get his wife back?" Web replied. "I didn't know she left."

"Yes — a few weeks ago already," said Davis.

"Do you think he was beating her, too?" Tyson massaged his temples. "This really doesn't look good."

"It doesn't seem like him, Web," Davis persisted. "Did Tammy say anything to you about this assault?"

Tyson paused. "No, but that would be just like her. She probably didn't want to worry me. Maybe she thought I wouldn't believe her. Maybe she flirted with him, and he just flipped out — I don't know."

Latner spoke up. "Regardless of the truth of this or not, it's gone too far. This guy is going to ruin our established reputation."

Tyson sighed. "Let him go."

"Just like that? They haven't convicted him of anything," Davis reported.

"Let him go! We can fall back on the 'dismissal without cause' clause in his contract. We don't have to have a reason. Just get rid of him!" Tyson huffed.

"What about the work?" Latner and Davis asked together.

"Find another surgeon. I know it won't be easy on you two, but we did it before, didn't we, Mark? Remember when it was just Tyson and Davis, Pediatric Surgery Associates?"

"I remember," Davis cringed. "I remember."

Latner rolled his eyes.

"Let's just get this done fast. We need to put some distance between our practice and this guy before he sinks us all." Tyson paused reflectively. "If this gets out beyond our own community, it won't look good for me. It looks like I made a bad choice. Not the wise Surgeon General I'm supposed to be, right?" He laughed nervously. "Anyway, let's cut the strings quickly before it gets any worse."

"I'll call him before the weekend's over," Latner responded.

"O.K., men. Carry on."

Latner cleared his throat and changed the subject. "So I guess your day in the sun arrives Monday."

"If you could call it that," Tyson chuckled.

"Knock 'em dead, boss."

Julie Forrest hadn't really known inner peace until the day her husband was picked up for questioning, an event of which she had no knowledge. After Bradley was asleep, she timidly climbed the stairs to the main level where the Mitchells lived. She could hear them in the kitchen.

"Sophie?" she said as she knocked on the door.

"Come on in, Julie. Door's open," Sophie called.

Julie walked in slowly. Sophie immediately put down her dishrag when she saw the tears in Julie's eyes. She sensed the Holy Spirit's convicting presence. "Julie?" She instinctively brought her friend close in a hug. "What's going on? Did you hear from Brad?"

"No, not that — not that at all." Julie backed away, wiping her eyes. "I've been reading the Bible you gave me. I read the verses you'd highlighted." She sniffed and wiped her eyes again. She looked up at her neighbor and friend. "I guess I'm a sight!" She dabbed the mascara from her cheeks. "I — I hardly know how to say it," Julie stuttered. "I've met Jesus."

Gerald, Sophie's husband, grinned as he shut the dishwasher. Sophie hugged her friend again.

Pretty soon Sophie was crying, and even Gerald wiped away a tear or two.

"I've known what I needed for a while," Julie began, "but I guess I just kept running. God kept softly calling me. First through Belle, but I didn't want to hear; then through Bradley, then Brad, and then I end up living here and find out that you two have met him too! After I heard your pastor, I knew I needed to surrender," she said. "And tonight I did."

Sophie's eyes glistened. "Praise God!" she said softly. "We've been praying for you. We could tell the Spirit was at work, particularly after hearing about what was happening in Brad's life."

"Thanks so much for opening your home," Julie responded. "It's made a real difference for me."

"What's next?" Gerald asked.

"I already resigned my library job this afternoon and talked to Bradley's teacher." She paused. "I'm taking Bradley home — home to his father. It's time we were a family again."

"Have you told Brad?" Sophie smiled.

"Not yet. I think I'll just ride up Monday morning and surprise him," she said reflectively. "We've got a lot of healing to do."

"Yes, but you've both made a new start. I know the Lord will guide you together," Sophie encouraged.

"Together. That even *sounds* right," Julie added.

In a first-rate, expensive Washington restaurant, Lenore held up her glass and touched Web's. "To you," she said softly.

"To us," he responded. He tipped his glass and swallowed his second round of champagne.

Lenore grasped his hand. "Can you believe this? This is just the beginning, Web. You are going to be one of the most powerful men in the world."

"I'm not there yet."

"It's only a matter of time now."

Web looked at her face. For a moment it seemed somehow familiar, like he'd known her before. She wore her hair down, the long black cascades falling on her shoulders. He touched her cheek and searched his memory. Nothing.

She looked at him curiously. *He thinks he's seen me before. If only you knew.* "What are you thinking, darling?"

He hid his thoughts and winked. "Just how much I owe to you."

"It's about time you realized that," Lenore responded with a tease. Web Tyson didn't think she was serious. When she realized that, she continued to playfully taunt him with the truth. "You're right, Web — I've put you where you are today. With my money and influence, I pretty much handpicked you for the job, then removed every obstacle to your obtaining it." She smiled thinly. *You don't realize how serious I am. You have been picked for this hour, Web Tyson. Soon you will understand. Soon you will understand just how much you owe me.* She rubbed her forehead.

Web coughed nervously and changed the subject. "Shall we walk around the mall?"

Lenore's headache had returned. "Let's get back to your room. I'm not really up for a walk tonight."

Web shrugged and stood to go. Lenore followed him, striking several chairs with her right leg as she walked. *It's like walking through a tunnel,* she thought. *I'm losing my peripheral vision. I've heard of visual changes during migraines. That must be it.*

Back at Crestview, evening rounds had turned into night rounds for Mark Davis. He looked at the small infant, Jordan Gaines, who was now post-op from a repair for duodenal atresia. He checked his bandage, his vitals, and his urine and gastric output and examined his IV. He looked at Alta. "Mrs. Gaines, you should get some rest. He's going to be fine."

Alta nodded. "How long will this have to stay?" She pointed to the nasogastric tube.

"A few days."

Leroy stood to his feet. "Thanks, Doc."

Mark Davis nodded. "Sure." He looked at the parents. "I'll see you in the morning."

CHAPTER 31

Sunday. A day with fresh meaning for new believer Brad Forrest. He attended a local church with Belle, his first such visit in three years when he'd gone to the wedding of a friend.

After dinner he took a nap and went for a jog, but nothing seemed to keep his mind from returning to his visit to the police station. Finally he got out his books and outlined a chapter on childhood malignant lymphomas. By forcing himself to write, he was able to keep his mind focused on something besides his current problems. By the time he finished the last page, the sun was setting.

Brad fixed himself a sandwich and looked for something to watch on TV. Nothing caught his eye. He was mindlessly channel-surfing when Belle brought him the portable phone.

" 'Phone's for you. A Dr. Latner." She held out the phone to him.

"Hi, George. What's up?" Brad's countenance fell. He listened for a few moments without speaking as Latner delivered the latest news. "But you can't believe all this stuff! It's all lies!" He listened again.

Belle watched him. His face was pale. For the remainder of the one-sided conversation, Brad only added a few "buts" and then a final "goodbye."

Brad flipped off the phone and looked at Belle. "He fired me."

Belle looked at Brad and shook her head without speaking.

Brad offered little explanation. "I told him the accusations were lies, but he says it has nothing to do with that. He didn't really give a reason. He just said, 'Look at your contract. We aren't required to give a reason.' "

Belle eased down into a wooden rocker. "I think it may be for the best. They want to free themselves from you. Perhaps you should be glad to clear yourself from them."

Brad walked to his room shaking his head. "Maybe you're right."

Mary walked out of the medical library and headed up the alley carrying an armload of textbooks. She looked ahead at a blue van wedged in between the dorm and the library. *Boy, some people will park anywhere!* She slowly picked her way around several puddles, noting that it seemed darker than usual. She looked up. *The streetlight is out, but at least there's still some moonlight.* As she stepped closer to the van, she saw that she had just enough space to squeeze by on the right. She edged her way forward. As she arrived at the van's bumper, a tall man appeared in between the van and the brick dormitory. "Oooh!" she gasped. "You scared me."

She could just see a coarse beard in the dim light. As the man stepped toward her, a second male grabbed her from behind. Her books scattered to the alley's surface, and a viselike grip pulled her to the rear of the van. A smothering hand choked her muffled screams away. The door opened, and the two assailants threw her to the floor. Her head struck the wall, and her body slumped to the floor. The door closed, and the van lurched forward. Mary's head spun. *What's happening? Where are they taking me?* As her thoughts began to clear, she felt the weight of her attacker on top of her, tearing at her blouse, ripping off her blue jeans.

"What are you doing?" the tall man screamed from the driver's seat.

"What do you think? I'm following instructions. Lenore said to make it look like a rape — a jealous affair turned sour."

Mary forced herself to alertness. *I've got to get away from here!* Her thought was stopped by the tip of a small, steel revolver.

"Decided to wake up, did we?" The short man backed slowly away and kept the gun trained on Mary's chest.

Mary studied her surroundings. The van had no windows in the back. Two doors opened at the rear, with a single handle in the middle to release both. The van was empty except for her and the two assailants, one driving and a smaller one holding the gun. She edged to a crouched position. She couldn't see the driver except for the back of his head, and she couldn't see where they were going, although the presence of occasional streetlights seemed to indicate they were still in the city. She bit her lip and held back a sob. *Help me, God. Help!*

Brad sat down on the bed and sighed heavily. *Maybe Belle is right. Maybe it's all for the best. I should be glad to dissociate myself from them. Start over.* He stood up and began to pace across the creaky wooden floor. *But where? With a bad recommendation by this group, I'm sunk.* He walked to his desk and picked up a small, hand-held Dictaphone that he used for doing clinic note dictations. *I guess they'll be wanting this back, too.* He looked at his watch. *It's getting late, but I sure don't want to return this during the day. Maybe I'll just go down there now. I could use the fresh air anyway.* He tossed the Dictaphone into the pocket of his windbreaker and headed down the stairs. "Belle, I'm heading down to Crestview for a few minutes, to return some equipment. I should be back in an hour."

Web huffed and swatted the newspaper with his hand. "I can't believe these reporters! I'm not even in office, and already they're speculating on the effect my decision-making will have on life in America." He held up the paper for Lenore to see. "Just look. Here are my views on everything from preventative medicine, child-care, and A.I.D.S. to embryo research, physician-assisted suicide, and abortion." He moved his finger to the next column. "Here is the way they predict my views will alter present legislation." He scanned further down the page. "And just look at this — here's a copy of my current stock-holdings. How do they get this stuff? This guy is scrutinizing my stocks to see if important decisions regarding health care could be tainted because of the economic effect on my own stock selection." He sighed.

"It's just the media, Web. Don't let the situation get to you." Lenore lounged on the king-sized bed.

Web continued scanning the paper for a few minutes before tossing it aside.

"It's going to be constant, you know," Lenore said bluntly.

"What?"

"The media's inspection. It will be constant. They will pick you apart. Everything you are, where you go, who you see — everything. You just need to decide to ignore it."

"I guess you're right." He sat quietly for a moment. "It's good I don't have stock in UBI," he said, smiling. "They'd probably say I made decisions that would benefit the company just so I could make money."

Lenore looked at him sharply. "If they see you and me together, they are likely going to say the same thing, except to say that your decisions were tainted by love, not money."

"But that's ridiculous! I wouldn't let that influence my objectivity." He was struck by the idea. He had never really thought about that aspect of his relationship with Lenore before. He eyed her suspiciously and smiled to soften his question. "You never thought that my feelings for you would influence policy that I make — policy that might affect the pharmaceutical or medical research industries, did you?"

She smiled thinly and said nothing. *I'll let him wonder about that for a while.*

Web looked at Lenore. *It's funny that you suddenly appear in my life after I've been chosen for political fame. Why didn't I think of this before? Have I been so blinded by my own pride that I couldn't see your intentions?* He shifted uncomfortably in his chair. *Was I so naive to think that you would be attracted to me under other circumstances?* He sat for a moment longer and then said, "Lenore, I would never compromise my objectivity for —"

"For love?" Lenore interrupted. "No, Web, I know you too well to believe that. I know you would never let your emotions get in the way of what is proper. You've never let emotions get in the way of your proper scientific decision-making in medicine. Why would you do it under other circumstances?" She glanced in his direction and then returned to looking at her magazine. "It would take more than emotion to be able to influence you."

Web sat quietly for a few minutes longer. He needed to process these new thoughts. *Does she only want me for what I can do for her?* He stood up. "I need some exercise before dinner. You up for a walk?" He picked up his coat and looked at Lenore.

"You go ahead. I'd like to freshen up a bit before we eat."

Brad noticed a vehicle in his rearview mirror after only traveling a few blocks from his home. He didn't feel like rushing. He looked up again. *I wish that guy would back off.* He put his hand out the window and waved. The vehicle wouldn't pass. Brad drove on for a few minutes. *Back off!* Brad tapped his brakes. *Maybe if I pull over, he'll pass.* He slowed down and pulled off the shoulder. The blue van drove on.

In a few minutes Brad approached an intersection. He could see the same blue van with its right turn signal on. *Why doesn't he go?* Brad pulled to a stop a few feet behind the van. *There's no one around, fella. You sure seemed like you were in a rush a minute ago. Why did you hurry up just to wait?*

Brad saw the reverse lights go on, but had no time to react. Tires squealed, and the van lurched backwards, slamming into Brad's car. His body snapped forward and caught in the shoulder harness. The van then pulled forward again until its bumper dropped down off the hood of the automobile.

What on earth . . .

A tall man with a graying, coarse beard jumped from the van and ran back to Brad.

"Are you O.K.?"

"I think so."

"I got the reverse mixed up with first." The man seemed extremely agitated.

Brad got out of his car and walked to the front to look at the damage. As he leaned over the hood, a second man jumped out of the van's rear door. Brad looked up in time to see a revolver shoved in his face. "Get in!" The assailant motioned to the van. Brad slowly stood up straight. When he held up his hands, the taller man elbowed him from behind. He felt a sharp pain in his kidneys and collapsed forward into the van. "Ow!"

That's when he saw Mary.

"Brad!"

"Mary! What are you —"

"Shut up!" The door slammed, and the younger, more agile assailant jumped in behind Brad. "We can kill you now if you like!"

The van pulled out, turning toward the Wanoset River.

As his eyes adjusted to the darkness, Brad began memorizing the details of his attacker's face. Dark, curly hair; medium build;

clean-shaven; tan jacket. They rode on in silence for a few minutes. Brad looked around the vehicle. Mary sat next to him on his right, closer to the rear door.

"I hope you're enjoying the ride." The man laughed.

Brad and Mary stared down the barrel of the revolver and stayed quiet.

The man continued to talk, taunting Mary about her appearance.

Brad slipped his hand into his windbreaker pocket. The Dictaphone! Quietly he pressed Record. *Keep talking, guy. Keep talking. Even if you kill me, someone might find this tape.* The man looked at Brad.

"Comfortable, Doc?"

"Quite," Brad snapped.

The man laughed and called to his friend, "The doctor's enjoying the ride. He says he's comfortable." He looked back at his captives, his gun trained on Brad's chest. "That's what you're used to, aren't you, Doc? From what I've seen, you doctors do all right." He laughed again, then cocked his head around as if he had a sudden memory. "Old Doc Southerly had a nice place. Hey, we're running a special this year!" he babbled on to his partner. "Doctors — two for the price of one! First him — and now you!"

"Shut up!" The driver yelled. "Quiet, you fool!"

The smaller man with the gun chuckled nervously and then became silent.

Just then the cassette in Brad's Dictaphone came to the end, and the recorder clicked off. Brad cringed.

The man looked up at him. He had heard the click. "What are you doing?" He pointed the gun at Brad's face. "Take your hand out of your pocket!"

Brad obeyed. The assailant reached in and pulled out the tape player.

At that moment the van drove onto the Nickel Bridge.

"Hey, he's taping us!" He held up the Dictaphone so his partner could see. He rewound the tape a few seconds and pressed Play. The recorded message was clear: "Doctors — two for the price of one! First him — and now you! Shut up! Quiet, you fool!"

"Let me see that thing!" The driver held out his hand. The smaller man moved to the front, keeping his eyes on Mary and Brad.

"Here." He handed the device to his partner.

He weighed it in his hand, lifting it up and down. "I'll take care of this," he said.

"The fish in the Wanoset can enjoy it." He flung it wildly out the passenger window. It struck a bridge railing and rebounded onto the bridge.

The younger man watched it fly. "You missed the river! It's in the road!"

"It's broken. Nobody can use it. Forget about it."

"It has a tape in it! We need the tape!" The younger man pointed the gun nervously at the captive duo. "Turn around. I'll get it."

The bridge was empty except for one oncoming car that passed just as the van did a 180-degree turn.

Brad looked at Mary, their silent communication understood. *He's going to stop.*

Rebecca Thomas pulled past the remnants of a dismantled toll booth and onto the Nickel Bridge. She was heading back to Bridgewater University after spending the weekend with her parents. Up ahead she saw a blue van veer wildly and spin around. She instinctively slowed. *He must be drunk.* She pressed the brake. *I definitely don't want to get too close to him on the bridge.*

"Slow down! It should be just ahead!"

"I can't see it!" The driver squinted.

"Fool! Go slower. There! Next to the pole! Stop!"

"There's too much glare. Which pole?" The driver slowed to a halt.

Mary's eyes met Brad's. He nodded slightly.

"I can almost reach it from the van." The smaller man edged into the passenger's seat, his gun still trained on Mary and Brad. He unlatched the door. As soon as he turned to retrieve the Dictaphone, Mary acted.

The back door flew open with a single kick to the handle. Mary leaped first, then Brad, both running from the back of the stopped van. Mary could see the lights of a car several hundred feet away. She waved madly. Brad, looking back, could just see the attacker raising his gun.

"Jump, Mary, jump!" Brad screamed. "He's going to shoot!" He overtook her with another stride and pulled her across the railing. Not knowing what would befall them, they lunged into the darkness.

Behind them, the gunman saw the approaching headlights and stepped back into the shadow of the van's interior.

As the van slowed to a crawl, Rebecca responded in kind. *What's this guy doing now?*

When the van stopped, so did she. *I'm not getting too close to that* — The rear doors flew open, and a partially clothed young woman jumped out. A man quickly followed. *That man's after her!* Rebecca squinted. The woman waved. The man struggled briefly to get her over the railing and then — they were gone!

Rebecca held her hand to her mouth. *I've got to get help!* She quickly negotiated the turn-around, with the bridge still empty except for the van. She punched the accelerator to the floor. *I've got to get help!*

With the car disappearing in the distance, the men quickly ran to where Brad and Mary had leapt over the railing. The gunman quickly emptied his weapon, firing into the murky blackness below. "They've got to be dead. I can't see anyone swimming down there."

They watched for several minutes before returning to the van. The older man cursed and hit the steering wheel.

"Don't worry," stated the younger man matter-of-factly. "They could never survive that. The bridge is so high, and the river is so strong, and the place where they jumped is so far from shore — man, they're dead for sure."

The van pulled away. "We're home free," the younger assailant crowed.

The older man wasn't so sure.

Caught up in the moment — one by pride, the other by fear, neither man thought to retrieve the Dictaphone.

Rebecca Thomas skidded into the parking lot of DeAngelo's. She bounded through the front door and ran to the hostess. "I need a phone. Some people just jumped from the bridge!"

The hostess handed her a portable phone that she lifted from the hostess station.

Rebecca frantically dialed 911.

She quickly told what she had seen. A few minutes later she met Bridgewater city policemen in the parking lot. Two units had responded, along with a rescue squad. She returned to the bridge, riding in the front police unit.

"Here — here's where they went over," she pointed to the railing. "The van was parked here." They stopped and got out of the car.

"Did you see anyone else?" Sergeant Dave Kowalski opened a notepad.

"No, only the two — the girl and the man chasing her."

The officers looked over into the water.

Their flashlight beams criss-crossed the rippled surface. "Nothing in the river, boss," another officer reported. "Can't see how anyone could still be alive down there. I sure don't see anyone clinging to a pole."

"Are you sure both bodies went into the water?" Kowalski squinted into the darkness.

"I think so. I mean, I didn't actually see them in the water, but it looked like they both went down." Rebecca scratched her head.

"The van is gone, so either one of them didn't jump or there was another person in the van."

Rebecca corrected her earlier report by adding, "It looked like the man threw her."

"And you think he went with her?"

"I think so."

The sergeant looked at the rescue squad captain. "I don't think we'll be needing you tonight. Why don't you have your unit call first thing in the morning? It looks like we'll need to start a river search, maybe drag for the bodies."

"Hey, what's this?" Richard Tidly picked up a scratched and cracked, black Dictaphone. Still legible on the side was a silver plate with the engraved words, Valley Surgeons for Children. "Somebody must have dropped this."

"Bring it along." The sergeant looked again at Rebecca. "Could you come back to the station?"

Rebecca shrugged.

"We'd like to solidify our reports tonight if we can. Can you describe the man to us?"

Rebecca nodded. "Sure."

Lenore didn't want the details. She only wanted the message she received.

"They've been taken care of."

"Thanks." She hung up the phone gently. She looked over her shoulder and smiled. Web wasn't listening.

CHAPTER 32

Lenore smiled at herself in the mirror and plugged in her curling iron. "Where do you want to eat tonight?"

"Your choice," Web responded, looking at his watch. "It's late enough — we shouldn't have trouble getting a table anywhere."

He walked in behind her and placed his hands on her shoulders. He looked at her in the mirror. "You look stunning." He kissed her hair, then studied her for a moment longer. At the roots of her hair he could see a hint of light color. He stepped back. "You never told me you dyed your hair."

She looked up sharply. "I don't." She could see he wasn't teasing. She leaned toward the mirror and pulled the hair away from the part. There, next to her scalp, the hair showed a barely perceptible color change. *Is it blonde? White?* She stood back and frowned. "Web, it's turning gray!"

He had never seen her like this. She was suddenly vulnerable, and for an instant she did not appear to carry the powerful, confident air he normally detected. "All at once?" He looked closer. "I — I was only teasing. No one will see."

Lenore remained silent.

"Maybe it's just a funny reaction to the shampoo," he offered, picking up the hotel's sample bottle. He shrugged.

"It's turning gray."

He had never seen her like this. Lenore pout? *She needs me.* He put his arms gently on her shoulders again. "It's really O.K. It makes no difference to me. You could have white hair for that matter. It's what's in here that makes a difference." He put his hand on his chest.

She returned his gaze and softened. *He really cares about me, doesn't he?* She looked at him a moment longer. *Maybe I could feel the same way about him — maybe.*

Mary kicked violently for the surface as her left shoulder screamed with pain. It wasn't easy with Brad holding a tight grip on her other wrist. She broke into the cool air and gulped it in before Brad could pull her under again. *What is he doing? I need air!* Brad swam for the bridge, dragging her behind him. *I'm going to drown! Let me go!* She kicked the water, propelling her body along next to Brad's. Her lungs burned. Suddenly her head broke the surface again. She pushed into the air and struck her forehead on an overlying board. *What?* Beside her, Brad pulled himself up beneath a wooden slat and slowly released the deathgrip he had on her wrist.

The night air reverberated as bullets torpedoed into the Wanoset around them. The snapping sound became deafening. *We're going to die!* Mary screamed silently. After a moment, a relative quiet resumed, and she could hear the waves licking the undersurface of their hiding place.

Mary explored the structure above her. They appeared to be beneath some sort of wooden platform that rested a few inches above the water. Brad's labored breathing reluctantly slowed to deep, irregular gasps. His fingers gripped a barnacled slot between two boards.

"Are you O.K.?" Mary whispered.

"I think so." Brad twisted around, his lips pursed to remain above the river. "What about you?"

"My shoulder hurts pretty bad." She took mental inventory and touched her forehead, which had been scraped on the barnacles.

She waited a moment for her eyes to adjust to the dim light. "Where are we?"

"Beneath an old scaffolding structure."

"But how did you know —"

"I've been here before with Bradley. We used to sit on these platforms when we went fishing."

"But how did you know where we were? This is a long bridge."

"There are structures similar to this every five or six poles beneath the bridge. I think they just got lazy and didn't dismantle the stuff. We jumped so fast, I couldn't really see," Brad whispered, "so I just obeyed a hunch." Of course, he had a suspicion where the hunch came from.

Web Tyson sipped his coffee as a waiter cleared the dessert dishes. The restaurant had thinned to one other couple as the clock approached midnight. He stared at Lenore as his memory returned to their previous conversations. He shifted in his seat as his insecurity prompted a question. "Why did you call me?"

She returned his gaze with an inquisitive one. "What do you mean?"

"When you first called me, why did you do it? Would you have come on so strong if they hadn't announced my appointment?"

"Are you worried?"

He stayed quiet for what seemed like a

long time. When Lenore saw his face twitch, she spoke again. "I've known you for a long time." She paused and sipped her coffee.

A vague dread pierced his memory. He looked at her face as she continued, "I've watched your progress, admired your positions." Her eyes locked with his. "I've studied you, Web. The appointment was only an excuse for me to act on my wishes. What better excuse to call than to celebrate your success?"

He took the line. All of it. He loved what she said, but . . . *What is it about her? What is it? Fear?* He shook it off. "You watched me?" He smiled.

"For a long time."

"You studied me?" He beamed.

"More than you'll know."

"You know me?" He sat up even straighter and took her hand.

"I know who you are." Her whispered words pierced his clouded memory, resurrecting his nightmare in full vengeance. He dropped her hand. His breath quickened with a cough. Sweat accumulated on his brow as he heard his heart pounding out the message again: *I know who you are!* Lenore's steely expression compounded his terror.

Web remained locked in her gaze, his

mouth open, as the shock erupted from his mind. *Delilah! Your hair — your face — older, yet similar!* He looked at her eyes. "Delilah," he whispered. She allowed a thin smile to come over her face as he uttered the name for the first time.

"And now," she said as her sinister smile broadened, "you know who I am."

Richard Tidly put the paper in the sergeant's hand. "Look at this, Dave. Ralph just called this in. They've found an abandoned car at an intersection about a mile from the river. Registered in the name of a Brad Forrest. His employer is listed as Valley Surgeons for Children."

Dave Kowalski's eyes brightened. "Like on the Dictaphone?"

"Exactly."

"Hmmm." Dave stood up. "Why don't you see if we can find this Forrest fellow in our computer. And get a picture. Let's show it to Rebecca here," he added, pointing to the student sitting to his left, "and see what comes up."

"I'll get right on it."

"Good." The sergeant looked at his watch. "Any report on missing persons?"

"Not yet," Tidly responded. "I'll keep you posted."

* * *

After waiting in the water for only a few minutes, the two refugees heard distant voices coming from the bridge. Mary bit her lip. "They're back!"

"Keep quiet and be still. It's nearly impossible to see this far under the bridge from up there," Brad whispered.

He held his breath momentarily as a spotlight crossed over the wooden slats. After a moment the darkness returned. In another few minutes, they heard a vehicle — or was it more than one? — leaving again.

"We've got to get to shore. Can you swim?" Brad looked at Mary. Blood oozed from the fresh barnacle scrape on her forehead.

"I can try." She rotated her left shoulder slowly. "I think I can."

"We need to stay under the bridge. If we're in open water and they return, they'll be more likely to see us," he instructed. "Stay away from the poles. The barnacles will cut."

"Tell me about it."

Brad submerged momentarily to remove his shoes and socks. He took another breath and pulled off his shirt. "I think I'll get along better without these." He looked at Mary. "Ready?"

"Let's go."

"We'll aim for the next platform as our first goal. We can rest there."

She nodded and ducked out from under the protective ledge. She tried a crawl stroke but found that impossible. She couldn't properly raise her left arm. *My shoulder!* She resorted to a modified dog paddle, using mostly her right arm. Brad swam ahead as they passed one, two, three sets of poles. Mary suddenly choked on the river water. "Ugh!" She coughed and resumed her struggle. At the sixth set of poles, they finally came to a ledge. She heaved a sigh and held on.

Brad pulled himself onto the platform and gasped for air. Mary's breath came in fast gulps. "I can't — do — it!" she sobbed. "I'll — never — make it."

Belle's old bed creaked. She looked at the clock and then at the porch light that she had left on for Brad. *Something's wrong! It's after midnight, and he's still not back.* She wobbled out of bed, pulled her robe around her, and headed for the stairs.

In a moment she was seated in her rocker in the kitchen alcove. *No grandson of mine is going to be out so late without some prayer coverage!*

Down at the Bridgewater City police station, the story continued to unravel at mind-bending speed. A missing persons report came in. A dental student reported that her roommate's books were found in an alley, and her roommate was long overdue. Tidly checked the computers. Forrest seemed clean, until he called the county police "just to check all the bases." Forrest, it turned out, had been picked up just the day before for questioning about a sexual assault accusation! A copy of Forrest's driver's license picture was faxed from the D.M.V. Now the wheels really spun. Sergeant Kowalski held three photographs up to Rebecca. She didn't hesitate.

"That's him."

Kowalski looked at Tidly and nodded. "It looks like Dr. Forrest had something on his mind besides surgery."

Just then another policeman, Jason Childs, walked in. "I got the report from the dental student. The missing girl is a medical student, Mary Jacobs. Here's a description and a picture." He handed the papers to Kowalski. "And get this! She was at the library studying pediatric surgery! She's been doing an elective with Valley Surgeons for Children!"

The sergeant bit his lower lip and shook his head. He passed the photograph to Rebecca. "Can you give us an I.D. on this one?"

She studied the picture. "Her hair was longer than this, but —" She hesitated, then nodded. "I think that's her."

Dave Kowalski paced through the small office. "But what about the blue van?" He walked back to his desk and looked at Rebecca. "Are you sure about that part?"

"Absolutely. I watched it pretty carefully after it spun around like that. I'm sure it was a blue van."

"Then we have to consider two possibilities. Either Forrest didn't jump and returned after throwing the girl from the bridge or he had help." Kowalski shrugged.

"Rapists are often solo artists. Another driver just doesn't fit the profile of a sexual assault," Tidly added. "Miss, tell me again what you saw."

Rebecca sighed. "I saw him grab her from behind and fling her over the rail. Then they were gone. Just like that. I didn't run to look for a splash. I just wanted to get help, so I rushed to DeAngelo's to call the police."

"He could have stayed out of sight over the rail and then returned to the van after you turned around," the sergeant hypothesized.

"I didn't see that," Rebecca said, shaking her head.

Kowalski sighed and summarized, "So we have a witness who places Forrest at the scene, and the Dictaphone as confirmatory physical evidence that links him with the assault. That, considering his past record, is something we can't ignore." He looked at the group and issued the orders. "Notify the state police. Give them everything we've got. Get 'em started on a search for the van and for Brad Forrest. If this guy's still alive, I want him. Let's get some men out close to the riverbank tonight. If someone crawls out of there alive, we should be there."

He looked at Childs. "I'm afraid we're going to have to get the media involved in this one. It's too dangerous to the public if Forrest is still running around out there somewhere. Talk to this Mary Jacobs's family. Let them know that a missing persons report has been filed. Keep Jacobs's name out of the news." He looked over at Tidly. "Better call Forrest's home. See if his wife knows where he is."

The team nodded. Dr. Brad Forrest was a wanted man.

Web stumbled into his room, his mind spinning. Lenore walked with him, holding his arm. He slumped on the bed and loosened his tie.

"How long have you known?"

"From the beginning." Lenore sighed. "What does it matter? I was a young girl then."

Web held his head. "Why didn't you tell me?" He studied her face. *Your black hair — your features.* "Age changed you, Lenore. I almost didn't recognize you."

"I saw from the start that you didn't remember me." She dabbed a dramatic but false tear. "I thought you'd hate me — that my past would drive you away."

He remained silent for a minute, unable to console his own soul or to quiet Lenore's apparent remorse. Finally he stood and walked to the window. *Maybe this can work to the advantage of both of us.* "Maybe you're right," he said slowly. "It happened a long time ago. We should let it go."

Lenore sobbed. This time Web responded. He placed his hands on her shoulders. "It's always been my buried secret. I never wanted anyone to know," he whispered.

She turned and faced him, her eyes brimming with theatrical tears. "Me too," she whispered. She placed her head against his chest.

"It's always been my secret," he repeated.

"Now it's ours," she said softly.

Brad and Mary had struggled slowly to the third platform. Brad looked at Mary. He had pulled her onto the wooden scaffolding beneath the bridge. Her head was still oozing, and she held her left arm at a funny angle. "It's dislocated, Mary," he said, feeling the top of her shoulder.

She caught her breath after a few minutes of rest. "I'm freezing."

"This wind isn't helping any."

Mary coughed and stated what appeared to be increasingly obvious. "You're going to have to leave me here. With my arm this way, I'll never make it all the way to shore."

Brad nodded soberly. "I'll bring back help." He looked at the structure, which rested four inches above the river's surface. "The tide's coming in. From the looks of these barnacles, this board must be underwater at high tide."

"Brad!"

"Don't worry. I should be back in an hour. I just need to get to shore and call the police. We can send a rescue boat." He leaned toward the water.

"Please hurry. I'm freezing."

Brad dove in and swam away into the

blackness. Mary lost sight of him when he passed the second set of poles. "O God," she prayed, "please h-help him br-bring back help."

The phone interrupted Belle's silent prayer. Brad? *Maybe that's my answer.* She picked up the phone. "Hello . . . Forrest residence."

She gasped at the caller's words.

"No, officer, he hasn't returned home. Is there a problem?" She paused.

"I see." She listened again.

"O.K. I certainly will."

She hung up the phone and looked at her watch. *Now I know it's time to pray!*

Tammy readied herself for bed. *If I didn't have to work, I'd be with Web right now,* she sulked. She looked at the clock. *It's late, but if I know Web, he's staring at the ceiling, worried about his Senate confirmation hearing tomorrow.* She smiled and thought of their last night together. *I'll bet he could use a little encouragement about now.* She took a small paper out of her purse and dialed his hotel. In a few seconds the phone began to ring.

One ring, two, three, four. *Come on, Web. Don't tell me I'm going to wake you up! Five rings. Are you out on the town, love?*

"Hello." The voice was feminine.

"I'm terribly sorry. I asked for Web Tyson's room."

"You've got it. Would you like to speak to him?" She handed the phone to Web without waiting for the answer.

Tammy stood up. *Lenore! The voice was unmistakable!* "Lenore? Is that you?"

"Hold on," Web responded and looked at Lenore. "It's for you, darling!" He handed the phone back to Lenore.

"What's going on? Lenore? What are you doing there?" Tammy shouted.

Now Lenore recognized Tammy's voice. She looked at the phone sharply and just hung up. She looked at Web and shrugged. "It was just dial tone," she lied. "Somebody just hung up."

On the other end, Tammy fumed. *That was Lenore! What's she doing with Web at this hour in his hotel room?* She slammed the phone against the nightstand. *And what did Web say? "It's for you, darling."* She huffed across the floor. *I even offered to quit my job so I could be with you! No wonder you didn't want me to do that! You wanted me to work so I wouldn't be in the way! @#$%&#!*

Brad gulped for air as his lungs burned. The tide pulled him continuously away from the pilings, and he was spending half his energy just struggling to swim in a straight line. He stopped three times for rest, and now, on his final leg, he decided to abandon his attempt at staying close to the bridge. The shoreline was his only goal.

It had taken longer than he'd hoped. His pants were heavy. The sky was beginning to color. *It will be dawn soon. The tide's coming in. I've got to keep going!* He struggled ahead a few feet more and then floated with the tide. *I've got to get my breath or I'm going to drown!*

After a few minutes he resumed his fight, alternating a slow crawl stroke with a modified dog paddle. And then, in another moment, his toes touched the muddy river bottom. *I made it!* He gasped and trained his eyes on the shore ahead.

Mary clung to the piling and prayed. She was shivering so violently that she was afraid she would fall back into the water. The wind had picked up, and the waves were cresting over the platform's surface. *Please hurry, Brad. I can't hold on much longer! O God . . .*

On the road to the south, Julie tapped the steering wheel excitedly. The thought of surprising Brad had driven her from sleep, and after packing the BMW she had shared the news with Bradley. "We're going home!"

"Now?" Bradley had offered sleepily.

It hadn't taken much to convince him that an early start would mean getting home a little faster. After a quick cup of coffee and a Pop-Tart for Bradley, they were on their way.

She watched the sun rise. She had a new life. She was going home!

CHAPTER 33

A few minutes later Julie Forrest drove across the Nickel Bridge. Even a momentary slowdown because of the police vehicles couldn't dampen her spirits. She was going home!

Bradley looked out the window. "Powise c-cars!"

For the next mile Bradley imitated a police siren. Julie looked over and tousled his still uncombed bangs. "O.K., captain! Enough of the siren. Mommy can't think."

Ahead, the traffic nearing the intersection slowed to a crawl. *What's this? It's too early for rush hour.* She looked at her watch. *I'd like to get home before Brad leaves for work. I can't wait to see him!*

As she waited, Bradley made the squeak of a siren noise again. A stern look from his mother cut him off. "Why don't we watch the cars, Bradley?" She looked at her watch again and tapped the steering wheel. "We might see Daddy if he's on his way to work."

"P-powise cars!" Up ahead on the left,

the police directed traffic around a stalled vehicle. Yellow police barricade tape surrounded the area. It looked like a photographer was taking pictures of the car. *That's Brad's car!* Julie had a sudden sinking feeling and pulled her car onto the soft shoulder.

She looked at her son. "Stay here, Bradley." Her lip trembled. She could see a dent in the hood of her husband's car. *Brad must have been in a wreck!* She stumbled along the road, looking for Brad. She approached a tall man in a police uniform. "Where's the driver of this vehicle?" She clenched her hands. "Is he O.K.?"

The officer looked down at Julie. "This vehicle was unmanned, ma'am. The driver's not around."

"Miss, you'll have to move your car!" A second officer directing traffic looked at Julie.

"He's gone?" Julie shook her head. *Maybe he walked for help?* She looked at the second officer. His glare intensified. *O.K.! I'll move my car!*

Julie pulled back onto the road. *Maybe he started walking for home.* "Look for Daddy, Bradley." She turned on the radio and mindlessly tapped the steering wheel. It wasn't until she pulled in the driveway that she paid attention to the announcer's words:

"A late-breaking story is developing. A Bridgewater University student is missing this morning and feared dead. An eyewitness reported a partially clothed woman being thrown from the Nickel Bridge early this morning. Chief suspect at this time is a Dr. Brad Forrest, formerly associated with Valley Surgeons for Children and questioned earlier this week on sexual assault charges. It is not certain if the suspect jumped from the bridge in an apparent suicide attempt after the assault. A search is underway for both bodies. If you have information on this or any other news items, please call the WLTK news hotline at . . ."

The announcer's words faded as a cold fear settled in Julie's mind. She looked around for Bradley.

He had already bounded out of the car, screaming, "Daddy! We're home!"

Lenore awoke as Web kissed her goodbye.

"Wish me luck," he whispered.

Lenore moaned softly and kissed him back. "I'll see you at the break."

With that, Web was gone, escorted to the Capitol building for an early-breakfast briefing before the hearings started.

Lenore moaned again, her head throbbing with agony. She slipped from bed and stumbled to the bathroom, her vision clouded, misting around a central, clear tunnel. She gulped two Tylox, paused, and swallowed a third. *What is happening to me?*

She collapsed back onto the king-size bed and punched the TV remote. *Let's see if the media are reporting Forrest's murder.* Once she found CNN, she rested, holding her aching head in her hands. She watched the news at the bottom of the hour and waited for headlines. She wasn't disappointed.

"A newsbreak from Green Valley reveals the sudden disappearance of Dr. Brad Forrest, former associate of the Surgeon General appointee, Dr. Web Tyson. Forrest is wanted on charges of assault. Eyewitness reports indicate that Forrest was seen throwing a partially clad college coed from the Nickel Bridge. It is unclear if Forrest also jumped from the bridge in an apparent suicide attempt after the assault. A search is underway for the bodies . . ."

Lenore smiled in spite of her pain. *My men did a good job. Those clowns really have people sucked into their story. I wonder how they set up the eyewitness account. I must remember to reward them appropriately,* she thought. *Now nothing will stop us. Everything is falling into place. The future belongs to me! My master has brought me success. He has kept every promise he made to me.*

A searing pain interrupted her thoughts, shooting from her head into her neck with the force of a knife. In another instant a second sensation reared. *I'm going to vomit!* She did not make it to the bathroom, stumbling to the floor beside the bed while she emptied her stomach's contents. A vise tightened around her forehead. *My head will explode!* As her anguish became unbearable, she was rescued by the onset of coma.

Seconds passed. Lenore's breaths were deep, fast, and erratic, followed by pauses even more horrifying. A series of violent seizures racked her twisted body until she stopped breathing.

At 6:35 A.M. the president of United Biotechnical Industries, a faithful follower of the master of deceit, was dead.

Brad swaggered through the chest-high water of the Wanoset River. Ahead of him, on the bank behind DeAngelo's restaurant, a group of rescue workers and police officials waited for full daylight. Brad coughed.

I'm saved. "Help! Help me!" he gasped.

An officer looked up and panned the water's edge with a spotlight. "There!"

Brad saw the group running toward him. "It's a man!" someone shouted.

"Help!" Brad pulled himself the last few steps before collapsing onto the mud-slicked bank. In seconds the police surrounded him.

"Brad Forrest?"

Brad smiled. *They were looking for us! Belle must have reported me missing!* He nodded. "Am I glad to see you!"

Four strong arms yanked him to his feet. Another man quickly cuffed his hands.

"Hey! What's going on here?" Brad demanded.

Sergeant Dave Kowalski snarled, "You're under arrest." He paused. "Kidnapping and assault." He stared at Brad, who was mud-covered and still heaving with exhaustion. "When we find the girl's body, we'll add murder." He looked at his team. "Let's go!"

Two men escorted Brad toward a waiting patrol car. Brad twisted around to get their attention. "There's been a terrible mistake! Stop! Mary's out there!" He flung his head toward the river. "Mary's out there!"

The sergeant walked behind him. "It's a

fine time to be remorseful after all you've done, Forrest." He looked at the two men carrying Brad along. "Get this maniac downtown!"

They pushed him onto the backseat of a police cruiser. As they pulled into the traffic lane, Brad continued to yell, "You've got to listen. A woman is out there — under the bridge! We need to help —"

"Save it for your attorney, pal," the driver interrupted. As they turned left out of the restaurant, Brad looked at the river. *Save her, God. Please save her!*

Above her, Mary could hear the morning traffic thickening. *If only they could see me!* Every few seconds she cried out, "Help!" again, but her screams evaporated in the wind and the traffic noise.

Below her, the water swirled at ankle level. She clutched the platform with her right hand and cringed with pain. *I can't hang on much longer.* She stared at the swirling water. *If I slip, it wouldn't be so bad. My suffering would be over.* Not convincing herself, she yelled out again. "Help!"

Nobody could hear.

The tide was rising.

Her cry weakened with a sob. "Somebody please help me!" *O God . . .*

* * *

Julie looked at Belle. *She's strong, but she's wearing out.* "Why don't you nap for a while. I'll call the station again in a few minutes. Maybe they'll have found something."

The grandmother shook her head. "I can't sleep," she argued. "There will be time for that later. Besides," she said looking at her watch, "the old folks at Patterson's should be up by now. The Stones too. I'm starting a prayer chain."

The Bridgewater police station hadn't seen this much activity in years. On the left, just beyond the entrance, a middle-aged man sat with his arm around his wife. They nervously asked questions and drank the coffee a detective had brought them.

Lilly Jacobs leaned over the front desk and looked at the slender female officer sitting there. "You must not be much older than our daughter," she remarked.

The woman looked up and smiled.

Roy Jacobs patted his wife's shoulder. She continued, "Did we tell you she is going to be a doctor?" She paused for a moment. "Have you heard anything else? Have they found her yet?"

The officer smiled again. "Mrs. Jacobs,

we'll let you know as soon as we hear —"

Ring!

"Bridgewater police. Oh, hi, Richard." She listened. "O.K." She hung up the phone and looked at the Jacobses. "They're bringing Forrest in. He's alive."

Mr. Jacobs stood up. The officer continued, "Still no word on your daughter." She sighed. "I'm sorry. Sometimes these things take time."

Mrs. Jacobs chatted nervously for a few minutes longer.

"Why don't you go on over to your motel? We can phone you as soon as we hear anything."

A commotion broke through the front doors as the team arrived with Brad Forrest. He twisted uselessly against his larger escorts and continued to yell about helping Mary.

Mr. Jacobs stood up and lunged at Brad. "You!"

"Get them apart!" Kowalski snapped. He shielded Forrest from the angry father, who seethed at Brad again. "Where is she?"

Brad was shoved from behind before he could speak. "Get this guy downstairs before he causes more trouble!" He stumbled ahead into a hallway. They carried him into a small room with a table and a single win-

dow next to another room. There they dropped him to the floor and shut the heavy door. In a few minutes he was joined by Sergeant Kowalski and another officer, Richard Tidly.

"We need to ask you a few questions. You've been read your rights. You can wait until an attorney is present if you like."

Brad nodded. *I've got to tell them! I've got to get help out to Mary.* "Can I give you my side?"

Tidly sighed and looked at Kowalski. He nodded.

Brad began. He started with his trip to Crestview and the attackers in the blue van. When Brad mentioned the Dictaphone and the recording of the two men who claimed to have knocked off Southerly, Kowalski's eyes widened. *I've caught you in a lie now, Forrest. You have no idea that I have your Dictaphone!*

Brad finished the story and pleaded again. "I know it sounds unbelievable, but you've got to listen. Mary's going to die!"

The two officers stood and left the room. As the door opened, a third officer threw in a pair of pants and a shirt. "Here! You could use a clothes change," he said with a laugh.

The door closed. Brad looked at himself.

No shirt. Bare feet. Muddy, wet pants. I'm not sure I'd believe me either! He looked at the shirt and pants. *I could use something dry.* He noticed the inscription on the front of the shirt and groaned. "Green County Correctional Facility."

Ben told Florence and Richard. Richard shared the prayer request with his wife, Alice, and with Craig and Sandy, who told Jen. In just a few minutes the prayer circle at Patterson's Nursing Home was launching a few missiles of its own.

Mary strained to hold on. She had stopped yelling. She had no strength left. In the distance she could see the faint outline of a boat, but it proved to be traveling in the wrong direction. *Where's Brad?* She squinted at the shoreline in the distance. *It's a long ways. Maybe he didn't make it.* Tears filled her eyes and fell into the river below.

She thought of her parents. *They're going to be heartbroken!*

Although the rising sun had warmed the air a few degrees, the wind and lack of clothing kept Mary from appreciating it. Her teeth chattered as she leaned against the bridge piling, the Wanoset River covering her knees. Quietly she closed her eyes and began to hum her favorite hymns.

The sergeant looked at the Dictaphone. The small cassette was still intact, but the door jammed as he tried to open it. After a few seconds he freed the cassette and looked at Tidly. "Hand me that tape player."

He placed the small cassette in the recorder and pressed Play. The message was clear:

". . . a four-year-old white male status post right inguinal and umbilical herniorraphies, here for a post-op visit. The mother reports no problems. The incision is healing . . ."

Kowalski pressed Stop. "This is just doctor talk."

"Sounds like his dictations," Tidly acknowledged.

"It looks like this Forrest has quite an imagination. Understandable, I guess. He's in some incredible trouble." The sergeant shrugged.

Jason Childs walked up just then. "The county's underwater equipment is being used over at Silver Lake. A kid's missing up there. They can't begin a river drag until this afternoon."

"That's O.K." the sergeant huffed. "I'm

not really looking forward to what we'll see anyway." He handed the cassette recorder to Tidly. "Anyone for some breakfast? I'm starved."

Ben Kreider sat in his rocker alone. He prayed aloud. It helped him to focus. "I pray that the truth will be revealed." He paused, discerning the point of attack. "In the name of Jesus, I bind all forces causing confusion and hindering the revelation of the truth . . ."

"Don't you think we should rewind this a little, just in case?" Tidly looked at Sergeant Kowalski.

"Suit yourself," Kowalski answered. Tidly rewound the tape and pressed Play. The group paused to listen.

"Comfortable, Doc? Quite." Laughter. "The doctor's enjoying the ride. He says he's comfortable. That's what you're used to, aren't you, Doc? From what I've seen, you doctors do all right." More laughter. "Old Doc Southerly had a nice place. Hey, we're running a special this year! Doctors — two for the price of one! First him — and now you! Shut up! Quiet, you fool!"

The room fell silent as Tidly stopped the tape.

"He's telling the truth!"

CHAPTER 34

The first two hours of the Senate confirmation hearings were history. Web Tyson walked a proud stroll through the hotel lobby. "See you in a few minutes, Jonathan," he called to his escort.

He pressed the Up button and waited for an elevator. *This isn't bad at all. Lenore was right. Just answer the questions. If Blackburn didn't think this would go smoothly, he wouldn't have picked me.* He smiled and stepped into the elevator.

When he arrived at his door, he could see the Do Not Disturb! sign still on the doorknob. *Hmmm. Lenore must have decided to sleep in. It was a late night last night, wasn't it?* He inserted his electronic card key into the slot and went in. A putrid smell hit him immediately. The bed was unmade. The TV blared. *Lenore!* He saw her sprawled in an awkward position on the floor. "Lenore! Lenore!" He turned her face. Seeing her deep cyanotic color, he felt for a carotid pulse. *Nothing!* He put his ear to her lips. *No respirations!* He tilted her head and put his lips to hers to begin resuscitation, but quickly drew back, repulsed by the coldness of her skin and the stiffness of her neck. *It's no use! She's been dead too long!*

He wiped his mouth and went to the bathroom to wash up. An open bottle of Tylox sat beside the sink. *She's overdosed!* He dumped out the pills. Seven remained. *Suicide?* Tyson heaved a sigh and walked numbly back into the room. *Maybe my knowing about her past really flipped her out.*

He felt strange. Numb. His elation over the morning's hearings had evaporated. He thought he should cry, but he felt little remorse. The enormity of the situation grew slowly, along with an unspoken relief. *She's gone! I don't need to fear her any longer.*

He stared out of the window for a minute and then called the front desk.

"Good morning."

"This is Dr. Tyson. I'm in Room —" He fumbled for his key.

"— 1703."

"Yes?"

He halted. "My companion has died. I'll need the police."

A paramedic leaned over the bridge railing. "I can see her! She's down there!"

Mary looked up to the man wearing a

blue uniform. "Help me!"

"Hold on! Help's here!"

In a few minutes the man appeared again, dangling by a rope. The rescue squad members slowly lowered him into position. "I can't reach her!" He looked at Mary. "Stay where you are," he said calmly. "I'll come to you." He called to those above. "Lower me into the water!"

The team responded, and he dropped into the Wanoset. He swam to Mary with a few strong strokes. Carefully he secured a harness around her waist. "Hold on."

Mary obeyed and gripped the man around his neck with her right arm. They stood in the river, the platform now covered by two feet of rising water. He pushed off the platform and into the Wanoset. As soon as they were out from beneath the bridge, the line tightened, and they were lifted slowly to safety.

In minutes Mary rested in the back of the Bridgewater Fire and Rescue unit number one. A paramedic covered her with blankets and took her vital signs. "Hey, Joe, we're right on the border of the county. The river's the dividing line. Shall we take her to the University or to Crestview?"

"Dealer's choice, Frank. Crestview may be a mile closer, so —"

"Please," Mary protested weakly, "take me to Bridgewater. I don't want to go back to Crestview for a while."

The paramedic looked at her and shrugged. "Let's go back to Bridgewater."

Mary was safe!

"I want to see my husband!" It wasn't a request. Julie stood in the sergeant's office and tapped her foot.

"You'll get to see him. Really, it's only a matter of time." He stood up and sighed. "We've been over all of this before, Mrs. Forrest. Until I get Ms. Jacobs's testimony, my hands are tied. If her story correlates with your husband's and she doesn't want to press charges, I'll release him to you, O.K.?"

Julie didn't have a choice. She returned to the lobby and sat down on the bench. In another moment Belle rounded the corner and hobbled to her place beside her daughter-in-law. "Where'd you go?" Julie inquired.

"Had to use the phone. I called Matt and Linda and the folks over at Patterson's and gave them the good news. I told them the police have found Brad and Mary, so it's only a matter of time before Brad is released."

Julie smiled. It felt good to know that people cared.

Sixty miles to the north, state police officer Billy Swartz called in a report to the Bridgewater police station. "Be advised we have in custody two male suspects who were occupants of a blue van, matching the description you have issued. The two were questioned in the parking lot of a local supermarket after an officer noted the vehicle to be in violation of inspection code. The left taillight appeared to be broken, and when the officer questioned them about it, the two men fled from the scene. They were apprehended a few minutes later after a brief chase."

Jason Childs inquired, "Any identification of the suspects?"

"Not as of this time." The radio cracked again. "There is paint on the rear bumper matching the description of Mr. Forrest's abandoned vehicle."

Childs shook his head and sighed. *And to think I moved to a small town to get away from all this!*

Tyson's hotel suite became a buzz of activity with police, paramedics, hotel security, a senator, and, of course, the media. Questions were fired. Pictures were taken.

Lenore's things were collected.

The confirmation hearings were postponed, and Tyson went with the police for questioning.

Lenore's body remained untouched until Tyson left. They then put her in a zippered body bag and took her to the coroner for an autopsy.

Tyson's emotional roller coaster had rolled from the highest peak to the lowest valley in a few short minutes. Elation, pride, and self-confidence were replaced by emptiness, the threat of scandal, and embarrassment.

The Bridgewater police waited patiently in the hallway while Mary was examined and warmed and had an IV started. The nurse cleaned her abrasions and gave her a tetanus shot. An X-ray confirmed a shoulder dislocation, and an orthopedic surgeon was consulted.

"The doctor's still in surgery, Ms. Jacobs. He should be over to see you in a few minutes."

Officer Tidly had overheard the conversation. "Could I ask a few questions while we wait for the physician?"

The nurse looked sternly at the officer and then at Mary. "Only if you're up to this," she said softly.

"It's O.K.," she said. "I'll talk."

Meanwhile, Belle's phone calls had stimulated quite an assembly in the lobby of the Bridgewater Police Department. First there were joyous introductions between Matt and Linda Stone and Julie. A few minutes later a Patterson's Nursing Home van arrived with the whole praising bunch. Ben Kreider came in first and held the door while an aide maneuvered Florence Tutweiller in with her wheelchair. The Nessselrodts and Yoders followed, and Jen Slabaugh walked in on her own, using her prosthetic leg and a four-footed cane. In a matter of minutes the whole place looked more like a sixty-year high-school reunion than a police station.

"I've never been to a police station before," Craig Nesselrodt snickered.

"Oh, you'd think it was exciting going to the grocery store!" his wife snorted.

"I seem to remember you getting pretty excited when they served peaches instead of applesauce the other day! Talk about someone excited over nothin'. You told three people about —"

Richard interrupted. "O.K., you two! We're all a bit excited about this." He paused. "Alice and I were up half the night with a prayer burden we didn't understand. When Belle called this morning, it all clicked. Brad was in trouble!" He looked at the group. "So we prayed again — all of us did."

"And look what happened," Ben reported slowly.

"He's safe." Julie smiled.

Everyone nodded. Lilly and Ron Jacobs stood up from the small bench where they had huddled for the last two hours. Tears filled their eyes. "We've heard what you said. We've been praying, too. Our Mary's been rescued!"

"To the honor of the Lamb!" Ben lifted his hands to the Lord.

Julie hugged Mrs. Jacobs.

Sandy blew her nose.

Richard started a tremulous song.

Their prayers were answered! Brad and Mary were safe!

Just as their praises quieted, Sergeant Kowalski lifted his voice. The group looked up to see him unlocking Brad's handcuffs. "We've talked to Ms. Jacobs. No charges." He looked at Julie. "He's a free man!"

Julie ran to her husband, collapsing in his arms. Tears, hugs, and shouts exploded through the small police station.

Not only was Brad free, but they were a family again!

CHAPTER 35

Two days later Randy Harris looked over the official autopsy report. The pathologist was sure Lenore hadn't died of an overdose as the media had speculated. "Death secondary to massive intracerebral hemorrhage secondary to pituitary tumor, pituitary apoplexy."

We should have gone slower! We should have waited to watch the Dalmatian group. I could have prevented this! If only . . . if only . . . !

He sat for a few minutes with his head resting on his desk. *My suspicions were too late to save her. I should have known. I should have told her as soon as I knew the Dalmatian surrogate was dead!* He wept for a moment, his tears spilling onto a data sheet in front of him. *Jimmy was right. Just because we can doesn't mean we should.* He rose slowly, shut down his computer, and picked up the phone. "Operator, connect me with Gardner Kingsley's office please."

Tyson was back at Crestview, attempting to lose himself in the work that absorbed him the fastest. He felt compelled to continue his important tasks, including that of relieving society of the burden of infants with an insufficient quality of life.

He pushed the stack of charts to the side and checked his watch. Tammy had bugged him for several days. Her words reverberated in his mind: *"We need to talk, Web. Come and see me on 5 north. I'll find a private place to talk."* He sighed as his beeper went off. *5 north again! O.K., Tammy, I'll come up.*

He walked to the elevators, dreading his first face-to-face encounter with Tammy James. *This isn't the way I wanted you to find out about Lenore — through the media!* He had no idea that her anger and hurt had been well established by the time CNN reported his little romance.

He walked up the hallway to the 5 north nursing station. "Dr. Tyson," the ward clerk responded, "Tammy's been asking for you. She just stepped back down the hall."

Tyson followed the nod of her head and trudged toward the back exit. He found her straightening the linens in Room 525.

"Hi, Tammy."

She looked up and moved behind him to close the door. "We can talk here since the room is empty."

"Tammy, I'm sorry you had to find out this way. I —"

"Don't apologize, Web!" She paused, hiding the anger she felt with a veneer of gentleness. "I knew it before." She spoke softly. "From the time we dined together, just the three of us." She looked at his eyes. *This is just the way I planned it.*

He shifted uncomfortably. She continued, "I was so jealous." She reached for his hand.

"Look, Tammy, I —" Web halted nervously. "It's too soon after Lenore's death to —"

"She was my friend, too, Web. Don't forget that." She paused. "We both need time to grieve."

Tyson relaxed and accepted her hand. "I've been pretty numb with it all. I feel so many things, and then I feel nothing at all."

She continued to gaze into his eyes. "I think I understand. Lenore was very powerful — very attractive." She stroked his hand. "I'd think less of your manhood if you weren't attracted to her," she lied.

Tyson nodded.

Tammy's eyes brimmed. "Oh, Web . . ." She fell into his embrace. "Hold me." She buried her head on his shoulder and wept. After a few seconds she pressed her face close to his, her eyes locked on his. Whispering, she used the very words he had spoken to her on many occasions before. "I want to make you very comfortable." Her words were barely perceptible. "Very comfortable," she whispered.

Web jerked back as he felt a sharp sting in his right thigh. He looked down in horror as Tammy emptied the contents of a syringe into his leg. "What are you —"

Her look hardened as she quickly pocketed the syringe into her lab coat. "Don't fight it, Web. You won't get halfway up the hall."

Tyson felt the effects almost immediately as the drug was quickly absorbed into his bloodstream. With his face petrified, he gasped, "Norcuron?"

"Of course. Just like all the babies, remember? We didn't want them to suffer."

The surgeon stumbled backwards to the floor as the paralyzing agent affected the large muscle groups of his legs. Quickly his respirations became shallow as the effect spread to his diaphragm. He managed one more word before he found himself unable to talk or breathe. "Why?"

Tammy crouched over him, her face only inches from his unblinking eyes. She knew he could hear, think, and feel, but could not move, breathe, or blink. "You used me, Web," she seethed. "Like a tool. First right here in this room, you used me to carry out your little infanticide schemes! You used me later, too, didn't you? I suited your fancy for a while, didn't I, Web?" She paused, continuing to stare into his immovable expression of pure fear. "Until someone prettier and more powerful came along, right? Then you thought you would toss me aside. You owned me, Web. I would have done anything for you." A thin smile came across her face. "Well, now I'm free!"

She lifted his hand above his face and dropped it.

Web felt the blow to his face from his own hand, his lip tearing on his incisors. His lungs burned. *I need air! Don't let me die! Help me breathe!* He lay motionless, unable to mouth his panicking thoughts. In another thirty seconds he slipped into a merciful coma.

Tammy took his pulse and watched the clock. One minute, two, three, four. His heart continued to beat, but was now slow and irregular. After eight minutes she stood up. *I guess it's about time to let someone see.* She swung the door open. "Help!"

John Beckler looked irritated. He was

holding a half-eaten turkey club sandwich.

"What's up, Conrad? What couldn't wait?"

Conrad ripped off the headset he wore and flipped a switch. "I was taking my turn listening to Tyson. I'm not sure what's going on down there. Listen!"

"Help! I need some help back here!" The voice was shrill and female, with a rising pitch of panic.

"What's going on, Tammy?" A second female voice was heard, deeper and distinct from the first. "Oh my!"

"He just clutched his chest and collapsed!" First voice again. "Web! Oh, Web, don't die on me!"

"He doesn't have a pulse! There are no respirations!"

The first voice cried hysterically. "Web, oh Web, oh Web!"

A male voice. "It's Dr. Tyson."

Second female voice. "Call the operator. Code Blue, Room 525!"

John looked at Conrad. "You hear that? Call Denise! We've still got video surveillance equipment in that room! Let's make sure she's gettin' this!"

Matt Stone pulled another chart from the rack on 4 north nurses' station. Overhead, the operator's message began to urge, "Code Blue! Room 525! Code Blue! Room 525!"

Matt sighed. *I'd better see what's going on up there. I'm so close by*. He pushed the chart back into the rack and jogged to the stairwell. In less than thirty seconds he was entering 525. "What's going on?" He looked at a short nurse with curly hair who had placed an oxygen mask over Tyson's face.

"Probable M.I.," she answered, using the usual medical abbreviation for a heart attack (myocardial infarction).

Tammy flailed over the patient hysterically.

Matt felt for a carotid pulse. "No pulse. Start chest compressions." A young man pushed a crash cart into the room. "Give me a laryngoscope!" The aide administered a few breaths via the ambu-bag and then removed the mask. Only then did he realize that his patient was Web Tyson. "Dr. Tyson?"

Tammy cried out and threw herself onto Tyson's chest, knocking the nurse doing chest compressions to the side. "Oh, Web! Don't die on me!"

"Tammy!" The other nurse grabbed her manager by the shoulders. A nurse aide resumed chest compressions as Matt slipped an endotracheal tube into the trachea.

"There!" He listened to the chest with his stethoscope. "Give me 100 percent oxygen!"

Two additional nurses arrived to help in the resuscitation. One started an IV while the other attached cardiac monitor leads to the patient's chest.

"It looks like fine ventricular fibrillation! Let me have the paddles!"

Tammy quieted down and looked on with real concern.

"Two hundred joules!"

"Ready."

"All clear!" Matt held the paddles to Tyson's chest and fired. He studied the EKG monitor again. "Still in V-FIB." He looked at the nurse with curly hair. "Give an ampule of epinephrine and lidocaine." To the aide he added, "Restart CPR."

After another minute he spoke again. "Four hundred joules!"

"Ready."

"All clear!" The thump jolted Tyson's paralyzed body. The monitor registered a regular beep. "Sinus tach!" He felt for a pulse. "He's got a pulse!"

A nurse pumped up a blood pressure cuff on his arm. "Pressure 70 systolic."

Tammy looked at Matt with a look that

personified the hatred she felt. *You can't save him!*

"Start a dopamine drip at ten micrograms per kilogram per minute," Matt ordered. "Let's get him down to the I.C.U." He stood and looked at the team. "Good work. I'm going to call a cardiologist."

A respiratory therapist continued ventilating the patient. He looked at Matt. "The patient isn't assisting respirations at all."

"Better keep breathing for him. Hopefully we got him back in time," Stone added soberly. "Let's get a stretcher in here."

As Matt walked toward the door, Tammy looked on in amazement. *He's alive?* She stared at the monitor. *He's alive! No!*

"How'd it go?" Julie greeted her husband with a kiss as he stepped out of the Bridgewater police station.

"O.K., I guess. It really wasn't that difficult." He shrugged and grasped her hand. "Let's get out of here." After they were outside, he continued, "As it turns out, I picked the same two guys out of the lineup as Mary did." He paused. "The prosecutor is confident he has enough to make the attempted murder charges stick. I guess between the Dictaphone, our eyewitness testimony, and the physical evidence of my car's paint on the van, he feels the case is winnable."

They shuffled hand in hand down the sidewalk. "What about Southerly?" Julie asked. "Any chance they'll get tried for his murder?"

"I'm not sure. The police seem to hope that one of the crooks will spill the story to another inmate once they're in the penitentiary. Sometimes they end up bragging to someone who is willing to work a deal with the law for a shortened stay. They do say they are reopening the file to see if any other evidence comes up." Brad paused. "But in the meantime at least they'll be off the street."

The two walked to their old green Nova, and Brad opened the door for his wife.

After he jumped in, he patted the seat. "It smells like it always did," he reflected.

"Yes," Julie giggled. "About a hundred too many fast-food meals in here with Bradley, I'm afraid."

Brad backed out of his parking spot. "It sure was nice of Mr. Wheatman to trade us back on the BMW." He looked around. "Maybe he thought it was a smart deal since I've joined the ranks of the unemployed."

Julie shrugged and scooted over to her husband's side. "At least this has a bench seat. I couldn't sit this close to you in the Beamer." She laid her head against his shoulder.

He smiled. "It's worth every penny we saved then." They drove along for a mile in silence. Finally Julie brought up the question they'd been avoiding. "What's next, Brad?"

He pulled up to a red light and stopped before answering. "I guess you know about Dr. Dixon."

"Belle told me he called."

"He wants me back at the U. He's heard all about my troubles at Crestview. He says my reputation hasn't suffered in his eyes, and he'll let me start anytime."

Julie bit her lip. "What was your answer?" she asked softly.

"I told him . . ." Brad paused for suspense. "No."

Julie breathed again — this time with relief.

Brad went on, "I knew that in no time I'd be back at it all the time — O.R., research, grant applications, lectures, clinics, call, and more call. I just knew we didn't feel good about it before. Why should it be right for us now? Especially," he added, "in light of our new commitments to the Lord and to each other. I just knew God must have something else in mind."

She smiled and watched the light turn green. "So that brings me back to my question — what's next?"

"I don't know. But I do know one thing. I've never been at peace like I am now. I know God has everything under control. It's time for us to pray and trust."

"You have changed!"

They laughed. "Just in time." Brad smiled. "Just before I lost it all." He slipped his arm around his wife. "Just in time."

The following morning cardiologist Stu Barnes spoke quietly with Jimmy Tyson. In the background, the intensive care unit buzzed with activity. Just inside the first I.C.U. cubicle, Tammy James could be seen clutching the hand of a lifeless Web Tyson. Alternatively she would cry out, spilling large theatrical tears, or sit motionless, almost catatonic, in her isolated silence. Web's body lay still, seemingly suspended beneath a tangle of monitoring wires and IV tubings, the only movement provided by the regular rise and fall of his chest as the ventilator forced oxygen into his lungs. "The tests are conclusive, Jimmy," Dr. Barnes reported with compassion. "I'm sorry."

"He's dead then?" Jimmy squinted sadly.

"According to the E.E.G., he is brain-dead. The resuscitation was successful at restarting his heart, but not before he suffered massive irreversible brain ischemia."

Jimmy nodded with silent understanding. After a pause he asked, "So what's next?"

"We take him off the ventilator."

Jimmy looked over at Tammy. "Have you talked to her?"

"Yes." Dr. Barnes looked the young man in the eyes. "Do you want to be there when I remove the breathing tube?"

Another nod by Jimmy. "Sure." He walked to his father's bedside. After finishing up a note in Dr. Tyson's chart, the cardiologist joined him there.

Dr. Barnes pulled the curtain and began gently removing the tape that secured the endotracheal tube to Web's flaccid cheeks. Once that was accomplished, he deflated a small balloon cuff that sealed the tube in Web's trachea. He slipped the tube from his mouth, turned off the ventilator, and pressed a red Silence button on the face of the cardiac monitor. He didn't want any alarms now.

The trio watched in silence as the monitor registered Tyson's last cardiac activity — a string of regular beats, followed by erratic, irregular, large, ventricular ones, ending in a terminal fibrillation with an eventual flat line. It had taken four minutes. Web Tyson was dead.

Dr. Barnes turned off the monitor as Tammy heaved herself upon the lifeless form. There she continued her dramatic display of emotional sobs as Jimmy excused himself from behind the curtain. Stu Barnes shook Jimmy's hand and offered his condolences. As Jimmy pulled the curtain, he nearly stumbled over two uniformed men standing just outside the I.C.U. cubicle. In the background Tammy glanced at the taller officer and winced.

"Ms. James?"

She turned back to the body and wept for a moment longer before answering the officer's second verbal prompt. "Ms. Tammy James?"

"Yes," she sobbed. Her eyes bounced from the face of Web to the police who now stood beside her. "He's dead," she cried. "He's dead."

"We understand that, ma'am," Kowalski snapped.

"What do you want? Can't you see how upset I am?" She stood and dabbed her eyes with a tissue.

Sergeant Kowalski lifted a pair of handcuffs. "Tammy James, you're under arrest for the murder of Web Tyson."

"What!" Tammy shrieked. "You must be out of your mind!"

The officer snapped the handcuffs into place, ignored her biting remarks, and led her from the scene.

John Beckler walked behind Ms. James and her two uniformed escorts, listening as the sergeant recited her rights. "You have the right to remain silent. Any words you say can and will be used against you in a court of law . . ."

Shortly after noon, Gardner Kingsley issued a sober statement to the media. He spoke in a manner that characterized the deep anguish he felt over the loss of his daughter. Slowly he approached a small podium set up in UBI's spacious lobby. "As many of you are aware, we remain shocked over the recent death of UBI's president and my daughter, Lenore Kingsley. The world will forever remain in her debt for the work she accomplished." He paused and cleared his throat. Although the lobby was filled with nearly fifty reporters, silence prevailed.

Gardner continued, "It is in regards to Lenore's death that I feel obligated to speak to you today. Information that I have received only yesterday has prompted my decision. Lenore's death, although originally reported to have been due to drug overdose, was confirmed by autopsy to be due to a rare brain tumor. Although we are awaiting final, confirmatory tests prior to Lenore's burial, we have strong suspicions that her tumor was caused by a virus used to perform experimental gene splicing in human embryos."

He paused as a ripple of murmurs spread across the standing crowd. Several reporters looked at the front door. "Do not be alarmed," he added, holding up his hand. "Lenore worked intimately with this research, and this virus is not one to which you are susceptible." Several sighs of relief followed. He made no mention of the nature of the experiments and purposefully did not define her role as a surrogate. "I am making this announcement only to clarify the media's continued questioning about Lenore's mysterious death, and to urge our government and other researchers to consider a moratorium on human embryo research. I know that Lenore was deeply committed to this research. I believe her dedication has cost her her life."

He cleared his throat again and sighed heavily into the microphone. "After talking with a top researcher directly involved with this controversial research, I am following his recommendations to end all germ cell line manipulation of human genes." He paused as several hands shot up and many other faces twisted with confusion.

"I am unable to answer your questions at this time. Look for full published data in the future in which UBI will give the details of our research." Slowly he moved away from the podium and disappeared through the locked doors at the rear of the lobby.

Before Matt arrived home later that day, the news of Tyson's death preceded him. Shortly after Tammy's arrest, the story riveted national news-watchers. As a second Surgeon General candidate lay dead, the police were holding a "jealous lover" as a prime suspect for murder. The normally sedate Green County reeled, tottering on the brink of control. First a local surgeon suspected of committing murder, then the death of a local pharmaceutical hero, and now this! People walked around as if they were dazed, unable to speak of anything else. Others couldn't speak of it at all, but only shook their heads numbly as if to say, "In our small county?" About the only one to benefit from the whole thing was Jake, who reported that his diner business increased by 30 percent as people gathered to compare stories and eat or drink.

Linda met her weary husband at the door with a kiss.

"I guess you heard —" Matt started without saying hello.

"Oh yeah."

He plopped onto the couch, oblivious to the table setting beyond. "This whole thing is incredible." Linda sat next to him. Matt went on, "I saw John Beckler down at Crestview just after the arrest. That's when it hit me! The F.B.I. must have picked up something because of the surveillance of Room 525. That's the very room Tyson coded in. They must have seen something that initiated Tammy's arrest."

"What did the F.B.I. say?"

"Nothing. John was pretty tight-lipped about the whole thing. I suppose they have to be."

"The news stories have been pretty sketchy on the evidence proving Tammy is responsible."

Matt sighed. Linda put her head on his shoulders. "Are you wearing perfume?"

Linda smiled. "A little."

"What's the occasion?" Matt shifted, finally noticing the table decorated with candles and a cheerful tablecloth.

"I just thought you might need a little cheering up." She kissed him.

"Is someone coming for dinner?"

"No."

Matt smiled. "That's pretty fancy just for the two of us."

"Just for the *three* of us," Linda corrected softly. Her eyes met Matt's. He instantly understood.

"Three?" His jaw dropped. "Y-you mean y-you're —"

Linda bit her lip to hold back a happy cry and nodded her head rapidly.

Suddenly Matt's focus on all of Green County's problems evaporated. He swept his wife into his arms and couldn't stop his own sweet tears. Life!

EPILOGUE

Four months later, life in Green County eased into a routine throb. At Jake's Diner and every other public waterhole, conversations still frequently turned to the summer's events and the trials that unseated those used to a quieter lifestyle.

Tammy James's trial unleashed a defensive outcry of unfair government intrusion that had people talking about Big Brother and the individual's privacy rights. The Blackburn Administration stood its ground and proclaimed that the broader public's protection was at stake if they were not allowed to investigate possible wrongdoing in public servants, even if that meant covert operations. In the end, the jury was allowed to view the F.B.I.'s tape, and Tammy's guilty verdict was sealed.

In the second trial absorbing the county's conversations, the jury found both the assailants of Brad Forrest and Mary Jacobs guilty of attempted murder. Paul Southerly's death gained increasing public speculation and continued to be shrouded in mystery. Although rumors abounded about additional information brought forward by Sally Southerly, a tight seal by the Washington, D.C., prosecutor prevented public knowledge about the possibility of any charges surrounding her husband's death.

Brad, Julie, and Bradley found a new home and a new job working for a small pediatric surgical practice outside Atlanta and joined a home group meeting weekly with Gerald and Sophie Mitchell. Belle chose not to move away from Green Valley and instead moved into the west wing of Patterson's Nursing Home.

Life for Matt and Linda Stone continued to unfold as an opportunity to stay on at Crestview Women's and Children's Health Center materialized. Matt accepted the temporary position as a chance to spend more time in prayer until he could secure a more permanent appointment. In spite of her husband's hospital affiliation, Linda sought prenatal care at Bridgewater University.

Meanwhile, the search for another physician for Valley Surgeons for Children persisted. It was a cold February day when Mark Davis bustled toward the clinic with another candidate to interview. He stopped momentarily when he saw Matt Stone.

"Hi, Matt. What do you hear from Brad these days?"

"He called the other evening. Seems like he

The American Secretary of State

AN INTERPRETATION

The American Secretary of State

AN INTERPRETATION

Alexander DeConde

FREDERICK A. PRAEGER
Publisher • New York

BOOKS THAT MATTER

Published in the United States of America in 1962 by
Frederick A. Praeger, Inc., Publisher
64 University Place, New York 3, N.Y.

Library of Congress Catalog Card Number: 62-13745

THE AMERICAN SECRETARY OF STATE
is published in two editions:

A paperback edition (U-520)
A clothbound edition

Printed in the United States of America

For Jeanne

A PRAYER ON BECOMING SECRETARY OF STATE

O God, my only trust was thou
Through all life's scenes before:
Lo, at thy throne again I bow,
New mercies to implore.

Thy aid, O Father, wilt thou lend?
My thoughts wilt thou inspire?
My heart to do thy pleasure bend?
My breast to virtue fire?

Thy gracious wisdom to fulfill
My constant aim incline,
Grant for my feeble, faltering will
Th' unerring strength of thine.

Grant active powers, grant fervid zeal,
And guide by thy control,
And ever be my country's weal
The purpose of my soul.

Thine be the purpose, thine the deed,
Which thou alone canst bless.
From thee all perfect gifts proceed,
Oh, crown them with success.

Extend, all-seeing God, thy hand,
In mercy still decree,
And make to bless my native land
An instrument of me.

JOHN QUINCY ADAMS
(Written when he assumed his duties as Secretary of State, September 21, 1817)

Preface

IN 1957, Dwight D. Eisenhower told newspapermen that the position of Secretary of State is "the greatest and most important job in the world." Although the President's statement was a deliberate exaggeration intended to stress his unflagging support of John Foster Dulles, then under attack in Congress and elsewhere, it was no more than accurate in recognizing that the shadow of the Secretaryship has become so big that it stretches around the earth. The Secretary appears to mankind a symbol of America, the official spokesman of the American Government on matters of foreign policy. His words and deeds have worldwide repercussions.

Despite the growth in importance of the Secretaryship of State, no one person, to my knowledge, has ever written a historical analysis of that office. Few, moreover, seem to have a solid understanding of the Secretary's role in the making of foreign policy. This study offers an interpretation of the Secretaryship—in effect, a brief biography of the office. It is more an introduction than a monograph and hence makes no claim to comprehensiveness. It concentrates primarily on the Secretary's power, his personal influence in the conduct of foreign relations and the influence he and his office have had and do have in government. It attempts to explain some of the Secretary's history and responsibilities and, most of all, his relationship to the President. This book does not deal with the details of the Secretary's diplomacy, his administrative functions, or his relations with other agencies in the government. Those aspects of the Secretaryship may be found elsewhere. I have tried in my analysis to combine the techniques of the historian and the political scientist, and in doing so, I have examined principles that may give some understanding of the Secretaryship as a historical institution.

My main theme is the conventional one that the power of the Secretary of State depends on his relations with the President and hence is personal more than institutional. I cannot accept the platitude that "every President must be his own Secretary of State"; power in the Secretaryship, in the sense that the Secretary participates in the making of high-level decisions, is flexible. Whether that flexibility derives from the Presidency alone or is intrinsic in the Secretaryship itself, it is clear that the Secretary of State often stands next to the summit of power in the American system of government. This analysis tries to show why this has been and is so.

A number of friends and colleagues, in history, political science, psychology, and in the Department of State, have helped me in clarifying my ideas and avoiding errors of fact and interpretation in the writing of this book. It is a pleasure to express publicly my deep gratitude to John R. Alden, John W. Atkinson, Thomas A. Bailey, David D. Burks, Mary P. Chapman, Richard N. Current, Donald F. Drummond, Russell H. Fifield, Sidney Fine, Hugh M. Hall, Harold K. Jacobson, John Tate Lanning, William L. Neumann, E. Taylor Parks, Marvin Zahniser, and Burton F. Beers, who shared some of his research on Robert Lansing with me. Since several of these gracious critics, who have read the manuscript at some stage of its development, disagree with some of the views I express, I must stress that all interpretations are my own. Remaining errors, of course, are mine too. I am indebted to the Horace H. Rackham School of Graduate Studies, of the University of Michigan, for a generous grant from its Faculty Research Fund that has aided me in my research and writing. Lastly, I wish also to point out that some of my time as a Guggenheim Fellow in 1960 was spent in condensing and revising this study for publication.

ALEXANDER DECONDE

Santa Barbara, California

Contents

I

Origins and Precedents

> The Congress have wisely put their finances into the hands of one intelligent person. I wish they would do the same with their correspondence, by appointing a single secretary for foreign affairs,
>
> —BENJAMIN FRANKLIN, 1781

WHAT may be called the beginnings of the Secretaryship of State were haphazard. Its domestic functions originated in the work of Charles Thomson, a fiery patriot of Irish birth known as "the Sam Adams of Philadelphia," who served as the Secretary of the Continental Congress throughout its life, that is, from 1774 to 1789. He promulgated the laws and ordinances of Congress, was the keeper of the Great Seal, the official mark of the nation's sovereignty, and served as the medium of communication between Congress and those affected by its acts. He was, in effect, a secretary for affairs of state, an administrator without power in the making of vital decisions.

No one individual at first held responsibility for the more important matters of foreign affairs. Congress itself controlled them but placed their operations in the hands of special committees. In November, 1775, more than six months before the thirteen American colonies made their final break with Great Britain, the second Continental Congress created the most important of those committees, the Committee of Secret Correspondence, to communicate with friends in Britain, Ireland, and other parts of the world. Since this standing committee of five was restricted only by the requirement that it had to place its correspondence before Congress when so directed, it theoretically could act on its own initiative. Its first chairman, Benjamin Franklin, carried the burden of its correspondence and of most of its other work. He may, therefore, be considered America's first executive official directly responsible for foreign affairs, a kind of embryonic secretary of state.

Franklin's committee held secret meetings with a French agent in December, 1775, to discuss possible aid to the rebelling Colonies, and Franklin himself wrote the instructions for America's first diplomatic agent, who went to France as a representative of the committee to seek an alliance. Yet neither Franklin nor the committee was able to gain any real power over foreign relations. Congress, either through other special committees or its committee of the whole, exercised a close control over foreign policy, even over minute administrative details.

In this condition of virtual impotence, with no permanent chairman, divided views, and a fluctuating membership, the Committee of Secret Correspondence survived until April, 1777, when, in keeping with the nation's proclaimed independence, Congress changed the group's name to the "Committee for Foreign Affairs" and appointed Thomas Paine its first secretary. As an organ for the conduct of foreign relations, the new committee proved as ineffective as its predecessor, for Congress would not augment its power along with the change of title.

Paine had hoped to become more than a mere clerk and even considered himself a kind of foreign minister. He frequently arrogated to himself the title "Secretary for Foreign Affairs," but his authority never matched his grandiose idea. As secretary, the pugnacious Paine lasted less than two years, being compelled to resign in January, 1779, for making public, in a quarrel within Congress, information his oath of office had pledged him to keep secret. During the controversy, Gouverneur Morris, a haughty conservative, stressed that Paine served solely at the pleasure of Congress.

James Lovell, a Boston schoolmaster and politician, next became the committee's guiding but faltering spirit. He monotonously complained of his difficulties—neglect by Congress, the obstacles to squeezing work from a committee whose members had other pressing obligations, and an inadequate staff. For months at a time, he himself was the committee, carrying on its affairs by what he called long hours of "quill-driving" at night after he had spent a full day in Congress. In one of his complaints, he admitted that "there is really no Such Thing as a Committee of foreign affairs existing, no Secretary or Clerk, further than I persevere to be one and the other."

Weary of Lovell's excuses for not maintaining correspondence, Benjamin Franklin, then the American Minister in Paris, sent him a piercing criticism of the committee system in the handling of foreign affairs, in which he said that they "would best be managed by one Secretary, who could write when he had an Opportunity, without waiting for the Concurrence or Opinions of his Brethren, who cannot always be got conveniently together."

John Jay, at the time on a special diplomatic mission in Madrid, was equally critical. "One good private correspondent," he wrote, "would be worth twenty standing committees, made of the wisest heads in America, for the purpose of intelligence."

Although in part responsible for Lovell's difficulties, Congress, too, had become dissatisfied with his work and the chaos in the management of foreign relations. Even before Franklin and Jay had expressed their criticisms, others had recognized that the committee system was failing and that a department of foreign affairs, headed by a responsible and respected minister, was needed. Alexander Hamilton, one of the most vigorous of the critics, wrote that "there is always more decision, more dispatch, more responsibility, where single men than where bodies are concerned."

The Articles of Confederation and Perpetual Union, the nation's first constitution, had not made provision for an office such as the critics desired. Yet the Articles stated that Congress could appoint such "committees and civil officers as may be necessary for managing the general affairs of the United States" —a power capable of broad interpretation. Congress, moreover, began to consider a reform before the states had ratified the Articles. In January, 1779, it instructed the Committee for Foreign Affairs to secure information on how foreign governments managed their executive departments.

Up to this time, the system used in the conduct of foreign relations had not followed foreign models. It had sprung by chance, as the need arose, from American roots. Hamilton and others who had studied the ministries in European governments had apparently been most impressed by those in France and England. The principle of control of an executive department by one man had advanced further in France than in England, and the example most often used to illustrate the advantage of centralized control was the work of the Duc de Sully, Henry IV's powerful minister.

Sometime in 1779, the Committee for Foreign Affairs obtained the information Congress had requested, but Congress did not act on it until May, 1780, when it appointed a special committee to consider a proper arrangement for a department of foreign affairs. The committee submitted a report in June, but Congress delayed consideration of it until December, when increased pressure in foreign relations made action imperative.

In its original report, the special committee had urged the grant of substantial powers to a minister of foreign affairs—probably patterned after the French model—who could formulate foreign policy. It pointed out that "the most effectual mode of conducting the business of the Department of Foreign Affairs would be through a minister vested with confidential powers after the example of other nations, responsible for his trust and under the immediate direction of Congress." Jealous of its own authority over foreign relations and unwilling to surrender any of it, Congress vetoed the suggestion.

The committee's plan, as modified and finally adopted by Congress on January 10, 1781, created the Department of Foreign Affairs headed by a Secretary for Foreign Affairs. The new office was neither that of a mere Congressional clerk nor that of a responsible policy-making minister. It fell somewhere between the two. The new Secretary was to be essentially a high-level administrative officer; he was to be elected by Congress, hold office at its pleasure, serve under its immediate control and supervision, and be responsible to it for his actions. His chief functions were to correspond with the American ministers abroad and to receive the communications of the ministers of foreign powers in the United States. To enable him to explain his reports and to keep informed of domestic developments, he was given the privilege of attending Congress, a privilege that might enable him to take part in the deliberations on foreign policy.

Divided by factional and sectional rivalry, Congress delayed seven months before filling the new post. In August, 1781, it finally elected Robert R. Livingston, lawyer, politician, and Chancellor of the state of New York, as the first Secretary for Foreign Affairs—a choice stemming allegedly from French influence in Congress.

Arthur Lee, the defeated candidate for the Secretaryship, was bitter. "Whatever you see or receive from him you may consider as dictated by the French Minister," Lee said of Livingston. "He made him what he is, and policy, or gratitude, keeps him from disobeying or renouncing his maker."

Having served as a member of the earlier Committee for Foreign Affairs, Livingston fortunately had had some experience with the demands of the new office. Nonetheless, he confessed that he felt unequal to the task, saying the subject was "new to me & foreign to the line in which my studies have lain."

Before accepting the post, Livingston asked for an explanation of its powers, particularly whether he would be given authority to appoint his own subordinates. The president of Congress assured him that his office was "one of the most honorable in the gift of Congress," and that "the liberty to attend Congress, and the constant intercourse with the Members, distinguish it from any other." In September, after Congress had satisfied his inquiry, Livingston accepted.

After three months, Livingston discovered flaws in the obligations and powers of his office and recommended changes. Since Congress was sovereign, he pointed out, an intimate knowledge of its sentiments was necessary if he were properly to carry out his duties, but he could not obtain that knowledge through its public acts or merely by attending its sessions and explaining his reports. In monarchical governments, he said, the minister of foreign affairs is "considered as the most confidential servant of the crown. In republics it is much more difficult to execute this task, as the sentiments of the sovereign sometimes change with the members who compose the sovereignty." He therefore requested the specific right to ask questions and explain his own views when his reports were being debated in Congress. He also asked for the power to act on his own in minor matters, and for more clerical help.

After examining the Secretaryship for Foreign Affairs, a special Congressional committee reported favorably on Livingston's suggestions. Among its recommendations, it urged that the Secretary be assigned a seat that would place him "officially in Congress" and allow him to initiate discussion and defend his policies. This last might have established the precedent for a responsible and politically powerful minister of foreign affairs, but Congress, unwilling to go that far, denied Livingston's basic request. Most of the committee's recommendations were embodied in a law of February 22, 1782, that repealed the act of the previous year establishing the office.

Although the new law made no basic changes, in some instances it enlarged the Secretary's powers and in others defined them more closely than before. He was obliged, for example, to submit correspondence concerning treaties or "other great national subjects" to Congress before sending it. Since the law entrusted him with correspondence on foreign affairs between Congress and the governors of the states, it in effect added a domestic responsibility to his duties. It also changed his title to the "Secretary to the United States of America for the Department of Foreign Affairs."

Despite the reform, the Secretary still found himself narrowly restricted. He had no power of independent action, and even in small matters of administration, Congress was to take the initiative and make the basic decisions. At times, it ignored him and corresponded directly with ministers abroad and with foreign diplomats in Philadelphia, the capital. It also gave special committees power over foreign relations, and those committees, too, often bypassed Livingston.

By disregarding the Secretary and taking the details of foreign policy into its own hands, Congress made his office little more than an administrative bureau. Except for employing his personal influence with Congress, Livingston could do little to shape the nation's foreign policy. The tenure of the first Secretary for Foreign Affairs thus set a precedent in that he suffered disabilities that were to plague some of the later Secretaries of State, particularly those serving under strong Presidents.

In November, 1782, Congress passed a motion, introduced by James Madison, to enlarge the Secretary's power by allowing him greater freedom in correspondence and in the selection of the information he was required to submit to it. Nevertheless, the next month Livingston offered his resignation, giving as his reasons the increase in his duties as Chancellor of New York, a post he had never given up, and a salary inadequate to maintain the dignity of his office. Madison and others suspected that the treatment Livingston had suffered under Congress had induced his resignation. Livingston left the department in June, 1783. Although hampered by severe limitations, he had tried to formulate as well as carry out policy. Even though he was unsuccessful in policy matters, he was a first-class administrator and brought organization to his department and stature to his new office.

Since Congress was still ridden by faction and some members had long been critical of Livingston, few seem to have lamented his departure. One critic wrote that "his Office was misterious, & secret to all those, who ought to have a perfect Knowledge of all it contain'd— It was undoubtedly public to all those, to whom it ought to have been a profound Secret."

Although a number of prominent men sought the office, which attested to its intrinsic importance, members of Congress appeared to prefer no Secretary for Foreign Affairs to one who might come from an opposing faction. They did not, therefore, immediately elect a successor to Livingston, and the duties of his office fell to the first Under Secretary, who soon resigned because Congress would give him no authority to act. The President of Congress then handled the routine matters and Congress itself managed foreign policy through special committees it appointed as specific needs arose. For a year, including the critical period when peace negotiations were being concluded with Great Britain in Paris, the nation had no officer directly responsible for foreign relations.

I.

Congress had for some time been receiving reports of the conspicuous skill John Jay had displayed in the peace negotiations in Paris. In May, 1784, it elected him the second Secretary to the United States of America for the Department of Foreign Affairs. Jay did not learn of his appointment until friends told him on his arrival home from Paris. Although only thirty-nine years old, he had acquired such broad experience that he was eminently qualified to endow the management of foreign relations with a prestige it had long been lacking. He had been President of the Continental Congress, an original member of the Committee of Secret Correspondence, and a key negotiator in the commission that secured England's recognition of American independence. Certainly, he appeared prepared for all aspects of his new post—political, diplomatic, and administrative.

In notifying Jay officially of the appointment, Charles Thomson stressed that "your country stands in need of your abilities in that office. I feel sensibly that it is not only time but highly necessary for us to think and act like a sovereign as well as a free people." The opportunities offered by the office, he said, "will I trust, greatly contribute to raise and promote this Spirit."

Despite this flattery, Jay deferred his decision, notifying Thomson that he would accept only if Congress would establish itself in one place and if he could appoint his own clerks. Congress met those conditions, and Jay assumed his new duties in December.

Interpreting his position as one of influence and authority, Jay was dissatisfied by the vagueness of the powers of his revived office. He believed that the Secretary should actually conduct foreign relations and have a voice in formulating policy. In January, 1785, he sought to clarify his status. "I have some reason, Sir," he told the President of Congress, "to apprehend that I have come into the office of Secretary for foreign affairs with Ideas of its Duties & Rights somewhat different from those which seem to be entertained by Congress."

To meet some of Jay's objections, Congress attempted a clearer definition of his responsibilities. In the following month, it resolved that all communications concerning foreign affairs should be made through the Secretary for the Department of Foreign Affairs. Congress thus conceded what it had previously been reluctant to do. By centralizing foreign relations in Jay's office, it had taken an important step toward making the Secretaryship a truly important organ of government, a step approved by those who wished to endow the office with stability and authority. "If the Office of Foreign Affairs be a proper one, & properly filled," James Madison wrote shortly after, referring to Jay's views, "a reference of all foreign despatches to it in the first instance, is so obvious a course, that any other disposition of them by Congress seems to condemn their own establishment, to affront the Minister in office," and to impair his usefulness in dealing with foreign governments.

Within the limitations of its power, Jay made the most of his office, trying to become a foreign secretary in fact as well as in name. Unlike his predecessor, he took full advantage of his privilege of attending Congress. He decided what papers should or should not be transmitted to it, brought before it any question of foreign affairs he thought necessary, frequently made recommendations as to what course it should follow in foreign policy, and did not hesitate to defend his own policies. In deference to his experience in foreign affairs, Congress listened to him with respect and usually followed his advice.

To outsiders, Jay's influence appeared great. The French consul in New York believed that the Secretary had acquired a "peculiar ascendancy over the members of Congress" and feared that since considerable important business passed through his office, they would "insensibly become accustomed to seeing only through the eyes of Mr. Jay." Two weeks later, he reported that "the political importance of Mr. Jay increases daily," and added, "Congress seems to me to be guided only by his directions, and it is as difficult to obtain anything without the cooperation of that minister as to bring about the rejection of a measure proposed by him."

Even though Congress did not, in fact, always guide itself by its Secretary's advice and suspiciously guarded its authority in foreign relations, it did release more of that authority to Jay than it had previously to any individual. In March, 1785, Jay had reported the form of a commission for John Adams as Minister to England. Although that important work had always been one of the Secretary's functions, it had usually been performed by special committees. This was the first instance in which Congress entrusted the Secretary with it. In July, Congress invested Jay with authority to make and sign a treaty with Don Diego de Gardoqui, an envoy from Spain. This was the first recognition of the Secretary as a negotiator of treaties, a task that had previously been assigned to special commissions. At the same time, Congress appointed a committee to receive communications from the Secretary, another recognition of the growing importance of his office.

In giving Jay the power of negotiator, Congress had stipulated that he would have to submit all propositions, his own and Gardoqui's, to it before acting on any of them. Irked by that restriction, he told Congress in August that "It is proper and common to instruct Ministers on the great Points to be agitated, and to inform them how far they are to insist on some, and how far they may yield on others— But I am inclined to think it is very seldom thought necessary to leave nothing at all to their Discretion." In such a case, he added, "the man ought not to be employed." Several days later, Congress rescinded its galling restriction, insisting only that he could conclude no treaty until it had been submitted to Congress for approval.

Nothing concrete came of the talks with Gardoqui, but Jay's determined efforts in those negotiations to take foreign policy into his own hands alarmed some members of Congress, particularly those from the South. They distrusted his independence and appetite for power, correctly fearing that he would, if he could, have bartered away the right to navigate the Mississippi River to its mouth in return for Spanish commercial concessions beneficial to the Northeast.

In the Gardoqui negotiations, as at other times, Jay suffered under the frustrating supervision of Congress. He believed that his office did not possess the power it should have or he himself deserved. Even though he was able to wield considerable political influence, he could not bring it into full effect because he could seldom swing the great majority of the legislative body to his views. In the case of the Algerian pirates who preyed on American commerce in the Mediterranean, for example, he preferred war to the payment of tribute, but in this instance, as in others, Congress refused to follow his advice.

Jay's experience as Secretary for Foreign Affairs contributed to his conviction that the Congress under the Articles of Confederation was a weak instrument and that the nation needed a stronger and more centralized government, especially for the guidance of its foreign policy. In collaborating with Alexander Hamilton and James Madison to produce the essays of *The Federalist,* in which Jay discussed the need for effective leadership in foreign relations, he lent his pen and the prestige of his office to those men who were bent on replacing the Confederation government.

Although Jay was clearly the servant of Congress, he had striven to become a responsible foreign secretary such as he had seen in his diplomatic work abroad, and he had partially succeeded. He had won greater power from Congress than had his predecessor. Under him the Secretaryship, despite its limitations, had become the foremost executive office of the Confederation government—a post of prominence and prestige. He had established precedents that were to make its successor, the Secretaryship of State, the highest nonelective office in the land.

II.

Drawing upon the experience of the Confederation era, the founding fathers at the Constitutional Convention in Philadelphia, in 1787, considered several proposals that would have surrounded the President with some kind of advisory council that included a secretary for foreign affairs. Yet the Constitution they framed provided for such a secretaryship only by implication. It stipulated that the President could require written opinions from the heads of the executive departments upon any subject relating to the duties of their offices. It was left to the first Congress of the new Federal Government, therefore, to establish an executive office for the management of foreign affairs.

In May, 1789, a month after Congress had assembled, it took up the question of creating and organizing executive departments. After considerable discussion, James Madison introduced a motion in the House of Representatives calling for the establishment of departments of foreign affairs, treasury, and war, each to be headed by a secretary appointed by the President with the advice and consent of the Senate and subject to removal by the President.

Objection immediately arose to placing the department of foreign affairs first and thus ranking its secretary ahead of the other executive officers. One member of Congress maintained that the treasury department was the most important and should be established first. On the basis of experience in the Confederation era, those who favored a strong government argued that the management of foreign affairs needed buttressing; they insisted that if there had been a sturdy department of foreign affairs during the Revolution, a great deal of trouble might have been avoided and the war shortened.

The most heated debate centered on whether the power of removal of a department head should be vested in the President alone or should be shared by him and the Senate. Madison saw danger in a dual control of the removal power, contending that the head of a department should be responsible to the President alone and, under that relationship, should have the highest degree of responsibility in the conduct of his office. "Now," he added, "if the heads of the Executive departments are subjected to removal by the President alone, we have in him security for the good behavior of the officer. If he does not conform to the judgment of the President in doing the executive duties of his office, he can be displaced. This makes him responsible to the great Executive power, and makes the President responsible to the public for the conduct of the person he nominated and appointed to aid him in the administration of his department."

If the President could not remove a Secretary without the Senate's consent, then the Senate would, in effect, share the President's responsibility for the Secretary's conduct. This, Madison said, "would abolish at once that great principle of unity and responsibility in the Executive department." In a dual control over the removal of executive officers, moreover, the people could not hold the Senate to any accountability.

Many Congressmen feared the surrender of too much authority to the President, particularly allowing him almost absolute power over his department heads. Such power, they held, would "make the President a monarch." Whether this faction believed that an executive officer, such as the secretary for foreign affairs, should be accountable by something similar to parliamentary responsibility is not clear. They were convinced, apparently, that the department heads had independent constitutional status and hence were not completely dependent on the President.

Madison's ideas prevailed. The House passed his motion and instructed a committee of eleven to prepare bills that would establish the three executive departments. In drawing up the bill for a department of foreign affairs, the committee used the laws of 1781 and 1782 as models. In fact, with some modification, it revived the department and secretarial office that had existed under the Confederation government.

In June, the committee reported bills for a war department and a department of foreign affairs. To give precedence to the department of foreign affairs, Congress considered its bill first. At once the debate on the removal power burst out again. One Congressman stressed that the head of that department "is as much an instrument in the hands of the President, as the pen is the instrument of the Secretary in corresponding with foreign courts. If, then, the Secretary of Foreign Affairs is the mere instrument of the President, one would suppose, on the principle of expediency, this officer should be dependent upon him." Nonetheless, the House struck out the clause explicitly making the proposed Secretary for the Department of Foreign Affairs removable by the President.

As passed by the House and Senate, and signed into law by President George Washington on July 27, 1789, the act created the Department of Foreign Affairs headed by the Secretary for the Department of Foreign Affairs, who was to perform such duties as the President entrusted to him. The few responsibilities it specified were those normally connected with the management of foreign relations. Moreover, the Secretary was to conduct the business of his department "in such manner as the President of the United States shall, from time to time, order or instruct."

The new Secretary was thus given responsibilities similar to those of his immediate predecessor under the Confederation, but instead of holding office at the pleasure of Congress, he did so at the pleasure of the President, for the basic law implied that the President had the exclusive power of removal; he did not need the consent of the Senate before acting. Since the Senate accepted this implication, the debate over the law creating the first of the executive departments resulted in an enhancement of the President's power and in making the Secretary for the

Department of Foreign Affairs his complete subordinate. Although Congress was later to challenge the President's power of removal, that power has always remained exclusively with the President and is one of the means by which he retains mastery over the machinery of foreign policy.

Although the power to remove all three of the original department heads had been vested in the President, all three were not equally subordinate to him. The law establishing the Treasury Department, for instance, did not mention the Secretary of the Treasury's dependence on the President in the conduct of his office. It also assigned that Secretary enumerated duties, whereas the law creating the office of the Secretary for the Department of Foreign Affairs indicated only the general scope of his duties. The Secretary of the Treasury, although dependent on the President for his appointment and tenure, was closer to Congress than was the Secretary for the Department of Foreign Affairs; the Treasury head was subject to the call of Congress, was more closely hemmed in by statutes, and had a greater freedom of action under the President.

To take over the functions formerly held by the Secretary of the Continental Congress, some members of Congress urged a fourth executive department, a Home Department headed by a Secretary of the United States for the Home Department. Since many other members considered the proposed office unnecessary and the whole idea thus met with scant favor, a compromise emerged whereby those functions that did not fall easily within the scope of the Treasury and War departments would be assigned to the Department of Foreign Affairs. The result was a law of September 15, 1789, that changed the name of the Department of Foreign Affairs to the Department of State, with its principal officer known as the Secretary of State.

In addition to his responsibilities in the conduct of foreign relations, the Secretary of State now acquired specific domestic duties, such as having custody of the Great Seal and responsibility for publishing the laws enacted by Congress. Thus, what had formerly been the duties of the Secretary for Foreign Affairs under the Confederation government and of the Secretary of the Continental Congress were now combined in those of the Secretary of State.

Since the founding fathers had studied and used the laws establishing the executive offices under the Confederation before creating new ones, it is not surprising that the Secretaryship of State inherited most of the duties and characteristics of its predecessors. There were, however, fundamental differences between the new Secretaryship and the old ones. In the new Federal Government, control over foreign policy was centralized in the President and, under him, in the office of the Secretary of State. The power of final decision in foreign policy, which during the Confederation had belonged to Congress, had now passed to the President.

In theory, the task of the Secretary of State was less difficult than that of the earlier Secretary for Foreign Affairs. The new Secretary, whose main task was to interpret and carry out the foreign policies of the President, was responsible only to one immediate superior, whereas his predecessor had been responsible to many. A strong Secretary of State, as the future would show, might gain such influence with a President that his, in fact, would be the decisive voice in the making of foreign policy, for a Secretary might more easily influence one man than a whole Congress.

Aside from the Secretary of State's complete dependence on the President, a distinctive feature in the founding of his office was that it had not been precisely patterned after models in other governments. Although the Secretaryship of State had European ancestors and a history before it was born, the foreign models that may have influenced its shaping had done their work before 1789. It had grown directly from the experience and precedents of the Confederation era, specifically from the Committee of Secret Correspondence of 1775 and the office of the Secretary of the Continental Congress. No other office in the world was quite comparable to the Secretaryship of State. It came into being as a uniquely American office to meet the specific needs of a new experiment in government.

2

Responsibilities, Powers, Limitations

> Although a Secretary of State confers with the President on important matters of policy and is the President's agent in the field of foreign relations, in practice he acts largely on his own initiative and responsibility.
>
> —CORDELL HULL, 1948

FROM the outset, as Congress had intended when it created his office, the Secretary of State was the nation's highest appointive executive officer. Thomas Jefferson, the first Secretary of State, held a vague but nonetheless real priority over the other department heads in what was to become the Cabinet. Since Jefferson's time, the Secretary of State has been entitled to take, and has usually taken, his oath of office before all other members of the Cabinet.

The Secretary of State's power does not derive, of course, from protocol. It comes from his influence with the President, from his ability to persuade the President and guide him properly, from his role as the President's chief staff adviser, and from his position as the only Cabinet officer who can devote his full time to foreign affairs. Next to the President himself, the Secretary has the heaviest responsibility for defending and promoting the nation's interests abroad. To do so effectively, he must, besides carrying out his other responsibilities, keep the American people aware of the nature of foreign policy and its objectives. He stands at the center of a web of constitutional, political, and administrative responsibilities at home that he must fulfill and defend against encroachment by other executive agencies that also deal with foreign relations. His position of primacy has long roots.

Tradition and the practice of Presidents have strengthened both the Secretary's official precedence and his *de facto* primacy. George Washington told Jefferson that the Secretary of State headed a "higher department" than did the Secretary of the Treasury. At another time, when incensed over certain allegations by Edmund Randolph, the second Secretary of State, whom he had forced to resign, Washington declared that "I made him Secretary of State, placing him at the head of my official council. . . . He occupied the chief seat among the guests at my table."

More than a century and a half later, in 1950, the question of precedence came up under unique circumstances. General George C. Marshall, who had earlier been Secretary of State, returned to Harry S. Truman's Cabinet as Secretary of Defense. Dean G. Acheson, who had been Under Secretary of State during Marshall's tenure, was now Secretary of State. "To all of us it was natural and proper," Acheson wrote, "that next to the President deference was due to General Marshall. But he [Marshall] would have none of it. The Secretary of State was the senior officer to whom he punctiliously deferred, not only in matters of protocol but in council as well." This practice was also in keeping with the view of President Truman himself, who believed that "the most important Cabinet officer is the Secretary of State."

Most Secretaries of State have been sensitive about the preeminence of their office. Edward Livingston, Andrew Jackson's second Secretary of State, was delighted with the prestige of his post. "Here I am," he wrote a month after becoming Secretary, "in the second place in the United States—some say the first. . . ."

Other Secretaries have gained satisfaction from the fact that on social and ceremonial occasions they took precedence over their Cabinet colleagues and others. Mrs. James G. Blaine, particularly, was pleased that her husband's position placed him socially above all but the President. Shortly after her husband had accepted the offer to serve at the head of James A. Garfield's Cabinet, Mrs. Blaine wrote to one of her sons that "all the world is paying court to the coming or expected Secretary of State. Socially you know it is about the best position."

The traditional pre-eminence of the Secretary of State was enhanced by a law of January 19, 1886, that made him second, after the Vice-President, in line in the Presidential succession, followed according to rank by other members of the Cabinet. Even though a new law of July 18, 1947, has placed the Speaker of the House and the President Pro Tempore of the Senate ahead of the Secretary of State, he still outranks the other department heads in the line of succession.

John Hay was twice the direct heir to the Presidency—after the death of Vice-President Garret A. Hobart, in November, 1899, and again after the assassination of William McKinley, in September, 1901. Stressing the Secretary of State's Cabinet rank, the newspapers referred to him as "the senior member" and the "ranking member" of the Cabinet. Theodore Roosevelt, the new President, made a special point of Hay's place in the Presidential succession by leaving him at the seat of the government while he himself accompanied McKinley's funeral party to Canton, Ohio. Since "I am the next heir to the Presidency," Hay explained, "he did not want too many eggs in the same Pullman car."

It is evident that in prestige, influence, and often even in power, the Secretary of State has long ranked second only to the President. Even so prominent and active a Vice-President as Richard M. Nixon had less stature than Secretary of State John Foster Dulles. Yet in the pay he receives and the legal authority that is his, the Secretary of State is not superior to the other members of the Cabinet. He is only the first among equals. Even in his own domain of foreign affairs, his voice has no greater authority than that of his Cabinet colleagues, unless the President decides that it should. Under Washington, for example, Alexander Hamilton, the Secretary of the Treasury, was the most influential member of the Cabinet, even in matters of foreign policy. His views usually carried more weight than did those of the Secretary of State.

One hundred fifty years later, in the relationship between Franklin D. Roosevelt and Cordell Hull, the same principle held. Roosevelt distrusted the Department of State, believing it incapable of conducting the nation's foreign relations during a time of crisis in the manner he desired. Secretary of State Hull, hence, attained less influence in the government, even in the conduct of foreign relations, than did some of Roosevelt's other advisers. Clearly, in the influence the Secretary of State wields in practice, he is not always the foremost Cabinet officer. His precedence may at times be little more than an expression of protocol.

Nonetheless, over the years the Secretaryship of State has grown steadily in importance, in part because the foreign relations of the United States have vastly increased, and in part because the power and influence of the Presidency itself have expanded. The Secretary of State is so close to the President that virtually any important development that affects the powers of the Presidency affects his powers too. By law, practice, and tradition, the Secretaryship of State is the office controlled most closely and directly by the President. It is, therefore, more an extension of the Presidency itself than are the other executive departments.

Explicitly, two of the basic functions of the Secretary of State are to assist the President in formulating foreign policy and to carry it out through the channels of the Department of State. Harry Truman, more than most Presidents, emphasized this role of the Secretary. In his view:

> The function of the Secretary of State is to be the President's personal adviser on foreign affairs. He has to run a department which should have skilled and experienced men to get the best information possible on any subject or problem that affects the relations with other governments. The Secretary of State obtains, if he can, the very best advice from the people who live with the problems of foreign affairs so that he may present it to the President.

Others who have worked closely with the Secretary have stressed the same responsibilities. "Ideally," a Chairman of the Senate Committee on Foreign Relations said, "the secretary of state should be the best-posted man in the country on foreign relations; he should keep the President apprised of what is going on abroad and he should advise him on formulating policies." In accord with the President's views, the Secretary should usually carry, in addition, the burden of high-level negotiations with other governments.

Technically, then, the Secretary of State is the President's chief adviser in foreign affairs and the department head responsible for matters related to them. Under certain conditions, he can be, as Truman implied, virtually the President's personal secretary in charge of foreign affairs. That, in effect, was Bainbridge Colby's status as Woodrow Wilson's Secretary of State.

Some Secretaries, however, have looked upon their relationship to the President as being a more impersonal connection. Henry L. Stimson, a Secretary of State with a flair for things military, and George C. Marshall, a soldier, viewed their relationship to the President as that of a soldier to a commanding officer. Even though they might disagree with their chief and might not like his orders, they would, like good soldiers, carry out his wishes.

Probably no Secretary of State has analyzed his relationship to the President, his own status, and the responsibilities of his office as thoroughly as did John Foster Dulles. He left a record of his analysis in a memorandum headed "More Important Duties of Secretary of State." Although the memorandum's sixteen points do not cover all the responsibilities of the modern Secretary, they do offer a useful and representative summary of what his job encompasses.

Dulles listed protocol first, pointing out that the Secretary of State has to meet foreign chiefs of state and foreign ministers when they come to Washington. Second, he must receive foreign ambassadors and accept their statements on matters pertaining to relations between their countries and the United States. Third, the Secretary has to visit foreign countries and attend international conferences connected with the United Nations, the North Atlantic Treaty Organization, security in the Pacific, and other matters. Fourth, he selects personnel for the highest posts in the State Department and the foreign missions.

In the fifth point, Dulles considered relations with Congress, receiving its members and testifying before its committees. Sixth, the Secretary has to prepare speeches for himself—and for the President, when they deal with foreign affairs. Dulles' seventh point concerned public relations, that is, the Secretary's press conferences and private meetings with newspapermen and radio commentators. Eighth, to maintain morale within the State Department, he said, the Secretary has to consult with his top-level associates and diplomats who have returned to the United States on leave. He listed social functions as the ninth item, pointing out that the Secretary has to attend dinners and receptions given by the diplomatic corps and American officials.

According to Dulles' tenth point, the Secretary of State has to establish policies for dealing and settling controversies with independent coordinate agencies, such as the departments of Defense, Treasury, and Commerce, and the Central Intelligence Agency, all of which are also concerned with foreign relations. The Secretary has to approve important outgoing cables and read important incoming ones as well as the memoranda of significant departmental conversations. In addition, he has to give personal attention to a portion of the department's correspondence and see at least some of the people who demand to speak to a top official.

Dulles' final three points touch on duties he considered most significant, those that involve the making of policy. The Secretary has to attend Cabinet meetings and general talks at the White House, consult with the President, and keep him informed of developments in foreign affairs. He also has to deal with crises that may arise suddenly anywhere on the globe and call for immediate reactions by the government, and lastly, he has to formulate long-range policies.

All Dulles' points relate to what he called "the Secretary's foreign policy functions," for only that, the most important feature of the Secretaryship, interested him. He wished to concentrate on the making of policy and had no interest in the Secretary's domestic responsibilities. These duties may often be delegated, but the foreign-policy function usually cannot. There is no substitute for the influence and authority of the Secretary of State in the meetings of the Cabinet. This is also true of the National Security Council, a special advisory body which is used by the President to coordinate foreign and defense policies and which often formulates basic decisions in foreign policy. No one else, moreover, can explain the Secretary's views to the President as well as he can himself or replace him in his relations with the President.

Another factor in the Secretary's job that Dulles did not emphasize, but of which he was acutely aware, is the obligation to reconcile the demands of foreign policy with those of domestic politics when the two seem to be, or are, in conflict. This calls for considerable finesse, a quality that few Secretaries of recent years have had in great measure. Without meeting this obligation, the Secretary may not be able to do full justice to all the responsibilities of his office.

The President needs a strong Secretary of State, one who is familiar with domestic as well as international politics, one who can carry his share of responsibility in dealing with Congress. John F. Kennedy, a President who has had long experience in Congress, has stated that he considers it imperative for a Secretary of State to be able to get along well with Congress. The relations of any Secretary with Congress so condition the degree to which he can execute his foreign policy that he has an obligation to gain the confidence of Congress. His effectiveness in dealing with Congress, of course, can be no greater than the strength of the support he inspires in the nation, which, in turn, depends largely on the President's own strength politically.

This does not, however, relieve the Secretary of the responsibility of marshaling public opinion in support of himself and his policies. He must, in fact, become master of these domestic political responsibilities before he can become truly successful in the management of foreign policy.

I.

The chief limitation on the Secretary of State is that he, like other Cabinet officers, has no special claim to consultation with the President, even in matters relating solely to foreign affairs. The President is under no obligation, legal or moral, to consult with him on issues of foreign policy, and the Secretary can claim no right to participate in the decisions affecting those issues. Yet, according to Dean Acheson, if the President "is to perform his duties in the wisest and most effective way, his Secretary of State must be his principal adviser in this field. The President will, and should, seek advice from whatever quarters he wishes. He will consult with and listen to many persons. But the Secretary of State should be privy to all his thoughts and to him should be given the last clear chance for advice before action."

At times, however, the President has not given the Secretary of State even the chance to offer information on foreign policy, let alone advice. If another member of the Cabinet interferes with foreign policy and the President supports him, the Secretary is almost helpless to prevent the invasion of his area of responsibility. This occurred in the original Cabinet, when Hamilton's meddling with foreign affairs infuriated Jefferson, and again a century later, when Benjamin Harrison's Secretary of the Navy, in a dispute with Chile, dictated a policy virtually the opposite of that advised by the then Secretary of State, James G. Blaine.

No President, however, so frequently undercut the authority of his Secretary of State as did Franklin D. Roosevelt. Assistant Secretary of State Raymond Moley was the first confidential adviser who had a weightier role in formulating a specific foreign policy than did Cordell Hull. Moley reported directly to Roosevelt, often without Hull's knowledge. At the World Economic Conference, held in London in 1933, Moley, acting as the President's personal agent, overshadowed and humiliated Hull.

None of the President's advisers, however, angered Hull quite as much as did Sumner Welles, the Assistant Secretary of State in charge of Latin American affairs. Roosevelt had brought Welles, an old friend, into the White House inner circle while at the same time excluding Hull. Once Hull told a Cabinet colleague that although he regularly spoke to the President by telephone, he seldom saw him. Welles, he pointed out, saw Roosevelt daily.

Hull later charged that Welles "abused his trust by going over my head to see the President without instructions from me and undertaking in one way or another virtually to act as Secretary of State." For instance, in the preparations for the Atlantic Conference, held in August, 1941, off the coast of Newfoundland, between Prime Minister Winston Churchill and Roosevelt, Hull had no part, but Welles did. Hull, in fact, did not learn of the conference until Welles told him.

Welles continually slighted Hull and acted as if he were the President's personal assistant, not amenable to the authority of the Secretary of State. In his memoirs, Hull explained with understandable bitterness:

> Welles was carrying on personal correspondence with our diplomats and with officials of other Governments which should have been carried on through the official channels of the State Department. He was sending personal notes to them and inviting personal responses from them on matters calling for Department notes handled in the regular way. The adverse effect of this was that he was gathering into his own hands items of negotiation or discussion that should have been of more general knowledge to me and to the Department officers directly concerned.

Hull also clashed with other department heads when they encroached on what he considered his exclusive domain. Several of them took a hand in foreign affairs because they knew that the President sometimes refused to accept Hull's ideas and would listen to and perhaps even act upon their own suggestions. Henry

A. Wallace, at one time Secretary of Agriculture and then Vice-President; Harold L. Ickes, Secretary of the Interior; and Henry Morgenthau, Jr., Secretary of the Treasury, were, Hull asserted, the most frequent trespassers on his field of responsibility.

Acting as the President's own representative, Vice-President Wallace took several special trips abroad, going to Latin America in 1943 and China in 1944. Those missions irked the Secretary of State. "I never at any time favored excursions into foreign affairs by Wallace," Hull wrote. "I was convinced that no person outside the State Department and the White House could break into these affairs without serious risk of running amuck, so to speak, and causing hurtful complications."

In trying to defend his jurisdiction, the Secretary of State clashed more often with Morgenthau than with any other Cabinet colleague. According to Hull, Morgenthau "often acted as if he were clothed with authority to project himself into the field of foreign affairs and inaugurate efforts to shape the course of foreign policy in given instances." Hull believed that the Secretary of the Treasury seldom lost an opportunity to meddle in foreign relations. He even conducted negotiations with foreign governments, Hull charged, "which were the function of the State Department." Morgenthau's plan for reducing postwar Germany to an agricultural state, which Hull opposed, and his work in "inducing the President to accept it without consultation with the State Department was," the Secretary of State said, "an outstanding instance of this interference."

Another limitation of the Secretaryship, one that has made a marked impression on foreigners, is the influence frequently exercised upon foreign affairs by unofficial Presidential advisers. Those advisers, in effect, displace the Secretary of State as the President's foremost consultant in the making of foreign policy. Secretaries who have been confronted with the problem of the unofficial adviser have seldom been happy about it. Regardless of how a President or anyone else may gloss over the status of the personal adviser, his mere existence reflects a lack of confidence in the Secretary of State.

Ulysses S. Grant, for example, had a penchant for old military cronies and kept some of them around the White House. Having direct access to the President, they would at times persuade him to embark on dubious ventures in foreign affairs, sometimes without consulting his Secretary of State, Hamilton Fish. Outraged, particularly by the influence of General Orville Babcock, Grant's private secretary, Fish protested the continual interference of the unofficial Grant family in his department and threatened to resign. He told the President:

> The State Department, above all others, cannot be administered except with the most unreserved confidence given to its head by the Executive. When that confidence is shaken, or when the influence of the head of the Department in the administration of its affairs, or the formation of its policy, is overshadowed by others, a sensible or a sensitive man will appreciate that the time for his retirement has arrived.

Fish thus made clear a basic principle governing the power of the Secretary of State. The Secretary can function best as a high government official only when he has behind him the President's confidence, personal influence, and prestige, when there is no man or other influence between the President and himself.

Fish demanded control over matters pertaining to his department, which, he said, is "necessary not only to a confident and satisfactory discharge of the delicate and complicated duties of the office, but also to the independence of feeling without which the high position which I have held in your Administration cannot be worthily occupied." There must be, he added, assurance "of the withdrawal of this Army influence—this back-stairs, Kitchen-Cabinet control over the affairs of my Department."

Grant gave the required assurance, saying there would be no more interference in Fish's domain, because he admired and needed Fish. The Secretary of State, therefore, by threatening to resign, was able to maintain control over the conduct of foreign policy. This is unusual; as a rule, Presidents who have resorted to unofficial advisers in foreign policy have been those who distrusted or had little confidence in their Secretaries of State. This principle can be seen in the cases of Secretaries who had to deal with two of the most noted of the unofficial advisers, Colonel Edward M. House and Harry Hopkins.

II.

Colonel House, a close friend of Woodrow Wilson, had direct access to him, enjoyed his confidence, acted as an executive agent, and exerted a greater influence over the formulation of foreign policy than did Secretaries of State William Jennings Bryan or Robert Lansing. House, not the Secretaries, usually acted as the President's most effective counselor and also as an unofficial spokesman in matters of foreign policy. So close was House to the President that at times it was difficult to distinguish House's ideas from those of Wilson.

House's unique power had grown in part out of Wilson's lack of confidence in his Secretaries of State. Apparently, the President could never fully overcome his feelings that Bryan was not competent to deal with great matters of state. At one time after World War I had begun, the President refused to trust Bryan even to act as the ordinary channel of communication between himself and the European belligerents. Without consulting his Secretary of State, Wilson sent House as his personal emissary on a peace mission to the belligerent capitals. When Bryan finally learned of the mission from House, he was keenly disappointed and probably deeply hurt.

Since Wilson and House shut out Bryan from important areas of foreign affairs, sometimes leaving him only with routine administrative duties within the State Department, it was natural that the Secretary resented House and his own humiliating status. Bryan accepted his subordination to House because, other than to resign, he could do little about it.

When Lansing succeeded Bryan in the Secretaryship, House continued as the President's intimate adviser. House, in fact, had urged Lansing's appointment partly because Lansing knew of his own relationship to the President and "tacitly accepted existing conditions."

Even though House continued to handle critical diplomatic negotiations for the President, the new Secretary of State gave no outward sign of resenting House's privileged position. "I bow to the political astuteness of Colonel House in most things," Lansing recorded in his diary. House himself apparently never detected resentment and usually found Lansing willing to cooperate with him. "I shall always remember with gratitude his attitude toward me," House wrote in later years, "for my position was unusual and without precedent, and it would have been natural for him to object to my ventures in his sphere of activities. He never did. He was willing for me to help in any way the President thought best."

Perhaps more powerful than House in matters of foreign policy was Harry Hopkins, Franklin D. Roosevelt's intimate adviser. Hopkins, a former social worker, was one of those "radical" New Dealers whom Secretary of State Hull disliked. While working for the New Deal, Hopkins had won Roosevelt's friendship and confidence in a way no one else had succeeded in doing since the death of Louis M. Howe, an earlier political adviser, in 1936.

In 1940, Hopkins moved into the White House, where he had well-nigh instant access to the President. "That kind of propinquity," another Roosevelt adviser wrote, "which enabled [him] to see the President at almost any time, was the greatest possible assurance of influence and power." Hull, in contrast, sometimes went weeks without a glimpse of the President.

During the last five years of Roosevelt's life, Hopkins was usually his most influential adviser in foreign affairs; he was called "Roosevelt's own personal Foreign Office." Hopkins even attended Cabinet meetings. He, not the Secretary of State, seemed to provide the readiest means of informal contact with foreign dignitaries and with the President himself in questions of foreign policy. Yet he had no legal status. He was only a private citizen without office, rank, or pay.

More than had Colonel House, Hopkins came to symbolize

the great personal power of the President in foreign relations and the insignificant role of the Secretary of State under certain conditions. Roosevelt gave Hopkins broad powers of decision in foreign policy, powers he denied his Secretary of State, because he liked and trusted Hopkins. While Hull bored the President with his solemn cautiousness, Hopkins, even more than Welles, was quick, direct, and bold in attacking a problem. That approach suited Roosevelt, who, in his lofty and lonely responsibility, felt the need of advice from someone whose judgment he trusted. Never being close to the President, Hull could not fill that need for informal personal advice suited to Roosevelt's patterns of thought. More than any of Roosevelt's other advisers in foreign affairs, Harry Hopkins was able to do so.

Unofficial advisers and official subordinates, such as Hopkins and Welles, are able at times to overshadow the Secretary of State in the shaping of foreign policy, not because of any inherent or technical flaw in the Secretaryship but because of the tremendous flexibility in the powers of the office, and, of course, in the Presidency itself. This flexibility, in fact, is a distinctive feature of the Secretaryship, one that we shall refer to again.

Roosevelt's informal advisers in foreign policy did not necessarily usurp the Secretary's jurisdiction; at times, they merely filled a vacuum. Since the President often did not use his Secretary in formulating important policies, Hopkins, Welles, Morgenthau, and others stepped in and supplied the counsel that might under other circumstances have come from the Secretary of State. This illustrates what is almost a truism—that a Secretary can make his greatest contribution to important decisions only if the President accepts and uses him as his chief agent in foreign affairs.

Hull himself attributed his awkward status to the fact that he was never a member of Roosevelt's inner circle and, hence, was at a disadvantage in defending his domain from assaults within the Administration. He believed also that the President did not consult him enough and allowed other officials to attack State Department policies, and that he himself had to fight for his department's policies without the President's backing. There is considerable truth in Hull's observation, for if the President makes it an obvious practice to consult the Secretary of State and uphold him in conflicts over policy, the other Cabinet officers are likely to accept the Secretary's *de facto* primacy.

Hull's, and hence the Secretary of State's, subordination during World War II is remarkable only because of the extremes to which Roosevelt went to keep important matters of foreign policy out of his hands. During wars, Secretaries of State have at times lost importance relative to the warmaking departments and have had few opportunities to bask in the limelight. The Presidents have retained a close control over foreign policy and the military men have won the glory and the public esteem. During the War of 1812, James Monroe, for instance, believed that he had little more to do than to write instructions to representatives abroad and care for routine administrative matters, and hence he became dissatisfied with the Secretaryship.

William H. Seward is an exception to the pattern of wartime impotence, but he was Secretary of State during a civil war, when the President's main energies were devoted to the domestic battles. Seward's power and influence, moreover, derived not solely from the fact that Abraham Lincoln had delegated broad powers to him in the area of foreign relations but also from his own status as the dominant personality in the Cabinet.

At times, the Secretary of State's power may be limited by the nature of the Cabinet. Unlike cabinets in parliamentary governments, the President's Cabinet does not have collective responsibility and is not a council of political colleagues. It is, instead, essentially a council of advisers, whose existence and influence depend on the will of the President. The foreign policies emanating from this purely Presidential institution become significant in terms of national policy only because the President chooses to adopt them. Since neither the Constitution nor Congress created the Cabinet, it has no legal status. It came into existence under President Washington as an experiment within the scope of his broad constitutional powers over his department heads. Its status, therefore, is anchored in tradition.

Some Presidents, such as Washington and Truman, discussed important issues of foreign policy in Cabinet meetings, often asked the department heads to vote on decisions affecting those issues, and acted upon the majority's wishes. Washington gave the Secretary of State's vote the same weight as that of the other department heads even in matters pertaining to foreign affairs. That procedure explains in part why Hamilton, who dominated the Cabinet, was able to direct foreign policy.

Under such conditions, the Secretary of State has no way of controlling foreign policy. Unlike a foreign minister in a parliamentary government, or even his predecessor in the Confederation Government, he cannot take his case to the national legislature and there explain or defend his policies. If the President uses the Cabinet to shape decisions in foreign policy, the Secretary, as a department head, has to make his case in the Cabinet. Otherwise, as is usually the procedure, he has to make it directly with the President.

Since the Secretary of State is not a responsible minister heading a foreign office, his actions and decisions must reflect the President's views, or if policy originates with the Secretary, his views must be accepted by the President as his own. In September, 1946, when Secretary of Commerce Henry A. Wallace publicly attacked the foreign policy that Secretary of State James F. Byrnes was carrying out, Byrnes protested in the name of the above principle. He asked President Truman to restrain Wallace, as a member of the Cabinet, from openly criticizing his policy, saying that "whoever is Secretary of State must be known to have the undivided support of your administration." Later, in the case of Dean Acheson, there was never any doubt that the Secretary of State was the President's spokesman in foreign affairs, for Truman went out of his way to support Acheson despite bitter attacks against him.

Truman had to defend his Secretary of State, for any foreign policy, whether it originates with the Secretary or whether he acts merely as an agent in carrying it out, becomes the President's policy. Technically, the Secretary of State has no policies of his own. All policies must be presented as coming from the President. When a Secretary does formulate a policy, it is assumed to have the President's support, for the President, as the founding fathers had intended, is officially responsible for the acts of his department head.

The Secretary of State, it must be emphasized, is the representative of the President—and not of the people directly—when carrying out foreign policy; the President—not the Secretary—is responsible to the people. No Secretary of State, as a result, can match the role of the President in the conduct of foreign relations, for no Secretary, regardless of how capable, can assume the authority of the President in representing the people and the nation.

III.

Since the Secretary of State acts in the President's name, it is virtually an unwritten rule that Secretaries who do not agree with the President must nevertheless carry out his policies faithfully or resign. In fact, mere want of mutual confidence can offer sufficient cause for a Secretary's dismissal.

Secretary of State Timothy Pickering, for instance, had no respect for John Adams. When Adams' foreign policy did not agree with Pickering's own ideas, he attempted to thwart it. Adams tried to force him to resign, but Pickering refused. The President then dismissed him. After that, the unwritten principle became so firmly established that although subsequent Secretaries of State have been forced from office because of disagreements with the President, none since Pickering has been fired outright. In no case since Pickering's, moreover, has a Secretary of State set out openly and deliberately to sabotage the foreign policy of his chief.

Although President Wilson accused Robert Lansing of disloyalty and forced him to resign, Lansing had not attempted to wreck the President's policies. Wilson demanded his Secretary's resignation because he realized that Lansing carried out his policies reluctantly, because his judgment differed from Wilson's, and Wilson preferred a Secretary of State whose mind would willingly go along with his own.

Lansing had subordinated his own judgments because Wilson cast aside or seldom solicited his opinions, even on issues of foreign policy. He had not attempted to resign earlier because he did not wish to give the impression of deserting the President in a time of crisis, but when Wilson demanded his resignation, he grasped the opportunity with a sense of relief because it finally freed him from the responsibility of having to carry out policies he disliked. "In hiding my feelings and subordinating my judgment I have felt a hypocrite," he confessed to his diary, "possibly I have been one, but what else could I do in these extraordinary conditions?"

Like Hull's, Lansing's ineffectiveness was unusual, for Secretaries of State more often have had broad responsibilities and have not been expected to confine their advice to foreign affairs. Most Presidents have invited their views on domestic matters as well. Such Secretaries as Martin Van Buren, William M. Evarts, and Jeremiah S. Black, in fact, were more valuable to Presidents Andrew Jackson, Rutherford B. Hayes, and James Buchanan, respectively, as political advisers than as managers of foreign relations.

Secretary of State Seward, too, under both Lincoln and Andrew Johnson, was more than a manager of foreign affairs. He helped write Lincoln's inaugural address, took a hand in military matters, worked on problems of internal security, and offered counsel on all kinds of domestic issues. He advised President Johnson on domestic politics and problems of Reconstruction and wrote some of his veto messages. And in the twentieth century, William H. Taft also relied on his Secretary of State, Philander C. Knox, for advice on internal as well as foreign affairs.

Some Presidents have relied so heavily on their Secretaries of State that instead of giving their own direction to foreign policy, they have accepted direction from their Secretaries. Such Secretarial dominance has usually come when a President has not been interested in diplomatic negotiations and the shaping of foreign policies, or when he has been beset by so many other problems that he has not been able to devote needed time to foreign affairs. Under these and similar conditions, if left to his own devices and if able, the Secretary of State has decided what matters shall be presented to the President for consideration, decision, or acquiescence. Such conditions prevailed during the Secretaryships of Daniel Webster under Tyler, Hamilton Fish under Grant, Charles E. Hughes under Harding, and John Foster Dulles under Eisenhower.

Fish's dominance, in view of his difficulty with back-stairs advisers, is particularly noteworthy. At the end of eight years, when he finally gave up his Secretaryship, he was recognized by contemporaries as the man who had virtually run the government and as the ablest of the twenty-five men who had held Cabinet posts under Grant. Far more than most Secretaries, he had won the President's confidence, the essential factor in the power of a strong Secretary of State. So highly did Grant come to esteem his Secretary of State that before he left the White House, he wrote a letter advising the nomination of Fish for President in case of a deadlock at the Republican convention. On a later occasion, when a friend listed those whom he considered the three greatest statesmen of the age, Grant insisted on adding a fourth—Hamilton Fish.

Dulles' dominance came during the tense years of the Cold War, years of seemingly perpetual crisis in foreign policy, years when the power of the Secretary of State seemed magnified beyond what it had been in the past, years when the President leaned heavily on him for guidance. Harry Truman gave his Secretaries of State considerable freedom, but President Eisenhower went beyond him. Although he never abdicated his power of final decision, he usually followed the practice of "leaving it to Foster," meaning that, in most instances, Dulles had practically a free hand in the conduct of foreign relations.

Eisenhower was convinced that Dulles had the ability and

experience to handle foreign policy as he, the President, wished it. He believed that since he had given his trust to Dulles in the first place, he should look to his Secretary for ideas and outlines of policy. Like Grant, Eisenhower had an almost boundless admiration for his Secretary, saying that Dulles had his unqualified support, behaved himself "like a master," supplied the heart and brains in the formulation of foreign policy, and was the greatest Secretary of State in the history of the nation. Few Presidents have relied as heavily on their Secretaries of State as did Eisenhower on Dulles. In effect, Dulles formulated foreign policy and Eisenhower made it his own.

Like John Quincy Adams and Seward, Dulles was a strong Secretary of State who dramatized his own status and hence the Secretaryship. A few days after taking over the State Department, Dulles spoke to the nation by radio and television, attempting to add stature to the Secretaryship and to gain public confidence by assuring the people that he would be devoted to their welfare. "You needn't be afraid," he said, "that we're working against you and for others." That broadcast, Dulles believed, was necessary, because the Secretary's prestige, owing to a situation he had inherited from Acheson, was at a low ebb and needed bolstering.

Unlike Truman, who had resented Byrnes's efforts to capture public attention, Eisenhower did not mind Dulles' frequent attempts to gain publicity and even seemed to encourage them. One of the distinctive features of Dulles' Secretaryship, in fact, was his frequent use of radio and television to talk directly to the American people. He was the most widely advertised Secretary of State in the nation's history. One friendly critic quipped that he used an Assistant Secretary of State as his personal press agent.

Again like John Quincy Adams and Seward, Dulles seems to have craved public approval, to have been keenly conscious of his place in history, and to have striven consciously to make a record. This can be seen in a special interview he granted to a reporter for *Life* magazine in January, 1956. The article, based on recorded conversations, portrayed Dulles as the Administration's genius, who valiantly preserved the peace after bringing the nation to the brink of war. The Secretary of State, it said, had given the nation "the greatest display of personal diplomacy since the great days of the Franklin-Adams-Jefferson triumvirate in the Europe of the 1790's"—a claim that Dulles did not deny.

Critics have pointed out that Dulles claimed too much and hence, in effect, revived an old argument running as follows: Since the Secretary of State is the President's instrument, all credit for achievement in foreign policy belongs to the President. Among those who have refused to accept such an assumption was Theodore Roosevelt, a vigorous Chief Executive who himself dominated the conduct of foreign relations. He wrote:

> To deny [Secretary of State Elihu] Root credit for what the Department of State has done because it has been done under me as President is a good deal like denying credit to Sherman and Sheridan because they were under Grant. The President is of course responsible for the general policy of the administration in foreign affairs, and here and there or now and then he must himself work out some given problem. . . . But in most things done by the State Department it is the Secretary of State, if he is a man like Root, who does practically all the work.

Some Secretaries, particularly the brilliant John Quincy Adams, have chafed under the knowledge that most of the credit for accomplishment in foreign affairs goes to the President. Adams feared that even though he had conceived the idea of extending the nation's boundary to the Pacific and had persuaded President James Monroe to act upon that idea, he would not get credit for it. "I record the first assertion of this claim for the United States as my own," he wrote in his diary, "because it is known to be mine perhaps only to members of the present Administration, and may perhaps never be known to the public."

From Adams' brain came most of the basic ideas in the foreign policy of the Monroe Administrations, and he executed the diplomacy that carried them out. He helped shape the Monroe

Doctrine, negotiated with Spain's Don Luis de Onís the treaty of 1819 that transferred to the United States both Florida and Spain's claim to a domain on the Pacific, and, in 1824, completed a treaty with Russia that recognized the American claim to the Oregon country. He could boast with considerable justification that "of the public history of Mr. Monroe's administration, all that will be worth telling to posterity hitherto has been transacted through the Department of State."

Strong Secretaries like Adams, Fish, and Dulles were in command of foreign policy, initiated it, built it up, and carried it out. Dulles, despite the controversy that swirled about him, was identified the world over as the master of American foreign policy more often than any other Secretary of State. Even Adams did not possess his far-flung influence.

The reasons for this are simple enough. Monroe did not surrender to Adams the extensive powers that Eisenhower ceded to Dulles, and the United States of Adams' day cannot be compared to the powerful nation of the 1950's committed to a world-wide network of alliances.

Nonetheless, whether it be Adams in the "era of good feelings" or Dulles in the era of hurtling missiles, the tenure of the strong Secretaries shows that the Secretaryship of State has been and can be an office of impressive power. Some Secretaries have even been surprised by the extent of their power. "I was not aware," John C. Calhoun told his daughter shortly after becoming Secretary of State, "until I took charge of the State Dept. of the immense influence, which may be exerted through it on foreign and domestic relations." The responsibilities, powers, and limitations of the Secretaryship, in other words, are so flexible that the office can sometimes bring frustration, but more often an eminence second only to that of the President.

3

Qualifications and Selection

. . . a Secretary of State ought to have pierced into the remotest Periods of ancient Times and into the most Distant Regions of the Earth: He should have studied the Map of Man, in his savage as well as civilized State. It is more necessary that a Secretary of State should be omniscient, than a President, provided the President be honest and judicious. Where can we find such Men? either for Presidents or Secretaries?

—JOHN ADAMS, 1811

IN practice, there are no formal qualifications for the Secretaryship, no technique or special training that would prepare one, and no standard of selection. Presidents and Presidents-elect have followed no rules and have selected their Secretaries of State for many varying reasons. Some have appointed personal friends, a few have sought good administrators, but most have chosen their Cabinet heads to hold or gain political support for their Administrations. Seldom has a President appointed a Secretary solely because he sought an adviser trained and experienced in diplomacy and the handling of foreign affairs.

As a result, when a man gains the Secretaryship it usually comes to him as an interlude in a career that has had little to do with foreign affairs, and not as the culmination or even an integral part of a professional career—a pattern different from that in the parliamentary system. In Great Britain, for instance, where the Foreign Secretary comes from Parliament and remains a part of it, the portfolio for foreign affairs can be the goal toward which a member of Parliament constantly moves. If and when he reaches that objective, it usually crowns a lifelong political career devoted to foreign affairs.

Disturbed by this lack of professional requirements, some men who have studied the Secretaryship have suggested qualifications. It should be kept in mind, however, that the selection of a Secretary in each instance involves a specific man, not an abstract principle.

John Adams, in the years of his retirement, wrote that the Secretary of State "ought to be a Man of universal Reading in Laws, Governments, History. Our whole terrestrial Universe ought to be summarily comprehended in his Mind." Adams even suggested that the Secretary should be more knowledgeable than the President.

Others have suggested qualifications less lofty but more obtainable. A Secretary of State, some have said, should be versed in international law, in the practice and procedure of diplomacy, should have a firm grasp of American foreign policy, and should know other peoples, especially from travel in foreign lands.

Some have argued that such professional qualifications are unimportant. Within proper limits, they insist, experience in domestic politics is more important, even essential. Since most problems a Secretary of State has to face are inherently political, he needs political perspective, insight, and wisdom more than technical training. In his relations with the President, Congress, and other members of the Administration, it has been pointed out, the Secretary has to deal with politicians. In selecting a Secretary of State, therefore, a President could rightly give more weight to political than to diplomatic experience, to ability and sound judgment than to specialized knowledge. The lawyer with political training who has risen to party chieftain and has been a candidate for high office, one student of the Secretaryship wrote, is well qualified for the post. Dean Acheson said that in selecting a Secretary, a President should simply be guided by his belief that the man he wants is the one who can help him more than any other in dealing with the problems he foresees.

Those who stress law and politics are moving with the tide of history, for most Secretaries of State have been lawyers or men who have had some legal training. This fact reveals something of the true nature of the office. From the beginning of the national government, the legal profession has offered the likeliest path to political preferment, and from the beginning, the alliance of law and politics has dominated the Secretaryship.

Most Secretaries have come from the higher ranks of political life, having been selected primarily for their status in the party controlling the executive branch of the government. More often than not they have come to the office possessing little experience in, or even knowledge of, world affairs. Although the main concern of the Secretaryship of State is foreign relations, the office is essentially political.

No one—not even men with considerable diplomatic experience, such as James Monroe, John Quincy Adams, or John Hay—has risen to the Secretaryship by virtue of having selected diplomacy as a career. No professional diplomat, in other words, has ever been Secretary of State, though John W. Foster, who served less than seven months, was an expert in international law and diplomatic practice. John Foster Dulles, too, had steeped himself in diplomatic experience but was not a career diplomat. Christian A. Herter had been a Foreign Service Officer, but with him, as with most of the others, political connections, not his training in and knowledge of diplomacy, had been decisive in his selection.

Most Secretaries have had political experience, generally in national affairs, before taking office. George Marshall, the only professional soldier to hold the Secretaryship, is the most familiar exception to this rule. He considered himself a nonpartisan Secretary of State, though he served a Democratic Administration, and even urged the appointment of a Republican as his successor so as to perpetuate the bipartisan foreign policy he had administered. Although President Truman deeply admired

Marshall and often followed his suggestions virtually without question, he did not do so in this instance and thus kept inviolate one of the most enduring traditions of the Secretaryship—that the Secretary of State must not come from the opposition party.

While it is true that Washington and Jefferson belonged to opposing parties, it should be remembered that when Washington appointed Jefferson to the Secretaryship, national political parties had not yet formed. Since he had been elected unanimously, moreover, Washington did not have to weigh political considerations in selecting his Secretary of State. Believing himself above political strife, the head of a nonpartisan government, he had no intention of selecting a Cabinet on the basis of political harmony.

Before the end of Washington's first term, all this had changed. National political coalitions, the Federalist and Republican parties, were forming under the leadership of his two major department heads, Hamilton and Jefferson. Those two also differed over foreign policy. Hamilton evolved a policy favorable to England, whereas Jefferson desired one friendly to France. Washington's Cabinet, in other words, was seriously split.

As Washington himself became more and more of a Federalist, the split grew deeper, for as Hamilton's ideas were transformed into policy, the Secretary of State found himself administering the foreign policy of a political enemy under the cover of an allegedly nonpartisan Administration. For a while, nonetheless, Jefferson stayed on, the only Secretary of State to carry out faithfully the foreign policy of an Administration to which he was philosophically opposed. He could maintain this unique status because at this early stage of Cabinet growth, there had not yet developed a precedent or clear obligation for a Secretary of State to be politically loyal to the President. As long as he performed his duties with due diligence and carried out policy as the President desired, he was technically free to follow his own political sentiments.

Later, as the Cabinet became an institution, political conformity became a requirement for anyone who would become

Secretary of State. Jefferson's successor, Edmund Randolph, learned this at great cost.

Considering himself a neutral in politics, Randolph told the President when he took over the Secretaryship that "let the consequence be what it may in this perilous office, no consideration of party shall ever influence me. . . ." Despised by both political factions, Randolph soon found neutrality untenable, and like Jefferson, he came to resent and oppose Hamilton's dominance in foreign relations. To Hamiltonians, therefore, he appeared disloyal to the Administration, and since he was the only non-Federalist who still held a high post in the government, they became eager to get rid of him.

In the summer of 1795, on the basis of inconclusive evidence supplied by the British, Randolph's Federalist Cabinet colleagues accused him of disloyalty to his country and the Administration through collusion with Republicans and the French Minister in the United States. Believing the accusers, Washington forced his Secretary of State to resign in disgrace.

Later, when Randolph published his *Vindication* of his conduct, the President held that it merely proved his guilt:

> While at the head of my cabinet, he has been secretly, but actively, plotting with the opponents of my administration, consulting and contriving with them for the defeat of its measures; he, the Secretary of State, to whose trust the foreign relations of the country are confided, has been conducting an intrigue with the ambassador of a foreign government to promote the designs of that government, which were to overthrow the administration of which he, Randolph, was a trusted member. . . .

More than the experience with Jefferson, the Randolph affair convinced Washington that he had to abandon the seemingly unworkable ideal of a nonpartisan Cabinet. More than once he pointed out that he would not knowingly appoint another Secretary of State "whose political tenets are adverse to the measures which the *general* government are pursuing; for this, in my opinion, would be a sort of political Suicide; that it would embarrass its movements is most certain."

There was no doubt about the political orthodoxy of Washington's third Secretary of State, Timothy Pickering. He was an impeccably stanch Federalist who wholeheartedly supported the foreign policy he was entrusted to carry out. Yet, in comparison with his predecessors, particularly Jefferson, he was ill-equipped to handle the responsibilities of his new post. Admitting his deficiencies, Pickering remarked in later years that "my life had been spent in business, not in study; the office required knowledge and abilities which I did not possess."

Following the disillusioning experience with his first two Secretaries, Washington had set the precedent of making professional qualifications secondary to political in the selection of a Secretary of State. Since his day, no President has knowingly appointed a Secretary whose politics differed markedly from his own. It was then that the Secretaryship clearly became a political office—and one with relatively short tenure.

When he took office, John Adams retained Washington's Cabinet. Since he and Pickering were both Federalists, there was no question of the Secretary of State's political loyalty, but Pickering proved to lack personal loyalty to the President. After dismissing Pickering, Adams chose John Marshall for his second Secretary of State, a man not only loyal to him and his policies but also one with diplomatic experience. Marshall himself was especially sensitive to the question of political loyalty and later explained that "no consideration could induce me to be the Secretary of State while there was a President whose political system I believed to be at variance with my own."

Marshall's appointment, moreover, illustrates what was to become a general principle in the selection of a second Secretary of State—he is more the President's own choice than the original Secretary. In seeking a second, or even a third, Secretary of State a President usually has greater freedom of choice than in making his original appointment. He is less restricted by forces beyond his control. Once he has launched his Administration and paid his initial political debts, he can choose the man he thinks best qualified for the post, be it for political, personal, or other reasons. His criterion can be the selection of someone who has his trust and confidence. A second Secretary, therefore, usually owes his appointment directly to the President and does not often have an outside following. He tends to be more loyal to the President and more eager to carry out Presidential policy without dissent than does a first appointee.

Although modified by individual circumstances, this principle can be seen in the following appointments. James Buchanan, in selecting his second Secretary of State, Jeremiah S. Black, turned to a friend he trusted and respected, one who would remain loyal to him as he struggled with the terrible secession crisis of December, 1860. Grover Cleveland virtually ignored political and diplomatic considerations when he chose Richard Olney for his third Secretary of State. Although Olney had been his Attorney General, he was a Democrat without high status in the party or experience in foreign affairs, but one whose judgment Cleveland respected. William McKinley selected William R. Day, an old friend, for his second Secretary and John Hay, another friend and skilled diplomat, for his third. "There is no politics in it," a former President said of Hay's appointment.

Theodore Roosevelt left no doubt that he alone decided on Elihu Root, his second Secretary, and that political pressures had little to do with the appointment. "I wished Root as Secretary of State," he explained, "partly because I am extremely fond of him and prize his companionship as well as his advice, but primarily because I think in all the country he is the best man for the position and that no minister of foreign affairs in any country at this moment in any way compares with him."

Roosevelt's third Secretary of State, Robert Bacon, an old Harvard classmate who served only thirty-seven days, received the office as a token of friendship, an appointment free of political complications. "I am so glad," the President wrote to his son, "to have had nice Mr. Bob Bacon made Secretary of State before I went out."

Woodrow Wilson chose his second and third Secretaries of State, Robert Lansing and Bainbridge Colby, without emphasis on political considerations. Stanch Democrats had objected to both. One critic complained of Lansing:

> He is wholly unknown in the country except as a son-in-law of [John W.] Foster and a beneficiary of Republican favors. I suppose he is a Democrat by inheritance, but if he has ever turned his hand over to strengthen the party I never heard of it, and if all Democrats were of his type, Taft instead of Wilson would be President. His appointment will add no strength to the administration or the party.

Lansing had acquired experience in the State Department and was trained in international law, but Colby had neither training nor experience in matters of diplomacy. Wilson felt that Colby, a former Republican who had joined the Democratic Party in 1916 and had campaigned vigorously for him, was a man he could trust, one who was devoted to his policies and to himself. Angry Democratic politicians believed that the elevation of a former Republican to the first place in the Cabinet was a blunder destructive to party morale in Congress. "He was a decided Democrat," one of them remarked, "but he only decided lately." Colby, it seemed, lacked what politicians value most—party loyalty.

When Calvin Coolidge picked Frank B. Kellogg for his second Secretary of State, there was great surprise, for except for Charles E. Hughes, Coolidge apparently did not consult his Cabinet officers or leading Republican politicians. Personal considerations, more than other factors, seem to have motivated the appointment. Kellogg, a friend, had been notably gracious to Coolidge when, as Vice-President, the taciturn New Englander had presided over the Senate and had been snubbed or ignored by other Senators. Coolidge, it has been asserted, repaid Kellogg's kindness with the Secretaryship. Nonetheless, Kellogg was a politician and had had diplomatic experience.

Edward R. Stettinius, Jr., Franklin D. Roosevelt's second Secretary of State, was essentially a businessman with only limited experience in diplomacy and politics. The vital factor in his appointment was not politics but his unquestioning devotion to the President—a quality he had shown while serving as Under Secretary.

George C. Marshall, the second Secretary appointed by Harry S. Truman, not only had no political record, but had never voted. Both Democrats and Republicans respected him as a nonpolitical Secretary, a status that Marshall himself stressed. "I'm assuming that the office of Secretary of State, at least under present conditions, is nonpolitical," he said when he took office, "and I will govern myself accordingly."

Marshall was thus remarkably well qualified to administer Truman's bipartisan foreign policy, a policy that needed Republican support for its execution. In this sense, in his ability to work with a Republican Congress, Marshall was a political asset to the Truman Administration. Nonetheless, the fact that Truman trusted and admired him was the most important factor in his appointment.

The third Secretary of State Truman appointed, Dean G. Acheson, was a loyal Democrat whom party leaders had supported for the post, but he was not a professional politician and had never held elective office. The decisive reason for his selection was his thorough knowledge of State Department organization and broad experience in shaping foreign policy. Truman, therefore, chose Acheson because by experience and technical knowledge he was qualified for the position. "There were few men who came to the Secretaryship as fully prepared for the job and as eminently qualified as Acheson was," Truman pointed out.

President Eisenhower's second Secretary of State, Christian A. Herter, though a successful politician who had held elective office, was also a man who had a lifelong concern with foreign affairs. In his youth, he had served abroad in the Foreign Service and before taking over the State Department had been Under Secretary for two years.

Acheson's and Herter's appointments appear part of a trend toward selecting Secretaries of State for their training and experience in the handling of foreign relations, toward placing greater emphasis on professional qualifications than on political considerations. Herter's predecessor, John Foster Dulles, had had broad international experience, both as a lawyer and a diplomat; he was not an office-holding politician who had obtained the Secretaryship only as a reward for political services. No available Republican seemed better qualified by training and experience for the post, and none had worked so long to obtain it. A reporter wrote that "Dulles was trained for diplomacy as Nijinsky was for ballet." President Eisenhower once told friends, "Foster has been studying to be Secretary of State since he was five years old."

The President's statement was true at least superficially. Dulles had had a lifelong association with the Secretaryship and diplomacy, and the attainment of the office marked the culmination of an old ambition. His grandfather was John W. Foster and Robert Lansing was his uncle. "I don't suppose," he told State Department employees shortly after taking office, "that there is any family in the United States which has been for so long identified with the Foreign Service and the State Department as my family."

Yet, as Dulles himself knew, Eisenhower, like most Presidents-elect, had given weighty consideration to political factors in selecting his Secretary of State. He had chosen Dulles, as he had other department heads, partly to conciliate factions within a divided party. Although Dulles had long been associated with the Eastern wing of the Republican Party, headed by Thomas E. Dewey, of New York, he also had connections with the midwestern wing, headed by Robert A. Taft, of Ohio. A major factor in his selection seems to have been that he had managed to remain on good terms with the leaders of both groups. Dewey and Taft had urged Dulles' appointment on the grounds that he was the one Republican who could take over the State Department without creating difficulties in the transition from a Democratic to a Republican regime, without aggravating dissension in Republican ranks, and with the hope of promoting Republican unity on foreign policy.

I.

The appointment of even so fully qualified a Secretary of State as Dulles thus conformed, in part at least, to an old principle that had grown out of experience. In making their first appointments, Presidents have usually sought to use the Secretaryship to build up and strengthen their own political positions rather than to place the conduct of foreign relations in capable and experienced hands. The filling of that office, the most coveted political plum, has also followed a pattern in the over-all composition of Cabinets, one by which Presidents strive to gain broad support by balancing geographic sections and political factions.

A variation of this principle is the bargaining for Cabinet posts in pre-election deals. In addition to honoring commitments made in his behalf by his supporters, a new President frequently has to recognize strong unsuccessful rivals even though no deals were made with them. Accordingly, tradition often reserves the Secretaryship of State as the prize to be bestowed on the man to whom the President is most indebted for his election, as a consolation for his outstanding rival for the nomination, or at least as a reward for a powerful party leader.

An early example of this principle, one that included most of the main elements, was Henry Clay's appointment to the Secretaryship. That appointment also shows that even a President as experienced in foreign affairs as John Quincy Adams could not ignore the pressures of domestic politics in seeking a Secretary of State. Nor could he escape the political consequences of his act, for the selection of Clay touched off one of the bitterest feuds in the nation's history.

When the election of 1824 was cast into the House of Representatives, Clay, himself a candidate, threw his support to John Quincy Adams instead of to Andrew Jackson, contrary to his instructions from the Kentucky legislature. When, as a result, Adams became President and appointed Clay to the highest office in his power to bestow, Jackson's followers were convinced that the two men were carrying out a plot that used the Secretaryship as the reward for Clay's action. Since they believed that this had deprived Jackson of the victory he merited, they immediately cried "Bargain and corruption," and kept it up for four years.

While undoubtedly there was some kind of a political bargain involved in Clay's appointment, there was no evidence of corruption. Adams maintained that he had given Clay the Secretaryship because the Kentuckian had been a prominent candidate for President, with a large Western following, and because he was qualified for the post. In effect, Adams said he had to recognize the new importance of the West in national politics and that Clay deserved a consolation prize. Privately, he admitted that he had offered the Secretaryship to Clay as a political reward.

Being a minority President, Adams had sought in fact to unite his political opponents and friends behind him and his party. Although seemingly sinister at the time, and the result of unprecedented pressures, the appointment of a prominent rival to head the Cabinet in payment of a political debt was to become a part of the American political tradition. In appointing Clay, however, Adams did more than any of his predecessors in setting that tradition.

Even Abraham Lincoln, who, on becoming President, faced the greatest crisis in American history, would not depart from this tradition. In constructing his Cabinet, he gave representation, on the basis of geography, to powerful groups within the new Republican Party. In the battle for his nomination, moreover, his managers had bartered Cabinet posts for convention support.

Although Lincoln himself denied making any bargains, he seems to have recognized his managers' commitments as binding by offering the ranking Cabinet post to his outstanding rival for the nomination, William H. Seward, a powerful politician from New York. Lincoln realized that his own debt for Seward's support in the election coupled with Seward's leadership of the Republican Party made him the outstanding candidate for the

Secretaryship. Another prominent Republican believed that Lincoln was "under moral, or at least party, duress, to tender to Mr. S[eward] the *first* place in the Cabinet," for if he did not "that would excite bad feeling, and lead to a dangerous if not fatal rupture of the party."

Seward's experience with foreign policy was limited to one year on the Senate Foreign Relations Committee. Lincoln's reasons for appointing him, obviously, were purely political. He needed the support and national prestige that Seward could bring to his Administration. In offering the post, the President-elect said that "It has been my purpose from the day of the nomination at Chicago to assign you, by your leave, this place in the administration." For Lincoln, foreign relations were dwarfed by the pressing domestic crisis. He wanted and needed a political adviser, not a foreign minister.

Thirty-six years later, William McKinley, virtually ignoring the effect of his action on the nation's foreign relations, went beyond Lincoln and, to pay off a political debt, juggled the Secretaryship as if it were a sinecure. No one had done more to guide McKinley into the White House than had Mark Hanna, a wealthy industrialist and politician from Ohio, and no one, in McKinley's view, more richly deserved the highest reward he could bestow. Hanna, however, did not desire the Secretaryship of State or any other Cabinet post. He coveted a seat as one of the Senators from his own state, but the next election was two years off. The only way Hanna could satisfy his desire immediately was if one of Ohio's Senators were to resign, and the Governor appointed him to fill the unexpired term.

To reward Hanna, therefore, McKinley made a bargain with Ohio's senior Senator, seventy-four-year-old John Sherman. If Sherman would resign his place in the Senate so that Hanna could take it, Sherman would be given the Secretaryship of State. Since Sherman had a strong sense of party loyalty, saw the Secretaryship as a post of honor and prestige that would serve as a fitting capstone to a long and distinguished public career, and was himself indebted to Hanna for political favors—particularly in his tight and costly campaign for the Senate in 1892—he agreed to the scheme.

Early in January, 1897, after Sherman had resigned from the Senate, knowledge of the bargain leaked to the press and led to sharp attacks on both McKinley and Hanna. Friends urged Sherman to back out of his commitment and critics charged that the plan to kick Sherman upstairs to pay off Hanna was a sordid deal that would injure the nation's foreign relations. Sherman, the critics insisted, was not fit to take over the heavy responsibilities of the Secretaryship, especiallly when relations with Spain were in crisis. Even though Sherman had the experience of ten years on the Foreign Relations Committee of the Senate, he was, they pointed out, senile, failing mentally and physically, and plagued by loss of memory.

To Henry Adams, whose main interest at this time was in foreign affairs, "the man in the State Department seemed more important than the man in the White House." He wrote of his shock on learning of the bargain between McKinley and Sherman:

> Grant himself had done nothing that seemed so bad as this to one who had lived long enough to distinguish between the ways of presidential jobbery, if not between the jobs. John Sherman, otherwise admirably fitted for the place . . . was notoriously feeble and quite senile, so that the intrigue seemed to Adams the betrayal of an old friend as well as of the State Department. One might have shrugged one's shoulders had the President named Mr. Hanna his Secretary of State, for Mr. Hanna was a man of force if not of experience, and selections much worse than this had often turned out well enough; but John Sherman must inevitably and tragically break down.

Even though aware that Sherman was too old and not fit to hold the Secretaryship, McKinley resented the slurs on Sherman's competence and the attacks on himself for his selection. In a letter to the Editor of the *Chicago Tribune* in February, 1897, the President-elect declared that "the stories regarding

Senator Sherman's 'mental decay' are without foundation and the cheap inventions of sensational writers or other evil-disposed or mistaken people. When I saw him last, I was convinced both of his perfect health, physically and mentally, and that his prospects of life were remarkably good."

Despite the criticism, McKinley and Sherman carried out their parts of the bargain. Mark Hanna thus received his seat in the Senate, and the President obtained an incompetent Secretary of State. As the critics had prophesied, Sherman could not handle the responsibilities of his office and a year later had to resign. Privately, Sherman was bitter, saying he had accepted the Secretaryship at McKinley's urging "with some reluctance and largely to promote the wishes of Mark Hanna. The result was that I lost the position both of senator and secretary."

Fifteen years later, critics attacked Woodrow Wilson as vigorously as they had McKinley for offering the Secretaryship of State to William Jennings Bryan, a politician from Nebraska and several times the Democratic candidate for the Presidency. Bryan's selection in fact has often been cited as the classic example of how Presidents have prostituted the Secretaryship to the exigencies of domestic politics. What particularly disturbed critics was that Wilson, a lifelong student of American government, understood as have few Presidents the theoretical qualifications for the Secretaryship; yet he had selected a man with no background or experience in foreign affairs, or even in government administration. Bryan, moreover, not only lacked understanding of international relations but also had never shown more than a casual interest in foreign affairs except as a political issue at the end of the Spanish-American War.

However, the reasons for Bryan's appointment fit into the political tradition of the Secretaryship. Wilson was not, as some have suggested, indebted to Bryan for his nomination, but he was grateful to the Nebraskan for support during the election campaign, and although Wilson had succeeded him as the leader of the Democratic Party, Bryan still had a large and devoted following, probably the largest within the party. From the beginning of his fight for the Presidency, therefore, Wilson knew that if elected, he could hardly avoid offering Bryan a high post. He even declared that "if Mr. Bryan does not take a place in the Cabinet the whole country must be told the reason why."

Wilson did not really want Bryan as his Secretary of State, for he considered the Nebraskan a dangerous demagogue. At one time Wilson had said that it was a pity "that a man with his power of leadership should have no mental rudder," but Bryan's strength within the Democratic Party was too great to be ignored. He could, at the head of the Cabinet, bring broad support and political prestige to the Administration.

Bryan himself exerted no pressure on Wilson for the Secretaryship. In an editorial in his newspaper, the *Commoner*, he even suggested that "Cabinet positions ought not to be regarded as currency with which to pay debts. The Presidents must look to the future and not to the past. We venture to hope that Governor Wilson will be governed by higher motives than gratitude in the selection of his official household."

Bryan's friends, however, were active in his behalf. Wilson, therefore, acting on the basis of political expediency, offered Bryan the Secretaryship of State "in order to have him at Washington and in harmony with the administration, rather than outside and possibly in a critical attitude." Mr. Dooley, the Irish wit, paraphrased this to say, "I'd rather have him close to me bosom thin on me back."

Although politically wise, Wilson's choice was unpopular with all except Bryan Democrats. "With all his abilities and possibilities," a New York newspaper said, "the Hon. William J. Bryan is about as well fitted to be Secretary of State as a cherub is to skate or a merman to play football. The intellectual make-up of the distinguished Democrat ends where the special faculties required for that particular post of usefulness and responsibility begin."

Few, if any, appointments to the Secretaryship were as ridiculed as was Bryan's, but Wilson turned aside the criticism. "How contemptible," he wrote to Bryan in February, 1913, "the efforts of the papers are, the last few days, to make trouble for us and between us—and how delightful it is—to me, as I hope it is to you—to know, all the while, how perfect an understanding exists between us! It has been to me, since I saw you, a constant source of strength and confidence." This assurance won Bryan's devotion.

With Bryan's cooperation, Wilson could establish party harmony and concentrate on needed domestic reforms. Those reforms were of foremost concern to both Wilson and Bryan, for when Bryan became Secretary of State, foreign affairs were not critical. Bryan himself, moreover, apparently looked upon his new post as being more important for its political influence than its management of foreign relations. Despite this emphasis on domestic matters, and the barbs directed against it, Bryan's appointment did no violence to the tradition of selecting Secretaries of State. Wilson's choice and his motive were no worse than those of many of his predecessors. Bryan, moreover, turned out to be a better Secretary than might have been expected.

II.

Thomas Jefferson, the earliest Presidential predecessor to whom Wilson's own party could lay claim, chose an old friend, James Madison, for his Secretary of State. Although inexperienced in diplomacy, Madison had demonstrated outstanding ability in politics, but, most important, his political principles fitted Jefferson's. In turn, when Madison became President, he selected his two Secretaries of State primarily for domestic reasons. Like Wilson, in fact, he catered to political expediency and appointed a man he did not want.

When Madison won the Presidency he wished to transfer Albert Gallatin, who had been his Cabinet colleague under Jefferson, from the Treasury to the State Department. When the Senate got wind of the plan, a hard-core opposition to Gallatin, a Swiss by birth, immediately formed. His political enemies alleged that it would be dangerous to entrust the nation's foreign relations to a foreigner.

A key figure in the opposition was General Samuel Smith, a Senator from Maryland and the brother of Robert Smith, Jefferson's Secretary of the Navy. The Senator sought a high post, the Secretaryship of State if possible, for his brother. Fearing a split in his party at the very start of his Administration, Madison appeased General Smith and other opponents in the Senate by appointing Robert Smith, a man he did not truly trust, Secretary of State.

Smith's appointment is unique—the only instance in which the Senate was able to impose a Secretary of State on a President. Most senators recognize the need for mutual trust and confidence between the President and his Secretary of State, and hence usually give quick approval to the President's nomination.

Madison was never happy with Smith, whose appointment he insisted had grown out of a "miserable intrigue," and finally got rid of him. Smith's removal alienated powerful factions within Madison's own party whose backing his Administration needed. To compensate for this loss of support, in Virginia at least, he offered the Secretaryship to James Monroe, who earlier had fallen out with him but who had remained a powerful force in the politics of the Old Dominion. Thus Monroe, a man with extensive if not always successful diplomatic experience, gained the Secretaryship because of the political support he could bring to the President, and not for his broad professional qualifications.

Even John Quincy Adams, the next Secretary, was selected mainly on the basis of domestic political considerations. Galled by the charge that his two immediate predecessors had chosen men from Virginia to perpetuate what came to be known as the Virginia dynasty in the Secretaryship and the Presidency, James Monroe was determined not to appoint another Virginian, or even a Southerner, as Secretary of State. To avoid making his Administration appear a sectional one, resting primarily on support from south of the Potomac, he decided to placate Northern discontent and to appoint a Secretary from the Northeast.

Of the available candidates, John Quincy Adams of Massachusetts fitted best the conditions Monroe had set. "I have thought it advisable," Monroe confided to Jefferson, "to select a person for the dept. of State from Eastern States, in consequence of which my attention has been turned to Mr. Adams, who by his age, long experience in our foreign affairs, and adoption into the republican party, seems to have superior pretensions to any there."

True enough; no man in the country was better qualified for the Secretaryship on the basis of diplomatic experience and training than Adams. His introduction to the ways of diplomacy had begun at age eleven at the knee of his father in Paris. At fourteen, he had accompanied the American Minister to Russia to St. Petersburg as private secretary. After that, he had held several diplomatic posts in the capitals of Europe and had helped negotiate the peace treaty that ended the War of 1812.

Despite Adams' outstanding diplomatic record, it must be remembered that Monroe would surely have passed him by if he had come from another region or if another New Englander had had stronger political, though weaker professional, claims to the office. As it was, Henry Clay, furious because he did not get the post, criticized Adams' selection on the ground that the former New England Federalist was not a true Republican.

A few years later, Andrew Jackson, who ignored diplomatic experience, contributed more than had Madison, Monroe, or any other President to the tradition of making political leadership the basis for the selection of a Secretary of State. After Jackson's time, it became relatively rare for a Secretary to have professional qualifications. Jackson offered the Secretaryship to Martin Van Buren, a politician from New York, a man he hardly knew, as the choice reward for political services. "I called him to the Department of State," Jackson said publicly, "influenced by the general wish and expectation of the republican party throughout the Union."

Jackson's next Secretary, Edward Livingston, a friend of Van Buren, was also strictly a political appointee, as was the next one,

Louis McLane. Old Hickory's last Secretary of State, John Forsyth, who retained the office under Van Buren, received it as a reward for supporting Jackson in his fight against the second Bank of the United States.

Other Secretaries of State before Wilson's time who had been selected mainly to pay political debts, bring support to the Administration, or merely to placate some section of the country or party, were Daniel Webster, James Buchanan, John M. Clayton, Edward Everett, William L. Marcy, Lewis Cass, James G. Blaine, Frederick T. Frelinghuysen, and Thomas F. Bayard.

A unique case is that of John C. Calhoun. A close friend and adviser of President John Tyler, who owed Calhoun a debt of gratitude, in effect offered the South Carolinian the Secretaryship of State without consulting Tyler beforehand. Although Tyler had serious misgivings about having Calhoun at the head of his Cabinet and was angered by the action of his friend, he decided against repudiating the indirect offer. To fail to nominate Calhoun after Calhoun and his friends had come to believe that he had been offered the Secretaryship would have created more enemies for an Administration that already had too many. Furthermore, Tyler lacked support from either Democrats or Whigs, and hence most prominent politicians, because they were concerned about their future, would not accept the office from him, particularly in the twilight of his Administration. Only Calhoun among the men of national stature was willing to take the post; he had already seen his greatest days; he had no political future.

Another President who appointed a Secretary of State he did not truly want because of political pressures was James K. Polk. In 1844, James Buchanan was a favorite son of Pennsylvania's Democrats, and when Polk won the Presidency, they expected to see their favorite rewarded handsomely. Pennsylvania's electors, in fact, went so far as to recommend Buchanan for the Secretaryship. Although Polk distrusted Buchanan, he could not ignore the claims of the powerful Pennsylvania party. Ironically, when Buchanan himself became President he was forced to place Lewis Cass of Michigan, a man he did not like, at the head of his

Cabinet because the Democrats of the Old Northwest demanded such recognition.

Similarly, Benjamin Harrison did not want James G. Blaine, the uncrowned king of the Republican Party, as his Secretary of State, but Blaine's supporters expected him to be paid off generously for his contributions to Harrison's campaign. A large majority of the leading Republicans, and almost without exception the rank and file of the party, expected him to be given the Secretaryship.

"The whole country knows," a friend told Harrison, "that the first great question before your mind in preparing the programme for your administration is as to the form in which you shall give consideration to the formidable personality of Mr. Blaine." Discerningly, he advised the President-elect to offer Blaine the Secretaryship, saying, "I should fear it would be accepted as a confession of self-distrust if you do not invite him." Finally, without overcoming his misgivings, Harrison offered Blaine the post, saying he did so to preserve party harmony and "to avoid anything that would promote dissensions."

III.

Presidents by accident, that is, those who have succeeded to their office through the Vice-Presidency—Tyler, Andrew Johnson, Chester A. Arthur, Theodore Roosevelt, Coolidge, and Truman—were also concerned about party harmony and hence frequently kept their predecessors' Secretaries of State. They wished to give the impression of carrying on the dead President's policies and hence hoped to inherit his political support.

Sometimes, as in the case of Millard Fillmore's appointment of Daniel Webster to the Secretaryship and even in Truman's replacement of Edward R. Stettinius, Jr., with James F. Byrnes, the accidental Presidents have acted on the principle that to escape the dead grip of their immediate predecessors, they must have a Secretary of their own choice. Incidentally, this principle can be stretched to cover most cases of a President succeeded by another of his own party. Only two elected Presidents, John Adams and Martin Van Buren, have continued with the Secretaries of State who were in office when they took over.

One President to whom political principle or tradition meant little was Ulysses S. Grant. Elected as a military hero, without knowledge of politics and affairs of state, he chose his Secretaries of State without concern for professional qualifications and in defiance of established political principles. Believing apparently that he was not obligated to politicians, Grant picked his Secretaries to suit himself and without consulting party leaders. He said he had appointed Elihu B. Washburne, a friend from his home town of Galena, Illinois, as a token of gratitude for favors and to give him prestige for a later appointment as Minister to France. Washburne held the Secretaryship for only ten days, and five of those were on sufferance while he awaited a successor to relieve him.

In his search for a permanent Secretary, Grant at one time considered John Lothrop Motley, a noted historian with diplomatic experience, but Motley's surface eccentricity doomed him. "He parts his hair in the middle, and carries a single eyeglass!" Grant told a friend after meeting Motley. Grant would have no monocled foreign-looking dandy at the head of his State Department.

Rutherford B. Hayes also flouted political principle in selecting his Secretary of State. Even before he was certain of his election to the Presidency, he wrote in his diary, "I am inclined to say, that I must not take either of the leading competitors for the Presidential nomination, nor any member of the present cabinet." Therefore, as a reform candidate, he appointed a leader of the liberal faction in the Republican Party, William M. Evarts of New York, to head his Cabinet.

The regular Republicans objected. One of the New York bosses told Hayes that "the working Republicans of the State would not have supported a man who had never shown his faith by his works, who had received wealth and honor from an Administration [Grant's] he has publicly abused and vilified, and whose record as a Republican has been more than doubtful." Hayes, the regulars believed, was defying the leadership of the party. Some of them even tried to organize a revolt against him and to kill Evarts' appointment in the Senate, but this failed.

Democrats raised similar objections in 1892, when Grover Cleveland, with no need to use the Secretaryship of State as a consolation prize to conciliate a prominent rival, offered it to Walter Q. Gresham, a Republican recently turned Democrat, a man without diplomatic experience. Apparently, Cleveland sought to hold in a kind of fusion the support of independents and disaffected elements of the Republican Party. "You are strong and represent a large class who have not heretofore stood with our party," he told Gresham in asking him to take the post.

Nonetheless, old Democrats and new associates alike regarded Gresham with distrust, believing that a prize as important as the Secretaryship should go to none but a highly placed regular Democrat. While recognizing that Gresham's support had contributed to Cleveland's victory, the regular Democrats believed that his contribution, though valuable, did not merit such a high reward.

Later Presidents, in most instances, followed the traditional pattern in selecting their Secretaries of State. Warren G. Harding, leaning on the advice of friends, appointed Charles E. Hughes, a nationally prominent Republican and former Presidential candidate without any background in foreign affairs, as his Secretary, an appointment that pleased most party leaders. Herbert Hoover, although solicitous about the political needs of his Administration, also showed some concern for the management of foreign relations. He finally selected Henry L. Stimson, a lawyer from New York, for his Secretary, because he appeared to be the only prominent Republican available who had some knowledge of foreign affairs.

To serve his domestic political needs, Franklin D. Roosevelt chose Cordell Hull, who had some Congressional background in foreign affairs but no experience in diplomacy, for his Secretary of State. Coming to the Presidency in a time of great internal crisis, Roosevelt knew he would need strong Congressional support to carry out a recovery program. In several particulars, Hull was an ideal candidate for liaison between the White House and Capitol Hill. Having served many years in both House and Senate and having been Chairman of the Democratic National Committee, Hull carried considerable prestige with the men who composed the Democratic majorities. They knew and respected him, and Southerners venerated him as their most distinguished representative in government. No President in Roosevelt's position, particularly one with his political sagacity, could overlook the assets Hull could bring to his Administration.

Hull's record, moreover, was good. In 1932, he was one of the first to jump on the Roosevelt bandwagon and had used his considerable influence among Southern party leaders to gain support for Roosevelt's nomination. He was one of the small group of preconvention Roosevelt supporters who believed that with victory they would be rewarded with high offices. From the outset, therefore, in recognition of Hull's part in the kingmaking, Roosevelt had marked him for a Cabinet post. When he finally offered the Tennessee politician the Secretaryship, he pleased old-line party leaders and assured himself the support of valuable allies in Congress.

Like Roosevelt, Harry Truman placed a Southern politician with a strong following in Congress in the Secretaryship of State —James F. Byrnes of South Carolina, a man who had also been his rival. In 1944, Byrnes had sought the Democratic nomination for Vice-President and when Truman, more acceptable to various factions within the party as a compromise candidate, received it instead, Byrnes was bitterly disappointed. "I thought," Truman wrote in explaining his appointment, "that my calling on him at this time might help balance things up." Truman also knew that Byrnes would bring far more political prestige to his Administration than could Stettinius, whom he was replacing, and would be an invaluable ally in working with the Southerners, who controlled the conservative coalition that ran Congress.

In his memoirs, Truman gives still another reason for appointing Byrnes. As the law of Presidential succession stood at the time, the Secretary of State was, in effect, also the Vice-President, and hence presented a special problem. Stettinius had never held an elective office; in fact he had never even been a candidate.

"It was my feeling," Truman wrote, "that any man who stepped into the presidency should have held at least some office to which he had been elected by a vote of the people." Truman wanted to change the law of Presidential succession so that a man who had been elected to office would replace the Secretary in the line of succession. "Pending a change in the law," he explained, "I felt it my duty to choose without too much delay a Secretary of State with proper qualifications to succeed, if necessary, to the presidency. At this time I regarded Byrnes as the man best qualified."

Thus, regardless of the variation in the pattern of selection, concern for the handling of foreign relations has seldom been foremost. Until the years of the Cold War, the Secretaryship of State had retained as one of its prominent characteristics one it had acquired in Washington's day; it was an office to be filled mainly by politicians to meet the domestic needs of the President. This need, of course, did not in theory preclude a concern for foreign policy, too, in making the appointment, but in practice it too often did.

In the years of the Cold War, when anxiety over foreign relations has become a foremost national concern, the appointment of such professionally qualified men as Acheson, Dulles, and Herter indicates that a dramatic change has taken place in the selection of Secretaries of State. Dean Rusk also can be called something of a professional, one with considerable diplomatic experience. He had served in the State Department for years in various capacities, and for a time as Deputy Under Secretary, before becoming the head of the department. When President-elect Kennedy offered him the Secretaryship, Rusk was President of the Rockefeller Foundation, a man knowledgeable in foreign affairs but without a national reputation or political following. In selecting Rusk, Kennedy passed over men like Adlai E. Stevenson and Chester Bowles, who had been rivals for the nomination, had strong political followings, and could claim experience in and knowledge of foreign affairs. The trend of selecting a Secretary of State mainly for his qualifications in the handling of foreign affairs thus appears to have become a new pattern.

4

Heir Apparent and Prime Minister

> By the superior real and inherent importance of the Department of State in the organization of this Government, and by the successive transfer of two Secretaries of State to the Presidency, a general impression has pervaded the Union of a higher consideration due to that Department, and that in the practice of the Government it is the natural introduction to the head of the Executive.
>
> —John Quincy Adams, 1819

THE first two Vice-Presidents, John Adams and Thomas Jefferson, both succeeded to the Presidency and seemed to have formed a precedent for Vice-Presidential succession, but Jefferson's rupture with his own Vice-President, Aaron Burr, destroyed the pattern. Then by designating Secretary of State James Madison heir apparent, Jefferson endowed the Secretaryship with a special political significance.

Thus, quite early in the history of the Republic, men entered the Secretaryship of State with their eyes fixed on the future, a future that lay only one step above them. The Secretaryship, in other words, was coveted as the steppingstone to the White House. Madison, James Monroe, and John Quincy Adams all rose directly from that office to the Presidency. Since the man who was chosen Secretary appeared to have a distinctive claim to the Presidency, men came to desire the Secretaryship not for its own virtues or as an end in itself, but for its political promise. So high did the prestige of that office rise that factions within the Jeffersonian party fought tooth and claw to control it.

Another reason for the Secretaryship's high repute was that in the early national period, foreign relations were a foremost concern in the councils of the government. Accomplishments in foreign affairs reflected glory on both the President and the Secretary of State. Most of those who held the Secretaryship, moreover, were men of exceptional ability. All these factors contributed to the status of the office as the steppingstone to the Presidency.

Sensitive to these factors, Madison's second Secretary, James Monroe, took over the Secretaryship determined to make use of it as the last step to the White House. Before accepting the offer of the office, however, he had written to two friends for advice. Both urged acceptance with almost identical arguments. The Secretaryship, they stressed, would keep him before the public and hence would offer a better opportunity to succeed to the Presidency than would his present post as Governor of Virginia. One of them advised:

> Our foreign relations seem to be drawing to a crisis, and you ought to be in the public eye when it happens, for your own sake, independently of the service you can render to your country. . . . This offer to you is an indication of a disposition in Mr. Madison to relieve himself of the burden [of foreign affairs]; and if you suffer yourself to lose the benefit of this disposition, another will gain it to your inestimable injury. Suppose this other should be a competitor for the Presidency, will it not be a decisive advantage over you?

Following this advice, Monroe accepted, became heir apparent, and succeeded to the Presidency.

Although the next Secretary, John Quincy Adams, entered the office concerned primarily with his responsibilities as a Cabinet officer and head of the Department of State, he and his friends also showed a sensitiveness to his special position in the Presidential succession. One friend told old John Adams:

> It seems to me that the office of secretary of state, the talents of the candidates being equal, is the stepladder to the presidential chair, at

least it has been so in the case of the last three presidents. Now as your son, the Honorable John Quincy Adams, is appointed to that station, if he makes the best advantage of his situation, it is more than probable that he may be the next president of the United States.

Six months later, though Monroe attempted to treat rival Presidential aspirants in his Cabinet with impartiality, rumor had it that he intended "to make his Secretary of State his eventual successor, and that he will in due time give evidence of such intentions." Such stories angered Adams' rivals, set him up as the target for politically inspired attacks, and led to assaults on the pre-eminence of the Secretary of State in the Cabinet. From the beginning of Monroe's Administration, in fact, the other department heads made it clear that they expected "an entire equality with the Secretary of State" and that they considered "as an offensive distinction in his favor" certain ceremonial priorities his office enjoyed.

"My office of Secretary of State," Adams himself complained, "makes it the interest of all the partisans of the candidates for the next Presidency (to say no more) to decry me as much as possible in the public opinion." The political influence of his office, the idea that almost by prerogative it would place him in the Presidency—and not its control of foreign relations—lay, Adams was aware, at the root of his colleagues' jealousy.

Adams' rivals were justified in fearing him, for he was ambitious and, as much as any man, wanted to become President, hoping that the Secretaryship would again lead directly to the White House. For him it did. Although not as popular as other candidates or as schooled in politics, he had the advantage of running on a record of accomplishment in foreign policy.

Despite the attacks on what the Jacksonians called the "Secretary dynasty," Adams' successor, Henry Clay, came to believe that the nation would continue to follow "safe precedents" and hence accepted the Secretaryship with the idea of using it to gain the Presidency. The circumstances of his appointment, which set the pattern for employing the Secretaryship as a consolation prize, and the public reaction to the cry "bargain and corruption," however, led to the breaking of the Secretarial succession. As Secretary of State, Clay became the main issue in John Quincy Adams' beleaguered Administration and never obtained the higher prize he so earnestly sought. Instead of clearing the path to the White House, the Secretaryship under Clay became a dead end for anyone with Presidential ambitions.

One reason for this change was Andrew Jackson's victory in 1828—a victory that marked the end of the caucus, the rise of the nominating convention, and the death of the "Secretary dynasty." Since Washington's day, every President had had experience in foreign affairs, either abroad as a diplomat or as Secretary of State. So important were foreign relations in those formative years that they had pre-empted a good part of the public life of those Presidents, but not so with Jackson. A soldier and frontier lawyer, he had had no diplomatic experience and had never held an administrative post that dealt essentially with foreign affairs. His primary interests, like those of the nation he headed, were domestic. Under him, therefore, the Secretaryship entered a new era, one that saw it descend from the heights of politics and statesmanship.

Jackson, who nurtured a deep hostility toward the "Secretary dynasty," laid down the rule that Presidential aspirants were ineligible for Cabinet appointments, meaning essentially that the Secretaryship of State henceforth would be closed to them. Since succeeding Presidents who adhered to the Jacksonian tradition adopted this principle also, the Secretaryship became in time an office that those who still aspired to the Presidency would try to avoid.

Nonetheless, Jackson's first Secretary of State, Martin Van Buren, accepted the post because, among other reasons, he believed it still might be used as a springboard to the Presidency. His appointment, he realized, symbolized the rising power of his state, New York, in national politics and the eclipse of Virginia, which had been the home of Secretaries of State as well as of Presidents. As a shrewd politician, he knew, therefore, that the

Secretaryship, despite its decline in status, retained considerable prestige.

When Van Buren resigned, he camouflaged his desire for the Presidency, however. He published a letter saying he was giving up the Secretaryship because Jackson had consented to accept a second term. Since he himself, because of the reputation of the Secretaryship but against his will, was considered the next successor to the Presidency, he could not properly remain in the Cabinet. To do so, he asserted, would draw attacks upon the Administration and its measures. He declared that he wished to set an example for the country by removing the politics of Presidential succession from the Cabinet; in fact, he left the Secretaryship for the same reason he had taken it: mainly because he thought the change would advance his political career.

Van Buren did succeed Jackson to the Presidency, but not from the Secretaryship or as a result of his work as Secretary. He did so from the Vice-Presidency.

William Henry Harrison, who won the Presidency from Van Buren, first offered the Secretaryship to Clay. Since Clay had never been happy in the State Department and knew from experience that the post was no longer the last step before the White House, he turned down the offer. Daniel Webster, however, accepted the office from Harrison, hoping it would once again open the door to the Presidency, if not immediately, perhaps later.

The next Jacksonian President, James K. Polk, like Jackson himself, wished to exclude Presidential hopefuls from the Cabinet but, for political reasons, violated this rule by appointing James Buchanan, a known aspirant, as Secretary of State. Polk, however, tried to protect himself against Buchanan's ambition by pledging him, as he did other Cabinet officers, to resign immediately if he were to become an active candidate for the Presidency.

Buchanan's acceptance of the Secretaryship, however, was so qualified that, in effect, he managed to evade Polk's conditions. While stating that "both patriotism & policy—the success of the party, as well as that of your administration, require that we should have repose from the strife of making Presidents," he also told Polk he "could and would not accept the high and honorable office to which you have called me, at the expense of self-ostracism." Nonetheless, Polk took Buchanan's statement as a pledge and placed him at the head of his Cabinet.

The arrangement was never a happy one. Believing that Buchanan had begun maneuvers to succeed him almost on the day he became Secretary of State, Polk never fully trusted him. Increasingly alarmed by his Secretary's ambition, the President wrote in his diary in December, 1847:

> I regret to be under the impression that for some weeks past Mr. B. seems to have been so much absorbed with the idea of being President that I cannot rely, as formerly, upon his advice given in Cabinet upon public subjects. My impression is that all his opinions are formed and controlled by the consideration of the means best calculated to enable him to succeed in getting the nomination as my successor. He seems to have lost sight of the success of my administration & to be acting alone with a view to his own personal advancement.

Several months later, shortly before the Democratic Presidential nominating convention, Polk gained the impression that his Secretary of State was guilty of treachery and weighed the idea of dismissing him. Friends had told Polk that Buchanan, fearing that Polk would run for a second term, had engaged a newspaper writer to attack the President and thus perhaps prevent his renomination. Polk's suspicions proved unfounded, but they reveal the depth of his concern over the succession and how little faith he had in his Secretary of State.

Although unable to use the Secretaryship as the final direct step to the White House, Buchanan ultimately gained the Presidency—the last Secretary of State to do so. Political considerations not connected with the Secretaryship, however, made him the Chief Executive.

Even though by Buchanan's day the belief that the Secretary would be elevated to the Presidency was virtually dead, the memory of that tradition lingered on in the late nineteenth and well into the twentieth century. In 1880, James A. Garfield, before offering James G. Blaine the Secretaryship, asked, "Please tell me whether you are or will be the candidate for the presidency in 1884. I ask this because I do not purpose to allow myself nor any one else to use the next four years as the camping-ground for fighting the next presidential battle." Believing that he could not obtain the Presidential nomination by soliciting it and that if it were to come to him, it would come seemingly unsought, Blaine answered that he "would not again seek the nomination," and accepted the Secretaryship.

A quarter of a century later, when Theodore Roosevelt appointed Elihu Root Secretary of State, rumors circulated that Root nursed Presidential ambitions and had now become heir apparent. Specifically, that gossip told of an agreement whereby Root had accepted the Secretaryship in return for Roosevelt's promise to aid him in securing the Republican nomination in 1908, but there is no evidence of such a bargain.

Some of Root's friends who wanted him to be President feared that by taking over the Secretaryship, which they considered a dead end, he would kill his chances for the higher prize. One of them sent him a telegram asking, "Would it not be best to wait three years for the substance rather than take the shadow now?" "My feeling," Root answered, "is that the things one has the opportunity to do are substance and the things one tries to get are shadow." But Root never became President.

More than a quarter of a century later, Cordell Hull held the Secretaryship believing that Franklin D. Roosevelt had designated him heir apparent and that he would move up to the Presidency after Roosevelt's second term. When Roosevelt ran for a third term, therefore, Hull felt betrayed. Since a Gallup public-opinion poll, whatever its worth, suggested that he was more popular than the President himself, Hull blamed what he called the "extreme left fringe" and its influence over the President for shutting him out of the White House.

Within the same decade, George Marshall's appointment to the Secretaryship aroused speculation that he would be a candidate for the Presidency in 1948, but Marshall scotched such talk. That, perhaps, was the last revival of the old tradition of Secretarial succession.

In the frustrating years of the Cold War, when foreign policy aroused public passions as seldom in the past, and the Secretary of State was compelled to uphold unpopular policies, even his "availability" as a Presidential candidate, if he had the other necessary qualifications and support, was practically destroyed. Few politicians who thought they had a good chance to win the Presidency, therefore, would eagerly take the Secretaryship.

With foreign relations demanding constant attention and occupying a Secretary's full energies, moreover, he did not have time for fence-mending with local politicians—an essential activity in the making of a President. Some students of American foreign policy even argue that the new urgency of foreign affairs demands a Secretary of State whose qualifications are so specialized that they would disqualify him from consideration as a Presidential candidate.

I.

After the Jacksonians had destroyed the "Secretary dynasty," a new concept of the Secretaryship arose. If they could not step from the State Department to the White House, some Secretaries of State reasoned, perhaps they could use their office as a prime minister would and actually run the government, or at least gain broad power. Apparently, the first Secretary to take office with this idea in mind, as well as with the hope of ultimately gaining the Presidency, was Daniel Webster.

In 1841, when William Henry Harrison, a military hero of advanced years, became President, Whig leaders, reacting against the strong executive leadership of the Jackson years, envisaged an eclipse of Presidential power. Looking upon Harrison as a figurehead, Webster planned to make most of the important decisions, in effect, to run the Administration as if he were prime minister. The Whig politicians, for instance, induced Harrison to bring administrative and policy matters before the Cabinet, which they controlled, for decision by majority vote. Under this scheme, the President, like the department heads, would have only one vote. Webster, as the leader of the Cabinet, was never able to carry out his part in controlling this experiment, for Harrison's sudden death after one month in office, followed by the accession of John Tyler, something of a political maverick not controlled by Whig leaders, threatened the Secretary's premiership.

Even though Tyler asked the department heads to remain, all but Webster resigned. The Secretary of State knew, however, that he could not take the part of a prime minister, for when he told the new President of Harrison's agreement to run the government by majority decision of the Cabinet, Tyler announced that "I, as President, shall be responsible for my administration." Yet Tyler allowed his Secretary to initiate policy and accepted his ideas and guidance in foreign relations. Since Webster made the most of his broad discretionary powers and actually formulated foreign policy, his brief but brilliant tenure as Secretary, though not that of a prime minister, contributed substantially to his reputation as a statesman.

Tyler's third Secretary of State, John C. Calhoun, overshadowed the President in political stature and statesmanship. In taking office, Calhoun, too, considered himself virtually a prime minister. Later, Calhoun claimed that he had chosen the means that had brought about the immediate annexation of Texas, the outstanding accomplishment of Tyler's Presidency. Referring to the South Carolinian as the "great I am," Tyler vehemently denied his claim for credit. "*If he selected,*" Tyler said, referring to the method used in acquiring Texas, "then Texas is not legitimately a State of the Union, for Congress gave the power *to the President to select,* and not to the *Secretary of State.*"

The next two Whigs, Zachary Taylor and Millard Fillmore, were weak Presidents who took as Secretaries of State men Whig politicians expected to function as prime ministers. Taylor, like Harrison, is reputed to have been a captive of his Cabinet, and his Secretary, John M. Clayton, was at first expected to be the Administration's strong man. Clayton, however, was never able to provide the Administration with the leadership it needed.

Taking over the Presidency after Taylor's death, in July, 1850, Fillmore gave Daniel Webster a second turn in the Secretaryship. In political stature, experience, and statesmanship Webster again outshone the President, and this time, when he was not sick, he took up the part of a prime minister. Since the most pressing problems were domestic, he devoted himself mainly to this area, bringing the Administration, for instance, decisive support in the Compromise of 1850.

Jeremiah S. Black, who took over the Secretaryship as a lame duck in the middle of December, 1860, after Buchanan's Administration had been repudiated and civil war threatened, also concerned himself almost wholly with domestic affairs. Although Black held office for less than three months, he acquired great power because Buchanan, confronted with a national crisis beyond his grasp, relied on him for guidance. When, for example, Black threatened to resign because Buchanan appeared to concede too much to the seceding South, the President pleaded with him to stay, saying, "I have leaned upon you in these troubles as upon none other, and I insist that you stand by me to the end." The Secretary stayed, and in the last three weeks of the Administration, he and three colleagues formed a Cabinet regency, which made the important decisions. Buchanan was reduced almost to a nominal chief of state and his forceful Secretary of State acted virtually as a prime minister.

From the day he was invited to join the Cabinet, the next Secretary of State, William H. Seward, expected to govern as a prime minister, to direct the entire government in the President's name. Believing that he alone could head off the disaster of civil war, he wrote to his wife in December, 1860, when he received the offer, "I have advised Mr. Lincoln that I will not decline. It is inevitable. I will try to save freedom and my country."

Seward told friends that Lincoln wanted him for his "prime minister." To a foreign diplomat, he explained that "there is no great difference between an elected President of the United States and an hereditary monarch. The latter is called to the throne through the accident of birth, the former through the chances which make his election possible. The actual direction of the public belongs to the leader of the ruling party, here as well as in any hereditary principality." Seward, of course, considered himself the chieftain of the ruling Republican Party.

Public opinion, North and South, seemed to concur in Seward's estimate of his expected status as Secretary of State. Since Lincoln was an unknown quantity, many assumed that he did not have the qualities needed to grapple with the secession crisis. They concluded that he had called on Seward, a man far more experienced in government than himself, not only to handle foreign relations and head the Cabinet, but also to run the government and make the vital decisions. The Secretary of State, many believed, would be President in fact.

In the three months before Lincoln's inauguration, the relationship between the President-elect and Seward seemed to give substance to these assumptions. Lincoln sought Seward's advice and assistance in various political matters. He asked Seward to keep him informed of the state of political parties and the temper of opinion among politicians in Washington and to offer suggestions on bringing loyal Southerners into the Cabinet so as to give it a broad geographical base. The public and politicians of both major parties, therefore, had reason to look upon Seward as the spokesman for the incoming Administration.

After the inauguration, Lincoln gave his Secretary of State a relatively free hand in foreign affairs and continued to consult him on other matters, but for Seward that was not enough. Less than a month after taking office, he made a bold bid for executive power. In a paper modestly headed "Some Thoughts for the President's Consideration," he suggested diverting public attention from the crisis over slavery by centering it on foreign grievances, evoking a surge of unity and patriotism, possibly with declarations of war against France and Spain. The heart of the plan, however, was Seward's offer to take over direction of the government.

"Whatever policy we adopt," the Secretary pointed out, "there must be an energetic prosecution of it. For this purpose it must be somebody's business to pursue and direct it incessantly. Either the President must do it himself, and be all the while active in it, or devolve it on some member of the Cabinet. . . . It is not my especial province, but I neither seek to evade nor assume responsibility."

Keeping the contents of this remarkable document to himself, Lincoln tactfully put his Secretary of State in his place and refused to abandon any of his own responsibilities. "Upon your closing propositions," he told Seward, "I remark that if this must be done, I must do it."

A month later, Seward wrote home that "a country so largely relying on my poor efforts to save it has refused me the full measure of its confidence needful to that end. I am a chief reduced to a subordinate position, and surrounded by a guard, to see that I do not do too much for my country, lest some advantage may revert indirectly to my own fame."

Despite this early rebuff and the fact that the President had made it clear that he himself would exercise the ultimate control in all matters, Seward succeeded in gaining vast power and, in the conduct of foreign relations, in retaining what seemed almost unlimited freedom. In time, Lincoln came to place such trust in his Secretary of State that when Seward sent him a document for approval he signed without question or asked merely where his signature should go. In certain areas of executive authority, Lincoln allowed his Secretary to act virtually as a dictator. Seward interfered in the work of other departments, conceived military and domestic policies, and had at his disposal a secret-service organization to carry out those policies, policies that Lincoln himself seldom questioned.

Seward appeared with the President constantly and frequently visited the armies with him. Since he lived near the White House, he spent a good part of each day with Lincoln and was always ready with ideas and proposals, but his influence with the President aroused the jealousy of his Cabinet colleagues. Gideon Welles, the Secretary of the Navy, wrote that Seward "has the inside track and means to keep it" and "is anxious to direct, to be the Premier, the real Executive."

Whether or not they liked it, most members of the Cabinet accepted it as a fact that Seward, next to the President, was the Administration's guiding spirit. Welles recorded that in the infrequent early Cabinet meetings, the Secretary of State "assumed, and was allowed, as was proper, to take the lead in consultation and also to give tone and direction to the manner and mode of proceedings. The President, if he did not actually wish, readily acquiesced in this."

To the public, too, the Secretary of State appeared the dominating member of the Administration. Even Mrs. Lincoln, who hated Seward and called him "a dirty Abolitionist sneak," believed that he ran the government. "He draws you around his little finger like a skein of thread," she said to her husband.

Both the public and Mrs. Lincoln overestimated Seward's influence; he did not dominate Lincoln. After his initial efforts to control, the Secretary recognized Lincoln's finer qualities, accepted him as the true and active head of the government, and reconciled himself to his own subordinate status under the President. "It was not Mr. Lincoln who conformed himself and his policy and general views to Mr. Seward," a Cabinet member explained, "but it was Mr. Seward who adapted himself with ease and address to Mr. Lincoln, and, failing to influence, adopted and carried out the opinions and decisions of his chief."

Lincoln trusted his Secretary of State and relied on him for policy and guidance more than he did on the other department heads because he found in Seward a loyal, resourceful, and intelligent assistant, one willing to take needed risks in a time of great crisis. In his reach for power and in the power Lincoln allowed him, therefore, Seward was able to extend his grasp far beyond control of foreign affairs and to become more than a Secretary of State. He viewed and attempted to use his office as a premiership, one that functioned with Lincoln's support, to gain access to all branches of the government.

"I am counselling with the Cabinet one hour, with the Army officers the next, the Navy next, and I visit all the troops as fast as they come," the Secretary of State wrote in 1861, describing his activities. "I dare not," he added, "because I cannot safely, leave this post from which all supplies, all directions, all inquiries must radiate, to armies and navies at home and to legations abroad."

Seward tended to inflate his own importance. Yet, in his record under Lincoln can be found precedents for tremendous power in the Secretaryship.

Under Andrew Johnson, as under Lincoln, Seward exercised a constant influence on domestic as well as foreign policy. He was close to Johnson, seemingly with him at all times, had unrestricted access to him, day or night, and was ready with advice on almost any issue. Like Lincoln, Johnson grew fond of Seward, whom he called "the old Roman." He relied heavily on him for advice, accepted his ideas readily, and delegated broad power to him. Seward, therefore, became the Administration's central figure, but the President did not abdicate his own responsibilities, and he himself exercised the power of final decision.

Under both Lincoln and Johnson, Seward tried to function as would a prime minister. He even wrote his diplomatic correspondence, which he promptly released to the press, in the style of political pamphleteers; he did so with the idea of influencing public opinion, thus showing a concern for the domestic political reaction which reflected his desire to create a premiership that could not in fact exist in the American system. Yet, in the sense that he was actively the leader of the official family, the department head entrusted to carry out major policies, Seward, perhaps more than any other Secretary of State, had acted as a kind of prime minister.

In the next Administration, Hamilton Fish did not accept the Secretaryship with the idea of becoming a prime minister, but if any one person provided the Grant Administration with leadership, he did. More than was necessary for a mere ceremonial head of the Cabinet, the other department heads deferred to him and accepted his leadership. Policies attributed to Fish created more interest than those of any other government official, for the public looked upon his policies as those of the Administration. Even newspapermen, in attempting to get at the inside of the Grant Administration, went to the Secretary of State; they constantly pressed him for interviews.

It was clear that Grant leaned heavily on his Secretary of State. On almost all matters, the President carefully weighed Fish's views and often pushed aside his own to accept his Secretary's. He allowed Fish full responsibility for the conduct of foreign relations, gave him unquestioned administrative authority, and in most other areas permitted him to exert a moderating influence, often a decisive one. So essential did Fish become as a policy-maker that Grant, upset by his Secretary's frequent attempts to resign, insisted that he could spare any member of his official family except Fish. At one time, with Grant's support, the Vice-President and forty-four Senators signed a letter urging Fish not to retire.

A man of recognized ability, Fish gave character to an otherwise tawdry and scandal-plagued Administration. As a Secretary of State, he is unique in that he did not crave great power and yet shaped policies beyond those of his own department. In effect, he too functioned as a kind of prime minister.

II.

In a few instances, the Secretaries of State who strove for the status of prime ministers believed that they, not their chiefs, deserved to be President. Blaine, like Seward, was one of those. No one else, he told Garfield in accepting the Secretaryship, could bring the Administration the political support he could. He accepted the office, moreover, with the idea in mind of running the government from the State Department, of functioning like a grand vizier. This desire surprised no one, for Blaine's lust for power was as well known as the bear's appetite for honey.

"Did your going into the State Department simply mean that you were to be Secretary of State," Blaine's eldest son wrote, "I do not think any of your friends would greatly desire it. But your taking that position will mean—and the country will so understand it—that you are the head of the administration under the President, and the chief counsellor of its policy."

Although Garfield thought that Blaine deserved the Secretaryship and wanted him to have it, this well-known desire to make policy worried him. "If you can only restrain his immense activity and keep him from meddling with the other departments," an old friend advised the President-elect, "you will have a brilliant Secretary."

As the dominant member of the Cabinet, Blaine from the first, however, refused to be restrained. He started out initiating and controlling foreign policy, and the President came to accept and approve the results. In all other matters also, Blaine offered his advice freely, in fact acted as the President's most intimate adviser, and seemingly considered himself the *de facto* head of the government. So close was he to Garfield that the Administration has been called the Garfield-Blaine administration.

Garfield's assassination, with Blaine at his side, abruptly ended the premiership. "I cannot help feeling a little blue over the loss of place," Mrs. Blaine wrote when her husband gave up the Secretaryship. "Do you suppose that a Prime Minister ever went out without a secret feeling that he was being deprived of a right?"

Eight years later, the fact that Blaine had overshadowed Garfield and held a dynamic view of the Secretaryship worried Benjamin Harrison, who reluctantly invited the "plumed knight" to a second term in the State Department. Harrison was determined to be master of his own government. In his offer, therefore, he had made it clear that he himself would make policy. Yet the public—Blaine's foes as well as his friends—expected him to dominate Harrison's Administration as he had done Garfield's. "First and foremost, James G. Blaine will be Premier of the

Harrison Administration," the *Chicago Tribune* said, "and the mugwumps can put that in their pipes and smoke it."

The newspaper pundits were wrong. Despite his experience, fame, and faithful political following, the Secretary of State could gain no power approaching that of a prime minister. Blaine was unable even to exercise a decisive control over foreign relations. The President himself shaped and controlled policy, foreign as well as domestic.

The next Secretary of State to take office thinking of himself as a prime minister was Philander C. Knox. He believed that William Howard Taft would look to him for guidance on internal as well as foreign affairs. The President did call upon him for general advice, more so than on the other department heads, but not frequently enough to please Knox, who felt that other advisers had greater influence than he.

Knox considered himself and his office important, in fact held a grandiose view of his own status. This was quite clear to those around him. "So you have noticed, too," Taft once told his military aide, "that Knox takes his office pretty seriously. I often think how Knox would enjoy playing the role of President."

Knox usually had full responsibility for the conduct of foreign relations, and the President admitted that he did. "To the record of a year's accomplishment under Secretary Knox in our foreign affairs," Taft announced to the nation, "I think I can point with pride, and yet with becoming modesty, for it is his work and not mine. All I can claim is the merit of selecting him for the task." Privately, Taft told Knox that "the comfort I have in your management of the State Department I cannot exaggerate." Nonetheless, though Knox was able to assume considerable authority on his own and was allowed more power than were most Secretaries, he was never able to become his own boss and to function as the prime minister he thought he should be.

Charles Evans Hughes, on the other hand, did not accept the Secretaryship with the idea of acting as Warren G. Harding's prime minister, but he did, in fact, become virtually his own boss. After the President-elect had named Hughes Secretary, a choice regarded by most observers as his best Cabinet appointment, newspaper reporters asked him what his foreign policy would be. "You must ask Mr. Hughes about that," Harding answered. "That is going to be another policy of the next Administration," he added, "from the beginning, the Secretary of State will speak for the State Department."

Although pleased that he would have actual control over the conduct of foreign relations, Hughes sought to avoid certain other responsibilities. Concerned over her husband's chronic inability to withstand political pressures, Mrs. Harding, for example, told Hughes, "You've got to help Warren resist these demands." Hughes, however, did not envisage his position as that of a special aide who would shield the President from political opportunists. In fact, he seldom intervened in domestic politics.

In other matters, too, the Secretary did not grab for power. Even though Harding, who preferred poker and drinking parties with his cronies to the details of foreign affairs, followed Hughes's lead in foreign policy virtually without question, Hughes did not transform his own ideas into policy without asking beforehand for the President's approval. Furthermore, he went to the White House practically every day to keep the President abreast of international affairs.

Later, explaining his relations with Harding, Hughes said:

> I realized that I must take a full measure of responsibility when I felt definite action should be taken. I did not go to him with a statement of difficulties and ask him what should be done, but supplemented my statements of the facts in particular cases by concrete proposals upon which he could act at once, and to which he almost invariably gave his approval.

A concrete example of how the Secretary exercised his control over foreign policy can be seen in the following blunder concerning the Four-Power Pacific Treaty of 1921 with Great Britain, France, and Japan. At a regular press conference, a reporter had asked the President if Japan's main islands were to be included in the treaty's "guarantee" of each signatory's territory in the Pacific. "As I see it," Harding replied, "the quadrilateral treaty does not apply to Japan proper. The mainland is no more included in the provisions of the treaty than is the mainland of the United States." This view contradicted Hughes's own interpretation of the pact and created a minor crisis. Some feared that the Secretary would resign, but instead he rushed to the White House to explain the embarrassing conflict in views to Harding.

"I shouldn't have said anything about it to the press," the President confessed. "But, Hughes," he added, "when they asked me about it, I didn't want to appear to be a dub." Both then agreed that Hughes should dictate a statement correcting the error in interpretation and that the White House would issue it. In the statement Harding confessed his ignorance and retracted his original comment. To Secretary of Commerce Herbert Hoover, easygoing Harding "seemed a little afraid of his stiff Secretary of State."

Harding's successor, Calvin Coolidge, also admired Hughes, calling him the backbone of the Harding Administration and "the greatest Secretary of State this country ever had." It was not surprising therefore that Coolidge, as ignorant of foreign affairs as Harding, a man without "an international hair in his head," retained Hughes in the State Department and gave him full responsibility for the conduct of foreign relations. Coolidge seldom initiated policy and, like Harding, usually approved unquestioningly what his Secretary presented to him. He also relied on Hughes for advice on various national problems.

Without striving to become a prime minister, Hughes therefore was able to make the most of the powers inherent in the Secretaryship. In his domain of foreign affairs, particularly under Harding, he functioned as one of the nation's powerful Secretaries of State. In this sense, Hughes may be classed as one of those who exercised some of the powers of a prime minister.

Two decades later, James F. Byrnes, like Seward and Blaine before him, took over the Secretaryship believing apparently that he was better qualified for the Presidency than his chief and should have the responsibilities of a prime minister. Although Harry Truman granted him considerable independence in the conduct of foreign relations, Byrnes, seemingly disdainful of Presidential authority, desired virtual autonomy. Moreover, the ranking Democrat of the Senate Committee on Foreign Relations pointed out, "As Secretary of State, Byrnes was secretive from the start. He tried to keep things to himself as much as possible." Byrnes viewed his office and his department as comprising the policy-making agency in foreign affairs.

Byrnes's attitude bothered Truman, who became convinced that his Secretary had come "to think that his judgment was better than the President's." Truman accused his Secretary of attempting to assume the responsibilities of the President. This led to a bitter break between the two men, and to the failure of Byrnes's efforts to play the prime minister.

Unlike Truman, Eisenhower did not feel affronted by the efforts of his Secretary of State to act, in part at least, the prime minister. Disliking the daily routine of keeping up with international developments on his own, Eisenhower at the beginning of his Administration said he would obtain his information on foreign affairs from John Foster Dulles. The Secretary of State, therefore, developed closer relations with Eisenhower over a long period than did any other department head. Seemingly, when he was not traveling, he was always with the President.

Eisenhower himself said that he met more often with Dulles than with any other member of his Cabinet. Dulles alone had the freedom of the President's office, being able to enter at almost any time. When in Washington, he went to the White House every day or used his direct phone connection to the White House to call Eisenhower once or twice a day; he conferred with him and other Presidential advisers in weekly sessions of the Cabinet and the National Security Council. When abroad, Dulles telephoned or cabled reports to the President as often as every day. In other ways, too, Dulles made himself the indispensable executive officer to Eisenhower, a President seemingly eager to delegate, but not abandon, some of the arduous responsibilities of his office.

In his conferences with Dulles, the President usually chose from alternatives the Secretary presented to him. Except in emergencies, he did not shape or carry out his own foreign policy. In most instances, Dulles initiated policy and carried it out. As a result, Eisenhower's heart attack in September, 1955, which largely incapacitated him for six months did not paralyze the conduct of foreign relations. As Dulles explained, "the policies and principles" of the Administration were entirely familiar to those charged with carrying them out, and hence the President's attack did not jeopardize "the steady prosecution of our national and international policies."

Democrats complained that there was no interruption in policy because even before the heart attack the President had delegated vital responsibilities of his office to a "regency" of his personal appointees. If so, no regent appeared more powerful in his own realm than did Dulles. No Secretary of State, not even Hughes, moreover, ever appeared more completely in command of foreign policy and none was more clearly identified the world over as the maker of that policy.

With his own people, Dulles' frequent appearances on radio and television strengthened his image as the maker of policy. Those appearances, too, reflected his desire to cultivate public opinion. Most Secretaries of State leave that task to the President, but Dulles, like a prime minister, believed that foreign policy began at home and that he needed a constituency for the support of his policies.

So well known did Dulles become that he was even made the subject of a song in a New York play, a ditty so bad, it was said, that it could have been part of the Democratic National Committee's anti-Dulles campaign. Next to the President himself, Dulles was regarded as the outstanding figure in the Eisenhower Administrations, the giant of the Cabinet. People, in fact, constantly referred to the Administration's foreign policies as the Dulles policies.

True enough, most policies did originate with Dulles. Although the Secretary seems to have had virtually a blank check in the conduct of foreign relations, it should be remembered that everything he did had the President's approval and that Eisenhower was informed in advance by Dulles himself of every action taken in foreign affairs. "Foster and I," Eisenhower said, "worked, as nearly as can be imagined, as one person." Except to be a prime minister in fact, the American Secretary of State can expect no greater power.

Such power, as Dulles' Secretaryship and that of other strong Secretaries shows, must come from the President. It is not inherent in the Secretaryship. The Secretary, of course, must have ability, intelligence, and certain aggressive qualities, but without the President's need or willingness to accept a "premier," he can attain no real power on his own. This is evident in the case of Secretary Blaine, who could be virtually a prime minister under one President and something quite different under another. The American Presidential system has no place for a prime minister in the true sense of the term, but if any executive officer has approached the powers of one, it is the Secretary of State.

An important reason for this is that much more than other Cabinet officers, the Secretary of State has responsibilities that cut across departmental lines. He should be able to bring to the President analyses and points of view that integrate military, economic, social, and other factors. He, unlike the others, should be able to offer the President a synthesis that gives due weight to all relevant data, whether in or out of the field of his department. In this broad sense of having a concern for developments in all areas that may affect the national interest, the Secretary of State, if he is a strong one, certainly shares some qualities in common with a prime minister.

5

The Figurehead

> The President is the only channel of communication between this country and foreign nations, and it is from him alone that foreign nations or their agents are to learn what is or has been the will of the nation.
>
> —Thomas Jefferson, 1793

Presidents who have allowed their Secretaries of State ministerial power comprise a minority. Other Presidents, particularly in times of crisis, have taken on themselves the conduct of foreign relations and have jealously guarded that domain against encroachments. Even though their Secretaries might be the true architects of foreign policy, most Presidents have usually seen to it that any substantial success in foreign affairs was theirs, or at least that they received credit for it.

Except for weak Presidents, or those unwilling to concern themselves with the details of foreign affairs, direct Presidential control of foreign policy is the rule in the American political system. Such control, in fact, is probably the most important single function of the Presidency, a power that the President, even if he should so desire, can never surrender entirely to his Secretary of State. In practice, therefore, some Presidents not only have retained a firm grip on the conduct of foreign relations but have also resented independent action by their Secretaries. A few, those who have sometimes been called their own Secretaries of State, have even relegated their senior department chief almost to the status of a figurehead.

The first President to attempt to reduce his Secretary of State practically to a figurehead was James Madison. Having spent eight years at the head of the State Department and thus being thoroughly familiar with the conduct of foreign relations, Madison as President expected to continue to keep their conduct in his own hands, leaving little more than routine administrative duties for his Secretary to perform. Moreover, when one considers the circumstances of Robert Smith's appointment to the Secretaryship and the fact that his relations with Madison while both served in Jefferson's Cabinet were not cordial, this limitation of Smith's status is not surprising.

Claiming that Smith was incompetent, Madison sometimes went so far as to write and rewrite his Secretary's official notes. He declared that the Secretary was incapable of handling the duties of his office. Whatever talents Smith may have possessed, the President said, they were not suitable to the Secretaryship of State.

Even if Smith had possessed the necessary ability, his chances for success in the Secretaryship were remote, owing partly to the ignominious status Madison gave him and partly to his own questionable conduct. Smith had been so eager to gain the Secretaryship that he accepted it knowing that he had been forced on a President who did not want him. Then after taking office, instead of trying to win the confidence of his chief, he earned further enmity by siding with Madison's enemies in the Senate. Understandably, until the President could rid himself of his unwanted Secretary, he gave him the title but not the substance of the office.

Andrew Jackson also denied his Secretaries of State real power. He took the view that a Secretary was "merely an executive agent, a subordinate," whom he could ignore if he chose. For guidance on almost all matters of policy, he relied on unofficial advisers, especially on a group known as his "Kitchen Cabinet." He even discontinued the regular meetings of the official Cabinet, thus shutting off the Secretary of State almost completely from the making of policy.

Jackson's reliance on unofficial advisers was not an innovation; nonetheless, the extensive use he gave the practice had the effect of reducing his Secretaries of State to administrative assistants, virtually to figureheads with practically no part in the shaping of foreign policy. Van Buren, of course, was an exception, yet he acquired a voice in the making of policy not because he held the Secretaryship but because he had gained admittance to the inner circle of the President's political advisers. Even though the rule that a Secretary was merely a Presidential assistant had been established before Jackson's time, it was he who anchored it deeply into the tradition of American politics.

James K. Polk, another Jacksonian who dominated the conduct of foreign relations, also lived by that rule. He wanted an administrator for his Secretary of State, one who would agree with his opinions and policies. For political reasons, however, he accepted a Secretary, James Buchanan, who frequently opposed his views. Although irritated by this opposition, Polk did not attempt to get rid of him.

"Though Mr. Buchanan differs with me on some points," Polk confided to his diary, "yet he had not in consequence of such difference embarrassed me but had shown a willingness to carry out my views instead of his, and I was desirous to retain him in the Cabinet." At another time, the President wrote of Buchanan, "He may differ with me in opinion on public questions, and when he does, having myself to bear the responsibility, I will control."

At still other times, Polk would interpret Buchanan's advice as obstructive. Once when the Secretary objected to having his views disdainfully disregarded, Polk said to himself, "Mr. Buchanan will find that I cannot be forced to act against my convictions and that if he chooses to retire, I will find no difficulty in administering the Government without his aid." Strewn throughout Polk's diary are passages equally harsh, all attesting to a strained relationship with his Secretary of State and to the President's determination to handle foreign policy as he alone saw fit.

So discouraged did Buchanan become with his menial status that in several instances he considered resigning. He never did because he feared that a break with the President would ruin his political career. Nonetheless, he did ask Polk to consult him:

> When I differ from you, it is always with reluctance and regret. I do not like to urge arguments in opposition before the whole Cabinet. I appear then to be occupying a position that is always painful to me. A little previous consultation with me on important questions of public policy relating to foreign affairs would always obviate this difficulty; because if I failed to convince you—there would then be no appearance of dissent.

Polk, however, did not allow his Secretary's views to shape his policy. Ignoring or overriding Buchanan's advice, he continued to act on his own. His brusque treatment of his Secretary, a man several years his senior, apparently opened old wounds left by the campaign of 1844, when Polk had been a "dark horse" and Buchanan a prime contender for the Presidency. Thinking himself a superior in talent and prestige, Buchanan probably found it difficult to subordinate himself and galling to be dominated, and ignominiously so, by Polk. He probably realized, too, that even outside the Administration it was known that he had no voice in policy. "Buchanan," one observer wrote, "is treated as no gentleman would treat a sensible hireling."

Thus it can be seen that if ever a President lived up to the Jacksonian principle that a Secretary of State is subordinate and should be kept so, it was Polk. He himself controlled not only the major policies, but also the details in routine matters. He would not allow his Secretary even the fiction of being responsible for foreign affairs. Under him, the Secretary functioned merely as an administrative clerk, at times almost as a lackey, a servile retainer whose main task was to carry out the President's policies regardless of his own feelings.

Buchanan's view of the Secretaryship as a burden, one he was eager to unload, is therefore, understandable. "The State Department has never been a pleasant situation for me," he wrote at the end of his term, "though it might have been so, and personally I long to enjoy the privilege of being once more a private citizen." Yet Buchanan's menial status, in part at least, grew out of his own timidity. If he had been a bolder man, a contemporary critic pointed out, the very nature of his post would have allowed him to wield more power.

Forgetting, perhaps, his own frustrating experience under Polk, Buchanan as President treated his Secretary of State as though he were a cipher. Such a Secretary, in fact, fitted Buchanan's plans. Taking the view that, with a record of important diplomatic experience and four years in the State Department, he was better qualified to conduct foreign relations than anyone he could appoint to the Secretaryship, Buchanan was from the first determined to initiate and carry out his own foreign policy. For his Secretary of State, therefore, he sought a man of national reputation who could head his Cabinet, give his Administration a respectable front, and accept the part of a figurehead gracefully. Although Buchanan was virtually compelled by domestic political considerations to offer the Secretaryship to Lewis Cass of Michigan, whom he had never liked and did not want, Cass in most respects met his requirements.

Cass, by then seventy-five, had lost his fire, but he still had awesome stature within the Democratic Party, based on a long and distinguished career in public life, and could bring prestige to the Administration, prestige that Buchanan sorely needed. At his advanced years, moreover, Cass no longer had high political ambitions and hence could offer no threat to Buchanan and the Presidency.

Before offering Cass the Secretaryship, nonetheless, Buchanan had tried to make sure that the old man would not take the office with independent ideas on the conduct of foreign relations. Using an intermediary, he asked Cass if he would accept an appointment hemmed in with restrictions. In effect, he told Cass that he could have the Secretaryship in name only, the title and honor but no real power, and that he would have to accept constant supervision. Cass agreed to Buchanan's conditions, because as a lame-duck Senator who had been defeated in 1856, he did not wish to return to Detroit a repudiated statesman. Doubtless, he also liked the idea of spending his last days in Washington holding the highest appointive office in the land—a fitting climax to his long career of public service.

The Secretaryship, however, brought Cass almost nothing but humiliation. To guide Cass's unsteady hand, Buchanan had appointed an old friend, John Appleton of Maine, Assistant Secretary of State. Working with the President, frequently independently of Cass, Appleton actually ran the Department of State. In other ways, too, whenever he could, Buchanan shunted aside his Secretary. Thus, Lord Clarendon wrote to Buchanan shortly after he took office: "I don't suppose there are many instances of the President of the United States & the English Foreign Secretary corresponding directly with each other, but if the practice is as agreeable to you as it is to me, I shall hope for its continuance."

As a result of his figurehead status, Cass had few responsibilities and accepted slights from the President that other men would have resented. In a short while, however, he apparently came to realize not only that he was excluded from the Administration's ruling inner circle but also that he had perhaps gained an empty honor at the cost of self-respect. That he was a mere figurehead had become common knowledge. "I think," Cass's predecessor wrote of him, "he begins to feel what others clearly see, that his condition is not what it ought to be or what he is bound to make it if he intends to sustain his reputation with the country."

The Secretary was incompetent, Buchanan charged, and therefore deserved to be treated as a cipher. Most of the dispatches that bear Cass's name, he explained after Cass had resigned, were written by himself, the Assistant Secretary of State, or the Attorney General:

> His original drafts were generally so prolix & so little to the point that they had to be written over again entirely, or so little was suffered to remain as to make them new Despatches. All this was done with so much delicacy & tenderness that, to the extent of my knowledge, General Cass always cheerfully & even gratefully assented. So

> timid was he & so little confidence has he in himself, that it was difficult for him to arrive at any decision of the least consequence. He brought many questions to me which he ought to have decided himself.

Buchanan was probably unduly caustic in his estimate of Cass. Since the President himself made most of the decisions, even the minor ones, Cass, even if he had been capable, did not have the opportunity to acquire any real power in the making of decisions. Only to very few who have held the Secretaryship does the term figurehead apply so aptly as it does to Cass.

I.

Although never a figurehead in the sense that Cass was, James G. Blaine functioned as little more than an administrative subordinate under Benjamin Harrison. He took orders from a President who jealously guarded his prerogatives, one who did not relinquish power or delegate authority easily. Aware that foreign relations was the field wherein a President could most likely build a lasting reputation, Harrison was determined that he, not his Secretary, would initiate and control foreign policy.

In foreign affairs, as in other major areas, Harrison studied important questions thoroughly and perused all pertinent documents. "I found the President here going over the Samoan despatches with your Father," Mrs. Blaine wrote, in a revealing letter to one of her sons. "He sat all crumpled up, his nose and his boots and his gloves almost meeting, but he was examining those despatches with care and great intelligence, and although I am not drawn to him, I cannot refuse him the homage of respect." So closely, in fact, did Harrison supervise the State Department that it was not unusual for him to know more of what was happening there than did the Secretary of State.

"My plan," Harrison explained, "was to give each of the Departments a stated day when the Secy would come with his papers and a full consultation would be had as to appointments and as to important matters of business." And, he added, "All matters of large concern were brought to my attention, and were settled in the conference I have referred to, or in the Cabinet meeting." Blaine, as a result, did not have full control of his own department.

When an important state paper was to be drawn up, the President usually discussed it with Blaine beforehand; sometimes he even prepared an outline for the Secretary to follow. He inspected papers drafted by Blaine, revised them, and at times discarded them for new ones he himself wrote.

Blaine chafed under such close supervision. His warm and affable personality rebelled against the President's cold and impersonal attitude. Precipitate and enthusiastic about his own ideas, Blaine never felt comfortable with the restrained and intellectual President. "Harrison," Mrs. Blaine said, "is of such a nature that you do not feel at all at liberty to enjoy yourself." Being older and better known than Harrison, moreover, the Secretary found it difficult to take orders from a younger man, particularly one who was not notably gracious in his assertion of authority and who wanted it understood that he had the whip hand. To Mrs. Blaine, it was almost unbearable to see Harrison, whom she considered a political novice and referred to as that "Indiana accident," ordering her husband to do his bidding.

The President, on his part, could not help resenting his Secretary's fame and continuing leadership in the Republican Party, of which he, Harrison, was titular head. Neither he nor Blaine, as a result, was happy with their relationship. Blaine, moreover, was never able to gain the President's confidence and, except for official functions, was usually excluded from Harrison's social affairs.

Since Blaine never had a decisive voice in the shaping of foreign policy, his status could hardly rise above that of a high-ranking administrative official.

The position of John Sherman, the next Secretary of State who had no control over his own department, resembled that of Cass more than it did Blaine's. Like Cass, Sherman was old and had accepted the Secretaryship under questionable circumstances.

Knowing that the senile Sherman could not handle foreign relations effectively, McKinley expected to use him merely as a respectable figurehead. As such, Sherman had value, for despite his acquiescence in Hanna's machinations, he still retained a national reputation, still had a political following, and could still bring some prestige to the Administration.

McKinley himself controlled the conduct of foreign relations, initiating important policies and even carrying on negotiations without Sherman's knowledge. His decisions, made without his Secretary's advice, were carried out by capable subordinates within the Department of State who frequently acted independently of Sherman.

In particular, the President relied on William R. Day, a close friend from his home town whom he had appointed First Assistant Secretary of State. Day, acting as the *de facto* Secretary of State, ran the State Department. Sherman often did little more than sign the papers that Day or other assistants brought to him for formal approval. Day, for instance, had charge of the negotiations leading to the annexation of Hawaii. The Secretary of State was called upon for consultation only when the treaty was ready for his signature. Sherman thus had practically no influence on policy or on the administration of his own department.

Finally, the crisis over Cuba placed such heavy demands on the State Department that Sherman could not carry even his limited responsibilities. Day took over virtually all his duties and, contrary to the usual practice, began to attend Cabinet meetings. Frustrated by his own inadequacies and humiliated by the fact that Day now openly represented his department in front of the other department heads, Sherman resigned immediately after the outbreak of the war with Spain.

A contemporary wrote:

> Poor Sherman makes everyone connected with the Department apprehensive. As Assistant Secretary of State, William R. Day has proved as great a diplomat in handling the situation within the Department as the International situation without. Upon Day has fallen everything of trouble from within and without. He has been compelled to

watch the venerable Secretary and guard the country from mistakes. The great career of John Sherman should have closed in some other way.

Sherman, obviously, served as Secretary of State in name only. For him the Secretaryship was a sad and inglorious twilight.

McKinley's next Secretary, John Hay, who continued in office under Theodore Roosevelt, is considered one of the outstanding Secretaries of State. His friend Henry Adams claimed that Hay was "the most imposing figure ever known in the office. He had an influence that no other Secretary of State ever possessed . . . and he stood far above counsel or advice." Hay's work under McKinley offered some basis for this extravagant estimate, for the President allowed him to shape some of his own ideas into policy. Under McKinley, therefore, Hay had a noteworthy part in formulating foreign policy, but under Roosevelt his status changed.

The relationship between Hay and Roosevelt, Henry Adams wrote, "was a false one." Hay, a friend and contemporary of Roosevelt's father, was twenty years older than his chief and was never really comfortable serving the exuberant young President, whom he remembered as the child he had once held on his knee. Roosevelt, who was fond of Hay, admired him, and at one time even called him "the greatest Secretary of State I have seen in my time," graciously tried to sweep away the difference in their ages, but he would not rely on Hay to the extent that McKinley had. He allowed Hay to administer the State Department and direct some negotiations, but he himself originated policy, often without consulting his Secretary of State. Disliking the formal channels of diplomacy leading through the State Department, Roosevelt frequently engaged directly in negotiations and other aspects of diplomacy, thus circumventing his Secretary. These attempts to monopolize power irked Hay.

Roosevelt justified his direct control of foreign affairs by saying that "when a matter is of capital importance, it is well to have it handled by one man" and that Hay was a weakling who sometimes could not be trusted. This criticism was partly true, for the Secretary was an Anglophile and something of a Germanophobe (he referred to William II of Germany as "His Awfulness"). "He had grown to hate the Kaiser so," the President remarked of Hay, "that I could not trust him in dealing with Germany." Later, he wrote that "Hay could not be trusted where England was concerned." At another time, Roosevelt said that in the work of the State Department, "I had to do the big things myself, and the other things I have always feared would be badly done or not done at all."

During Hay's last two years in office, the President was compelled to take over direct control of foreign affairs because the Secretary was frequently sick. In fact, in the months before his death, Hay was Secretary in name only. As Roosevelt explained, "for a number of months now I have had to be my own Secretary of State, and while I am very glad to be it so far as the broad outlines of the work are concerned, I of course ought not to have to attend to the details."

After Hay's death and a private printing of his letters in which there were comments Roosevelt disliked, the Rough Rider reversed his earlier estimate, saying that Hay "was not a great Secretary of State." His Secretary's usefulness, he wrote, "was almost the usefulness of a fine figurehead." Hay, he insisted, "never initiated a policy or was of real assistance in carrying thru a policy; but he sometimes phrased what I desired said in a way that was a real service; and the respect for him was such that his presence in the Cabinet was a strength to the administration."

Even though Roosevelt's evaluation of Hay is excessively harsh, the Secretary obviously did not possess much power over the conduct of foreign relations; he was more a diplomat than a statesman. Thus, we have another example of a Secretary of State who stands out as a maker of policy under one President and is reduced almost to the status of a polished administrative assistant under another.

II.

Like Theodore Roosevelt, Woodrow Wilson was a President determined to act as virtually his own foreign minister, one who found it difficult to delegate authority. "He is," one of his Cabinet members observed, "one of those men made to tread the winepress alone. The opportunity comes now and then to give a suggestion or to utter a word of warning, but on the whole I feel that he probably is less dependent on others than any President of our time." Two of Wilson's Secretaries of State, in part at least as a result of his independence, functioned, in many instances, practically as figureheads.

Although Wilson consulted his first Secretary, William Jennings Bryan, on various subjects and even allowed him independence in shaping some policies—in the Caribbean and in a project to advance peace through a world-wide network of conciliation agreements, or "cooling-off" treaties—in most matters, he did not permit Bryan the power of initiative. Wilson himself exercised a tight control over the conduct of foreign relations, a control that Bryan at first did not question. Unlike some other Secretaries, Bryan accepted his subordinate position gracefully and seemed pleased merely with the honor of the Secretaryship. Those who knew him said he was "deferential to the office" or "highly appreciative of the position to which he had been appointed."

Bryan's honor appears an empty one, for Wilson apparently could never fully overcome his feeling that his Secretary was incapable of dealing adequately with great matters of state. Moreover, he distrusted the career officers of the State Department and often used executive agents to circumvent the department and the Secretary himself.

Wilson's personal control of foreign relations became more marked as international affairs, after 1914, came to dominate his Administration. He entered diplomatic negotiations himself, without using or even consulting his Secretary. At one time, when he sent Colonel House abroad to seek some way of mediating the war in Europe, he told House to explain to Sir Edward Grey, the British Foreign Minister, that "while you are abroad I expect to act directly through you and avoid all intermediaries."

In May, 1915, after the sinking of the British passenger liner *Lusitania*, with a high loss of American lives, Wilson, on his own initiative and without outside consultation, prepared a strong protest to the German Government. When he read it to his Cabinet, only Bryan objected. Although Wilson then softened the note a bit and Bryan signed it, that signature meant little, for the note remained Wilson's in thought and word.

The second *Lusitania* note was also Wilson's. Bryan was convinced that this note would lead to war with Germany. Rather than accept the President's policy, he resigned in an act of conscience to take the issue to the people.

In later years, Bryan resented the charge that as Secretary of State he had been a figurehead and maintained that the President had consulted him "on every proposition." Yet a Cabinet member reported being told by Mrs. Bryan at the time of her husband's resignation, "that her husband had been unhappy in his position for some time on account of the President's habit of preparing important papers himself. He had come to feel, she said, that he was not consulted as he ought to be, and that he was playing the part of a figurehead." When Bryan offered his resignation, Wilson recalled, "he had remarked with a quiver in his voice and of his lips, 'Colonel House has been Secretary of State, not I, and I have never had your full confidence.' "

The fact seems to be that Bryan was far from being the "Mr. Prime Minister" his friends had called him. Although a kindlier chief than Polk, Wilson, too, in many ways had reduced the Secretaryship almost to the status of a high-level clerkship.

Under Robert Lansing, the next Secretary of State, the office seemingly became even more of a clerkship than it had been under Bryan. Ironically, Wilson had at first opposed Lansing because he lacked imagination and initiative, but Colonel House urged his appointment. "I have a feeling," House had told the President, "that if Lansing is at all acceptable to you that he could be used to better advantage than a stronger man."

House, in fact, had suggested a reorganization of the State Department that would give it two new assistant secretaries. "These with Lansing," he explained to Wilson, "would be able to do the details intelligently, and you could direct as heretofore and without half the annoyance and anxiety that you have been under." It was most important, he advised, "to get a man with not too many ideas of his own and one that will be entirely guided by you without unnecessary argument, and this, it seems to me, you would find in Lansing."

Wilson agreed, but Lansing himself was convinced that the President appointed him because he thought they were of the same mind concerning international affairs. Others believed Wilson had told Lansing that as Secretary he would function essentially as a legal clerk. Wilson's son-in-law, Secretary of the Treasury William G. McAdoo, said that Lansing "accepted his post with a distinct understanding that all negotiations with foreign powers were to be carried on by the President." Postmaster General Albert Burleson pointed out that "Wilson is going to be his own Secretary of State. Lansing is the very man he wants—a good lawyer, without outstanding personality, who will be able to carry on the regular duties of the office and be perfectly willing for the 'Old Man' to be the real Secretary of State."

Even outsiders, *The Nation*, for example, held similar views. "Every President," it said, "has to be, in the big matters, his own Secretary of State, and Mr. Wilson will undoubtedly continue to determine for himself the main features of our foreign policy."

These estimates of Lansing's status proved fairly accurate. He came to be the silent man of the Cabinet. In meetings, he rarely spoke, did not attempt to influence policy openly in any area, except possibly foreign relations, and was so deferential to the President's views that the other department heads were convinced he had no ideas of his own. Lansing did have his own ideas but usually could not persuade Wilson to accept them.

The relations between Lansing and Wilson were always more or less formal, and the Secretary never knew what went on in the President's mind, in fact, never understood him. Wilson seldom sought his Secretary's advice on matters of policy and continued to write some of his own notes, but, as expected, he relied on Lansing's expert knowledge of international law and his other technical skills in the drafting of most notes and documents. Lansing's lack of influence on important issues was so obvious that it led the German Ambassador to declare that "since Wilson decides *everything,* any interview with Lansing is a mere matter of form."

In the diplomacy of World War I, and especially the peace-making, Wilson practically ignored his Secretary of State. In drawing up his Fourteen Points for peace, in January, 1918, for instance, the President obtained his ideas and information from the "Inquiry," a group of experts that had been organized by Colonel House to deal with the problems of the peace. Wilson did not show his Secretary the Fourteen Points address until the day before he was to deliver it and then allowed Lansing to make only a few slight changes that did not affect its substance. Later, Colonel House, not the President, informed Lansing of the general plans for the Paris Peace Conference.

Wilson would even have excluded the Secretary from the Peace Commission that went to Paris if he had not felt that he had to include him because the other foreign ministers would be active in their delegations. To have left Lansing at home, moreover, would have been an unpardonable affront.

At the conference, Lansing took virtually no part in drawing up the Treaty of Versailles or in shaping the League of Nations. Before the Peace Commission had left for Paris, he did not even know of Wilson's plan for the League. The President, he wrote, "neither asked my advice as to any provision of the [League] Covenant nor discussed the subject with me personally." Lansing was able to gain some information from Colonel House, but his first basic knowledge came from the President in a conversation on the ship that carried them to Europe.

On one occasion in Paris when the Secretary tried to take the initiative, the President rebuffed him. Without consulting Wilson beforehand, Lansing asked the legal advisers to the American Commission to prepare an outline treaty for the Commission's use. When the President learned of it, he told his Secretary, "I don't want lawyers drafting this treaty."

"I was deeply incensed at this intemperate remark," Lansing recorded, "as he knew I was a lawyer. . . . I never forgot his words and always felt that in his mind my opinions, even when he sought them, were tainted with legalism."

In February, 1919, when Wilson had to return to Washington before the close of Congress, Lansing as Secretary of State stood to inherit the official leadership of the American delegation, but the President acted so as to place actual authority in the hands of Colonel House and to make Lansing merely titular head *ad interim*. Wilson not only distrusted his Secretary, he also wished to retain direct control of negotiations. Consequently, he wanted decisions postponed until he returned to Paris. "It showed very clearly," Lansing wrote, "that the President intended to do everything himself and to allow no one to act for him unless it was upon some highly technical matter."

Seven months later, after Wilson's collapse at Pueblo, Colorado, Lansing was left in sole charge of the State Department, but again he was allowed no power of decision in matters of policy. The sick President either refused to answer his Secretary's recommendations or vetoed them. "He is certainly well enough to interfere with or nullify everything I attempt to do," Lansing complained.

The Secretary said that if it were not for the President's illness, he would have resigned. "I want to be free and my own master," he wrote. "I am sick of being treated as a school boy or a rubber stamp." When he finally did resign, he explained that he had been conscious of the fact that Wilson did not welcome his "advice in matters pertaining to the negotiations in Paris, to our foreign service, or to international affairs in general."

So bitter did Lansing become over his ignominious status that he denounced the President as "a tyrant, who even goes so far as to demand that all men shall *think* as he does or else be branded as traitors or ingrates." We can see, therefore, that Wilson had made a mistake in selecting Lansing for the part of a figurehead. Few Secretaries of State, in fact, have suffered such frustration and helplessness as did Lansing. He left office detesting the man who had raised him to the highest appointive post in the land.

III.

Even more than in the case of Lansing, the conditions under which Cordell Hull—the next Secretary of State who at times had merely nominal authority over the conduct of foreign relations—accepted office are clouded with contradictions. According to one story, he was advised to accept only on the condition that Franklin D. Roosevelt would allow him to make his own appointments in the State Department. "The Secretary," he was told, "should at least be given every chance to have the personal loyalty of his assistants." Hull appeared to take this advice but then accepted the post without insisting upon control over appointments. This, the story goes, was a fatal mistake.

Hull himself asserted, however, that he did lay down conditions before taking Roosevelt's offer. He said that he sought and was able to obtain a complete understanding that he would be more than a mere administrative clerk. "If I accept the Secretaryship of State," he told Roosevelt, "I do not have in mind the mere carrying on of correspondence with foreign governments." He insisted upon being consulted and having a share "in the formulation and conduct of foreign policy." Roosevelt, according to Hull, agreed to the conditions and assured him that "we shall function in the manner you've stated."

Whether or not Hull accepted the Secretaryship under firm conditions that he himself had set, his record reveals that he came to have only a small part in the shaping of major foreign policies. He claimed that the President allowed him considerable independence and "that in the majority of cases I had to make my own decisions," but critics maintain, with some exaggeration, that he was in fact little more than an "imposing white-haired figurehead." It is true that in some matters, such as in a program for reciprocal trade agreements, in Latin American affairs, and in negotiations with Japan prior to the attack on Pearl Harbor, the Secretary had substantial influence; in most instances, however, his power of decision appears to have extended mainly over administrative procedure and the mass of detail that daily flowed into the State Department. Roosevelt, the evidence shows, often chose to act as his own foreign minister.

From the beginning, the President himself made the basic appointments in the State Department and Foreign Service. He corresponded privately with diplomats in the field, carried on direct negotiations with foreign statesmen, and made most of the important policy decisions on his own. In effect, he frequently acted without seeking the advice of his Secretary of State.

At the World Economic Conference, in London, in the summer of 1933, the Secretary of State was the *ex officio* chairman of the American delegation, but Roosevelt had chosen the delegates without consulting him. Hull had no real power over them and could not instruct them or prevent them from making embarrassing statements to the press. His role was so humiliating that even though he had been in office only a few months, he considered resigning.

In that same year, against Hull's wishes, Roosevelt sent an invitation directly to the President of the Soviet Union calling for negotiations over the terms of American recognition of the Communist regime. When Hull's negotiations deadlocked, the President stepped in, and in what he called man-to-man talks with the Russians, concluded a recognition agreement.

Direct diplomacy became something of a habit with Roosevelt. In September, 1938, when Adolf Hitler threatened Czechoslovakia, William C. Bullitt, Ambassador to France and one of the several friends of Roosevelt who did not hesitate to go over Hull's head, urged the President to attempt to preserve peace by appealing directly to the heads of the governments involved in the crisis. Sumner Welles also urged the appeal. Hull opposed it, saying later that "Welles kept pushing the President on while I kept advising him to go slow." Siding with Bullitt and Welles, the President made the appeal.

Seven months later, after Benito Mussolini's Italian Blackshirts had invaded Albania, Bullitt telephoned Roosevelt from Paris urging him to ask Hitler and Mussolini to guarantee specific countries against attack. As before, Hull opposed the idea. "It was another of the direct appeals to the heads of Government, in which practice," he wrote, "I had little confidence." Again the President ignored the advice of his Secretary and made the appeal.

The fact that the advice of subordinates like Bullitt carried greater weight with the President than did the Secretary's weakened Hull's influence in the Cabinet and in his own department. The fact that his subordinates could correspond directly with the President had the same effect. Admiral William D. Leahy, for example, regularly wrote directly to Roosevelt, and thus circumvented the Secretary of State, when he was Ambassador to the Vichy Government of France.

Roosevelt's direct diplomacy also eroded his Secretary's influence with foreign statesmen. Shrewd ones, like Russia's Constantine Oumansky, were convinced that Hull meant well but had no control over policy. Oumansky, therefore, attempted to channel important matters directly to the President.

No other foreign statesman, however, went over Hull's head as often as did Winston Churchill, who all during the years of World War II carried on high-level diplomacy directly with Roosevelt—much of it unknown to the Secretary of State. He and Roosevelt, for instance, handled the details in the exchange of British bases for American destroyers in 1940. Almost up to the time the executive agreement was completed, Hull, in fact, opposed it, arguing "that the President had no authority to give away Government property."

Roosevelt and Churchill also planned the Atlantic Conference of 1941 without Hull's knowledge. When the Secretary returned to Washington from a vacation, he found that "the President was already en route to his rendezvous."

Later that year, when the Prime Minister visited Roosevelt in Washington, he and Hull clashed over British and American policy toward the Free French Government of General Charles de Gaulle. The Secretary felt that the British were undermining the policy he had established toward the Free French, but Hull's anger did not disturb Churchill. The Secretary, Churchill wrote, "did not seem to me to have full access to the President."

To Hull's consternation, the President also deliberately excluded him from the other wartime "summit" conferences—Casablanca, Cairo, and Teheran. Hull protested his exclusion: "I'm not looking for increased responsibility, but I do believe the Secretary of State should attend these meetings." To strengthen his case he pointed out that the British Foreign Secretary participated in various war councils.

The President replied that the British governmental system differed from the American in that the British Cabinet constituted the government. Under the parliamentary system, the Foreign Secretary had stronger claims than had the Secretary of State to participation in the war councils, particularly when vital diplomatic problems were considered. Roosevelt pointed out, in effect, that under the Presidential system, he could do virtually as he pleased in the conduct of foreign relations.

Roosevelt did not, however, completely disregard Hull's feelings. He stressed that the wartime conferences were essentially military, not diplomatic, and hence did not require the Secretary's presence. Yet, he did not inform Hull even of the diplomatic developments, leaving him in ignorance of what went on at the meetings. "I learned from other sources than the President," the Secretary wrote, "what had occurred at the Casablanca, Cairo, and Tehran conferences." Discussing with Henry Morgenthau what would follow the Teheran Conference, in 1944, Hull gasped, according to Morgenthau, and said, "Henry, this is the first time I have ever heard of this. . . . I have never even been permitted to see the minutes of the Tehran conference!"

So determined was Roosevelt to deprive Hull of any tangible reason for attending the summit meetings that he sometimes went to extremes. One of the reasons he kept his advisory party small at those conferences was to freeze out his Secretary of State. When Churchill, for example, agreed to the Casablanca Conference, he told Roosevelt that he wanted to take Anthony Eden with him because of his position as a member of the British War

Cabinet as well as the fact that he was Foreign Secretary. Realizing that if Eden were included, Hull would have a good excuse to attend also, the President objected and made it a firm condition that Eden be excluded.

Hull's exclusion from the conferences fell in with Roosevelt's general design of subordinating the State Department to other agencies involved in wartime diplomacy. Before the United States had entered the war, Hull had been a member of the War Council—a small inner group composed of the President; the Secretaries of State, War, and Navy; the Chief of Staff; and the Chief of Naval Operations—and had regularly attended its meetings. After the attack on Pearl Harbor, the President shut him out of the meetings concerned with military matters and never informed him, for example, of the atomic-bomb project.

Realizing that there could be no war council that did not in some way deal with diplomatic matters, Hull occasionally questioned his exclusion, but he could bring about no change in his status.

Another technique that Roosevelt used in circumscribing the authority of his Secretary of State was to create new agencies and entrust them with responsibilities in foreign affairs. He neither consulted Hull in forming them nor allowed him control over them. Often administrators of the agencies clashed with the Secretary in various jurisdictional disputes.

One of those agencies, the Office of Lend-Lease Administration, became a vital bond in America's relations with the other Allied governments and with some of the neutral nations, as well. Increasingly, therefore, foreign missions in the United States directed or tried to direct much of their important business to the head of that agency rather than to the Secretary of State. Furthermore, Lend-Lease ignored the Foreign Service by sending its own representatives abroad.

W. Averell Harriman, for instance, went to London as "Expediter" of Lend-Lease with the rank of Minister. He had direct access to Churchill and Roosevelt and did not even use State Department channels to report to his chief, Harry Hopkins.

Occasionally, Hopkins sent Hull polite notes with enclosed cables marked "For your information." Being brought up to date on foreign relations in this manner did not soothe Hull's injured pride.

Thus, many of the important matters of policy did not go to the Secretary for decision, and much of the President's diplomacy never went through the State Department. Many of the department's upper-level career officers, Roosevelt believed, had been abroad too long, had lost the feel of their own country, and were not truly representative of the American people or the objectives of his Administration.

Hull, on the other hand, accepted the State Department as he found it and became its ardent defender. He also often opposed the President's views or was slow in giving them support. It was for these and other reasons that Roosevelt frequently excluded his Secretary from the formulation of important policies. Furthermore, he lost patience with Hull's conservatism, especially during the war, when he felt that quick daring action was needed in the management of foreign relations. Paradoxically, therefore, as foreign relations became increasingly vital, the Secretary of State became less important in their conduct.

Hull's lack of pervasive influence can also be seen in the fact that his relations with Roosevelt were largely official and devoted mostly to routine State Department affairs. The President usually did not discuss domestic affairs with him. Since he was not in the inner circle of advisers, Hull's social contacts with the President were also limited. "I was frankly glad," the Secretary wrote, perhaps with a sour-grapes attitude, "not to be invited into the White House groups where so often the 'liberal' game was played on an extreme basis."

The Secretary, moreover, was unable to use the Cabinet to influence policy, for Roosevelt seldom discussed international affairs in the Cabinet meetings. "Roosevelt Cabinets are really a solo performance by the President," one department head explained, "interspersed with some questions and very few debates."

Hull himself wrote that "no decisions on foreign policy were taken by Cabinet vote during my tenure."

Although Hull resented his status, he did not hold the bitterness toward Roosevelt that Lansing felt toward Wilson. He apparently realized that he held an office of great prestige but without the full power that should have gone with it. Having held office most of his life, he also realized that some of the indignities he suffered were inevitable in public life and hence apparently bore them as occupational hazards.

Hull told a friend at the end of his Secretaryship:

> When I accepted this office, I knew that I would be misrepresented, lied about, let down, and that there would be humiliations that no man in private life could accept and keep his self-respect. But I made up my mind in advance that I would accept all these things and just do my job. I have suffered all these things but have just kept right on.

He kept on, in fact, for almost twelve years, longer than any other Secretary of State.

Despite Hull's sometimes nominal control over foreign relations, he was not publicly reduced to a figurehead and was never denied control over his own department—because he had considerable political influence. He was, in fact, the most popular department head in the Roosevelt Administration (especially with conservatives), as a Gallup poll published in 1938 indicated. Roosevelt, moreover, always publicly treated him with respect, acclaiming him the "father" of the United Nations and recommending him for the Nobel Peace Prize. Hull's tenure shows that the Secretaryship, under certain conditions, can bring distinction even to one who seems almost a figurehead, and that even so dynamic a President as Franklin D. Roosevelt was not truly "his own Secretary of State."

Roosevelt's next Secretary, Edward R. Stettinius, Jr., was expected to carry out the President's own policies without objection and to advance no ideas of his own. In urging his appointment, Harry Hopkins had argued, in effect, that since the President would continue his high-level personal diplomacy and would manage foreign relations on his own, he needed only a figurehead in the Secretaryship and that Stettinius would fit this role graciously.

Although Stettinius did not attempt to initiate policy, by the time he took office, the gulf between the President and the State Department had become so great that he decided to appoint a career officer for liaison between the department and the White House. "This was an effort by Stettinius," one of Roosevelt's advisers wrote, "to get in closer contact with the President, who had been handling much foreign affairs business without consulting the Department of State."

Although it seemed strange for the Secretary to need an intermediary between himself and the President, Stettinius did manage to develop a closer relationship with Roosevelt than had Hull. He was told about the secret atomic-bomb project and was taken to the Yalta Conference, but had no truly important function there. In the eleven months that Stettinius held the Secretaryship, he served, as Hopkins had predicted, mainly as an agent who faithfully carried out the President's own policies.

Unlike Stettinius, Dean Rusk is not a figurehead and is respected by the President for his grasp of foreign affairs. Yet within a few months after Rusk had taken office, critics began pointing out that he apparently was not the central figure in the shaping of foreign policy. For instance, he was reported to have opposed American support for an ill-fated invasion of Cuba, in April, 1961, but the President apparently preferred the views of others. To the public, Rusk in his first year in office seemed overshadowed by a coterie of White House advisers on foreign policy and by politically powerful princelings in his own department. Some argued that these advisers stood between President Kennedy and Rusk and hence encroached upon the power that should belong to the Secretary. The dynamic Kennedy himself, moreover, on most issues seems to take direct command of foreign relations and hence keeps his Secretary of State in the shadows.

Regardless of the cause, lack of power in the Secretaryship is not unusual. The very nature of the office allows the President to use his Secretary of State almost as a figurehead if he so desires and if the Secretary accepts such a status. If the President contents himself with such a Secretary, he adds immeasurably to the burdens of his office and deprives himself of normal assistance in the conduct of foreign relations, the area of his gravest responsibility. If he does not accept the Secretary of State as his principal adviser, primary executive agent, and trusted confidant in foreign affairs, one of the basic relationships in the American system of government will not function as effectively as it should. In other words, a President who insists on acting as his own Secretary of State is like a pilot who fails to obtain maximum power from his airplane because he refuses to use all of its engines.

6

The Partnership

> The foreign affairs are in their inception and management exclusively executive, and nothing decisive can be done in that important field except with the President's personal knowledge and official approval. So entirely confidential has the relation of the Secretary to the President been held that questions relating to foreign affairs are brought to the attention of other members of the Cabinet by the Secretary of State *only* as directed by the President.
>
> —James G. Blaine, 1889

Some Secretaries of State have managed to remain on good terms with the President without becoming figureheads and, in effect, to control the conduct of foreign relations without attempting to act as prime ministers. This, recent analysts maintain, is essentially what the intensely personal relationship between the President and the Secretary should be—one of partnership. It cannot, of course, be a partnership of equals, but rather of a junior and a senior colleague.

Nevertheless, in the case of John Marshall, the first strong Secretary of this type, critics have charged that he had gained an unhealthy ascendancy over the President who came to rely heavily on him for aid in domestic as well as foreign affairs and who, they said, would accept his Secretary's ideas without realizing that he did. John Adams, it seemed, had such confidence in Marshall that almost from the time the Virginian took over the Secretaryship, he received a mandate to run other parts of the government as well as the State Department, and hence became a Secretary who carried a larger share of responsibility than had his predecessors.

Marshall came to assume this broad responsibility not only because Adams trusted him, but also because soon after he became Secretary, the President left the seat of government for his home in Quincy, Massachusetts, and remained there during most of the eight months Marshall held office. The Secretary, therefore, seemingly ran the government like perhaps a viceroy, taking his orders from a distance. He did not, however, attempt to use this circumstance indiscriminately to make his own ideas policy or to impose his will upon the President, but instead trimmed his ideas to fit his chief's policies. Marshall, in fact, had faith in those policies and carefully carried them out as Adams desired—a key factor in his success, one that gave him power, brought strength to the Administration, and won favor with the President.

The next Secretary of State, James Madison, was much closer to Thomas Jefferson than Marshall had been to Adams. Madison was one of Jefferson's old friends, whom the President could trust to carry out his policies as he desired. Few Secretaries and Presidents have been able to work together with so intimate an understanding of each other's views as did Madison and Jefferson. So close did the collaboration appear that certain contemporaries believed that Jefferson had formed the habit of trusting "almost implicitly in Madison," and that the Secretary had "acquired a compleat ascendancy over him." To some, it seemed that the President scarcely consulted the other department heads.

It is improbable that Madison enjoyed the ascendancy alleged to him, for although the President listened to his advice and frequently changed his views as a result, Jefferson made his own decisions, and the policies Madison directed were clearly the President's. Madison proved himself a valuable administrator and adviser, one who offered counsel when needed or requested, in domestic as well as foreign affairs, but who functioned as a Secretary who realized and accepted his subordination to the President's will.

In this capacity, Madison had responsibility for the conduct of the nation's foreign relations for eight years—the first Secretary of State to complete two full Presidential terms. When his Presidency closed, Jefferson declared that "Mr. Madison is justly entitled to his full share of all the measures of my administration. Our principles were the same, and we never differed sensibly in the application of them."

Eight years later, John Quincy Adams took over the Secretaryship, also clearly realizing that he must function as a subordinate and that his duty required him to support, and not in any way counteract, the President's policies. This, he believed, would not be difficult, for he was convinced that his views coincided with the President's. He wrote of the relationship he envisaged:

> The President, I am sure, will neither require nor expect from me any sacrifice of principles inconsistent with my own sense of right, and I hope I shall never be unmindful of the respect for his character, the deference to his sentiments, and the attachment to his person, due from me to him, not only by the relative situation which he has placed me to himself, but by the gratitude with which his kindness ought to be requited.

Despite this deference to the President, Adams is one of the few Secretaries of State who has been given most of the credit for what was accomplished in foreign affairs during his term. This recognition of his talent seems especially remarkable when one considers the fact that James Monroe had had extensive diplomatic experience, nearly six years in the Secretaryship himself, and was not a President who readily surrendered control of foreign policy to anyone.

Although Monroe listened to his Secretary's views and frequently was swayed by them, he made it clear that he alone was responsible for the foreign policy of his Administration, a responsibility he willingly assumed. He read most of the important dispatches that came into the State Department and went over Adams' drafts, modifying, enlarging, or cutting them down. In some instances he drafted notes himself or told his Secretary exactly what he wanted written. In effect, he kept his finger on every diplomatic decision of consequence. "This sifting and revising of every important paper that I write," Adams once complained, "is not flattering nor very agreeable."

Monroe also maintained a tight control over appointments, causing Adams to lament his lack of influence. "The President," he said in reference to the pattern of appointments, "kept it very much in his own hands. There had not been a single appointment of any consequence, even in my own Department, made at my recommendation, nor one that I approved."

Yet, Monroe never ignored his Secretary's opinions and, within the limits mentioned, allowed him broad power in the conduct of foreign relations. Adams knew what was going on in the Administration and frequently his ideas became policy. Even though he maintained that, with few exceptions, he deferred to the President, he expressed his views forcibly, fought for his own policies, and held firmly to them against competing advice. Furthermore, particularly when he considered an issue important, he did not hesitate to offer unsolicited and independent advice. These are the qualities of a dynamic Secretary of State, but not necessarily of one who functioned like a prime minister. Only when a President delegates big areas of his power to a Secretary of State, which Monroe would not do, can the Secretary be considered something of a prime minister.

All in all, Adams and Monroe made an effective team. "They were made for each other," Jefferson is said to have observed. "Adams has a pointed pen; Monroe has judgment enough for both and firmness enough to have *his* judgment control." The secret of this successful relationship seems to be that from the beginning, both Monroe and Adams understood who was President in fact as well as in title—a principle basic to a really effective partnership.

The next Secretary of State who came to hold an influential place in government without aspiring to the power of a premier was William M. Evarts. He never approached Adams in accomplishment and, in fact, is one of the lesser-known Secretaries, one who dealt with no great international problems. Political opponents, nonetheless, deplored his alleged influence. One of them claimed that "his dreamy doctrines have captivated the President and led him into many of his unfortunate ways that have done much to alienate his friends." Others pictured him as the Mephistopheles of the Cabinet, who held Rutherford B. Hayes—whom they called "His Fraudulency the President"—his captive.

Although in domestic as well as foreign affairs Evarts' views carried weight with the President, they were not decisive. Hayes himself usually controlled the conduct of foreign relations and made the decisions in policy. Evarts, moreover, wisely did not attempt to force his ideas upon the President. In general, he and Hayes respected each other and enjoyed each other's company. When Evarts took office, he and the President hardly knew each other, but they soon got along so well that by the time he gave up the Secretaryship, he and Hayes had become close friends.

Like Hayes, Grover Cleveland got along well with his Secretaries of State. In his two terms in the White House, he had three Secretaries and not one functioned either as a figurehead or as a prime minister. In working with all three, Cleveland accepted and often followed their advice, but he himself took a hand in all important questions of foreign policy and, depending on the Secretary, made most of the decisions. He also decided on most of the diplomatic appointments himself and, if he believed such action necessary, did so without consulting his Secretary.

Thomas F. Bayard, Cleveland's first Secretary, frequently influenced foreign policy, but usually acted as the instrument of the President's wishes instead of an initiator of policy. He was one of Cleveland's favorite companions, one who constantly visited the White House and was consulted on many matters besides foreign affairs. Cleveland greatly admired Bayard and once said, "I think he is one of the most complete men, mentally, morally, and politically, I ever met."

The next Secretary, Walter Q. Gresham, acquired more power over foreign relations than had Bayard. Cleveland developed a strong affection for him and consulted him on almost all matters pertaining to international affairs and on many domestic problems. Gresham's influence was such that Cleveland more often than not followed his suggestions, and the Secretary thus in effect initiated policy.

Cleveland relied more for advice and guidance on his third Secretary, Richard Olney, than he had on either Bayard or Gresham and allowed Olney considerable freedom in the conduct of foreign relations. For instance, when Olney drew up his first important state paper as Secretary of State—a bold note dealing with a sensitive boundary dispute between Venezuela and British Guiana—Cleveland commended him for preparing "the best thing of the kind I have ever read."

The President, in fact, left the details of the diplomacy of the Venezuelan controversy "wholly in Mr. Olney's hands." The Secretary antagonized Great Britain and drafted a warlike message that the President revised and sent to Congress in December, 1895. Despite the criticism the message evoked, Cleveland defended it and praised his Secretary.

Cleveland later told a friend:

> I do not think that, in all my experience, I have ever had to deal with any official document, prepared by another, which so entirely satisfied my critical requirements. . . . It was vigorous, but it caught the national spirit perfectly. I have never been able to express my pleasure and satisfaction over this assertion of our position, and the country has never shown that it fairly understood or recognized the debt it owes to Richard Olney.

Even though Olney exerted substantial influence on the President in both external and internal affairs, he did not seek the power of a prime minister. He regarded himself as the President's personal adviser, a zealous and important member of Cleveland's official family. Not being a professional politician looking forward to greater rewards, Olney took the Secretaryship as an end in itself. He often ignored political considerations in arriving at decisions and made no effort to placate party factions, but instead tried to make the most of the Secretaryship within the scope of its limited powers. Although he served only twenty-one months, Olney showed that even under a strong President, a forceful Secretary of State need not function as a prime minister in order to have a decisive voice in the shaping of foreign policy.

Unlike Olney, John Hay cannot be considered a forceful Secretary of State, but under McKinley he, too, had a hand in shaping foreign policy without assuming himself a premier. Ironically, he accepted the Secretaryship unwillingly, as a duty he would gladly have avoided if he could have done so gracefully, or at least he went out of his way to give that impression. "I am a soldier," he said, "and go where I am sent."

Yet, Hay looked upon McKinley with affection and respect and worked amiably with him. In fact, the two men were quite close. Often they would make decisions in conference, and would work together on diplomatic notes, correcting and polishing each other's drafts. Although the President kept a firm control over the general direction of foreign policy and did not hesitate to make his own decisions, he usually followed his Secretary's advice and allowed him broad discretion in the conduct of foreign relations. "He has been most generous and liberal ever since I have been here," Hay said of his chief; "he has allowed me an absolutely free hand in the important work of the Department, supporting and sustaining me in the face of all sorts of opposition in Congress and elsewhere."

The President, however, did not share his control over appointments. "As to appointments under the State Department," Hay wrote, perhaps in exaggeration, "it is clear that I am to have nothing to say. I could not appoint even my Private Secretary." At another time he remarked, "I have not controlled a single appointment in the State Department since I entered it."

Hay did, however, express his own views on some appointments and the President listened, for he respected Hay. So highly did McKinley esteem his Secretary that in March, 1900, when Hay offered his resignation over a quarrel with Congress, the President refused it and returned it the day it was submitted. "Nothing could be more unfortunate than to have you retire from the

Cabinet," McKinley wrote privately. "The personal loss would be great but the public loss even greater. Your administration of the State Department has had my warm approval." It was under this kind of a relationship with the President, essentially that of a partnership, that Hay acquired his reputation as one of the nation's distinguished Secretaries of State.

Elihu Root, who had been an outstanding Secretary of War, never achieved Hay's distinction in the Secretaryship of State, but he too was a Secretary who was able to win more than the usual share of the President's confidence. That confidence was based on a close friendship and mutual respect between himself and Theodore Roosevelt. Root did not insist upon launching policies of his own, did not appear to push pet policies that were clearly distinguishable from the President's, and accepted Roosevelt's close control of foreign relations without resenting it. In directing those foreign relations, Root worked mainly as the agent who carried out the President's own policies.

Roosevelt, however, did not use Root merely as an administrative assistant. He relied upon his Secretary for careful advice. In later years, moreover, Root himself declared that Roosevelt "was the most advisable" man he ever knew. In some areas, in Latin American affairs, for example, Root had virtually unhampered responsibility for matters of policy. "My part in it," Roosevelt said, "has been little beyond cordially backing him up." Furthermore, Root did not hesitate to speak, and when he did, he gained the President's ear. Roosevelt himself pointed this out. Once when an editor asked him which of his Cabinet officers had been most valuable, "Elihu Root," Roosevelt replied. "He is the only one who will fight with me."

When Root left the Secretaryship, Roosevelt told him "that in my judgment you will be regarded as the greatest and ablest man who ever filled the position of Secretary of State." Although an exaggeration, that statement apparently expressed Roosevelt's true sentiments at the time.

The source of Root's success in winning Roosevelt's confidence seems to be that he did not allow the President to see in him a political or intellectual rival. Root accepted the Secretaryship for what it was under Roosevelt, a junior partnership, did not attempt to make it a premiership, and did not overreach himself in any grab for power.

I.

Calvin Coolidge, who seldom took the initiative in matters of foreign policy, left Secretary of State Frank B. Kellogg with the major responsibility for handling almost all problems in foreign affairs. Like Root, however, Kellogg did not attempt to seize more power. He usually originated policy and controlled its conduct, and Coolidge generally merely approved. Although nervous and upset by some of the demands of his office, Kellogg apparently was content with his status, authority, and relationship to the President. In later years, he said that the Secretaryship had given him the best and most interesting period of his life.

In contrast to Coolidge, Harry Truman was extremely sensitive to any encroachment on what he considered the responsibilities of the President, particularly in foreign affairs. Yet he allowed his Secretaries of State freedom in shaping foreign policy. He believed that the Secretary should run his own department, "but all final policy decisions," he insisted, "would be mine." He also held that "the Secretary of State should never at any time come to think that he is the man in the White House, and the President should not try to be the Secretary of State." This principle, he believed, worked exceptionally well in his relations with two of his Secretaries, George C. Marshall and Dean G. Acheson.

As far as Truman was concerned, Marshall was the ideal Secretary. It is doubtful that any President has admired his Secretary of State as deeply as did Truman. More than once, he publicly referred to Marshall as the greatest living American and wrote that the "General is one of the most astute and profound men I have ever known." Regardless of contrary pressures, Truman invariably followed Marshall's advice, often without question.

Marshall, in turn, respected Truman and, like Truman, revered the Presidency. In 1948, when Truman began his lonely whistle-stop election campaign against great odds, Marshall was one of the loyal department heads who saw him off and wished him well. During that campaign, as at other times, the Secretary resisted the suggestions of some of his career subordinates that foreign policy was independent of the President. Unlike some of the other Cabinet officers, he remained loyal to Truman the man as well as Truman the President.

Truman never forgot this loyalty. He depended on Marshall because he could rely on him, knowing that the Secretary would carry out policy as he desired. He knew, too, that Marshall, unlike some of his other appointees, did not covet the Presidency. Nor did the Secretary, as Truman believed Byrnes had, consider himself a premier.

Even though in a few instances Marshall and Truman differed over details of foreign policy, their relations were never marred by fundamental disagreement or personal conflict. More than most Secretaries of State, Marshall directly influenced the formulating of foreign policy, and far more than most Presidents, Truman went out of his way to follow his Secretary's advice. Marshall had a voice in every major decision and through his staff usually initiated policy. The President, for instance, insisted that the European Recovery Program be called the Marshall Plan because, he said, "I wanted General Marshall to get full credit for his brilliant contributions to the measure which he helped formulate."

Marshall's authority stemmed mainly from the President's unbounded faith in him, not from any desire of his own to augment his power or that of his office. As a result, even Secretaries who have aspired to the power of a prime minister could seldom match Marshall's influence over the making of foreign policy. Under him, the Secretaryship was part of a true partnership.

Like Marshall, Acheson was another of those Secretaries of State who had a decisive influence in the making of foreign policy without trying to be a premier. Since Truman himself lacked broad experience or training in foreign affairs, he came to rely heavily on Acheson, even more so than on Marshall, to keep him informed and to guide him. Acheson saw the President at least four times a week on business, and sometimes every day. At least twice a week, and more often in times of crisis, he brought or had sent to the White House carefully prepared reviews of international developments. His reports were full and clear, designed only for the President and written specifically to hold his attention. Acheson went out of his way to demonstrate that he knew and respected the fact that the President and not the Secretary of State was responsible for the conduct of foreign relations.

This constant concern for the President's sanction is one of the distinctive features of Acheson's Secretaryship. Far more than most Secretaries, as a consequence, he became the President's advocate and came to incur all the responsibilities and liabilities that such a specialized relationship entailed. Although many criticized Acheson, few, as a result, doubted his authority to speak for the Administration. He, and no one else, was the President's spokesman for foreign affairs.

On almost all issues, moreover, even where he might have disagreed, Acheson supported the President. Truman wrote, with only slight exaggeration:

> There was never a day during the four years of Dean Acheson's secretaryship that anyone could have said that he and I differed on policy. He was meticulous in keeping me posted on every development within the wide area of his responsibility. He had a deep understanding of the President's position in our constitutional scheme and realized to the fullest that, while I leaned on him for constant advice, the policy had to be mine—it was.

Thus, although the President delegated wide authority to Acheson in the conduct of foreign relations, the Secretary appears to have no truly personal record. Few knew which decisions were his, which belonged to the President, or which came from State Department subordinates. It is clear, however, that the President and his Secretary worked closely, as a partnership should. During the Korean War, the most important single crisis of Acheson's

Secretaryship, the President usually followed his advice in matters of policy despite intense pressures to do otherwise. Even when the Secretary spoke within the National Security Council, he often led the discussions and offered the advice that the President acted upon.

Truman accepted Acheson's counsel because he had faith in his judgment and ability and, like many Presidents who were pleased with their Secretaries of State, praised him without restraint. "History, I am sure," Truman wrote, "will list Dean Acheson among the truly great Secretaries of State our nation has had." And, he added, "his keen mind, cool temper, and broad vision served him well for handling the day-to-day business of the great issues of policy as well as the Department of State." Acheson, like Marshall, furthermore, had given Truman loyalty as well as service.

That loyalty worked two ways, for in his final news conference before leaving the Secretaryship, Acheson expressed deep gratitude for the complete loyalty Truman had given him. Truman had also given him power, for through Acheson's persuasive influence on the President, the Secretaryship in effect had been the source of most foreign policy.

Acheson's deference to Truman illustrates a principle that usually governs the relationship between a competent Secretary of State and a sensitive President. If the Secretary wishes to remain on good terms with such a President, he should not attempt to overshadow him. He should not try to dramatize his own actions and accomplishments and thereby steal headlines from the President; he should not act as though he were the senior partner. Violation of this code can be, and has been, a source of friction between the two men.

John C. Calhoun, for instance, tried to buck the tradition that the Secretary exists only in the shadow of the President, and in so doing caused trouble. He took office not with the idea of serving the President but mainly with the intention of advancing his own philosophy of government. After leaving the Secretaryship, moreover, he claimed credit for the outstanding accomplishment of the Tyler Administration—the annexation of Texas—a claim that the President vehemently disputed.

That determination not to be overshadowed by a prominent Secretary of State lay, in part at least, behind Polk's harsh treatment of Buchanan and Benjamin Harrison's tight control over Blaine. When Blaine was sick, as he was frequently, Harrison himself took over his duties. The President expected gratitude, but Blaine, bitter because Harrison carried out policies he disliked, offered none.

In May, 1892, Harrison aired his grievances, complaining that for over a year he had himself carried the burden of the State Department, even to preparing documents in his own handwriting. Yet, he said, Blaine had boasted of what had been done in the department and had taken all the credit. The President told a Senator that he was "perfectly willing, to use a familiar figure, to carry a soldier's knapsack, when the soldier is sore of foot and tired, and all that he wanted in return was acknowledgment of the act and a show of appreciation." Someday, he vowed, he would disclose the "true conditions" of his relations with Blaine.

A similar friction ultimately came to mar relations between Herbert Hoover and Henry L. Stimson, two men who started out their partnership with the highest respect for each other. Although Stimson did not attempt to acquire the power of a prime minister or to overshadow his chief, he did at times compete with Hoover for recognition as the maker of certain policies.

Hoover looked upon the nonrecognition doctrine of January, 1932—a doctrine that said the United States would not recognize territorial gains that violated the peace treaties—as his personal accomplishment and as the most important principle in foreign affairs advanced during his Presidency. The note announcing that principle, he told his Secretary, "would rank with the greatest papers of this country." He resented efforts, he said later, "to stamp this as the 'Stimson Doctrine' with the implication that I had no part in it."

The President was so proud of the principle that he wished to exploit it in his campaign for re-election in 1932, pointing to it as his own unique achievement. He asked Stimson, therefore, to make a speech proclaiming the nonrecognition principle as the Hoover Doctrine. Stimson would not do so, arguing that it was improper for members of the State Department to make political speeches. Moreover, he consistently refused to champion the "Hoover Doctrine," believing that the international acceptance of the nonrecognition principle, usually called the "Stimson Doctrine," was perhaps the greatest constructive achievement of his public life, an achievement he did not wish to share even with the President. "It would hurt his feelings terribly to have this called the Hoover doctrine," the Under Secretary of State noted, "because he thinks of it as one very important star which history will put to his credit."

Hoover could never overcome the feeling that his Secretary of State was trying to take credit that rightfully belonged to him. At the close of his Administration, he even obtained statements from his other department heads attesting that he, not Stimson, had been the true author of the nonrecognition doctrine.

Truman, too, felt that one of his Secretaries of State was vying with him for publicity. This feeling toward James F. Byrnes, in fact, was one cause of the break between the two men. Of the other reasons for the rupture, Truman observed:

> More and more during the fall of 1945 I came to feel that in his role as Secretary of State Byrnes was beginning to think of himself as an Assistant President in full charge of foreign policy. Apparently he failed to realize that, under the Constitution, the President is required to assume all responsibility for the conduct of foreign affairs. The President cannot abdicate that responsibility, and he cannot turn it over to anyone else.

In particular, Truman was irked by Byrnes's failure to keep him fully and privately informed of developments at a conference of foreign ministers held in Moscow in December, 1945, saying that he could learn little from his Secretary's reports that did not appear in the newspapers. After the conference, Byrnes had cabled a request to the White House to arrange time over all the radio networks so that he could explain the results of his diplomacy directly to the American people. Then he had released information on the conference to the press before reporting to the President.

According to Truman's version, one with which Byrnes disagrees, when the Secretary finally reported to him, he read the "riot act" to Byrnes.

> I told him that I did not like the way in which I had been left in the dark about the Moscow conference. I told him that, as President, I intended to know what progress we were making and what we were doing in foreign negotiations. I said it was shocking that a communiqué should be issued in Washington announcing a foreign-policy development of major importance that I had never heard of. I said I would not tolerate a repetition of such conduct.

In contrast, Eisenhower did not resent John Foster Dulles' efforts to capture attention. Indeed, he seemed to encourage them. In May, 1955, for example, Dulles reported the results of a foreign ministers' conference in Paris to the people by radio and television directly from the President's office. The President appeared with him but took only a minor part in the program. Moreover, Eisenhower tried every trick of radio and television to assure his Secretary a large audience and a chance to advertise his accomplishments in top-level diplomacy. The other members of the Cabinet, as if to emphasize the importance, pre-eminence, and unique relationship of the Secretary of State to the President, formed a mute background for Dulles' talk.

In this instance, as in others, there was never any danger that the Secretary would overshadow the President, for Eisenhower commanded such prestige that Dulles himself could gain full attention for his own accomplishments only with the President's active assistance. No Secretary of State, in fact, has profited from a President's popularity to the extent that Dulles did.

II.

The wise Secretary of State, regardless of his own fame or political influence, and even though his chief may not be the popular hero that Eisenhower was, will devote as much care to cultivating good relations with the President as he will to the policy and administrative functions of his office. He will, if he can, avoid quarrels, for it is virtually an unwritten rule that if a fight betwen a President and his Secretary becomes public knowledge, the Secretary's political career is destroyed. Seldom can the Secretary expect to wield great political influence or hold high office again.

Edmund Randolph's quarrel with Washington, for instance, ruined him. When he appealed to the public for support against the President by publishing a *Vindication,* moreover, he made his situation worse, for no Secretary, or former Secretary, can compete with the influence of the Presidency, and Randolph could not make a dent in Washington's amazing popularity. In all such cases, where the Secretary has chosen to bring the issue of his differences with the President before the public, the result has been similar. The Secretary has been the loser.

Robert Smith's case illustrates the point. He foolishly sought revenge for his dismissal by publicly attacking President Madison and seeking to overthrow him. Mistakenly, he believed the course he took "will lead to the injury of Mr. Madison and to my advantage." His attack, published as a pamphlet entitled an *Address to the People of the United States,* caused the President much concern, as it did old John Adams, who, seeing in the quarrel a similarity to his difficulties with Timothy Pickering, asked: "Must a President publish a justificatory Proclamation containing all his Reasons, for dismissing a Secretary of State?"

In addition, the feud between Smith and Madison touched off a newspaper battle joined by partisans of both men. The President became so disturbed that he commissioned Joel Barlow, poet and politician, to refute Smith. Barlow publicized Madison's charge that Smith had obtained his appointment through intrigue, that he had long shown a "want of capacity and integrity," and that he was in general unfit for the Secretaryship.

Despite Smith's spirited defense of his conduct, he lost the fight. Because of the nature of the relationship between the President and his Secretary of State, there could have been no other result.

Wishing to avoid a public feud such as Smith precipitated, some Presidents have retained Secretaries with whom they have quarreled. John Adams, for instance, at first hesitated in dismissing the disloyal Pickering because he feared that the removal would arouse "a turbulent session" in Congress and perhaps split his own party. In later years, Pickering defended his conduct as Secretary of State, questioned Adams' motives in removing him, and carried on a debate with Adams over those points. As in the Randolph and Smith cases, Pickering had the weaker side and showed that in an argument with the President, the Secretary has few weapons.

James Buchanan understood this principle well. He accepted his humiliating status under Polk because he realized that if he resigned as a result of a difference with the President, his political career might collapse. Later, when his own Secretary of State, Lewis Cass, resigned on a note of righteous protest because of a difference of opinion with him, Buchanan also learned that in a quarrel with a politically powerful Secretary, a President can expect some discomfort. Cass's friends rallied around him and an aroused Northern public showered abuse on Buchanan. For a while Cass was a popular hero and Buchanan almost a villain. Later, Cass tried to return to the Secretaryship, but Buchanan would have nothing to do with him, and again the President ultimately emerged on top.

Unlike Smith and Cass, William Jennings Bryan knew that his quarrel with Wilson over policy toward Germany would ruin him once his resignation made it public. Such action, a friend pointed out to Mrs. Bryan, "would be bitterly resented by the country; and he would be condemned . . . because the American people would believe that he had resigned for the purpose of embarrassing the President." He told Bryan himself, "I don't want you to destroy yourself."

Bryan replied, "I believe you are right; I think this will destroy me; but whether it does or does not, I must do my duty according to my conscience. . . ." Later, in his last luncheon with the other department heads, he said, "as I leave the Cabinet I go out into the dark . . . the President has the prestige and power on his side."

True enough; Bryan's resignation created a sensation in the press, aroused public opinion against him, and won widespread sympathy for the President. Pro-Allied newspapers and other journals dubbed him mentally incompetent, an unthinking pacifist, a pro-German, and practically a traitor. In his long political career, Bryan had been abused frequently, but never with the viciousness that followed his resignation from the Secretaryship. The general reaction was that the Secretary owed it to his party and country to stand by the President in a time of crisis, that Wilson was right and Bryan wrong. "He was quitting under fire," men said.

The quarrel and resignation broke Bryan's power within the Democratic Party and crushed him personally. With his personal and political popularity gone, his resignation became an ineffective gesture.

Robert Lansing's quarrel with Wilson, on the other hand, did not rally public sentiment behind the President. Wilson had demanded his Secretary's resignation because during Wilson's illness, Lansing had convened the Cabinet without consulting him and, thus, ostensibly had usurped Presidential authority. "It would relieve me of embarrassment, Mr. Secretary," Wilson said, "the embarrassment of feeling your reluctance and divergence of judgment, if you would give up your present office and afford me an opportunity to select some one whose mind would more willingly go along with mine."

When Joseph Tumulty, Wilson's private secretary, first saw this demand, he tried to dissuade the President from sending it, arguing that it would not strike the public in the right way. "Tumulty," Wilson answered with a show of fire, "it is never the wrong time to spike disloyalty. When Lansing sought to oust me, I was upon my back. I am on my feet now and will not have disloyalty about me."

To make matters worse, Wilson published the correspondence between Lansing and himself. That correspondence and the resignation shocked the nation. "It seems," one of Wilson's friends wrote, "the petulant and irritable act of a sick man." Public and press opinion this time sided with the Secretary of State. Many came to regard Lansing as a martyr. It was not the dismissal itself that aroused public sentiment in favor of Lansing, but Wilson's abruptness and the reasons he gave for ridding himself of Lansing.

"My greatest expectations have been more than satisfied," Lansing naïvely confided to his diary. "I never for a moment dreamed of having the whole country rise to my support. I knew that in the exchange of letters I had the better of it, but I did not realize how much the better of it until the people spoke."

Wilson, too, sensed that he had acted hastily. After the initial public reaction to the Lansing resignation, Wilson asked, "Well, Tumulty, have I any friends left?"

"Very few, Governor," Tumulty replied.

Wilson then observed:

> . . . in a few days what the country considers an indiscretion on my part in getting rid of Lansing will be forgotten, but when the sober, second thought of the country begins to assert itself, what will stand out will be the disloyalty of Lansing to me. Just think of it! Raised and exalted to the office of Secretary of State, made a member of the Peace Commission, participating in all the conferences and affixing his signature to a solemn treaty, and then hurrying to . . . repudiate the very thing to which he had given his assent.

Although Wilson himself did not come out well in this feud, it is clear that when the furor died, no one could truly question the right of the President to rid himself of a Secretary he disliked. Again, as in the past, the Secretary of State had come out second best in the long run.

The same was true of Byrnes in his feud with Truman. After Byrnes had left office, the President brought the quarrel into the open by allowing a letter of his to Byrnes to be published in which he had accused Byrnes of insubordination while the South Carolinian had held the Secretaryship. Byrnes struck back through an article in *Collier's* magazine in which he denied the charge and asserted that he had never seen the letter until it was published.

Regardless of the merits of the Byrnes case, or of any of the others, the Secretary of State can never gain the attention for his side of the argument that the President can for his. Most Secretaries know this and hence try to keep their differences with the President to themselves, for arguments with the President are never disagreements between equals.

In summary, if the partnership is to work smoothly, the Secretary of State should not arouse any fear in the President that he is being overshadowed; he should not assume powers that belong to the senior partner without the President's sanction; and he should be wise enough to avoid quarreling with his chief. He should keep the President fully and immediately informed on all important matters so that the President has all the freedom of decision a given situation permits in carrying out his Constitutional duty of directing foreign policy. The President, on the other hand, can contribute to the partnership by using his Secretary's advice, whenever appropriate, in shaping policy and by sharing his power in arriving at decisions, though the ultimate decision is always the President's.

7

Statesmanship and Politics

> Every Secretary of State, second only to his President, and alone among appointive officers of the Government, stands before the world as the representative of the United States of America. No man who holds this office can fail to feel the extraordinary responsibility he carries for service to the country and its peace. No man has a greater right to ask the sympathetic support and cooperation of his fellow-citizens, and none is more properly exempt from the ordinary trials of politics.
>
> —Henry L. Stimson, 1950

If, over the years, Americans have fashioned a popular image of the Secretary of State, one that sets him apart from other executive officers, it is that he, second only to the President, is a statesman, an official who deals with issues and policies on the highest level. In contrast to other officeholders whom they might class as politicians, the people apparently see the Secretary as a statesman who functions on the level of prime ministers, incorrect though this view may be. They see him as a powerful official responsible for the management of affairs of state, one whose views carry considerable weight in the making of decisions that affect the whole nation, one who is or should be immune from the ordinary stresses of domestic politics.

Yet, historically, the Secretaryship has been as thoroughly meshed into the American political system as any other office in the executive branch and its control has been governed more often by domestic considerations than by concern for broad statesmanship. The popular image and the historical pattern are not contradictory, however, for the office has been hospitable to both the statesman and the politician, and from the beginning men who have taken the office have done so with the idea of becoming statesmen though they may not have been such previously.

When Thomas Jefferson accepted the newly created Secretaryship, for instance, he expressed distaste for its domestic responsibilities and alarm at "the extent of that office, embracing as it does the principal mass of domestic administration, together with the foreign." He wished to be a statesman and hence was assured that as Secretary of State he would not be encumbered with trifling duties.

One of the first to define his own idea of the Secretaryship before he took office and, like Jefferson, to seek assurance that he would be allowed to function as a statesman was James Monroe. He told President Madison that he would join the Administration only if its foreign policy were not so inflexible as to bar his own views from consideration, for he wanted the direction of foreign relations placed in his hands. In effect, he also brought up the issue of whether or not a Secretary and a President, even though of the same political faith, could work together when they held differing views on foreign policy.

"It would not become me to accept a station, and to act a part in it," Monroe explained, "which my judgment and conscience did not approve, and which I did not believe would promote the public welfare and happiness. I could not do this, nor would you wish me to do it. If you are disposed to accept my services under these circumstances and with this explanation, I shall be ready to render them."

Without promising a free hand in foreign policy but nevertheless giving the impression that the new Secretary would be treated as a statesman and enjoy a considerable independence, Madison accepted Monroe's services. "With the mutual knowledge of our respective views of the foreign as well as the domestic interests of our country," the President said, "I see no serious obstacle on either side to an association of our labors in promoting them." Differences of opinion on foreign policy, he added, "must be looked for, even among those most agreed on the same general views. These differences, however, lie fairly within the compass of free consultation and mutual concession as subordinate to the unity belonging to the Executive department."

At first, the Secretary and the President gave the appearance of having overcome their differences. "On public affairs," Monroe wrote, "we confer without reserve, each party expressing his own sentiments, and viewing dispassionately the existing state, animated by a sincere desire to promote the public welfare." Soon, however, the old conflict burst to the surface. Monroe, in effect, urged a policy friendly to Great Britain whereas Madison persisted, seemingly, in favoring France. The President, moreover, tried to keep control of foreign policy in his own hands, refusing to delegate major responsibility to his Secretary.

Monroe, of course, was not happy, particularly with the policy that led to the War of 1812. He explained to an old friend that his Secretaryship was turning out far differently than he and his supporters had expected. "I have been afraid to write to you for some time past," the Secretary said, "because I know that you expected better things from me than I have been able to perform." In fact, he reversed himself. Instead of replacing the President's foreign policy with his own, as he had planned, he found himself not only committed to the President's policy but also to supporting a program he had previously opposed. We can see, therefore, that Monroe was a statesman not in the sense that he was able to shape policy from his own ideas but in the sense that he was able to manage affairs of state planned by others.

John Quincy Adams, the next Secretary of State, took office determined to act the statesman, and also to accept and not to attempt to change the President's policies. In his words:

> For myself, I shall enter upon the functions of my office with a deep sense of the necessity of union with my colleagues, and with a suitable

impression that my place is *subordinate.* That my duty will be to *support,* and not to counteract or oppose, the President's administration, and that if from any cause I should find my efforts to that end ineffectual, it will be my duty seasonably to withdraw from the public service, and to leave to more competent persons the performance of the duties to which I find myself inadequate.

Adams proved himself a statesman in the best sense of the term. He was able to work closely with the President and through him to make his own ideas policy. He was, in fact, more the statesman in the Secretaryship than in the Presidency.

So great did Adams' reputation as a statesman become that some seventy-five years later, John Hay, another Secretary of State who gave deep thought to the powers and meaning of his office, studied Adams' diary seeking a guiding thread or ideas that would help him to understand the Secretaryship. His search probably was not rewarding, for his conclusions were bitterly negative. "The real duties of a Secretary of State seem to be these," he wrote: "to fight claims upon us by other States; to press more or less fraudulent claims of our citizens upon other countries; to find offices for the friends of Senators where there are none."

One reason for Hay's sour evaluation is that he held an exalted view of the Secretaryship, seeing the Secretary, and hence himself, as a statesman who should not be trammeled by political compromises. Government by experts seems to have been his ideal, a concept that ran counter to the history of his office and for which there was no firm basis in the American tradition. Politics in foreign policy and the functioning of the Secretaryship irked him, and he scathingly denounced those to whom politics provided the meat of statesmanship. In all, Hay had a high sense of the dignity of his office but cherished a distorted ideal of its prerogatives.

So elevated did Hay's view of the Secretaryship become that he came to believe it should be above politics. This can be seen in his reaction when Theodore Roosevelt asked him in the spring of 1904 to speak in New York to aid the Republican campaign there. "It is intolerable," the Secretary wrote in his diary, "that they should not see how much more advantageous to the Administration it is that I should stay at home to do my work than that I should cavort around the country making lean and jejune orations."

Hay eventually agreed to speak, but complained that the Secretary of State should not participate in political campaigns. To do so, he said, would create a bad effect on the diplomatic corps and injure his precarious relations with the Senate. Roosevelt replied bluntly that if Hay would not make a political speech, the election might be lost and then he would no longer be Secretary of State.

In other ways, too, Hay's appraisal of his office was unrealistic. "If a Secretary of State could work in a vacuum," he once told a friend, "and only do the things which would be of advantage to the country, I could imagine no place more delightful than this, but the unconditioned and the absolute are beyond the reach of mortal men, and everything we do must pass the ordeal of a thousand selfish interests and prejudices and spites."

As unrealistic as any of Hay's views was his conviction that the Senate was virtually the natural enemy of the Secretary of State. He hated Congress for its alleged interference in matters of foreign policy, and his writings abound with denunciations of the Senate. The following is typical of his complaints:

> We are so handicapped by the Senate and the House that there is nothing to do but follow a policy of makeshifts and half measures. I see absolutely no chance of any improvement. The President himself is unable to carry out the measures he thinks best. He is unable even to make the appointments he thinks best, and as for the Secretary of State, he is extremely fortunate if he can bring to pass one tenth of the measures for the public good that the Department has elaborated.

So contemptuous of Congress and so concerned with the importance of his office did Hay become that he came to consider it beneath the dignity of the Secretary of State to appear before

Congressional committees. His main concern, however, was the Senate's power over treaties. He once told a friend that "the irreparable mistake of our Constitution puts it into the power of one third + 1 of the Senate to meet with categorical veto any treaty negotiated by the President, even though it may have the approval of nine tenths of the people of the nation." Such bitter complaints, of course, did not make him popular with members of Congress and politicians.

Hay's hatred of the Senate was foolish. He should have realized that a wise Secretary of State does not attempt to reform Congress, but tries instead to learn to live with it, for without reliable support in Congress he usually can accomplish little. This, for instance, was particularly true of Henry Clay. Throughout his term, he and John Quincy Adams had to face a hostile Congress and hence Clay served as a kind of foreign minister to a beleaguered Administration. With anti-Administration forces running Congress, especially the Senate, there was little he could do to carry out Administration policy.

Hay's friend, the historian Henry Adams, lamented this relationship of the Secretary to Congress, saying:

> The Secretary of State has always stood as much alone as the historian. Required to look far ahead and round him, he measures forces unknown to party managers, and has found Congress more or less hostile ever since Congress first sat. The Secretary of State exists only to recognize the existence of a world which Congress would rather ignore; of obligations which Congress repudiates whenever it can; of bargains which Congress distrusts and tries to turn to its advantage or to reject. Since the first day the Senate existed it has always intrigued against the Secretary of State whenever the Secretary has been obliged to extend his functions beyond the appointment of Consuls in Senators' service.

I.

Other critics have maintained that one of the reasons for the Secretary's difficulties with Congress is that he usually has no way of expressing himself politically except through the President. Unlike the foreign secretaries in the parliamentary system, he cannot appear before Congress to explain and defend his policies or even the activities of his department. It is the President who has to defend the Administration's foreign policy. He, not the Secretary of State, reports to Congress and to the people on the state of foreign relations, usually in his regular or special messages on the state of the union.

The Secretary of State reports only to the President; he is the only department head not required by statute, or the traditions of his office, to report or give information regularly to Congress on the policies of his department. This is the President's responsibility. Moreover, if either house of Congress passes a resolution demanding information on foreign relations, the Secretary of State may refuse to comply with it if he deems the release of the information contrary to the "public interest." Congress, therefore, makes its request with the proviso that the release will not endanger the national interest. When the Secretary does forward the information, he does so through the President.

Keen politicians, such as Theodore Roosevelt, realized that they needed the support of Congress for their foreign policies and sought its cooperation. Roosevelt was bothered by Hay's notoriously poor relations with Congress and appointed Elihu Root as his successor at least partly because he thought Root could remedy the difficulty between the State Department and Capitol Hill. During his years in the War Department, Root had learned to get along well with the Senate. "He has managed Congress better than any Cabinet Minister I have known," a friend told the President of Root, "and I know he will manage the Senate better than any Secretary of State I have known."

Roosevelt and his friend were right. Root had become a master in dealing with Congress. To cement cordial relations, he regularly attended meetings of the Senate's Committee on Foreign Relations. "In fact," one Senator remarked, "he became so constant and punctual in his attendance at the meetings of the Committee that we grew almost to regard him as a regular member."

Later, particularly in the years after World War II, the direct contacts between the Secretary of State and Congress on questions of foreign policy increased. As the demands on the President became greater and more complex, the Secretary came to assume the enlarged responsibility of acting as his agent in dealing with Congress on questions of foreign policy. This task required him to use the President's prestige as effectively as possible in gaining support without at the same time downgrading his own status.

The Secretary and his staff now appeared before various Congressional committees to explain, defend, or plead for Administration policies. At times, the Secretary even conferred with the Senate Committee on Foreign Relations in advance of important diplomatic negotiations. This seemed a wise procedure, since under the committee system in Congress, committee assent, particularly in the case of a treaty, was tantamount to Senate approval if the matter were negotiated as the committee desired.

When seeking support for a treaty or for particular legislation, the Secretary of State now at times went before Congressional committees at his own request. Usually, however, Congress asked him to appear. In the years of the Cold War, Congress came to take a greater interest than before in foreign affairs and members of both houses, usually in committees, sought to be "briefed" on international developments by the Secretary himself. Sometimes the Secretary testified before the committees in executive session, where he could speak freely and frankly present his case. When, however, he appeared before public sessions, he could not speak with the freedom he might desire.

The Franklin D. Roosevelt, Truman, Eisenhower, and Kennedy Administrations have all considered close liaison with Congress so important that the Department of State assigned one of its ranking officers the task of maintaining that liaison. Still, the Secretary's relations with Congress have not been smooth, or, as Acheson's and Dulles' Secretaryships show, even cordial. The nature of the Secretaryship, virtually independent of Congressional control, is in part responsible for this.

At the same time, though he usually has no independent political influence, the Secretary, as the President's agent, is a political official whom the men in Congress can attack or defend as they would any political appointee. Few Secretaries, moreover, had extensive Congressional experience and hence many of them could not fully understand or gain the confidence of Congress. Furthermore, a Secretary can seldom separate his Administration's politics from foreign policy.

In trying to maintain cordial relations with Congress, actually in attempting to bridge the gap in part created by the separation of powers, the Secretary of State has had a checkered experience. Until the change of recent years, he usually approached Congress directly only through committees dealing with legislative matters concerning his department, mainly the foreign-affairs committees of both houses. Only as the appropriations committees came to deal with his own budget did the Secretary appear before them. After World War II, when economic foreign policy became critically important, the appropriations committees became virtually his regular channels of communication with Congress. At the same time, Congress' expanded participation in foreign affairs made it imperative that he be concerned with the activities of some of the committees that seemed thoroughly domestic in their work, such as those on agriculture. Actually, the disposal of enormous farm surpluses abroad, often the result of Congressional action, certainly has an impact on foreign relations.

Dulles' record illustrates the increased demand of the Congressional committees on the Secretary's time. In his first three years in office, he met with committees or subcommittees of Congress one hundred and twenty times. From 1955 to 1958, he met on an average of six to eight times a month with important Senators and Congressmen, and two or three times with representatives from foreign-affairs, appropriations, and other committees. When Congress was in session, he appeared before its various committees concerned with foreign affairs about six times a month, and some months as often as twelve times.

Dulles also attended some of the occasional conferences that the President had with leaders from both houses, meetings that have now become almost an established practice. In time of crisis in foreign relations, the President has met with Congressional leaders on what has appeared to be almost a regular schedule, often on a weekly basis. A wise President would do well, whenever possible, to have his Secretary of State at his side during these conferences.

Never, until Cordell Hull's time, however, did a Secretary of State appear before the whole Congress to make a personal report. Hull's speech before a joint session of Congress in November, 1944, after his return from a conference in Moscow, was unprecedented. It reflected his unique personal influence upon Congress.

Although he lacked Hull's political background, Dean Acheson went as far as any Secretary of State in trying to build good relations with Congress. He experimented with an unofficial conference with members of Congress for the purpose of answering questions on the Administration's foreign policy. After speaking to an informal joint session of Congress in the Coolidge Auditorium of the Library of Congress, he submitted to an unprecedented questioning. This unusual experiment was ostensibly to bring Congress into the making of foreign policy and make it possible for the Secretary and Congress to meet on neutral ground, but it failed. Since Acheson was himself under fire from Congressional critics, he could not remove the Secretaryship from political warfare.

Acheson's and Dulles' difficulties with Congress led some political analysts to contend that a Secretary of State must have political experience to be effective. Only with political influence in his own right, such as Hull or Herter had, they have said, can a Secretary conduct foreign relations free from political attacks at home. Without such support, the argument goes, a Secretary cannot fully meet the demands of his office.

This argument, of course, runs counter to John Hay's idea, one shared by Henry L. Stimson, that the Secretary of State should be above politics. In 1932, President Hoover collided with this idea when he asked Stimson to make a speech attacking Franklin

D. Roosevelt, the Democratic candidate for President. The Secretary refused, saying "he considered such partisan polemics improper in a Secretary of State." He maintained that "to use the great office of Secretary of State to launch a purely personal attack on Roosevelt is quite inconsistent with my dignity and that of the office." Stimson, who had at one time also been Secretary of War, believed that the Secretaryship of State was "the most nonpartisan in the Cabinet."

Hoover disagreed with his Secretary's view. "Secretary Stimson who had taken part in Republican political campaigns for many years past," he wrote, "felt that he must, as Secretary of State, be neutral. He was the first Cabinet leader in history to take that view."

Although mistaken in detail, Hoover was right in principle. Stimson's idea of a nonpartisan Secretary has no strong historical foundation. The refusal of a Secretary of State to campaign for his President, in fact, contradicts one of the traditional rules governing his selection. Presidents have generally expected their Secretaries to bring them political strength and, at times, have even retained Secretaries they did not want because they desired the support those Secretaries could give the Administration.

Seward's national prestige and high status within the Republican Party were assets that Lincoln wanted and needed. Andrew Johnson, in turn, retained Seward in the Secretaryship because he wished to identify his Administration and his Reconstruction problems with plans bequeathed by Lincoln. Seward, who had been a vital instrument in the Lincoln policies, furthered that identification. In other words, he was able to bring Johnson political support.

Years later, Theodore Roosevelt kept John Hay, even though he preferred a new Secretary of his own choice, because "his name, his reputation, his staunch loyalty, all made him a real asset of the administration."

Similarly, Wilson needed Bryan in the Secretaryship primarily for the political strength the Great Commoner could bring to his domestic program. Bryan's support, for instance, proved invaluable in obtaining Congressional approval for the Federal Reserve Act.

Bryan's successor even hesitated in accepting the Secretaryship because he lacked political influence. "Such influence," Lansing wrote, "was and is an important qualification for a Cabinet officer in carrying through a general legislative program, a fact which had been proved by Bryan during his two years as Secretary, and without which some of the important legislation sought by the President would undoubtedly have failed." Bryan's tenure thus illustrates that a politically powerful Secretary of State can be an asset in a way that a nonpartisan Secretary, if there has ever truly been one, can never be.

This principle can also be seen at work in the case of Cordell Hull. With him at the head of the Cabinet, Roosevelt could keep Congress, mainly the Southern Democrats there, loyal to his Administration and its policies.

Hull frequently threatened to resign, particularly when he heard that one of his subordinates was attempting to evade his authority with "backstairs business" at the White House. Harry Hopkins got so tired of Hull's periodic threats that he hoped that the President would someday accept the Secretary's offer to resign, but Roosevelt never did. In a showdown, in fact, he invariably supported his Secretary of State.

For instance, though Roosevelt preferred Sumner Welles to Hull in the handling of foreign affairs, in 1943 when the feud between the two men became so intense that he had to choose between them, he sided with Hull. Political influence won out over his own desire.

Roosevelt could never forget Wilson's crushing experience with the Senate a quarter of a century earlier, when the League of Nations was defeated. He realized that he would need Hull's potent influence in gaining the Senate's approval for postwar treaties, and if he should seek re-election in the following year. Hull, moreover, was one of the most popular members of the Administration, one who had a following of his own. Rather than risk the loss of any kind of political support that Hull could give him, Roosevelt reluctantly let Welles go.

Like some of his predecessors, furthermore, Roosevelt dreaded the political repercussions likely to flow from Hull's resignation, even though he could have weathered the tempest. A number of Presidents, Polk, for example, have retained Secretaries they did not want because they feared the political reaction of a removal. So valuable a political asset did Roosevelt consider Hull, in fact, that in October, 1944, when the Secretary said he must resign, the President persuaded him to withhold the resignation until after the November elections. He did not wish to lose Hull's prestige in the midst of his fourth-term battle. Few Presidents understood the importance of a politically influential Secretary of State as well as did Roosevelt and probably none used him as effectively in obtaining support for Administration policies.

Despite his independent influence and popularity, Hull was not a powerful Secretary of State. His Secretaryship, therefore, contradicts the conviction held by some politicians that, to be truly successful, a Secretary must be popular. Seward's political mentor, Thurlow Weed, for example, told him, "In the position you are to assume all the qualities that won men and made you popular are required. To be successful you must be a popular Secretary. And this popularity depends largely upon manner and temper."

II.

Seward was not a popular Secretary of State; neither was Acheson or Dulles. Yet all three, in the sense that they were statesmen who shaped foreign policy, were more powerful and hence more successful than Hull. All three suffered slander and vilification from political opponents. One reason for Acheson's difficulties—a factor beyond his power to control—was that he, more than any other person in the second Truman Administration, came to symbolize American foreign policy. Those who hated that policy, or the Administration itself, attacked him, for unlike Hull, he had few defenders in Congress. Since he had no independent following, even within his own party, he became a practically defenseless prey for those legislators hunting for political issues.

Acheson's troubles also stemmed from the fact that during his time, the early years of the Cold War, the Secretaryship came to assume greater importance, at home and throughout the world, than ever before. People had a vague idea that perhaps he might be the cause of difficulty in uncertain times and some blamed him for the President's policies. Unlike the President, or the men of Congress, but like his predecessors, he was not under constant surveillance by reporters. The reporters, and consequently the people, saw him only occasionally, and when they did, as in his press conferences, he usually delivered prepared statements and occasionally seemed condescending.

By the very nature of his office and the vagueness of his powers, the Secretary of State may give the impression of being a mysterious figure, one who invites suspicion, mainly it seems, because he appears at times not sufficiently ardent in his defense of "national" policies against foreign interests. Sometimes if, like Hull, a Secretary has a good press or a strong political following, he may even receive credit for accomplishments that are not his own. If he has neither, as in the case of Acheson, people may blame him for policies or blunders that are not his own. Then, as they did with Acheson, politicians can use the Secretary of State as a scapegoat for policies they do not like.

Acheson was never able to popularize himself or to achieve a respected status with the masses or the politicians. His predicament seems to demonstrate that a Secretary of State without political support, no matter how well qualified in the conduct of foreign affairs, in a time of intensified and frustrated concern over foreign policy, faces grave difficulties at the hands of politicians. The Secretary's helplessness in the face of Congressional attacks is in part imbedded in the American political system and in the structure of his office. He does not have at his own disposal, as do the President and other department heads, the usual political weapons of reward and reprisal with which to blunt Congressional opposition or to gain Congressional support.

More than any other, the politician who attempted to take advantage of the national frustration over foreign policy during the early days of the Cold War was Senator Joseph R. McCarthy, a Republican from Wisconsin who touched off a debate on the political complexion of the State Department in February, 1950, by charging that it was honeycombed with Communists. Before he was through, McCarthy was able to make the character of the Secretary of State himself a foremost political issue.

The Senate held long hearings on McCarthy's charges against Acheson and his department and, despite the fact that no evidence of disloyalty was uncovered, the gunning for the Secretary continued until he went out of office. "The charges against him had no foundation whatever," a prominent Senator wrote, "but unfortunately they served to undermine the administration's foreign policy and to gain publicity for Acheson's critics."

Although few voices, in Congress and elsewhere, rose to Acheson's defense, he did have some defenders, among them Henry L. Stimson. Although almost at the point of death, Stimson expressed resentment and alarm over the attacks on the Secretaryship. "It seems quite clear that the real motive of the accuser in this case is to cast discredit upon the Secretary of State of the United States," he said. And, he added, "In any test of personal confidence the men of honor, in both parties, will choose to stand with the Secretary."

The Secretary of State, he pointed out, has the right to expect the sympathy and support of the people, and then referred to an old idea, that the Secretary should be exempt from the ordinary trials of politics. "The man who seeks to gain political advantage from personal attack on a Secretary of State," he declared, "is a man who seeks political advantage from damage to his country." At that time, however, Stimson's voice was that of a minority, for the campaign against Acheson continued, leading to demands for his resignation.

"The blunt fact is," a newspaper editorial said, "the most important post in Mr. Truman's administration is filled by a man who does not enjoy general or congressional confidence." Even a former Cabinet colleague, Harold L. Ickes, demanded Acheson's resignation. "I will go further," he said of the editorial, "and affirm that, on the basis of knowledge that I possess, he does not 'enjoy the confidence' of many who are prominent colleagues of his in the Administration, to say nothing of Democratic political leaders throughout the country."

Finally, the attacks against his Secretary of State so angered Truman that he lashed out in defense of Acheson. "How our position in the world would be improved by the retirement of Dean Acheson from public life," he said, "is beyond me." He insisted that the charges were false and pointed out that Seward had suffered from similar slander. As Lincoln refused to dismiss Seward, the President announced, "so do I refuse to dismiss Secretary Acheson."

Later Truman wrote that "the men who struck out against Acheson were thus in reality striking out at me." He was right, for since the Secretary technically has no personal responsibility for policy and is the spokesman for the President's policy, it is almost axiomatic that one way to attack the President is through his Secretary of State. "In other words," Truman said, "they wanted Acheson's scalp because he stood for *my* policy."

Acheson's tenure spanned a period when the opposition party attacked Administration foreign policy, and hence the Secretary of State, as savagely as any policy or Secretary has ever been attacked. Acheson himself wrote that "in 1950–52 the ferocity of the Republican attack knew no limits." Nonetheless, Acheson was not driven from office, and thus he gave strength to the principle that if a President stands by his Secretary and chooses to support him in the face of partisan political onslaughts, the Secretary of State can withstand almost any kind of pressure or criticism.

This principle can also be seen at work in the case of John Foster Dulles. Acheson, at least, was admired abroad, but Dulles was distrusted not only by the opposition party but also by his country's allies. In England, one member of Parliament attacked him, perhaps unjustly, saying that never before had a man "spent so long in preparing himself to be Foreign Secretary and made such a fool of himself when he finally got the job." At home, Democrats disliked him, particularly for his inconsistencies and apparent efforts to wring political advantage from foreign policy.

The most powerful attacks on Dulles came after the Suez crisis of 1956, which nearly ruined America's Middle Eastern policy and her alliance with Great Britain and France. The British and French, who had invaded Egypt and were forced to withdraw in part because of American pressure, felt that Dulles had betrayed them. Friends as well as critics, therefore, pointed out that a Secretary of State who is distrusted by his country's major allies cannot be effective. "How long," one newspaper asked, "can the United States afford the luxury of a Secretary of State in whom there is so little confidence at home and abroad?"

By this time, the Secretary had succeeded in alienating nearly the whole Democratic Party in Congress. Even some influential members of Dulles' own party shared this lack of confidence in him, though Republicans rallied to his defense as Democrats in Congress had not to that of Acheson. More important, Eisenhower stood by his Secretary's side just as Truman had rushed to the defense of Acheson. The President made it clear that he wholeheartedly supported Dulles and was responsible for his policies, which, he said, "have my approval from top to bottom."

Some observers, remembering Acheson's ordeal, now concluded that the bitterness between Congress and the Secretary of State in a time of international tension is not unusual. It is almost inevitable, they said, because the Secretary cannot avoid dealing with Congress in his role as a representative and even defender of the Administration in power. He frequently does not have the luxury of choosing between a partisan or bipartisan approach to Congress.

Students of government have also pointed out that the new controversial and intense concern with foreign affairs makes it practically impossible for a Secretary of State to be popular and still do his job well. James F. Byrnes, in contrast to Thurlow Weed almost a century earlier, stated that "one of the functions of a good Secretary of State is to be unpopular," for the Secretary has become a symbol and personification of the international frustrations that Americans could not escape or resolve. The fact that the Secretary offers a ready target for the pent-up anger produced by these frustrations, it was said, is merely one of the unpleasant occupational hazards of the modern Secretaryship.

Although it is true that some of Dulles' difficulties seem inherent in the problems he had to face, he also created certain of his own handicaps. Despite a formal espousal of bipartisanism in foreign policy, he was himself as Secretary of State a narrow partisan. He paid close attention to the needs of the Republican Party in foreign affairs and seldom hesitated to blame Democrats for some of his predicaments. His partisanship, however, was not merely a personal trait. It reflected the times. The new controversy over the nature of foreign policy made the Secretary of State a partisan to a degree that had no clear historical precedent. Indeed, as one political writer pointed out, at times the main issue in foreign policy between the Democrats and Dulles seemed to be Dulles himself.

Dulles, moreover, seems to have had a knack for plunging into controversy. Critics quipped that he was born with a silver hoof in his mouth. One source of controversy stemmed from his conviction that foreign policy begins at home and should be based on domestic political considerations, on what he called the realities of American politics. When domestic and international considerations clashed, his theory held, domestic politics should take precedence. This attitude led to compromises with hectoring politicians, such as Senator McCarthy, who continued to attack the State Department even though it was now controlled by his own party.

Dulles' concern for domestic political support grew out of his determination, among other things, not to repeat Acheson's failure to gain the support of Congress and of the press, just as Acheson had been determined not to repeat Byrnes's failure to hold the President's confidence. Despite his precautions, Dulles failed. In many ways, he had a less favorable press than Acheson and though his record of getting along with Congress was at first better than Acheson's, it too was poor. He seems to have had a passion not to offend Congress, and yet did. Only Eisenhower's popularity saved Dulles from any harsher criticism than he received.

As a general rule, opposition to a Secretary of State is just another means of attacking the President, but Eisenhower was so popular that few politicians openly attacked him or attempted to force his Secretary from office. His second Secretary, Christian A. Herter, offered no problem. Having served several terms in the House of Representatives, Herter had many friends in Congress. He was, in fact, one of the most popular men to take over the Secretaryship. His popularity and political record probably saved him from Congressional flailings for several blunders, notably for his part in the U-2 fiasco and in Japan's humiliating last-minute cancellation of Eisenhower's visit to Tokyo in the summer of 1960.

More than a century earlier, those who mercilessly attacked John M. Clayton, thinking he ran the Administration, did so to strike at President Zachary Taylor, even though, like Eisenhower, he took office as a war hero. Clayton's seventeen months in the Secretaryship, therefore, were unhappy. Unpopular and subjected to savage criticism for policies that were not his own, he was politically helpless, having no official means, no political influence of his own, that he could invoke to defend himself or Administration foreign policy. That defense had to come from the President himself. All Clayton could do was to absorb the criticisms or act as a shield for the President.

When Taylor died in office, despite his grief over the personal loss, Clayton was grateful for the opportunity to resign gracefully. "The situation I have filled," he wrote, "was during the period of President Taylor's administration more difficult, more thorny and more liable to misrepresentation and calumny than any other in the world, as I verily believe."

III.

Even though the Secretary lacks legal responsibility for foreign policy, sharing the criticism of that policy has become one of the traditional burdens of his office. When the policy is an unpopular one or thought to be shaped by the Secretary, the public frequently holds him responsible for it. The public, therefore, at times attacks the Secretary of State instead of the President himself. Moreover, attacks against the Secretary may bring immediate results. Since the Secretary has no fixed term or direct political power, he can be driven to resign, whereas the President cannot.

This political vulnerability, as early as the cases of Thomas Jefferson and Edmund Randolph, accounts in part for the relatively brief service of the Secretaries of State. Only four Secretaries have served eight years or more. The average term has been about three years. Seldom has a short term been the result of problems in foreign policy itself, or of the inability of a Secretary to master the responsibilities of his post. Serving at the pleasure of the President, a Secretary has no claim to any kind of tenure. Subject to the winds of domestic politics, Secretaries have had to be concerned with their relations with Congress and politicians, as well as with the President. It is little wonder that many of them have been even more concerned with domestic issues than with their main responsibility, foreign relations.

For example, so closely was Seward identified in the public mind with Lincoln and Administration policy that on the night of Lincoln's murder, one of the assassins forced his way into the Secretary's house and tried to kill him also. In the Johnson Administration, the public credited Seward with responsibility for many of Johnson's unpopular policies, and the Secretary therefore lost influence with the public, with politicians of his own party, and with his friends.

John Hay, on the other hand, feared that attacks on himself would injure the Administration. This was evident in March, 1900, when the Senate had saddled one of his treaties with distasteful amendments and he offered his resignation. "The action of the Senate," he told the President, "indicates views so widely divergent from mine in affecting, as I think, the national welfare and honor, that I fear my power to serve in business requiring the concurrence of that body is at an end. I cannot help fearing also that the newspaper attacks upon the State Department, which have so strongly influenced the Senate, may be an injury to you, if I remain in the Cabinet." McKinley refused to accept the resignation and said that he would "cheerfully bear whatever criticism or condemnation may come."

Like Seward rather than like Hay, Charles Evans Hughes deliberately drew criticism upon himself to protect the President. He believed that the Secretary of State, whenever possible, should shield the President from attack for unpopular decisions in foreign policy by absorbing the criticism himself. In 1924, for instance, Hughes wished to spike a movement calling for the recognition of the Soviet Union. He prepared a terse statement to the effect that negotiations would be futile without evidence that the Russians were willing to modify their conduct. When he brought the statement to Coolidge for approval, the President asked, emphasizing the personal pronoun, "Why shouldn't *I* say that?"

"Of course you could," Hughes answered. "But would it be wise to expose yourself to the criticism that will rain on the head of the person who makes this statement public?" The President agreed and Hughes issued the statement.

Hughes understood that the Secretary of State, to function properly, had to play several roles. Often that of politician is the most useful, but usually that of statesman is the most impressive. The latter role is the one that draws greatest attention and causes the deepest concern.

In 1947, for instance, President Truman established a special Commission on Organization of the Executive Branch of the Government, under the chairmanship of Herbert Hoover, which urged a reorganization of the Secretaryship. The Hoover Commission's recommendations called for a reassignment of responsibility and an expansion of the Secretary's staff at the top so that his own authority was clear and unencumbered. In effect, they provided for strengthening the Secretary's role of statesman by enlarging his power over the formulating of policy. After considering the Hoover Commission's report, Congress passed a law in May, 1949, that confirmed and enlarged the Secretary's authority over policy and freed him from certain routine administrative duties by giving him additional assistant secretaries.

Despite this concern for statesmanship, the history of the Secretaryship shows that a Secretary of State to be effective must be a politician as well as a statesman. In fact, it is difficult to draw a line between the two. The Secretary cannot work in a sphere of foreign affairs isolated from political developments at home, for the conduct of foreign relations requires political leadership of Congress as well as statesmanship. In the years of the Cold War, moreover, when the Secretary is the center of public attention as he has never been before, his personal and political ideas have attained unprecedented public importance. Many have come to recognize that he is a politician as well as a statesman.

It is as a statesman, nonetheless, and not as a politician, that the Secretary of State usually appears before the American people and the world. If he is to fill that role properly, he should be allowed the power to make decisions, and he must make them; he cannot be content merely to transmit to the President the views and raw ideas of his subordinates. He should use the experts in his department to inform him and stimulate him, but he himself ought to put together the pieces that go into the making of policy. In fact, he should draw on other departments and agencies, as well, for support, information, and ideas. From this unique wide-ranging position that cuts across departmental lines in the hierarchy of government, he has to arrive at his own conclusions and make his own synthesis in formulating the advice he offers the President. When he can persuade the President to use this advice as the basis for action, and when he receives a mandate to carry out the decisions thus arrived at as national policy, the Secretary functions as a statesman in the true meaning of the term in the American system.

8

The Administrator and Diplomat

> As a maker and executor of foreign policy, whatever the appearances, the Secretary of State is not an individual performer. He is part of an institution, another essential part of which is the personnel of the Department of State and the Foreign Service, from which flow to him his initial analyses of problems and recommendations for dealing with them.
>
> —Dean G. Acheson, 1955

Like the other members of the Cabinet, the Secretary of State is the head of an institution—in his case, the Department of State—which forms the foundation of his office. This institution acts in his name and feeds him most of the information and recommendations on which he usually bases his own advice to the President. The Secretary, therefore, functions not only as an individual, but also as part of an organization, as an administrator.

Until the sudden expansion of the State Department during World War II, the Secretary's administrative problem, despite the complaints of various Secretaries about their heavy administrative loads, was not truly acute. Now, however, it is imperative that the Secretary be enough of an administrator to control and use his vastly expanded department effectively.

Despite the considerable technical skill that administration may require and the large amount of time that it may absorb, no Secretary of State has achieved a lasting reputation for concentrating on efficiency in administrative detail and departmental routine. Secretaries such as Louis McLane, John Forsyth, and

Edward R. Stettinius, Jr., who carried out major administrative reorganizations within the Department of State, are scarcely remembered, except perhaps by academicians specializing in American diplomacy.

Even so capable a statesman as John Quincy Adams, in a day when the State Department's administrative responsibilities were light, felt despair over the pressing nature of his own daily administrative duties, fearing they would so overwhelm him that he would be able to leave behind him no record of substantial accomplishment in the Secretaryship. Administrative changes, such as one in 1823 that made the Secretary responsible for granting passports to Americans who wished to visit foreign countries, merely added to his burden. Few Secretaries, in fact, have been content to act merely as administrators, and virtually all have considered themselves something more.

Henry Clay, Adams' successor, for instance, detested his administrative responsibilities. In his day, the Department of State was still little more than a collection of clerks, and most of the routine tasks that required decisions fell to the Secretary of State. In retrospect, in part because he clashed with President Adams over policy and appointments, but more because of the administrative duties that bored him, Clay could say that his Secretaryship gave him four of the most miserable and uninteresting years of his life.

Clay's experience, though extreme, is not unusual, for some Presidents, such as Polk, wanted nothing more than administrators as Secretaries of State, men who were capable of handling routine matters on their own but who would not shape policy. "As long as he will carry out my policy and act faithfully," Polk said of Secretary Buchanan, for instance, "I am willing he shall remain in the office of Secretary of State; when he ceases to do so, he must cease to occupy that position."

A quarter of a century later, William L. Evarts thought so little of his administrative duties that he ignored them or left them almost entirely to his subordinates in the State Department. Once, when the President questioned his neglect of administrative matters, Evarts replied, "You don't sufficiently realize the great truth that almost any question will settle itself if you only leave it alone long enough." So lightly did he take his responsibilities that he continued to practice law while in the Secretaryship. Even friends criticized him for this cavalier attitude toward his office. Hamilton Fish, for example, complained that shortly after Evarts took office, before he had had time to acquaint himself with his new responsibilities, he rushed off to New York to plead cases.

Another who accepted outside employment while in the Secretaryship and therefore pushed aside administrative duties, but who also came to feel the lash of savage criticism, was William Jennings Bryan. As he had done for years, Bryan while in office continued to give lectures for pay. In the summer of 1913, while on the Chautauqua circuit, for example, he gave speeches in West Virginia, Maryland, Pennsylvania, and other states. To critics, particularly in the Eastern press, the Secretary of State had "disgraced his office" by stripping it of proper dignity and had descended to the level of a mere entertainer, "a barnstormer, playing one-night stands, preceded by the magic lantern and followed by the hurdy-gurdy man and his dancing bear." Although unprepared for such humiliating attacks, Bryan shrugged them off as best he could and went on with the lectures, for the controversial publicity pulled in larger crowds than before.

Bryan explained that he could not live on the Secretary of State's annual salary of $12,000 and had to lecture for additional income. "Mr. Bryan's attitude in this matter," one critic wrote, "is fundamentally wrong. If a Cabinet officer cannot live on his salary, and is unwilling to use his private means to make up the difference, he has no business to retain the office an instant."

Foreigners, too, joined the criticism. "It is a pity," the British Ambassador wrote, "that Bryan has given so much occasion for Europe to ridicule the State Department. He has, after all, attended to business more in the intervals of his lecturing and golf than Knox did in the intervals of his touring and golf. . . ."

Philander C. Knox, incidentally, detested the administrative duties of the Secretaryship and whenever possible shunned them. He wished to deal only with high policy, not with routine or technical matters. It was probably this attitude that persuaded President Taft that his Secretary of State was lazy. Yet, under Knox, the State Department went through its most thorough reorganization since that carried out by Hamilton Fish in 1870.

John Hay, too, disliked administrative tasks and complained constantly of being overworked. At the end of a year in the Secretaryship, he wrote that "it is impossible to exaggerate the petty worries and cares which, added to the really important matters, make the office of Secretary of State almost intolerable." At another time, he said that "the worst of my present job is that I can delegate so little of it."

Hay did exaggerate his plight, for he was able to delegate administrative responsibilities, relying heavily on Alvey A. Adee, his Second Assistant Secretary of State, who had been in the State Department for twenty-one years and understood virtually every detail of administrative and diplomatic procedure. Adee, a bachelor who would work at night and sleep in his office when the department's work load could not be handled in a normal day, drafted instructions, went through the morning mail, signed official correspondence, and performed other administrative duties. He served until 1924, when he died in harness at the age of eighty-two. Altogether, he had spent forty-seven years in the State Department, easing the administrative burden of twenty-two Secretaries of State.

In fact, it is the work of men such as Adee that has given administrative management in the department an essential continuity. William Hunter, Adee, and Wilbur J. Carr, administrative assistants for various Secretaries of State, served without a break from 1829 to 1937, a period of more than a century. They were professionals whose knowledge of administrative procedures made the problem of administration a manageable one for all Secretaries, regardless of party or policy.

Hay's successor, Elihu Root, who apparently liked administrative tasks and is remembered as a capable administrator, by practical standards was not a sound one because he himself took on too much of the routine work that might better have been delegated to reliable subordinates such as Adee. By the same criteria, Frank B. Kellogg's concern for petty details, his truculent attitude and bursts of temper, which earned him the nickname "nervous Nellie," made him a poor administrator.

Some men have seemed concerned mainly with their administrative responsibilities and have served in the tradition that the Secretary of State is the President's personal administrative officer in foreign affairs. Frederick T. Frelinghuysen, for instance, seems to have considered himself the head of an organization staffed by competent subordinates, the holder of an office that ran itself and required little of him. Others, such as John W. Foster and William R. Day, also apparently considered themselves mainly administrators.

Few Secretaries of State, however, have been as concerned with effective administration as was Charles E. Hughes. His thinking helped to inspire the Rogers Act of 1924, which improved the diplomatic service through salary increases, the merging of the diplomatic and consular services, and the basing of appointments and promotions on merit. "You will find, I believe," he told his successor, "that the Department is more effectively organized than it has ever been."

Cordell Hull took administrative problems seriously. He immersed himself in the mass of routine data that flowed through the State Department, but he cannot be called an able administrator, in part because he accustomed himself to the department's bureaucracy instead of mastering it.

Edward R. Stettinius, Jr., was essentially an administrator, experienced in the management of large corporations. His successor, James F. Byrnes, on the other hand, looked upon administrative obligations as barriers to the Secretary's true responsibilities, believing that the Secretary should be free of purely administrative duties so that he could concentrate on the making of policy. "The amount of time a Secretary of State must give to decisions on carrying out operating functions," he said, "necessarily is taken away from the important questions of foreign policy."

The next Secretary, George C. Marshall, had a deep interest in efficient administration, having been Chief of Staff in control of the nation's military establishment in a time of unparalleled growth. In one of his first chores as Secretary of State, therefore, he reorganized the top command in the State Department so as to clarify the lines of authority. As he had in the army, he entrusted almost all administrative problems to subordinates, to what he called his staff. Like an army commander, furthermore, he demanded orderly staff procedure and kept himself remote from the workings of the department. Under Secretary of State Dean Acheson functioned as his chief of staff and ran the department. Only major questions were submitted to Marshall for decision.

In the War Department, Marshall had been concerned with long-term, centralized planning, which he felt the State Department lacked. Therefore, he created the Policy Planning Staff, a small group of specialists who would work directly under him but outside the usual departmental hierarchy. That group would analyze trends in foreign affairs from the point of view of the Secretary of State's world-wide responsibilities and formulate policy recommendations for some twenty-five years into the future for his guidance and for others who must make the decisions. Under Marshall, perhaps more than under any other Secretary, policy emerged from staff planning. Critics thought he was excessively influenced by his staff, a captive of his own administrative devices.

Like Marshall, Dean Acheson, too, relied heavily on his staff for assistance in formulating policy and administering the State Department, but by experience, he was better qualified than Marshall had been to run the department. Probably no Secretary, in fact, has been as well prepared as an administrator upon taking office as was Acheson. He had served in the State Department continuously for six and a half years, worked under four Secretaries of State and two Presidents, and, as Vice-Chairman of the

Hoover Commission, studied the department. Under Marshall, he had actually administered the department and, moreover, is the only Secretary who was both an Assistant Secretary and an Under Secretary. He knew the internal workings of the department as no other Secretary has.

One of Acheson's first moves as Secretary of State was to carry out a partial reorganization of the State Department along lines recommended by the Hoover Commission. Among other changes, the reorganization relieved the Secretary of some of his administrative responsibilities, for his duties had become so complicated that at times he could be little more than an administrator.

When Dulles was offered the Secretaryship to replace Acheson, he expressed distaste for the Secretary's administrative obligations, saying that he doubted that any Secretary would have time to think clearly if he were to try to administer the State Department and to meet the other routine demands of his office. When he took office, therefore, he indicated that he intended to confine his attention to large issues of policy while leaving the details of administration to subordinates. That was why almost the first piece of legislation President Eisenhower requested of Congress was authorization for two Under Secretaries of State instead of one. Dulles asked for this change because he wanted the second Under Secretary to handle administrative details within the State Department so that he himself could devote most of his time to diplomacy and the making of policy.

Like Stimson, moreover, Dulles virtually ignored the career men in the Department of State and the Foreign Service. Although he delegated administrative responsibilities, he did not do so when such matters touched the making of policy. In fact, he rarely accepted advice from his subordinates and, unlike Acheson, seldom used the Policy Planning Staff. His thinking alone, he appeared to assume, generated foreign policy. As a consequence, he was never popular with his subordinates, most of whom considered him a poor administrator. In contrast, Herter, who tried to give the top officials in the State Department a share in formulating foreign policy, was admired by his subordinates for being a team worker.

I.

Popularity within the State Department and effective administration, however, have had little effect on the reputation of a Secretary of State. Even political power and achievements in domestic affairs, unless they led to the Presidency, have brought no lasting recognition. Those who stand out are the Secretaries who made notable records in the conduct of foreign relations, mainly the diplomats who were also statesmen. Even the lesser figures have gained recognition for their connection to some special idea, to some doctrine, and most of all, to some noteworthy achievement in diplomacy. Such achievement has usually so firmly captured public imagination or so overshadowed all else in a Secretary's tenure as to stamp him with an enduring distinction.

The list of such Secretaries and their accomplishments is long, but a brief mention might refresh faded memories and should illustrate the point. Few can think of the Monroe Doctrine and the Transcontinental Treaty of 1819, which reinforced the claim of the United States to a foothold on the Pacific and took Florida from Spain, without bringing to mind John Quincy Adams, or of the Webster-Ashburton Treaty of 1842, which settled the Maine-boundary dispute with Great Britain, without recalling Daniel Webster. Seward's name is forever linked to the skillful diplomacy of the Civil War and to the purchase of Alaska, Hamilton Fish to the Treaty of Washington in 1871, which settled a number of grievances with England and Canada, Blaine to Pan-Americanism, John Hay to the Open Door Policy, Olney to an extravagant expansion of the Monroe Doctrine related to a boundary dispute between Venezuela and British Guiana, Knox to Dollar Diplomacy, or economic expansion in Asia and Latin America, and Hughes to the Washington Disarmament Conference of 1921–22 which temporarily eased tense relations with Japan.

Kellogg gave his name to the Kellogg-Briand Antiwar Pact and received the Nobel Peace Prize for his part in it. Stimson is best remembered for the nonrecognition doctrine that bears his name and Cordell Hull for his Reciprocal Trade Agreements Program and his work in the founding of the United Nations—a task that earned him a Nobel Peace Prize. George Marshall, too, won a Nobel Peace Prize, mainly for his part in the European Recovery Program, also known as the Marshall Plan. Acheson is noted for his work on the North Atlantic Treaty and for the diplomacy of the Korean War, and Dulles for the idea of "deterrence" and the building of a world-wide network of alliances, one of which is the Southeast Asia Treaty Organization, or SEATO.

We can see, therefore, why the popular image of the Secretary of State is that of a statesman, at least in the sense of being the nation's foremost diplomat. It has not been, however, a constant image. Until the twentieth century, the Secretary conducted practically all his own diplomacy, or personal negotiations, quietly in the United States. In 1791, Thomas Jefferson and the first British Minister to the United States negotiated in Philadelphia for the removal of the British from posts they occupied in the Northwest; later, John Quincy Adams and Spain's Luis de Onís bargained for Florida in Washington, and Seward obtained Alaska from the Russians in a treaty signed in Washington. When, as in the case of the Jay treaty of 1794 with Britain or the Louisiana Purchase, negotiations had to be carried on abroad, the Secretary stayed at home and sent special commissioners to conclude the agreements. In those instances, the special emissaries, not the Secretary, captured whatever glory the negotiations offered.

In the twentieth century, the Secretary of State has become a traveling negotiator, a diplomat on the move. Unless the President himself takes over, the Secretary participates in almost every important negotiation or international conference affecting the United States, no matter where it might be. Using fast ships and streaking airplanes, he has established a new pattern of secretarial conduct.

Lansing attended the Paris Peace Conference, in 1919, Kellogg went to Paris to sign his antiwar treaty, and Stimson went to the Naval Disarmament Conference in London in 1930 and participated in other negotiations abroad. Within a few months of taking office, Cordell Hull headed the American delegation to the World Economic Conference in London and several months later led a delegation to an International Conference of American States in Montevideo. In 1943, even though he had never set foot in an airplane, was seventy-two years old, sick, and suffered from claustrophobia, he was so determined not to be excluded from another major international conference that he suppressed lifelong fears and insisted on making a long arduous flight to Moscow for a conference. The results, he felt, were worth the danger, for at Moscow he obtained the Four-Nation Declaration, signed by the United States, Russia, Great Britain, and China, which laid the basis for the United Nations and gave him his greatest personal triumph as Secretary of State.

The next Secretary, Stettinius, held office only seven months but spent more than half of that time away from the Department of State participating in various international conferences or negotiations. Such extensive travel now began to alarm some students of government, who argued that the Secretary had to concentrate so much on negotiation that he was forced to neglect his administrative and political responsibilities, but more important, he had no time to participate in the making of policy.

While traveling, despite the advanced technology of rapid communication, critics pointed out, the Secretary of State could not keep in close touch with the developments in Washington that went into the shaping of policy. He could not be in a position to make important decisions on the basis of seeing and weighing all the evidence, nor could he make an effective case with the President against competing agencies that had a part in molding foreign policy. This peripatetic diplomacy, some analysts argued on the other hand, merely reflects the President's traditional dominance of foreign policy and the use of the Secretary as his personal agent. One powerful Senator, for instance, called Stettinius "the presidential messenger."

No one could rightly accuse the next Secretary, James F. Byrnes, of being merely a Presidential messenger, yet three days after taking office, he had packed his bags for a "summit" conference at Potsdam. He, too, had no time to take part in the collective policy-making in the Cabinet, for he kept up a fast pace of travel, being away from the State Department conducting negotiations with foreign powers some 62 per cent of the time he held office, or 350 out of 562 days.

George Marshall, Byrnes's successor, followed a similar pattern, spending most of his time as Secretary abroad attending conferences or negotiating with foreign statesmen in the United States. Almost as soon as he took office, he had to prepare himself for a meeting with Russian, British, and French foreign ministers in Moscow. Up to October 15, 1948, he had devoted 228 days out of 633 in office to the diplomacy of international conferences.

Dean Acheson, too, had to commit himself to a schedule of travel and negotiation, but John Foster Dulles, more than any other Secretary of State, became a traveling negotiator, conspicuously the nation's foremost diplomat. So much did he like to travel and negotiate that it was said that to him an airplane was not merely a convenience, it was a temptation.

Dulles started his travels early. Less than ten days after taking office, he jumped over to Europe to persuade our allies to hasten unification for defense. At the end of his six years in office, he had logged some 560,000 miles on affairs of state, more than the distance of a round trip to the moon. He traveled farther, visited more countries, met more statesmen than any other diplomat in history. He considered himself a roving negotiator or trouble shooter, who represented the President's Constitutional authority to conduct foreign relations. He worked out problems directly with foreign statesmen and then left his subordinates to administer his policies in his absence.

"It's silly," Dulles told a television audience after one of his trips abroad, "to go at it the old-fashioned way of exchanging notes, which take a month before you get a good understanding," when by overnight flight and "talking a few minutes face to face," you can do so at once. "I don't think we'll ever go back to the old-fashioned way." After another trip, he spoke of the importance of talking intimately with foreign leaders and asserted that "talking face to face is the best way yet invented for enabling men to understand each other."

There were many, however, who were critical of this approach to the conduct of foreign relations. Since Dulles did all the negotiating himself, critics said, he was reducing ambassadors and other subordinates to mere executors of his policies without diplomatic powers of their own. Others insisted that he should remain at home in full command of the State Department to make decisions when crises arose, particularly since he did not rely on subordinates for aid in the making of policy and appeared to carry the nation's foreign policies in his vest pocket. For a one-man State Department, they insisted, Dulles was traveling too much.

Actually, it was not Dulles alone who had reduced ambassadors to mere symbols, or funnels of information, but also the times—an age that demanded a roving Secretary of State and the technology that made rapid travel possible. Dulles was an agent, not the sole cause, of change in the work of the Secretary.

When Christian Herter, Dulles' successor, took office he told reporters, "I will travel if I feel it is necessary to travel. But as you know I have always been a pretty strong team worker." Yet Herter spent 80 out of his first 115 days away from Washington involved in personal diplomacy.

Kennedy's Secretary, too, announced that he would try to avoid travel, indicating that he believed the Secretary of State should remain at his desk as much as possible. Yet the pressing demands of America's world-wide responsibilities were such that within four months after taking over the Secretaryship, Dean Rusk was away from Washington about as often as he was there, flying to various high-level conferences in Bangkok, Ankara, Oslo, and Geneva.

The use of peripatetic diplomacy is not unique with the Secretary of State. Other foreign ministers, heads of state, and especially the President, have also become globetrotters. The great surge in personal diplomacy and travel on the highest levels has come mainly from the staggering changes in the climate of opinion and the political structure of the world and, for the Secretary, from the vastly expanded responsibilities and world-wide commitments of the United States. Statesmen and peoples all over the world now demand emissaries on the highest levels; they are no longer content to settle important matters through ordinary channels and ambassadors. The extreme sensitiveness of foreign policy to the vagaries of world opinion, to publicity, and to propaganda, seemingly are making the Secretary's globetrotting, and even summit conferences, necessary.

Touching on this theme, a controversial article in *Life* magazine of January, 1956, claimed that Dulles had "altered drastically the basic concept of the job of Secretary of State." He did not, it said, work in the so-called traditional pattern of the administrative executive. He regarded too much time spent in Washington as neglect of American leadership in world affairs, and hence devoted himself fully to personal diplomacy. In contrast to Acheson, Marshall, and Herter, who were team men despite their travels, Dulles seemingly had a romantic view of the Secretaryship, envisioning the Secretary of State as an individual performer on the international stage, a master diplomat who had perfected the art of settling world problems through negotiation.

Actually, Dulles did not fundamentally change the nature of his office. Even though most Secretaries have been politicians and few have had the diplomatic experience he brought to the office, the Secretaryship has always been basically the post of the nation's foremost diplomat. Its link with the diplomacy of the past, in fact, has given it a stability that time and bewildering technological changes have not destroyed. Secretaries such as Jefferson, Monroe, and John Quincy Adams were all skilled diplomats.

Early in the twentieth century, John Hay came as close to being a professional diplomat as anyone who has ever filled the Secretaryship.

Virtually all Secretaries, particularly in the twentieth century, have had to be diplomats regardless of their lack of previous experience, for all have had to meet and negotiate with foreign statesmen, even if they did not travel halfway round the world to do so. Without leaving Washington, Hay, for instance, negotiated the treaties that led to the building of the Panama Canal, Root concluded an important executive agreement with the Japanese, Bryan signed a series of conciliation treaties with foreign governments, and Hughes concluded one naval and two Far Eastern pacts. It can be seen, therefore, that the Secretary of State, regardless of his own deficiencies or the restrictions placed upon him by the President, cannot avoid diplomacy; not even the senile and powerless John Sherman could do so.

II.

In the years of the Cold War, however, the Secretary's diplomacy has received more publicity than ever before, and his own stature has appeared to increase because his power over the shaping of foreign policy seems to grow with the extent of his travels. Actually, the Secretary's relative importance has grown because the President himself can take cognizance of only a small part of the nation's vastly expanded international activities. He is often compelled, therefore, to rely on his Secretary of State and others for help in formulating foreign policy and sometimes for the policy itself.

Seldom, actually, is the Secretary of State alone responsible for abrupt or radical changes in foreign policy. From Secretary to Secretary, Administration to Administration, decade to decade, foreign policy usually manifests a fundamental continuity and a movement so gradual as to seem almost glacial. This is so because foreign policy does not usually spring only from the brain of the Secretary but also emerges from the collaboration of many minds, from time, from experience, and from *ad hoc* situations. In the words of Dean Acheson, "the springs of policy bubble up; they do not trickle down."

It may be convenient to speak of the foreign policy of a Secretary of State, but to do so is frequently misleading, for the day-to-day decisions of the Secretary are often of little consequence in the development of major policies. An idea does not become national policy, as the unthinking believe, merely because the Secretary approves it. The making of foreign policy is one of the highest functions of the state, and in the United States, that power belongs almost exclusively to the President, a power that few Presidents would totally delegate. Most strong Presidents, therefore, tend to deal with major issues and fundamental foreign policy themselves. They usually make the great decisions and leave the lesser ones to their Secretaries of State.

It is frequently this unwillingness of the President to share his power and the desire of the Secretary to grasp power that has led to friction between the Secretaries of State and the Presidents who appointed them. Usually this struggle for power, mainly over the conduct of foreign relations, grows out of a clash of personalities, for, after all, the drive for power is embedded in personality. Only one Secretary was dismissed outright, and this case, that of Timothy Pickering, involved a personality conflict as well as friction over policy and politics. The forced resignations, such as Robert Smith's and Robert Lansing's, also usually hinged on personality conflict.

Out of the fifty-three men who have held the Secretaryship, at least fifteen either quarreled with the President or differed seriously with him over matters of policy. This number excludes those Secretaries who differed with their Presidents in the normal give and take of shaping policy or in the heat of small arguments. In about thirty-five cases, the relations between the President and his Secretary can be described as generally harmonious.

Even though this analysis, admittedly based on limited evidence, may have a disquieting margin of error, the uncomfortable fact remains that the ratio of friction to harmony between the two men who have the major responsibility for the nation's foreign policy has been high. It suggests, too, that the conduct of foreign relations may have suffered at times more from personality conflicts than from technical or professional deficiencies in the Secretary. In fact, only three Secretaries, Jefferson, Pickering, and Bryan, left office over an issue of foreign policy, and Pickering's case turned more on personality.

This analysis also suggests that the intangible factor of personality may at times outweigh a Secretary's intellectual and professional competence in convincing a President that he should share his power over foreign relations with his Secretary of State. A President, like anyone else, is more likely to trust and work comfortably with a man whose personality pleases him than with one whose temperament he finds uncongenial.

Although this conclusion implies that compatible personalities are important in the relationship between a President and his Secretary of State, because that relationship is intensely personal as well as official, it does not indicate that personality should be the decisive factor in the selection of a Secretary. Indeed, Secretaries whose main virtue is that they please the President may do him and their country a disservice, for nothing can substitute for intelligence, professional competence, independent judgment, and ideas in the Secretaryship.

That independence, even though a Secretary acts in the President's name, makes the Secretary of State more than an administrator or a mere figurehead. As a result, despite his reliance on the President and his sometimes humiliating status, the Secretary not infrequently deserves greater credit than anyone else for shaping and carrying out foreign policy. Most Secretaries, in fact, have left an imprint of some kind on the office, on the nation's diplomatic history, and on the foreign policy that has been woven into its diplomatic tradition.

Regardless of the limitations of the Secretaryship, moreover, it can be an office of vast power, one that gives the Secretary a broad opportunity, second only to that in the Presidency itself, to translate his ideas into policy and to play a grand role in world affairs. He, more than any other department head or the Vice-President, has the best chance to attain lasting fame, for he, next to the President, has the largest stage on which to perform. Under a weak, or permissive, President, a bold competent Secretary, one with a strong personality to match sweeping ideas, can achieve a greatness second only to the President and a distinction above that of any other foreign minister.

This, consequently, might lead one to ask by what criteria do we measure effectiveness and accomplishment in a Secretary of State. Although there are more complicated means, for our purpose it seems appropriate to advance the theory that an outstanding Secretary is one who has great ideas and principles, that is ideas that transcend immediate and local problems, one who has been given the power to participate in the making of important decisions and to mold his ideas into policy, and who has the diplomatic skill and statesmanship to carry out that policy in international affairs.

At the same time, the outstanding Secretary is one who retains the over-all direction of foreign policy against the parochial interests of other agencies dealing with foreign affairs. He is one who can establish and maintain his authority within his own department, in the Cabinet, and in his relations with the President. He is one who can keep those with independent political support, from inside his own department and without, from stepping between himself and the President. He is one who realizes that he can refine and enrich decisions, can persuade the President to take action, but does not have to be reminded that he does not himself possess the power of final decision. He is one who is jealous of his prestige and that of his office, for he understands that such prestige is an important tool in carrying out foreign policy.

Finally, the truly great Secretary of State will give style and cohesion to foreign policy as a whole. Even though we have broken down the obligations of the Secretary into categories for purposes of analysis, the outstanding Secretary will always realize also that no one part of his duties, or his office, can be wholly isolated from the other parts, that all belong inseparably to an interacting whole.

The listing of these criteria leads logically to the question: Who are the Secretaries who have come closest to fulfilling them, the Secretaries who stand out above the others? This, in turn, leads to an old game of diplomatic historians and political scientists, that of ranking the Secretaries of State, a game second in popularity only to that of ranking the Presidents. Even though experts are bound to disagree over any listing, we shall nonetheless boldly rank ten of the Secretaries, but not on the usual basis of effectiveness in diplomacy alone. We shall do so only in accordance with the standards in our theory.

Most historians and students of government reserve the first position for John Quincy Adams, and according to our criteria, he deserves it. From his mind sprang the idea of continental expansion, from his diplomacy emerged the Transcontinental Treaty of 1819 that helped make it possible, and from him came the noncolonization principle of the Monroe Doctrine. Moreover, despite great odds, he persuaded President Monroe to make a unilateral pronouncement of the doctrine, and Adams was allowed the power to carry out the policies he advanced. His brilliant accomplishments as Secretary of State are outstanding in a notable public career. He is a great Secretary.

William H. Seward conducted a masterful diplomacy during the Civil War, skillfully helped maneuver the French out of Mexico after Maximilian had established a shaky empire there, almost alone acquired Alaska, and was prominent and powerful in the making of foreign and domestic policy in two crisis-ridden Administrations. He, too, is a great Secretary and merits second place.

Third place goes to Dean Acheson for helping to guide the nation through the perilous and frustrating Korean War, when a diplomatic misstep might have led to a nuclear Armageddon. In his advice to President Truman, he helped to maintain the supremacy of the civil authority over the military leader and courageously refused to allow foreign policy to become secondary to immediate objectives on the battlefield. His contributions to the policy of containment and the making of NATO, and his ability to originate policy and to carry it out despite searing political criticism, all mark him as a Secretary of unusual ability and accomplishment.

John Foster Dulles, despite the gusts of controversy that he and his policies started, originated foreign policy and carried it out. There is no doubt that he was the dominant figure in the Eisenhower Administrations, a man whose intellectual grasp was greater than that of his contemporaries in government, a man who brought the modern Secretaryship virtually to the summit of its power. He helped conclude the Korean War and despite his "brinkmanship," or what critics called a reckless flirtation with war, helped keep the nation at peace in times of crushing crises, and built up a network of alliances to safeguard the nation. More than most Secretaries, he showed growth in office and devoted his life to his work. He fits into fourth place.

Hamilton Fish ranks number five because he, also, was the leading figure of the Administrations he served. He, too, helped to keep the nation at peace when war seemed logical, mainly by diverting President Grant from a determination to free Cuba from Spain. In addition, he negotiated the monumental Treaty of Washington. He was the outstanding statesman of his time.

Daniel Webster ranks sixth and Charles E. Hughes seventh because they clearly commanded foreign relations, were the sources of ideas in foreign policy, and each was associated with an outstanding diplomatic accomplishment, the Webster-Ashburton Treaty and the treaties of the Washington Conference of 1921–22.

George C. Marshall takes eighth place for helping to save Europe from misery and perhaps from Communism with his Marshall Plan, and John Hay, ninth, for his skilled diplomacy.

Although Henry L. Stimson at times quarreled with President Hoover over foreign policy and did not have the power in shaping policy that the others on this list had, he was a man of ideas and gave his office a mark of dignity. As a statesman and thinker, he takes tenth place.

Ironically, this list includes only one of the three Secretaries who won Nobel Peace Prizes. We must remember, however, that those prizes are awarded for special achievement and not for one's power and ideas in the Secretaryship.

Even though every Secretary cannot be outstanding, from the criteria we have used it should be clear that the Secretaryship should not be offered as a political plum and that the Secretary should not be merely a figurehead. Ideally, a man with experience in politics, diplomacy, and administration should hold the office, but under the new urgency of foreign affairs in an age of weapons of unprecedented destructiveness, the specialized ability in international matters, in the art of diplomacy, is more important than the others.

The modern Secretary should, above all, be a statesman and a diplomat in the finest sense, the active head of an organization equipped to act quickly in foreign relations in keeping with the stepped-up tempo of international affairs, a person the President can trust with impressive delegated powers, one so loyal to his chief that he may be allowed to initiate and shape policy. This relationship is essential, for in the American system the making of foreign policy cannot usually be successfully delegated beyond the Secretary of State, and in times of great crisis cannot be delegated at all.

This standard does not mean that the President should abdicate any of his power over foreign affairs or that the Secretary of State must or should take on the full characteristics of a foreign minister, as in the British system. The Secretary can carry on effectively in the traditions of his own unique office, an office whose traditions grow more impressive with each passing year, an office of such dignity that it sheds luster on whoever holds it. This holds true even though a few Secretaries have appeared to have practically no power, for the record of the American Secretary of State compares favorably with that of foreign ministers of virtually any other country.

The Secretaryship, in other words, is flexible enough to be one of the great offices of the world. A President, therefore, should not attempt to be his own Secretary of State, but should use his chosen Secretary to help ease his own immense burden. He should go beyond tradition and assign the Secretary preeminent influence in the government in fact as well as name, especially in the light of the new pressing importance of foreign policy in the nation's welfare. The old boundaries between domestic and foreign policies, we are told, have virtually disappeared. Domestic and defense policies, in fact, are being shaped in large measure by the requirements of foreign policy. Hence, the selection and proper use of the Secretary of State, Americans should realize, is one of the most compelling of their President's duties.

Bibliographical Note

This book rests on a selected use of manuscript sources and a mass of printed works, letters, diaries, memoirs, other personal accounts, biographies, and monographs. Most of the manuscript collections consulted, such as the William McKinley, Whitelaw Reid, John Hay, Theodore Roosevelt, Elihu Root, Philander C. Knox, Woodrow Wilson, William Jennings Bryan, Robert Lansing, and Charles Evans Hughes papers, are in the Manuscript Division of the Library of Congress. I have also used microfilm copies of the Timothy Pickering Papers, in the Massachusetts Historical Society in Boston, material from other collections examined in my earlier researches on the Federalist period, have gone through the Lewis Cass Papers, in the William L. Clements Library of the University of Michigan, have sampled the Herbert Hoover Papers, in the Hoover Library at Stanford University, and have examined a small file of material pertaining to the Secretaryship of State in the Historical Office of the Department of State.

The secondary and printed materials, as well as serials and files of newspapers such as *The New York Times,* may be found in any of a number of good research libraries. The interested specialist should not have difficulty tracing most of my sources from the text, but since this broad study has no formal documentation, the following selected general titles may prove helpful to the reader who may wish to pursue this subject in greater detail.

For almost anyone, the starting point should be Samuel F. Bemis, ed., *The American Secretaries of State and Their Diplomacy* (10 vols., New York: Alfred A. Knopf, 1927-29). This indispensable work covers the individual Secretaries from the beginning of the nation through the Secretaryship of Charles E. Hughes. It has been supplemented, down through the Secretaryship of John Foster Dulles, by Norman A. Graebner, ed., *An Uncertain Tradition: American Secretaries of State in the Twentieth Century* (New York: McGraw-Hill Book Company, 1961), a book of essays by fourteen authors. These essays are valuable because they concentrate more on power, ideas, and key issues in the Secretaryship itself than do the studies in the Bemis series. The only book that offers an analysis of the Secretaryship itself is Don K. Price, ed., *The*

Secretary of State (Englewood Cliffs, N.J.: Prentice-Hall, 1960), another collection of essays. Written by scholars and former government officials, such as Dean Acheson, these essays served as background reading for the Eighteenth American Assembly in 1960. They include more data on the State Department, the making of foreign policy, and other related matters than on the Secretaryship itself. A brief but stimulating analysis of the office is Paul H. Nitze, "'Impossible' Job of Secretary of State," *The New York Times Magazine*, February 24, 1957, p. 9. E. W. Kenworthy, in "Evolution of Our No. 1 Diplomat," *The New York Times Magazine*, March 18, 1962, p. 31, deals with the Secretaryship of Dean Rusk and stresses that President Kennedy "has learned that he cannot be his own Secretary of State."

Graham H. Stuart, *The Department of State: A History of Its Organization, Procedure, and Personnel* (New York: The Macmillan Company, 1949), briefly describes the main contribution of each Secretary to foreign policy and to the history of the State Department but is most useful for information on the administrative responsibilities of the Secretaries. The most recent analysis of the department and its administration, Robert E. Elder, *The Policy Machine: The Department of State and American Foreign Policy* (Syracuse, N.Y.: Syracuse University Press, 1960), concentrates on policy-making procedures. Another recent study, Henry Field Haviland, Jr., *et al., The Formulation and Administration of United States Foreign Policy* (Washington, D.C.: Brookings Institution, 1960), deals with various agencies, besides the State Department, involved in the making of foreign policy. It urges, among other proposals, the creation of a super Secretary of State, "a secretary in the sense that Washington regarded Jefferson or Hamilton." An older but still valuable study of the State Department, which, like the Stuart history, also stresses administration is Gaillard Hunt, *The Department of State of the United States: Its History and Functions* (New Haven, Conn.: Yale University Press, 1914). For an analysis of the British equivalent of the State Department, see William Strang *et al., The Foreign Office* (London: Allen & Unwin, 1955) and Donald G. Bishop, *The Administration of British Foreign Relations* (Syracuse, N.Y.: Syracuse University Press, 1961). For diplomatic practice, see Graham H. Stuart, *American Diplomatic and Consular Practice* (2d ed.; New York: Appleton-Century-Crofts, 1952); Warren F. Ilchman, *Professional Diplomacy in the United States, 1779–1939: A Study in Administrative History* (Chicago: The University of Chicago Press, 1961); Charles W. Thayer, *Diplomat* (New York: Harper & Brothers, 1959); and Katherine Crane, *Mr. Carr of State: Forty-Seven Years in the Department of State* (New York: St Martin's Press, 1960). Power as a political concept, and the shaping and sharing of power, are analyzed in Harold D. Lasswell and Abraham Kaplan, *Power and Society: A Framework for Political Inquiry* (New Haven, Conn.: Yale University Press, 1950).

The standard work on the American Cabinet system is Henry B.

Learned, *The President's Cabinet: Studies in the Origin, Formation and Structure of An American Institution* (New Haven, Conn.: Yale University Press, 1912). See also Mary L. Hinsdale, *A History of the President's Cabinet* (Ann Arbor, Mich.: George Wahr Publishing Company, 1911), and for the later period, Richard F. Fenno, Jr., *The President's Cabinet: An Analysis in the Period from Wilson to Eisenhower* (Cambridge, Mass.: Harvard University Press, 1959). Stephen Horn, *The Cabinet and Congress* (New York: Columbia University Press, 1960), concentrates on the relationship between the legislative and executive power in the government.

There are a number of books on the Presidency that may be consulted with profit. Edward S. Corwin, *The President, Office and Powers, 1787–1957: History and Analysis of Practice and Opinion* (4th rev. ed.; New York: New York University Press, 1957), has long been the standard work in the field and is especially strong on Constitutional questions. A unique study of personal power, that is, of the President's problem of obtaining power for himself, of keeping it, and of using it, is Richard E. Neustadt, *Presidential Power: The Politics of Leadership* (New York: John Wiley and Sons, 1960). Sidney Hyman, *The American President* (New York: Harper & Brothers, 1954), is a readable and perceptive popular analysis; Harold J. Laski, *The American Presidency: An Interpretation* (New York: Harper & Brothers, 1940), is well written and provocative. Dean Rusk, in "The President," *Foreign Affairs*, XXXVIII (April, 1960), 353–69, discusses the problem of summit diplomacy and the Presidency. Also useful are Clinton Rossiter, *The American Presidency* (New York: Harcourt, Brace and Company, 1956) and Wilfred E. Binkley, *The Man in the White House: His Powers and Duties* (Baltimore: The Johns Hopkins Press, 1959). For an account of the President's unofficial advisers and biographical studies of several, such as Edward House and Harry Hopkins, see Louis W. Koenig, *The Invisible Presidency* (New York: Holt, Rinehart and Winston, 1960).

For a detailed history that places the Secretaryship in the broad context of administrative problems within the Federal Government, see Leonard D. White's study, which earned him a Pulitzer Prize, *The Federalists: A Study in Administrative History* (New York: The Macmillan Company, 1948); *The Jeffersonians: A Study in Administrative History, 1801–1829* (New York: The Macmillan Company, 1951); *The Jacksonians: A Study in Administrative History, 1829–1861* (New York: The Macmillan Company, 1954); *The Republican Era, 1869–1901: A Study in Administrative History* (New York: The Macmillan Company, 1958).

Although there are many biographies of individual Secretaries of State, three of them, all of which won their authors the Pulitzer Prize, stand out: Samuel F. Bemis, *John Quincy Adams and the Foundations of American Foreign Policy* (New York: Alfred A. Knopf, 1949); Allan Nevins, *Hamilton Fish: The Inner History of the Grant Administration*

(New York: Dodd, Mead and Company, 1936); and Tyler Dennett, *John Hay: From Poetry to Politics* (New York: Dodd, Mead and Company, 1933). Another prize-winning study that throws light on the Secretaryship from the point of view of a personal adviser to the President is Robert E. Sherwood, *Roosevelt and Hopkins: An Intimate History* (New York: Harper & Brothers, 1948).

For insights on the Secretaryship in later years as recorded by insiders, the following memoirs are among the most useful: Henry L. Stimson and McGeorge Bundy, *On Active Service in Peace and War* (New York: Harper & Brothers, 1948); *The Memoirs of Cordell Hull* (2 vols., New York: The Macmillan Company, 1948); *Memoirs by Harry S. Truman* (2 vols., Garden City, N. Y.: Doubleday & Company, 1955–56); and Sherman Adams, *Firsthand Report: The Story of the Eisenhower Administration* (New York: Harper & Brothers, 1961).

Index